"LOOK AT ME, VELVET, MY LOVE."

She turned her passion-glazed green eyes to Alex's lionlike golden ones. With featherlike touches he stroked a tender breast, his fingers gently encircling it slowly with a delicious mesmerizing action. Velvet felt a lovely warmth begin to suffuse her limbs. She sighed, and Alex smiled. His fingers moved upward and began to tease the sensitive nipple until she thought her flesh would burst. Velvet understood that the pleasure was only beginning. Suddenly she was no longer afraid . . .

"LOOK AT ME, MY ROSE."

Akbar pulled Velvet into his arms, and his mouth crushed bruisingly against hers. Unable to restrain her inflamed emotions, she wrapped her arms about him and returned the kiss as passionately. For some time they kissed hungrily and without ceasing, one deep kiss blending into another. His tongue made its first penetration of her, plunging between her lips and into her mouth to meet her tongue, which leaped with shock at his touch and fled, only to be pursued until the two were entwining together with ever-mounting ardor.

ALSO BY BERTRICE SMALL

The Kadin

Love Wild and Fair

Adora

Unconquered

Beloved

Enchantress Mine

Blaze Wyndham

The Spitfire

A Moment in Time

THE O'MALLEY SAGA

Skye O'Malley

All the Sweet Tomorrows

A Love for All Time

This Heart of Mine

Lost Love Found

Wild Jasmine

This HEART of MINE

Bertrice Small

BALLANTINE BOOKS • NEW YORK

 Published in the United States by Ballantine Books, a division of Random House, Inc., New York, and simultaneously in Canada by Random House of Canada Limited, Toronto.

Library of Congress Catalog Card Number: 85-90564

ISBN: 0-345-32639-3

Cover painting by Glen Madison
Cover design by James R. Harris
Text design by Ann Gold
Manufactured in the United States of America

First Edition: September 1985
10 9 8 7 6 5 4 3 2

To two Great Ladies of Romance:
Nancy Coffey, who got me into
this fix in the first place;
and my dearest friend, Kathryn Falk,
who keeps the pot constantly boiling.

The Players

THE FAMILY, THOSE CONSIDERED FAMILY, AND RETAINERS

Skye O'Malley, Lady de Marisco–A fabulously wealthy Irishwoman (See: *Skye O'Malley, All the Sweet Tomorrows*)
Adam de Marisco–Her husband, Master of Lundy, and *Queen's Malvern*
Velvet de Marisco–Their only child, born May 1, 1573
Ewan O'Flaherty–Velvet's half-brother, born March 28, 1556
Gwyneth Southwood O'Flaherty–His wife, Robin's half-sister
Captain Murrough O'Flaherty–Velvet's half-brother, born January 15, 1557
Joan Southwood O'Flaherty–His wife, Robin's half-sister
Willow Small Edwardes, Countess of Alcester–Velvet's half-sister, born April 5, 1560
James Edwardes, Earl of Alcester–Her husband
Robert (Robin) Southwood, Earl of Lynmouth–Velvet's half-brother, born September 18, 1563
Deirdre Blakeley, Lady Blackthorn–Velvet's half-sister, born December 12, 1567
John Blakeley, Lord Blackthorn–Her husband
Padraic, Lord Burke of Clearfields–Velvet's half-brother, born January 30, 1569
Sir Robert Small of Wren Court–called Uncle Robbie, the business partner of Lady de Marisco
Dame Cecily Small–His elder sister who has helped to raise Skye's children
Captain Bran Kelly–A captain in the O'Malley-Small trading company fleet
Daisy Kelly–His wife, Skye's tiring woman
Pansy Kelly–Their daughter, Velvet's servant

The English

Elizabeth Tudor–Queen of England, 1558–1603
Sir William Cecil, Lord Burghley–The English Secretary of State, and the queen's greatest confidant
Henry Carey, Lord Hundston–The queen's chancellor, her first cousin
Robert Dudley, Earl of Leicester–The queen's oldest friend, and favorite
Lettice Knollys Dudley, Countess of Leicester–His second wife, the queen's cousin and rival
Robert Devereux, Earl of Essex–Her son by a prior marriage, Master of the Queen's Horse, and one of the queen's favorites
Sir Walter Ralegh–A gentleman of Devon, and one of the queen's favorites
Elizabeth (Bess) Throckmorton–A maid of honor
Angel Christman–A royal ward
Christopher Marlowe–Playwright, actor, rake, and rogue
Will Shakespeare–A young actor and aspiring playwright
Lady Mary de Boult –A lady of the court
Alanna Wythe–A London silversmith's daughter
Sybilla–Her daughter

The Scots

James Stewart–King of Scotland, heir to England's throne
Anne of Denmark–Queen of Scotland, his wife
John Maitland–Chancellor of Scotland
Francis Stewart-Hepburn, Earl of Bothwell–The king's cousin, called "The Uncrowned King of Scotland"
Catriona Leslie, Countess of Glenkirk–Bothwell's mistress, but coveted by the king (See: *Love Wild and Fair*)
Alexander Gordon, Earl of BrocCairn–Velvet's betrothed husband, a cousin of both Bothwell and the king
Annabella Grant–His sister
Ian Grant, Master of Grantholm–Her husband
Dugald Geddes–Alex's servant

Jeanne Lawrie–A former playmate of Alex's who is living in his village
Ranald Torc–An outlaw of Clan Shaw

THE CLERGY

Michael O'Malley, "The O'Malley"–The bishop of Mid-Connaught, brother to Skye O'Malley
Bearach O'Dowd–His childhood playmate, now a Jesuit priest living in Paris
Father Ourique–A Portuguese Jesuit stationed in Bombay
Father Jean-Paul St. Justine–Adam's nephew, and the family chaplain

THE PORTUGUESE

Don Cesar Affonso Marinha-Grande–Portuguese governor of Bombay

THE INDIAN COURT

Akbar, The Grand Mughal–The emperor of India
Rugaiya Begum–His cousin and first wife
Jodh Bai–A Rajput princess; also Akbar's wife, the mother of his heir
Ramesh–The royal household steward
Adali–A zenana eunuch

This Heart of Mine

Prologue

January, 1586

"*Christ's bloody bones!*" The oath exploded like a thunderclap from Elizabeth Tudor's mouth. She stopped in midstride and, whirling about, fixed an angry stare upon the only other woman in the room. "You dare to say No to *me*, madame? I am your queen!"

"I have no queen," came the calm reply. "In fact, thanks to you, I have no country."

"*Bitch!*" the queen hissed. "You have ever been a thorn in my side! Did I not give you and your husband a home? Are your children not welcome at my court? Is this the gratitude you show me for all my many kindnesses?" She glowered at the men who attended her as if enlisting their support.

"*Kindnesses?*" The other woman emitted a sharp bark of laughter. "Let me think back, Majesty, over our long association. There was the time when you condoned Lord Dudley's rape of my person because you weren't woman enough to love him totally. Then there was the time you forced me into a foreign marriage promising to protect my infant son's lands, which you then quickly gave away. And I seem to remember another time when, needing my help, you kidnapped my daughter to ensure my cooperation."

"And I remember that you pirated my ships, costing England much-needed revenues!" shouted the queen, stung by the reference to Lord Dudley.

"A deed you were never able to prove," was the quick reply.

"A deed we both damn well know you committed!"

The two men in the room watched this exchange with admiration. One was the queen's most loyal servant, and the other, husband of her antagonist.

The women are well matched, thought Lord Burghley, Queen Elizabeth's secretary of state, but the bickering must stop, for time was of the essence in this matter. The queen had not been well of late. The constant plottings that surrounded her imprisoned cousin, Mary Stewart, Scotland's exiled monarch, were taking their toll on her health. The Spanish would not give up their holy vendetta against Elizabeth Tudor, and she was forced to work long and hard to keep ahead of their wickedness.

William Cecil, Lord Burghley, sighed softly. It was very late at night, and the queen had been ready for bed when her guests had come. She had insisted on seeing them immediately upon their arrival at Greenwich, and despite her deshabille they had been brought to her. She had greeted them clad in a quilted white velvet robe embroidered with gold threads and small garnets. The elegant red wig she wore to cover her graying and thinning hair had been affixed to her head, but even it could not compensate for her lack of makeup, and, at that moment, the queen looked every bit her fifty-two years. Lord Burghley's prim mouth crinkled in a momentary smile, for he suspected that part of Elizabeth Tudor's anger stemmed from the fact that she realized it too, while the woman standing before her looked ten years younger than her forty-five years.

"Madame, if I may speak," he requested of his mistress. She nodded. "This anger between you is not solving our problem." He turned to the queen's guest. "Lady de Marisco, as you know, we have already sent one expedition to the East Indies."

Skye O'Malley de Marisco's mouth curled up in amusement. "Aye, my lord, I know. William Hawkins, a London merchant, in the company of a sometime jeweler and a painter of pictures. A most interesting choice of ambassadors." Her voice held the faintest hint of scorn.

"We felt it best to be discreet in light of the fact that the Portuguese are fast solidifying their hold on the Indies," was William Cecil's reply.

"The Portuguese be damned!" shouted the queen. "'Tis the Spanish, for they call the tune in Portugal now! They mean to have the riches of the East Indies as they have all the wealth now pouring forth from the silver and gold mines in the New World. Well, I won't have it! The East Indies must be England's!"

"I wonder if the prince who rules those lands will agree with your sentiments, madame," observed Skye wryly.

Elizabeth Tudor looked at her longtime adversary and then said something that no one had ever thought to hear her say to this great rival of hers. "I need your help, dearest Skye! No one else can do what I need done but you."

The two men in the room glanced at one another, one more surprised than the other. Skye looked to her husband, Adam de Marisco, and saw in his gaze what she knew she would see. The queen had come as close to begging for her aid as she was ever going to. Adam's smoky blue eyes looked steadily into Skye's, and she could hear his silent voice as clearly as if he were actually speaking to her. *You cannot refuse her now*, his eyes told her quietly. *Give over, little girl. Be gracious in your victory.*

"Madame, may I have your permission to sit?" she asked. "Our journey was a long road traveled in a short time. I find that I can no longer spend so many hours in the saddle without suffering from it."

The queen nodded, graciously motioning Skye to a comfortable chair by the fireside. Elizabeth Tudor sat opposite her old foe, leaning forward almost girlishly upon her elbows, and said with a grin, "After so many years, one would think our bottoms would grow hardened, but alas they do not. I find that I cannot hunt as often as I once did without suffering also."

There was a momentary silence, and then Skye asked, "Why did John Newbery, William Hawkins, and their party travel overland, madame?"

"Hawkins thought to appear less conspicuous."

"More than likely he thought to save himself the cost of mounting a proper expedition and thereby gain a greater profit," said Skye. "Upon the sea he was not likely to encounter many ships if the voyage was planned carefully, but upon the land Englishmen traveling in foreign climes, however simply, cannot help but appear objects of curiosity to the local population, a fact that would be quickly brought to the attention of the local authorities. Still, he has not been gone for so long that he will not be successful, madame. Why this haste to launch another expedition?"

"Our agents in Spain send word that our dear late sister's husband, Philip, seeks to send a great armada against England. The cost of this war is to be borne by the bounty Philip wrests from the Indies. India is ruled by a mighty prince who willingly trades with Portugal and hence with Spain. The Portuguese are a heavy-handed people, however, and I will wager that if we could but get our foot in the door of India, their emperor, Akbar, seeing the difference between our two countries, would more willingly trade with us, and Spain's revenues would be badly cut.

"William Hawkins and his little party may eventually attain the Indies, but your ships can reach it far more quickly, dearest Skye. You have ever been adept at accomplishing the impossible. 'Tis Irish luck, I suppose, but you and Sir Robert Small together seem to be an invincible pair where trade is concerned."

"Robbie is getting too old for this sort of thing, madame," Skye protested.

"I should like to be present when you tell him so," Elizabeth said, chuckling, "but if that concerns you then go yourself. In fact I should far prefer that you go, for no one else has your knack for diplomacy, when it so pleases you."

"I have a family, madame. I cannot simply pick up and leave them."

"Your children are grown."

"Not Velvet. She is still a little maid, not yet thirteen."

"Send her to me here at court," the queen suggested. "She is my godchild, and I shall be happy to have her."

"Never!" said Skye vehemently. "Forgive me, madame, but my child is yet an innocent, and I would she remained so for the time being. Your court is a wondrous place for those who are wise in the ways of the world, and you, madame, are the most virtuous of women, but my child would be fair game for those whose high-mindedness is not as great as Your Majesty's. If I do this for you, Velvet must remain in her own home in the care of Robbie's sister, Dame Cecily Small."

"*If*, madame?" The queen's gray-black eyes narrowed.

Skye sighed. "We must leave almost immediately if we are to catch the proper winds across the Indian Ocean. It does not give us much time to mount and provision the ships."

"You will have our utmost cooperation, dearest Skye," the queen promised.

"What else will I have?" Skye demanded. "Favors between us have never come cheaply, madame."

Elizabeth Tudor laughed, then nodded. "Do you fancy being a countess again? Do this for me and I will create for you the earldom of Lundy."

"The inheritance of which will pass down through the female line of our family," said Skye. "The title must belong to Velvet in her own right one day as we have no son, nor the hope of one. I will expect a share of any profits accrued by my efforts also."

"Agreed!" said the queen, and her smile was one of admiration.

"How much of a share?" demanded William Cecil, ever mindful of his mistress's interests.

"Robbie and I will work it out, my lord," said Adam de Marisco. "The queen will, as always, receive the lion's portion. I do not believe you have ever found fault with our accounting."

"Nay, my lord," Burghley agreed. "Never have we missed so much as a groat in our dealings with you."

"Then it is settled," the queen said, pleased. "Pour us some wine, Cecil, and let us celebrate. One last thing, however—this voyage must remain a secret, for if Philip's spies get wind of it too soon your chances of success will be destroyed."

"Aye," Skye agreed, taking the goblet that was offered her.

The four occupants of Elizabeth Tudor's private closet drank to the success of the planned expedition, and then with the queen's gracious permission Lord and Lady de Marisco took their leave of Her Majesty.

"Their chances of success are not very good," observed William Cecil when the queen's two guests had departed. "Even if they can leave England without arousing Spain's suspicions, there is the long voyage to India, and once there they must evade the Portuguese to get to the emperor Akbar."

"I know," replied Elizabeth, "but I truly believe that our best hope lies with Skye O'Malley. Ah, my dear *Spirit*, what would I have done all these years without you to look after my best interests?"

"There are many eager to serve Your Majesty," replied Lord Burghley, but he was nonetheless touched by her gratitude. Her use of the private nickname she had given him further warmed his old bones.

"None like you, William. None like you. The others would have called me mad for summoning Skye O'Malley after all these years. How long has it been since I exiled her to *Queen's Malvern*? Nearly eleven years, William. In all that time I have not laid eyes upon her. Christ's bloody bones!" She grimaced. "The woman has hardly changed, and yet she is already a grandmother many times over! It must be living in the country and raising horses that keeps her young, my *Spirit*. Still, I saw the look in her eyes. She is eager for the chance to go to sea once more. Oh, yes, she is most eager!" The queen laughed.

She would have laughed even harder had she been aware that her very thoughts were being echoed by Adam de Marisco, Skye's husband.

A royal barge had taken Skye and Adam upriver to their London house, Greenwood. They were silent during the trip, for both were well aware that the royal bargemen, like all servants, loved to gossip. It was not until they were safely in their own home, alone within their private apartments, that Adam burst out, "I thought you were happy at *Queen's Malvern*, sweetheart."

"I am," Skye replied. "Loosen my bodice for me, Adam. I am fairly exhausted and longing for bed."

"You *want* to go." His fingers nimbly undid the buttons on her gown.

"Of course I want to go!" She shrugged the bodice off and turned to face him. "For over ten years now I have been kept from the sea. I am happy at *Queen's Malvern*, but the thought that we are to have the opportunity once more to go adventuring . . . Oh, Adam!" She flung her arms about his neck and kissed him.

He laughed. "Adventuring is it, little girl? And here I thought you had grown up. 'Tis a staid and proper wife you've been to me since we came to live at Queen's Malvern."

"Not too proper, I hope, my darling." She chuckled. "Oh, Adam, do you mind? I could not really refuse the queen, could I?"

He sighed deeply. "Nay, we couldn't refuse her though I would to God that we might have. I do not like the idea of leaving Velvet, Skye. She is overyoung yet."

"We might bring her with us," Skye suggested. "After all, she is half O'Malley."

"Nay, sweetheart, we should not do that. 'Tis a dangerous voyage that we plan for all you make light of it. We have kept her safe all these years, and by the time we return her marriage to the son of my old friend, the Earl of BrocCairn, will be nearly due. Let her remain here in England in our good Dame Cecily's care, learning all the things she must know to be a good wife to young Alexander Gordon, who will one day be the Earl of BrocCairn himself."

Skye chuckled. "All those duties that I've neglected to teach her myself, you mean. But I've taught her other things, Adam. She's a well-educated child and will be no shame to her husband when he takes her to Scotland's court."

Adam smiled. He knew how much value Skye put upon knowledge even for her daughters. Had Dame Cecily not been a part of their household all these years, he wondered if the girls would have ever learned how to manage a household. That skill was the lowest on Skye's list of priorities.

"Nay, Velvet will be no shame to BrocCairn, sweetheart," he agreed, "but in the time we are away she will learn how to care for a large estate and all of its people. Though you dislike that duty, even you can perform it, but Velvet cannot, and in just a few short years she will be wed."

Skye sighed. "I know, and that is one reason I am so loath to leave her. We shall miss at least two years of our daughter's life, Adam. There is nothing Elizabeth Tudor can give us to compensate us for that loss." She looked up at him and touched his cheek. "We have been so happy, haven't we, my darling? As much as I long for this adventure, I am reluctant to break the spell that *Queen's Malvern* has woven about all our lives. There is so much happiness to come. We shall not be here to help Robin and Alison celebrate little Elsbeth's first birthday, and there is the new baby Alison carries that will be born soon. Ewan and Gwyneth promised to bring the children from Ireland this coming summer, and we've not yet seen their new child, Ualtar. Murrough will want to come with us, and I promised Joan I would not send him off upon another long voyage so soon. Do you realize that when the twins were born last summer it was the first time he was home for the birth of any of his children? He has been off so much that the twins are their first babies in five years."

"You're becoming a matriarch, sweetheart," he teased her.

"I became a matriarch at seventeen when my father thrust the title of "The O'Malley" upon me. Thank God I have been relieved of that burden these past years! Oh, Adam! I want to go to India, and I don't!"

"But go we must, Skye. The family will survive without us though I will allow they will miss you."

"And you also, my darling! Though Velvet is your only child of my body, all my other children love you as they would their own fathers. If I am the matriarch of this family, then you are its patriarch, and we shall celebrate our fourteenth anniversary in the Indies come September."

He laughed happily. "I can always trust you to see the bright side, sweetheart. So it is settled then. Velvet will remain safely with Dame Cecily at *Queen's Malvern*, the rest of our children shall go on as usual, and we, my sweet Skye, shall go off on a final adventure in the queen's name before we settle into a rather comfortable and quiet old age."

"Old age?" She looked up at him, outraged, and then a wicked smile lit her features. "I shall never be old, Adam de Marisco," she said, her fingers nimbly undoing his shirt. "I shall never be ready to become *that* comfortable and quiet." Her warm lips spread little kisses across his furred chest, causing a shiver of excitement to race through his veins. Then she eyed him mischievously. "Shall we begin our adventure tonight, my darling?"

His laughter rumbled about the room. "Our little daughter would be quite shocked," he said, smiling at Skye. "She considers us a most respectable and staid couple."

"And so she should," replied Velvet's mother. "She is much too young to be considering the ways of a man and a woman. There is plenty of time for her to think about those things after we return from India. Let her have her childhood first."

"She is betrothed, Skye."

"She has long since forgotten BrocCairn's son, Adam. The betrothal took place when she was five, and you will remember I allowed it only because you swore to me she might make her own choice when the time came. I will not force Velvet into a marriage as my father forced me. Besides, although BrocCairn corresponds with you, his son has shown no interest in Velvet at all over the years. There is plenty of time yet to worry about such things. In the meantime, let

Velvet be a little girl without a worry or care beyond her horses and the sweetmeats she constantly manages to weasel out of you and her brothers. She is really quite spoilt."

"You're right," he agreed with her, smiling as he thought of his only and much-beloved child. "There is time for Velvet. More than enough time."

Part One

Lord de Marisco's Daughter

Now is the month of May, when merry lads do play!
Fa la la la la la la, la la!
Fa la la la la la la!

Each with his bonnie lass, a-dancin on the grass!
Fa la la la la!
Fa la la la la la la, la! la la! la la!

—*Sixteenth-century tune*

Chapter I

"What the hell d'ye mean by 'marry without delay,' Father?" Alexander Gordon glowered down from his great height upon his bedridden father, but the Earl of BrocCairn was not intimidated by his son's look. It was a look he'd often worn upon his own face in his younger days when someone more powerful than he was dictating to him. God, he thought, looking up at Alex, he looks just like I once did. He has the same height and lanky frame, a face that looks as if it was hewn from rock, and my black hair. Why, up until I had this damned accident, we were often taken for brothers.

Angus Gordon sighed deeply. He hated admitting his own weakness, but gritting his teeth, he said, "It should be clear to ye, Alex, that I will not survive to see the spring. Each day I find myself growing weaker, unable to do even the simplest things for myself. Hell, man! I can't even stand to piss! I don't want to live like this, and the physician from Aberdeen says I will get no better. I know I'm dying."

"Damnation!" The younger man shifted his feet, obviously made quite uncomfortable by his father's bluntness.

"I will be dead within a few weeks, Alex, and ye're my only male heir," continued the Earl of BrocCairn. "Wi' yer mother and brother, Nigel, gone in last year's epidemic, I have no one but ye and yer sister. I would rather not pass *Dun Broc* on to Annabella and her weak-willed husband who does not bear my name. Ye have a betrothed wife, Alex. *Marry her!* Get me a grandson on her body!"

"God's foot, Father! A little English girl I haven't seen in years? A child barely half grown, let alone capable of mothering a bairn of her own! Yer illness has addled yer wits!" Alexander Gordon's voice was full of pity.

"Aye," his father retorted sharply, "ye've not seen the lass since the day of yer betrothal. Whose fault was that, my son? Are ye aware of how long ago it took place? Almost ten years have passed, and de Marisco's lass is full grown now and ripe for wedding. Ye have but to claim her!

"Is there another, perhaps, who has captured yer heart?" Angus Gordon went on suddenly. "If there is, I'd not force this match upon ye, for I want ye to be happy with yer wife, Alex, as I was with mine. Yer mother was the love of my life, and as sad as I am to be leaving ye, I'll be glad to be wi' her again. It's been a long year since my Isabelle left me." His voice trailed off sadly.

Alex could feel unbidden tears pricking the back of his eyelids, and he fought to prevent them from overflowing his eyes. "There's no lass, Father," he said quietly. "Ye know it."

"Then go to England and wed wi' the girl I chose for ye. She is yers for the asking, and both Adam de Marisco and I always hoped to unite our families by this marriage. It is my dying wish, Alex. I would not take ye from another, but if there is truly no other, then ye *must* honor this betrothal to my friend's daughter. Ye've never before objected to it. Do this final thing for me, my beloved son."

In the last of the icy, howling winds of winter that roared about the dull gray stone turrets of *Dun Broc*, Alexander Gordon heard again the voice of his dead father importuning his speedy marriage. Seated at the high board in the Great Hall of his castle, he looked at his brother-in-law, Ian Grant, and knew he had no other choice but to marry. He had but lately overheard one of his nephews saying to the other, "Papa says that one day this will all be mine. I will be the earl."

The innocent, yet prideful words spoken by his sister's eldest child had suddenly brought home to Alex his father's desperate dying wish. *A Grant the next lord of BrocCairn? Never!*

Alex understood why his father had made an English match for him. The English queen was, despite her age, a maiden, and no issue of hers would inherit the throne of England. It was her cousin, and his, young James Stewart, the king of Scotland, who would one day rule England.

Although Alex had spent as little time at the Scottish court as possible, even he could see Jamie Stewart's eagerness to have his inheritance and flee south to a more civilized clime. The English nobility were less fractious than their Scots counterparts. The English kings had the kind of longevity a royal Stewart could not seem to count upon. Not one Scots king since the time of the first James Stewart had lived longer than forty years, and not one had died a natural death. The current Jamie must wish as would any normal man for a long life, but Scotland was not the place for it. When he inherited the throne of England and went south to claim it, those who went with him, and those already married to good English connections, would be the ones to prosper. That was why Angus Gordon had made an English match for his son.

Alex sat back in his chair and watched Ian Grant through narrowed eyes. Ian was a nice-enough fellow, but it was high time he made his own way. He had grown soft living at *Dun Broc* with all its small comforts. It was past time for him to return to his own holding in the glen below—a holding that he badly neglected—and made something of it. Forced back there, Alex thought with a wicked smile, his sister Annabella would be sure to ride her spouse hard to improve her lot.

"I'll be leaving for England in a few weeks' time," Alex began.

"Why on earth are ye going there?" demanded his sister, stuffing a piece of pigeon pasty into her mouth. Bella had grown plump of late, Alex noted. Was she breeding again, or was it simply too much good living?

"I'm going to claim my bride, Bella. It's high time I married and started a family. It was our father's dying wish."

Annabella Grant choked on her mouthful of pasty, looking stunned at her elder brother's surprising revelation, but before she could swallow and speak, her husband was actually taking the initiative and speaking for them.

"Marry? Ye're near thirty, man! If ye must wed, then why not wi' a good Scots family? Why would ye blend yer blood with that of a damned Sassenach?"

"Because I was betrothed to the girl ten years ago, Ian, and there's no one in Scotland I care enough to wed. Honor demands that I keep my word. Besides, she is the daughter of one of Father's old friends."

"Who?" Annabella had finally recovered enough to ask.

"A man by the name of Adam de Marisco. Father, it seems, spent time in France as a youth. Although de Marisco had an English father, his mother was French. It was at the home of her second husband, a chateau called *Archambault*, that Father and Adam de Marisco met. They were both boys at the time, but there seems to have been a correspondence of many years' standing between them after that. Ten years ago—it was the summer that Ian was courting ye, Bella, and ye'd no time for anything else—Father and I went south to England for a short time. There I was formally betrothed to de Marisco's daughter who was then just a wee lass of five. I can barely remember the ceremony myself, and I remember less of the lass except that she was strong."

"Strong?" Bella looked puzzled.

"She was the littlest, yet she was the leader of all the bairns."

"So." Bella sniffed. "Because of a dying wish made by a sentimental old man, ye're going to get on yer horse and ride down to England to claim yer bride, are ye? Why this de Marisco man has probably forgotten all about ye and that silly betrothal! They'll set the dogs on ye!

"Och, brother, marry if ye must, but marry a good highland lass," she went on. "Oh, I'll admit I thought to see my oldest laddie in yer place here at *Dun Broc* one day, Alex, but if that's not to be 'tis not to be. Just don't make a fool of yerself over something long forgot."

"Aye," put in Ian Grant. "Don't make a fool of yerself before the Sassenachs, brother."

Alex felt a bolt of irritation shoot through him. He loved his sister, but though Annabella was five years his junior, she had been born an old woman, and her husband was not much better. Neither he nor Bella had ever left the vicinity in which they had lived all their lives. They were two ingrown people who knew nothing of the outside world, and they were content to remain exactly as they had always been.

"Father has been in correspondence with Lord de Marisco without cease all these years, Bella," Alex explained patiently. "There are two boxes in the library. One contains the letters they wrote to each other. I have recently browsed through them. Their friendship remained strong, as was mine, with de Marisco's stepson, the Earl of Lynmouth, my betrothed's half brother. Remember, we studied together in Paris? The other box contains miniatures of the de Marisco lass, painted each year immediately after her birthday. The betrothal is quite secure, Bella, and now with Father gone I must marry without delay. I think it's time that ye take yer sons and go home, sister. *Dun Broc* will be very much unsettled while I am away for I have already given orders that it be cleaned and freshened from towers to dungeons. The countess's chambers will be redecorated for my bride. Yer own house must stand greatly in need of yer sure touch, Bella. Ye've not been there in over a year."

"Are ye sending me from my home?" His sister looked aggrieved.

"No, sister, I am sending ye *to yer home*. *Dun Broc* ceased to be yer home the day ye married Ian Grant, and my castle can only have one mistress: my wife. I am sure that yer husband misses his own house as well, eh, Ian?"

Ian Grant thought about the damp pile of dark gray stones in the glen that was called *Grantholm*, and he shuddered. There was never enough money to make all the repairs it needed, nor enough wood to heat it, and it had a ghost that wailed and threw crockery when annoyed. Ian thought that perhaps a bog would be preferable, but then he caught his brother-in-law's fierce look and stammered, "Oh, a-aye!

'Twill be good to get home a-a-again, Alex. I-indeed i-it w-will!"

Bella threw her husband a disgusted look. Ian was such a cowardly worm where Alex was concerned. Sometimes she questioned why she had ever married him, but immediately laughed inwardly, knowing the answer to that. *No one!* No one, she was certain, could love a woman the way her Ian did. It was his one talent.

She rounded on her brother. "So!" she snarled angrily. "I am no longer welcome in the house of my birth. I would have never guessed that ye felt that way, Alex, for ye hid it well from our parents. Our mother would shed bitter tears to see it, and our father would turn in his tomb if he but knew."

"Mother wouldn't let ye stay more than a week at a time before she died, Bella, and Father would have thrown ye out a month after that, but he was too ill to do so, and 'twas not my place then." Alex's voice was filled with amusement. Her guilt tactics might work well on Ian, but the new earl was made of stronger stuff. "Ye're always welcome as a guest to *Dun Broc*, but I'll not have ye moving in on me so that yer weak-willed husband and yer snot-nosed sons can lord it over my inheritance. Father would have lived a long life had it not been for that hunting accident, and I am a young man yet, sister. I'll have an heir within a year of the wedding ye can be sure, and another son for every year of the first five I'm wed. They'll be plenty of Gordons for *Dun Broc*! We've held this small scrap of Highland territory for over three hundred years, and we'll hold it another three hundred! The Grants will have to be content with *Grantholm*, unless, of course, Ian, ye're of a mind to go to court and serve Jamie Stewart."

Ian Grant looked mightily uncomfortable, as Alex had known he would. Alex often wondered what it was about him that bound his ambitious sister to this rather cowardly fellow. He shrugged.

Annabella glared at her brother, and he smiled back at her. She was a pretty woman with dark brown hair and sharp gray-blue eyes. In face, form, and coloring she reminded him of their mother though she had not their mother's sweetness of nature. "So," she said archly, "so yer off to claim yer bride. I can only hope the lass is willing, brother dear."

"Willing?" He looked at her as if she'd gone mad. "She's betrothed to me, Bella. Her father is willing, and that is the important thing. The lass has no choice in this matter."

His sister began to laugh softly. "Oh, Alex," she said to him, "how much ye've got to learn. How the lass feels is most important. This is the sixteenth century, brother! She may be betrothed to ye, but if she's nae willing . . ." Bella laughed again. "What's her name?" she asked.

"Velvet," he replied, still puzzled by his sister's laughter as well as her mocking words.

"Velvet," repeated Bella. "'Tis a soft cloth, a most biddable fabric. I can only hope yer lass is the same, brother."

"What is it ye hint at, sister?" he demanded irritably.

"I don't hint, Alex, I say it plainly. Ye know nothing of women! *Nothing at all*!"

"Christ's bloody bones, woman!" he exploded at her, and Ian Grant sat back so hard he came near to tipping his chair over. "Christ! I bedded my first wench when I was barely twelve! Not know women, indeed! Ye're daft, Bella! Pure daft!"

"Oh, ye know how to bed a lass, 'tis true, Alex," she shouted back at him, "but bedding a woman and knowing how to love one are two very different things! I just hope that yer Velvet is a patient lass and can teach ye that!" Bella stood up, her dark skirts swirling about her legs. "Come, Ian! We've a great deal of packing to do over the next few days!" Then she strode from the room, her husband following quickly in her wake.

With an impatient snort, Alex got up and stamped from the hall. Behind him the servants smiled conspiratorily at each other. They could barely wait to spread the news that the young earl was going to get married at long, long last. Oh, they, too, might have wished the bride to be a good Scots lass, but then new blood was always good for an old family like the *Gordons of Dun Broc*. Still, there would be many a broken heart in the district, for Alexander Gordon had always been generous with his favors as the many bairns with Gordon features attested to. The servants wondered if he'd continue that custom or if he'd be true to his wife. Only time would tell, but none of them thought that the earl was the sort of man to confine himself to one woman.

Alex hurried to his library to open the box containing the miniatures. He was eager to see what the girl looked like. Though he had been bold in his speech to Annabella with regard to marrying the little English lass, what did he actually know about her? And whose fault was that, for he'd not given the child a thought in ten years' time. It discomfited him to realize that he was nervous. He hoped that the miniatures would give him some small advantage.

With clumsy fingers he yanked the lid open to reveal a tray lined in heavy black silk and fitted with oval indentations. Within each oval was a small miniature enclosed in a gilt frame. He picked up the first of the tiny paintings and, turning it over, saw written upon its back the words: *Velvet de Marisco, aged 5, 1578 A.D.* Turning the miniature back over, he stared at the child's face. It was an adorable one, still baby-round, with dimples at either corner of the mouth.

Alex smiled suddenly, remembering how the child had shyly hidden behind her beautiful mother's skirts until he had lured her out to sit upon his lap, his bait a fat sugarplum. She had thanked him in a soft, lisping voice, her eyes round and curious, before slipping from his knee and hurrying back to her mother. Later, however, he remembered seeing her playing with her cousins, ruling them all with a mixture of charm and temper, stamping her little kid-shod feet, her curls flying. A curious little minx, he had thought, amused.

Returning the miniature to its place, he picked up the next one in line and read the legend on the back. *Velvet de Marisco, aged 6, 1579 A.D.* The tiny paintings were obviously arranged by Velvet's age and the year. The last miniature in the top tray showed Velvet at age nine, and it was here he could note the beginning of a difference. The infant plumpness was fully gone from her face, and her hair, which had been so dark when she had been a wee girl, was somewhat lighter, as were her eyes.

Alex lifted the first tray out of the box, suddenly impatient to view the last miniature, painted almost a full year ago after the girl's fourteenth birthday. Seeing it, his mouth dropped open and he caught his breath, though not so much from surprise, for it had been obvious from the beginning that Velvet de Marisco would be a beauty. What he found so marvelous was the strong character in her face. It was a proud young face that clearly stated: *I know who I am;* and when her natural beauty was added—the fair skin with the wild-rose cheeks, the auburn hair, the clear, unwavering green eyes—the effect was somewhat overwhelming!

What kind of a lass was this? Alex wondered. He longed to hear her voice in speech and raised in laughter—and, he was startled to realize, in passion too. Was she educated? Was she a good rider? Did she enjoy music? He found he was anxious to know all these things and more, things that he could not even put into words yet. The correspondence between his father and Adam de Marisco had told him little, for once the two men had accomplished their goal of matching their children, they seemed to have lost interest in the entire situation. Here and there was a mention of Velvet, but not enough for Alex to learn the sort of person she might be.

He groaned to himself. Why had he not visited England since their betrothal? He might have taken the opportunity to get to know Velvet gradually, and she might even have fallen in love with him, or, at the very least, learned to like him.

Alex shook his head to clear it. The girl was betrothed to him and would be his wife whether they liked each other or not. It was proper that a father matched his daughter to suit himself, and that the daughter did her parent's bidding unquestioningly. Once she was his wife Velvet would bear his children uncomplainingly, and do his bidding without question as she had done her father's. That was a woman's lot.

Women needed a tight rein or else they ran wild. God only knew his sister, Annabella, was proof of that. He need have no regrets that he had neglected Velvet. It was enough they were betrothed.

Oh, he had visited Italy and France where the men often made fools of themselves over the women they loved; but that was not a Scotsman's way. A woman was made for a man's comfort: to bear his bairns so that his name might not die, to give him pleasure, and to warm his backside on a frosty night. His own mother had been a sweet and biddable woman who had openly adored his father and willingly done all that Angus Gordon had asked. With such an example to follow Alex wondered why Bella was so headstrong, but then that was Ian Grant's fault. If his brother-in-law had taken a switch to Bella's backside at the beginning of their marriage, she'd not be so forward today.

Alex didn't intend to make that mistake with his young wife once they were wed. He didn't actually hold with beating a woman, for he considered himself a civilized man; but he fully intended to impress upon his bride immediately at the start of their union that it was he would be master here at *Dun Broc, and* in every other aspect of their married life. He would never be ruled by his woman.

His amber-gold eyes strayed to the miniature he now held in his hand. Damn, but she was a beauty! This latest portrait showed dark auburn curls tumbling about soft shoulders and a budding young bosom. He smiled to himself. Her beauty was just another advantage to be enjoyed. He would write to Adam de Marisco tonight and send the message south tomorrow with one of his own people. He would follow his own messenger within the next few weeks since there was no use in delaying. The lass would be fifteen on the first of May, and although at the time of the betrothal the wedding had been set for the summer of Velvet's sixteenth year, that would now have to be changed. His father's untimely death made it imperative that he marry immediately. He needed a son and heir now! It was past time to claim that which had been promised to him that sunny English summer of 1578.

Alex smiled with self-satisfaction at the thought of the lovely girl who would soon grace his house, while about the towers of *Dun Broc* the last snowflakes of winter capered madly in the wild wind in silent celebration of what was to come.

The prospective bride was not nearly so welcoming of her proposed future. To begin with she could not even remember having a betrothed husband, since she had been so young when the match was formally made, the contracts signed, and the event celebrated. Staring at her beleaguered Uncle Conn, her mother's youngest brother, she angrily shouted her frustration with the topsy-turvy muddle her complacent life had suddenly become when the messenger from *Dun Broc* had arrived.

"*Betrothed husband?* What betrothed husband? I do not understand this at all, Uncle! I have no betrothed husband!" Velvet de Marisco looked furiously at Lord Bliss as if he were personally responsible for her high dudgeon.

Aiden St. Michael put a restraining hand on her husband's velvet-clad arm. "Let me, Conn," she pleaded softly.

He was openly relieved to have her take over. Velvet in a temper was far too much for him to handle.

"Velvet dearest," said Lady Bliss quietly, "perhaps you do not remember the incident, but I want you to think back. Think hard. When you were barely five years old, your parents betrothed you to the heir of the Earl of BrocCairn. The earl was an old friend of your papa's from his childhood, and the two of them thought it would be a wonderful thing if their families could be joined by blood. It was the summer that your grandparents came from France with practically all of your French relatives. Willow went into premature labor during the celebration and delivered your nephew, Henry, right here at *Queen's Malvern.* A few days later at the christening the Earl of BrocCairn was the baby's godfather, and you were allowed to carry the holy oil. Don't you remember? They say it was such a lovely family party!"

"Were you and Uncle Conn married then?" said Velvet. "Were you at this party?"

A shadow passed over Aiden's face for a moment, but then smiling, she said, "Yes, Velvet, Conn and I were married then, but we were not able to come to your betrothal party. Your mother often spoke of it, however. Try and remember."

Velvet furrowed her brow in genuine concentration. "I do remember Henry being born and carrying the oil, and that Grandmère and Grandpère were here. But, Aunt Aiden, I remember no betrothal! It cannot be true! Mama has always said that I should never marry without love!"

"I am quite sure the new earl will love you, Velvet," said her uncle helpfully, and his wife bit her lip to prevent her laughter.

"But I may not love him!" came the explosion. "Oh, why are Mama and Papa not here now? They have been gone over two years! They *must* come home soon, Uncle! I shall marry no one until they do! And even then I shall marry no one unless I am in love!" With a flounce of her silk skirts, Velvet stamped from the room.

"Oh, Lord." Aiden St. Michael sighed. "Your sister Skye *would* be away. What are we to do, Conn? I don't have to tell you what your niece is like when she sets her mind against something. Why did Adam and Skye plan such a long voyage, before Velvet was settled in her own home?"

"They didn't *plan* the trip, my love. They were asked by Her Majesty to undertake this voyage in order to ascertain the possibility of England's opening trade with the Grand Mughal. The Portuguese have a very strong grip on India right now, and its riches are beyond belief. Why should only the Portuguese, and the Spanish, who control them, profit? They are rich enough!"

"But why not send one of the large trading companies? Why the O'Malley-Small fleet?" Aiden was curious for she was descended from a family of London merchants.

"There were several reasons, I suspect," Conn replied. "For one thing the O'Malley-Small shipping company is small and wealthy, but holds no official position with Her Majesty, so they won't arouse the Portugueses' suspicions.

Also, the fact that Skye is a member of the old faith may be an advantage since the Jesuits are strongly involved in the Portuguese colony in India and have even insinuated themselves in the Grand Mughal's court."

"I still don't understand why Skye and Adam had to go. Robbie Small has been doing all the voyaging for years now."

Conn smiled at his sweet wife. "Robbie is growing old, and my sister had been landlocked since her return to England," he said. "Up until they came home from France, Skye always lived near the sea, but a condition of her return was that she must live here in the heartland of England. The queen, wily wench that she is, would never again allow my sister to be a threat to her. Still, when this voyage was proposed, Her Majesty insisted that Skye go. Bess must have needed her badly." Conn chuckled.

"More than likely the queen felt such a voyage with a beautiful noblewoman in evidence wouldn't be considered threatening by the Portuguese, or even taken seriously," Aiden remarked wisely.

"By God, you could be right!" Conn said. "Ah, William Cecil and the queen are a clever pair. But then Skye probably knew their motives but cared not as long as she could feel a deck beneath her feet again and smell the salt breeze in her nostrils. Besides, my sister always loved a good adventure, O'Malley that she is."

"Her absence, however," noted Lady Bliss, "leaves us with the problem of her wayward daughter. What are we to do, Conn?"

"Go after Velvet, my love, while I think this thing out," Conn said, pouring himself a healthy dollop of good Archambault Burgundy, then lowering himself into a large comfortable chair by the fire so that he might consider this thorny new development. He didn't even hear Aiden close the door behind her as she hurried off to find Velvet.

Lord Bliss ran a big hand through his hair and sighed. When his sister, Skye, and her husband, Adam de Marisco, had asked him to keep an eye on their only beloved child more than two years ago, it had seemed a simple enough thing. He knew that although Velvet was spoilt and headstrong she would be safe here on her parents' estate. She had, in fact, spent most of her life at *Queen's Malvern*, except for several long summers in France at her father's chateau, *Belle Fleurs*. It hadn't even been necessary for Conn to bring Velvet into his own home, the lands of which bordered those of *Queen's Malvern*. The child had stayed on in her own house with Dame Cecily, Robbie Small's sister, her nursemaid, and all the servants who had known her since babyhood. Everything had run smoothly until that blasted letter had arrived!

Conn swallowed the remaining wine in his goblet, then absently twirled the bejeweled gilt cup in his hands as he puzzled out what to do next. He was a big, bluff man with midnight black hair and gray-green eyes. Born an O'Malley of Innisfana, he had come to England with his sister almost fifteen years ago. As the youngest O'Malley of them all, he had been wise enough to realize that there was nothing for him in Ireland. So with no more than his extraordinary good looks, his charm, and a quick wit to recommend him, he had arrived at Elizabeth Tudor's court. These small assets had been enough, however, to earn him the queen's favor, for Bess Tudor appreciated a handsome man with a silvery tongue. Conn had been appointed to the queen's own personal guard, the *Gentlemen Pensioners*, and from there he had begun his climb up the social ladder. The little share of gold he received from his elder brothers' privateering ventures was invested in his clever sister Skye's trading company. Soon he was a wealthy man.

Money and his position in the *Gentlemen Pensioners* overcame the drawback of his Irish heritage in the minds of the members of court. Conn held the queen's favor so strongly that even when he addressed her as "Bess" he was never reprimanded. He was charming and roguish without being unscrupulous. He was considered a very eligible fellow and actually had his pick of any number of lovely young ladies and restive matrons. But Conn, rather like a large bumblebee, spent a great deal of his time flitting from flower to flower rather than settling down.

Overconfidence, however, has brought many a man down, and suddenly Conn O'Malley found himself in the center of a rather naughty scandal involving a noble lady, her twin daughters, and an ambassador's wife. With the injured gentlemen involved both demanding the queen's justice, Elizabeth Tudor had no choice but to send "*the handsomest man at court*," as Conn was known, from her charmed circle. Before she did so, however, she tempered her judgment with a final kindness. She married Conn to a royal ward, Mistress Aiden St. Michael.

Aiden was at court as a maid of honor, having been placed in the queen's custody at her father's death. When Elizabeth Tudor wanted a bride for her favorite, she had remembered that Aiden's lands bordered those of Queen's Malvern, the estate to which she had exiled Conn's sister, Skye, and her husband, Adam.

The St. Michaels were not of the bluest blood, nor were they considered of first-class eligibility in the marriage market. Aiden's great-grandfather had been a wealthy London merchant who had done a great personal favor for Henry VII, and had been rewarded with a title and estate for his troubles. Three generations later Aiden St. Michael was all that was left of her family, and the one condition that her dying father, Lord Bliss, had begged of the queen was that the bridegroom she eventually chose for his daughter would take over his name. The queen had agreed, for it was not an unusual request, and as far as Conn O'Malley was concerned, it was a reasonable one. There were, after all, shiploads of O'Malleys. Conn would not be missed at all, and he would have a title in the bargain.

Aiden St. Michael was not a great beauty. She was taller than the average woman, and somewhat bigger boned. Her skin was fair, and she had copper-colored hair and gray eyes. She was educated far beyond most girls of her day, even more than her bridegroom. But Aiden was bright and amusing, and she loved Conn O'Malley with her whole heart. Their early years together had been difficult, but now they lived the kind of life Conn had always dreamed of living. They were wealthy and the parents of a fine family.

Life had gotten *too* comfortable for them, he thought somewhat wryly. So comfortable that when they had agreed to look after his niece, he had believed that it wouldn't disturb their peaceful existence. Conn grinned to himself. He really should have known better. Velvet was, after all, Skye's daughter, and hadn't his big sister been the hell-raiser of all time?

He shifted himself in the chair. The message addressed to Lord de Marisco had arrived only yesterday. Dame Cecily had brought it to him herself, for, having recognized the seal of BrocCairn, she suspected that it was an important communiqué. The old woman well remembered Velvet's betrothal ten years before and how worried Skye had been about it. Skye, remembering her own childhood betrothal, which had culminated in a disastrous first marriage for her, hadn't wanted to risk the chance that her daughter would suffer as she had. Still, Adam had wanted it so very much, and he had promised his wife that should Velvet and young Gordon not suit once she was grown, the match would be called off. Velvet was, he reminded his wife, *his only child, his beloved daughter.* Skye had at last agreed, for she loved her husband and knew he would never hurt Velvet.

Conn had debated about opening the missive addressed to his brother-in-law. Adam was probably still some months from returning, and the communiqué might be important. Conn felt that Adam would certainly understand. Breaking the seal Conn opened the parchment. Quickly scanning the message, he was shocked to learn that both the old earl, his wife, and his second son were all deceased. He was equally disconcerted to learn that Alexander Gordon, now twenty-eight, wished to marry Velvet as quickly as possible so that he might sire a male heir, there being no others in his family to carry on the Gordon of BrocCairn name. The letter was almost brusque in its tone.

Astounded by this turn of events, Conn nonetheless understood the gentleman's position. Still, he didn't feel he had the right to force Velvet into marriage with a virtual stranger. He was not her parent, and at that thought he heaved a mighty sigh of relief. He knew his sister's feelings on the subject, and he also knew that Adam would not want his only child married off willy-nilly despite the official betrothal agreement. It was not Conn's responsibility, and yet it was.

The earl would be arriving from *Dun Broc* within the next few weeks, but Adam and Skye were most inaccessible. The earl was within his rights to press for an immediate wedding, the betrothal having been officially celebrated. It was all very neat and quite legal. The only thing not considered or taken into account in the situation was Mistress Velvet de Marisco, a most unwilling bride.

"Uncle Conn?" Velvet had slipped quietly back into the room, and, coming across the floor, she settled herself into his lap as she had done so often when she was just a wee girl. He noted that she was no longer so wee, for she stood five feet nine inches tall in her stockinged feet.

"Ah, Velvet lass. Now don't go trying to wheedle me, poppet. I'm in a quandary about what to do as it is."

"But I don't want to get married, Uncle Conn! I want to stay at *Queen's Malvern* with Mama and Papa." Her reasoning still sounded like that of a protected child.

"All girls marry eventually, Velvet. You're going to be fifteen in a week, sweeting. Remember that your mama was first married at fifteen. 'Tis no great thing."

"Mama hated her first husband!" Velvet said explosively. "She says he was a horrible beast, and that is why I should *never* marry without love! Mama promised me, Uncle Conn! I will not marry without love, and I will not marry without my parents here!"

Conn shifted his niece in his lap so that he might look at her. God's bones! he thought, startled. Her logic was childish, but she certainly didn't look like a child! When had she gotten so beautiful? She had always been a pretty little girl, but the face now before him was incredible in its perfection. There was no sweetness about it as there was with his sister's face. Velvet's was elegant and oval in shape; her forehead and sharply sculpted cheekbones high; her nose her father's long Norman one; her well-spaced eyes almost almond-shaped and green. They were marvelous eyes with sooty lashes so thick that they tangled amongst themselves; eyes that threatened to snare any man foolish enough to gaze into them too deeply.

Velvet's chin was small and square, Conn noted. Her mouth was wide and sensual like her father's, but she had Skye's fair skin. He marveled at her hair, for though she had been dark as a child, it had become a deep rich auburn as she grew older. Her French grandmama allowed that her own mama had had auburn hair. Velvet's hair was a luxuriant mop full of long, silky tresses that was greatly admired and envied by her cousins. Conn decided that though she had the family features she frankly looked more like herself than like either of her parents. He was also suddenly very discomfited to notice that she had developed a rather lush female form for all he still thought of her as a child.

"I'm sure your mother never meant for you to marry without love, Velvet. As I remember the marriage agreement, you were not to wed until you were sixteen. But the earl, because of the deaths of his father and brother, must marry quickly now and beget heirs," Conn explained.

"*Marry? Beget heirs?* Uncle, I haven't even been to court yet! I know that Mama meant for me to have a little time at court before I married. I've never been anywhere or done anything in my entire life! My whole world has been here at *Queen's Malvern*, or at *Belle Fleurs*, or at my grandparents' chateau at *Archambault*. My whole social life has consisted of family parties. I've never been to London, nor have I even seen Paris! I will not be rushed willy-nilly into marriage before I have had a chance of doing these things! This wild Scotsman will not carry me off to that cold, wet land of his to imprison me in some damned dank castle simply to have babies! I won't go! I won't! You cannot let him take me! We *must* wait until Mama and Papa get back. It won't be long now, I'm sure!" Her young voice was edged with panic.

Conn understood her plea. She had been very sheltered by her parents who adored her so very much. Velvet's very birth had been a miracle, and until this trip neither Skye nor Adam had been content to let her out of their sight.

"We will explain everything to the earl when he comes to *Queen's Malvern*, Velvet. I'm sure he'll understand and be reasonable," Lord Bliss promised, silently hoping that he was right.

Velvet kissed her uncle's smooth cheek, then slipped from his lap. Though she led him to believe otherwise by her docile submission, she had no intention of sitting quietly and waiting for fate to sweep her up. She knew very well that if she allowed the earl to make the decision he would insist on celebrating the marriage immediately. She had seen how men looked at her of late, and it would be no different with this betrothed husband she had suddenly found she had. She was not that big a fool! Men thought they owned women.

"I am not getting married," she muttered mutinously to herself. "At least not yet, and not ever unless I love the man!" Then she smiled mischievously. Uncle Conn had seemed so very relieved, innocently believing that everything was settled. Sweet old Dame Cecily thought Velvet was an angel, and would never suspect that she could be devious. There was no one to bother or interfere with her for several days, of that she was certain. It was time enough to put into action the plan she had been thinking of ever since she had digested the news of the Earl of BrocCairn's impending arrival.

Although Velvet's sister, Deirdre, was six years her senior, they had always been very close. Deirdre and her husband, Lord Blackthorn, lived just a few miles away at *Blackthorn Priory*. On the first of May they would be entertaining the queen, who was beginning her annual summer's progress. Velvet had never met the queen that she could remember, although her mother said Elizabeth Tudor had seen her as a baby. The English queen was one of her two godmothers, the other being Queen Margot of France.

Deirdre had been half-promising for months that Velvet could come and get a peek at the queen when Elizabeth stopped overnight at *Blackthorn Priory*. Velvet's scheme involved meeting the queen and becoming one of her maids of honor. The Earl of BrocCairn could scarcely go against Elizabeth Tudor's wishes and take a royal maid of honor from court without the sovereign's permission, and Velvet knew the queen's attitude toward gentlemen stealing her maids away. She chuckled to herself, quite pleased with her own cleverness. In the queen's service she would be safe until her parents came home and the matter of this betrothal was straightened out.

"I'm going to ride over to *Blackthorn Priory* to get a glimpse of Her Majesty," Velvet told Dame Cecily on the morning of the first of May. She had just come in from gathering an armful of flowers, and they were still wet with the dew. "Perhaps I may be of help to my sister, for she is surely very busy right now."

"What a love you are, Velvet pet," returned the old lady, "but have your forgotten, child? It's your birthday. Do you want to spend it helping Deirdre with last-minute chores?"

"Deirdre is breeding again, Dame Cecily. She has been very tired of late, and I am sure she will welcome my help today. Besides, I really do want to see the queen. I never have, and here I am fifteen!"

Dame Cecily chuckled. "Run along then, child, and have your look at Bess Tudor," she said. "With your parents still away 'twill not be much of a birthday for you again this year, I fear."

Velvet almost shouted with joy as she rode the few miles between her home and her sister's. It was an incredibly lovely morning, a perfect May day, and her big chestnut stallion galloped along easily. She reached the hall without incident and, slipping down from her horse's back, tossed the reins carelessly to a waiting groom.

Inside, the priory was just as she had expected. Chaos reigned everywhere, and in its midst was Deirdre Blakeley, Lady Blackthorn, looking harassed and forlorn by turns, her fair skin flushed, her black hair half undone from its chignon.

Deirdre's blue eyes lit up at the sight of her youngest sister, and Velvet felt a twinge of sadness, for Deirdre looked so very much like their mother.

"Velvet poppet, thank goodness you've come! I'm at my wit's end, and the queen is due by two o'clock!" Deirdre exclaimed.

Velvet flung an arm about her older sister. "I came to help, sister. You have only to tell me what it is you need done and I will do it."

Deirdre lowered her slender form, with its very distended belly, into a chair. "I'm not sure where to begin, Velvet. I've never entertained the queen before. I don't even know how she knew of *Blackthorn Priory*, but her secretary wrote that she had heard of our fine gardens and wished to see them. How could she have heard of our gardens? We are not a part of the court and neither is anyone else in the family except for Robin, and he withdrew from it after Alison's death. I doubt Robin made any remarks to the queen about our gardens. Gardens are not our brother's métier."

"Don't fuss so, Deirdre. 'Tis a great honor the queen does you and John. She rarely ventures out of the home counties to come to Worcestershire."

"Better she hadn't decided to venture this far!" said Deirdre irritably. "Do you have any idea what it costs to entertain royalty? Nay, how could you? You're just a child!"

"I wish that Scots earl claiming to be my betrothed understood that," muttered Velvet, but her elder sister didn't hear her for she was too concerned with her own problems.

"It will cost us a small fortune to have the queen and her court here. Of course, John wrote to Her Majesty's household controller, Sir James Crofts, that we could not entertain the entire court. The priory is simply not big enough for all those people. Do you know what he wrote back? That Her Majesty would only expect us to put up fifty or so of her people within the house and that the rest would be housed in tents upon our lawns! Can you imagine what the lawns are going to look like after five hundred people, their horses, and baggage trains have trampled upon them? It will take us five years to restore them!" She shook her head in an agitated fashion. "I don't mean to sound inhospitable, Velvet, but what will we get out of all of this besides debts—and the privilege of saying that the queen stayed in the Rose Bedchamber, which of course will have to be renamed the Queen's Room now. She won't even be sleeping in the bed there since she travels with her own and will sleep in no other."

Velvet listened to her sister with a sense of growing amazement. She had never known Deirdre to be this way. Deirdre was the serene daughter. She had never fussed like Willow or Velvet herself.

"It's all too much," wailed Deirdre, "and I'm sure that we have neither enough food or drink for such a huge gathering. We shall be disgraced, I am certain."

"Tell me what's been done so far, Deirdre," Velvet said soothingly. She could see that her sister was growing more nervous by the minute.

"The whole house has been turned out," Deirdre began. "The Rose Bedchamber has been completely redone. Heaven only knows where I'm going to put the rest of her attendants! Thank the Lord they will only be here for one night. God's bones! I only hope I have enough food for the whole company!"

"What have you laid aside?"

Deirdre furrowed her brow in concentration. "There are six dozen barrels of oysters packed in ice, twenty-four suckling pigs, three wild boars, trout from the river, twelve legs of lamb, another dozen sides of beef, six roe deer, and six stags; two dozen hams, five hundred lark pastries for tonight, capons in ginger sauce, goose, at least three dozen, larded ducks, pigeon pies and rabbit pies, a hundred apiece. Every house in the neighborhood has baked for us." She stopped to draw a breath. "There will be bowls of new lettuce, cress, radishes, scallions, artichokes in white wine, carrots glazed in honey, and enough bread to feed an army! There are molded jellies; marzipan of every imaginable color; fruit tarts from dried apples, peaches, apricots, and plums; custards; and the first strawberries of the season with clotted cream!" she finished triumphantly. Then her brow puckered. "Will it be enough?" she fretted.

"'Tis not elegant, but I suspect 'twill serve," Velvet teased. "You've not forgotten the wines?"

"Nay, there are a full two hundred casks each of both red and white from *Archambault*, bless your grandparents, as well as a hundred barrels of Devon cider, which Robin sent from *Lynmouth*. Then, too, we have our own October ale."

"Well," observed Velvet, "if they don't stuff themselves with all the foods you're offering, they will most certainly drown in the drink!"

"Oh, how I wish Mother were here instead off in the Indies!" Deirdre wailed.

"You don't need her, sister. You have done everything just as Mother would have if the queen were visiting her."

"Oh, Velvet! What would I do without you, little sister? You will stay overnight, won't you?"

Velvet's heart skipped a beat. "But where will you put me, Deirdre? I would love to see the queen, but let me just peek at her from among the servants and then be on my way home."

"No! You must stay with me Velvet! I can't get through this without you, especially in my present condition. You can sleep in my dressing room."

"Who is to sleep in your dressing room?" demanded John Blakeley as he came into the sunny morning room where the two sisters were seated.

"Velvet," replied his wife. "I want her to stay for the queen's visit, John."

"By all means, my dear," replied Lord Blackthorn as he bent to place a kiss upon Deirdre's brow. "The queen is Velvet's godmama as I recall, and it would not hurt for her to renew her acquaintance with her now." He walked over to the table and poured himself a goblet of wine from a crystal decanter. "A friend at court cannot hurt a lass." He looked up and smiled at Velvet.

"Thank you, my lord, and I believe you are correct in your observations," Velvet answered demurely, curtsying to her brother-in-law. Lord Blackthorn grinned at her over his wife's head and winked conspiratorily. God's bones, thought Velvet, what does he suspect? He can't possibly know what I plan! *He can't!* Her brother-in-law's next words gave her cause for more worry.

"When is the earl arriving at *Queen's Malvern*, Velvet?"

"His letter only said he would arrive within a few weeks' time, my lord. It did not give a date. Most thoughtless."

"Well, I do not imagine it will be within the next day or so, little sister, so you are quite welcome at *Blackthorn Priory* for the queen's visit. It will do Deirdre good to have you with us." He turned his attention back to his wife. "Come, my dear, I want you to rest before we must greet our royal guest. I have personally inspected all of your arrangements and, as always, Deirdre, everything is perfection. You are a fine wife."

"You see!" Velvet crowed with delight. "Did I not tell you, silly goose?"

Deirdre blushed with pleasure at her husband's words, then said to her younger sister, "Send one of the grooms to *Queen's Malvern* to bring back proper clothes for you, Velvet." She stood up heavily, her seventh month of pregnancy weighing upon her. "I think I shall rest, John."

He escorted her from the room, and Velvet, after writing a hasty note to Dame Cecily, dispatched it with a *Blackthorn* groom. She then sat down to gloat quietly. She felt no remorse at using her sister to gain her way in this matter. Someone had to take the situation in hand, and her Uncle Conn was obviously not about to do so. Despite her logical protests against this marriage, she sensed she would still find herself wed to the arrogant-sounding Earl of BrocCairn before her parents returned from their voyage, by which time it would be too late. She needed a powerful protector, and there was none more powerful than England's own queen. She smiled at herself, a grin of smug satisfaction.

"Ah, I knew that you were planning some mischief," Lord Blackthorn said as he reentered the room.

"You imagine it, my lord," came her quick denial.

"Nay, Velvet lass, I do not imagine it. I hope you do not think to appeal to the queen in this matter of your marriage. Elizabeth Tudor is a firm believer in parental authority and the keeping of contracts." He looked closely at her, but Velvet's face was devoid of expression.

"John, you must think me appallingly ill-bred to believe that I should attempt to involve Her Majesty in a family matter," Velvet said tartly. "I have no intention of discussing my marriage with the queen. I came to *Blackthorn* today to help Deirdre if I could; and, if I may remind you, my sister promised me months ago that I could come to see the queen when she stopped here. If you think I seek to cause some sort of scandal, however, then I shall tell Deirdre that I have a headache and go home to *Queen's Malvern.*"

Lord Blackthorn could not rid himself of the feeling that his young sister-in-law had some scheme in mind, but Velvet was not a liar, and if she said she would not discuss her marriage with the queen then he believed her.

"Nay, lass, I want you to stay. I simply don't want to find myself in the middle of a family argument. I don't want to endanger my position with your parents. You know that they worried at first that I was not right for Deirdre."

Velvet felt a small twinge of guilt at his words. Her family had come to *Queen's Malvern* when she was barely two years of age. Deirdre had been eight then, and John Blakeley twenty-eight. His first wife was still living and his life was a misery. Maria Blakeley was totally mad, and had been since the stillbirth of her only child ten months after her marriage. For the past eight years, she had been confined to her apartments where she raved and wept but showed no signs of either recovering or dying.

At first Lord Blackthorn was drawn to Deirdre because the child his wife had miscarried was a girl and would have been Deirdre's age. Deirdre's own life had been a rather topsy-turvy one, and though it had finally become settled, she who had been fatherless for most of her life suddenly discovered that she now had two father figures. Adam de Marisco was a loving stepfather, but he was unable to conceal that Velvet, his only child, was the light of his life. Had John Blakeley not been there for Deirdre, her life would have been a sadder one. When his love turned from paternal to passionate, and her love grew from a child's to a woman's, neither was ever sure.

Maria Blakeley escaped from her captivity and drowned herself in the estate lake at the priory when Deirdre was thirteen. A year and a day later, Lord Blackthorn asked Deirdre to be his wife and was joyously accepted by her.

Deirdre's mother and stepfather, however, were not pleased, and at first refused their permission. They felt John Blakeley was far too old for Deirdre Burke. Lord Blackthorn pleaded desperately, for he was a man in love. Deirdre pined away as more suitable suitors were paraded before her, only to be weepingly rejected. In the end the lovers' persistence won out, and they were married four months after the bride's sixteenth birthday. For a time afterwards Skye and Adam de Marisco worried that Deirdre might not be happy. Only just before they had sailed had they become convinced that John Blakeley was the perfect man for the gentle Deirdre.

"I swear to you, John, that I shall cause you no trouble," Velvet promised him now.

"Go along then, lass, and see to your sister. She's too excited to sleep, but she's lying down."

With great control, Velvet walked calmly from the room, then fled up the staircase to Deirdre's apartments. To her great relief, her sister had finally fallen asleep, and Velvet settled herself quietly in the dressing room. Mama and Papa weren't going to be angry at her for avoiding a quick marriage to the earl. *They* would understand why she had done what she was going to do. After all, she hadn't said she wasn't going to honor her betrothal. She simply wanted time to get to know the earl, and she wanted to wait until her parents returned from their voyage to make her decision. It wasn't a great deal to ask, despite what her uncle and her brother-in-law thought. Velvet closed her eyes and dozed.

She was awakened by a maidservant bringing her clothing into the room. "Is it time to dress?" she asked groggily.

"Aye, Mistress Velvet. Lodema has prepared baths for both you and m'lady." Lodema was Deirdre's fiercely protective tiring woman.

Velvet arose and the servant girl helped her to disrobe so that she might wash. Deirdre was already happily splashing in her oaken tub by the fire in the other room, while Lodema grumbled fussily at her.

"All this washing, and in your state. 'Tis unhealthy, I tell you, m'lady."

"Nonsense!" The nap had restored Deirdre's good humor and confidence. "Hurry, Velvet, or your water will be chilled," she called to her younger sister.

Velvet came shyly from the dressing room, somewhat embarrassed by her nudity. She quickly got into the tub, then wrinkled her nose in delight. "Gillyflowers! Oh, Deirdre, you remembered!"

"Hyacinth for me and gillyflowers for you. Of course I remember. I was twelve when Mama gave me my own scent, and you cried and cried until she chose one for you also, even though you were much too young for a fragrance."

Velvet giggled. "I remember," she said, "but I only wanted to be like my big sister, and you had a perfume and I didn't."

"Fiddlesticks!" replied Deirdre firmly. "You were a spoilt minx, Velvet, and you still are!" Then she chuckled. "But, damn me, little sister, if you don't have charm! I've never known anyone so able to get people to give you your way and yet never feel resentful about it."

"Are you planning to greet the queen in your shift, m'lady, because that's all you're going to have time to get into unless you get out of that tub!" Lodema grumbled at her mistress, and when Velvet giggled again, the tiring woman turned a baleful eye on the girl. "As for you, mistress, you'd best wash yourself quickly, or you'll be joining your sister in a chemise! Hurry along now, both of you!"

The two finished bathing quickly, then left their tubs to be dried and powdered by two waiting undermaids. Velvet dressed in her silken undergarments swiftly, not liking to be nude before unfamiliar servants. She glanced at her sister's protruding belly and thought that even so Deirdre was the most beautiful creature, almost their mother's mirror image.

Their gowns were brought; both sisters had chosen to wear velvet as the day was cool. Deirdre's dress was a rich ruby red with an underskirt of white satin embroidered in silver thread. Silver and white puffed and slashed sleeves also showed through the rich velvet. About her neck was a strand of marvelous pearls to which was fastened a heart carved from a single large ruby, and in her ears Deirdre wore pear-shaped pearls that dangled from small rubies. Her black hair was simply dressed in a French chignon at the nape of her neck and fastened with jeweled pins; upon her slender fingers were several beautiful rings.

Velvet's gown was similar to her sister's in design, with a charming bell skirt. It was a rich forest green in color, its satin underskirt a lighter green embroidered in gold thread; the chemisette showing through the sleeve slashes was a golden color. The dress was a birthday gift from her aunt and uncle, and was the only really fashionable one she possessed. Her lovely auburn hair fell in tempting ringlets about her shoulders, and around her neck she wore a gold chain from which dangled a carved and heart-shaped gold pendant that was actually a locket.

Deirdre loaned her little sister delicate little freshwater pearl earbobs, for Velvet, being considered too young, had little jewelry. Lodema, casting a critical eye upon her mistress's sibling, directed an undermaid to bring her two full-blown golden roses from a vase. She then twisted the flowers together with green ribbons and affixed them on one side of Velvet's head.

Standing back, she noted sharply, "There now! You'll not disgrace us."

Deirdre and Velvet hurried from the apartment and flew downstairs to where Lord Blackthorn awaited them. Velvet felt like an intruder upon an intimate moment as her elder sister brushed an imaginary piece of lint from her smiling husband's deep blue doublet. John was a very handsome man, Velvet thought, and obviously in his full prime. He stood just a head taller than his wife, and had a well-molded figure that was devoid of fat. If anything he was a bit on the slender side. He had a full head of deep brown hair that was well sprinkled with silver, and he kept it close-cropped. His eyes were of a much lighter blue than Deirdre's; his face was very narrow and aristocratic with a slim nose, well-spaced eyes, and thin lips. Despite he austere appearance, he was a man who smiled easily and appreciated a good jest better than most.

John Blakeley's family had owned *Blackthorn Priory* since the days of William the Conqueror. The priory and its lands had been given to the nobleman who had captured it for William from its inhabitants, rebellious Saxon monks. He was the Sieur Blakeley. The Blakeleys were loyal Englishmen who loved their land and protected it fiercely. They had fought for England alongside Richard I and Edward, the Black Prince, but never had they involved themselves in any court or its politics. It had been their salvation.

Never had an English monarch visited *Blackthorn Priory* until Elizabeth Tudor had learned—Heaven only knows how, thought John Blakeley—of *Blackthorn Priory*'s beautiful gardens, which were justly famous throughout the countryside. The gardens, begun over two hundred years ago, had been lovingly tended and added to by each Lady Blackthorn right down to Deirdre, who, like her late grandmother O'-Malley, was a lover and collector of rosebushes. The gardens, however, contained not only roses but every flower known to the English, including some beds of rare Persian and Turkish tulip bulbs smuggled in from the East by O'Malley ships. There was also a wonderfully clever boxwood maze, and the queen was known to enjoy mazes. At this moment, the gardens were colorfully ablaze with late tulips, narcissus, primroses, and columbine. Elizabeth should not be disappointed.

Suddenly, up the carefully raked gravel driveway of *Blackthorn Priory* raced the head gardener's barefoot son, crying out: "Her is coming! Her is coming!"

"Get off the drive, boy! Get off the drive!" shouted the priory's fussy majordomo, and the lad scooted onto the green lawn, making a rude noise in the direction of the majordomo as he went.

The younger maidservants, lined up in order of importance, giggled, only to be silenced by a severe look from the housekeeper. The entire staff of *Blackthorn Priory*, from highest servant to the lowly potboy, stood washed and waiting for a glimpse of the queen and her court.

For what seemed a long moment, there was no sound, not even the chirp of a bird, but then faintly on the wind came the sound of jingling bells and laughing voices. The servants tensed and strained their necks to get the first sighting of the court. At last, as if by magic, around the curve in the drive appeared Elizabeth Tudor and her court, and those waiting and watching let out a collective sigh of delight.

The first rider was mounted on a fine chestnut gelding and bore before him the ceremonial sword of state. Next came the queen riding upon a magnificent snow-white stallion with the Earl of Essex, her Master of the Horse, who rode a beautiful black gelding and held the queen's bridle as part of his duties. All around Elizabeth were members of her guard, who were followed by the lord treasurer, the lord chancellor, and other officers of the state: the household treasurer; Sir Francis Knollys, the queen's favorite cousin; Lord Hundston who was lord steward; Sir James Crofts, the household controller; the other household officials and menials; and of course the court.

The queen was attired in the most elegant fashion. Her overgown was of black velvet edged with tiny pearls along the hem and the sides of the gown separation. Interspersed along the rows of pearls were red silk bows tied with jet beads, alternating with black silk bows tied with garnet beads. Her shoulder rolls were similarly decorated, as was her stomacher, which was festooned at its point with a red silk bow from which hung a large teardrop-shaped pearl. Beneath the overgown was a white satin undergown edged in lace. The same white satin showed through the slashes in her black velvet sleeves. About the queen's neck was a small starched white lace neck ruff, beneath which hung eight rows of pearls that dripped down the black velvet gown front with its merry cherry-red bows. The queen wore a bright auburn wig that was topped by a soft, round black velvet cap from which bravely fluttered white feathers held down firmly by a bright red ruby clip. Her hands upon the reins of her mount were sheathed in perfumed white leather gloves embroidered with pearls, garnets, and jet.

Around Elizabeth Tudor, upon equally spirited and prancing horses, were her gentlemen and ladies, all clothed just as luxuriously and colorfully as if to complement their monarch. On either side of the queen rode gaily clad gentlemen, Sir Walter Ralegh and young Essex being nearest her. Ralegh was currently the captain of the Queen's Gentlemen Pensioners, her personal bodyguard. Essex, as her Master of the Horse, held the position once performed by his stepfather, the Earl of Leicester, Robert Dudley. Dudley, though still the queen's dear friend, had lost some of her favor on his marriage to her cousin, Lettice Knollys, though she still held a deep fondness for him.

As the horses came to a stop before the priory, Lord Blackthorn stepped forward to lift the queen from her mount and, having done so, knelt to pay his homage. Both Deirdre and Velvet curtsied low.

"As pretty a pair of pigeons as I've ever seen," murmured the Earl of Essex to Sir Walter. "Sisters, d'you think?"

Ralegh said nothing, seeing the queen's head stiffen as she caught Essex's words, but he did grin at the earl, his moustache waggling in appreciation.

"Welcome to *Blackthorn Priory*, Your Majesty," said John Blakeley. "We know not what we have done to deserve such honor, madame, but may your stay be a pleasant one." He signaled to his head groom, who immediately led forth an exquisite rare Arabian mare, pale gold in color. Upon the mare's back was a silver saddle bejeweled with pearls, topazes, blue zircons, rubies, and small diamonds. The horse's bridle was also silver. John Blakeley arose and said, "For you, madame, with devotion and great admiration. I count myself fortunate to be living in your reign."

The queen's eyes swept over the mare and her accoutrements, warming at this Midland lord's great generosity. His flattering tongue had also given her pleasure, for she believed his words to be from the heart. He had naught else to gain from her by them, not being a member of the court. Graciously, she held out her hand and said, "Our thanks for your most beautiful gift, my lord."

John Blakeley kissed the hand presented to him. "My wife has a way with animals, madame, and has schooled the beast herself. You'll find she has an excellent gait and is a fine jumper. She seems to have been created by almighty God Himself for the sole purpose of hunting. 'Twas why I chose her."

Elizabeth Tudor smiled, well pleased, for there was nothing she enjoyed better than the hunt. "Present me to your family, Lord Blackthorn!" she commanded him. "I would meet this lady who can school horses so well."

John Blakeley took Deirdre by the hand and led her forward to the queen. "My wife, Deirdre, Your Majesty."

Deirdre curtsied again.

"God's foot!" Elizabeth Tudor swore, staring hard at Deirdre. "You're Skye O'Malley's daughter, Lady Blackthorn, aren't you?"

"Her daughter, and Lord Burke's," said Deirdre, "but I remember not my father, madame. He died when I was quite young." She smiled. "I should like to present my youngest sister to you, Mistress Velvet de Marisco."

Velvet stepped forward and curtsied prettily, making sure to keep her eyes modestly lowered.

The queen reached out and gently raised Velvet's head up, cupping the girl's chin in her elegantly gloved hand. "Rise, dear child, and let me look upon you. What a pretty thing you are! I have not seen you since you were a tiny baby, but then you would have been too young to remember. How old are you now, Velvet de Marisco?"

"I am fifteen today, Your Majesty," said Velvet sweetly.

"Today?" the queen exclaimed. "*This* is your birthday?"

"Aye, Your Majesty, and I might have been May Queen in our village, but I far preferred to come to the priory to meet you." It was said with such a lack of guile that Elizabeth Tudor smiled.

"We must give you a gift then, child. I am your godmother, Velvet de Marisco. Before you were born in France I was much angered by your parents' behavior, for they had not obtained my permission to wed. Your clever mother made me your godmother in an effort to placate me, but I never knew your exact birthdate. Tell me, my dear, what can I give you?" The queen smiled more broadly at Velvet's wide eyes and little gasp.

Velvet was stunned. Here was incredible good fortune, and she could scarcely believe it was hers. Now she would not have to find a way to wheedle the queen, but she must still be quick and clever. Her hands flew to her cheeks in a gesture of innocent surprise. "Madame," she gasped, "Oh, dear Majesty, I cannot think!"

Elizabeth Tudor smiled once again and patted the girl in a kindly fashion. "Within reason," she teased gently. "Remember I am merely queen of England."

Velvet composed herself and looked adoringly at the queen. "Madame, I have everything I could possibly want in this life but one thing. My parents have always been more than generous with me and of material treasures I lack none; but all my life I have dreamed of serving you, Your Majesty, of being one of your Maids of Honor. Can you give me my dream, madame? If you would truly gift me, then gift me with the privilege of serving you."

Lord Blackthorn squeezed his wife's hand to prevent her from speaking. He was filled with genuine admiration for his young sister-in-law's astuteness. She had not broken her promise to him and yet she was going to get her own way nonetheless.

"Dear child!" The queen's face was wreathed in smiles.

By tradition Elizabeth Tudor had eighteen female attendants. There were four Gentlewomen of the Bedchamber, older, married women of rank; eight Gentlewomen of the Privy Chamber, also married women of noble birth; and six Maids of Honor, young girls of noble families whose ambitious parents believed that by serving the queen honorably they might increase their value on the marriage market. These eighteen saw to the queen's wardrobe and toilette, her food, and all of her creature comforts within her private apartments. They were her closest companions.

The position of Maid of Honor was greatly sought after, and under normal circumstances the queen would have been forced to turn her godchild away since there would have been no opening available. By merest chance, however, one of the queen's maids of honor had just given birth to a child in the Maiden's Chamber. Enraged, Elizabeth Tudor had clapped both mother and child into the Tower along with the unfortunate father. The fact that the young people had been secretly wed for over a year did nothing to improve the queen's temper, or ease her outrage. Both sets of parents were in equal disfavor with Her Majesty for having spawned and raised such disobedient offspring.

The valued post the girl had forfeited would have been swiftly filled, but the queen was so annoyed by this latest episode of what she considered rampant immorality amongst her ladies, that no one dared broach the subject. Now here was this sweet and unspoilt child begging her innocent birthday boon of the queen.

Elizabeth Tudor, of course, did not let her sentimentality override the humor she saw in the situation. This child was the daughter of Skye O'Malley. Skye O'Malley, that outrageous, prideful, rebellious, stubborn, haughty, and unsubmissive woman who had dared to do battle with England's queen. That impossible creature who had had the effrontery to bargain with Elizabeth Tudor! That damned woman who two years ago had turned down Elizabeth's offer to take her child under royal protection. The queen smiled, quite broadly this time. What a fine jest!

"Of course you may be one of my Maids, Velvet de Marisco!" she said. "When we leave here you will come with us. With your mama away I feel a moral duty to take you under my wing. Still, I would have you accept a small, tangible token of this our first meeting on your fifteenth birthday." The queen drew from an elegant finger an emerald ring, square-cut and flanked with diamonds on either side. The stones were set in red gold, and the setting was engraved both in the front and the back in a design of graceful filigree. "Wear it always in remembrance of Elizabeth Tudor, my dear girl," she said effusively. Then, taking Lord Blackthorn's proffered arm, she moved forward into the priory.

Velvet slipped the ring onto her little finger and gazed down at it wonderingly.

"It matches your eyes, sweetheart," came a deep, masculine voice, and she lifted her eyes to look directly at the speaker.

"We have not been introduced, sir," Velvet said primly, though thinking at the same time that with his curly red hair and sparkling bright black eyes he was a divinely handsome young man. He was tall and well formed with a long face ending in a slightly weak chin. That, however, did not detract from his overall good looks. He was dressed in deep blue velvet trimmed in silver lace.

The man laughed and, turning to his equally well appareled companion, said, "Introduce us, Wat."

The elegant gallant complied by making a leg to Velvet and saying, "Mistress de Marisco, may I present to you, Robert Devereux, the Earl of Essex, Master of the Queen's Horse. My lord earl, Mistress Velvet de Marisco."

The Earl of Essex bowed gracefully to Velvet, his black eyes twinkling mischievously.

"But, sir," Velvet protested to the other gentleman, "I do not know you either!"

"That's easy," Robert Devereux said. "Since we have now been properly introduced, may I introduce to you, Mistress de Marisco, Sir Walter Ralegh, the captain of the queen's Gentlemen Pensioners. Wat, Mistress de Marisco. There! We've all been properly introduced and may now be friends."

"My lord," Velvet scolded Essex, "I am not such a country mouse that I don't know the queen dotes upon you. If you make her jealous, I shall be forbidden to accompany her, and then I shall have to . . ." She stopped herself just in time. "My lords, the queen will miss you shortly. You had best hurry into the hall." Then she moved to brush past them and catch up with her sister.

"Ah, fresh sweet meat," murmured the earl, blocking her path. "Perhaps the progress shall not be so dull this summer."

"Robin, you're mad! The maid is right, and well you know it." Ralegh admonished. "The queen does dote upon you, though why I cannot see when she has a far brighter fellow in me. Besides, I have heard the stories of this girl's mother and father. Either one of them could have you for supper, my lord earl, and not even belch daintily afterwards."

Velvet gazed at Ralegh with interest. He was older than the handsome earl, yet still a youngish man. Far more stylish than Robert Devereux, he wore a doublet of deep brown velvet richly embroidered with copper threads. It complemented his dark amber eyes and ginger-colored hair and beard. He was sturdier than Essex, but, though not as tall, he was even better proportioned with supremely elegant legs. She had never seen boots that fit so beautifully.

Suddenly mindful that her place was with Deirdre, Velvet boldly gave the earl a shove and hurried past him. Essex looked startled that she had laid hands upon him, but then he laughed.

"God's foot, the de Mariscos seem quite fierce, Wat! Perhaps 'twould be best if we were just friends with the maid. Besides, virgins are so emotional." He chuckled, and then, arm in arm, the two courtiers made their way through the crowd entering the priory, in order to regain their places by the queen's side.

Elizabeth Tudor was already in the Great Hall being offered refreshments by her host while the hostess had found her sister and was angrily reproaching her.

"How could you, Velvet!"

"How could I *what*, Deirdre?"

Deirdre sighed. "What are we to tell the Earl of BrocCairn when he arrives, Velvet? He is coming to marry you! You knew that!"

"Why is it," Velvet demanded, "that everyone is so concerned with the earl and his feelings, and no one thinks of me or mine? Mama and Papa made the match for me when I was just a child. I can't even remember the man! Mama has said I should not marry without love, and, Deirdre, I will not! You certainly refused to do so. I will also not marry without my parents by my side, and it is several months until they will return. Perhaps I shall fall in love with the earl, but then again perhaps I won't. Whether I do or not, I won't be hustled willy-nilly down the aisle before I have at least been to court. I shall have my time at court, Deirdre, and this wild man from Scotland will be forced to wait upon me until my parents return, for it is a well-known fact that the queen does not like gentlemen poaching among her maids. I shall be safe with my royal godmother!" She looked archly at her elder sibling.

"I am going to tell the queen, Velvet! You cannot embarrass us like this!"

"If you tell the queen, Deirdre, I shall flee to my grandparents in France and cause a great scandal! The betrothal will then be broken, and it will be all *your* fault! If my parents truly desire this match, they will not thank you for your meddling. I am as determined to have my way in this as you were to have yours in the matter of your marriage to John! We are sisters—with different fathers it is true—but the blood of our mother runs fiercely and hotly through both our veins. Why should I be any different in my desires than you were in yours?" Velvet look searchingly at Deirdre. "Wouldn't you rather I remained in England, safe with the queen?" she wheedled, a small smile tugging at the corners of her mouth.

"Damn you, you minx!" Deirdre muttered. "Oh, all right! The earl doesn't have to know that when you learned he was coming you practically begged the queen to become a Maid of Honor. Although you will give Uncle Conn a fit, sister!" Then she giggled. "I should not like to be our poor uncle and have to tell the earl that you are not at *Queen's Malvern* but rather with the queen, and therefore at the moment unavailable to wife. Lord, what a tangle!"

Conn St. Michael was, however, strangely unperturbed when he was told that evening of Velvet's tactics. "She'll be safe with Bess," he noted dryly. "Bless the little vixen for finding a way out of this herself."

"Why, Uncle, you sound as if you approve of Velvet's behavior," Deirdre replied, not a little shocked.

"Frankly, Deirdre lass, I didn't like the idea of giving our Velvet over to BrocCairn in marriage without Skye and Adam here. Velvet's actions have solved the problem for me. The queen will only give up her new Maid of Honor to her parents, certainly not to a Scots earl, especially with the maid objecting." The matter settled in his mind, Lord Bliss escorted his wife and niece down to the Great Hall for the feasting.

Elizabeth Tudor was just arriving as they hurried into the big room, which was lined with arch-shaped windows. The spring sunset turned the hall crimson, a brilliant hue echoed by the bright red flames in the four big fireplaces that took the chill from the room. Stepping forward, Conn knelt and raised the queen's hand to his lips to kiss it slowly. A warm light sprang into her gray-black eyes.

"Conn, you devil," she murmured, remembering a romantic evening they had spent several years back before he had married Aiden.

"Bess, you're as beautiful as ever," he said softly. "Still breaking hearts, lass?" He stood, relinquished her hand, and glanced at Essex and Raleigh.

Elizabeth Tudor shook her head wonderingly. "God's foot, Lord Bliss!" she said. "You're still an Irish rogue with a quicksilver tongue."

"And a quicker wit," he parried, to the queen's delight. "I hear my niece is to become one of your Maids of Honor."

"Ah, Velvet. A lovely child! I am delighted to have her."

"She has never been to any court, madame," he said softly. "She has never even been to London."

"Nor Paris either?" the queen queried him.

"Nor Paris either, madame. She is, despite her beauty, an innocent maid. She has been most sheltered."

"Is she betrothed?"

"Aye, to the son of a friend of Lord de Marisco's, but the wedding is not scheduled until after her sixteenth birthday."

"I will be most careful with Velvet, my lord," said the queen, understanding his fears. "I will treat her as I would my own child, and in a sense she is just that, being my goddaughter. Did I not take good care of your wife, Aiden, when she was in my charge?"

"Aye, and thank you, madame," Conn said quietly. He had now done all he could, and they would simply have to wait for his sister and Adam to come home from their voyage. The responsibility was no longer his, and he sighed almost audibly in his relief.

Across the hall, Velvet had suddenly found herself swept up in the society of the court. Her head whirled from all the outrageous compliments she was bombarded with from the gentlemen of the royal party, who were intrigued by this new Maid of Honor. She did not simper like the other girls, but was rather outspoken in her speech without being forward or suggestive. Add to this the fact that she was extravagantly beautiful and an heiress to boot, and the gentlemen were willing to brave the queen's wrath—at least as long as Elizabeth was across the room. Just when Velvet thought she could bear no more of the courtiers' silliness, Sir Walter Ralegh and the young Earl of Essex arrived to take her away from the noisy crowd.

"So sorry, gentlemen," Essex said, laughing, "but Wat and I have taken it upon ourselves to protect this maiden and her virtue from all of you. Be warned that we think of her as we do our own dear sisters and woe to any of you who should dare to trifle with her. Unless, of course," he amended to general laughter, "she wishes to be trifled with!" Taking Velvet firmly beneath the elbow, he hustled her off to sit with Ralegh before the fire.

"You're mad," she proclaimed.

"Aye, Mistress de Marisco, but admit that all those silly popinjays were boring you to death. I promise you that Wat and I shall be far more fun. Are you betrothed?"

"Why?" Velvet demanded, looking at him suspiciously.

"Because, you silly puss, I would like to know what my chances are of being called out."

"He's in Scotland, my lord, and for your information I haven't even the faintest idea of what he looks like, so to be overly discreet about you and Sir Walter would be a waste of my good time!" Velvet replied pertly.

The two gentlemen laughed delightedly, and then Ralegh, who was Essex's elder by some fifteen years, said, "Will you give us leave to call you Velvet? And you must call us Wat and Robin."

"I have a brother, Robin, so, my lords, I shall call you Wat, and you Scamp, for you my lord earl I suspect of being a wicked fellow." She pierced Robert Devereux with a sharp look, and he had the good grace to flush.

Ralegh chuckled. "You are young, Velvet, and I suspect far too innocent for this fast and sophisticated court of Elizabeth Tudor's; but you have a sharp eye to go with your quick mind. You are, I think, a survivor."

At that moment, two young women came hurrying up to them, one a sweet-faced girl with long, poker-straight dark blond hair and calm gray eyes; the other a glorious creature whose thick golden blond curls ran riot and who had incredible turquoise-colored eyes. The darker-haired girl smiled shyly at Velvet and curtsied politely.

"I am Elizabeth Throckmorton, called Bess, one of the queen's Maids of Honor. Her Majesty has put you in my charge, Mistress de Marisco. This is my friend, Angel Christman. We welcome you to court."

Velvet returned the curtsy, saying, "Please call me Velvet, and I hope we shall be friends."

"Lord, have mercy, what an innocent!" cried the beautiful blonde.

"Angel! You must not frighten Velvet, for this will be her first time away from home."

"Are you a Maid of Honor, too?" Velvet asked the blonde.

Angel laughed. "Nay," she said. "I am merely a royal ward. My father was the younger son of a fairly respectable noble family who married the younger daughter of an equally respectable noble family. Sadly, they had no money, and when Papa discovered my mama engaged in less than circumspect behavior with a wealthy farmer, he killed her and her lover, then killed himself. He provided for me by asking in his will that the queen take me under her protection. Of course she could not refuse, and so I have been raised very nicely at court, and I shall have a much better dowry than if my parents' families had taken me in. Positions such as you have obtained, Velvet de Marisco, are reserved for far nobler lasses than I."

"Ah, but you've a noble spirit, Angel love," murmured Essex, lecherously slipping an arm about her tiny waist.

Angel harrumphed and slapped his arm away. "Unhand me, you satyr, lest you destroy my chances for a decent marriage. Strange as it may seem to you, my lord earl, no respectable man wants your leavings!"

"*Angel!*" Bess Throckmorton looked shocked.

"Well, it's true, Bess. You've a powerful family to protect you, but I must guard my own virtue and good name!"

"No man wants a shrew with a sharp tongue," countered Essex, "and that, my dear Angel, is what you are in danger of becoming." He looked extremely put out by her words, and Velvet hid a smile.

In an effort to change the subject, Bess Throckmorton said, "The queen has asked us to accompany you to your home tomorrow so that we may aid you in packing what is necessary for court. Is it far?"

"Nay, just a few miles. Do you ride?"

"Aye," both girls chorused.

"Good! Let's start early then," said Velvet enthusiastically.

"We shall accompany you," Sir Walter promised. "Three maids riding alone is not wise."

A contradiction sprang to Velvet's lips, but then she considered how marvelous it would look to return to *Queen's Malvern* in the company of two elegant gentlemen of the court. "Are you used to getting up so early?" she teased them gently.

"Getting up? We shan't even go to bed, sweetheart! Sleep is something one catches when one can at court. You'll get used to it."

Dame Cecily, warned by a message from Deirdre of what Velvet had managed to gain from the queen, was waiting along with Velvet's nursemaid, both wearing a disapproving frown as Velvet rode up to *Queen's Malvern* in the company of the earl, Sir Walter, Bess, and Angel the next morning. Small and plump, Dame Cecily was a neat little soul, with sharp blue eyes and silvery curls. Still, she could be quite formidable and even now her foot tapped irritably.

"Your mama is going to be very angry at you, Velvet, and what are we to say to his lordship when he comes?" she scolded as the girl dismounted from her stallion.

"Nonsense, dearest Dame Cecily," returned Velvet. "Remember, she promised me that I should not marry without love."

"How can you know if you will love your betrothed or not if you are not here to get to know him? You were well aware of his impending arrival when you left for your sister's home. Now I hear of this business of going to court as a Maid of Honor!" Having helped to raise Velvet, as well as most of her siblings, Dame Cecily was looked upon as a grandmother by Skye's children. That, she felt, gave her the right to speak out and to interfere where she thought necessary.

"I could scarcely refuse the queen," said Velvet innocently.

"You *asked* the queen for it, and well I know it!" came the sharp reply. "You are a wicked lass, and your papa should have taken a switch to your bottom from the beginning. But no! Adam de Marisco simply dotes upon you, and look where it has led us!"

While she fussed on, Velvet's companions listened with interest until suddenly, realizing their presence, the old lady stopped in midsentence.

Velvet sweetly introduced them in a sugary voice. "The Earl of Essex, Sir Walter Ralegh, Mistress Bess Throckmorton, and Mistress Angel Christman; and this is Dame Cecily Small, the sister of Sir Robert. She is as a grandmother to me."

"You are all welcome to *Queen's Malvern*," said the dame politely, dropping a scant curtsy. "Come into the house for biscuits and wine, my lords, ladies." Turning, she led the way.

"Why, what is this, Velvet?" teased Ralegh. "You have not met your betrothed husband? How old-fashioned, an arranged marriage."

"It is not important," Velvet muttered, feeling reduced to a child once more by the old dame's scolding. "I was matched with the son of my father's friend when I was so little I cannot even remember the gentleman. Besides, my mama said I need not marry him if I do not love him."

"Yet," persisted Ralegh, "your Dame Cecily says he is coming shortly, and you won't be here to greet him, will you?" He began to chuckle. "You are rather a sly puss, aren't you, Velvet de Marisco?"

"I rather admire her spirit." Essex grinned. "Give me a lass with a mind of her own!"

"Give you a lass, period!" snapped Angel. "I never knew you to be particularly discriminating in your appetites, my lord earl!"

"My lords, Angel! Stop this instant," cried the gentle Bess. "Angel, you and I have come to help Velvet and to advise her what she will need at court. You gentlemen will sit quietly and have your wine while we do so," she finished firmly.

Both men smiled agreeably, and then followed the rapidly disappearing skirts of Dame Cecily down the hall. Elizabeth Throckmorton was one of the queen's favorite ladies, both well liked and respected. At twenty-four, she had been at court some years and was the oldest Maid of Honor. Now she turned to her new charge and said, "Will you take us to your room, Velvet?"

Velvet nodded, then led the way upstairs to her chambers.

Angel Christman slipped an arm through hers and said, "If Bess has decided to take you under her wing, you're a lucky lass. She is so very nice and most of the others aren't—but then you'll find out soon enough." Angel was only two years older than Velvet, but her life at court had given her a worldly-wise look that made her seem much more mature.

Velvet was soon to realize how fortunate indeed she was to have the friendship of Bess and Angel. Examining her wardrobe, they declared it outdated for the most part and much too countrified. She would, they said ruefully, be laughed out of court, and first impressions were so very important. She would have to stay behind when the court left *Blackthorn Priory* and then join them in a week after her wardrobe had been refurbished.

"No, I can't!" Velvet cried. "He might come in that time and then I would never get away! I would rather be laughed at by the court than . . ." She stopped as she realized that she had been close to disclosing her innermost fears.

"Well," said Bess, not one to pry though she was curious, "perhaps we can have your seamstress redo several of your gowns tonight. Then you can come with us tomorrow while she makes you some new gowns to send along after us. The seamstress will have to sew you several gowns all in white. The queen prefers her ladies in black and her Maids of Honor in white when they are on duty with her."

"Can the white gowns be trimmed with anything?" Velvet queried.

"Aye." Bess laughed. "'Tis the only way we're able to avoid looking like little French nuns. Sometimes our gowns are white with another color in the underskirt or in a pattern with a white background. Don't fret, though, Velvet. You'll get to wear your most beautiful and colorful gowns at the fetes and the masques. It's just that Her Majesty sometimes has her moods."

"What Bess is too nice to say is that the queen is growing old, and resents it," said Angel astutely. "By keeping those attending her in either black or white, she can appear even more glorious than her legend makes her."

"She is a kind mistress!" defended Bess.

"To those who don't displease her, but she is jealous, too, Bess, and well you know it. She hates for any of her Maids to leave her to make happy marriages, for she will not marry herself. Woe to any girl fool enough to wish for a husband in the queen's presence."

"There are those who have married with her blessing," Bess said.

"Girls who came to her long betrothed by their families, like Velvet, but the lasses who have found love at court have been cruelly handled by the queen, and you know I speak the truth, Bess. Why else would *you* be so careful?"

"Angel!" Bess's face was anguished.

"Oh, very well, but 'tis right glad I am to be only a humble royal ward." Angel turned to Velvet with an impudent grin. "Are you excited to be leaving your country nest, little mouse, and coming with us?"

"Yes, yes," agreed Velvet, greatly relieved and more at ease now that the conversation was off marriage.

They entered Velvet's bedchamber, and, to her surprise, Daisy, her mother's tiring woman, was awaiting her there.

You've already been in the dressing room, I can tell from the look on your faces," Daisy said.

"Oh, Daisy! Most of my things are so . . . so . . ."

"Old-fashioned and childish," supplied Daisy pertly. "Aye, and that's the truth, but don't you worry none, Mistress Velvet. Your mother's gowns are always in the height of fashion no matter that she doesn't go to court anymore. Since she's away and they're just hanging there in her wardrobe, I don't see any reason why we shouldn't refit some of them for you."

"A most sensible solution," remarked Bess. "Might we see the gowns you think would suit Mistress Velvet, Daisy?"

"I'll bring them in," came the reply. "No one is allowed in my lady's wardrobe but me." She hurried from the room.

"What an old dragon," Angel said. "I imagine she's been with your mother forever."

"Almost thirty years," Velvet supplied. "She was very annoyed because Mama wouldn't let her go along on her voyage this time, but then Daisy never really liked to travel with Mama anyway. She has an enormous family, for every time her husband, Bran Kelly, came home from the sea he used to give her another child before going off again." Velvet giggled.

"How many children do they have?" Bess queried.

"Ten. She's really an amazing woman, Daisy. All her babes lived, and all have grown up healthy and strong. There are seven sons and three daughters, whose names are Pansy, Marigold, and Clover."

Before Velvet could divulge any more, however, Daisy returned to the bedchamber carrying several gowns, a young girl following behind her with more. "Pansy and I have brought you five, Mistress Velvet," Daisy said. "These colors should suit you best. We'll see what bolts of fabric are in the storeroom later and you may choose several to be made into additional gowns."

The dresses drew gasps of admiration and not a touch of envy from both Bess and Angel. They were richly made, encrusted with gems, and embroidered with gold and silver threads. Three were jewel colors: sapphire blue, aquamarine, and amethyst; two were pastels: apple green and rose pink. It had not occurred to her new friends until this moment that

Velvet de Marisco was a young heiress with the kind of wealth that is only fable in most cases. They had not associated her with that kind of wealth, for she was so unspoiled, innocent, and totally unpretentious.

Daisy quickly had the girl out of her riding clothes and into one of her mother's gowns. She eyed her charge critically, walking slowly about her, nodding and muttering to herself. "Pansy!" she said sharply to her daughter. "Pansy, fetch the seamstress this minute!"

"Aye, Ma!" The girl ran off.

"I'm going to send her with you as your maid," Daisy told Velvet. "I've taught her everything she knows, and she'll do a good job for you."

"But what of Violet?"

"Surely you wouldn't expect a nursemaid to be a good tiring woman, Mistress Velvet? Oh, she's been fine as long as you were here at *Queen's Malvern* or in France with your grandparents, but at the Tudor court? Nay! Besides, Violet is with child and is to finally marry."

"The assistant coachman!" Velvet exclaimed gleefully.

Bess Throckmorton and Angel Christman looked at each other and giggled. Each was thinking that country gossip was really no different from court gossip.

Daisy looked somewhat mortified. She didn't like feeling foolish before these two fine ladies. After all, she had been at court before either of them was ever born. "There now," she fussed at Velvet, "such things are not your concern. Your papa would have a fit if he thought you knew about them!"

Mercifully, Pansy had been quick and returned with Bonnie, the manor seamstress, who went to work at once to alter the gowns. Velvet was an inch taller than her beautiful mother, but each gown had a generous hem so that the length could be adjusted. The waist and bustline of the gowns, however, needed to be taken in as Velvet was more slender than Skye and far smaller in the bust. The seamstress marked the adjustments to be made on each gown, and then, gathering up the garments, took them away.

Daisy then dressed her charge in a silk chamber robe and led the way to the manor storeroom, where she displayed the many and exquisite fabrics kept there to the three girls.

"God's foot!" swore Angel. "You could outfit the entire court for a year and a day with all of this."

"Aye," Daisy noted proudly.

It did not take Velvet long to decide, for she knew exactly what she wanted. She did not fancy heavy velvet fabric for the summer and early autumn. She chose instead a marvelous silk in topaz gold and another in sea green. For her duty gowns she chose half a dozen whites of various fabrics. Some were plain, some designed with colored and metallic threads and jewels. Then, seeing the gorgeous Angel almost salivating over a turquoise silk and Bess looking longingly at a bolt the color of red poppies, Velvet said, "Take those two also, Daisy." She pointed at her friends' choices. "Have Bonnie measure both Mistress Throckmorton and Mistress Christman before they leave and make them gowns to send along with mine."

"Oh, no, Velvet!" Bess protested. "'Tis much, much too generous of you."

"Don't be silly," Velvet replied. "There is, as Angel pointed out, enough fabric here to clothe the entire court. Please, Bess! You and Angel are the first friends I've made at court. I would so like to share my bounty with you."

Quick tears sprang to Bess Throckmorton's eyes. What a lovely child this was, she thought. She blinked the dampness away and said, "We thank you for your great kindness, Velvet de Marisco."

"Amen!" breathed Angel somewhat irreverently, and when Bess sent her a chiding look, the blond girl answered most matter-of-factly, "Well, I thought you weren't going to let us have them, Bess. That's all right for you with a family to aid you, but a royal ward has precious little!"

Bess Throckmorton shook her head. "Nay, Angel. Were I a maid of wealth I should have long been married, but my brother lost my dowry in a poor investment. I am no better off than you for all my high connections."

"Then thank God for the queen's court, which houses and clothes, though not too generously, us poor but well-connected church mice." Angel chuckled good-naturedly.

Mistress de Marisco soon found that though she might be a princess at *Queen's Malvern*, she was most lowly in rank in the hierarchy of the royal court. Among all the ladies and greater nobility, the heiress of Lundy, as she was known, was a very small fish indeed. Still, she was well liked by those who took the trouble to get to know her, for though Velvet was young, she was amusing and well read, and though she had a temper there was no meanness in her.

Because Velvet was the youngest and the newest of the queen's Maids, the simplest of tasks was assigned to her. It was her duty to see that the many-colored silks in the queen's workbasket were always in perfect order, untangled, and free of knots, the colors lined up as neatly as the colors in a rainbow. She had to be sure that the queen had the proper needles and that her cutting tools were sharpened. When Elizabeth Tudor wished to work on her tapestries or to embroider, the workbasket was quickly fetched by the heiress of Lundy, who was now totally responsible for it as once her Aunt Aiden had been when she was at court.

The pace of court life was quicker than she was used to, and Velvet was grateful for the friendship of Bess and Angel. She would have felt quite alone without them, for the other Maids of Honor were not as willing to be friendly. Some had great names but small funds to support them. Others of both wealthy and titled families were nowhere near as lovely as Velvet. Most were jealous of her.

"The queen's godchildren are a ha'penny a baker's dozen," said one high-born lady sneeringly.

"And most are of no account," put in another girl. "The queen is chosen by the parents in hopes of currying favor for an otherwise undistinguished child."

Velvet felt her cheeks burn with the insult. Her instinct was to fly at the girl and scratch her eyes from her ugly face, but feeling Bess Throckmorton's warning gaze upon her she held her temper.

"It is true that my mother's family were only humble Irish chieftains, but my father, whose ancient name I bear, is a nobleman. My sister, Willow, is the Countess of Alcester; my brother, Robin, the Earl of Lynmouth; my sister, Deirdre, Lady Blackthorn; my brother, Padraic, Lord Burke, of whom you all seem so fond." She glanced demurely at them. "Padraic certainly speaks well of all of you," she finished, and then bent to her task again.

Bess Throckmorton stifled a giggle and sent her protégée an approving look. Velvet had neatly put them all in their place, without even raising her voice.

"Your brothers are Robert Southwood and Padraic Burke?" demanded one young woman.

"Aye."

"Lord Burke of *Clearfields Manor* and Robert Southwood, the Earl of Lynmouth?"

"Aye."

There was a long silence as this piece of information was digested by the queen's Maids. Finally the girl who had spoken said, "We are going to *Lynmouth Castle* shortly."

"Are we?" Velvet replied. "Oh, it's so lovely in the summer. I do love Devon, don't you?"

"Your brother is a widower still?"

"Aye," said Velvet. "He felt very badly about Alison dying during her last lying-in. He swears he'll not remarry ever, but I think it's just a matter of meeting the right lady." Then Velvet turned her smile on those about her, a smile of such bland innocence that none would suspect the wicked thoughts that danced about her head as she gazed upon her companions of these last few weeks. What vain and shallow creatures they were for the most part. They would, she had not a doubt, begin a not-so-subtle currying of her friendship now that they knew she was the sister of two eligible gentlemen of wealth and land.

As she studied the other Maids of Honor from beneath her long lashes, Velvet decided that neither Robin nor Padraic would find even good sport among the queen's maidens. Bess was the best of them all, and of late Velvet had begun to suspect that her friend's heart was engaged by Sir Walter Ralegh, though neither Bess nor Wat showed the slightest interest in each other publicly.

The court left *Blackthorn Priory* and traveled south again toward London. The Spanish threat to English security was said to be most serious this year, and it was rumored that a large fleet was being assembled to attack England. The queen's councillors had insisted that she return to London where she might be properly protected, so the summer progress came to an abrupt halt.

The Earl of Lynmouth, upon learning that his royal guest would not be visiting Devon after all, raised a troop of men for her defense and came up to London to entertain her in his beautiful home, Lynmouth House, which was located on the Strand.

Velvet, hearing that her brother had arrived in London, begged time off from her duties so that she might go to see Robin. She was going to need all the allies she could get in the matter of her betrothal. She had no doubt that both Dame Cecily and Deirdre had already written to him.

Dressed soberly in black and white, the queen's colors, she hailed a common wherry from the landing of Whitehall Palace and was easily transported to Lynmouth House, which also sat on a bank of the river. A Southwood servant was there to help her from the little cockleshell and to pay the wherryman. Velvet hurried up through the vast gardens to the house and, seeing her brother on the terrace, called to him.

"Robin!"

Robert Southwood, the Earl of Lynmouth, looked up, and the corners of his mouth turned up in a smile. He was dressed casually, his silk shirt open to reveal a smooth expanse of chest. His lime-green eyes took in her long silk cloak of alternating black and white stripes with silver frog fastenings studded with black agates. The open cloak blew in the light breeze to show off her very fashionable gown of white silk with its silver lace ruff. The youngest of his mother's children, she was, next to his older sister, Willow, his favorite.

"Hallo, you minx!" he said, giving her a hug and a kiss.

"Oh, Robin, not you too?" Velvet wailed. "Are you going to lecture me also? Why doesn't anyone understand *my* point of view in this matter?"

The earl put an arm about his little sister and led her to a nearby bench beneath a late-flowering apple tree, where they both sat down.

"Suppose you tell me your side of the tangle you've woven, and then I shall judge whether or not to scold you. I have had two very frantic letters, one from Dame Cecily and the other from our Burke sister."

"I didn't know that I was betrothed," said Velvet miserably. "Then this letter came from Scotland from an earl."

"The Earl of BrocCairn," supplied Robin.

"Oh, yes, BrocCairn. It's such a funny name, I keep forgetting it. It was then that Uncle Conn told me of the betrothal, and he said that although the wedding wasn't supposed to be celebrated until after my sixteenth birthday, the earl suddenly found himself the only male in his direct line, and needed to marry now and beget heirs."

"Those things can happen, Velvet. It is not an unusual occurrence, and I can see BrocCairn's point."

"Robin, until a month ago I didn't even know that I was promised to this stranger! I don't want to go off to Scotland without knowing this man, and I am most certainly not ready to beget his heirs! I won't marry without love! That much our mother promised me, Robin. And I won't marry without my parents by my side when I finally decide to do so!"

"Couldn't you have told the earl this, my sister? He cannot be totally insensitive to a young girl's fears. I am sure he would have acceded to your request to wait until our mother and Adam return in a few months' time.'

"Uncle Conn did not seem to think so, Robin, and what if I had waited to ask him and this earl refused me? By law

I would have had to marry him. By becoming one of the queen's Maids of Honor I am protected until our mother returns. It is not so terrible a thing I've done, my lord brother. This Earl of BrocCairn can hardly be offended that his betrothed wife is one of the queen's honored maidens."

Robin shook his head. "You're far too clever for a maiden, Velvet," he said. He grinned at her. "'Tis just the sort of thing our mother would have done when she was a girl, but never say I told you so! Tell me now, how do you like the court?"

"It's the most exciting place I've ever been, Robin! I never thought I could exist on so little sleep and so much hurly-burly, but I can, and I do! I have two best friends now. One is Bess Throckmorton, and she has been ever so kind to me, Robin. Not like all the others who are, for the most part, proud as peahens and very shallow. They wanted nothing to do with me until they discovered I had two very wealthy and eligible brothers."

He smiled at her enthusiasm. "And who is your other friend?"

"Her name is Angel Christman, and she is absolutely beautiful, Robin! She's a royal ward and as poor as a church mouse, as she puts it, but she, too, is ever so nice. When Bess and I can get away from our duties, we go with Angel, Wat, and Scamp into the city. I have been to the theater, Robin!"

He smiled again. "What play did you see performed?"

"It's a new one, called *Tamburlaine the Great*, by Master Christopher Marlowe. Wat says he is the finest playwright England has ever seen."

"Indeed," replied Robin, "and just who is this Wat who is such an authority on our drama?"

"Why, Sir Walter Ralegh, Robin. I think he is in love with Bess, although neither one of them ever dares to look at the other in the queen's presence. Scamp says the queen would clap them both in the Tower if she suspected there was anything between them."

"Again you mystify me, little sister," said Robin. "You have twice referred to 'Scamp,' but I know not who you mean."

"The Earl of Essex, Robin. Everyone else calls him by your name, but I told him I would not, for there is only one Robin in my life."

Robert Southwood stiffened. The Earl of Essex had a reputation for womanizing similar to that of his stepfather, the Earl of Leicester. Robin knew how that gentleman had so sorely tried his mother after his father, Geoffrey Southwood, had died. "So, Velvet," he said, in what he hoped passed for a calm voice, "you have become friends with Essex, have you?"

"He's so very nice," she replied. "He says I am like his sister, Dorothy, and he and Wat warned all the gentlemen of the court that they were not to trifle with me. Oh, Robin! We have such good times together, Wat and Scamp, Bess and Angel, and me!"

"Then he has not been forward with you, Velvet?"

"Who?"

"Essex."

"No." She laughed. "He is far too busy courting the queen's favor to bother with me. Frankly, I'm rather disappointed, for I think I should like him to kiss me. One should always be kissed for the first time by someone one likes, don't you think?" She cocked her head at her brother.

"Yes," Robin answered his sister quietly, charmed by her genuine innocence and yet at the same time worried for her. How could their mother and Adam have raised her so unaware of the world? He stood up and, taking her hand, raised her to her feet. "Let's go into the house, Velvet. You have not seen Lynmouth House, never having been to London before. I want you to familiarize yourself with it, for you are to be my hostess when the queen comes in a few days' time."

"*I am to be your hostess?* Oh, Robin! I assumed that you would ask Willow."

"I would have, except that my charming youngest sister has just arrived in London and, being newly fledged, should have the experience of hostessing a large party for royalty. You may be called on to entertain King James one day, Velvet."

A small cloud of annoyance passed over Velvet's beautiful face, but its passage was so swift that he did not notice it at all.

"It's not certain that I will marry that Scot, Robin. Remember our mother's promise."

"I remember it, Velvet, but you must not be so unkind as to judge the Earl of BrocCairn before you have met him, *and* before you have had the opportunity to know him. You are now safe as a Maid of Honor, at least until your parents return home in a few months. You have won the first skirmish. Be generous in your victory, little sister."

Chapter 2

Robert Geoffrey James Henry Southwood, the Earl of Lynmouth, had held his title since before his third birthday. He had no real memory of the father whom he so startlingly resembled. By choice, he had gone to court at the age of six to be a personal page to Her Majesty, the queen, and he had taken to court life with an ease that was his birthright. When he was sixteen his mother had sent him to study at Oxford University. When he was eighteen he had been sent to the Sorbonne, and from there he had traveled throughout Europe. It was at the Sorbonne that he had met Alexander Gordon, the heir to the Scottish earldom of BrocCairn.

Alex was three years older than the blond English earl, but the two had taken to each other like long-lost brothers. They decided to pool their resources and share living quarters. Even that hadn't spoiled their friendship. They studied together, drank together, and even wenched together; sometimes, when their funds were low, they shared the same pretty whore who, far from being offended at being paid only once, was ecstatic at having two such virile lovers. Alex and Robin had known each other for well over a year when the matter of marriage came up.

Robin had explained to his friend that he had been betrothed since childhood to the daughter of a friend of the family, and when he finally returned home he would marry her. Alex admitted to a similar situation, but explained that the lass involved was younger than he by thirteen years, and the agreement between them did not allow him to wed her until she was sixteen. Still, he said, he was in no hurry to settle down. Mistress Velvet de Marisco could take her time growing up as far as he was concerned.

"Whom did you say?" Robin suddenly sat up on the bed where he say lounging. "What is the name of your betrothed wife?"

"Velvet. Velvet de Marisco," came the answer.

"Good Lord! Velvet de Marisco!" Robin began to laugh.

"Do you know her?" Alex was now looking curiously at his friend. "Has she become pockmarked or has her nose grown overlong? I remember naught but that she was a pretty child."

"Aye, I know her! She's my sister, Alex! My half-sister, and she's outrageously fair. That's why you have always looked so familiar to me. We originally met several years ago at your betrothal feast at my mother and stepfather's estate of *Queen's Malvern*."

Now it was some six years later, and Robin had married his betrothed wife, Alison de Grenville, had sired three daughters with her, and had buried her almost two years past. He could still not think easily about Alison, that sweet, foolish, and headstrong young girl who had given him his first daughter, Elsbeth, nine months to the day after their wedding; Catherine, ten months later; and then against all advice died while birthing Cecily within a year of Catherine. Alison had been so proud of her children, but she had felt a strong, almost fanatical responsibility to give her husband sons. He had known that it was his responsibility to protect her, for his seed was strong and his wife very fertile. He had tried avoiding her after little Catherine's birth, but she had mischievously gotten him drunk one night, and in his wine-induced stupor he had thought one time could not hurt.

Robin had used his mourning as an excuse to withdraw from court life and from all social contact in his Devon neighborhood. After a year his sister Willow began to fuss at him to remarry, but he could not be moved. Logic told him he was not entirely responsible for his wife's death, but his emotions told him another tale. Had he been mature enough to control his baser nature, Alison would be alive today. He had not been in love with her, but they had been good friends.

Now Robin found himself drawn back into the world by a combination of events. The queen's proposed visit to Devon had necessitated an invitation on his part, for his father's hospitality had been famous, and as Geoffrey Southwood's son he could do no less. Then when it was decided that the queen should return to London because of the Spanish threat, he had felt duty-bound to travel to the capital with his troop of men for England's defense and to entertain the queen anyway. As he had told Velvet, Robin had also received several frantic communications from various members of his family complaining about his youngest sister's behavior. With their mother and stepfather away, Robin's siblings, older and younger, looked upon him as the head of the family by virtue of his high rank.

He had been in London just a short time when he received a rather droll letter from Alexander Gordon, now the Earl of BrocCairn. The earl had arrived at *Queen's Malvern* to find an apologetic Lord Bliss in place of the blushing bride he had expected. He would need an entrée to the court if he was to catch up with his reluctant betrothed. Would Robin help him?

Robin had answered immediately, telling his old friend to come directly to London to stay with him, and together they would work out the mess that Velvet had made. She wasn't really like their mother, Robin thought, but still there was enough of Skye in her to make her willful.

Alex had arrived quietly in London riding his own horse and accompanied only by his valet, a rather wicked-looking rogue named Dugald. With one smooth motion, he slid from his mount and turned to greet his host, who had hurried from his house, a smile upon his handsome countenance. Seeing Robin's face again reminded Alex that in Paris women had called the pair of them the *Archangel* and *Lucifer*, for the contrast between the tall, fair Englishman and the tanned, dark-haired Scot had been that sharp.

"Alex! Damn me, you look just the same. Welcome to London, my friend," Robin greeted him.

The Earl of BrocCairn grasped and shook the outstretched hand offered him. "I'm glad to be here, Robin. When can I meet yer sister?"

Robin grinned ruefully, remembering Alex's way of always coming directly to the point. He led his guest into the house, directing Dugald to follow the majordomo. After settling Lord BrocCairn in his library with a large silver goblet of strong Burgundy, he said, "It's not going to be as easy as all that, Alex. You cannot march into the queen's court, introduce yourself to Velvet, and carry her off to church."

"Why not?"

Robin had to laugh. He simply could not help it. Alex had always known how to wield his weapon well with the ladies, but he had absolutely no finesse or tact to use on the fair sex. He knew nothing of how to court a woman, for he assumed his prowess in bed would be enough. The problem, Robin decided, was that his friend had never known a virgin. He spoke carefully. "Alex, my sister is an independent wench by nature. She is very much her parents' child, and despite the betrothal made between you two, my mother has always promised her that she could marry for love."

"A damn fool promise, if ye ask me," came the surly reply. The Earl of BrocCairn cast Robin a black look.

Robin hid his smile. "Perhaps," he said, "but my mother's first marriage was arranged when she was in the cradle. They did not suit, and her life was a hell on earth until he died. My mother has never forgotten that. Velvet was born out of a great love and is extremely precious to both her parents. I know that they meant for you to come for Velvet's sixteenth birthday next year, to spend some months getting to know her, and letting her get to know you. She has been very sheltered her entire life and, in all likelihood, would have easily fallen in love with you. This sudden change in your life, your urgent desire to marry her has frightened her. She doesn't know you, Alex. You have never even been to see her since the day of your betrothal. With her parents away she felt almost hunted when your message came. Particularly since our Uncle Conn was at a loss as to what to do."

"I *must* marry, Robin! I am the last of my line, and the thought that my brother-in-law, poor weak-kneed idiot that he is, could inherit *Dun Broc* infuriates me. I cannot wait!"

The strain in his friend's face was apparent, and Robin's voice softened. "Listen to me, Alex. I inherited *Lynmouth* when I was barely out of the cradle. My father and my younger brother had died in a late-winter epidemic, and I was the last male of my line. Yet it was almost twenty years before I wed and had children.

"You must cultivate patience, Alex, because if you are to win my sister over, and you must if you want a happy married life, you, my old friend, are going to have to court her properly. My mother and stepfather will return to England in a few months' time, and I know they will espouse your cause. Unless, of course, Velvet takes a violent dislike to you."

"By 'court' I suppose you mean I shall have to practice yer precious Sassenach ways with the lass."

Robin chuckled. "Don't grumble at me, Alex. I'm not the one who sent an abrupt note to *Queen's Malvern* demanding my bride. You're bloody lucky Velvet didn't ask to serve her other godmother, Queen Margot of France! Please, I beg of you, don't be a pig-headed Scot with me over this. Your King Jamie will one day be England's king, and then we shall all be united."

"Hell, Robin, I've never courted a woman properly in my life. When we were at the university in Paris and traveling in France and Italy, there was no need to court. There was only the need for ready coin to pay a wench for her favors. At *Dun Broc* I don't even have to bother with that. Because I was my father's son the wenches were willing, and now that I am the master they are even more so."

"Then it's time, nay, past time, that you learned how to court a respectable lass, Alex. 'Tisn't really hard, you know. Poetry and posies, clever little gifts and a quick wit, sweet words meant for her alone."

"She is so very beautiful," Lord BrocCairn said, almost to himself, as he slipped the miniature of Velvet from his doublet and gazed upon it.

"Aye, she's beautiful," Robin agreed, fighting to keep his mouth from breaking into a grin. "She's also extremely intelligent, independent, and totally spoilt."

"God's blood, man, ye're scaring me to death!" exploded Alex. "How the hell am I, a simple Highlander, supposed to handle that?"

"God almighty, man, don't let her know you're afraid of her," Robin fretted. "She's a lass, a virgin, an innocent. Court her gently but firmly. She's not been wooed before, for her mother and her father were most strict with her."

"I wish she didn't have to know who I was, Robin. Not at first. If only I could meet her without her knowing that I'm the Earl of BrocCairn."

Robin's lime-green eyes narrowed a moment, and then he said, "According to my uncle she didn't want to know anything about you, she was so panicked by the thought of a sudden marriage. She might remember BrocCairn, but I'll wager she doesn't know that BrocCairn is Alexander Gordon. Let me introduce you as Lord Gordon, and if she doesn't recognize the name, then you'll be safe to court her for a time. If Velvet doesn't know who you are, then perhaps she will feel comfortable with you and allow herself to get to know you."

"But if she doesn't know I'm BrocCairn, will she allow a man, not her betrothed, to court her?"

"'Twill be nothing more than a harmless flirtation, Alex, and all maids enjoy a summer flirtation." Robin laughed lightly. "'Tis good for them to think they are sowing wild oats before settling down. They are then more content in their marriages."

Now it was Alex Gordon's turn to laugh. "How in hell did ye get so knowledgeable these last few years?" he teased his friend. "I thought that I was the elder."

"Aye, you are my elder by three years, Alex, but I've been wed, a father, and a widower in the time we've been separated." Robin sighed deeply. "Experience makes for knowledge."

"I was sorry to hear about Alison," Alex said quietly. "I wish I had known her, for she must have been quite a lass that ye mourn her so deeply, Robin."

"She was a good girl," his friend replied. "If you hadn't been in France when we wed, you might have met her."

"Aye, but my trip to France was for the crown, and I do precious little for the Stewarts as it is." He smiled encouragingly. "Ye'll find another lass someday, Robin."

"Nay, I'll not wed again," came the firm but quiet reply.

Alex did not press his friend further, but instead asked, "Are ye not going to show me this London town of yours, Robin?"

"Aye, I'll show you London, Alex, and once I've entertained the queen, you'll go to court too. In a few days' time I'm scheduled to give a huge fête. I don't believe there has been one in this house since my father's time. He always gave an enormous Twelfth Night celebration, a masque that every dressmaker in London both dreaded and delighted in, for the costumes were incredible to behold. Since his death, though, my mother has rarely used the house. She has one of her own next door that I suspect will go to Velvet one day."

"When will I meet Velvet?"

"She's coming to stay with me the day before the queen's fête. Courage, Alex! I've known Velvet to throw things and to shriek, but I've never known her to bite. While his friend glowered at him, Robin chortled mischievously.

Now, a few days later as he ushered his sister into Lynmouth House, Robin wondered if Alex could learn to court her and if Velvet would even give him the opportunity. She was so full of the delights of the court and of London, which was to be expected considering the quiet life she had led heretofore.

Velvet was enchanted by the elegance of her brother's ancestral house, and her open admiration brought many smiles to the faces of the staff she encountered, most of whom had been there in her mother's time.

"I have a guest staying with me, Velvet," Robin said casually.

"Who?"

"Alexander Gordon, my Scots friend from the Sorbonne. You may remember me speaking of him. We met at the university, shared quarters, and then went on through Europe together."

"Umm," said Velvet, not particularly interested in her brother's friend and far more concerned with the translucent porcelain bowls filled with red damask roses that adorned the main hall of the mansion.

"You will probably meet him tonight at dinner, Velvet."

"Who?" Velvet suddenly realized that she had not been attending to her brother's words closely enough.

"Alex Gordon, my friend."

"I am sorry, Robin. Your house is so beautiful that I cannot stop looking. I promise by tonight I shall be more attentive, and I shall certainly be polite to your friends. Did Pansy come from Whitehall yet?"

"I'll ask the housekeeper, and then I'll show you to your apartments." He led her into the library, poured her a light and fruity pale gold wine, and, ringing for a footman, sent him for the housekeeper. When she arrived a moment later, the housekeeper bobbed a curtsy and assured Mistress de Marisco that her tiring woman had indeed arrived safely with her mistress's wardrobe, and was even now preparing a bath for her lady.

Velvet arose and, kissing her brother, allowed herself to be led off by the beaming housekeeper who was already regaling Velvet with stories of when her mama was a young bride in this house.

Velvet's apartments were most spacious, consisting of an anteroom, a lovely light bedchamber that looked out over the river and the gardens, a dressing room, and even a small, separate, windowed room for Pansy. Pansy, though just fourteen, had been well trained by her mother. She was so clever with hair in fact that when her skill was discovered, Pansy became in great demand amongst the Maids of Honor. She would, to their annoyance, do none of them without her mistress's permission, which meant that those in Velvet's bad graces could expect no help from the loyal Pansy.

Velvet almost cried aloud in her delight at the sight of the steaming tub. Baths at court were few and far between. Even when she had a little time to herself, which wasn't often, there was the matter of bribing the queen's footmen to haul water, hopefully hot, to the tiny cubicle assigned to her when she was not on duty, or to the Maiden's Chamber.

The air in this bedchamber at Lynmouth House was redolent with the scent of gillyflowers, and Pansy was hanging two large, soft towels before the fire to warm.

"Oh, I wish I could live here at Robin's house whenever we were in London, Pansy! Just to be able to bathe every day again would be heaven."

"Aye," agreed Pansy. "I don't think much myself of those fine ladies at court who use perfume to cover the stink of their bodies instead of good honest soap and water. Come now, Mistress Velvet, and I'll help you to undress."

Velvet stood as her tiring woman quickly and efficiently stripped the clothes from her slender form. "Did you bring along the new sea-green gown, Pansy? I should like to wear it tonight. I want Robin to see how grown-up I've become." Velvet now stepped into her tub and sat down. "Umm," she murmured, closing her eyes as a blissful look spread over her face.

Pansy smiled merrily at her mistress and chattered on, "Aye, I've brought the sea-green and the topaz gold silk for the earl's fête when you'll be his hostess. Y'know, mistress, I will wager that his lordship would want you to make this fine house your home when you're in London with the court. Why don't you ask him? I've never known him to be ungenerous, and next to your sister, Lady Willow, you've always been his favorite."

Velvet nodded. Kneeling, Pansy took up a cake of hard-milled cream-colored soap and began to bathe her mistress.

When she had finished, she washed Velvet's hair, dumping several buckets of warm water over her to rinse it. Velvet then stepped from her tub, to be wrapped in a large, hot towel. She sat down on a small wooden stool in front of the fire while Pansy dried her hair and perfumed it with her personal scent. Slipping into a rose silk chamber robe, Velvet lay down in the lovely big bed with its plump feather pillows to sleep until it was time for dinner.

When Pansy woke her, she felt more refreshed and relaxed than she had since she left *Queen's Malvern*. She put on her silken undergarments; outrageously extravagant pink silk stockings embroidered with heart-shaped leaves, with silver lace garters; several petticoats; a small farthingale; and finally her new sea-green gown. The tight bodice slipped over her torso like a second skin, its neckline coming just barely to the tops of her small, full breasts. Velvet stared, blushed, and then said in a hesitant voice, "Pansy, do you think this neckline too low?"

Pansy stepped back and viewed her mistress critically. "Nay, 'tis just as the fashion dictates. You're simply not used to it."

Velvet continued to stare into the glass for a minute longer. The gown really was lovely. The sleeves were embroidered in tiny paler green glass beads that formed ivy leaves and vines, as was the lighter green underskirt. The hem of the overskirt was decorated with small silver bows. She wore no jewelry except the large pearls in her ears that her parents had sent from the Indies for her last birthday. They had not arrived until recently, however, and had been sent down from *Queen's Malvern* by Dame Cecily.

Seating herself at the dressing table, Velvet silently watched as Pansy did her hair: parting it in the middle, wrapping it into a soft chignon at the nape of her neck, and teasing the little side curls about her beautiful face. Velvet then daubed on her perfume, enjoying its heady fragrance as she did so.

"His lordship will be amazed at you," Pansy said worshipfully as Velvet stood up and slipped her feet into her green silk shoes.

"I would not want Robin to be ashamed of having asked me to be his hostess for him tomorrow. He really is a very elegant gentleman. Tonight I shall try out my best manners on him and his friend, Lord Gordon. Perhaps I shall even attempt flirting with the gentleman."

"I would have thought you got enough of that at court," Pansy replied.

"Ha!" snapped Velvet. "With Wat and Scamp protecting my virtue so assiduously? Most of the gentlemen are afraid to come near me for fear of provoking a duel."

Pansy chuckled. "'Tis just as well, mistress. You're a betrothed young lady, if you'll remember."

As she was leaving her apartment, Velvet turned and made a rude face at her tiring woman. *Betrothed!* God's blood, how she hated the very thought of it! She wondered if the wild Scotsman had arrived at *Queen's Malvern* yet and what his reaction to her absence had been. Well, he had his nerve thinking that a highborn young Englishwoman would just sit there waiting for him to marry her! Never since they had been betrothed those long years ago had he ever been to see her, or written to her. No small presents on her birthday or New Year's or Twelfth Night. And now! A cold, abrupt letter announcing *his* arrival a full year in advance of the prearranged date, saying that *he* desired an immediate marriage. It was not to be borne! He was obviously a rude clod, a bumpkin. The nerve of the fellow! He could damned well go to the devil!

Velvet had no idea how her silent outrage heightened her color as she descended the staircase, making her look even more beautiful this evening than she usually did. Watching her come down, Robin was stunned. Where was the charming *little* girl he had so loved? There was something about this Velvet, perhaps the tilt of her head, that reminded him of their mother once long ago when she was angered over something.

Alexander Gordon, seeing Velvet come nearer and nearer to him, felt his heart quicken with excitement. She was a thousand times lovelier than any painting, and seeing her he realized that he *must* have her. He could not allow any other man to possess her. Suddenly he wondered if he would be able to speak, for he felt his voice had disappeared. My God! Was he a green boy to be so affected by a little wench?

Stopping two steps from the bottom, Velvet focused her gaze on the two men and smiled. "Well, Robin," she teased, "do you look so surprised because I look most presentable or because I look most unpresentable?"

The Earl of Lynmouth laughed. "Dearest Velvet," he said, "you are more than presentable. You are outrageously fair, sister, and far more grown-up than I ever expected you to be."

"'Twas time for me to grow up, was it not?" Velvet said softly.

"I cannot help but wonder whether our mother and Adam will agree to that, sister. You are their precious babe, and this change has come about in the time that they've been away."

For a moment brother and sister stood looking at each other in total silence, and then Velvet said quietly, "Will you not introduce me to your friend, Robin?"

Recalling his duties as a host, he replied, "Velvet de Marisco, may I present to you Alexander, Lord Gordon. Alex, my sister, Velvet."

From her place two steps up the staircase, Velvet regally stretched out her slender hand as she had seen the queen do. When Alex had kissed it and straightened up once more, Velvet was somewhat startled to find that he was at eye level with her. Then with a gentle pressure on her fingers he drew her down those last two steps, and she discovered that she had to look up at him despite her own height.

His amber eyes, gazing into her green ones, twinkled mischievously as he fully realized his advantage and felt the confidence flow back into his veins.

"Why, fie, my lord, do you seek to flirt with me?" Velvet inquired with equal mischief. She fluttered her thick eyelashes at him.

"It is impossible not to flirt with you, mistress," was his swift reply, and Velvet laughed.

"You will be a great success at court, my lord, for you are quick," she said, and then feeling Alex's grip relax she gracefully freed her hand.

Robin Southwood breathed a soft sigh of relief. Velvet had not recognized "Lord Gordon" as the Earl of BrocCairn, and she seemed to tolerate him. Moreover, it was immediately obvious that Alex was totally besotted with the minx, the Lord God help him.

When the rest of the evening went equally well, Robin could not believe his good fortune. They ate an excellent dinner, just the three of them, and the conversation around the table was amusing and witty.

Velvet flirted shamelessly with Alex. They played at cards, and she then went to bed early feeling quite satisfied that her female powers were potent and in excellent working order.

"Do you think we might tell her who I am?" Alex asked later as he and Robin sat before the library fire drinking some excellent peat whiskey that he had brought his host. "She is a sweet girl, not at all the formidable creature I envisioned."

"No," Robin replied. "If you tell her, she will feel trapped once more and flee you. You only met tonight. Give her time to know you."

"But she seemed to like me, Robin, and she is a most charming flirt."

"She is a young girl trying out her skill at seduction for the first time, Alex. I know you are enchanted with her, for I can see it in your eyes, but be patient, my old friend. She is so damned innocent and idealistic that she will feel terribly betrayed if you tell her now. Let her know you better first."

Alexander Gordon sighed, but nodded his agreement. It would not be easy to practice patience now, having met Velvet. Why, several times tonight, he had come perilously near to sweeping her into his arms and kissing her enticing mouth. He wondered what she would have done had he given in to his desires. Would she have melted into his embrace, or would she have grown angry at his apparent boldness? After all, she was his by virtue of their betrothal. *She was his*, and no other man could have her! Hot and irritable with sudden jealousy, he slept restlessly that night.

The following morning it seemed as if Lynmouth House was erupting. The footmen hurried purposefully about seeing that all the silver, gold, and crystal was polished and gleaming. Every candle from simple sticks to those that lit the great chandeliers were replaced with fresh beeswax tapers. Tables were carried out into the gardens where supper would be served to the court. There were maids running to and fro setting the tables, and others who were set to washing, sweeping, and polishing. The guests would start to arrive in the late afternoon, and all must be in readiness.

Robin wanted this great fête to be especially enjoyable for Elizabeth Tudor. She had been a great friend of his father's, and for Robin's whole life, despite the constant battles of will she waged with his mother, England's queen had been his friend and his patroness also.

These last months had been filled with personal tragedy and trauma for the queen. She had finally had to admit to herself that her cousin Mary Stewart meant her serious harm. She had been forced to end that threat by ending Mary's life. It had not been an easy decision, and it was one that still haunted her.

Now her brother-in-law, Philip of Spain, had amassed a monstrous naval armada and was preparing to send it against England. From all reports, Spain's position was impregnable and they stood a good chance of conquering England. Still, the queen was determined that no foreign power would prevail over her kingdom. Recently she had avoided several assassination plots thanks to Sir Francis Walsingham's excellent secret service, but the strain was beginning to show. Tonight at least, thought the young Earl of Lynmouth, the queen can feel she is safe among friends, and enjoy herself.

Robin smiled as he gazed over his exquisite riverside gardens hung with lanterns that by evening would be twinkling like golden fireflies. The trees were filled with silver cages containing songbirds of various species. The tables were covered in snow white damask cloths with bright green silk runners, the Tudor colors. There were silver bowls filled with pink damask roses up and down the board. A musicians' gallery painted silver had been built in the center of the gardens so that everyone could easily hear the music, and Robin had hired a company of players to act in scenes depicting the great moments in the queen's reign to date. Master Marlowe, London's current favorite playwright, had written the sketches and would also perform in them. Robin had arranged with an Italian fireworks maker for a magnificent display of fireworks to delight the queen and her court at midnight. It would be a perfect evening.

"Oh, Robin, how beautiful you are!"

The earl turned and smiled warmly at his young sister. "Then you approve of my garb, poppet?" He was dressed in cream-colored velvets and silks embroidered with gold threads, small diamonds, pearls, and pale blue zircons. His golden blond hair was like his late father's in its silken texture and its natural wave. He wore it neatly cropped, but one recalcitrant lock fell over his forehead.

"May I return the compliment, Mistress de Marisco? Your gown is exquisite!" Robin's lime-green eyes sparkled with approval.

Velvet pirouetted proudly for him. "The gown was made at *Queen's Malvern* after I left and then sent on to London. I chose this fabric from the storage room."

Robin smiled. "You chose well, my dear," he said, and Velvet preened beneath his approving gaze.

It was indeed the most grown-up dress she had ever worn, and she was no longer uncomfortable with the very low neckline that fashion seemed to dictate these days. The gown was entirely made of topaz gold silk, the underskirt embroidered with copper threads, small freshwater pearls, and tiny topazes in a pattern of flowers and butterflies. The full sleeves were trimmed with gold lace at the wrists, and small, gold cloth bows were scattered up and down their fullness. There were matching bows strewn over her bell-shaped skirt. Her beautiful auburn hair had been dressed in an elegant chignon, and there were tiny gold bows decorating it.

"You have no jewelry," Robin noted.

"Only the pearl earbobs Mama and Papa sent me for my birthday," Velvet answered.

Robin signaled to one of his footmen. "Find Master Browne," he said, "and tell him I wish a single rope of black pearls for Mistress de Marisco."

"Oh, Robin! How can I thank you for the loan of such pearls? They will make me perfect, and so I should be, standing by your side, my lord Earl of Lynmouth."

"They are not a loan, Velvet. They are a gift. I did not send you a gift this year, or last year either for that matter, and never before have I forgotten your birthday."

Velvet kissed her brother's cheek. "You were mourning Alison, Robin, and there was no room in your heart for anything else. I knew that. We all did." Then she threw her arms about him and hugged him hard. "Thank you, dearest brother! The pearls will be a most wonderful present!"

"There, Will, have I not told you? Offer a wench a pretty bauble and she'll reward you with a kiss, *or* perhaps even more," came a mocking drawl.

The earl and Velvet stepped back from each other and turned to see who it was that spoke. Robin's face crinkled with pleasure at the sight of one of the two men who stood there.

"Damn me, Kit Marlowe, you haven't changed, have you? Still totally disrespectful of your betters, aren't you?"

"Aye, Robin Southwood, for I don't hold any of the gentry to be my betters. Who's the lass?"

"My youngest sister, Velvet de Marisco. Velvet, this scoundrel is Master Christopher Marlowe. Do not believe a word he utters, for he is a playwright, and worse, he is an actor."

The gentleman before them flashed them a blinding smile, a smile that was ivory white against his rather swarthy face. His eyes were like black cherries and sparkled with irreverence. "This is the second sister of yours I've met, and both have been beauties." He made Velvet an elegant leg, sweeping off his small, soft black cap with its rather jaunty feather. "Your slave for life, Mistress de Marisco. Ask what you will, and I will obey."

Velvet giggled. "I think you are rather mad, Master Marlowe," she replied, and he grinned again.

"Totally," he agreed, "but 'tis where my genius comes from."

"Introduce us to your friend, Kit," the earl commanded gently, noting that Marlowe's companion was hanging back, looking somewhat uncomfortable.

Without even looking, Marlowe reached casually back and drew forward his hesitant friend, a tall, slender man with a serious and sensitive face. "These country bumpkins," he lamented. "When they first come to London, they are so shy and meek, but within a year he'll be as irascible as I am, I guarantee. This is Will Shakespeare, newly come from Stratford-upon-Avon. Like me, he has pretensions of being a writer, but, for the moment, he's but a simple actor."

"I hope you will find London everything you dreamed it would be Master Shakespeare," said Robin graciously.

Will Shakespeare bowed politely, replying, "Thank you, my lord."

"This is my first time in London, too, Master Shakespeare," said Velvet, following her brother's lead in attempting to set the actor at his ease. "I am one of the queen's Maids of Honor."

"Until your parents return from a voyage and help you to celebrate your forthcoming marriage," Robin reminded his sister.

"Oh, bother my unknown betrothed, Robin Southwood!" Velvet said irritably. "I will not marry without love!"

"My lord, you sent for these pearls?" Master Browne was at their side, a small red morocco case in his hands.

"We'll see you later, Rob," Kit Marlowe said. "I hope that you'll enjoy the scenes I've written for the queen. Mistress de Marisco, keep your sweet and honest ideals. Come, Will!" Then he strode off with his companion by his side.

Robin reached out and took the proferred jewel case. "Thank you, Master Browne." He opened the case and lifted out the rope of smoky dark pearls, then handed the box back to the waiting man. "Give the box to my sister's tiring woman. I am gifting Mistress de Marisco with these pearls."

"Very good, my lord," said Master Browne. He bowed and backed away.

Robin held out the pearls. "For you, poppet, with many happy returns."

Velvet's flash of temper had quickly cooled, and she took the jewels her brother proferred, her beautiful green eyes round with delight. She looped the rope about her neck once and let the rest of it fall. It reached two thirds of the way down her stomacher. "How do they look?" she asked, trying to keep her voice calm.

"Perfect," said her brother.

"But not half as lovely as you are, Mistress de Marisco," said Alexander Gordon as he joined them. Dressed in black velvet, there was an almost severe elegance about him.

Velvet's eyes swung between her brother and his friend. "You look like an archangel and Lucifer standing here together," she said softly.

"A comparison that has been made many times before, Mistress de Marisco," said Alex as he took her hand up and pressed a warm kiss upon it. His eyes glowed with a warmth that was both flattering and frightening.

Velvet took her hand back with what she hoped was not unseemly haste. "I think you might call me by my name, if my brother thinks it not too forward."

"I think it would be permissible," Robin said quietly.

"My lord, the guests are beginning to arrive," the majordomo announced.

"We will greet them here on the terrace leading to the gardens," replied Robin, and, nodding, the man went about his duties. "Some will come by the river and others by coach," Robin explained to his sister. "This is the middle ground between the two. Besides, Her Majesty will be coming from Whitehall on her barge, and I would be prompt in welcoming her."

It was as if some secret signal that could be heard only by the favored had been sounded. Suddenly the guests were arriving, one party quickly followed by another, coming from both the river and the road in a seemingly never-ending procession of brilliantly colored gowns, doublets, and jewelry, and of fragrances that ranged from the simplest to the overpowering. Velvet thought that her face would crack from the strain of smiling, and her cheeks began finally to ache. Her hand felt both limp and permanently damp from all the kisses it had received. As she stood there receiving her brother's guests, she realized for the first time in her life the responsibilities that her beautiful mother had carried in the days before her discreet banishment from court. She also knew that as the wife of a great lord these same responsibilities would one day be hers. It was not a position for a child; that realization gave Velvet some pause for thought.

Finally a cry rose from the edge of the gardens as the queen's barge was sighted coming around the bend in the river heading in toward the Lynmouth House landing. Taking his sister's hand, Robin made his way through the gardens and past his guests down to the quay. Seeing the brother and sister waiting to greet her, Elizabeth Tudor had an incredible sense of déjà vu. The young earl was without a doubt his late father's mirror image, and, although she had known Robin his whole life, it was never more apparent to her than now. Dear little Velvet reminded the queen of Skye, although she really didn't look that much like her mother. Yet there was something there. Perhaps it was that arrogant tilt of her proud, young head. For a moment Elizabeth felt that time had stood still. Seeing them standing there brought back to the queen memories of well over twenty years past, when her dear *Angel Earl*, Geoffrey Southwood, and his beautiful countess, her one-time friend, Skye, had reigned at Lynmouth House.

"Do you see it, Rob?" she demanded of the aging Earl of Leicester who accompanied her.

He knew instantly what she meant. "Aye," he answered. "There is a likeness."

"We are growing old, Rob," said the queen.

He took her hand in his and pressed it to his lips. "Nay, Bess. I am growing old, but you never shall."

She looked at him with a faintly cynical gaze, but then her gray-black eyes softened. They had been together a very long time, since they were children. They even shared the same birthday. She patted the hand that still held hers. "Do you know what young Southwood wrote to me this morning? He said that tonight I should be safe among only those who loved me. That I need not fear Spain." She laughed softly. "He is every bit the courtier that his father was, but he is not quite as tough as my *Angel Earl* yet. Then, Rob, I opened the dispatches that my secretary had brought to me, and, lo, I learned that the Spanish fleet is preparing to sail." She laughed again, this time more harshly. "Is it not ironic, my lord? This could be the last fête I ever attend as England's queen if King Philip has his way."

"Nay!" Robert Dudley answered her fiercely. "The Spanish will not prevail over England, Bess. The only chance they had was in Mary Stewart, but they persisted in encouraging her in her treasons and her deviltry. Now that she is dead, Catholic Englishmen will rally to no one but you. Given a choice between Bess Tudor, who has ruled them so wisely and so well all these years, and Philip of Spain, there is no choice." He kissed her hand again. "Spain persists in making this a religious crusade, but there is no such thing in this day and age."

The queen's barge gently bumped against the landing and was made fast by a Lynmouth footman. Elizabeth Tudor stood up, shaking the folds from her bright crimson gown. Before her on the quay Velvet was curtsying and the earl bowing. As he straightened up, Robin held out his hand and helped the queen from her vessel.

Then he kissed her beautiful hand, saying as he did so, "Welcome to Lynmouth House, Your Majesty!"

The queen smiled and looked fondly about her. "It has been many years since I was entertained here by a Southwood," she said. "I don't believe I have been here since your father's time. Everything is as lovely as I remember."

Offering the queen his arm, the earl escorted her from the quay up into the gardens where all her courtiers awaited her. The Earl of Leicester climbed from the boat and offered his arm to Velvet. She took it coolly, avoiding his bold gaze.

"Ah," he murmured softly, "your mama has undoubtedly told you about me, my pet. I regret that I was not at court when you came. I am Dudley."

"I am aware of your identity, my lord. If I do not look directly at you, it is because your gaze is far too intimate for so short an acquaintance. My mother has never spoken of you in my presence."

Her tone was somewhat severe, but the earl was not offended. Rather, it amused him, for she was so very young. He was somewhat put out that Skye had never mentioned him to her, but then considering his relationship with Lady de Marisco that was to be expected. "Are your parents still away?" he asked, moving to what he hoped was a safer subject.

"Yes, my lord. They are expected back by the autumn."

"Pity," said the Earl of Leicester thoughtfully. "We could use your mother's ships now against the Spanish."

Velvet's eyes came up sharply. "O'Malleys," she said, "do not involve themselves in politics."

"Are O'Malleys not loyal to the queen?" he demanded softly.

"I, my lord, am not an O'Malley, so how could I possibly know the answer to such a question? I am loyal to my lady godmother, and my parents are certainly loyal to the crown, but other than that I cannot say. After all, my lord, I am just a maiden newly come to court. I do not know the way of the world, having been protected from it all of my life."

Robert Dudley laughed harshly, then, stopping, took Velvet's chin in his hand, forcing her head up. "I would say, my pet, that though you're newly come to court you are learning most quickly. There is, I can see, a great deal of your mother in you."

She pulled away, her eyes blazing. "Sir, you take liberties!"

Dudley laughed again. "My pet, you haven't, I can see, the faintest idea of what *liberties* can involve. Alas, I am too old and sick now to initiate you, but there was a time, Velvet de Marisco, ah, yes, there once was a time." His voice died away.

"Ah, Steppapa! I should have known you would snatch the fairest lass away this evening, but you cannot have Velvet all to yourself! I am afraid that Wat and I have a previous engagement with the lady." The Earl of Essex stood before them, and Velvet's scowl smoothed into a smile.

"Scamp! Where have you been? The queen is already here! You are insufferably rude to be so late," she scolded him.

"The queen has already forgiven me, Velvet darling, and I should not have been late but that Wat was unhappy with the way his doublet had been made, and nothing would do until it was fixed. He is such a damned popinjay!"

"Since when are you and Ralegh such bosom friends?" demanded the Earl of Leicester.

"The threat of war and a beautiful woman makes strange bedfellows, Steppapa. By the way, where is my mother?"

"Lettice? Humph! Look for your friend, Christopher Blount, and there I will wager you will find your mother, simpering like a girl of seventeen, though she be past fifty," replied Dudley sourly.

"*Mille mercis*, Steppapa," said Essex brightly, and, snatching Velvet's hand, he pulled her away. "Come on, Velvet! There is dancing to do, and I must pay my respects to your brother."

"Please enjoy our hospitality, my lord," Velvet said to Dudley as she moved away.

The Earl of Leicester stood watching her go, a world-weary smile on his face, then moved off himself to join the queen. Elizabeth was surrounded by all her favorites, both old and new. Sir Christopher Hatton was saying something that obviously amused her very much, and even old Lord Burghley had a faint smile upon his severe face. There was Burghley's second son, Robert Cecil, who was being trained to be his father's successor if the old gentleman ever died. Walsingham was there, too. Leicester wondered what news his vast network of spies had brought about the Spanish fleet. The Bacon brothers, Anthony and Francis, were in the group along with the foppish and impossible Earl of Oxford. Conspicuously missing at the moment were Dudley's stepson Essex and Sir Walter Raleigh whom he could see across the gardens speaking with Velvet and young Southwood. Dudley pushed through the group surrounding the queen and moved to her side. Wordlessly the queen reached out and stroked his hand.

The late afternoon slipped into evening, a clear one, and warm for an English July. In the trees, the caged birds sang on, oblivious to the twilight because of the bright lanterns that bobbed gently in the faint breeze. An incredible array of foods was served up for the guests, who did more than justice to the Earl of Lynmouth's board. There were several sides of beef that had been packed in rock salt to preserve their juices while they turned over open spits. There were one hundred legs of baby lamb dressed with garlic and rosemary; sixty suckling pigs prepared in a sauce of honey, oranges, and black cherries, each holding a green apple in its mouth. The pigs had been roasted to a fine, juicy turn, their skins crackly and crisp. There were ducks and capons in a lemon-ginger sauce; sweet pink hams flavored with rare cloves and sauced in malmsey; salmon and trout on beds of cress decorated with carved lemons; and prawns cooked with white wine and herbs in silver dishes. Three fine deer also cooked over open fires, and there were pasties containing rabbit and small game birds. There were many platters, quickly eaten, of small and succulent crabs with dishes of pounded mustard, garlic, and vinegar in which to dip them, as well as other platters containing quail, partridge, and larks roasted golden and set in nests of green watercress.

Then there were dishes of artichokes from France, delicately braised and served with olive oil and a tarragon-flavored vinegar; large bowls of peas, honey-glazed carrots, lettuces, radishes, and small green leeks. Breads were in plentiful supply, along with tubs of butter and wheels of sharp English cheddar and soft Brie imported from Normandy. There were fresh cherries, peaches, early pears, and apples along with small individual bowls of late strawberries. There was creamy egg custard dusted with grated nutmeg, next to tiny cakes soaked in claret or sherry. There were large tarts of peach, apple, rhubarb, and strawberry accompanied by bowls of clotted cream. Wines, both red and white, as well as claret and beer were available to quench the guests' thirst.

As the company began to grow bored with the eating, Master Marlowe and his players appeared to entertain them with the scenes he had written depicting the various triumphs of Elizabeth Tudor's reign. The queen was shown as a kind, benevolent, and wise monarch. She preened visibly beneath the lavish flattery. It was a soothing balm to her troubled mind and spirit. Kit Marlowe and his players were applauded with great approval when they finished.

The night sky was now black satin studded with bright stars as the dancing began. Elizabeth Tudor loved to dance, and so Robin had chosen talented and tireless musicians to play for her as she would wear out many partners before the evening was done. Her host was her first partner, and Robin acquitted himself well. Sir Christopher Hatton, her lord chancellor, was the second chosen. It was said by those less than charitable that Sir Christopher owed his position to his dancing feet. It was not true. He might originally have brought himself to the queen's attention by cutting a better caper than most, but he was competent and able in his position as England's lord chancellor.

Velvet did not lack for partners. She enjoyed dancing as much as her godmother, the queen, did. She was naturally skilled, quick, and light on her feet. Finally, however, she was able to slip off to catch her breath, and, seemingly unobserved, she walked slowly down to the riverbank where the graceful, green willows grew, teasing the water with their delicate branches. It was the most exciting party she could ever remember attending, and being her brother's hostess made her the second most important woman here tonight. It was a heady experience for a young girl newly entered into society. Leaning back against a tree, she listened to the music coming, faintly from the garden and watched the moonlight that was now playing on the Thames.

"Come live with me, and be my love, and we will all the pleasures prove," came the sudden murmur of a deep, masculine voice by her ear.

Velvet jumped and, turning, saw Kit Marlowe. "God's foot, Master Playwright, how you startled me."

Marlowe reached out to steady the girl whose foot, he noted, was perilously close to slipping off the mossy bank. Gently he drew her into the circle of his arms, smiling winningly down at her. "Careful, my love, you are near to falling." His arms tightened slightly. There was an almost untamed gypsy look to him, she thought.

Velvet felt her heart accelerate. It was very exciting to be held in such a close embrace, but there was something about Master Marlowe that made her nervous. He was far too bold for a respectable girl to tolerate. That thought gave her courage. "My thanks for your timely rescue, sir," she said sternly, "but had you not startled me 'twould not have been necessary. You may release me now."

The actor-playwright laughed softly. "What a prim little puss you play at being, mistress, but I know all about the queen's Maids of Honor. You're a merry bunch of jades, and eager for loving, cooped up as you are with such a strict mistress. Do you think you're the first of the queen's ladies I've ever approached?" His mouth dipped toward hers, but Velvet managed to avoid his intent, turning her head so that his lips wetly brushed the side of her neck.

She had wanted to be kissed, but not in this manner, and certainly not by this man. She shuddered with revulsion, but he mistook her emotion for budding passion and urged his suit onward over her very vocal protests.

"Sir, unhand me this instant! I shall inform my brother of your outrageous behavior!" She pressed her palms against his chest and pushed at him.

Marlowe laughed, delighted by what he considered her feigned resistance. "Damn me, you adorable wench, if you don't make me hotter to possess you with all your protesting!" His knowledgeable fingers were undoing the laces of her bodice.

Velvet gasped with surprise, never realizing that a man would be so very bold with a maid. She could feel the night air on her bared breasts, and in that moment Marlowe, seeing her shock, took complete advantage of the girl, burying his face in her cleavage, inhaling the intoxicating fragrance of her perfume. Velvet shrieked, extremely frightened and equally outraged as she struggled unsuccessfully against her attacker. She felt tears of frustration beginning to slip helplessly down her cheeks. Maddened by his lust, he attempted to force her down to the mossy bank, but just as maddened with her fear and the realization of what could happen to her, Velvet fought him wildly, trying to fend him off with flailing fists and sharp nails. Drawing in a breath, she tried to scream, but, seeing it coming, Marlowe put his hand over her mouth. Infuriated, Velvet bit him as hard as she could, and was rewarded with his yelp of pain as he pulled his bleeding hand away.

"You bit me, you little bitch!" he exclaimed, outraged. "'Tis my writing hand, too!" He held the injured digit away from him, looking at it dramatically, as if he had been mortally wounded, yet his other hand still firmly held her captive.

"Release me this instant!" Velvet sobbed indignantly. "The queen shall hear of this, Master Marlowe. Release me!"

"I think not, mistress, for you now owe me, having injured me so grievously." His grip tightened again. "I shall have a sweet forfeit from you!"

"Damn me, Marlowe," drawled the amused voice of Alex Gordon as he stepped into view. "I had heard you were a ladies' man, but I did not think you would stoop to rape, and especially the sister of your host. Loose the lass, or I'll be forced to really injure your precious writing hand, perhaps even remove it entirely." Outwardly, Lord Gordon appeared calm, but inwardly he raged at this low, roguish fellow who dared to lay his hands upon BrocCairn property. Still, he had interrupted Marlowe in time, and instigating a brawl, even in defense of Velvet's honor, would not aid his case with the English queen.

"The jade lured me down here and then turned coy," the playwright proclaimed, but his arm dropped from around Velvet's waist.

Angrily, she pulled away from him. "'Tis not so!" she cried. "I left the gathering for a moment's peace, and he followed me."

Alexander Gordon's amber eyes narrowed dangerously as he looked at Christopher Marlowe. "Your reputation for debauchery and dueling is well known, sir, but I doubt your career could stand another scandal, particularly as the queen is present. I suggest you leave quietly. *Now!*"

Marlowe digested Lord Gordon's words, and then laughed. "You're wiser than I, m'lord. Ah, well, no wench is really worth all that trouble." His black eyes snapped boldly as he took a final look at Velvet's half-bared bosom. Then, with a mocking bow, he turned and walked away.

There was a long silence, then as Alex moved before her, Velvet cried out in a frightened voice, "What are you doing?" His hands were on her bodice.

"Relacing you, my dear. I think that is the first order of business, lest someone stumble upon us and your reputation be compromised." His fingers skillfully redid her gown as she watched him with big eyes. When he had finished, he quietly gathered her into his arms and said, "Now you may cry, Velvet," and she did so, sobbing softly into the fabric of his doublet.

"I d-didn't lure h-him," she said, weeping. "I didn't."

"I know that, lass," he said. "He's a brilliant writer, but basically a low fellow. He has a terrible temper that will one day be the undoing of him, and a worse reputation where women are concerned. I have not a doubt that, seeing you slip away, he followed to take advantage of your innocence."

"I've never even been kissed," Velvet whispered.

"He wanted more than a kiss, lass. You know *that*, don't you?"

"Aye." She looked up at him for a moment, and then, lowering her eyes, blushed, embarrassed by his meaning.

"Surely you've run into this problem before, Velvet. At court, perhaps? What did you do then."

"I have never been accosted so boldly, and certainly not at court. The queen does not appreciate gentlemen who tamper with her ladies, though I know there arc those, both men and women, who brave her wrath for a tryst, a kiss, and a cuddle. I am not, however, one of them, and, besides, none would dare approach me in such a manner knowing my parents' fierce reputation." She had begun to feel better now, snuggled as she was in this big man's arms. "I am better protected than the Spanish infanta herself, my two stern duennas being Sir Walter Ralegh and the Earl of Essex." She chuckled, a small, merry sound that delighted him. "They have warned off all who would approach me in any less than a respectful manner."

Now Alex understood, and he shook his head in admiration. Velvet had a way about her that appealed to the gallant knight hidden in most men whose paths she crossed. They wanted to protect her even as he was now protecting her, as she had been protected all her life by her family. She was much too innocent to be at court. Tonight she had been lucky. He had been out walking to escape the crush for a moment when he had heard her cry for help, then Marlowe's yelp of pain, followed by a smothered oath. He had known instantly what was afoot. What he had not known was that the lady in distress was Velvet. What if he was not there the next time to rescue her?

Before he could seriously digest this thought, however, she, now fully recovered from her fright, said woefully, "I'm fifteen years old, and no one has ever kissed me. *No one.*"

"You are betrothed, or so your brother tells me," Alex said cautiously.

"Aye, I am betrothed!" Velvet said fiercely. "Betrothed at five years of age to a man who didn't bother to acknowledge my presence until just a few weeks ago. For ten years he has ignored me, but now he suddenly finds himself the only male in his line, and he has written to say he is coming to marry me so that he may immediately beget sons!"

"He obviously finds himself in a difficult position, Velvet," began Alex.

"He finds himself in a difficult position?" Her voice dripped scorn. "What of me? My parents promised me that I should never have to marry without love. But they are away! Will a man who has never had the delicacy to even remember my birthday consider that I do not want to marry a perfect stranger, and particulary not without my mother and father by my side? I strongly doubt it!"

"Is that why you came to court?" he asked, knowing the answer she would give; what her brother had dared not say to him.

"Aye! I'm safe from this unknown, unwanted *betrothed* of mine with the queen. When my parents return, the matter will then be settled for good and all."

"Yet the gentleman is within his rights wanting the marriage now, Velvet."

"I'll wed no one until my parents return, and I'll wed no man unless I love him!" she repeated firmly. Then she cocked her head and looked up at him. "Let us speak no longer about this unpleasant matter, but rather let us speak of how I may go about getting my first kiss. You are a man, Alex, and you are surely far more sophisticated than I am. Tell me, then, how does a maiden encourage a gentleman to kiss her?"

"Velvet, lass," he protested, "'tis not a thing you should be discussing with a man."

"Why not?" she demanded. "Every one of the queen's maids has been kissed but me. Why does no one want to kiss me?" She stared up at him and he was hard put to answer her. It gave him secret pleasure to know that whether she realized it or not, she belonged to him. It delighted him to know that no man had yet tasted of her sweetness. But then, as he basked in his smugness, it occurred to him that she was suddenly very ripe for loving, and if he did not pluck her then someone else was going to brave Elizabeth Tudor, Walter Raleigh, and Robert Devereux to possess Velvet de Marisco.

"The first kiss is a very special one," he said reflectively. "It should be given by someone of experience."

"You are qualified, I am certain of it," she said softly.

"Are you asking me to kiss you, Velvet?"

"Should I have to?" she countered, then blushed again.

He laughed low, suddenly realizing that their entire conversation had taken place while she stood within the protective circle of his arms. Drawing her closer with one hand, he gently raised her chin with the other so that she looked him full in the face. "No, Velvet lass, you don't have to ask me to kiss you. 'Tis something I've been wanting to do ever since I first laid eyes upon you."

He lowered his head, and Velvet's heart seemed to leap from her chest as his golden gaze captured her emerald one. Slowly his mouth descended to meet with hers, and her stomach knotted and reknotted in a half-fearful, half-pleasured frenzy of excitement. Unbidden, her eyes closed, and she shivered with delight as his lips came down over hers in that first tender embrace. For a moment Velvet wasn't sure that she was breathing, almost certain that she was perishing as the strength drained from her limbs. Her arms reached up to cling to him, and he pulled her closer against him.

Alex had never known a woman's mouth to be so pliant, so tender. He had been gentle at first, but when she showed neither fright nor resistance his kiss deepened until finally her lips softened and parted beneath his. He shivered with his rising ardor and realized that it was his responsibility to cease their embrace now before it went any further. Reluctantly he drew his head back and looked down into her pale oval face. Slowly her eyes opened and she gazed up at him.

A smile lit his eyes, and he gently touched her cheek. "I hope it was a satisfactory first kiss, Velvet," he said quietly.

Struggling to stand on her own again, she nodded silently at him. It was not necessary to say anything, for he could see her eyes had darkened with her awakening passion. She took several deep breaths that seemed to clear her befuddled brain.

Noting that she was regaining her equilibrium, Alex said calmly, "When you are ready, I shall escort you back to the festivities, Velvet."

Finally she managed to find her voice again. "Is it always like that?" she asked.

"Like what?"

"So . . ." She struggled for the correct word. "So tempestuous!"

He was charmed by her honesty. "I cannot say what a female feels, Velvet, but for me our kiss was tempestuous also. You are a very sweet lass." Then, taking her hand, he began to draw her back through the gardens to where the others were still dancing.

"Will you want to kiss me again?" she surprised him by asking.

He stopped and, taking her by the shoulders, looked down at her, somewhat concerned. "Yes, I will kiss you again, Velvet, but you must promise me something in return."

"What?"

"I would prefer that you did not go about asking other gentlemen to kiss you also."

"Do you fear for my reputation, my lord, or is it that I am not expert enough in kissing yet?" she demanded saucily.

"Both." He grinned, amused by her pertness.

Velvet chuckled. "I like you, Alexander Gordon," she said. "Will you be my friend as well as Robin's?"

"Aye, lassie, I'll be your friend." He felt warmth suffuse through him at her words. Robin had been right in making him wait. Velvet liked him! Soon he would teach her to love him.

"I'll kiss no one else but you, Alex," she said softly. "At least not until I'm good at this kissing," she amended with a laugh.

Alex noted that Robert Devereux eyed him somewhat jealously as they returned to the gathering. The Earl of Essex saw with rising irritation that Velvet's cheeks were pinker than normal and that her mouth had a sudden lushness about it. Moving next to Lord Gordon, he murmured in a low voice, "You know that the queen frowns upon those who trifle with her ladies, my lord. Besides, the girl is betrothed."

"I am aware of all that, my lord earl," was Alex's calm reply. "Remember, I am a friend of Velvet's brother, and I would not strain that friendship by harming his sister. The lass is safe in my company."

"God's foot!" exploded Velvet. "You are worse than a parent, Scamp. Considering your own reputation with the ladies, this constant defense of my virtue becomes burdensome! I came to court to have some fun before I must settle down and become an old married woman! I will have no more of this watchdogging from you!"

"I only seek to protect you from those who would despoil your character and reputation," said Essex sulkily.

Velvet instantly felt contrite since she knew that the man she called Scamp, one of England's most powerful courtiers, was a true and good friend to her.

"I know that," she said, "but sometimes you are overly diligent, dear Scamp. Lord Gordon is to me as you and Wat are. He is my friend, and I am glad of it." She put her hand on Essex's arm. "Come now and let us find some refreshment. I am being a bad hostess, and Robin will be most put out with me."

Essex, immediately restored to his good humor by her gentle wheedling, allowed himself to be led off.

Walter Ralegh smiled at Alexander Gordon. "She is a most winning maid, isn't she, my lord earl?"

Alex stiffened. "Sir," he began, "I think you mistake me for someone else."

"Nay," replied Ralegh. "I have a memory for name and titles. You are the Earl of BrocCairn, Velvet's betrothed husband, and she doesn't know it, does she?"

Since denial would have been useless, Alex simply replied, "Nay, she does not. Her brother and I felt it would make things easier if we could become friends without the strain of our betrothal standing between us."

Ralegh nodded. "She had never met you, then?"

"She was five the last time I saw her."

Ralegh stared. "In ten years' time you have not seen the girl? I realize that you live in the north, Lord Gordon, but don't you think in all those years you could have spared some time to see Velvet? Now I understand her reluctance."

Alex flushed. "I spend a great deal of time in France and Italy; and then there were small errands to perform for my king; and my father needed me. The time seemed to slip by so quickly. My father's dying wish was that I marry Velvet and perpetuate our family."

"So," remarked Walter Ralegh dryly, "good son that you were, you hurried to do your father's bidding without so much as a thought for the maid's feelings in the matter. You've not a great deal of tact about you, have you my lord?"

"Nay." Alex grinned somewhat ruefully. "Robin has taken me greatly to task about it. I'm afraid I allowed my grief for my father to rule my common sense when I sent the message south demanding my bride. Now I shall have to work all the harder to win Velvet over before I dare to tell her who I am."

"I'm going to reveal your identity to the queen," Sir Walter said. "In order to woo Velvet, you will need her cooperation. She guards her maids jealously, but if she knows that your suit is an honorable one, and that you have the right, she will subtly aid you. You can have no better friend than Elizabeth Tudor, nor a worse enemy."

"What of Essex?"

"Robert Devereux is a young hothead," Raleigh said quietly. "Normally he and I have little to do with one another. There is no need for him to know who you really are, Lord Gordon. He could easily in a temper give you away and cause damage without meaning to do so. Robert is not deliberately thoughtless, but he is thoughtless nonetheless. Let me go and speak to the queen now, and then with her permission I shall introduce you to Her Majesty." Walter Ralegh moved off, and Alex went to find his host.

Ralegh slipped easily into the circle about the queen, working his way cautiously through the press until he was next to her. The queen was listening to a rather clever story being told by one of her favorite young men, Anthony Bacon, but, as always, she saw everything that went on about her. Quietly she slipped her arm through Ralegh's and gave him a smile without ever turning her attention from young Bacon.

"I need a moment in private," he said softly in her ear, and she nodded her assent.

When the storyteller had done with his tale, which was greeted with pleased laughter, the queen began to move off through the gardens still holding Ralegh's arm. Behind her the gentlemen followed until she turned and said coquettishly, "Keep your distance, sirs, for I wish to be alone with my Wat-er." Then she walked on, the disappointed courtiers now well behind them and out of hearing.

"Thank you, madame," Sir Walter said.

"What is it you would beg of me this time, sir? I often ask myself if you will ever stop being the beggar," the queen teased him.

"I shall stop being a beggar when you stop being so generous, madame," he quickly riposted, and the queen laughed heartily.

"God's nightshirt, Wat-er, you are quick!" Then she grew serious again. "'Tis not the Spanish threat, is it? Dear God, not another plot!"

"Nay, dearest lady," he hastened to reassure her. "What I have to tell you is a love story in which Your Majesty could play an important role toward arranging a happily-ever-after ending for the lovers involved." Then Ralegh explained the situation between Velvet and the Earl of BrocCairn, being very careful to ensure that the queen did not suspect that Velvet had begged for her position as a maid of honor only to escape Alex.

As he spoke, Elizabeth Tudor's face softened. She had grown extremely fond of Velvet in the few weeks she had known her. The child was bright, amusing, and generally loveable without being one of those sickly sweet misses who annoyed her so. The queen could understand Velvet's fright at being told that a stranger was coming to wed her and carry her off, especially with her beloved parents half a world away. She was young and eager for the joy of living, and she should have some pleasures before settling to become a man's charge for the rest of her life.

The queen knew that her own lot and the fates of the few independent women in her realm were rare. Most women belonged to their fathers until they were wed, and afterwards they belonged to their husbands. Elizabeth Tudor knew better than most what a man's power over a woman could be. She had seen her father destroy so many women. Only two of her stepmothers, Anne of Cleves and Catherine Parr had escaped Henry Tudor. The princess of Cleves had willingly agreed to a divorce, and thus avoided the fate of Elizabeth's own mother, Anne Boleyn. Queen Catherine Parr had only avoided an unhappy end by outliving Henry Tudor. Yes, Elizabeth understood well a woman's position in relation to the men of this world.

Still, as represented by Ralegh, the Earl of BrocCairn did not appear to be a bad fellow, and Velvet was eventually going to have to marry him. The betrothal was a firm agreement made many years prior and approved by Lord and Lady de Marisco. That the Scots earl had come to London to woo Velvet greatly weighed in his favor with the queen. There was, however, no reason why he could not wait until her parents returned to wed the bride. It would allow Velvet her interval at court while at the same time preserving the legalities of the situation, and that seemed a good solution to the queen.

"Let me meet this gentleman, Wat-er." The queen loved giving the broad Devonshire accent to Walter Ralegh's name. She called most of those close to her by pet names. Leicester was her *Eyes*; Hatton, *Lids*; Cecil; *Spirit*.

"I will fetch him directly to Your Majesty!"

"Nay, send one of the others. You stay with me," she commanded.

Ralegh turned to the other gentlemen who were following at a discreet distance. "Bacon," he called, "the queen requests that you fetch Lord Gordon. He is the Earl of Lynmouth's houseguest. A rather tall fellow with a craggy face."

"An interesting description," observed the queen. "Is he then so rocklike, this Scotsman?"

"He has a rather handsome face that appears to have been carved from the granite of the Highlands itself," replied Ralegh. "I've not a doubt the ladies of the court will all vie for his favor."

"Hmm," said Elizabeth Tudor.

"He knows nothing of fashion, however," Ralegh continued. "His garb is woefully plain."

The queen chuckled, then stepped back to let her eyes play over Sir Walter Ralegh's peacockish finery. His doublet was embroidered in so many gold beads, pearls, and topazes that the queen could barely see any fabric. Ralegh was indeed the fashion plate of her court, and it was said he would have made his tailor a wealthy man by now if only he would pay his bills.

"Wat-er," she said, "there is no one ever come to my court who could hold a candle to you for style. I doubt not your earl will well suit me, however, and all the shameless jades of my court, too. They will be mightily disappointed to find his attention is for my godchild, Velvet, alone."

They chatted lightly for the next few minutes with all the familiarity of old and good friends. Then suddenly the queen's attention was taken by the sight of Anthony Bacon returning in the company of a wonderfully attractive gentleman. The Scots earl, she thought, and had a moment's regret that she was not a simple maid like Velvet. How nice to be courted seriously for one's self. Bacon and his companion reached her, and Elizabeth Tudor shook off her self-pity to assess frankly the young man.

Her gaze was direct and frank, and she liked what she saw. She was not impressed by his outward good looks, but rather by what she glimpsed in his serious amber eyes. There she saw steadiness, loyalty, and reliability. His big hands with their elegant, long fingers were the strong hands of a horseman, not of some soft fop. What she liked best, however, was the fact that he met her piercing gaze without flinching. Elizabeth Tudor instinctively trusted a man who could look her in the eye, and few could, or dared.

"Madame," said Ralegh, "may I present to you the Earl of BrocCairn, Alexander Gordon, the gentleman of whom I spoke."

"You are welcome to my court, my lord," said the queen quietly. "How is it with my young cousin, James of Scotland?"

"I cannot give you a firsthand account, madame," said Alex, "for I choose not to frequent the Stewart court. My family's business interests keep me at *Dun Broc* or in Aberdeen, but I have heard that the king is well." So this was the woman who had ordered Mary Stewart's death, thought Alex. How different the two women were, though he had never met the late Scots queen. His opinion stemmed only from what his father had told him.

Angus Gordon had been intensely loyal to his half sister, Mary Stewart, but he had thought her rash, a woman ruled by her emotions, not her intellect. When he had learned of her death just before his own, he had shaken his head wearily, saying, "It was bound to come to this in the end—but hold no grudges against England's queen, Alex, my son. Scotland will be the final victor, for 'tis Mary's son who will one day rule England."

Now, as Alex mouthed civilized words to Elizabeth Tudor, he realized that he harbored no ill feelings toward her. Rather he sensed a magnificent intelligence and a sharp wit housed within her frail body, and he knew he was going to like her very much.

The queen took his arm and they began to walk along a torchlit path. "Tell me, when were you betrothed to my godchild, my lord?" she said quietly.

"It was the summer of her fifth year, madame. I came with my late father down from *Dun Broc* to *Queen's Malvern*. My father and Adam de Marisco had been boyhood friends in France. It was their hope that this marriage would unite our families. When my father passed away, I found myself the sole surviving male in my family, and I realized that I must marry at once. I sent word to Lord de Marisco, but he was away. Lord Bliss opened my message and informed Velvet of her impending marriage. I'm afraid she was most put out."

The queen chuckled. "And fled to me," she remarked wryly.

"Aye, she fled me," he admitted. "I must admit to feeling extremely chagrined by her conduct, madame, and I can assure you that she has dealt my pride a hard blow. Nonetheless, I believe if Velvet could learn to know me, perhaps she would not fear our marriage so greatly. I do want her to be happy, madame."

"I think that my godchild will be fortunate in her husband, my lord," Elizabeth said quietly. "Very well, sirrah! You may court the maid with my permission, and I shall not reveal your secret to anyone. I see the wisdom in the plan devised by you and Robin Southwood. In the short time I have known Velvet, I have learned that she is indeed stubborn. It is better that she come to know Alexander Gordon for himself and not resist him merely because he is BrocCairn. I will, however, give Velvet one small advantage. I will not release her from my service until Lord and Lady de Marisco return. The latest news has them arriving some time in the autumn. I think you might wait until then to claim, and to bed, your bride."

Alex stopped, and, turning to face the queen, he caught her hand up and raised it to his lips. "I am grateful, madame," he said.

She smiled at him, and for a brief moment he saw the young girl inside the aging woman. Then, offering her his arm, they strolled in the beautiful midsummer gardens of Lynmouth, and he made Elizabeth Tudor forget for a few short minutes the terrible Spanish threat that hung not only over her beloved England, but over her own frail person.

Chapter 3

Robin Southwood was totally confused. Never in his life had he felt this way. His fête for the queen had been a tremendous success, and yet he felt despondent. When the last guest had left, he flung himself into a chair by the crackling fire.

Joining him there, Velvet and Alex were so full of high spirits themselves that at first they didn't notice Robin's depression.

"I've never been to such a gathering before," Alex said enthusiastically. "You're a fine host, Rob!"

"God's nightshirt, big brother, 'twas a great success. The house and gardens looked magnificent, and the food and entertainment will be talked about for weeks. Her Majesty said that she has not attended such a party since your father was alive! I am the most envied girl at court because you are my brother!"

"I met Sir Walter Ralegh tonight, Rob," Alex put in. "He's planning a voyage to the New World, and he wanted to know if any of my ships might want to go along. Do you know what an opportunity it would be for us?"

"Scamp is quite envious of you, you know, Robin. I think he may try to steal away your chef the next time he himself entertains Her Majesty." Velvet giggled. "Oh, Robin, how can I thank you for letting me be your hostess and for these lovely pearls? You are just the best brother a girl ever had!"

Suddenly the Earl of Lynmouth sat bolt upright in his chair. *"Who was she?"* he demanded. "Who was the incredibly beautiful creature you introduced me to tonight, Velvet?"

"What!" Both Velvet and Alex were taken aback.

"That utterly exquisite blonde in the wonderful turquoise silk gown! Never have I seen such perfection! Who is she? You *must* know, Velvet, and *I* must know as well!"

For a moment, Velvet was totally baffled. There had been several beautiful blond women at the fête tonight. "Robin," she said slowly, "I am not sure who you mean. There were a number of blondes, and at least three of them were in blue."

"Not blue, turquoise! You must know her! You said she was one of your best friends at court when you introduced her, but I could not linger and find out more because the queen's barge was sighted then."

"Angel! You mean Angel!"

"Angel? Is that her name? My God, how fitting!" He sighed deeply.

Velvet resisted the overwhelming urge to burst into a fit of giggles, though the fact that Alex grinned conspiratorily at her over her brother's head didn't make it any easier. Swallowing, she said in a somewhat strained voice, "Her name is Angel Christman, Robin. She is a royal ward, and has been raised at court. Her parents are deceased."

"I want to meet her," Robin said firmly.

"You did meet her," Velvet protested.

"I want to meet her properly, Velvet. I realize that you must return to court tomorrow, but the next time you come to Lynmouth House I want you to bring Mistress Angel Christman with you."

Again Velvet fought back the urge to laugh. Robin was behaving so foolishly. Then, looking at him, she realized, somewhat startled, that her brother had fallen in love! Love at first sight was something that happened only in fairy tales, wasn't it? Had Robin really fallen in love with Angel? What would Angel think of it when she told her? No, she couldn't tell her! What if Angel didn't really love Robin back and only accepted his suit because of his vast wealth? Mama had always said a woman should marry only for love. She would have to keep silent and wait and see if Angel responded to Robin's suit.

Without warning, Velvet felt very tired, and she realized that it was almost dawn. She was due back at court that very evening, and if she did not get some rest, she was going to disgrace herself by falling asleep on her feet in the queen's presence.

"Go to bed, Velvet," Robin said as if reading her thoughts. "I remember what it was like to be at court in the queen's service."

Velvet curtsyed to her brother and Alex, then moved slowly and sleepily from the library.

As the door closed behind her, Alex looked at his friend. "When will Velvet be coming back to Lynmouth House, Rob?"

"I'll tell her tomorrow before she returns to her duties that she's to treat my home as her own whenever she's in London. Mother would want it that way, I know," Robin said.

"When do you think she'll have another day free?"

"We'll have to join the court, my friend, if you're going to woo my sister and if I'm going to pay my addresses to Mistress Christman. Maids of Honor take their pleasure when and where they can, for the queen is an exacting mistress. I well remember my own days as her page."

"God in His heaven, I nae thought to find myself at Elizabeth Tudor's court. I'm no courtier, Robin." Alex shook his head.

"As long as you're honest with the queen and Velvet grows fond of you, Alex, you've no need to play the royal game. I could not help but notice tonight that several of the ladies were most taken with you."

Alex chuckled softly. "I must say I've nae had such imaginative offers since our days in Paris, Robin. With such a virtuous queen, I am surprised she tolerates such licentiousness around her."

"She tolerates it as long as it is not out in the open. Let a liaison become a scandal and there is hell to pay, you may be sure."

The Scotsman nodded, then said, "Well, I'm off to my bed, too." He stood, stretching his long frame.

"You should have pleasant dreams," Robin teased, "or were you unsuccessful this evening with my sister?"

Alex grinned back. "A gentleman, even a wild and rude Scot such as myself, never kisses and tells, Robin." Before Lord Southwood could pursue it further, Lord Gordon was quickly gone.

Robin smiled after him, thinking that there had been a day when Alex Gordon had most certainly kissed and told. His smile broadened into a grin as he remembered those long-gone times they'd spent in Paris, the whores they shared, and the lies they told each other about their prowess. He chuckled, then grew somber. Those were the days before his marriage to Alison de Grenville.

Alison. Foolish, foolish Alison. He had never loved her, but he had been very fond of her. He had never been *in love* at all until tonight when he had seen the exquisite Mistress Angel Christman. He had spoken but few words to the girl. He hadn't even danced with her, yet he knew, or rather his heart knew, that she was the woman for him. He had sworn to himself that he would never marry again, but this was an entirely different matter altogether.

His mother had once tried to explain love, true love, to him. She had even asked him if he wanted to call off the betrothal that she had made with the de Grenvilles when he was a little boy. He hadn't allowed her to do so, for he knew he had to marry someone and Alison was pleasant enough. He had known her all his life. "But you don't love her!" his mother had fussed at him, and he'd smiled with the superiority of youth. His mother had spent her whole life *in love*, it seemed, and although she claimed to have found great happiness with the last of his stepfathers, Adam de Marisco, she had suffered greatly for her love. Robin had often questioned if love was worth all the pain, and had decided early it was not. He had wanted an orderly life.

Mistress Angel Christman, he suspected, was going to change all that. He had never meant to return to court, preferring a quiet life on his Devon estate with his children. His marriage to Alison had brought about his gradual withdrawal from the queen's circle, and her death had been the best excuse of all to stay away. Now he found himself being drawn back by a pair of meltingly gorgeous blue eyes, a head of blond ringlets, and a smile that touched his heart so strongly he almost wept remembering it. His duty as the queen's host had prevented him from pursuing Mistress Christman this evening, but he was going back to court to do so. His first move, however, would be to inquire about her background from Lord Hundston, who would know all.

The queen's chancellor was very surprised the morning after the Earl of Lynmouth's fête to receive a message from that gentleman regarding the background of one Mistress Angel Christman, a royal ward. England was facing the most serious threat of invasion since the Normans. Everything Elizabeth Tudor stood for, everything England stood for, was in mortal danger, and Lord Southwood wanted to learn about a chit of a girl. These hedonistic courtiers, thought Hundston, and then he remembered who the request came from and reassessed the situation. Robert Southwood was a serious young man who had been deeply and genuinely grieved by his wife's death. That there was a royal ward with some quality to attract this nobleman was in itself interesting.

Lord Hundston looked into the matter and was disappointed by what he found. Mistress Angel Christman, age seventeen, had been a royal ward since the age of five. She was the granddaughter of two minor barons from the northwest counties and the child of a younger son and daughter. She had been left in the queen's charge by her father, who had murdered her mother after finding the lady in another gentleman's bed. The girl had no fortune, no influential relations to aid her, and therefore no prospects. One thing Lord Hundston did learn was that Mistress Christman was radiantly beautiful, which might possibly stand her in good stead if she were clever as well. So far she had not given evidence of such quality, and there was absolutely no gossip connecting her with any gentleman. Her closest two friends seemed to be Bess Throckmorton and Velvet de Marisco.

"Of course!" Hundston spoke aloud to himself. That had to be the connection. Mistress Christman was involved with Mistress de Marisco, who was a younger sister to the Earl of Lynmouth. With her parents away, the earl was looking after his sister's interests, and rightly so. He but sought to know about her favorite companions. Bess Throckmorton was a known quantity coming as she did from a highly placed family, even if she herself was poor; but Mistress Christman, an unimportant royal ward from an undistinguished family, was, of course, unknown to Robert Southwood. Lord Hundston dictated a message to his secretary presenting the girl's background and informing the Earl of Lynmouth that, according to the information available to him, Mistress Christman was a proper friend for his sister. Then he turned to the far more serious matters of state.

The night before warning beacons had sprung up on every hill in Devon and Cornwall. This was the signal that the great Armada of Spain had been sighted off the *Lizard* at dawn, and it was now close to Plymouth. The signal fires had spread the word from Devon to Dorset to Wiltshire to Surrey to London. The news had been kept from the queen on Lord Burghley's orders, however, until after the Earl of Lynmouth's fête.

The queen had had a very traumatic year and needed this small bit of pleasure, William Cecil had decided. He had been with her since the very beginning, and he knew her better than anyone. The next few weeks would tell the fate of the Tudor dynasty, and the queen would need to be strong.

Once the fête was over, however, he had told her, and the news had spread like wildfire throughout the court. The gentleman courtiers had not even bothered to sleep. They had returned to Greenwich only long enough to change from their silks and velvets into more practical clothing. Then they were off for the coast. Charles Howard, the lord admiral, was already in Plymouth, and had been for some time. So was Sir Francis Drake, John Hawkins, and Martin Frobisher, the other great admirals of the fleet.

There had been several earlier sightings of the Spanish. In late June a Cornish bark bound for the French coast had spotted nine large ships with great, blood-red crusaders' crosses on their sails cruising the seas between the Scillies and Ushant. Another coastal trader out of a Devon port was startled to come upon a small fleet of fifteen ships. Chased, he had come ashore in Cornwall and ridden hell-bent for Plymouth with his story.

Francis Drake had, of course, realized what these sightings meant. The previous year he had surprised the Spanish at Coruña, and burned their fleet, thus postponing King Philip's attack on England. Now the Armada was rebuilt, refitted, and revictualed. Drake convinced the lord admiral to seize the initiative, sail south, and strike at the Spanish again before they could reach England. Within a day's sail of Coruña, however, the wind veered about and blew strongly from the south. The English had set sail short of victuals, and now, even shorter of rations, there was nothing for them to do but turn about and sail home. There was always the distinct possibility that the Spanish would take advantage of the south wind and reach England before they did. Such a thing was too awful even to contemplate.

The day that the English fleet had returned to Plymouth, the Spanish had set sail from Coruña and, with a southerly wind behind them cruised northwestward across a sunshine-filled Bay of Biscay, not usually noted for its pleasant weather. The skies then turned dark for several days, slowing the Spanish down before it had become fair once again. The great Armada continued ever northward toward England. Then on Saturday, July 20, 1588, Lord Burghley had word that the Spanish had at last arrived.

England had responded in an overwhelming fashion to the queen's earlier request for aid. The city of London had asked how many men and ships they were expected to supply, and were told five thousand men and fifteen ships. Two days later London's aldermen produced ten thousand men and thirty ships for Her Majesty's service.

England's Roman Catholic Cardinal Allen sent an "*Admonition to the Nobility and People of England.*" They must support the invasion, he counseled, the purpose of which was to restore the Holy Mother Church and to rid them of that monster of impiety and unchastity, Elizabeth Tudor. This incredible plea was sent from the cardinal's lodgings at the Palace of St. Peter in Rome.

The English Catholics were not interested. They were content, and had become prosperous under Harry Tudor's brat. They were English to the soles of their feet, and they had no intention of replacing an honest-born English queen with a Spanish infanta, for Philip of Spain had said he would give England to one of his daughters. All England rallied to the cause. The dispatches came fast and furious from the coast to Lord Burghley and the queen.

While Robin's fête was in full swing, the English navy had worked furiously to warp their ships out to sea again. Caught on a lee shore with the enemy at their gates, they strove through the night to tow their ships to safety.

On the morning of July 20, the wind against them, the English worked their way laboriously out of Plymouth Sound into the open sea. By noon, fifty-four vessels, in an incredible feat of pure skill and superb discipline, were close to the Eddystone Rocks. The Spanish, twenty miles to windward, were unaware that the English fleet lay smack in their path.

The Spanish had been given a plan of action by their king, and come what may they would adhere to it. Was not God on their side? The English, however, had been given an order by their queen. *Win.* How they fought their battle was up to the admirals. Elizabeth Tudor was only interested in the successful results of their naval decisions. She knew that God helped those who helped themselves. As she had said so many times, "There is but one lord, Jesus Christ. The rest is all trifles."

By evening, a hazy moon scampered devilishly amid high, fair-weather clouds. The Armada was anchored in the close battle formation that it was to maintain until it reached its rendezvous with the Duke of Parma off Calais. During the night, the watches on the many decks of the Spanish fleet occasionally noticed shadowy forms passing in the mist before them and moving westward toward the Cornish coast. At dawn, the surprised Spanish discovered that they had been outflanked, and their outnumbered enemies were sailing a mile or so to windward. The English now had the battle advantage.

The great Spanish Armada—its huge ships top-heavy with turrets; some of them weighing more than a thousand tons with towering masts and superstructures; their sails bright with paintings of saints and martyrs; their great hulls painted a forbidding black; packed with soldiers and great grappling irons hanging from their yardarms—bore down on England's defenders. The English ships, by contrast, were trim and far smaller. Their pure white sails bore a simple design: St. George's Cross. Their hulls were painted in the queen's colors, green and white, in a geometrical pattern. They lay low in the water, their ports bristling with guns.

The battle was fierce and hotly contested, but by one in the afternoon when the action was concluded, neither side could claim a victory. The Spanish had come prepared for a close-in fight. Their new fifty-pound iron round shot was capable of destroying the rigging on an opponent. The English, however, had greater mobility with their sleeker vessels, and their expertly handled English culverins were far superior at long range. They whisked in and out of the Armada, attacking like small dogs nipping at the heels of fat sheep. After several hours of battle, and finding themselves unable to gain the advantage, both sides wisely retired. The English, however, had not lost one ship.

The Armada continued on its ponderous way, moving majestically in the summer sunshine across Lyme Bay. Upon the coastal hills spectators peered anxiously through the haze for a glimpse of Spain's mighty fleet. Meanwhile, a host of small ships poured out from the little seaside towns of Dorset, bringing the English fleet supplies of fresh food and ammunition as fast as the authorities could requisition them.

By Saturday, July 27, the Armada had anchored off the French port of Calais. Here the Spanish admiral, the Duke of Medina-Sidona, could communicate with the Duke of Parma, the Spanish general who was to command the landing forces. The Armada's shadow, the English navy, was now joined by the remainder of the fleet commanded by Lord Seymour and Sir William Winter, a seasoned veteran.

In London, they waited. The rumors were wild and many. Drake had been captured, went one. Another tale was that there had been a great battle off Newcastle and the English flagship had been sunk. In the face of these rumors the English people had only one thought: the coming battle. Wednesday, August 7, was the date of the highest floodtide at Dunkirk, and it was expected that Parma's troops would embark across the channel that day and swarm onto English soil, probably in Essex.

The Earl of Leicester, Robert Dudley, had been put in charge of the army and named lieutenant general. The queen had wished to go down to the coast to see the battle, but Leicester would not permit it. He wrote to her saying:

Now for your person, being the most dainty and sacred thing we have in the world to care for. . . . A man must tremble when he thinks of it, specially finding your Majesty to have that princely courage to transport yourself to your utmost confines of your realm to meet your enemies, and to defend your subjects. I cannot, most dear Queen, consent to that, for upon your well-doing consists all and some for your whole kingdom, and therefore, preserve that above all!

The queen chafed, fussing at her ladies, irritable and moody by turns. She hated being cooped up in London.It was the gentle Bess Throckmorton who finally suggested to her, "Perhaps Your Majesty might go as far as Tilbury and review your troops. Just the sight of you would hearten them greatly."

"God's nightshirt, Bess! You are absolutely right! We shall go to Tilbury, for surely Leicester, old woman that he has become, will not object to that."

Leicester gave in gracefully, for he understood her concern better than most. He wrote: *Good sweet Queen—alter not your purpose if God give you good health*!

The queen came down the river Thames to Tilbury on August 6. Her great barge with its green and white banners was filled to overflowing with her ladies, certain chosen courtiers, and minstrels who sang and played gaily as they wanted to take their mistress's mind from the business at hand if only for a short while. Behind the royal vessel floated several others, carrying servants, the royal coach, and the horses.

Though Ralegh had now joined the fleet, Essex was with the queen. She would not suffer to have him gone from her, much to his embarrassment and anguish, for Robert Devereux was no coward. Velvet, being the least of the queen's ladies, had offered to ride in her brother's barge so that there would be more room in Elizabeth Tudor's vessel. She had invited Bess and Angel to ride along with her. Bess was gowned in rose pink, but she had been pale and wan of late, and now Velvet was even more convinced that her friend was in love with Walter Ralegh who was in danger. Velvet would not dare to suggest such a thing out loud, however, for if the older Bess wished to confide in her she would do so. To pry would be unforgiveable, especially since Bess's friendship had smoothed Velvet's way at court.

The cruise down to Tilbury had an almost holidaylike atmosphere to it despite the seriousness of the situation. Everyone was wearing their best clothes, and the barges' storage areas contained vast picnic hampers filled with cold chickens, rabbit pasties, freshly baked breads, cheeses, peaches, cherries, and fruit tarts. Behind the Southwood barge bobbed an openwork wicker basket. Through its slits could be seen several stoneware bottles of wine cooling in the river.

"Do you really think the Spanish will invade us tomorrow, my lord?" the beauteous Angel asked Robin. She was wearing a gown of sky blue silk that was somewhat faded and perhaps a bit tight across her bosom, for royal wards, especially poor ones, were not often given new gowns. The besotted Earl of Lynmouth did not notice. All he knew was that she was the sweetest girl he had ever met.

"God forbid it," he answered, "but you need have no fear, Mistress Christman. I will protect you."

Angel blushed rosily, and Velvet was amazed to find her usually quick-tongued friend so maidenly and at a loss for words. What on earth was the matter with her? Velvet's eyes met Bess's, and Bess smiled, understanding her thoughts.

"Are you afraid, Velvet?" Alex asked her.

"Nay!" came her quick reply. "I'll take a sword in my own hand to defend England before I'd let the damned Spanish have it!"

"Bravo, *petite soeur*!" approved Robin. "You're as loyal an Englishwoman as any. Your father would be proud of you."

Just after noon, the royal barge arrived at Tilbury, approaching the dock near Block House where Leicester and his officers were on hand to greet the queen. As Elizabeth set her elegantly shod foot onto land, cannons were discharged and a fife and drum corps began to play. Awaiting her was Sir Roger Williams with two thousand mounted knights. A thousand of these were sent ahead to *Ardern Hall*, the home of Master Rich where Elizabeth would be staying. The other thousand horsemen escorted the queen's carriage. The queen was in high spirits, here among the people she loved. Though she feared an invasion, she truly believed that the spirit and courage of her people would prevail over the dark might of Spain's vastly superior forces. Never at any time would she even consider failure, though no word had yet come from the fleet.

Beside her in the coach sat the Earl of Leicester. Like Elizabeth herself, he had not been well this last year, but he had mustered what strength he had to command the army for her. Time had mellowed Robert Dudley somewhat, and his genuine affection for Elizabeth could not be doubted. It was as strong as his ambition. He had waited many years after his first wife's death for the queen to marry him, but when it became apparent that she had no intention of doing so, he had, in a fit of pique, married her cousin, the widowed Lettice Knollys. It had been a secret marriage, for neither the bride nor the groom wished to destroy their positions at court. The queen, however, found them out and was furious. The earl and his countess were banned from court for a period of time, but Elizabeth missed Dudley and he was soon recalled. Lettice was not so fortunate and was forced to cool her heels for several years.

At first the marriage had been successful, but then, like so many hasty marriages, it began to fall apart. Dudley truly loved the queen inasmuch as he was ever capable of loving anyone. Then, too, he loved the power and the favors that only she could bestow. In that attitude, Lettice was her husband's equal, but Elizabeth could not forgive her cousin for marrying the man that she herself loved above all others, even if she would not marry him. Neither of the Dudleys were the most admirable of characters, but both were unquestioningly loyal.

Bess had gone with the queen to *Ardern Hall*, but the queen, ever indulgent of her godchild, had told Velvet that she would not need her that night. Velvet and Angel were to stay with the Earl of Lynmouth and Lord Gordon at one of Tilbury's better inns, the Mermaid. Robin had been wise enough to send one of his men ahead several days prior to their departure from London to request the two best bedrooms and a private parlor for dining.

The Mermaid was located amid a green lawn on the banks of the river. A whitewashed building set with dark timbers, it had lovely diamond-paned windows and red and white roses by every door. To one side of the main building was a stable, to the other a lovely garden, its flower beds filled with spicy marigolds and gillyflowers, fragrant blue lavender and sweet rosemary. Symmetrically set within the small garden were little green shrubs, trimmed into fancy shapes like urns and birds. Nearer the back door of the inn was a small kitchen garden growing beans, carrots, peas, parsnips, leeks, and salad greens. There were also several fruit trees—apple, plum and pear—as well as currant and gooseberry bushes. It was nothing at all like the beautiful gardens at *Queen's Malvern* with its two mazes, hundreds of rosebushes, and rare lilies brought back from the Americas. Nonetheless, it was a pleasant place to walk after a fine meal.

It was twilight, and the busy river was at last calm, a faintly discernible haze hovering above it, the momentarily calm waters reflecting the mauve sky above. Swallows swooped over the surface in the pinkish light. Despite her privileged place on her brother's barge, it had not been possible to bring many changes of clothing. Velvet was still wearing the apple green silk gown she had put on that morning, but though he knew she was annoyed at being unable to change her gown, Alex thought she looked fetching.

Velvet was surprised to find herself alone with the handsome Scot. Her brother, it seemed, had managed to move to another part of the inn garden with Angel. Determined not to show her nervousness, she turned to Lord Gordon, saying, "You have told me nothing of yourself, my lord. Speak to me of your home."

"I thought we had agreed that you would call me Alex," he said in his deep, warm voice.

She blushed and silently fussed at herself for doing so. "Tell me of Scotland, Alex. Until I joined the court I never lived anywhere but at my homes in England and France. Tell me of your land. My betrothed husband is a Scot, and if I do wed with him, I shall be living there."

"My family has a small castle in the Highlands to the north and west of Aberdeen. They also have a town house in Aberdeen."

"Do you not have a house in Edinburgh? Surely you follow the court?"

"Nay, lass, I've not the time or the inclination to involve myself in the Stewart court. Stewart monarchs invariably borrow money from their nobility, never pay it back, and are incredibly ungrateful. The king, however, is a cousin. We share the same grandfather, James V."

Her green eyes widened, impressed by this revelation. "Your grandsire was the king of Scotland?"

"Aye. My grandmother, Alexandra, was the heiress to"— He hesitated an instant, realizing that he had almost said BrocCairn, then, recovering, he continued—"our family's estates. She claimed a handfast marriage with the king, but as she died birthing my father, Angus, nothing was made of it. The king recognized his paternity, but my father bore the Gordon name. It was said that my grandmother loved her Jamie Stewart very much."

Velvet sighed dramatically. "How wonderfully romantic! If only I could fall in love!"

It was pure madness that led him to say it, but Alex could not contain himself. "I think I'm falling in love with you, Velvet," he said quietly.

She stopped in midstep and turned to look up at him. "You must not, Alex," she said with utmost seriousness. "I am betrothed, and you know it."

"Yet you tell me you fled this betrothed, that you will not have him."

"I have not said I would not have him. I simply will not wed him until I know him, and until my mother and father return home from India. I would not, however, compromise my family's good name, Alex. Surely you don't think that I would?"

"Nay, lass, I do realize your honor would not allow you to shame your family, but, Velvet, would you break my heart? The heart that I would so willingly put into your gentle keeping?"

She looked so confused, and his heart rejoiced. Then she said with total candor, "I have never been courted by a man before. Are you courting me, Alex?"

"Would you welcome such a suit, Velvet?"

Her beautiful young face was grave, and for a long moment she considered. Finally she spoke. "I have said that I would marry only for love, yet how can I know what love is if I accept my parents' decision blindly? The one freedom they have always given me has been the freedom of choice, and though they be far from me now, I know that they would allow me that same freedom in this case. Yes, Alex, I will welcome your suit provided that you understand that it may lead to nothing more than a simple flirtation. I cannot mislead you. My family's honor binds me legally to this unknown earl though my heart might be drawn elsewhere."

Pulling her into his arms, he kissed her roughly, leaving her blushing and breathless. She slid her arms about his neck, and his big hand tangled in her auburn hair, holding her face up while he covered it with kisses. "Ah, lass," he murmured thickly, "you make me a very happy man!"

Velvet, suddenly filled with an unexplained joy, laughed up at him, her eyes shining brightly as she said, "You make me happy also, dear friend!"

While they continued on down the riverbank, a far more intense scene was being enacted in a secluded part of the inn garden. Robert Southwood had waited from the instant he had laid eyes upon Angel Christman to be alone with her like this. His gentle manner was deceptive, for like his father before him, he took what he wanted. Without any preamble, he declared himself. "I love you," he said in an intense voice. "I have loved you from the first moment I saw you!"

Angel stopped, shocked by his words. She had not believed that Velvet's brother was the kind of gentleman who would make mockery of a poor girl. She was confused and, for a minute, unsure of what to say to him. Then realizing that to play the simpleton would only encourage his cruelty, she said briskly, "You make fun of me, my lord, and that is unkind of you. Your sister loves you dearly, and she is the best friend I have ever had. Would you endanger the one thing I prize most, Velvet's friendship? For shame, my lord earl!"

"But I do not mock you!" he cried. "*I love you, Angel!*"

"Then you are a fool, my lord, for you do not even know me!" she snapped, her patience gone. I may be poor and unimportant, she thought to herself, but how dare he tease me in this fashion!

"Your father was Witt Christman, the son of Sir Randor," said Robin. "Your mother, whom you favor strongly, was

Joanne Wallis. Your family seat is near Longridge in Lancaster. Your parents died when you were five, and although your paternal grandparents would have taken you in, your father left your wardship to the crown. You will be eighteen on your next birthday, which is December fifth."

"How do you know all this?" Angel demanded, furious at having her privacy invaded.

"I asked Lord Hundston," came his honest reply.

"Why?" She glared at him.

"I have told you why! I love you, Angel!" Dear heaven, how fair she is, Robin thought.

"My father killed my mother, who was unfaithful to him, and then took his own life," she said bluntly.

"Unfortunate," he answered, "but those things happen even in the best of families. My mother and Velvet's was in a Moroccan harem once."

"*That* doesn't happen in the best of families," Angel answered quickly, and a small smile tugged at the corners of her lush mouth. "You are teasing me, aren't you? Trying to make me feel better?"

"No," he said. "'Tis true."

"What do you want of me, my lord?" she queried him, still confused as to his motives. In her heart, she knew he was going to suggest something she could not countenance and she would offend him by refusing. How angry would he become? Would he forbid her to remain friends with his sister? Oh, Lord! He was so handsome. He was the most beautiful man she had ever seen.

"I want you to be my wife," Robin said quietly.

"My lord, that is cruel!" she cried, and, to her surprise, her eyes filled with tears. Damn him! she thought. Damn him! Embarrassed she hid her face from him.

Southwood, however, would have none of it. Gently he turned her so that she was forced to face him. "Look up at me, my sweet Angel," he said softly. "I love you, dearest heart."

She stared at him as if he had gone mad. "You can't love me," she said. "Knowing facts about me is not really knowing me. Besides, you are the Earl of Lynmouth, one of England's most powerful and wealthy men. I am nothing in light of your family. What is the daughter of an impoverished second son of an unimportant baron to the Southwood family?"

"I am Southwood, Angel. There is no one to tell me yea or nay! I am my own master."

"You should marry a lady of equal wealth and family, my lord," she said softly. "Even I know that."

"I should marry the girl I love," he answered her, "and, my beautiful Angel, I love you beyond life itself! Marry me, my darling! Make me the happiest of men!"

Angel was now totally disconcerted. She had always thought that the queen would eventually make some sort of match for her, for she could not remain a royal charge forever. Angel had believed that the only asset she had to her name was her beauty. Her face, she had hoped, would win her a wealthy merchant, or perhaps an unimportant but pleasant nobleman. It had never occurred to her that someone like Robert Southwood would fall in love with her, and Angel, being the practical girl that she was, had never even considered aspiring to such heights.

Her heart was hammering in her chest, and her normally muted color was high in her excitement. She looked at Robin and said, "I don't know if I love you, and like Velvet I believe a girl should have some feeling for the man she marries." She bit her lower lip with some vexation. "This is totally unthinkable, my lord! What will your mother say to such a match? The queen will certainly not countenance it. Speak no further about it, I pray you. I shall forget you have even mentioned such a possibility, and then perhaps you will allow my friendship with your sister to continue. I will not embarrass you by repeating this incident. I promise."

Robin came perilously close to hugging Angel right then and there. "My mother married my father when she did not even know who she really was," he said quietly. "She had suffered a loss of memory. My father, however, loved her no matter who she was, and he married her. She might have been a murderess, but it mattered not to him. What did matter was that he loved her even as I love you, Angel. As for Her Majesty, my love, she will give her consent. Come with me now and we will ask her."

Angel looked aghast. *"Now?"* she cried. "At this time of evening?"

Robin grinned at her. "Yes, Angel Christman. Now! At this time of evening. You can ride pillion behind me to *Ardern Hall*." He took her firmly by the hand to lead her off, but Angel hung back.

"Velvet," she said. "Please ask Velvet to come with us."

"Very well." He smiled down at her. "Where do you think the minx has gotten to?" He shaded his eyes with his hand and looked down the garden. "Ah, there they are by the riverbank. Velvet! Alex!" he called.

They came toward him hand in hand, and Robin noted silently that his youngest sister was pleasingly flushed and his friend, Alex, looked relaxed and content. "Is everything all right, Robin?" Velvet inquired of him as they finally reached him.

"I have asked Angel to marry me, and, being the sweet child she is, she fears it is not at all a good enough match for me. She thinks the queen will not allow me to wed her, but I have explained that our mother wed my father under even more difficult circumstances with the queen's blessing. We are going to *Ardern Hall* now, and Angel wants your support."

"Do you love my brother?" Velvet was suddenly very protective of Robin. Men were such fools when it came to women. Dame Cecily had said it often enough.

"I-I don't know, Velvet," Angel answered honestly. "How can I know such a thing? I hardly know Lord Southwood."

"It's not important," said Robin with a wave of his hand. "I love her, and most matches do not take into account whether the parties involved love each other. Alison and I didn't love each other."

"You knew Alison all her life, Robin," said Velvet. "You have only just met Angel. Understand it is not just you I fear for, but also my dear friend, Angel. If this is some whim on your part, Robin, I shall be very angry."

"When have you ever known me to be deliberately unkind, Velvet?" he chided her gently. "I realize that love at first sight is a rare phenomenon, but it has happened to me with Angel. I will devote my life to making her happy if she will but give me the chance." His lime-green eyes were filled with such emotion that for a moment Velvet looked away in embarrassment. She had never known her brother to be this way.

She swallowed the little lump that had risen in her throat and, looking back at him, said, "Then, dammit, Robin, why are we standing here when we should be on the road to *Ardern Hall*!"

Alex looked from one to the other, amused. What charmingly willful people they were, these children of Skye O'-Malley. Both assumed that all was settled because it suited them. Neither had bothered to consult the other person most definitely involved. He looked at the beautiful blond girl and said quietly, "And what say you about all of this, Mistress Angel Christman? Are you content to rush off into the night to ask the queen's permission to wed with the Earl of Lynmouth?"

"I think it is all madness, my lord," she replied with a smile, "but if the earl be serious in his intent toward me, I could not receive a better offer. It is indeed a *magnificent* offer for a maid in my position. I suppose I must be practical in any event."

Velvet looked somewhat shocked. "You would be practical in the matter of marriage, Angel? What of love? This is a lifetime we are speaking about!"

Angel sighed and smoothed her palms down over her rather plain gown. "Velvet, you were born an heiress. I do not have your choices. Yes, I want to love the man I marry, but if the queen gave me to a stranger, I could not refuse. In the little time I have known your brother he has shown himself to be a kind and gentle man of the most delicate breeding.

He says he loves me, and I do not believe he is a man easily confused by his own feelings. In time I believe I can learn to love him, and that is as good a basis for a marriage as any maid in my position has ever had."

Robin put a protective arm about Angel and softly kissed the top of her golden head. "Thank you, sweetheart, for giving me your trust. I shall endeavor not to disappoint you. Now, little sister, if you are satisfied as to our intentions, may we be on our way?"

"Oh, no, my lord," said the blushing bride-to-be. "Not until I have changed my gown. I cannot appear before Her Majesty in this travel-worn garment. Will you help me, Velvet?"

"Aye," came her friend's reply. Then Velvet said to her brother, "I assume you can arrange a coach for us?"

"A coach?" Robin laughed. "I had thought to have you ladies ride pillion behind Alex and me."

"Pillion? Nay! We would arrive at *Ardern Hall* so covered with dust they would take us for gypsies! Angel and I have but one other dress apiece, and we will need them again tomorrow. You must find us a coach! I shall leave it to you, Robin. Come, Angel!" Her eyes twinkling, tossing her curls, Velvet took her friend's arm and led her back into the inn.

In the short time it took for Velvet to help Angel from her worn blue gown and relace her into the magnificent turquoise one that matched her eyes, Robin did manage to find them a coach. He also learned that the queen was supping with the Earl of Leicester in his tent in the middle of the army's camp.

It was but a few moments' ride from the Mermaid Inn to the encampment. Upon arriving, the young earl requested a brief audience with the queen, and a few mintues later the four were ushered into Dudley's quarters.

The queen was gowned in a magnificent black and gold dress, the bodice of which was covered with pearls. She smiled graciously and extended her hand to Robin and Alex. Once the men had paid their homage, it was the girls' turn to curtsy, which they did prettily and in unison.

"Well, now, my lord of Lynmouth," said Elizabeth, "what is so very important that it cannot wait until this business with the Spanish is over and done with?" She peered at him, genuinely curious.

Robin smiled warmly at his queen. "Do you remember, madame, when I first came to court to serve you and I cried for my mother? You told me then, in order to stop my weeping, that I might have anything of you that I desired. I was so enchanted at the time by the prospect of my queen giving me anything I wanted that I could not decide."

The queen laughed at the memory. "As I recall, my lord Southwood, I then said that the offer was an open one; a promise from me to thee that might be claimed at any time. 'Tis that not correct?"

"Aye, madame. Your memory does not fail you."

"I should hope not!" The queen chuckled. "I am not yet so old that I grow forgetful." She peered at him again. "So you have finally decided after almost twenty years have passed what it is you would have of me, Robert Southwood. Is that not it?"

"Aye, madame, I have finally decided, and I come before Your Gracious Majesty to ask for the hand in marriage of your royal ward, Angel Christman."

The queen's surprised glance swung to Angel as she attempted to exercise her memory once again. There were several royal wards. Who was this one? Ah, yes! Her eyes lit up. "You are aware that the maid is penniless, my lord. She will bring you nothing but her maidenhead if you have not stolen it already."

Angel flushed crimson, and Robin quickly said, "Nay, madame! I have far too much respect for Angel's reputation to compromise her."

The queen smiled, a trifle bitterly, Velvet thought, and said, "You may look like Southwood, but you are your mother's son in many ways, my lord. I believe you when you tell me that you have had a care for the girl's honor. It is an incredible offer you make to Mistress Christman. What, however, will your mother say to such a match when she returns from her voyage? Will she approve? I wonder."

"Yes!" he said firmly.

The queen laughed again. "Aye, you are right. She will be glad, I have not a doubt, to see you happily settled, for Skye O'Malley has always been a woman for a happy ending. Very well, Robert Southwood, Earl of Lynmouth, you may marry my royal ward, Angel Christman. When may we expect to be invited to your wedding?"

"I would wed Angel as quickly as possible, madame. I see no point in waiting. Neither of us have parents here to satisfy, and there is no dowry to be worked out."

Elizabeth Tudor nodded. "Tonight!" she said. "You will be married tonight by my own chaplain, and my lord Dudley shall give the bride away! Yes! *Tonight!* It shall be a good omen for England! A beginning, not an end!"

"Madame!" Robin was astounded. "You are most gracious!"

"Dudley!" the queen snapped. "Get off your skinny backside and fetch my personal chaplain! Then find some posies for this child to carry!"

Angel stood, stunned with surprise. It was all happening so quickly. Less than an hour ago she had found herself facing a proposal from a wealthy and powerful man. Now she was to find herself married in less than another hour. What was happening to her? She began to tremble with fright until Velvet pinched her fiercely.

"Courage, you little ninny!" her friend hissed. "The queen honors you. Where is the feisty sparrow I knew when I first came to court? If you swoon, I shall never forgive you, Angel!"

"Look who advises me about marriage!" Angel snapped back, the blood beginning to flow hot in her veins once more. "The runaway bride herself!"

Velvet grinned mischievously at her friend. "Good!" she said. "You have returned to yourself again. I hope you're not going to be one of those wives who hangs on to every word her husband says. God's nightshirt, Angel, be yourself! Alison was one of those simpering idiots!"

"Perhaps that is why he is in love with me," replied Angel in a slightly stricken voice.

"Nay! You're nothing like Alison de Grenville. Dying was the wisest thing she ever did," Velvet said harshly. "Robin was already beginning to be bored with her though he knew it not at the time."

"Come here to me, child," said the queen, beckoning to Angel. When the two girls had moved to the queen's side, she asked, "How long have you been a royal ward, Angel Christman?"

"I came to court when I was just a little past five, madame. I shall be eighteen my next birthday."

"So young," murmured the queen. "You were so young to lose your parents, but then I was younger when I lost my mother. I hope you have not been lonely, my child."

"Oh, no, madame! Your court was a wonderful place in which to grow up. Had I not been at court, I should not have had any of the wonderful advantages that I received by being part of it. I have been taught to read, and to write, and to figure. I can both speak and read Latin, French, and Greek. I am proficient with the lute although I have never owned one. The strings are so expensive."

"You like music?" The queen was suddenly interested in this lovely girl who was about to rise from the ranks of the unimportant royal wards to the station of an important noblewoman.

"Oh, yes, madame, very much. I would like to learn to play the virginal, although I dare not aspire to Your Majesty's talent."

The queen smiled. The girl was quick despite her fluffy beauty. That was good, for she would be an asset to Lord Southwood. "'Tis said I have a talent for the virginal," Elizabeth remarked dryly.

At that moment Lord Dudley returned, bearing with him a small bouquet of pale pink wild roses, daisies, and some sprigs of lavender. "'Tis the best I could do, Bess, stamping about the edges of the camp in the dark looking for flowers!" He thrust them out to her.

The queen removed a gold ribbon from her sleeve and tied it around the bouquet. Then, taking it from the Earl of Leicester, she presented it to Angel. "There, my child, though your own beauty far outshines that of the flowers. Now, dammit, where is the chaplain?"

"Here, madame." The cleric stepped foward.

"I wish Lord Southwood and his betrothed to be wed here and now," said the queen. "Waive the bans."

"Of course, madame," came his smooth reply. "Might I have the names of the parties involved?"

"Robert Geoffrey James Henry Southwood," said the queen with a chuckle. "He is one of my many godchildren, and Lord Dudley's also. It has been more years than I care to remember since he was baptized, but, nonetheless, I do."

Robin smiled. "You are truly amazing, madame," he said.

"Humph!" said the queen with a little snort. Then she turned to the bride. "What is your full name, child?"

"Angel Aurora Elizabeth, madame. I am told my grandmother insisted I be called Angel because she thought I looked like one. Aurora was my mother's suggestion because I was born at dawn. Elizabeth was for Your Majesty."

"You were named for me?"

"So I remember being told, madame."

The queen nodded, pleased, and then said, "Well, Father, let us begin."

What a funny place to have a wedding, thought Velvet as she stood listening to the cleric droning the marriage service. Here they all stood, in the middle of the lieutenant general's tent on a potential battlefield. The startled servants had cleared away the table where the queen and Dudley had eaten earlier. It now stood against one side of the tent. Above, the lamps cast warm golden shadows. The hurriedly summoned cleric was plainly garbed without vestments of any kind. The bride stood in the only decent gown she possessed, clutching a hastily gathered bouquet. Thank heavens Angel had refused to come before the queen before she changed, thought Velvet.

It really was a lovely gown, and Velvet was especially glad of the impulse that had caused her to share her own bounty with Angel and Bess. Bonnie had made the dress as if she had been doing it for Velvet herself. The underskirt was striped in narrow bands of gold and turquoise, the bodice embroidered with freshwater pearls and tiny crystal beads, the sleeves beribboned with silk bows. What no one but Velvet knew was that beneath the gown the bride's stockings were darned neatly in several places and her shoes were almost worn through. Just before the simple service began, she had thought to loose Angel's long golden hair so that it hung unbound almost to her waist. It was like a shimmering veil. Angel really was an exquisite bride.

"I pronounce thee husband and wife," said the queen's chaplain.

For a long and silent moment, Robert Southwood looked down into Angel's radiant face, and then, smiling, he kissed her lips sweetly and briefly. Angel then found herself kissed by Lord Dudley, the queen, and Lord Gordon. She blushed rosily. Velvet gave her friend an enormous hug, whispering as she did so, "I am so glad we are now sisters, dear Angel!"

The queen's servants hurried forth with goblets of sweet Malmsey wine and thin sugar wafers, which they passed to all assembled. "It is a poor wedding that does not offer its guests a loving cup," declared Elizabeth.

"I am a poor bride," Angel said, but she smiled as she looked down at her husband's ring with the Southwood family crest now on her finger. When the cleric had asked for the ring, they had suddenly realized they hadn't one, and Robin had drawn his own ring from his finger to use as the wedding band. Later, he had promised, she would have a proper one.

"Nay, child. You must be dowered properly, and since you have been my royal ward all these years, it is my duty to see it done," the queen told her. "For each of the thirteen years you have been in my care and charge there will be a hundred gold pieces, plus an additional two hundred as my bridal gift to you. Finally, my lady Southwood—" and here the queen smiled at the sudden look of delight that passed over Angel's face—"I present to you this necklace." The queen reached up and unfastened from about her own neck a small, exquisite necklace of pale pink diamonds set in gold. "For you, child," she said, and, turning Angel, she fastened it about the startled girl's throat.

Angel's hands flew to her face, and then one hand stole to her neck to feel the necklace now lying there. "Madame . . . madame . . ." she stammered, feeling totally foolish at her inability to say thank you. No one in her entire life had ever been so kind to her. *Never!* The queen reached out to pat her cheek, and then, raising her goblet, said, "Once long ago I raised my glass to Geoffrey Southwood on the occasion of his marriage to Skye O'Malley. As I recall, I arranged that wedding, too! It seems to be a royal custom of mine seeing that Southwoods are married off safely. Good health, long life, and many children to you both. God bless you, my dears!" Then she drank, and the others drank with her.

Shortly afterward, the queen departed back to *Ardern Hall*, and the four young people returned to the Mermaid. This time Robin insisted that Angel ride before him on his horse, so Velvet was left to herself in the coach. The moon was waning, but the night sky was bright with myriad stars. Alex rode discreetly ahead of his friend, giving the newlyweds some measure of privacy.

Robin Southwood couldn't ever remember being so happy in his entire life. All of his days he had been privileged and pampered, but marriage to this lovely creature who was now nestled in his arms meant more to him than anything else he had ever had. He could feel her trembling ever so slightly against him and it distressed him that she was afraid. He would not openly address her fear, for he knew it would embarrass her, and so he sought to distract her.

"When we go back up to London, we shall go to my mother's warehouses along the river and find all kinds of wonderful materials to be made into gowns for you, my darling. You are surely the most beautiful girl ever born, and a beautiful gem should have an equally beautiful setting. You will let me help you choose, won't you? I picture you in jewel colors, for they will be perfect with your exquisite pink-and-white complexion."

"You are most kind, my lord," came her soft reply, but her head remained turned away.

"Look at me, Angel. Do you know that you have never looked me directly in the eye? Look at me now, my lady Southwood."

She turned and blinded him with the flash of her marvelous turquoise eyes. There was a small smile on her lips. "Lady Southwood," she said softly. "I am, aren't I? I really am!"

He grinned back at her. "You are, Angel. You are most assuredly my lady, Angel Southwood, Countess of Lynmouth, married in the sight of God, Her Majesty the queen, *and* by the queen's chaplain."

"Oh, my lord, what have we done?"

"Nothing yet," he replied mischievously, then chuckled as she colored a most becoming rose. "Now, madame, I shall issue you my first husbandly order. Will you please call me Robin, my darling wife?"

"Are you sure we haven't made a dreadful mistake . . . Robin?"

"No, my lovely Angel, we have not made any mistake. Even the queen knew this rather hasty marriage was right. I love you, and I hope in the days to come that I can teach you to love me. You must never be fearful of me, Angel. You must never be afraid to speak your mind or to ask of me what you will. I will always listen to you. Now before we arrive back at the inn I would discuss tonight with you."

"Tonight?"

"Our wedding night, but, dear Angel, if you prefer, it is a time that may be postponed until you learn to know me better. The choice is yours to make, sweetheart."

She was silent for what seemed to him a very long time, and then she spoke in a soft voice that he had to bend over her to hear. "I know you a great deal better than you would believe, Robin, for Velvet loves you dearly and has always spoken of you. I know that you will not hurt me, for you have always been wondrously kind. I cannot, however, think of a more fitting way," she finished mischievously, "for us to get to know one another better than to celebrate our wedding night as it should be celebrated. One thing I would warn you of, however. Despite my years at court, I am truly a virgin, and not particularly knowledgeable. I only ask that you be patient with me."

"It never occurred to me that you would not be a virgin, Angel," came his quiet reply.

It was at this point that they arrived at the inn, and, quickly dismounting, Robin lifted his bride from the saddle. Hand in hand, they entered the building and made their way upstairs to the rooms that the earl had booked earlier. It had been planned that Velvet and Angel would share one of the bedchambers while the gentlemen slept in the other. Now Robin led his wife into that second room, stopping only long enough to remove Alex's saddlebag and place it in the small parlor where they had eaten earlier. Once in the bedchamber with Angel, he closed the door and threw the bolt.

"I—I have no nightgown," she said.

"There is no need," he answered, and then, pulling her into his arms, he kissed her passionately, not even hearing the door to the parlor open and close outside.

"They can't be here already," said Velvet. "Surely they would have waited for us, Alex."

His eye lit upon the saddlebag. "They are here, Velvet."

"Oh, good! Let us have the innkeeper make a caudle cup, and we shall drink to the bridal couple's good health!" She moved to the door, but he blocked her path.

"Nay, lass. The bedchamber door is shut, and I do not think Robin would welcome our intrusion at this time."

"But there's been no caudle cup! 'Tis a poor bridal ceremony without a celebration."

Alex smiled. "Many a couple has done without the caudle cup, Velvet. There are other things more important to a bridal couple on their wedding night."

She snorted, but then a slow flush crept up her neck and into her face. "Oh," she said helplessly.

Alex chuckled. "Go to bed, lass. The queen reviews the troops on the morrow, and that should be something to tell your granchildren one fine day."

"Where will you sleep?" she asked, realizing his predicament.

"Out here on the floor by the fire," he said. "I've laid my head in worse places in my time, lass. Good night."

The night had grown chill, and Velvet wasted little time in unlacing her gown, removing it and creeping beneath the covers wearing only her chemisette. Outside the tiny window she could hear the cricket songs, soothing and cheerful. Beyond her door she heard Alex moving about for a short while and guessed from the friendly crackle that he had built up the fire in the little fireplace. She smiled wryly, considering the possibility of changing places with him: her cold bed for his floor by the fire.

She was just dozing off when a short, piercing cry rent the quiet. Trembling, she sat up, listening intently. It had been such a piteous cry. Where had it come from? Then she heard a low moaning and realized that it came from the other bedchamber.

With a little sob, she leaped from the bed and fled out into the parlor straight into a protective pair of warm arms. She couldn't seem to stop shaking. Alex gently lifted her up, then cradled her in his arms as he sat down in a chair by the fire. He said nothing, waiting instead until she had quieted. Finally she gazed up at him, saying, "Did you not hear that terrible cry, Alex? Then I heard moaning through the wall. It gave me such a fright. Is this place haunted?"

"Nay, lass. 'Tis not haunted. I imagine the cry you heard was your friend, Angel."

"Why would she cry out as if hurt? Robin would never hurt her!" Velvet protested.

"'Tis not a hurt a man inflicts willingly upon a maid, lass."

"I don't understand," was her reply. "What do you mean?"

There was simply no delicate way for him to put it, and besides, he thought somewhat irritably, he should not be the one to have to explain such things to her, yet now he had no choice. "Your friend cried out when Robin pierced her maidenhead," he said matter-of-factly.

"Oh, God," she whispered, and he could hear the fear in her voice. Then she began to tremble again.

"It only happens once, Velvet," he said, helplessly attempting to calm her fears, and his arms tightened about her.

"I am so afraid, Alex," she said. "I am so afraid of this wild Scots earl who demands marriage of me. My mother has never explained to me how it is between a man and a woman. Oh, I've watched the animals at the farm mate, but 'tis not the same for people, is it? Oh, Alex! I feel such a fool!"

"Velvet, Velvet," he murmured at her soothingly. "'Twill be all right, lass, you're nae a fool for not knowing what lovemaking is. You're but a maid, and your earl will be glad of it, sweetheart."

She looked up at him, her face streaked with tears. She looked so very young and woebegone that his heart almost burst with the love he felt for her. Her next words startled him.

"Make love to me, Alex," she said softly.

"Velvet lass!"

"Make love to me," she repeated. "You're my friend, Alex. You showed me kissing. Now I want you to make love to me so that I will know what to expect." She was very serious, and he resisted the urge to chuckle bubbling within him.

"Sweetheart," he said patiently, "it would not be right for me to take what is rightfully another man's. A maidenhead can be only lost once."

Now it was Velvet's turn to giggle. "I didn't mean *that*," she said. "Surely there is more to lovemaking than just *that*." She looked at him questioningly.

Alex felt his heart leap with excitement within him. Every time he was with her now, he found himself wanting more than just the sweetness of her lips. "Do you trust me enough, Velvet, to accept my word when I tell you we have gone far enough along Eros's road?"

She nodded, her eyes wide, her face solemn as a small owl's.

Deep inside, he repressed a hard shudder. She was so damningly innocent and so incredibly tempting a tidbit. He envied Robin, who was now making love to his bride. This lovely girl in his lap was his betrothed wife under the law and he longed to tell her the truth, to take her into the other bedchamber and initiate her into the many arts of Venus. Instinctively he knew she would be an apt pupil.

"Well?" Her voice pierced his consciousness, and she looked up at him curiously.

Brazen little minx, he thought, amused. Then, with a swift motion, he opened her chemisette and, sliding it over her silky shoulders, bared her to the waist. Velvet gasped with surprise at this bold maneuver, and Alex's head swooped down as his mouth found hers in a blazing kiss. A ball of fire burst within her stomach and spread flaming throughout her whole body. His lips worked on hers, teasing them open, and, with a swift movement, his tongue touched hers. Her heart hammered wildly in her ears as his tongue's warm smoothness caressed the inside of her mouth, touching her sensitive flesh, running along her teeth. He had never kissed her like *that* before, and Velvet, though a little bit frightened, found it wildly exciting.

Then his big hand began to caress her satiny flesh, smoothing the roundness of her shoulder, sliding down her long arms, moving up her bared torso to cup a breast. She thought that she would faint right then and there. An incredible, aching warmth began to seep through her veins. When Kit Marlowe had touched her, she had wanted to die from the shame and frustration of her anger and helplessness, but this was different. Alex's hand was gentle, loving. She knew that should she ask him to stop at any moment he would comply with her wishes. She did not, however, want him to stop, and that in itself was puzzling to her.

"Dear heaven, lass, but ye are so beautiful!" She heard his voice mutter thickly in her ear. Her head fell back, and his lips slowly kissed the long line of her throat; his hand tangled in her auburn hair, cupping her head as his lips found hers once more. She was conscious of his hand touching her breasts again, his fingers gently teasing her nipples until they thrust forward, throbbing with the sweet torment he was inflicting upon them.

Velvet shivered with pure excitement. If this was lovemaking, it was wondrously sweet. With a sigh of rapture, she tried to move closer to him. The arm that had been cradling her head moved down to encircle her waist. The hand that had played with her young breasts now slipped down beneath her chemisette. Then he slowly began to move it upward again, sliding it easily along the smooth skin of her long legs. For a moment, she considered the rightness of his actions, but honeyed heat once more raced through her veins, rendering her helpless to impede his movements. Her consciousness became peopled by a thousand small, fluttering butterflies, and she was only aware of the pleasure he offered her.

As he stroked the softness of her inner thighs, Alex knew that he must stop. Already he was perilously near to losing his own control. His manhood ached with longing for Velvet, and he was regretting that he had ever let the wench tease him into this. Better he had waited until their marriage, when the natural conclusion of such loveplay could be effected. Slowly he removed his hand from beneath her garment and held her close.

"Enough, lass," he said quietly. "I can bear no more and keep my promise to preserve yer honor. Ye're ripe as a peach, Velvet, and I am hungry to pluck yer fruit."

"Please, Alex, just love me a little while longer. I hurt with such a strange wanting."

He kissed her gently. "Nay, sweetheart. Remember yer promise to me. We must stop now." Quietly he redid her chemisette, pulling it up and tying the little silk ribbons.

She signed. "Will you love me again soon, Alex?"

"Aye," he whispered, and then with a sigh of his own, he rose to his feet, holding her against his heart. Without another word, he returned her to her bed and, tucking the coverlet about her, left the room, firmly closing the door behind him.

Velvet lay in the darkness for what seemed a long while, reliving over and over again his every touch, his every kiss. She wanted to rise from the bed and run back to him, but she knew she couldn't. She could barely await the morning when she might see him again. Dear heaven! she thought. Am I falling in love with Alex? It was her last conscious thought before sleep overtook her.

The innkeeper called them early in the morning, for the queen was to address the troops, and all the court was to be present. As a Maid of Honor, Velvet had to be in attendance on Her Majesty that day. As the new Countess of Lynmouth, Angel would be by her husband's side in a prominent place amongst the courtiers. In their hurry to get ready, they needed to help each other dress, and any awkwardness that might have been between them was forgotten in the rush. Neither girl could eat the sumptuous breakfast that had been ordered, although Alex and Robin both ate with fierce appetites the eggs poached in heavy cream and marsala wine, the thick slices of pink ham, the loaf of hot bread that each slathered with freshly churned butter and plum preserves. Green apple cider, freshly pressed from the early apples, served to wash their meal down.

"How can you eat like that?" grumbled Velvet at the two men. "It's positively disgusting at so early an hour!"

"Sun's up," said Robin with a grin, "and besides I find I have a monstrous appetite this morning for some reason." He sent Angel a passionate look, and she blushed furiously and scolded him.

"Fie, my lord, to tease me so!" But her voice was sweet, and the look she sent her bridegroom equally so.

"And what is your excuse, Alex Gordon?" demanded Velvet, somewhat irritably. For some reason she did not share their good humor.

"When one cannot satisfy one appetite, one satisfies another," he said calmly as he buttered another piece of bread. "More cider, Rob?"

Velvet retreated to her small bedchamber and, flinging open the tiny window, leaned out. It was a glorious summer's day, this eighth day of August. She sighed deeply.

"Are you all right, Velvet?" Angel had come into the room behind her and gently shut the door.

Velvet turned from her view of the inn garden. "Are *you* all right?" she demanded a trifle nervously.

"Why, yes!" Angel exclaimed. "Why would you worry about me?"

"I heard you . . ." Velvet blushed scarlet. "I mean after last night . . ." The color came into her face and neck once more. "What I mean is, did my brother hurt you?"

Angel's eyes suddenly lit with understanding. Poor Velvet. She was so innocent, but then so had Angel been until last night when her bridegroom had introduced her to delights not even previously imagined. Angel put an arm around her friend's shoulders. "Robin would never hurt me. He is the kindest, gentlest man alive."

"Are you falling in love with him?"

"Velvet, it is much too soon for me to know such a thing, but I believe that I shall be able to love him in time. For now, I respect him, and I am grateful that the good Lord has given me such a good and kind husband." She smiled at Velvet. "What a dear sister you will be to me, Velvet, and having never had a sister I shall appreciate you very much."

"Am I a fool, Angel?"

"Nay, my dearest. I love you for worrying and caring."

The two girls then saw to their last-minute toilette as, outside the bedchamber door, Robin exhorted his wife and sister to hurry. Arm in arm, they exited the inn, both looking beautiful, Angel in her turquoise gown and Velvet in an exquisite creation of yellow brocade, the underskirt and the sleeves embroidered with black butterflies. Today the queen was allowing her maids to wear their most elegant gowns instead of their usual virginal white.

Outside the inn they found not the coach that Velvet had expected her brother to supply, but four fine mounts that would take them to Tilbury Plain where the army had assembled to hear the queen. The Earl of Lynmouth assured his sister that as they would be riding slowly there would be little danger of the dust ruining their lovely gowns. Then Robin lifted his bride up onto the saddle of a gentle bay-colored mare, smiling as he did so. Velvet saw a soft, intimate look pass between them.

As she turned away, Alex put his hands about her tiny waist and lifted her into her own saddle. Their eyes met for a long moment, and she felt herself quiver ever so slightly beneath his firm grip. He said nothing, but in his eyes was a look she could not fathom. Then he reached up as she settled herself and gently touched her cheek. Velvet felt suddenly and unaccountably shy of this man whom she claimed as a friend, with whom she had shared a first kiss, and far more. Her brother and his bride, however, noticed nothing, for they were far too involved in themselves.

The gentlemen mounted their own horses, and together the two couples began the short ride to Tilbury Plain. A quarter of a mile from the encampment they met with the queen's party, and Velvet detached herself to join the other maids of honor. Bess, looking pretty and spirited in her scarlet gown, greeted her gaily.

"Is it true?" she demanded.

"Is what true?" Velvet replied.

"Is it true about Angel? That your brother has taken her for his mistress? 'Tis all over the court this morning!"

Velvet was shocked. "My brother, the Earl of Lynmouth, and Angel Christman were *wed* last night."

"Is that what they told you?" One of the Maids of Honor, Leonore D'Arcy, rumored to be a particularly promiscuous girl, laughed. "Lord bless me, Velvet, you are still a country mouse if you believe that! One can hardly blame Mistress Christman as your brother is wealthy and handsome. With no fortune or great name such as we have, the poor girl could hardly be expected to make an advantageous match." She laughed again.

"I would not speak that way before the queen if I were you, Mistress D'Arcy, for my brother and his bride were married in the queen's own presence by the queen's own chaplain," snapped Velvet. How she disliked these catty young courtiers. "I should know for I was there!"

"They were?" This was chorused by all the Maids of Honor who now crowded around Velvet's mount.

"Indeed they were," replied Velvet sweetly. "The Earl of Leicester was also there, as was my brother's friend, Lord Gordon. Angel Christman is now Angel Southwood, the Countess of Lynmouth."

"God's nightcap!" said Bess, who rarely swore. "How did this all happen?"

"For Robin, it was love at first sight. He saw Angel for the first time several weeks ago at his fête for the queen, and he would not rest afterward until he had made her his wife."

"Oh, how romantic!" Bess said soulfully. "How very fortunate they do not have to worry about offending the queen, for if they were married by her own chaplain then she must approve the match."

"Why, Bess, do you have some secret love who is the queen's favorite perhaps?" mocked the D'Arcy girl. "You daren't set Wat-er afire, I'm told."

Bess Throckmorton whitened and glanced forward to where the queen rode with Leicester and Essex. She was terrified lest Elizabeth Tudor hear the thoughtless words of Leonore D'Arcy. Bess was hopelessly in love with Walter Ralegh, and he with her, but neither dared to jeopardize their position at court, for their very livelihoods depended upon the queen's favor and goodwill.

"I wonder if Her Majesty knows that you've been tumbling Anthony Bacon?" murmured Velvet innocently, never even glancing at the D'Arcy girl.

"That's a foul lie!"

"Not according to the Earl of Essex, my dear. He says you are a most prodigiously hot piece, but you sell your favors far too cheaply considering your ancient and powerful name."

The other girls in the queen's train began to giggle. This was a delicious piece of gossip, and Leonore D'Arcy wasn't particularly well liked while Bess Throckmorton was loved and respected. Most had guessed Bess's secret, but never discussed it amongst themselves, fearing to spoil what they all considered a sweetly tragic romance. Silently they applauded Velvet's wickedly sharp words, though none would have dared to challenge the D'Arcy heiress themselves.

"I'd expect you to defend Bess," sneered Leonore D'Arcy. "She may be poor, but her family is influential, and yours is certainly not, though they be vulgarly rich. You need her influence here at court, for your own father is of little importance, and your mother, I am told, is a common Irish pirate forbidden to even come to court."

"You confuse my mama with our cousin, Grace O'Malley, who is most definitely not common, though she be called a pirate," Velvet said brightly. "As to needing anyone's influence, I don't. Money, dear Mistress D'Arcy, is the mightiest influence. I choose my friends for their amiability. Since I am a great heiress, I have that option."

"Please," pleaded Bess, "let us not quarrel amongst ourselves in this time of such great mortal danger for our dear queen and our beloved England."

A murmur of assent arose from the other girls, and, outnumbered, Leonore D'Arcy ceased her sniping. Velvet looked fondly at Bess and, leaning over, patted her friend's hand. Bess smiled gratefully back at the younger girl.

Ahead, Elizabeth Tudor rode like an Amazon queen. She was mounted upon a huge white gelding with dappled gray hindquarters. The animal had been a gift to her from Robert Cecil, Lord Burghley's younger son. Cleverly the queen had chosen to wear virginal white. The velvet gown had a satin underskirt embroidered with silver Tudor roses, and the sleeves were festooned with white silk bows that had Indian pearl centers. As her hair was beginning to thin, she wore a fiery bright red wig into which she had stuck two white plumes. Because of her council's fear of assassination, she also wore a decorated silver breastplate over the bodice of her gown, and in her right hand she carried a silver truncheon chased in gold. There was no doubt that she was a most inspiring and queenly sight to all who saw her, and the men cheered and shouted themselves hoarse, particularly when they saw that she meant to come amongst them without fear, accompanied by only a few gentlemen. The rest of her train had now stopped, remaining on the edge of the vast crowd of soldiers.

Erect and proud upon her beautiful mount, Elizabeth Tudor advanced, reining her horse in every now and then to accept their wild and fiercely loyal acclaim. Finally, deep within the center of her army, she stopped. Around her was a sea of English faces, faces representing every walk of life from the highest to the lowest. Great lords rubbed elbows with merchants and butchers, farmers with cobblers, blacksmiths with rich landowners. There were old and young faces that looked adoringly up at her, and the queen felt a surge of pride for these wonderfully loyal Englishmen who were assembled to defend her, to defend their homeland. She let them cheer for several long minutes, then, with a dramatic gesture, she held up a gloved hand, the sunlight flashing off her truncheon.

On Tilbury Plain it grew deathly quiet, and the queen of England spoke from her heart to her army.

"My loving people, we have been persuaded by some that are careful of our safety, to take heed how we commit ourselves to armed multitudes, for fear of treachery; but I assure you, I do not desire to live in distrust of my faithful and loving people." Elizabeth paused and glanced with some amusement at her breastplate. *"Let tyrants fear! I have always so behaved myself that under God, I have placed my chiefest strength and goodwill in the loyal hearts and goodwill of my subjects; and therefore I am come amongst you, as you see, at this time, not for my recreation and disport, but being resolved, in the midst and heat of the battle, to live or die amongst you all; to lay down for God, my kingdom, and for my people, my*

honour and my blood, even in the dust. I know I have but the body of a weak and feeble woman; but I have the heart and stomach of a King, and a King of England too, and think it foul scorn that Parma or Spain, or any Prince of Europe, should dare to invade the borders of my realm; to which, rather than any dishonour should grow by me, I myself will take up arms, I myself will be General, Judge, and Rewarder of every one of your virtues in the field.

*"I know already for your forwardness you have deserved rewards, and crowns; and we do assure you, on the word of a Prince, they shall be duly paid you. In the meantime, my Lieutenant General shall be in my stead, than whom never Prince commanded a more noble or worthy subject; not doubting but that by your obedience to my General, by your concord in the camp and your valour in the field, we shall shortly have a famous victory over these enemies of my God, my Kingdom, and of my People!"**

As she finished, she thrust her truncheon upward and the field erupted in a roar of cheers. Hats were thrown skyward, men clapped each other on the shoulders, thrilled by Elizabeth Tudor's words. Now even the poorest, weakest Englishman could face the proudest Spaniard and totally destroy him. There wasn't a man there that day who would not have willingly laid down his life for the queen. Religion played no part in this for any of them. Catholic or Protestant, they adored her to a man. That day more than any day in her reign, Elizabeth Tudor was England!

Though impressive in their drilling and unsurpassed in their loyalty, as it turned out Elizabeth Tudor's soldiers were not called upon to fight the invading Spanish that day. After almost two weeks of anguishing suspense, word finally reached the queen that her navy had successfully broken the Armada in a fiery battle that had taken place on the twenty-eighth and twenty-ninth of July.

That Sunday night, a single gun had been fired from the British flagship *Ark Royal*. Silently, manned by volunteer

* Elizabeth Tudor's actual speech on Tilbury Plain.

crews, fireships had set off from the English fleet, towing behind them the little dinghies that would evacuate the brave crews when their work was done. With wind and tide both running fast behind them, the blazing ships bore down on the Spanish, creating total panic. Though the Duke of Medina-Sidona kept his head and took orderly evasive action, the majority of Spanish captains panicked, cut their anchor cables, and fled out to sea. Many collided in the darkness and were swept onto the beaches of France, where they were plundered by English and French alike, and their unfortunate crews killed.

To the east of Calais, off the Flemish coast, lay a line of concealed sandbars, the Banks of Zeeland. It was here that the Spanish Armada had found itself at daybreak on Monday, July 29. Drake, most familiar with the area, led the attack from the west to the Armada's rear. Again and again they passed the defending Spanish galleons, exposing them to heavy fire from the fleet's guns. Almost half the seamen on Medina-Sidona's flagship, the *San Martin*, were killed; the ship's decks were strewn with the dying.

Over and over again the English pounded the Spanish: Drake in his ship *Revenge*, Hawkins in *Victory*, Frobisher in *Triumph*, Seymour in *Rainbow*, Winter in *Vanguard*, Fenton in *Mary Rose*, Lord Admiral Howard in *Ark Royal*, and that amazing old gentleman from Cheshire who had been knighted upon the lord admiral's flagship with Hawkins and Frobisher only three days prior, eighty-nine-year-old Sir George Beeston in his ship *Dreadnought*. Fiercely, England's brave and gallant captains, amid the dense smoke and deafening gunfire, ravaged the mighty Armada. It had been an incredible victory, and by day's end not a single Spanish ship remained capable of fighting. The English ceased their firing, however, only because they had run out of ammunition. They had no real idea of the fantastic victory they had just won.

That night the wind shifted, blowing the Armada back onto the dreaded Zeeland banks. The Spanish were in danger of being totally wrecked. By dawn, the Spanish pilots were sounding depths of six fathoms, and all could see the waves breaking over the ever-closing shoals. In order to save the lives of the twenty thousand men still alive aboard the remaining Spanish ships, an offer of surrender had been prepared, to be carried by pinnace to the English. Close to midday, however, the wind shifted to the southwest, and the battered Spanish ships, their tattered sails filling with wind, were able to turn northward, running past the approaches to the river Thames and the port of Harwich. All the while, as the broken Armada made its escape, it was shadowed by the English fleet. On Friday, August 2, the winds shifted to the northeast. Short on rations, practically out of water, the English turned back for home, convinced that further pursuit was unnecessary. From the bodies of the drowned livestock thrown overboard by the Spanish, it was concluded that their enemy was also crucially short of rations and water.

In England no one had any idea of the great defeat visited upon the Spanish. The English fleet had sent no word of their victory to Elizabeth, for even they were not entirely certain that they had fully overcome the Armada. No one, it seemed, wanted the responsibility of crying success lest failure overtake them yet. Instead, they had continued to pursue their enemy, driving them farther from England, farther toward their ultimate destruction, while in England preparations had continued for war, for invasion, until at last the news of her navy's triumph reached the queen.

Chapter 4

When the English finally learned the extent of their impressive victory over the Spanish and the great Armada, the country went wild in a frenzy of rejoicing. For a good week, bonfires blazed on every hill throughout the land during the late-summer evenings. Before leaving Tilbury, the queen rode to every corner of the encampment to bid her faithful soldiers farewell and to thank them for their loyalty. Riding through the lines of cheering men, she was accompanied by Leicester and young Essex.

As they escorted her to her barge, Robin Southwood could not help but notice that Leicester did not look particularly well. His hair and beard were suddenly white, and his too-florid complexion coarse. He had also grown fat with too much good living and his many personal indulgences. Remembering how a once slender and elegant Leicester had long ago abused his mother and misused his position as Robin's godfather, the Earl of Lynmouth could feel little pity for the man. True, he was ever loyal to the queen, but in his favored position he had often misused that power. Robin stepped forward as Elizabeth Tudor approached the quay and, bowing with a little flourish, kissed his sovereign's hand.

"Ah"—Elizabeth smiled warmly—"my lord Southwood. Are you for London then?"

"Aye, madame, but only for a short while. Merely long enough to visit the O'Malley-Small warehouses in order to choose fabrics for my bride. I am anxious to take her to *Lynmouth* to see her new home and to meet my little daughters."

"Will you not stay in London long enough to await your mother's return, my lord?"

"Mother's last letter this past spring said that she would come to Bideford first, madame. It is my daughters, I suspect, who draw her to Devon."

"The beautiful Skye, a grandmother!" said Leicester with an exaggerated sigh. "'Tis not to be borne!"

"We all grow older, my lord," Robin returned.

Robert Dudley looked sharply at the younger man, but Robin turned a bland face to him and smiled pleasantly.

"Bring your bride to court when you next come to London, my lord Southwood," the queen said graciously. "We shall be happy to receive her."

"As always, madame, you are too kind. God grant Your Majesty a safe trip."

The queen passed on to her barge, and Robin moved down the quay to his own vessel. The incoming tide swept them swiftly up the Thames to London, which was already celebrating the Armada's defeat at the hands of England's brave seamen. The streets, draped in festive sky blue silk cloth, were packed with people hoping to catch a glimpse of Elizabeth Tudor so that they might cheer and salute this bold queen, defender of England. Arriving from Tilbury, she was transferred into a great gold coach decorated with a lion and a dragon holding up the arms of England at its front, while four gold columns held up a canopy in the shape of a crown over her head. Beneath it, the queen in her white velvet gown sat accepting her people's homage, a relaxed smile upon her face, her hand waving in salute to the happy crowds.

Services of thanksgiving were held at both St. Paul's and at St. Paul's Cross, where the banners of the captured Spanish fleet were displayed to the delight of the crowds. There were bonfires, dancing, feasting, and tournaments to celebrate the miraculous victory. The formal services of thanksgiving would be held on November 17, 1588, a day that would also mark the anniversary of the queen's thirtieth year as England's ruler.

The queen in her good humor was overly indulgent of her young goddaughter, Velvet de Marisco. So it was that Velvet found herself spending more time at Lynmouth House than at court. She was helping Angel to pick out fabrics for all the gowns that Robin was having made for his bride. Never had the young Countess of Lynmouth been faced with such incredible bounty. Never in her life could she remember having more than two dresses at one time, and usually they were either remade from someone else's outgrown garment or of the plainest fabric. Angel was stunned by the profusion of gorgeous fabrics presented to her. Amazed, she watched as Velvet, heiress born and raised, chose bolt after bolt of the incredible stuffs.

"That ruby red velvet, that emerald brocade, the pink silk, and, of course, the violet. No, no! Yellow is not Lady Lynmouth's color, dolt! Now that amethyst with silver stripes has possibilities." Velvet turned to her sister-in-law. "What do you think, Angel?"

Angel laughed. "I think it's too much, Velvet. We've already enough fabric for a dozen dresses."

"Dearest Angel, you are the Countess of Lynmouth, not some little royal ward now," Velvet teased her friend. "You will need dozens of gowns."

"I give up! You and your brother are totally incorrigible. I shall never in a million years wear all the gowns you insist on having made, nor the jewelry Robin has lavished upon me."

"Yes, you will," Velvet said with great assurance. "Oh, it's true you're going down to Southwood for a while, but I guarantee that once Mama is back from her voyage, you'll be invited to *Queen's Malvern*, and Her Majesty has already insisted that you and Robin return to court. You'll need everything we're having made and more!"

"What is she like?" Angel asked.

"Who?"

"Your mother. I've heard . . . Well, everything said about her is so contradictory."

Velvet chuckled. "She is the most marvelous woman alive, Angel, and she will love you as Robin and I do. I don't doubt everything that you've heard is contradictory. Mama is so fabulous that there is no other woman like her in the world. My father is her sixth husband, and she has had healthy children by all but one of them. For many years she was head of her family in Ireland and took care of them all. Along with Sir Robert Small, who has been my mother's partner for many years, she built up a huge trading empire. O'Malley ships have been bringing spices to England for years, although now that the Portuguese have a stronghold in the Indies it is much harder. That is one reason my mother undertook this voyage. She wanted to obtain for England the same privileges that the Grand Mughal has given to the Portuguese. Still, despite her many activities, none of her children has ever been slighted, or felt unloved, and we are all close.

"Of course, Robin holds the highest rank of us, although he is the fourth born. We have two O'Flaherty half brothers: Ewan and Murrough. Then comes our half sister, Willow, the Countess of Alcester. Then there are our Burke half brother and sister, Deirdre and Padraic. My father has been married to Mama longer than any of the others. They have been wed sixteen years."

"What are Robin's little girls like?" Angel was obviously concerned that her stepdaughters like her.

"Beth has just turned three this year, Kate was two in January, and little Cecily will be two in December. They are dear little things with Alison's blue eyes and Robin's blond hair. They don't remember their mother at all, even Beth for she wasn't even two when it happened. You are their mother now, Angel, and for them you will always be. You need have no fears in that direction."

Suddenly the door into Angel's bedchamber was flung open, and as they looked up, startled, Willow, Countess of Alcester, stalked into the room. "Is *this* the bride, Velvet?" she demanded. Willow was an extremely beautiful woman with Skye O'Malley's black hair and her father's amber-gold eyes and skin. There was an exotic look to her for all her English ways.

"*Willow!* Oh, I'm so glad to see you, and yes! This is Angel, Robin's new wife!"

"Could you not have informed me, Velvet? James and I hurried to London to celebrate the queen's great victory, and after we had paid our respects to Her Majesty, I was accosted by Lord Dudley, ooozing with his usual sly innuendos, this time about Southwood's bride. Have you at least had the decency to inform the others, or is there some reason it is to be kept secret from the family? Will Mama approve?" Though Willow was several inches shorter than her younger sister, there was a regalness about her that was intimidating.

"We have been back in London but two days, Willow," Velvet said calmly. "Scarce time to inform the family. 'Twas far more important to Robin that Angel be clothed decently and as befits the Countess of Lynmouth. After all, Mama will be returning any day now."

"Mama will not be returning until next spring, Velvet. Robin has had word this very day."

"What?" Velvet looked as if she were about to burst into tears. "What has happened? Why is she delayed?"

"I don't know," snapped Willow. "You will have to ask Robin, for it is he who received the communiqué. Besides, 'tis not as important as this marriage." She turned and fixed Angel with a searching gaze. "*Who are you?* Are your people landed? I know nothing, but I intend to know all!"

"I must go and find Robin," Velvet said. She turned to her new sister-in-law. "Don't be afraid of Willow, Angel. Her bark is far worse than her bite, and she has always been our little matriarch. Tell her everything. She will love you as the rest of us do." Then, picking up her skirts, she hurried from the room, her elder sister's voice echoing in her ears as she ran.

"Impudent chit!"

A little frown upon her face, Velvet moved swiftly down the stairs to the next floor of the house and along a hallway to her brother's library. She burst in without even stopping to knock. Both Alex and Robin were there bending over a map. They looked up, annoyed, as she barged into the room.

"Is it true? Is it true that you received a message from Mama? That she is not to be home until next spring? Why didn't you tell me, Robin? What shall I do when this damned betrothed of mine arrives on the scene, which he is bound to do any day now?" Then she began to sob. "I want Mama and Papa, Robin!"

Alex strode across the room and gathered the weeping girl into his arms. Looking over her head at Robin, he said in an even voice, "Enough of this charade, Robin! I will not have Velvet terrorized any further. Sweetheart, look at me. I am the Earl of BrocCairn, your betrothed husband, and I love you. Please don't be frightened any longer, I beg you!" He kissed the top of her head, making soothing noises at her.

Safe in his arms, it took a moment or two for his words to penetrate her brain, but then Velvet shrieked with outrage and pulled furiously away from him. She looked angrily at her brother. "You knew of this, Robin? You knew who he was?"

"Of course I knew, Velvet. He is an old friend."

"You lied to me!" she shouted at him. "Both of you lied to me!"

"What lie?" demanded Robin. "No one lied to you."

"You said he was Alexander, Lord Gordon!" She angrily stamped her foot, and her midnight blue skirts shook with a furious hiss of silk.

"He is, you little virago. He is Alexander Gordon, the Earl of BrocCairn. There was no lie told to you."

"But not the full truth either," she accused. "Oh, I will never forgive you! Never! *Neither of you!*"

Robin's lime-green eyes narrowed in sudden anger. Grasping his sister by her upper arms, he shook her, enraged at her behavior. "You spoilt little minx, do you know how lucky you are in Alex? He has all the rights, Velvet. *Not you!* It is his right to demand an immediate marriage with you, and if I were wise, I am thinking, I would insist upon it, for I am convinced it is past time you had a lord and master to teach you a woman's proper place. God knows Mother and Adam never have. They have spoilt you to the point of ruination! Alex, however, felt if you had the time to learn to know him, you could be brought around. He has been far more sensitive of your feelings than you have been of his."

Velvet pulled away from her brother. Rubbing her arms where he had bruised her, she drew herself to her full height and said, "I shall return to court immediately, Robin. I thank you for your hospitality. I have aided your wife in the choosing of fabrics, but now that our elder sister, Willow, is here she can take charge. She is far more knowledgeable than I in matters of the latest fashions."

"You will remain here if I have to lock you in your rooms, Velvet! I shall ask your release from the queen, and we will celebrate your marriage as soon as possible so that you and Alex may return to *Dun Broc* before winter." He glowered at her icily, every inch the great lord.

"Go to hell, my dear brother!" she spat back at him. "Try to force me to the altar and I will create a scandal the likes of which the Tudor court has never seen!" She turned to gaze scornfully at Alex. "And what have you to say about all of this, *my proposed lord and master*, my betrothed?"

"My dear, I am of a mind to release you from the agreement our parents made ten years ago. I have never had to force a woman to my bed yet, and frankly I am not sure you are to my taste with your russet hair, your bad manners, and your temper. I seek a woman for my wife, not a spoilt brat."

"Oh!" Velvet looked outraged, and Robin hid a small smile of amusement.

"Nevertheless," Alex continued, "the uniting of our families was a dream of both my late father and your father. Let us wait until the spring when your parents return home to make any irrevocable decisions."

He had stung her and Velvet now retaliated wickedly. "Very well, my lord, but you understand that we are both free to seek our pleasures where we may until then."

"Of course, madame," was his equally cool reply.

Throwing him a final outraged look, Velvet turned on her heel and exited the room, slamming the door behind her.

"She ought to have her bottom paddled," said Robin angrily.

"Thank you for telling her it was I who suggested giving her time to accept our marriage."

"It was the least I could do under the circumstances, Alex. Why did you think now was the moment to tell her who you were?"

"In the fiew weeks Velvet and I have gotten to know one another, I believed we had become friends. I realize now that I have miscalculated."

"Hell, man, you should have let me arrange the wedding and be done with it. Velvet would have settled down once she realized she had no other choice. She is a stubborn chit, but not a stupid one," Robin said.

"Nay, she's not stupid, but you would have miscalculated if you had tried to force the marriage now, and I would be the fellow who had to live with the consequences, Robin."

"What will you do then, Alex?"

Alex chuckled, and it was a deep, rich sound of pure mirth. "I think, Robin, my friend, the time has come to give Mistress Velvet de Marisco a lesson in tactics. I love her, Rob, and I believe she is beginning to love me. But I shall teach her a lesson that will have her begging for our marriage within a very short time, I promise you."

"In that case," Robin said with a slow grin as he poured them out generous goblets of golden wine, "I think we should drink a toast to your wedding, Alex. When do you think I can anticipate the festivities?"

"I imagine I can bring your sister to heel by midautumn," came his confident reply. "Although I forced my sister and her weak-kneed spouse from *Dun Broc*, I want to get back before Bella takes it into her head to move back again.

Neither Alex nor Robin, of course, took into account that if Alex Gordon was stubborn, Velvet de Marisco was even more stubborn. Returning to court and her duties as a Maid of Honor, she threw herself into the social life that surrounded the queen with surprising vigor. The hitherto shy maiden that Velvet had been disappeared, and in her place emerged an amusing and beautiful young woman with a distinct penchant for fun. It was she who suddenly became the instigator of the games and the practical jokes that the youth of the court delighted in so much. If the women at court were no friendlier than they had originally been, the gentlemen were most assuredly delighted.

At first Alex and Robin watched Velvet with tolerant amusement, but as the weeks went by they became less enchanted with her behavior. It was not that there was any real gossip about Velvet, for she was no fool, and if she was flirtatious, she was still careful of her reputation. Her coterie of gentlemen, however, did not include either her brother or her betrothed, which made it difficult for either of them to know exactly what she was doing. Everything they learned was by hearsay, and both were becoming increasingly nervous. Robin and Angel paid a hurried visit to Devon, then returned to find Velvet becoming more unbridled as each day passed.

"I thought you had a plan to control my sister," Robin complained to Alex one evening after they had spent a good hour watching Velvet and her friends play a particularly wild game of hide-and-seek. There had been much shrieking, open tickling, and even a quick kiss observed as the Earl of Essex cornered Velvet, who quickly escaped him, throwing her brother and his friend an arch look as she did so.

"I do," Alex said somewhat smugly, "but I wanted to give her time to amuse herself first. Now, however, *I* shall make *her* jealous."

"Jealous?" Robin was incredulous.

"Aye, Rob. Jealous! I am going to suddenly find myself enamored of a lovely lady of this court. One, of course, of experience who cannot possibly accept any serious addresses on my part, but one who will flirt with verve."

"Oh, Alex," Angel cautioned, "I do not think that very wise. In the short time I have known Velvet, I have learned one thing. She never does the obvious. You will only make her angrier, I fear."

"Now, sweetheart," Robin soothed his lovely wife, "Alex is right, I am certain. Velvet may be angry at us now, but she is basically an innocent. Let her believe that her betrothed husband, whom I know she must care for, is interested in another woman, and she'll come around quickly enough."

Angel shook her head worriedly. Men were sometimes very dense when it came to understanding women, and yet they were supposed to be the superior sex. She sighed deeply. Velvet was not going to come running like a chastised puppy if Alex annoyed her further. She would instead seek to retaliate. If, however, Velvet knew what Alex was planning . . . Angel brightened. That was it! She would tell her sister-in-law and, thus warned, Velvet would not react so violently.

Velvet, however, to Angel's dismay, chuckled wickedly when she learned what her betrothed was planning. "So he seeks to make me jealous? Ha! Until now, all I have done is amuse myself. *Now* I shall endeavor to make him jealous instead while ignoring his little amour. Do you know whom he has singled out, Angel?"

Angel hesitated, then said, "Lady de Boult."

Velvet whooped with glee. "*That drab!*"

"She's very beautiful," ventured Angel.

"'Tis also said she's entertained every cock at court at one time or another," was Velvet's quick reply.

Angel laughed. "Shame on you, Velvet de Marisco! A maiden should not know such things even if they are true!"

"You did!" Velvet countered. "Besides, I'll have far better taste, I assure you, in *my* choice of a lover."

Angel's eyes widened, and her voice was shocked. "You don't really mean to take a lover, Velvet, do you?"

"Nay!" Velvet quickly reassured her best friend. "Alex, however, shall never be certain of it until after our marriage! 'Tis payment enough for his perfidy, I think."

"You love him!" Angel accused.

"Perhaps, though he's scarce given me the chance."

"Nor you he," Angel reminded Velvet.

"Nay," Velvet agreed. "In the beginning it was my fault, but I was so fearful of being forced into a marriage without my parents. Alex, however, must shoulder part of the blame now, for he and Robin should have told me from the start who he was, and then quickly reassured me that he would be willing to wait. We are both, it appears, quite stubborn."

"If you are wise enough to know that, then stop this foolishness before it goes any further, Velvet. Say to Alex what you have said to me and let us end the enmity now," begged Angel.

"Not yet, Angel. If Alex thinks he has bested me in this, then he will always try to keep the upper hand, and our married life will be one battle after another. No. Let him win me, and he shall then appreciate me much more than if he simply married me because I was his betrothed wife. Remember that for ten years he has ignored me in his arrogance! Let him fight a little to regain my affections. It will be a great lesson for him since I shall never allow any man, even my husband, to take my love for granted."

There was a great deal of wisdom in what Velvet said, and Angel was greatly reassured that her sister-in-law would do nothing foolish.

To be wise is one thing, however, but to be jealous is another. Knowing that Alex meant to enrage her by his attentions to Lady de Boult, Velvet did not expect to find herself plagued by what the ladies surrounding the queen referred to as "the green-eyed monster." She could not, however, avoid the gossip that was gleefully reported by the other maids of honor, and Lady de Boult did nothing to discourage the talk surrounding her affair. Indeed she added to it by openly discussing her liaison with her cousin, Audrey, who was one of the queen's ladies.

On the afternoon of the queen's fifty-fifth birthday, Velvet had been listening for over an hour to increasingly idle talk until she thought she would shriek with annoyance. She could not leave because the embroidery threads in the queen's basket were in an incredible tangle. It had taken her most of the afternoon to separate the reds, pinks, roses, and light blues. The greens, darker blues, yellows, and purples were still hopelessly enmeshed, and the queen liked to do busy work in the early evening. Head lowered, she worked to separate the bright colors and ignore the silly chatter, but Audrey Carrington's irritating voice suddenly cried out, "Oh, Mary, how lovely you look! Where did you get those marvelous earbobs? They're new, aren't they?"

Lady de Boult glided into the Maiden's Chamber, a small, feline smile upon her pretty face. She was a tiny, full-figured woman with a delicate, brunette beauty about her. She had milky white skin and large dark eyes that seemed to take up most of her face. She wore a garnet red silk gown, and her hair was contained in an exquisite gold net, a new extravagance from France that allowed her new earbobs to show to their greatest advantage.

Tossing her head, Lady de Boult asked, "Do you like them, Audrey? Lord Gordon gave them to me."

"Are they rubies?" Audrey was quite impressed.

"Aye. Beautiful, aren't they? He said their color reminded him of my lips."

"Oh, how romantic!"

"Aye, he's the most romantic man I've ever met," purred Lady de Boult, looking smugly about her.

"He's a crude Highlander," murmured Velvet, "and more than likely the stones in your ears are either glass or garnets of poor quality."

"How would you know?" Mary de Boult sneered, tossing her head so that the red stones glittered.

"He's my brother's friend and is staying at Lynmouth House," replied Velvet sweetly. "I suspect he's a fortune hunter, m'lady, for earlier this summer he tried to sweep me off my feet, and I'm a betrothed lass. Robin says he has very little but an old stone castle in the mountains west of Aberdeen. More than likely he's come south for a rich wife to rebuild his tumbling-down manse."

"Well! I should certainly not qualify to be his wife," said Lady de Boult huffily, "after all, I have a husband."

"Then why do you accept gifts from another man? I doubt very much the queen would approve such conduct," Velvet retorted primly.

"You know very little about the world, Mistress de Marisco," Lady de Boult replied scathingly.

"True, madame, but is yours an example I should follow? I may be young, but I am not so young that I misunderstand either your shameless behavior or Lord Gordon's base motives."

"How dare you!" Mary de Boult's fair complexion became mottled with outrage, and she raised her hand to slap Velvet, but at that moment the door to the Maiden's Chamber flew open violently.

"Where is the queen?" Robert Devereux entered, an urgent and distressed look about him.

"I'll tell her you're here," said Bess Throckmorton, and, catching Velvet by the hand, she drew her away from Lady de Boult. Together the two young women entered the queen's bedchamber where Elizabeth lay sleeping, for she had had the ague recently. "Majesty, please awaken," Bess said gently, touching the queen lightly.

Instantly Elizabeth woke. "Yes, Bess, what is it?"

"The Earl of Essex with an urgent message, madame."

The queen sat up. "Velvet, hand me my wig and help me with it. Bess, give me but a moment and then tell the earl I shall be with him."

Quickly Velvet aided the queen in setting the beautiful red wig upon her head. The queen's hair had grown thin and gray with age, and she did not feel it suited her at all. The wig was a vanity she readily admitted to, but she cared not who knew as long as no one she considered important saw her own naturally steely locks. Once the hairpiece was affixed atop her head, she stood up, and Velvet helped her sovereign into a beautiful white velvet chamber robe embroidered with gold threads and pearls.

"Thank you, child," murmured Elizabeth kindly to Velvet. "I am so very glad to have you with me."

Bess held the door open as the queen passed through into the Maiden's Chamber. Robert Devereux knelt and, taking the queen's hand, kissed it.

"Madame," he said, his voice low and choked. "Madame, I do not know how to tell you this without hurting you, and hurting you is the one thing I would not do."

Elizabeth Tudor stiffened. "Say on, my lord, for your procrastinating will make it no easier."

"I have come to you from my mother at Cornbury. She wishes you to know that her husband, my stepfather, Lord Dudley, departed this life on September fourth. She said I was to tell you it was a peaceful death, and that Lord Dudley's last thoughts were of Your Majesty." Essex caught at the hem of the queen's gown and kissed it fervently. "God forgive me for having to be the one to bring you this news, for I shall never forgive myself."

For a long moment Elizabeth Tudor stood very still and remained very quiet. She was whiter than her gown, and Velvet was almost afraid that the queen would die right where she stood, seemingly rooted to the floor.

Then Elizabeth Tudor took a deep breath and said in a tight, controlled voice, "Get up, Essex." When he had risen, she continued, "I forgive you, for someone had to tell me, and I had as lief it was you. Now leave me, all of you!" Then, turning, she moved swiftly back into her private closet.

"Come along." Bess Throckmorton hurried them all from the Maiden's Chamber, but not swiftly enough, for they all heard the sound of Elizabeth Tudor's bitter weeping. Shock coursed through them for never in the memory of anyone present had the queen been heard to cry.

It was said that though Elizabeth was sorry about the Earl of Leicester's death, no one else was. The court was too worried over their sovereign's grief, however, to stop and mourn even had they had the desire to do so. The queen locked herself in her rooms for some days, weeping until her eyes were virtually swollen shut and vastly irritated by the salt from her tears. Food was brought in upon trays only to be taken out barely touched as the ladies-in-waiting and the

Maids of Honor huddled, whispering worriedly, with the queen's councillors in the palace corridors.

Finally, when several days had passed, and the queen was still prostrate with her grief, Lord Burghley's concern for Elizabeth Tudor overcame his respect for the privacy of the woman he had served for more than thirty years. Pounding on her bedchamber door, he shouted, "Madame, you must cease your grieving now! I understand your sorrow, but it will not bring my lord of Leicester back to life again, and it would pain him to know that you neglect your duties in this way!"

"He would love every minute of her grief," muttered Ralegh irreverently.

Lord Burghley sent Sir Walter a fierce look, effectively silencing him. "Madame, I beg you," William Cecil continued. "You must give up your sorrow now. We need you. England needs you!"

There was no sound from within the queen's closet now, and after a few moments Lord Burghley took it upon himself to order the door broken down. It was the smashing of the wood that finally brought the queen to her senses. Rising from her bed, she admitted her ladies into the room. She was queen of England, and there was no further time for sorrow. She would have to face the rest of her days without her *sweet Robin*.

Her grief was stirred afresh however, several weeks later when the Earl of Leicester's will was read. In it he wrote:

> *First of all, and above all persons, it is my duty to remember my most dear and gracious Princess, whose creature under God I have been and who hath been a most bountiful and princely mistress to me.*

The queen was then presented with a rope of six hundred pearls from which hung three great bright green emeralds and a large diamond set amidst them. Dudley had left the necklace to Elizabeth, his parting gift to her. A single bright tear rolled down the queen's face before she firmly recovered herself.

When Leicester's widow, Lettice Knollys, quickly remarried Sir Christopher Blount, the queen sued the Dudley estate for all of the thousands of pounds he owed the crown. She would have forgiven the debt but for her cousin Lettice's lack of respect for Leicester's memory. Now she would rather impoverish Lettice than see the money go to the Blounts.

Robert Devereux, the Earl of Essex, was mortified by his mother's lack of respect for her late spouse. There were times, he thought, when Lettice could be an embarrassing liability, and this hasty marriage to a man young enough to be her son was certainly one of those times. Besides, he had come to like his stepfather.

He grumbled about it to Velvet one afternoon as they stole a few moments from their duties, seated together in a secluded, windowed alcove. "Blount, of all people, Velvet! What in God's name does she see in him?"

"He's very handsome," Velvet ventured.

"Handsome!" Essex was forced to laugh. "That's just the sort of answer I would expect from an inexperienced girl."

"I am not inexperienced!" Velvet huffed.

Essex chuckled and slipped a bold arm about her waist. "You're certainly not experienced, Mistress de Marisco," he teased her fondly, and then stole a lingering kiss.

"Fie, sir!" she scolded him breathlessly, but she dimpled and colored becomingly, totally unaware of how very lovely she was at that moment, of how she glowed, flattered by his attention.

It would have added greatly to her pleasure to know that across the room, unobserved by the pair, Alexander Gordon seethed with impotent rage. He could not hear what they said, but it mattered not, for it was obvious that Velvet was flirting shamelessley with the Earl of Essex, and Alex could do nothing about it.

The court that autumn was a dull place, for the queen would hold no revels nor allow any gaiety until the official thanksgiving for the Armada victory, which was to be held on November 17. Nonetheless, the younger members of the court managed to find their way to the bear gardens, the theaters, and the autumnal fairs during the afternoons when the queen was less apt to notice their absence.

Alexander Gordon kept up his seemingly ardent pursuit of Lady de Boult. One warm autumn afternoon Velvet came upon the couple in an arbor by the river. The sight of his hand down her well-filled bodice enraged Velvet.

"Lecher!" she shrieked at him as Mary de Boult looked stunned, caught between the two of them. "So you court her to make me jealous and to bring me to heel, do you? Liar! Liar! Liar! You could not possibly have known that I would choose to walk at this hour along this path! You but use our estrangement as an excuse to pursue any bitch who is willing to lift her tail for you!" Then she slapped him with all her might and, turning on her heel, stalked angrily away.

"Madame!" His voice roared after her, and when she did not stop, he leaped the space between them and, grasping her arm, spun her about.

"Unhand me, lecher!" she snapped, "else I'll tell the queen of your behavior with this woman!" She tried to pull away from him, but his fingers tightened cruelly about her flesh.

"You're jealous," he said flatly.

"Never!" She shouted the hollow denial.

"Aye, you're jealous, Velvet, and I've been jealous, too, each time I've seen you cuddling with my lord Essex." His grip loosened enough to pull her toward him, while his other hand tipped her face up toward his. "Come, sweetheart, enough of this warring between us. We have both been wrong. Now let us make peace and begin afresh. Your parents will be home in the springtime, and we will celebrate our marriage then. Let us spend the winter learning to love one another." He bent to kiss her, but Velvet turned her face from his.

By this time Mary de Boult had recovered her surprise and, glaring at them, demanded to know, "Are you to marry this, this chit, my lord Gordon? How dare you lead me on, then! I have never been so insulted in my entire life!"

"Nor as amply rewarded for your infidelity!" snapped Velvet. "If you feel so abused, my lady, then I suggest you complain to your husband!"

"Ohhhh!" Lady de Boult was a picture of perfect outrage. With an angry, futile, "Well!," she glowered at Alex, and then, to his surprise, she also slapped him before stamping off toward the palace.

With a rueful grin, he rubbed his twice-injured cheek. "You English lasses have hard hands," he said.

"Go to hell!" was Velvet's furious reply. "If you think I intend to kiss and make up with you, you're mistaken, my lord."

His brow darkened, and then he said in a seemingly calm voice, "What I think, Velvet, is that you're a spoilt brat. I admit I was wrong in ignoring you in the years between our betrothal and now, but when that contract was made between our families you were a child and I already a man."

"You might have sent the child a doll, my lord. You might have remembered her occasionally on her birthday, or Twelfth Night, or even the anniversary of our betrothal, but you did not! The truth of the matter is that you did not remember me at all until your dying father reminded you of your obligations. Only then did *you* decide *you* needed a wife, a creature upon which *you* might breed the next generation of Gordons of BrocCairn. Well, my lord Earl of BrocCairn, I am not a brood mare, and I have decided that I will not marry you ever! You're far too fickle a man to suit me!"

Alex was stung by the truth of her words, yet if she would not give in, neither would he. The right was his, he told himself firmly. "I was willing to wait until yer parents returned home, Velvet," he said in an ominous voice. "I have played, or tried to play, the suitor for these four months, but ye're an impossible little shrew! I will wait no longer! Not for yer parents, not for ye, not for anyone! I need a wife now, and ye're contracted to me by both God's law and man's." Taking her firmly by the hand, he dragged her along behind him down the queen's garden toward the river.

"Stop! Where are you taking me?" Velvet demanded of him.

"To Scotland, madame! To be my wife! To be the mother of my children! By this time next year, the first of our sons will be at yer breast, Velvet, and this nonsense will be long forgotten!"

"Never!" she cried. "*Never!* I would sooner be dead!"

He ignored her cries and her frantic struggles as, reaching the quay, he called out to hail a boatman. Shoving her down into the small boat, he directed the man to Lynmouth House. When she looked as if she might scream, he glowered at her and said in a low, threatening voice, "One word, Velvet, and I'll toss ye in the river to drown! I swear it!" She believed him, regretting bitterly that she had ever driven him so far. It was symptomatic of her own childishness, she realized, that she had been so wrapped up in herself she hadn't stopped to consider him or his feelings in this matter. Perhaps she might reason with him.

"My lord," she began softly, "please, I beg of you, do nothing foolish. We are too much alike, I fear, to make a successful match. I cannot believe that there are not any number of girls who would be honored to be your wife."

"*Ye* are my betrothed wife," he growled at her. "Now be silent! I don't wish to share our problems with all of London."

She opened her mouth to protest further, but then closed it again. Better not to aggravate him. They were going to Lynmouth House, and Robin and Angel would be there. They would help her reason with him and it would all be resolved. Meekly, she folded her hands in her lap and waited to reach their destination.

The Earl and Countess of Lynmouth, however, were not in residence when they arrived. A message had come up from Devon late the day before saying that the earl's little daughters were ill, and nothing would do, the majordomo told them, but that her ladyship hurry down to *Lynmouth Castle* to minister to her stepdaughters. Naturally his lordship went with her.

Velvet was horrified, realizing that without Robin and Angel to mediate this quarrel she had no control over Alex. Turning, she whispered, "I can't leave without seeing my brother, my lord."

"We're leaving within the hour," he said coldly. "I want to be free of London and well on the road north before nightfall. We have maybe four hours of daylight left today. Pack only essentials. I'll arrange to have the rest of yer things sent later on."

"I cannot leave the queen, my lord. She will never forgive me if I go without speaking to her first."

"Once we're in Scotland, Velvet, Elizabeth Tudor will no longer matter in yer life. Ye'll have a king then. A Stewart king."

"What about Pansy? I can't travel without my maid!"

"Aye, ye'll need the girl. Where is she?"

"Back at the palace."

"I'll send Dugald for her." He grasped her arm again and led her up the stairs of Lynmouth House to his apartments. "I want ye with me, madame, for I'll not have ye upsetting the servants with any caterwauling." They entered his rooms. "Dugald! Get back to St. James and fetch Mistress de Marisco's tiring woman, Pansy. Be quick, man, for we're off for home this day!"

Dugald's face split into a wide grin. "Aye, my lord! I'll not be long in fetching the lass, and 'twill be good to go home at last." He hurried out the door without so much as a look in Velvet's direction.

"Sit down," Alex commanded, and in order not to anger him any further, she obeyed.

For some minutes they sat in silence, and then Velvet said pleadingly, "Please, my lord, you can't do this."

He looked coldly at her. "I am doing it, Velvet, and if ye were to challenge me in the courts over this I should win. Ye are legally my betrothed wife, and unless either I or yer parents dissolve the contract made between us, ye have no other choice. Yer parents are away, and I wish to marry now. Yer brother would support me if he was here as he is yer guardian. Ye know that, so resign yourself to our marriage."

"Wait at least until Robin returns from Devon, my lord!"

"Nay, Velvet. If I sent a messenger after Robin it would be several days before we had a reply. Winter is coming, and in the north it's nearer than it is here in yer soft England. Even the few days it would take to obtain Robin's official permission could mean the difference between our getting back to *Dun Broc* before the snows or being caught in the first storm of winter. I have the right, Velvet, and we leave before sunset."

Once again silence descended upon the room. Why, thought Velvet to herself, why could I not have walked away when I saw him fondling that overblown de Boult creature? *Because you love him*, came the answer, and she cried aloud, "No!"

"No?" he questioned.

"'Tis nothing, my lord. I but had a thought that distressed me."

"What thought?"

She shook her head.

"What thought?" he repeated, and now he came and knelt by her chair so that he might look up into her face. "What thought, Velvet, distresses ye so greatly that ye cry out against it?"

"I but merely wondered why I had not left you to your pursuit of Lady de Boult instead of interfering," she said honestly. "Had I not disturbed you, I should not now be in this position."

"And why did ye interfere, sweetheart?" His voice had gotten softer, and his amber eyes were suddenly gentle and even a touch amused.

She shook her head. If he thought to cozen her with sweet words, then he was very much mistaken.

"Oh, Velvet," he said quietly, "why do ye refuse to admit that perhaps ye care a trifle for me?"

"Nay!" Her denial was too quick, and she flushed quietly.

He sighed. "I think ye lie, lass, not only to me, but to yerself also. Never mind, for we shall become reacquainted again on the road where we will have no one but each other. I had thought, though, that perhaps ye were beginning to care a little."

"And you, my lord? Do you care, even a little?" she asked.

"Aye, lass," he answered her without hesitation, and to her great consternation. "I do care."

Velvet swallowed hard, but refrained from answering him. For ten years he had ignored her existence, and then, upon entering her life, he had falsely represented himself. He had flaunted another woman at her, no matter that she had known it was only to make her jealous. She strongly suspected that he had enjoyed himself, and that was totally unforgiveable!

The silence about them deepened. Lord Gordon arose from his knees and, going to a table, poured himself some wine from the decanter. "Are ye thirsty?" he asked her, holding out a goblet. She shook her head, so he drank deeply of it himself. The minutes ticked slowly by, and the tension about them was so thick that she thought she would scream. Finally, when she believed she could bear it no more, the door of the apartment opened, and Dugald entered with Pansy, who ran directly to her mistress.

"This brigand dragged me from the Maiden's Chamber where I was awaiting you, mistress. He says we are going to Scotland. Is it true then?"

Before Velvet could answer, Alex spoke for her. "We will leave as soon as ye can pack, Pansy. We are riding. There will be no carriage. Lord Southwood's servants can pack yer mistress's things for shipping later on, but she will need some necessities for now. I expect ye can ride?"

"Yes, m'lord."

"Very well then, go along, lass, and hurry."

"I must go with her," Velvet said.

"Why?" he demanded harshly.

"My lord, have you no delicacy?"

He flushed. "I beg yer pardon, Velvet. Of course, go with yer woman, but Dugald will accompany ye."

"As you will, my lord," was her cool reply.

Ignoring the grinning Dugald, Velvet left Alex's apartments and, with Pansy following, hurried through her brother's house to her own rooms. As Dugald attempted to step into the apartment after them, Velvet firmly barred his way. "I will have my privacy!" she said sharply.

"The earl said I was to stay wi' ye, mistress."

"There is only one way into or out of my rooms, and we are three stories up," Velvet snapped. "You'll stay here in the hall, or I'll scream the house down! Lord Gordon will not thank you if I create a scene." Then she firmly slammed the door in his face.

"What is happening?" Pansy begged to know.

"It is all my fault," Velvet said, distraught. "I came upon the earl and Lady de Boult this afternoon. He was caressing the creature most ardently. It was infuriating. I could not help myself, Pansy. I created a terrible fuss. When my temper had cooled, the earl's temper had heated considerably. He dragged me back here, and insists that we leave for Scotland today to be married. I had hoped that Robin and Angel would intercede for me, but they have gone to Devon. What am I to do?"

"It appears, mistress, that there is nothing to do but go with the earl," replied Pansy. "He is your rightful betrothed. Don't be afraid, for I shall come with you."

"Nay, Pansy! You must ride for Devon and send my brother after us! 'Tis my only hope!"

"I'll do no such thing, Mistress Velvet! Why, me ma would have the hide off me if I left you now. She would, and that's a fact! Always stay with your mistress, she's told me. Why, she would be with m' lady Skye this very minute had not her ladyship forbidden her the voyage. If, however, you'll write a note for Lord Southwood, I'll see that it gets delivered. Me cousin, Elvy, is a footman here in the house."

"I'll write it immediately!" Velvet hurried to the desk.

"And I'll pack for us, for we're off to Scotland whether we will or no," replied Pansy, beginning to gather up the necessities.

While Velvet frantically scribbled a plea for help to her brother, Pansy got together a small parcel containing some changes of linen, several silk shifts, a warm nightshift, a comb, and a brush for her mistress. For herself, she put together a similar packet. Then she went to the door of the apartment and, opening it, told the waiting Dugald, "Fetch the housekeeper, so I may explain what things of me mistress's are to be shipped north."

"I canna leave her ladyship," Dugald replied. "Ye know the earl's orders."

"Then you'll not mind if I speak to the housekeeper meself," said Pansy.

"I dinna see any harm in it, lassie. Run along, but dinna dawdle, fer his lordship's anxious to be off."

"I'll run like there's wings on me feet," replied Pansy pertly. "Let me tell me mistress first though." She popped back into Velvet's rooms, closing the door once more behind her. "Give me the note, mistress. I'll get it to Elvy now, and when I get back, I'll help you change into your riding clothes."

Silently Velvet handed Pansy her missive, which the tiring woman slipped into her bodice, and then Pansy was quickly out the door, hurrying down the hall.

Dugald grinned after her and licked his lips. There was something English he'd like to get familiar with, and just mayhap on the trip north he'd have the opportunity. She was a fine-looking little lass. He liked them small and buxom, and he'd never seen such blue eyes, like bluebells they were. He even liked her rich chestnut-colored hair and her freckled face. Aye, she looked like a lass who could warm a man's bed very well of a winter's night.

Pansy, unaware of his thoughts, hurried to seek the housekeeper. Finding her, she explained that Mistress Velvet would be leaving shortly for the north, and that it was imperative that her clothing followed her within a day or two. Since she herself must accompany her mistress, she did not have time to pack it.

The housekeeper nodded with an understanding smile. Young lovers were always so impatient, though my lord Southwood would certainly be disappointed that his sister had not waited until the spring to get married, when her parents returned home.

Pansy dared say nothing. Instead she thanked the housekeeper for her kindness, and then asked if the good woman knew where her cousin, Elvy, was so that she might bid him farewell.

Elvy was in the pantry cleaning the silver and looked very surprised when Pansy told him that she and Mistress Velvet were leaving that very afternoon for Scotland. "'Tis a quick decision, it is," he said. "Is she then with child that a wedding must be celebrated so soon?"

"Nay, dunce!" snapped Pansy, outraged. "He's forcing her to come with him." She reached into her bodice and drew out Velvet's note. "Take this to me lord Southwood in Devon, as quickly as you can, Elvy. Wait until after we've gone and then ride like the wind. With luck, Lord Southwood will catch us before we reach the border. Me mistress and the earl had the most terrible argument, Elvy, and now in a temper Lord Gordon insists the marriage be celebrated without further delay. Me lady would wait until her parents return home in the spring. What is the harm in that, I ask you?"

Elvy shook his head. "None that I can see, Pansy. She's a good girl, Mistress Velvet is, and has ever been loving of her parents. He's unreasonable, this Scotsman is. I'll never understand why Lord de Marisco betrothed her to a foreigner anyhow."

"The whys and wherefores of the gentry aren't for us to wonder about, Elvy. Just get the note to me lord Southwood. Now I'd best get back lest they leave without me. I don't want me lady to ride alone." She left him and flew back upstairs.

"That didn't take long," Dugald remarked as Pansy hurried back to the apartment door.

"I'm a swift worker," Pansy replied.

"Aye, and I'll just wager ye are." He chuckled.

"Mind your manners, you grinning baboon," she snapped at him, then pushed past him into Velvet's rooms. As soon as the door had shut behind her, she said to her waiting mistress, "'Tis done now, and you need have no further worry. Lord Southwood will catch up with us before we are too far from London, I'll vow!"

Velvet nodded. "We had best hurry, Pansy. I don't want to be dragged off before I can change into comfortable clothing."

The two women quickly donned their travel garments. They knew they would be expected to ride astride, for Lord Gordon would be in a hurry, so they both put on split-legged skirts like the ones that Velvet's mother had designed for herself years before. With them they wore shirts, Velvet's of silk, Pansy's a more sturdy linen, and over this warm cloaks. Both had boots, Velvet's of fine leather that came to her knee, Pansy's made of a less elegant leather that only came to her ankles.

With a sigh Velvet looked about her bedchamber and wondered if she would ever see it again. Oh, why was Robin away when she needed him? And why couldn't Alexander Gordon accept the fact that she didn't want to be married to him—at least not yet. With another little sigh she picked up her cloak. "Come along, Pansy. I imagine his lordship is very impatient by now."

"Aye," replied the girl, "but me mother says 'tis a good thing to keep a man waiting lest he become too sure of you." She gave Velvet a cheery smile. "It's a lovely time of year to go north, Mistress Velvet, and I've not a doubt Lord Southwood will have caught up with us before we even get to Worcester. Take your gloves now, else you ruin your beautiful hands." She handed her mistress a pair of soft beige kid gloves.

Together they left the apartment, Pansy picking up the two packets that would be stuffed into their saddlebags. She wasn't sorry to be leaving London, and if the truth were known she wasn't sorry that her mistress was finally going to settle down. Pansy had grown up with her mother's stories of Mistress Skye, and she decided that she would far prefer being settled in one place, even if that place was Scotland. I'm not a lass for adventuring, she thought to herself.

There were four horses waiting outside of Lynmouth House in the drive. Lord BrocCairn's mount was a large gray stallion at least eighteen hands tall, with a black mane and tail. Dugald and Pansy had smaller, sturdier brown geldings while Velvet's mount was a fine-boned elegant black mare who danced nervously awaiting her mistress.

"Where is my chestnut stallion?" Velvet demanded.

"There can be only one stallion in my stables," Lord Gordon replied, "and Ulaidh is that stallion. I have arranged to have your horse returned to *Queen's Malvern* as he is a valuable breeding animal. I knew you would not want him sold."

"You are too kind, my lord," she said dryly. "Have you named my mare?"

"Her name is Sable," he replied. "She is a daughter of Ulaidh." Without warning, he boosted her into the saddle. "If you wish to discuss my stables, Velvet, we can do so as we ride. The day wanes already."

They rode out from Lynmouth House and took the road north toward St. Albans, where Alex said they would stop for the night. "I do not wish to hire post horses at inns along the way, and so we must rest our own animals daily and see that they are well fed and watered," he stated

Velvet might find many things to disagree with when dealing with Alex Gordon, but his care of their horses was not going to be one of them. She had been raised to have a great respect for horses by her parents who, once they had been removed from their seafaring activities by Elizabeth Tudor when they were forced to make *Queen's Malvern* their home, had raised horses during most of the years of her youth.

Travel, even in this enlightened day and age, was not easy. Velvet was rather surprised that Alex would undertake such a long journey with two women along without an armed escort. The farther you journeyed from London, the less safe the roads became. Two men, two women, four horses. It seemed dangerous, even foolish. The horses would be their most precious possession. No, Velvet wasn't going to argue with him this time. Besides, the slower they went, the faster Robin could catch up with them.

Velvet settled herself in her saddle and concentrated on learning the whims and ways of her new mare. She quickly found that Sable was beautifully trained, needing only the lightest touch of the rein to bring her to obedience. "What a lovely little creature Sable is," she exclaimed. "Her manners are perfect. Who trained her?"

"I did," Alex replied. "She's very spirited, but then I've always had a way with skittish females, I'm told." He grinned rather impudently at her.

Velvet tossed her head. "We'll see, my lord, how good you really are," was her sharp retort.

They rode the twenty miles between London and St. Albans, stopping after sunset at the Queen's Head Inn. St. Albans was a lovely town on a hill overlooking the Ver River. Although there had originally been a Roman settlement on the site, the present town had grown up around the great abbey that had been built by Offa, king of Mercia, after the departure of the Romans. He had used the stones from the Roman town to raise up the religious house, and then he had named it after Britain's first Christian martyr.

Velvet, however, was in no mood to remember her history. It had been a long time since she had ridden for such a long distance, and she found her legs, and other more delicate parts of her anatomy, quite sore. There were only two things that she wanted: a bath and a soft bed. They were fortunate in that the inn, although a popular one, was not crowded. They were able to obtain two rooms and a private parlor in which to take their meals. While Dugald saw to the horses, Pansy saw that her mistress had a good hot bath. She then wrapped Velvet in the silk nightshift she had packed and tucked her into bed.

"Tell his lordship that I shall not be joining him for supper, Pansy. I shall take a bit of capon and some wine right here."

Pansy curtsied, then informed the earl that her mistress was extremely fatigued from their ride and would be dining in her bed.

Alex smiled to himself. Obviously being a Maid of Honor, and one of the darlings of Elizabeth's court, did not prepare a lass for a long ride. She'd be well used to it, he thought, by the time they reached *Dun Broc.*

The following day dawned wet and dreary, but despite the weather they reached Northampton by nightfall. The rain continued for two more days during which time they passed through Leicester and Derby. The fourth day of their journey dawned bright and sunny, and they rode farther that day than they had in the previous two.

That evening at Sheffield's Rose and Crown inn Alex told Velvet that this ancient English town, famous for its cutlery, had been the place where Mary, Queen of Scots had been imprisoned for fourteen years. Looking up at Sheffield Castle as they rode away from the town the following morning, Velvet shivered, thinking of that wretched queen.

It was five and a half days since they had left London. They were nearly two hundred miles from the city and Velvet was growing increasingly nervous with each mile that passed. *Where was Robin?* Then she soothed herself with logic. Traveling at top speeds, it would take at least two days for the footman to reach *Lynmouth.* It would take two days for Robin to return to London, and two to three days more for him to catch up with them. However, each mile they traveled was another mile for him, too. It would be a losing battle unless she could get Alex to stop somewhere along their route, thus giving her brother time to reach them.

They arrived at York and put up at the Bishop's Mitre Inn. It was a luxurious place overlooking the junction of the Ouse and the Foss rivers just outside the walls of the medieval part of the town. Velvet, who had taken her supper in bed since they had begun their journey, this night made the effort to dine with Lord Gordon.

"I am embarrassed to come before you dressed in my riding clothes, but I suspect I am a great deal more respectable than if I wore my only other garment, my nightshift. She smiled wryly at him.

"You are growing used to our pace now?" he questioned her.

"Aye, my lord. My poor bottom is well used to my saddle by now."

He chuckled at her small attempt at humor. Perhaps she was becoming more tractable although she had hardly spoken to him at all during their journey.

"It would be nice to have a day out of the saddle, however," she continued. "Might we stay in York a short while? I am told the cathedral is magnificent, with more stained glass than any other church in all of England."

"We have several more days ahead of us, Velvet, before we even reach Scotland. I have told you that winter comes early in the Highlands."

She sighed deeply. "Would just one day matter?"

He thought a moment. One day could matter very much, and yet she looked so disappointed. He wanted to please her. He wanted them to have that same relaxed and pleasant relationship they had once had. Perhaps humoring her would help. "Very well," he said, "but just one day."

Early the following morning, Pansy was up and out to an open-air market where she managed to purchase secondhand a respectable dark green velvet skirt that her mistress could wear and that would cover Velvet's riding boots as she walked about York. It was a plain garment, but her mistress certainly could not wear her riding skirt in town.

After a breakfast of steaming oat porridge that had been served with heavy cream and honey, a hot cottage loaf that was offered with a crock of sweet butter, peach jam, or cheese, brown ale for Alex, and watered wine for Velvet, they left the inn to visit the cathedral. Despite her anger at being dragged from London, and her fear of marriage to this strong, fierce man, Velvet was as excited as any sightseer. Educated in the history of her country, she knew that next to Canterbury, York Minster, originally called St. Peter's, was the most famous cathedral in all of England. It was built between the twelfth and fourteenth centuries, but its soaring towers only dated from the previous century. It was one of the loveliest examples of Gothic architecture in all of Christendom.

Velvet, who, unlike most of York's pilgrims who came simply to pray to the saints, had a rare appreciation of beauty in art, found the north transept of the cathedral with its magnificent stained-glass windows beautiful beyond all. She was in transports over the wood vaulting in the nave of the cathedral and simply fell in love with the exquisite Lady Chapel. Alex, who had seen York Minster before, now saw it through her eyes with a new enthusiasm, and was enchanted at this different aspect he had found in this child bride of his.

Leaving the cathedral, they walked through the old part of the city with its narrow and winding medieval streets. This ancient part of York was surrounded by the original wall of the city with its four gates. It was a lovely, cool autumn day, and Alex found that he was glad he had stopped their journey in midflight. Velvet was more relaxed and chatty than he had seen her in weeks. Rather than return to the inn at midday, they bought sausage, bread, and cider from street vendors and sat by the banks of the river. Each carefully avoided the subject of their marriage: Alex, not wanting to fight with Velvet again, and Velvet, not wanting to spoil the day lest he insist they go on their way once more. Every hour they remained in York was an hour closer to her rescue by her brother. Surely Robin would come tomorrow or the next day.

Velvet's heart sank when Alex announced that they would retire early that night because he wished to ride out before sunrise.

"We can't make up for this lost day, but we'll be a bit farther on than if we started later," he said.

"How far will we ride tomorrow, my lord?" she asked him, afraid of the answer.

"I should like to make Hexham. If we do, then we shall be able to cross the border into Scotland the day after tomorrow."

Alone with Pansy, Velvet fretted, "Where is Robin? It is a week since we left London. He should be here now!"

Pansy looked unhappy, and then she said, "Perhaps he is not coming, mistress."

"*Not coming!* Why wouldn't he come to my rescue?" She stamped her foot to emphasize her point.

"Mistress Velvet, you are betrothed to Lord Gordon, and your mama and papa did approve the match. Perhaps Lord Southwood feels that now that the earl has taken things into his own hands, it is better to have you marry and be done with it."

Velvet's face crumbled. "*No!*" she whispered. "I don't want to be married now! I don't want to be a mother yet! I am just barely past my own childhood, dammit! It isn't fair! It just isn't fair!"

Pansy sighed deeply. Life wasn't always fair, she thought, but there it was. You took what was handed you and made the best of it. At least that's what her mother had always said, and her mother knew. Pansy's charming Irish father, one of Lady de Marisco's captains, on the other hand, was more like Mistress Velvet. Always seeking the impossible, always anxious to see what was over the rainbow. He was a dreamer and a romantic, just like the young girl she served. Pansy couldn't understand why Mistress Velvet was making such a fuss. If she had been given a handsome, wealthy, and kind man for a husband, *she* would be on her knees thanking the blessed Mother!

"We will run away!" Velvet said dramatically.

"*What?*" Pansy was startled from her reverie.

"We'll run away," Velvet repeated. "Tonight, when Lord Gordon is snoring snugly in his bed, we will escape him and make our own way back to London. When I tell the queen that he kidnapped me, she'll have his arrogant head!"

"Mistress Velvet! That's the silliest idea I ever heard," Pansy declared bravely, for she had no right to speak to her mistress in such a fashion. "Frankly, we have been lucky to get this far without being assaulted by robbers, traveling without an armed escort as we have been doing. Only the fact that Lord Gordon and Dugald are well armed, and look like the type of men that will not be trifled with, has saved us, I've not a doubt. Two women, however, are a totally different matter! We'll not get five miles from York before we are set upon, murdered, robbed, and heaven only knows what!"

"There is no other way, Pansy. Perhaps we could dress as boys?"

Pansy looked down at her full bosom and shook her head ruefully. "I could never disguise these," she said. "Mistress, listen to me. Let the earl bring you to Scotland. 'Tis true you're his betrothed wife, but only a priest can unite you in the holy bonds of matrimony. If you refuse the marriage, there can be no marriage, can there? Lord Gordon will have to send you back to England and wait until your parents return next spring, won't he?"

The smile that suddenly lit Velvet's face was like the sun returning after a gray day. "Oh, Pansy! You're right! You're absolutely right! Why didn't I think of it in the first place? The worst that can happen is that we'll be stuck in Scotland for the winter. What matter as long as we return to England in the spring?" Impulsively Velvet hugged her tiring woman. "Oh, what would I do without you?"

Pansy sighed with relief. Her mother had always said she had a quick mind. If her mistress had persisted in attempting an escape from Lord Gordon, Pansy would have had to side with the earl for Velvet's sake, but she knew that her mistress would never have forgiven her, and she would have been sent home in disgrace. What would she have said to her mother then? Pansy was certain that Lady de Marisco couldn't have been like Velvet or else Daisy would not have been able to cope so well.

Two days later, the Earl of BrocCairn's party crossed over the invisible line that separated England and Scotland and rode into the Cheviot Hills. It was a clear mid-October day, and the air was sharp and crisp. Alex had put aside the elegant garb of the gentleman that morning, and he now rode dressed as the Highlander he was in a belted plaid consisting of a piece of Gordon tartan, plaited in the middle and wrapped around his back, leaving as much at each end as would cover the front of the body, the ends overlapping each other. The plaid was held in place with a wide leather belt that had a silver buckle jeweled with a reddish agate. The lower part of the tartan fell to the middle of his knee joints while the upper part was fastened to his shoulder with a large silver brooch engraved with a badger and the BrocCairn motto, "*Defend or Die.*"

With the tartan he wore a white silk shirt, knitted green hose, a doeskin vest with horn buttons, and black leather brogues. On his head was a blue bonnet with a pheasant's feather set at a jaunty angle. He was armed with his broadsword, a dirk, and a sgian-dubh in his right stocking.

Dugald was dressed similarly, and Pansy openly eyed him with approval, for he was a fine figure of a man in his plaid, she suddenly decided.

Velvet was now more uncomfortably aware of Alex than she had ever been. He was, she noted, extremely handsome in his tartan, and seeing his bare knees gave her a shiver. There was something almost savage about him that had not been there before. She began to wonder if perhaps she shouldn't have fled him in York when she had the opportunity. Any softness he had shown was gone with his English clothes.

They stopped during the noon hour to rest the horses and to eat the lunch that the innkeeper's wife had packed for them that morning. There were slabs of fresh bread with sharp cheese and sweet pink ham, a cold chicken, a skin of cider, and some pears. The day was quiet, the air warm and still. Velvet was taken by the beauty of the Border country. The hills stretched into the purple distance, seeming almost softly smudged in the clear autumn light.

"Where are we to stay tonight, my lord?" Velvet asked as they mounted up to ride again.

"I am heading toward *Hermitage*, the Border home of my cousin, Francis Stewart-Hepburn. He is the Earl of Bothwell, and even if he is not in residence, they will offer us hospitality. I am hoping to stay a few days while I send Dugald on to *Dun Broc* to bring back an escort. We have been lucky so far, but I will bring ye no farther without my men at my back."

"Is it so dangerous then? We have had no difficulties, and we are closer to *Dun Broc* now than we are to London."

"Are ye anxious then, Velvet, to see yer new home?"

She flushed at his reference to *Dun Broc* as her home. "My lord, you have kidnapped me from the queen's court, and though it is true that we are betrothed, you cannot compel me to marry you. I have told you that I will not marry you until my parents return home."

He smiled. "I thought ye weren't going to marry me at all," he gently teased her.

She would not look at him, instead staring straight ahead, her hands clenching her reins. "It is not that you are not suitable, my lord, it is just that I am not yet ready to wed. Why can you not understand that? I am being neither coy nor coquettish."

"Ye were correct when ye said that we are alike, Velvet, for if I do not understand yer attitude, ye do not understand mine. I have courted ye and tried to be patient."

She snorted derisively, and he was forced to laugh in spite of himself.

"There is no way you can force me to the altar without my family about me," she said firmly.

Before he could answer her, Dugald said urgently, "Riders, my lord! Up ahead, and they've already seen us." His hand reached for his broadsword.

"Rein in!" Alex commanded sharply, and then he directed his words to the two women. "Even at this distance I can tell Borderers. Pray God they are Bothwell's men, but, in any event, keep yer mouths shut! Velvet, I am deadly serious when I tell ye that this is a matter of life and death."

"I understand, Alex," she replied softly, and he looked sharply at her. It was the first time since they had left London that she had called him by name.

He smiled a quick, encouraging smile back at her. "Good girl!"

They moved forward at a slower pace, allowing the large party of riders ahead of them to come toward them. As the troop came nearer, Alex's tense face relaxed as he realized that they indeed wore the plaid and the badge of the Earl of Bothwell. As the two parties came abreast of each other, the Earl of BrocCairn saw Francis Stewart-Hepburn's bastard half brother, Hercules Stewart, riding in the forefront. Hercules, like the hero he was named for, was a huge man with a shock of black hair. He also had a handsome Stewart face.

"Hercules, my friend," called Alex.

Hercules Stewart's face broke into a friendly smile. "My lord Gordon! What brings ye into the Cheviots?"

Alex reined his horse in, facing Hercules. "I'm just over the border after several months spent in England. Is Francis at *Hermitage*? I would ask his hospitality for several nights. We have ridden hard from London these last ten days and my lady is weary."

Hercules let his gaze roam to Velvet, and his eyes widened with approval at what he saw. "Aye, my lord Bothwell is in residence and will welcome ye. We'll escort ye there now. Have ye come all this way without any escort? Christ, man! Ye're braver than I!"

Alex laughed, saying, "When did any Scotsman need an armed escort among the English? However, I dinna think it safe to continue north without my own men. Dugald will leave tomorrow for *Dun Broc*."

Hercules nodded. "Aye, 'tis best. The northern clans have been roused to a fever pitch pillaging the Spanish ships driven ashore in the late-summer storms. Travel is even worse than usual."

"'Twas a great victory for the English," Alex remarked.

"'Twas God's own luck," rejoined Hercules. "They were badly outnumbered, though I'll grant they're better sailors than King Philip's men." At this point his band had moved around and behind Alex's party. "Come along now, my lord, and I'll take ye to *Hermitage*. Yon bonny lass looks as if she'd welcome a bath and a soft bed."

"She's my betrothed wife, Hercules," Alex said quietly.

"I congratulate ye, my lord," was Hercules' reply, then he raised his hand as a signal, and they moved forward.

Within the hour they had reached *Hermitage*, the favorite residence of the Earl of Bothwell. A thirteenth-century castle, it was the strongest of the Border strongholds and sat atop a hill, allowing its inhabitants a view of the land below and for miles around. Above its main entry were the Hepburn lions, and Velvet noticed as they rode in that *Hermitage's* heights were well patroled.

Dismounting within the castle courtyard, they followed Hercules into the building. It was late in the day now, near to sunset, and the Great Hall of the castle was alive with activity as the dinner hour approached. The four fireplaces were already blazing with hearty fires that took the chill from the large room. There wasn't a woman in sight except for a few serving wenches, but the hall was filled with Lord Bothwell's male retainers who lounged about chatting, drinking, and dicing while they awaited the arrival of their master for the meal.

"I'll get my brother," Hercules said. "Ye'll be comfortable here." And then he was gone up a flight of steps.

"I've heard of the Earl of Bothwell," Velvet said. "Wasn't he wed to the late Queen Mary?"

"'Twas his uncle," Alex replied. "It was James Hepburn who tried to be king. Sadly, he left no legitimate heirs, and so the title passed to his sister's son, my cousin Francis. He added the Hepburn to his own Stewart name in honor of his mother's family. He's an interesting man, Velvet. Educated and highly intelligent. The king is terrified of him." Alex chuckled. "But, then, Jamie Stewart is terrified of his own shadow."

"How are you related to the earl?" she asked, curious.

"I'm afraid ye'll be shocked, Velvet, but we are all related through a common grandfather, King James V of Scotland. The Stewarts are a loving family, but they've nae been known to confine their loving to their legal spouses. Both my grandmother, Alexandra Gordon, and Francis's grandmother were mistresses to the king at one time. My father was the result of my grandmother's liaison with James, and Francis's father, John Stewart, the prior of Coldingham, was the result of his grandmother's passion."

"Aye," said a deep, amused voice. "We Stewarts have always been a passionate clan, and generous with our favors. Good day, my cousin of BrocCairn, and who is this fair creature ye bring into my castle?"

Velvet turned and saw before her one of the handsomest men she had ever laid eyes upon. He stood well over six feet in height, and had the lean, hard body of a man who spent a great deal of time out of doors. He had a sculpted, sensitive face with bright blue eyes. His hair was a deep auburn like hers, his short, barbered beard the same. His smile was quick and extended as far as his eyes.

Alex laughed, "Ye never change, Francis! Always an eye for the wenches, but this one is mine, and I've brought her all the way from England. My betrothed wife, Velvet de Marisco. Velvet, this is my cousin, the Earl of Bothwell, Francis Stewart-Hepburn."

Bothwell bowed low over Velvet's hand, raising it to his lips and kissing it. "Madame, if I had known that England held such an exquisite treasure, I should have long ago stolen ye away like the Border raider I am," he said.

She blushed, yet she was delighted by his words, and he knew it.

"My lord," she returned, "if all Scots earls were as charming as you are, I should have come to Scotland long since." She cocked her head at him and asked mischievously, "May I please have my hand back now?"

Bothwell laughed, delighted by her quick tongue. This was certainly no silly miss. "I return yer hand wi' regret, sweetheart," he told her. "When is the wedding, Alex?"

"As soon as we return to *Dun Broc*," came his answer.

"In the spring," came hers.

"What is this? A reluctant bride?" demanded Bothwell.

"Velvet, dammit! When will ye learn that I will be master in my own house?"

"'Twas you who kidnapped me from court and stole me away to Scotland, my lord of BrocCairn! I have told you a hundred times: There will be no wedding until my parents return home!"

About them the men in the hall had grown quiet, listening with keen interest. Here was something that might prove to be amusing.

"Velvet de Marisco, are ye or are ye not my legally betrothed wife? Do ye mean to wed wi' me or nae?" Alex asked her, and Francis Stewart-Hepburn suddenly realized just what his cousin was doing. He looked to the English beauty.

"Aye, Alex, I am your betrothed wife," she answered him angrily. "And well you know it! You infuriate me beyond all, but, aye, I will wed with you. Not, however, until my parents return home to England!"

"Ye heard her?" Alex looked to his cousin.

"Aye," came Bothwell's level reply.

"And ye?" Alex looked to Pansy, Dugald, and Hercules Stewart. "Did ye hear her?"

"Aye," they chorused.

The Earl of BrocCairn turned to Velvet and said quietly, "Under the laws of Scotland, Velvet, we are now married. Ye're now my wife."

She paled, then shrieked at him, "*What?* What trick is this you play on me, Alex?"

"No trick, sweetheart. The law of handfast requires only that a man and woman publicly state their intentions to wed in order to be wed. We have done that in the presence of a hall full of witnesses and are therefore married."

"Never!" she hissed, and then, with a speed that surprised them all, she snatched his jeweled dirk from his belt. "I'll carve your heart out before I'll let you do this to me, Alex

Gordon!" She held the dirk in a distinctly threatening position toward him.

"God in His heaven!" roared Bothwell. Then he turned to Velvet. "Gie me the dirk, lass. 'Tis no use really, ye know."

Her mouth trembled. "Nay," she whispered.

It was a mouth meant for kissing, Bothwell thought, and he sighed. "Lassie, be reasonable. Do ye intend to hold us all here forever, for that is the only choice I can see ye have. Gie me yer weapon, and we will discuss this privately. I am the law here and along the entire border, nae my cousin of BrocCairn."

Two bright tears rolled down her cheeks, and, reaching out gently, Bothwell took the dirk from her. "Trust me, lass," he said softly.

"I ought to beat ye black and blue for that," Alex snarled.

"Touch me, and I'll kill you, I swear it!" Velvet retaliated, her tears gone.

Bothwell was forced to laugh. The lass reminded him of a small, spitting kitten, while his cousin was as belligerent as a large dog. "How long have ye two been betrothed?" he asked.

"I was matched with him when I was five, but he was a man grown and couldn't be bothered with me in these last ten years!" Velvet said indignantly. "Then his father and brother died, and suddenly he must hurry to England, for he *must* marry and have an heir."

"It's a reasonable request!" shouted Alex. "I am the only male left in my direct line!"

"I told you we would be wed in the spring when my parents return from the Indies, but nay! Nothing would do but that you kidnap me and drag me to Scotland, and attempt this mockery of a marriage!"

"I love ye, dammit! I don't want to wait!"

"You love me?" She looked surprised.

"Aye, ye stubborn jade! I love ye though I don't understand it myself." He turned to Bothwell. "Dammit, man, isn't there somewhere private where we might speak?"

The Border lord hid a smile. Love was a powerful emotion. With a nod of his head he led Velvet and Alex to his library. "If I leave ye alone, can I trust ye nae to kill each other?" he asked, but they didn't hear him, for they were already too involved in their argument. He left the room, closing the door behind him.

"Velvet, I adore ye, but I can't wait any longer," Alex said. "I lay awake nights aching for want of ye. What difference does it make if yer parents are here to see us wed if we love each other? 'Tis a match they planned themselves."

"I love my parents, Alex."

"'Tis good that ye do, sweetheart, but ye're no longer a child. All that sweet love ye possess should now be directed toward a man, toward me." He moved next to her and slipped his arm about her tiny waist. She quivered and tried to pull away, but he would not allow it. "Sweetheart," he murmured against her ear, kissing it. "I mean to have my way in this, Velvet. Ye love me. I know ye do, though ye will nae say it."

"Without a priest there is no real marriage between us in my mind and heart, Alex."

"We dinna need a priest, sweetheart. We are already wed by law, and I mean to bed ye this night."

"Your sons will be bastards then, my lord of BrocCairn, for whatever anyone may say, I will deny that any marriage ever took place between us. I can imagine how that will delight your sister and her husband, for I suspect they look to your lands for their own sons."

"Very well, ye damned little hellcat, I'll find us a priest, but ye'll wed wi' me before him tonight or I swear I'll gie yer pretty little maid servant to Bothwell's Borderers for their evening's amusement! Do ye understand me?"

"Aye," she snarled back bitterly at him.

Alex slammed from the room, leaving her alone and not a little frightened. She had never in all her dreams of her wedding day imagined that the event would take place in a gray Border fortress filled with men, without any of her beloved family about her, or that she would be forced to marry in a travel-stained riding skirt. "I'll never forgive him for this!" she muttered mutinously.

She didn't hear the door open, but turned, startled, as Lord Bothwell said, "I'm afraid there isn't a priest of the old kirk to be found in these parts, lass, but I've sent for a parson of the new kirk."

"'Twill be no true marriage for me then," she said sadly.

He came into her line of view and, tipping her face up with gentle fingers, said, "A marriage isn't made by words spoken by any man, be he holy or not, lass. A marriage is in the heart and in the soul. I know, for I had a proper marriage in every sense of the word, and yet my wife and I haven't lived together in years." There was a sadness in his eyes that Velvet saw, though he quickly masked it.

"Is there no one you love, my lord?" she said shyly, yet curiously.

"Aye, there is someone I love, though she knows it not. I canna speak of it for she is the loveliest and most virtuous of women." Again there was a sadness that touched Velvet, but then Bothwell sighed deeply and said, "Ye canna be wed without a proper dress, lass. I've asked one of the serving wenches to help ye prepare."

"But, my lord," Velvet protested, "I've nothing suitable. Alex really did kidnap me from London, and I've nothing but what I am wearing and an old velvet skirt that is no better."

Bothwell smiled. "But, lassie, ye're in a Border brigand's castle. I've all sorts of booty available if ye dinna mind choosing a gown from amongst such stuff. Come along, and I'll take ye to yer rooms."

He led her from his library and up a narrow, curving flight of stone stairs to a spacious apartment. There they found a woman waiting, and the Border lord said, "Maggie, this is Mistress de Marisco, who will very shortly be the Countess of BrocCairn. Find her something suitable and lovely to wear to her wedding, and have the men bring a tub, for I'll wager the lass wants a bath."

"Oh." Velvet sighed with pleasure. "You're an intuitive man, Francis Stewart-Hepburn!"

"Aye, 'tis what all the lasses tell him." Maggie laughed, and then she was gone from the room before he could reach out to swat her bottom.

Bothwell chuckled. "I think that my cousin is a very lucky man, sweet Velvet. Damn me, if I dinna think ye're a lass made to love!" Then to his surprise Velvet suddenly began to cry softly. "Why, lassie," Bothwell protested, and found himself taking her into his arms, "what is it?"

"My lord," she said, sobbing, "I do not know how to love a man!"

"Why, lass, there is no crime in that. In fact I suspect that Alex will far prefer it that way, for a man likes to school his own wife in matters of that sort." He reached for the silken handkerchief that was tucked into his sleeve and tried to wipe her tears away.

"My brother wed but a little while back, and I slept in the room next to his and his bride's on their wedding night," Velvet said. "She cried with pain when he made love to her, and Alex said it was because he had pierced her maidenhead, that it would only hurt once. Did he tell me true, my lord, or did he say it to calm me? What did my brother do that hurt his bride? I do not understand, and my mother never spoke on it, for she believed me too young before she went away. Do a man and a woman mate like the animals do? I have seen the stallions in my father's stables mated with the mares. I have seen his hounds with the bitches. I can't believe it, but is it the same?"

She nestled against him, and Bothwell wondered how he had gotten himself into this predicament. He had always thought of himself as an elegant and debonair man. He saw nothing about himself that should remind an attractive young woman of a mother hen, and yet here was this adorable female who, on the barest of acquaintances, was asking him questions that her mother was far more suited to answer than he. Then she trembled against him, and Bothwell, ever a gallant where the ladies were concerned, began to speak.

"'Tis something like the animals, lass, but nae really. The beasts feel a need to mate while a man and a woman feel something entirely different. For a man and a woman, the mating is nae simply a physical act but an emotional one as well, though a man can take a woman physically simply because he desires her body. There is pain the first time a maiden is mounted, but the amount of the pain depends upon how tightly the maidenhead is lodged. 'Tis over in an instant, though, and then there is naught but sweetness. Alex has never been known to mistreat a lass, Velvet. He loves ye and will be gentle wi' ye, I've nae a doubt." He stroked her hair and said, "Now dry yer eyes, lass. There is naught to fear, I promise ye."

She took his handkerchief and wiped her face. "I have no other choice, do I?" she said softly, realizing he had actually told her nothing.

"Nay, lass, ye don't," he agreed.

The door to the room opened and several sturdy, kilted Borderers came in carrying a huge oak tub, followed by others bearing steaming buckets of water. The tub was quickly filled, and Bothwell followed his men from the room, saying as he went, "We'll have to fill the other tub in the kitchen, lads, for if the lass bathes, then so should the bridegroom." The door slammed noisily behind them, and for a minute Velvet found herself alone. Then the door burst open again, and Pansy ran into the room.

"Oh, Mistress Velvet! A tub, and 'tis hot, too! Here, let me help you. That Maggie is bringing the loveliest dress you've ever seen for you to wear. She's just behind me now."

"Och, good! The men filled the tub," said Maggie as she reentered the room carrying a gown. With a smile she held it up for the bride's inspection.

Velvet's eyes widened, for when Bothwell had offered her a dress, she had not expected it would be something as incredibly lovely as what Maggie now proffered. The gown was of a heavy candlelight-colored satin, its bodice and underskirt embroidered with pearls and crystal beads. The leg-of-mutton sleeves were tied by many small, pearl-encrusted ribbons; the cuffs, which were turned back, were of rich antique lace. The neckline was shockingly low but totally fashionable. It was the most beautiful dress Velvet had ever seen, and it was obviously brand new.

"It's glorious!" Velvet exclaimed. "Where did he ever find such a gown?"

Maggie laughed. "When a Borderer gies ye a gift, lassie, 'tis nae wise to ask where he got it." She dug into her pocket and pulled out a necklace that blazed with diamonds and pearls set in rose gold. "These are Hepburn family jewels, and he says for you to hae the loan of them for yer wedding."

"Oh, Maggie, please thank Lord Bothwell for me!"

Maggie smiled and nodded, then went about the task of helping Pansy to ready the bride. The serving woman had seen the woebegone expression on Mistress de Marisco's face earlier, and the men were already talking of the fierce argument between Lord Gordon and his betrothed wife. His lordship must have seen her look, too, and had obviously comforted the lass before sending along the jewelry. He was a man who knew how to make a woman smile, was Francis Stewart-Hepburn, thought Maggie, who had known him all her life.

Stripped of her filthy riding clothes, Velvet climbed into the high oak tub and sighed blissfully. Then suddenly she sniffed. "Gillyflowers!" she exclaimed.

"Aye," said Pansy. "I may have had to pack light, mistress, but there was no need to forget the essentials. I slipped a small vial of your scent into the pack."

Together the two women soaped Velvet, then washed her long auburn hair. There was no time to dally, Maggie said, for the wedding was set for eight o'clock. The men were already decorating the hall, delighted at the diversion. Half a dozen of Lord Bothwell's men had ridden into the nearby village to bring back the preacher. She chattered on, Pansy joining in, while Velvet only half listened to them.

Married. She turned the word over in her mind. *Married*. She still felt as strongly about her situation as she had five months ago when she had first heard of Alexander Gordon.

It was not that she didn't care for him, for to her discomfort she found that she did. Whether or not it was love she couldn't be sure, never having been in love before. What she did know was that she felt trapped. She was willing to marry Alex, but not quite yet. I'm not even sixteen, she thought.

Her mother had been married for the first time at fifteen, and Velvet knew that that was precisely why she had wanted her youngest child to have more time. Somehow Velvet didn't believe that she would be like her mother with several husbands and so many adventures, but it would have been nice to have had a little more time at court. She was also unhappy about Alex's tricking her into a handfast marriage, followed by this hurried religious ceremony by a Calvinist preacher. She had been raised in the holy Catholic church, and although she was not particularly religious, she knew in her heart that until she was wed in her own church, she would feel slightly wicked.

Pansy and Maggie worked quickly to prepare the bride who silently obeyed their orders. Another serving wench arrived with a tray containing a small meat pie, steaming hot from the oven, and a tall goblet of heady, sweet red wine. Velvet ravenously wolfed the meal down, for she was very hungry. Then she suffered her face and hands to be rewashed. Silken undergarments and charming silk stockings with gold roses embroidered on them were brought and put on her. Somewhere a pair of shoes that fit her were obtained, and finally the gown was dropped over her head. The fastenings were neatly done up, then Pansy sat her on a chair and brushed her long, auburn hair until it shone with dark red and gold lights. The hair was left unbound to signify her virgin state and her head crowned with a wreath of wheat, symbolizing fertility. Then Pansy carefully fastened the necklace about Velvet's neck. As the young tiring woman stepped back, she gaped in awe when Velvet stood and turned to face her.

"Oh, mistress! You're absolutely beautiful!"

Maggie's face was also soft with admiration. "I dinna believe that Hermitage has ever seen a more beautiful bride," she declared.

There was a knock on the door, and Maggie opened it to admit Lord Bothwell. He was dressed in the elegant red and green Hepburn plaid and a black velvet jacket. His blue eyes swept approvingly over the bride as he said, "Christ almighty, lass, ye're the most beautiful thing I've ever seen. With each minute that passes I further envy Alexander Gordon." He held out his hand to her. "Will ye gie me the honor of escorting ye?"

"With pleasure, my lord," Velvet answered. "Since my own dear papa isn't here, I cannot think of anyone else I would prefer but you."

Bothwell winced at the mention of her father. Dear Lord! He certainly wasn't old enough to be the lass's father—or was he? He dismissed the thought immediately with a grimace and sent Maggie a black look, for he had heard her muffled chuckle. Her gray eyes danced with merriment.

Velvet put her hand into Francis Stewart-Hepburn's, and together they walked from the room and down the narrow stone stairway into the Great Hall. Velvet's eyes were round with amazement at the transformation that had taken place in just the few hours that she had been at Hermitage. The hall was decorated with pine, red whortleberry, and white heather. At the entry to the Great Hall Lord Bothwell said something low to one of his retainers, and the man hurried away to return a moment later with a small bouquet of white roses and white heather.

"The very last of the roses." Bothwell smiled at her. "One of the serving girls found them by a sheltered wall and cut them for ye."

"You're so very kind, my lord," Velvet said. "You almost make me feel guilty for being such a reluctant bride."

"Captive brides are a tradition here on the Border, lass," was his reply, "but I believe that within a few short days yer anger will have cooled. He's a good man, ye know."

"Aye, the queen said that of him," Velvet replied.

"Did she now? Well 'twas never said that Bess Tudor was a stupid woman." Bothwell stopped a moment and lifted her face with his hand. "Gie us a wee smile now, Velvet de Marisco, for I can see ye love the man, even if ye're too stubborn to admit it. Pride is something I well understand." She smiled up at him, and he said, "Aye, lassie, that's it! Now, come forward, and we'll meet yer fate head-on. Never fear to meet yer fate!"

Then he led her into the Great Hall, and a mighty cheer went up from the Borderers gathered there. Before the high board stood the hastily summoned preacher of Scotland's new kirk and Alexander Gordon, the Earl of BrocCairn, freshly scrubbed, and with a black velvet jacket borrowed from Lord Bothwell to wear over his dark green, blue, and yellow Gordon plaid. On his shoulder he sported a magnificent gold clan crest, identifying him as the chief of his clan, the Gordons of BrocCairn. On the pin was the raised and snarling badger with red ruby eyes, and around the beast were inscribed the words "Defend or Die."

The pipes began to skirl softly as the bride was led forward. Lord Bothwell placed Velvet's hand in Alex's, and without further ado the preacher commenced reading the marriage ceremony. Where are the beeswax tapers in the gold candelabrum, the sweetly singing choir, and the family priest in his glorious white and gold vestments? thought Velvet. For a moment she almost cried, for she so wanted her parents, her sisters and brothers, Uncle Robbie, Dame Cecily, Uncle Conn, and sweet Aunt Aiden. Instead she found herself in the stone hall of a Border castle surrounded by men, being married by a Calvinist preacher to a man she half feared.

"Say aye!" Alex hissed at her, and she said, "Aye," as he pushed his own chieftain's heavy gold ring upon her marriage finger. She had been paying absolutely no attention to what was happening at all. This was her wedding. Was she going to tell her children and her grandchildren one day that she didn't remember the ceremony because she had been daydreaming? She giggled, and the preacher looked sourly at her, making her want to laugh all the more. Alex squeezed her hand in warning, and Velvet got a grip on her emotions though she was becoming nearly hysterical.

"I pronounce ye husband and wife," the preacher said, and another mighty cheer went up in the hall.

Alex pulled her into his arms roughly and kissed her with a passion that left her breathless. When he let her go she was blushing, and his eyes mocked her. "Now, m'lady, ye're most truly wed wi' me," he said softly. "Wedded, and soon to be bedded."

"I will never truly feel wed with you until we are married in our own church and my family is about me," Velvet said stubbornly.

"God's blood, madame! How many weddings do ye want?"

"I think," said Bothwell, interrupting what seemed to be another storm brewing between the Earl and Countess of BrocCairn, "that it is my turn to kiss the bride."

Velvet held up a cheek for him to kiss, but Francis Stewart-Hepburn laughed mischievously and said, "Nay, lass," as he took her lips. It was but a moment, and it was a sweet kiss. As he let her go he said, "'Tis the only time I've an excuse to sip yer honey, lass, and ye're far too sweet to resist."

The preacher had disappeared, and the lord of the castle led them up to the high board. "I must apologize for such a simple wedding feast, my lady," Bothwell continued, "but I was not expecting to gie a bride away tonight." Then he signaled the servants to bring in the meal. There was venison, boar, pheasant, quail, duck, and capon. There were platters of salmon and trout dressed with cress, bowls of peas and carrots and beans, as well as hot breads and tubs of butter and cheese. Ale and wine were both served.

Velvet ate sparingly, taking a bit of capon and another slice of trout, some vegetables, bread, and cheese. She was very nervous now, and her stomach was rolling. Only the wine seemed to settle it, but she drank sparingly even of that. She had been placed between Alex and Lord Bothwell, both of whom took delight in filling and refilling their plates and goblets until she thought that they would surely burst. A large apple tart with heavy cream was the last thing to be presented and it was the only dish that tasted good to her, so she ate two large pieces of it.

The pipes started up again, and the men began to dance upon the gray stone floor. The fireplaces and the tapers smoked as the wind had risen outside, somehow managing to slip through cracks in the stone walls. Above Velvet were many colored banners and pendants. Francis leaned over to tell her that they were taken in various battles over the centuries by the Hepburns and their allies. The skirling bagpipes, the kilted clansmen dancing a dance she was told was the sword dance, the orange firelight shadowing the hall as it leaped in time with the pipes—all combined to create a savage splendor that she would not soon forget. This was what she would tell her children and grandchildren. It was all really quite exciting.

Then Lord Bothwell said quietly, "Maggie is outside the hall, Lady Gordon. She will escort ye to yer bedchamber."

Velvet started at the address "Lady Gordon."

"Is it time so soon?" she asked him plaintively.

"Aye, but remember what I told ye to do, lass. Face yer fate bravely and squarely. Alex has told me of yer parents, and I suspect beneath yer maiden fears ye're their daughter well and true." He took her hand and kissed it. "Go along now, my lady Gordon. I'll be sending ye yer man in a few minutes."

As Velvet stood to leave the high board, Bothwell raised his goblet and cried out, "The bride!" His words were echoed by the hundred men who were in the hall. *"The bride!"* was their toast. Her head held high, she acknowledged them with a return toast. "A Bothwell!" she shouted, and they cheered her as she drank. And then she made her way out of the hall to where Maggie and Pansy awaited her.

"God, she's bonny!" Francis Stewart-Hepburn said admiringly after she had gone.

"Aye," replied Alex. "And stubborn, and beautiful, and maddening, but, damn me, I want her!" He sighed. "I'm not so sure I should not have married a more biddable female."

Bothwell laughed somewhat bitterly. "Biddable females breed up weak sons, cousin. This little wench of yers will give ye a litter of fire-eaters for BrocCairn. Have another cup wi' me, and then go to her."

While they drank of Lord Bothwell's excellent Burgundy, Velvet was shown to the bedchamber she would share with her new husband. There she was divested of her finery by Maggie, while Pansy brought her a silver basin in which to wash her face, hands, and teeth.

"Have you eaten?" Velvet asked her tiring woman.

"Aye, mistress, I mean, my lady Velvet."

"Where will you sleep?"

"Maggie is letting me stay with her, me lady."

"Steer clear of Dugald, Pansy. He means to seduce you, I suspect."

Pansy giggled at her mistress's words. "I may be a country girl, me lady, but I'm wise to the likes of Dugald. He'll get naught without a wedding ring for me finger first."

Velvet was completely nude now and she looked surprised when the two women led her to the big bed. "My nightshift, Pansy," she scolded the servant.

"Nay," said Maggie. "'Tis the custom in the Border that ye greet yer new lord in yer bed without a shift, but as God has made ye, m'lady." She tucked Velvet beneath the lavender-scented sheets and the soft fur coverlet. Then she plumped up the fat goosedown pillows behind her back. "There! Now ye're ready, and just in time, I vow!"

In the hallway outside they heard men shouting, and then the door was flung open and the room filled up with laughing clansmen. Velvet clutched the covers to her bosom, drawing them almost to her chin.

God's blood, Lord Bothwell thought as he looked at her gardenia skin, wide green eyes, and auburn hair. She's exquisite! I'd best get my men from this room before there's a riot. He shoved his cousin forward. Alex had been stripped down to just the lower half of his plaid. "Yer husband, Lady Gordon!" Bothwell announced. Then he said to his men,

"Come, lads! There's a troupe of gypsies outside *Hermitage* walls this night, and I'm thinking we should invite some dancers in to entertain us." He moved out of the room, and thus diverted, the two serving women and his retainers followed him.

The door closed behind them, and Alex, swiveling, shot the bolt before turning back to Velvet. He gazed at her for a long moment, and she reddened beneath his close scrutiny. Then he moved about the bedchamber blowing out the candles until only the one on the table by his side of the bed remained. A small, cheery fire burned in the fireplace. Without a word he pulled off his plaid and climbed into bed before she even had a chance to see him, except for a flash of taut buttocks.

Her heart was hammering wildly as she sat stiffly in the bed, next to him. She wasn't sure she was even breathing. There was a fluttery feeling of anticipation in her stomach, and yet she was also afraid. She desperately wished now that her mother had not believed her to be too young to discuss the marriage bed before Skye had left for India. Velvet didn't know what to do, or even if she should do anything, and she felt like a perfect fool. Her fingers clutching the bedcovers were white with her tension.

"Lower the bedclothes, Velvet." Alex's voice in the heavy silence startled her and she jumped. Gently he broke her death grip on the sheets and the coverlet, and her hands fell into her lap. She stared straight ahead, for she was terrified of looking at him.

Alex felt his breath catch in his throat. That one time all those long weeks ago that he had caressed her lovely body had not prepared him for such perfection. Free of any restraints, her beautiful young breasts sprang forth, as smooth and as round and as firm as young apples. Her skin was smooth in texture and creamy in color.

Velvet felt herself blushing again under his warm gaze. She wished he would hurry and do whatever it was he was going to do, and then leave her be. But when Alex reached out to caress one of her breasts, she was unable to restrain the little cry of fear that struggled from her tight throat as she tried to push his hand away.

"No, sweetheart," he said softly, "don't, for I love ye."

"I am so afraid," Velvet whispered.

He knew what that admission must have cost her. "Why are ye afraid, lovey? Ye know I won't hurt ye."

"I don't know what I'm supposed to do," she said miserably.

Laughter bubbled up in his throat. "*Do?* God's blood, Velvet, the marriage bed is nae a performance."

"Don't you dare to laugh at me, Alex Gordon!" she cried. "From the moment I first heard your name, all I have been told is that you must breed sons quickly to protect your damned direct line of descent. Well, my mother has been gone from me for over two years, and she did not think me old enough before she left to discuss adult things with me. I know nothing of how sons are bred up, you arrogant ass! I asked Lord Bothwell earlier, but he told me naught. In fact I think now that I probably embarrassed him."

Alex could not help it. He howled his laughter. The thought of the elegant and urbane Earl of Bothwell being asked to mother-hen his bride was too delicious. "Y-you asked Francis about t-the, t-the marriage bed? Ah, ha! Ha! Ha! Ha! Ha! *Ouch!*"

This last came as Velvet, desperate to retaliate, grabbed a handful of his thick, black hair and yanked.

"Dammit, ye little vixen, let go!"

"Don't you dare laugh at me!" she raged at him. "Don't you dare!"

She tried to slap him, but Alex, now realizing that she was deadly serious, grabbed for her. Fiercely they wrestled across the bed, she trying to smack at him; he trying to prevent it. They battled back and forth for several minutes until suddenly Alex found her beneath him.

Her eyes widened with sudden realization as she felt his hard body pressed atop her. She groaned in defeat as his mouth captured hers in a deep and tender kiss.

In that moment Velvet knew that she was lost. His lips moved gently and sweetly against her own, coaxing her to respond, willing her to meet his passion with her own. Hungrily he kissed her, sending the blood racing through her veins and into her head with a pounding roar that left her dizzy. She had the feeling that she was falling, and she clung to him desperately.

"Ah, lovey, how ye intoxicate me," he murmured against her mouth, kissing her again, this time parting her lips to plunder its sweetness. For a moment this new intimacy drained her will completely. Only once before had he kissed her like that and then but briefly. Now his tongue probed deeply with slow, exaggerated movements, stroking and caressing the satin of her tongue until small flames of undiluted desire began to burn deep within her.

Alex thought he would go mad from the pleasure that her lips presented. He had never believed that any woman could offer such delights, and he was in no great hurry to rush them into the final act of consummation. As her head fell back against his arm, he trailed his slender fingers down her graceful throat, lingering a moment to touch lightly the visibly beating pulse in its blue-veined hollow. Then he bent his head and kissed the quivering throb.

He lay back a moment, his dark head next to her auburn one on the pillows. "Look at me, Velvet, my love."

She turned her passion-glazed green eyes toward his lionlike golden ones, which now gazed down on her. With feathery touches he stroked a tender breast, his fingers gently encircling it slowly in a delicious, mesmerizing action. Velvet felt a lovely warmth begin to suffuse her limbs. Without realizing it she sighed, and Alex smiled softly. His fingers moved upward and began to tease the sensitive nipple until she thought the flesh would burst open and pour forth a liquid sweetness. But then, when he twisted his body and, lowering his head, took her little nipple into his mouth, Velvet understood that the pleasure was only beginning.

Suddenly she was no longer afraid. She realized that she hadn't understood anything about this marvelous thing called lovemaking. She still didn't understand what was expected of her, or exactly what the act of consummation would involve, but she was content for now to trust in Alex Gordon. After all, she reasoned for one brief, sane moment, he was her betrothed husband and she certainly could not deter him from his intent. A great burst of tenderness overcame her and, reaching up, she caressed his thick hair with her hand.

He felt her touch, and his heart quickened with delight, for he recognized that at least for the time being she was free of fear. When he turned his attention to her other breast lest it feel neglected, she moaned low, and the passionate sound sent a shiver through him. His curious hand slipped down her torso to her belly, and he tenderly rubbed it, sending a small dart of delight through her.

Then to his surprise she said, "May I touch you, Alex?"

"Aye, lovey, for if I gie ye pleasure wi' my touch, so can ye gie me pleasure wi' yers." He lay back, barely breathing lest he startle her.

Velvet raised herself onto an elbow and gazed down at him. He was lean and muscled, and upon his broad chest was a wide mat of dark hair that narrowed as it traveled down his belly. She followed the dark line, her green eyes widening suddenly, her gaze flying back upward as her cheeks reddened. Then, shyly, she caressed his shoulder, her hand running down his chest, tangling in the soft fur of him. Her touch inflamed him, and his own heart beat wildly as she indulged her virgin's curiosity.

Reaching up, his arm encircled her neck and drew her back down so that her firm, young breasts were pressing against his chest. Their lips met again, and this time Velvet did not simply receive his homage. This time she kissed him back. He rolled her onto her back, enfolding her in his hungry embrace. She could feel his long body matching hers: his legs against her legs, his long torso pressing into her soft flesh.

His lips became more frantic as desire rose from deep within him. He kissed her eyes, the tip of her nose, her stubborn little chin, and her mouth again. "Tell me that ye want me, Velvet," he almost pleaded with her. "Tell me that ye want me as much as I want ye!" And he shuddered with his desperate need.

She shivered, too, feeling the hard length of him that had not been there before. It pressed insistently against her thigh, almost a separate entity of its own, seeking entry into her young body. Suddenly she was afraid again, and she sobbed her fear.

"Dear God, Velvet, dinna put me off now when I long so desperately for ye!" Shifting his weight, he slipped his hand between her legs and, moving swiftly up, touched her in that most secret of places.

"No!" She twisted beneath him, her fright evident.

He groaned. "I won't hurt ye, sweetheart. I swear it!"

"Liar!" she whispered. "Do you not remember my brother's wedding night? I do!"

"The pain is sweet, my darling, and 'tis only once. For God's sake, let us have done with this damned virginity of yers!" He caught her hands and, pulling them above her head, pinioned her firmly. Then his knee nudged her resisting thighs apart while with his other hand he guided his manhood to the mark.

Feeling him gain a small entry, she cried out as the swelling pressure invaded her and she begged him to stop. Maddened now with his own needs, he barely heard her. Carefully so as not to give her any more pain than necessary, he slowly pushed himself into her virgin sheath. She could feel him filling her with a fullness that shattered her, and then, before she could protest his actions further, he thrust through her maiden barrier with one swift movement.

She felt but a single stinging pain and cried out sharply, but her cry was more of a lament for something lost rather than from any serious hurt she had received.

He lay very still within her, allowing her tender body to adjust itself to his invasion, and then he said softly, "There, sweetheart, 'tis over. Now let me teach ye the honeyed sweetness that two bodies can create."

There was a little discomfort as he began to move in her, but with each stroke of his manhood it lessened. His breathing became labored, then suddenly he shuddered and lay still once again.

"God's blood!" he swore angrily, and, curious, she asked, "What is it, my lord? Have I displeased you in some way?" She didn't understand why, but suddenly she wanted to make him happy.

He rolled off her and, laying next to her in the big bed, said, "Nay, sweetheart, ye've not displeased me. I am angered at myself, for I was so damned hot for ye that I was only interested in my own pleasure and gae ye none. 'Twill not happen again, Velvet, I promise ye. I behaved like a green boy, spilling my seed so quickly."

She really didn't quite understand what he meant, and so, innocently, she soothed him. "You didn't hurt me greatly, Alex. After the first pain it was rather pleasant. Really it was!"

He laughed gently. "Pleasant, Velvet, is not quite what it should have been. There should have been a lovely melting feeling, and I know that ye did not receive that, did ye?"

"Nay," she answered him, puzzled. "A melting feeling? Nay, I had no melting feeling. Is it necessary, this melting feeling?"

"Not necessary, but wonderful, sweetheart. Gie me time to recover myself and then we shall love again. Ye hae made me very happy, lovey, and I would make ye happy also." He put an arm about her and said gently, "Sleep now, sweetheart. 'Tis been an exciting day for us both."

When Velvet opened her eyes again, the gray dawn was just beginning to filter through the narrow windows of the room. For a second she forgot where she was, but then Alex snored lightly beside her and she remembered. Curious, she sat up and stared down at him. It was the very first time she had really looked hard at him, and in sleep there was a vulnerability about him he did not have when awake. Just above his left eyebrow was a tiny scar that she had not noticed before. Gently she reached out and touched it, letting her fingers trail softly down his jawline. He was really quite attractive, this man who was her betrothed husband, even if he was totally impossible to get along with and far more stubborn than anyone else she had ever known in her whole life. *Her husband.* This man was her husband. Nay! She was betrothed to him, but he was not her real husband yet, and neither a handfast marriage nor a Calvinist preacher could make it so if she would not accept it. When her parents returned from the Indies, when they were properly wed in a church by a priest of their own religion, *then* she would accept him as her husband.

"Ye're even beautiful when ye frown," he remarked, opening his wonderful eyes.

She smiled at him, noticing that his speech had become even more Scots in character since they had crossed over the border yesterday. "How did you get the scar over your eye?" she asked him.

"When I was a boy, my brother Nigel and I were practicing with swords and his foot slipped. My father beat him for it, and me also. He said we should have been better swordsmen." He reached up and pulled her down. "I want ye, lass," he said thickly, and then he was kissing her.

She had no fear of the unknown this time, and her body softened against him. She felt his hands smoothing down her back to cup and caress her buttocks, and then he turned her onto her back, finding her breasts once more and loving them with both his hands and his mouth. Velvet found his touch delicious and murmured her approval of his actions. Her lovely young breasts grew swollen with her longing as the nipples began to ache, becoming tiny and tight.

His hand slipped down her body, sliding between her legs, and she tensed slightly, but he kissed her ear and whispered, "Nay, sweetheart, but trust me." His fingers were incredibly gentle, and for a moment she hardly realized that he was stroking her soft secret. Then without warning that little jewel began to tingle with such an intense feeling that very quickly the only thing she was conscious of was the fierce throbbing.

"Oh." She gasped softly. "Oh! Oh!"

Twisting his big body, Alex swung over Velvet and, in one smooth motion, drove into her. Again she gasped, but the sound was one of pleasure. His hands rested on her hips, holding her firmly as he moved upon her, and this time it was far different than it had been the night before. Her senses were awash with pleasure, and behind her closed eyes images whirled in a pinwheel of kaleidoscopic colors.

Velvet met passion head-on for the very first time, her head thrashing wildly. She was lost in a blazing world, and, sure now of her pleasure, Alex took his own.

When afterward she became aware of herself and her surroundings again, Velvet lay quietly next to Alex, waiting for her breathing to even and her heart to stop pounding wildly. Finally she said, "'Twas more like an explosion than a melting, my lord."

Reaching out, he took her hand in his and squeezed it. "I love ye, my Velvet Gordon, Countess of BrocCairn. I love ye very much."

"I—I love you, too, Alex," she admitted finally. "Oh, but please understand how I feel about our wedding! I know now that my fear of you, of the marriage bed, was nothing but maiden foolishness, but I honestly do not feel married to you, and I won't until we are wed before my family by a priest of our own church. Take me back to England and let us wait until the spring when my parents will return. I am yours, Alex. I am yours now and for always! Do this for me, my lord . . . husband."

"Nay, Velvet! Nay! We are home in Scotland. We are far closer to *Dun Broc* than we are to London. By spring ye could be wi' child, our child!"

"A bastard child!" she flung at him. "Would you bring that shame upon me? You say you love me!"

"He'll be no bastard, Velvet! We are wed under the laws of Scotland and in the eyes of the new kirk!"

"But not in the eyes of the church in which we were both raised, Alex!"

He had no answer to give her. Angrily he flung himself from their bed and, pulling on his clothes, slammed wordlessly from the room.

Velvet lay silently for a long moment, and then she felt a tear slide down her cheek. "Damn you, Alexander Gordon," she whispered to herself. "You're the most impossible man I've ever met! I'll not be beaten though, my fine love! I'll get back to England, and you'll marry me properly before any child of ours is birthed. That I can promise you!" Then, yanking the crumpled covers back up over her naked shoulders, Velvet snuggled down in the bed and fell asleep.

Part Two

The Earl of BrocCairn's Bride

My true Love hath my heart, and I have his,
By just exchange one for the other given:
I hold his dear, and mine he cannot miss;
There never was a better bargain driven.

—Sir Philip Sidney

Chapter 5

James Stewart, the sixth of his name and king of Scotland, glared at his cousin, the Earl of BrocCairn, saying, "Ye've got to take her back to England, Alex! What in hell possessed ye, anyway?"

"I do not have to take her back, Jamie. We're married," replied the earl sullenly.

The king's face grew mottled with his anger. They were always arguing with him, these nobles of his! It made no difference that, thanks to his grandfather, he was related to half of Scotland. Even blood ties made no difference here. Scotland's nobility were headstrong and determined to defy their rulers.

"Dammit, Alex, don't ye realize the seriousness of what ye've done?" he growled. "Ye've kidnapped one of Elizabeth Tudor's Maids of Honor! Her entire family is in an uproar and are demanding her return. More important, my cousin England is demanding that you bring her back."

"Since when have Scotland's rulers obeyed England's orders?" mocked the Earl of BrocCairn.

"Scotland will one day inherit England, Alex, and I would be welcomed by the English when that day comes. I look to my future. I have no desire to engage England in even a small war. Particularly over a wench, however pretty," he amended with a small smile toward Velvet.

Her green eyes twinkled back at him, and she said, "I am only too happy to obey the queen's order, Your Majesty, and to return home."

"Did ye truly marry this rogue, Mistress de Marisco?"

"Nay, sire."

"Christ's bones!" The oath exploded forcefully from Alex's angry mouth. "Ye're wed wi' me well and true, Velvet!" He turned back to the king. "She's twice wed to me. Once by handfast admission, and the second time by a parson of yer new kirk."

"I most certainly don't accept your handfast marriage," Velvet snapped. "And since we are both members of the holy Catholic church, I do not accept a ceremony performed by a preacher of the Calvinist faith."

"Just where was the ceremony performed?" demanded the king.

"At *Hermitage*," replied Bothwell, and he smiled blandly.

"At Hermitage?" The king looked somewhat surprised. "Why in hell at *Hermitage*?"

"Ye could hardly expect me to allow Alex to bed her without the proprieties, Jamie." drawled Bothwell. "Yer advisors, including yer sour-faced chaplain, are always accusing me of being immoral, but even a reprobate like myself recognizes a respectable virgin."

The king laughed in spite of himself. "I'm surprised ye were able to get a man of God to step into *Hermitage*, Francis."

"Only the very ignorant or, worse, the very superstitious, believe the gossip that I'm a warlock, Jamie," came Francis Stewart-Hepburn's disconcerting reply. The Earl of Bothwell knew full well that his cousin, the king, was secretly terrified of him and believed everything detrimental that was said about him. On the other hand, James admired the man they called the Border lord, "the Uncrowned King of Scotland," for Francis Stewart-Hepburn was everything James Stewart wished he could be.

"Ye delight in the damned controversy that always swirls about ye," muttered the king, and Bothwell smiled, amused by his royal cousin's sudden astuteness.

James looked at Alex. "Take her back to London, Alex. I will nae accept a refusal from ye in this matter! The Earl of Lynmouth and a party of the queen's own Gentlemen Pensioners will be waiting for ye just over the border to escort ye back to my cousin England's court. The queen says that ye're welcome back despite yer rather wild behavior." The king chuckled in spite of himself. "Dammit, Alex, ye behaved just like an ancient Scot. Bride-stealing is no longer the fashion."

"Yer majesty sets the fashion, and I'm told ye seek a bride," commented Alex. "I only sought to emulate yer good example."

"Ha!" The king snorted. "Ye sought to have yer own way, cousin. Ye wanted the lass now, and so ye took her! Nay, dinna deny it, for I know ye well! Ye've ever been a stubborn man, even when we were lads together."

Velvet stood quietly watching the three men. For a moment they had forgotten her, and she was frankly relieved. They were cousins, and there was a definite family resemblance amongst them. The king and BrocCairn had the amber-gold eyes of the Stewarts; Bothwell and James had the auburn hair of their clan. All three had the Stewart nose. There, however, the resemblance ended, for although the king was a total Stewart in face and form, Bothwell was obviously more a Hepburn and Alex more a Gordon. The two earls had strong, determined faces, whereas the king's features bespoke a weakness that even Velvet could see.

"Let us stay a few days here at court, Jamie," Alex pleaded. "Velvet is exhausted wi' all our traveling."

"And would ye like that, Mistress de Marisco?" The king looked sharply at her.

To refuse would have been ungracious and Velvet knew it. She smiled sweetly at James Stewart and replied, "Aye, Your Majesty. I should very much like to stay for a few days before my return to England."

"Very well, Mistress de Marisco, ye shall have yer visit wi' us." Having gotten his way, the king was feeling more gracious now.

"Dammit, Jamie, she's Lady Gordon now. Whether she is willing to recognize it or not, surely ye must. Unless, of course, ye're saying that the new kirk is nae Scotland's church. I am certain some of the earls would be quite fascinated by this recent change of heart of yers. Do ye lean back toward the old and true faith then?" Alex smiled wolfishly at the king.

Bothwell hid a grin. Here was a man after his own heart! He suspected that whatever church Alex had been raised in made no difference to him at all, but he would play on the king's fears in order to get his own way. He smothered his laughter for he had done exactly the same thing on many an occasion when dealing with their cousin James. Fear was Jamie Stewart's sharp spur.

The king shot Bothwell an angry look, for he had heard his low chuckle. Then he looked to his cousin of BrocCairn, saying, "Ye've developed unpleasant habits the few days ye've been in Francis's company, Alex. Remember that I am yer king."

"I nae forget it, Jamie, but ye canna have it both ways. If ye're to have any credibility wi' yer English cousin, ye'll have to tell her that Velvet and I were married legally and lawfully, else ye deny yer own church and a law that goes back centuries. I dinna think ye will want to do that, cousin. If ye do, ye'll have all the ranting preachers of fire and brimstone tearing yer kingdom apart with the earls joining in as they did in yer mother's time."

"You're not married to me until we are wed in our own church," Velvet interrupted.

Alex shot her a quelling look. "Hush yer mouth, lass! This is politics we're talking of, nae religion. Ye can rest assured that I'll wed ye a third time in our own church. Yer family will hae it no other way, I've nae a doubt. In the meantime, however, ye're my wife in the eyes of both Scotland's church and Scotland's law, and ye'll behave as such."

"Indeed, my lord? Am I to suppose you'll use force if I do not?" Her glance was pure defiance.

"If ye do not, I will take great pleasure in beating yer bottom, fetching as I find it, until sitting is the farthest thing from yer clever mind. Mark me well, Velvet! I dinna jest wi' ye." Alex's black look matched her own in spirit.

The king and Bothwell looked at one another, their previous disagreements momentarily forgotten in light of the battle between the bride and groom. Each was delighted in his own way by BrocCairn and Velvet.

"When I tell my brothers how you've abused me, Alex Gordon . . ." she began.

"They'll undoubtedly either cheer me or challenge me, Velvet, but I think the former rather than the latter," he replied dryly.

"Now, lass," said Lord Bothwell, grinning, "I think ye've certainly won this round in yer ongoing battle wi' Alex. However, ye're going to go back to England in a few days' time. Be gracious in victory. Ye two are going to have to learn how to get along sooner or later."

"When she accepts the fact that I am the master," blustered Alex.

"Master, is it?" Velvet shrieked. "Why, you pompous idiot! Do I look like a horse or a dog to you that you would *master* me? I am a woman, Alexander Gordon! I have a damned good brain and I am as well educated as you are for all your French university. I will be respected by you for my intelligence or, believe me, your life will be one long hell, I promise you!" Her eyes blazed green fire at him.

"Is this how yer mother speaks to yer father?" he demanded, outraged. Both had again forgotten the king and Bothwell.

"My father respects my mother as well as loves her. Their marriage has been a partnership of love, trust, and mutual admiration. I will accept no less in my own marriage. If you had waited until my parents returned home from India, you would have understood that by knowing me better. But no! You had to carry me off like some Border plunderer!" She glowered at him. "Now, having taken my innocence, you're bound to wed with me in our own faith, but mark me, Alex. I will be no man's slave or brood mare!" She drew herself up to her full height and, with an unflinching gaze, stared proudly at him.

"Christ almighty!" swore the king. "I can only hope the lass I wed is not as fiery as ye are, *Lady Gordon*! I am of a mind to have a quieter life than my cousin Alex is likely to have."

"Your Majesty appears to me to be a gentleman of breeding and sensibility," Velvet said softly. "I doubt were I your wife that I should have to resort to violence as I very well may have to do with my wild Highland husband." She gave him a dazzling smile, and James was again enchanted by her.

Bothwell laughed, shaking his head, and remarked, "Well, Alex, I suspect that the next move is going to be up to ye. Think well first is my advice. Dinna act rashly wi' such a hot-tempered lass."

Realizing that he had been bested in this bout with Velvet, Alex smiled good-naturedly, saying, "I'm not of a mind to hae my brains bashed in today, Francis, and I can see that her ladyship has a dangerous look in her eye."

"Why, my lord," said Velvet sweetly, "violence is not my habit at all. Is not the Gordon motto 'By Courage Not Craft'?"

"That is the motto of the main branch of the family, the Gordons of Huntley," he answered her, "but we Gordons of BrocCairn have our own motto. It is 'Defend or Die.' We keep what we take, Velvet." His meaning was boldly plain.

"Enough!" said the king, whose head was beginning to ache with the argument between these two.

With a charming blush, Velvet curtsied to James. "Your pardon, my liege. You must think that Alex and I know not how to communicate other than by shouting. I promise you that I am far better bred than that."

The king was once more charmed by this lovely young girl. "I think my court will be a livelier place for yer presence, Lady Gordon. Will ye join us for the evening meal?"

"I should be honored, sire."

The dining room at *Holyrood Palace* where James Stewart was in residence was not particularly large. The room was paneled with a coffered oak ceiling. Upon the walls were beautiful French tapestries, some of which had been brought from France by James's grandmother, Mary of Guise. Others she had worked during her years in Scotland, and later her daughter, Mary, Queen of Scots had taken them up. The scenes depicted upon the tapestries were pastoral in style. There was a large fireplace in the room, and it now burned with pine and aspen logs.

The king's high board ran almost the width of the room, the side tables taking up the rest of the floor. There was a small center space between the tables where the servants were able to squeeze in and out with the dishes. It was a great deal less sophisticated than the Tudor court, but there was a warmth about it that was lacking, Velvet decided, at the English court.

Alex and Velvet had been seated with the king as his personal guests and the new Lady Gordon found herself the center of many curious looks. She was a little uncomfortable at being the subject of such close scrutiny. Gentlemen, she knew, were always interested in a pretty face, the ladies in her clothes. She was sorry she had none of her own gowns to wear, for they were the height of fashion. Instead, she had on another borrowed gown from Lord Bothwell's treasure room, and only that because Francis understood enough about women to know that Velvet would want to wear something attractive when meeting the king for the first time. Alex had argued with her saying that Jamie wouldn't care if she appeared before him in her riding clothes, but Bothwell had interceded for her, and she was now more grateful than ever. In her tawny orange gown with its heavy gold embroidery she felt the equal of any woman at the Scottish court even if she was bare of jewelry.

"Well, Lady Gordon" said James, turning to her, a haunch of venison in his hand, "what think ye of my court when compared to that of my cousin England?"

"One cannot possibly compare them, sire. I mean no offense, but the queen's court is possibly the most elegant in the world. Even the French have not such a court! Still, I am not certain that I do not prefer yours, for although it's not as sophisticated, its informality offers charm and warmth. When we return to Scotland next year, I shall enjoy being a part of your court."

"Ye'll be one of its shining stars, madame," James complimented her.

"We'll nae be able to come to court until Velvet has borne me several bairns, Jamie," said Alex. "I would take no chances wi' her health."

"My mother bore eight children with no difficulty," Velvet said sweetly. "She took sea voyages and even rode while she carried my brothers and sisters. I am sure I shall be as hardy."

"Eight bairns!" The king was impressed. "How many lived to adulthood, Lady Gordon?"

"Seven, sire. My half brother, John Southwood, died before his second birthday in the same epidemic of white throat that took his father, the Earl of Lynmouth."

"How many sons did yer mother bear?" the king asked.

"Five, sire."

"Ye'll be a good breeder, I've nae a doubt, Lady Gordon," the king approved.

"Aye." Alex smiled. "I'll see to it with great pleasure, Jamie."

Velvet also smiled across the king at her husband, but when James's attention was attracted by someone else, she mouthed the word *beast* at the Earl of BrocCairn. Alex grinned back. He was anxious to leave *Holyrood* and get back to Bothwell's town house where he might take his wife to bed. She drove him wild with lust, a condition he had never before experienced. He could feel his blood begin to rise at the sight of men like Patrick Leslie, the Earl of Glenkirk; George Gordon, the Earl of Huntley, who was a kinsman of his; and the handsome Lord Home as they gazed upon his wife with undisguised admiration. He wanted to take her to *Dun Broc* where she would be safe from such hot eyes.

She sensed his jealousy and mischievously set out to enrage him even further. When the meal was over, the tables were cleared from the room, and in the little minstrel's gallery above the musicians began to play for dancing. The king led Velvet to the floor first and danced a slow and stately pavane with her. This first decorous dance, however, was followed by a galliard, the waltzlike lavolta, and a coranto jig. The Earl of BrocCairn could not get near his bride, for she was clearly the most popular woman in the room. Her cheeks were flushed a soft rose from her exertion, her green eyes sparkled merrily, and her neat chignon had come loose in the middle of the lavolta. Now her auburn hair tumbled in a devilishly attractive fashion about her shoulders as she laughed happily up at Lord Home. Francis's warning hand on Alex's arm only just prevented him from challenging Lord Home, for Sandy Home was boldly leaning over the lovely Lady Gordon and ogling her exposed bosom.

"Easy, man! Ye'll make a fool of yerself," Bothwell cautioned. "Sandy means no harm. The lass seeks to provoke ye, or don't ye see it?"

"I know she does it deliberately, Francis, but I canna help it! I love the wench, and, worse, she knows it."

"She's still young, Alex, and like any thoroughbred she is headstrong. Be gentle wi' her. Women like a man who is gentle."

"How can I be gentle when I want to strangle her?" Alex asked.

Bothwell laughed. "I've never met a woman who could drive me that far," he said.

"I dinna know whether to hope ye will, so ye'll know my agony, or hope ye never do, so ye won't know such pain, Francis."

For a moment a sad look passed over the Earl of Bothwell's handsome face. He had a wretchedly unhappy marriage, and he and his wife did not live together. It had been a match of powerful families, not one of love. He sighed. "I have already met a woman who makes me feel hungry wi' love, Alex," he said, "but she is a decent woman and does not suspect the depth of my feelings. She must not, for she is happy in her own marriage."

The Earl of BrocCairn stared, surprised by his cousin's words. Then Bothwell shook himself as a wet dog might, and Alex realized that the Border lord was embarrassed to have confided in anyone something so personal. To ease Francis's chagrin he changed the subject. "What do I do to reclaim my wayward lass without causing a scene?"

Bothwell's good humor restored, he grinned and said, "Let me aid ye, Alex." Then, stepping out onto the floor, he intercepted George Gordon, the powerful Earl of Huntley, who was dancing with Velvet.

"Gi'e over, Geordie," he said good-naturedly. "Alex wants to take his lass home to bed now, and who can blame him, eh?" He grinned engagingly.

George Gordon chuckled. "Aye, I see yer point, Francis." He let his eyes run boldly and approvingly over Velvet. "We Gordons are a hot-blooded bunch." Kissing Velvet on the cheek, he said graciously, "Good night, fair cousin. Ye're a lovely addition to the family!" Then he handed her over to Lord Bothwell, who led her off toward her husband.

"But I don't want to go," she protested softly.

"Aye," Bothwell drawled, and his blue eyes danced with mischief. "Ye'd much rather stay here and drive poor Alex wild wi' jealousy. Ah, ye're a wicked lass, Velvet, but ye're still an innocent. A little more whiskey, another hour or two, and half the men in the hall would brave Alex for a taste of yer pretty lips. Do ye really want to cause a brawl, lass?"

Velvet shook her head. "Nay," she admitted.

"Then smile prettily at the poor, besotted man ye've wed, and he'll be yer slave, I promise," Bothwell teased her.

She made a little moue with her mouth. "He's worse than a mule," she muttered.

"And ye're no better!" he said quickly.

"Francis! 'Tis not so!" She pouted prettily, and he chuckled.

"Aye, Velvet, it is. Both ye and Alex are determined to have yer own way. Ye're selfish. One of ye has to grow up if the other is going to."

She sighed. "I know you're right, but, dammit, Francis, why must it always be the woman who gives in?"

"Because possibly women are a gentler and more patient sex."

Velvet laughed. "I'm not sure that I'm either, Francis. All I know is that when Alex grows stubborn and pompous with me, I want to smack him! He simply infuriates me with his old-fashioned ideas. He refuses to even consider change."

"Gi'e him time, Velvet. He expected a sweet, young thing who was anxiously awaiting his arrival; a lass who would come meekly back to Scotland glad that he wed wi' her, who would eagerly bear his bairns without complaint."

She looked at him, amused. "I know, and instead he got a wench who ran *from* him instead of *to* him. If I was such a disappointment, why was he so determined to marry me, Francis?"

"Pride for one thing," came Bothwell's reply. Then he stopped and looked down at her. "Love for another, Velvet. Do ye doubt it, lass?"

"Nay."

"And ye love him." It was a flat statement.

"Aye," she answered shortly. "I do love him, but we'll have no peace until he can treat me fairly as my father treats my mother, and not as a possession, Francis. Is that so hard a thing?"

"Velvet, my sweet," said the Earl of Bothwell, "ye suffer from the same ailment that I do. Ye were born in advance of yer time. Yes, it is a hard thing for Alex to accept! Who ever gave ye such ideas?"

"My mother."

"Jesu, I should like to meet her! She must be a fascinating lady."

"She is." Velvet smiled. "I wish she would come home."

Alex leaned over as they reached him and slipped a possessive arm about her waist. With a sigh Velvet leaned against him. "Ye're tired, hinny," he said, concerned. "Let us go home."

"Aye," she answered him. "I am tired, my lord."

Bothwell smiled. For the moment there would be peace between the battling BrocCairns. Velvet even dozed in the coach that took them from *Holyrood* to Bothwell's house in the Highgate. His eyes met those of Alex as they rode, and he nodded his approval of his cousin's calm behavior.

When they reached Lord Bothwell's mansion, Alex carried his wife into the house and up to their chamber. There he expertly played lady's maid to her as she stood sleepily before him. His hands fumbled with the laces of her gown, undoing the beautiful bodice and the skirt. Carefully he laid them over a chair. Yawning, she helped him to undo her petticoats and her chemise, to slide from her silken undergarments. Kneeling, he peeled off her stockings as she kicked off her shoes.

He caught his breath as she stretched lazily, yawning again. He could feel himself hardening as his eyes swept her slender form. "Jesu, Velvet, ye could tempt a saint!" he muttered huskily.

For some reason she felt more relaxed with him now than ever before. It did not even bother her that she stood naked before him. She suspected that her little talk with Francis had acted as some sort of catharsis. Her eyelids were heavy, but she smiled softly at him. "Come to bed, my lord," she said. And, turning, she held out her hand to him.

He stood rooted to the floor, completely surprised by her sudden softness. He was even more surprised when with a smile she moved to undo his kilt. "Velvet," he managed to murmur, tongue-tied and feeling like an idiot. A small smile played at the corners of her mouth as her eyes caught his for a brief moment. Then she went back to her task of disrobing him. Within a very short time he was as naked as she, and his desire was obvious. He almost blushed for she had actually made him feel shy.

Reaching out, he caressed one of her lovely breasts. "Ye're so beautiful," he whispered reverently.

Stretching her hand out to stroke his swollen manhood gently, she whispered back, "So are you, Alex."

They came together, their bodies touching lightly while their lips kissed tenderly. With a soft cry of triumph, he swept her up in his arms and carried her to the large bed with its red silk hangings. The sheets, scented with lavender, had already been drawn back by the maidservant. They felt cool and silken against her back and buttocks. Kneeling next to her, he bent his head to kiss her delicate rose-colored nipples. The touch of his mouth rendered them rigid with rising desire. Lovingly he teased each one in its turn, kissing it, licking at it, sucking sweetly and strongly upon it until she moaned low, an almost sobbing sound. His hand smoothed down her quivering torso, his fingers seeking eagerly for the tiny jewel of her womanhood, finding it, taunting it with delicate little touches until her head began to thrash upon the plump down pillows. How his slender fingers sought to take the edge off her passion, thrusting into her softness while his thumb continued to rub against her sensitivity.

Velvet gasped with each new sensation. They had been wed but four days, and tonight was the first time she had willingly participated with him in this marvelous sport called lovemaking. She realized that by not fighting him she was allowing him to give her the most incredible pleasure. Why had she not thought to ask her sisters about all this?

His lips moved with fiery kisses down the slender column of her neck to her shoulder, where the kisses turned to gentle nibbles of his sharp teeth. Velvet shivered with delight, and he moved his head up again to kiss her ear, growling softly into it, "I like my English rose without her thorns, lass."

She wound her fingers into his thick dark hair and tugged playfully at it, answering, "I love you best when you are gentle, my lord husband."

He swung himself over her, imprisoning her between his two thighs, and his hands moved upward to cup both of her breasts. He handled them like prized possessions until he felt Velvet's eyes upon him, and then he bent to kiss each nipple tenderly. She laughed softly, and Alex flushed guiltily, muttering, "Ye canna expect me to change much in four days, if I can change at all."

"I think I *may* learn to love you forever," she answered him mischievously, her heart soaring with her small victory.

He saw the triumph in her eyes, and, still needing to be master, he thrust into her very soft and very willing body almost harshly. Surprised, Velvet gasped once again, but suddenly in a burst of clarity she understood him. Instead of challenging him further, she pushed her hips up to meet his downward movements, at the same time taking his head between her two hands and whispering, "Aye, Alex Gordon, my lord of BrocCairn, *forever!*"

His mouth covered hers in a blazing kiss of such incredible intensity that it left them both breathless. Hungrily he moved on her, drawing her forward with him into a web of passion that he wove about them both so tightly that for Velvet there was no beginning and no end to this lovely moment. She felt her own identity slipping away as her emotions became all, and then she could no longer prevent her descent into the fiercely throbbing vortex that reached up to claim her. With a little cry of sweet surrender, she offered herself completely into his keeping.

Afterwards they lay together talking, her back against his chest, his hands playing lazily over her breasts. A bond had been formed between them now. He kissed the top of her tousled head, saying as he did so, "Dare we disobey yer queen and my king and go home to *Dun Broc*, lass?"

She sighed. "Oh, Alex, please understand," she begged him gently. "I must go home to England. We must be wed with my family about us. I shall never be happy with you if we do not." She turned her head up to him. "You know that you can be sure of me now, my wild Scots lord!"

"I had hoped to have our first child born at *Dun Broc*, as all its lords have been born in past memory." Then he sighed. "If we obey our rulers and return to England, it is very likely that our son will be born in England."

"My lord, you have yet to give me a wedding gift. If I could choose anything I desired it would be that we would return to England. If I bear a child for you in the next year, Alex, at least my mother would be with me. As you have stolen her right to be at our wedding, you owe us both that much, my lord."

He knew that she was right. She had been angered to learn that her brother's friend was actually her dreaded betrothed, but never had she really considered refusing his suit, and he knew it. He had been the one who had stolen her from London and tricked her into her marriage vows. If his first son was not born at *Dun Broc* he had no one to blame but himself. "We'll be wed in England in our own church with yer family about us, Velvet. How can I refuse ye now, lass? I love ye so very much!"

Her face lit up, and she twisted about so that she was facing him. "Thank you, Alex! Oh, thank you!"

She was the most beautiful thing he had ever seen in his entire life, this thorny English rose. With a helpless groan he kissed her, feeling his desire begin to rise once more. She melted against him, her lips parting, her little tongue teasing his in a surprisingly bold action. "Tell me ye love me," he murmured against her mouth. "Tell me!"

"I love you, my wild Scot!" she whispered back, and then he swept her away into a world of exquisite sensation, their passions being their only guide.

Two days later they left Edinburgh on their way south, this time traveling with a large party made up of Bothwell's Borderers and Alex's Gordon retainers, who had arrived the following day from *Dun Broc*. They broke their journey again at *Hermitage* but only stayed a night. The next day the Earl of Bothwell, at his cousin the king's orders, escorted the Earl and Countess of BrocCairn over the border to meet with the Earl of Lynmouth and his party of the queen's Gentlemen Pensioners.

Robert Southwood did not seem happy, his sister noted as they rode toward him. He sat upon a white stallion that danced nervously as he held it tightly in check. Lord Bothwell's midnight-colored Valentine whinnied a challenge and was also reined in tightly by his master.

Velvet winced delicately. "Robin looks angry," she whispered to Alex. "Which one of us do you think he is angry at?"

"I suspect both of us," came his answer, "but as long as we stand together I have no fears, lass."

"Greetings, my lord!" Bothwell called as they came abreast of the English party. Technically they were now over the border, but in the Cheviots national boundaries were extremely fluid. "I am Francis Stewart-Hepburn, His Majesty's most loyal cousin. Which one of ye is the Earl of Lynmouth?"

Robin moved his mount forward. "I am, my lord Bothwell. I am Robert Southwood, Mistress de Marisco's brother."

Bothwell grinned lazily. The young man reminded him of the angels he had seen portrayed in the stained-glass windows of French cathedrals. He was absolutely gorgeous, and yet Francis noted the hard line of the Englishman's mouth and his wary, lime-green eyes. "Then 'tis to ye I am instructed to turn over Lord and Lady Gordon, for I am bound to tell ye that yer sister and Lord Gordon were legally wed at my own castle of Hermitage. His Majesty, King James, expects to see the Earl and Countess of BrocCairn returned safely within a reasonable time, y'understand, my lord?"

"I am not privy to any agreements made between Her Majesty and your own king, my lord. I only know I am instructed to bring my sister and Lord Gordon back to London with dispatch," came Robin's cool reply.

Bothwell turned to Velvet. "Does he ever smile, this brother of yers, m'lady?"

"Often, but, Francis, I suspect he is angered at me now for taking him from his own bride of but two months," Velvet replied.

"You're damned right I'm angry!" snapped Robin. "There is a chance that Angel is breeding already, and I've had to leave her down at *Lynmouth* to come tearing after you two!"

"How are my nieces?" Velvet queried sweetly, hoping that her concern for Robin's daughters would soften his wrath.

"A bloody false alarm! They had eaten green apples was all, the little gluttons! We hurried all the way from London, and they were as merry as drunks when we arrived! One cannot follow the court and raise children successfully. After you and Alex are settled, I shall retire to Devon again."

"Then we are to be *settled*?" She looked anxiously at him.

"Aye, you baggage! I'd have let you go to *Dun Broc*, Velvet, believe me, but the queen would have none of it. She has planned your wedding herself, and the ceremony will be performed the day after the Armada thanksgiving, on November eighteenth. Then you and Alex are to remain at court until Mother returns in the spring. After that you're free to go your own way."

"Then having safely delivered ye, lassie, I shall return to *Hermitage*," Lord Bothwell said. "I regret I cannot be at yer grand English wedding, but I shall think of ye on that day and remember that I had the privilege of being at yer first wedding. Break yer journey next spring at *Hermitage*. I shall happily welcome ye both." Then, leaning from his saddle, he kissed her cheek. "Godspeed, fair Velvet."

She returned the kiss graciously. "Thank you, Francis." She hesitated a moment, then said, "For everything!" He alone would understand what she meant.

Alex and his cousin shook hands, their eyes meeting in a look of understanding, and then Bothwell whirled Valentine about and galloped off, his men riding behind him, shouting, "A Bothwell! A Bothwell!"

"So that was the famous Wizard Earl," said Robin. "Impressive chap! Far more so than King Jamie himself, I'm told. What think you, Alex?"

"James was born a king," he said, "but our cousin Francis is more a king born. Still, the Bothwells make enemies as history has proven. They could no more rule Scotland than the Stewarts can."

Robin nodded. "Let's go!" he replied. "We have a long way to ride. Once we get farther south I can arrange for a coach for Velvet."

"Nay! You'll not stuff me in one of those swaying, hard-sprung vehicles," she protested. "I'd sooner ride!"

"What of Pansy?" came her brother's answer.

"Not to worry, m'lord. My bottom's tough as leather now anyhow," was Pansy's saucy reply.

"Pansy!" Velvet attempted to look shocked, but she was as amused as her brother and her husband were.

"It's almost like being with Mother, isn't it, Pansy?" teased Robin.

"Aye, m'lord, but then me mum did warn me what life was like with Mistress Skye. They say a daughter is most like her mum, and if me lady is like Lady de Marisco, then I hope I am like me own mum and can keep up with her." She smiled her gap-toothed grin, and Lord Lynmouth chuckled, for she was so very much like a young Daisy, and he remembered Pansy's mother when she was not much older than Pansy herself right now.

They rode south into the heartland of England, and Velvet suddenly noticed that the days were growing shorter and the air cooler. The trees were almost bereft of their leaves now, and the land was beginning to have a wintry look about it. For two days they rode in freezing rain, and the road was awash in a sea of mud that eventually froze into deep, hard ruts that would undoubtedly remain until spring, thawing and refreezing over and over again. Velvet did not know which was worse, the mud or the dust they had encountered on their earlier journey to Scotland.

Although the pace was quick, they stopped each evening in a suitable place, either a respectable inn or the house of one of Robin's many friends whose homes were scattered throughout England. There the horses were rested and well fed, as were their riders. The queen had sent twenty-five Gentlemen Pensioners along with Southwood to escort Velvet and Alex back to London. There were also the fifty clansmen who had come from *Dun Broc* to be with their chief. Such an enormous party was certainly safe upon the darkest and loneliest of roads, but it was not easy to house them all.

Several days after they had left Scotland Velvet suddenly began to recognize the landscape about her. "We are near *Queen's Malvern!*" she cried.

"We're going to stop there tonight," said Robin. "Father Jean-Paul will marry you and Alex there."

"But I thought we were to be married in London on the eighteenth in the queen's presence," Velvet protested.

"By the archbishop of Canterbury," replied her brother. "If, however, you are to be married in the faith in which you were raised, little sister, it will be at *Queen's Malvern* by your old confessor. I sent word to him before I came to fetch you, and by now the banns have been properly published."

"Jesu!" said Alex. "Two marriages in Scotland and two in England! Surely we'll be the most married couple of all time, Rob."

"It all could have been avoided if you had but waited for our mother to return in the spring, instead of taking matters into your own clumsy hands, Alex," replied Robin sharply.

"Ye're three years younger than I am, Rob, and ye've three children already, and the possibility of another on the way. I have no bairns to bear my name."

"I have three daughters," came Robin's grim answer, "and the possibility of more. My father's first wife bore him six girls before she died and he married my mother who gave him sons."

"There was a son from the first marriage, too," Velvet reminded her brother. "Mama told me that he died in the same epidemic that killed your father's first wife and three of his daughters."

"Are you defending this plunderer of your virtue?" Robin demanded. "I thought you hated him."

"He is to be my husband," Velvet answered primly, although her green eyes were dancing with mischief. "Is it not proper for a wife to cleave to her lord, brother?"

"Dammit, Velvet, make up your foolish female mind! Either you love him or you don't."

"Of course I love Alex. How could you even think otherwise?"

Robin glowered at her. "I wish to heaven Mother had not left England leaving me charge of our damn difficult family.

"Ah, but she's in my charge now," said Alex.

"I am my own mistress," countered Velvet.

The two men glanced at each other across the distance that separated them. Then they both looked at Velvet, who rode between them, her eyes straight ahead, her hands light on her reins. She raised her head, turned first to Alex and smiled sweetly, and then turned her face to her brother, smiling again. Both gentlemen burst out laughing and laughed until the tears ran down their faces.

"God help you!" Robin chortled.

"Aye, God help me, brother, for no one else will!" wheezed Alex.

In that moment their old relationship was completely restored, and by late afternoon when they sighted the chimneys of *Queen's Malvern* it was as if they had never quarreled. Riding up to the door of her childhood home, Velvet felt a lump insinuate itself into her throat, and then the door was flung open and dear old Dame Cecily came hurrying out. Several quick tears slid down her cheeks, which she swiftly wiped away. Slipping from her saddle without waiting for aid, Velvet wordlessly flung herself into the old woman's open arms. Dame Cecily hugged her tightly, tears running down her worn face as well. Velvet pulled away at last and wiped the old lady's face gently with her hand.

Dame Cecily finally mustered a smile and, regaining control of herself, said briskly, "Well, now, you bad thing, you're home again!" Her eyes moved to Alex, who had dismounted with Robin and stood waiting to be introduced. "And is this great craggy man your husband?" she demanded, and Velvet nodded. "He doesn't look at all like a devil to run from, child, but then you always were willful and would have your own way."

"I haven't had it this time." Velvet chuckled. "He kidnapped me off to Scotland and tricked me into marriage before I knew what was happening."

"You don't look any the worse for wear," remarked Dame Cecily. Then she looked with snapping eyes at Robin. "Introduce me, you mannerless scamp, fine milord though you may be!"

Robin laughed warmly. "Alexander Gordon, may I present to you Dame Cecily Small, sister to our mother's trading partner, Sir Robert, and adoptive grandmother of all the children of Skye O'Malley. Dearest Dame Cecily, the Earl of BrocCairn, Velvet's husband."

Dame Cecily curtsied as low as her stiff joints would allow her to, but Alex put out his hand and raised her up. Kissing the old, gnarled hand with its beautiful diamond and sapphire rings, he said, "I can see ye're one of the few good influences my wife has had, madame. I hope that even though we will live in Scotland ye'll continue to be a part of our lives."

Dame Cecily's eyes sparkled with delight. "You're a rogue, my fine Scot! That I can certainly see! Nevertheless, I suspect you're well matched with my girl. Come in now! Come in! 'Tis far too cold out here, and I've several warm fires going in the house."

Her eyes lit on Pansy. "You, girl! Your mother wants to see you, and then hurry and draw a hot bath for your mistress. They'll be time enough later on to flirt with that evil-looking Scot with the naked knees you keep eyeing!"

With a mumbled "Yes, ma'am!," Pansy scrambled from her pony and hurried around the side of the house, out of sight.

"Take your animals to the stable," Dame Cecily commanded the waiting horsemen. "Then come into the house. It will be crowded, but there's ale and meat for all." Then she led Velvet and the gentlemen into *Queen's Malvern*.

Inside, the house was toasty and fragrant with the smell of applewood fires. From the small family hall came a tall man, and Velvet ran toward him, her arms outstretched. "Uncle Conn!"

Lord Bliss hugged his wayward niece, muttering, "You get more like your mother in temperament every day!"

"Have you come for my wedding?"

"Aye, and your aunt Aiden, too, *and* all your little cousins."

"*All* my cousins? How lovely," Velvet replied, but her tone of voice lacked sincerity. "'Tis only to be small ceremony! Alex and I have already been wed twice."

"Surely you don't consider what happened in Scotland as a true marriage, Velvet?" Conn asked.

"I will not be happy until I have been wed in my own church, Uncle Conn, but perhaps we had best consider the Scots ceremonies, should I already be carrying a child." Her eyes danced merrily.

"Velvet!" He was shocked. She was far too young to be saying such things, wasn't she? Then he realized that she was quite shamelessly teasing him. "You're impossible!" he grumbled.

Velvet laughed while Conn St. Michael looked at her closely. The half-grown girl who had left *Queen's Malvern* six months ago was gone. This was an incredibly beautiful and headstrong woman. He looked at the Earl of BrocCairn and was startled to see in the amber eyes of that craggy-faced Scot a look of pure love and devotion directed toward his niece. God help Alex Gordon, Conn St. Michael thought to himself. Velvet has her mother's magical allure.

"Come along, come along!" Dame Cecily fussed at them all. "If there is to be a wedding here tonight, then we must all work together. Robin, my lad, take your Scots friend to the Tapestry Room, and I'll send his man and a bath along." She fixed Alex with a sharp gaze. "You've something respectable to wear, I trust?"

"My kilt, madame," he replied soberly.

For a moment they all thought that she would argue with him, but Dame Cecily finally nodded, saying, "'Twill serve quite nicely, my boy. Get along with Robin now."

Alex's eyes were dancing with delight. It was plain that he liked the tart-tongued Dame Cecily mightily. He bowed elegantly and then, turning, followed Robin upstairs.

"Now as for you, Velvet de Marisco, go directly to your room. Pansy should be there by now. Daisy and I have a surprise for you," Dame Cecily said.

"Aren't you coming?"

"Nay, child. I have a great deal to do before Father Jean-Paul weds you and your Alex in the chapel."

"Will you give me away, Uncle Conn?" Velvet asked.

"Aye, sweetheart," came his heartfelt reply. "If Adam cannot be here to do it, then I'll be proud to stand in his place."

Velvet felt tears start, and Dame Cecily snapped at Conn, "You've no sense, Conn St. Michael! No sense whatsoever!" Then she gathered Velvet to her bosom. "There, child. I know you wish your parents were here, but your wild Scot has taken that choice away from us. Don't cry. There, there!" She held Velvet close as she waved Lord Bliss away with her other hand.

"I'm all right." Velvet sniffed. "Just for a moment I had the most terrible longing for Mama and Papa. Oh, Dame Cecily, what would I do without you?"

"A pity you didn't think about that before you went running off to court, Mistress Willful! Go along now and get ready for your wedding!"

The old lady released Velvet and hurried off down the hall toward the kitchens. With a little sigh, Velvet climbed the stairs and followed the familiar route to her bedchamber. As she drew near she could smell the lovely fragrance of her gillyflower bath oil and knew that Pansy was awaiting her. Entering the room, she found both Daisy and her daughter bustling about.

"Welcome home, Mistress Velvet," said Daisy, coming forward to give her a hug. "I have a lovely bath ready for you, but before you bathe come and see our surprise." Taking Velvet's hand, she led her into the dressing room. There spread out in magnificent array on a pair of chairs were two of the most exquisite dresses Velvet had ever seen.

One was an apple-green silk, with a low bodice embroidered with gold thread and tiny pearls that matched the panel of the slightly darker underskirt. The leg-of-mutton sleeves were held by a profusion of tiny gold ribbons, the wristbands turned back to form cuffs with gold lace ruffs. The bodice of the gown had a long, wasp waist that ended in a pronounced peak, and the bell-shaped skirt separated in front to reveal the elegant undergown.

The second gown was of a rich, heavy, candlelight satin that was mellowed with age. Its simple bodice was cut low and embroidered with seed pearls. The puffed sleeves, which ended just below the elbows, were slashed and the openings filled with delicate cream-colored lace. Below the elbows the sleeves hugged the arms in alternating bands of satin and lace, and the wrists were ruffled with wide bands of lace. The underskirt was embroidered with delicate seed pearls and tiny diamond flowers. The dress had a small, starched, heart-shaped lace collar edged in tiny diamonds that rose up behind the neck, and the skirt shape was that of a bell.

"Daisy! Where did you find such marvelous gowns?" Velvet demanded.

"The green was your mother's wedding dress when she married your father. I thought perhaps you'd like to wear it tonight. There's gold roses for your lovely hair. As for the cream, your mother wore it when she wed Lord Southwood at Greenwich Palace twenty-five years ago! Dame Cecily and I hoped that you would take it with you to London when you marry before the queen."

"Oh, Daisy!" Velvet was astounded. "My sisters never wore mother's dresses. Do you think she'd mind if I did?"

"Mistress Willow wanted her own gown so that she could pass it on down to her daughters one day. She puts great store by tradition as you know, particularly those she starts herself. As for Mistress Deirdre, she was so relieved when your parents allowed her to marry Lord Blackthorn that she cared not what she wore. Your mother didn't feel that these gowns were suitable for Lord Burke's daughter. Besides, she's not as tall as your mama, and has more bosom than my lady did at her age. Mistress Skye wanted Mistress Deirdre to have everything new. I know, however, that she would fully approve of Dame Cecily's and my choices. You, however, may not want to wear them."

"Oh, yes, I do! If I have Master Hilliard paint my miniature in each gown, Mama and Papa will know how I looked on my wedding day! If Robin doesn't mind my wearing the cream-colored gown, I should love to take it to London, but tonight for the ceremony with Father Jean-Paul I want to wear the gown in which Mama married Papa."

Daisy smiled. "Then let us hurry and get you ready, though I never thought I'd see the day I'd be preparing your mother's youngest child for her wedding!"

Velvet hadn't had a bath in several days, and the hot, scented water was wonderful. She loved the hard-milled soap, perfumed with the elusive gillyflowers scent, that Daisy and Pansy used with the boar's-bristle brushes when they scrubbed her back and with which they lavishly lathered her dusty auburn hair. Velvet regretted that there was no time to soak, but it had been close to sunset when they had ridden into *Queen's Malvern*. The evening meal was being held up until after the wedding ceremony.

Stepping from her tub, Velvet stood quietly while she was first dried, then perfumed and powdered. Her beautiful long hair was toweled with warm linen, then brushed and rubbed with silk. Pansy held out a pair of green silk stockings with vine leaves embroidered on them with gold thread.

"I made them for you using your mother's originals for models," Daisy said, "and I had Bonnie lower the hem on the green gown. We weren't sure whether or not we would have to edge it in fur to give you enough length, but it turned out there was enough material. 'Twas French made, the gown, and there's no doubt they're fine seamstresses. Bonnie did have to edge the cream satin with a bit of lace though to lengthen it enough, you being taller than your mama."

Pansy held out Velvet's silken undergarments and a pair of gold garters. Velvet was beginning to feel better than she had in days. It was amazing, she thought, what good a hot bath could accomplish. Daisy then slid the apple-green silk gown over Velvet's head. It fell gracefully, and as the tiring woman laced it up, Velvet was astounded by the perfect fit. It molded her waist and made her young breasts more sensual than she had ever believed they could be. Her eyes widened with surprise.

Then Daisy's voice broke her thoughts. "I had Bonnie take the silk in, for your mother was a trifle thicker in the waist than you are when she finally married your father. The cream satin, however, should fit you perfectly, but we'll try it on tomorrow and have Bonnie make any alterations necessary. Now sit and let Pansy do your hair."

Carefully adjusting her dress, Velvet sat down. Behind her Pansy took up the boar's-bristle brush, and parting her mistress's hair in the center she drew it back carefully over Velvet's ears. Then, working swiftly with the brush and a mouthful of gold hairpins, she fashioned the thick, rich auburn hair with its coppery-gold lights into an elegant chignon. Looking critically for any wisps of hair that might have escaped her vigilance, she nodded, satisfied to find none and affixed the cloth-of-gold and silk roses upon the top of the chignon.

In the mirror Velvet could see Daisy bobbing her head in approval. "Lovely!" she pronounced. "I never saw your mother in this dress, for I wasn't in France when she and your father were wed, but she couldn't have looked any more beautiful than you do, Mistress Velvet. The apple-green suits you with your gorgeous hair."

There was a knock on the door, and when Pansy answered it the de Mariscos' chaplain, Father Jean-Paul, entered the room. With a smile he said, "Good evening, *ma petite cousine.*"

With an answering smile, Velvet arose and went to him with her hands outstretched. "Père Jean-Paul! How happy I am to see you!"

Jean-Paul St. Justine was the second son of Adam's younger sister, Clarice, and her husband, Henri, Comte de St. Justine. From childhood he had known that he wanted to be a priest, and he had entered the seminary on his thirteenth birthday. He had done brilliantly in his studies, and upon his ordination he had, to his family's pride, been appointed to the staff of a prestigious bishop. Eight years ago, however, he had taken the part of a young peasant girl cruelly raped by her master's sons. She had sought sanctuary in the village church, but the nobleman's sons had broken into the church and dragged the hysterical girl from her refuge at the feet of the shocked old priest. It had been at that moment that Père Jean-Paul had ridden by, and using the weight of his office he had managed to rescue the girl.

The noble father of the miscreants, had complained to the bishop, to the cardinal, and finally to the king himself. Père Jean-Paul St. Justine had been relieved of his post and sent to England to act as family chaplain to his Uncle Adam. He had arrived at *Queen's Malvern* the year Velvet had been six. Among all people in the rural region in which *Queen's Malvern* was located, he was most beloved, for he had a strong sense of justice and used his own personal wealth to ease the sufferings of many, be they Catholic or Protestant. He was that rarest of men, a true Christian, and he possessed a wonderful sense of humor.

Father Jean-Paul took the two lovely hands presented to him and kissed them warmly. "You are absolutely radiant, *ma petite*," he said. "I am pleased that you have come home to be married. I have already heard your betrothed's confession, Velvet, and I am quite shocked." The priest's blue eyes danced with mischief. "I expect your confession shall shock me equally."

Used to his teasing, she countered quickly, "But, *mon cousin*, what can I possibly have to confess, for was it not I who was wronged by this wild Scot my parents chose to husband me?"

"And you have not enjoyed one moment of your carnal encounters?" he said innocently.

"As a good daughter of the church, *mon père*, how could I?" she returned demurely. "Such things are but for the procreation of the faith only, I have been taught."

"Strange," he mused. "'Twas not what Lord Gordon believed. He was most contrite for having compromised your virtue without benefit of clergy, yet he soothed his conscience with the thought that he gave you pleasure."

"Then he was mistaken, and most ungentlemanly to boot!" replied Velvet, but her lips were twitching with amusement.

The priest tucked Velvet's hand through his arm. "I have never seen you look so beautiful, *ma petite*. I would not make you sad, but I truly regret that your parents cannot be here. Sometimes it is difficult to understand God's will, eh?" He patted her hand. "Come, *ma petite*, and we will go to the chapel where I will listen to your confession. I have taught you that marriage is a sacrament, and you must purge yourself of your sins before a holy sacrament."

"Oui, mon père," Velvet said quietly, and she allowed him to lead her from her chamber.

The family chapel was a small, square room in the northeast corner of the house. Jean-Paul St. Justine had consecrated it upon his arrival from France. It was a beautiful room with a coffered oak ceiling and a polished oak floor. The small double doors were carved with twin archangels with outspread wings in raised relief, painted and gilded in bright colors and gold leaf. Facing the doors was a creamy marble altar with a lace cloth. Upon the altar sat a beautiful gold crucifix set with precious stones flanked by candlesticks. Above it was a small round window stained in rich shades of red, blue, gold, rose, and green. To the left of the altar were three tall arched windows, the first of which depicted the temptation of Eve, the second the baptism of Jesus, and the third the Resurrection. Only red, blue, and gold had been used in these windows.

The altar rail was carved round with grape vines, and upon either side of the single altar step were long red velvet cushions. At the back of the chapel, and to the right of the doors, was a small carved oak confessional. To the left of the entrance stood a marble baptismal font with a silver ewer. There were but four carved oak benches with high backs in the chapel, two on the right and two on the left side of the room. The chapel was not really large enough to contain the entire family of Lord and Lady de Marisco, but on the occasions when they all came together, they had somehow managed.

Velvet entered the confessional, and after offering her cousin the traditional salutation she began to speak. Her confession, however, consisted mostly of small wrongs and uncharitable thoughts she had had while she had served the queen at court. Jean-Paul St. Justine was amused when he realized that she felt not one moment of remorse for having tried to hold off Lord Gordon for so long. Her main concern seemed to be for her parents.

He offered her absolution and a mild penance, for her sins were small if, in fact they existed at all. Then he left her to say her prayers before the marriage ceremony and went to his own quarters to change into more splendid and festive priestly garments.

When Father Jean-Paul returned to the chapel a half an hour later, the gold-and-jeweled candlesticks flanking the matching crucifix had fresh beeswax tapers in them and were already alight. The young boy from the nearby village who served as his altar boy was dressed in his red cassock and embroidered white lace surplice.

"The earl says we're ready to begin, Father," the boy piped.

"Open the doors then, lad, and let the family come into God's house," the priest said quietly.

The altar boy hurried to do the cleric's bidding and flung open the two doors to admit first Dame Cecily and Aiden St. Michael, and her children who were followed by Lord and Lady Blackthorn, Daisy, Pansy, and Dugald. Next came all the servants belonging to *Queen's Malvern*, many of whom had been there ever since Skye and Adam de Marisco had first made the house their home. Velvet's old nurse, Violet, sniffed audibly. They had all seen the young mistress grow from child to woman, and they felt a strong sense of personal attachment to Velvet, as if she had been one of their own. In fact most of the servants considered that she was. When the four pews were all filled to overflowing with the de Marisco retainers, the Earl of BrocCairn's clansmen entered the chapel and lined the walls of the small room.

Lord Gordon, with Lord Southwood acting as his groomsman, entered and came forward to stand just below the altar step. Robin was garbed in an elegant velvet suit of sapphire blue; Alex was dressed as he had been in Scotland, in his dark blue, green, and yellow plaid kilt and dark velvet jacket.

Now came the bride, radiant on her uncle's proud arm. With great dignity Lord Bliss led his niece down the center of the chapel to where the Earl of BrocCairn awaited her. He put her hand into Alex's, and Father Jean-Paul began to intone the ages-old Latin words of the marriage ceremony. Mentally Velvet sighed with relief. She loved Alex Gordon, of that she had no doubt, but in her heart and her mind she had needed this ancient ceremony in order to feel truly wed. Her only regret, of course, was that Alex had not waited for her parents to return home.

How often had Velvet and her mother spoken of, and planned for, the day when she would marry. Each detail had been gone over and over again, from exactly what she would wear, down to the very wines to be served at the bridal banquet. The wines would come from *Archambault*, her French grandparents' great chateau and vineyard in the Loire Valley. Grandmère and Grandpère! Here was another regret, for they, too, were absent on this her day of days. They and all the *tantes* and *oncles*, and not to be forgotten, all her wonderfully voluble and fashionable French *cousins* and *cousines*, were woefully absent, except, of course, for Père Jean-Paul. He, she knew, would write to his parents and grandparents in France announcing her marriage. He would leave out no detail, though they would think it a poor affair, she thought, with no bridal cake or guests other than Dame Cecily and the St. Michaels, and only one brother, one sister, and one brother-in-law. There had been neither the time nor the opportunity to invite Alex's sister and her husband, as well as Velvet's own far-flung relatives.

She forced her mind back to the ceremony and was surprised to find that Père Jean-Paul was to the point where they would take their vows. Paying closer attention, she played her part, answering in a clear, calm voice. She had waited all her life for this, even if it wasn't quite right. The vows spoken, the priest moved on to the mass, and Velvet's mind wandered once more.

She wondered where her mother and father were at this exact minute. Were they still in India, or had they already embarked upon the long voyage back to England? She wished that there was a way in which she might communicate with them so that even if they couldn't be here with her at this time, they might at least know she was wed and share in her happiness. *Mama. Papa.* She tried to reach out to them in her mind. *Mama, Papa! I love you both!* She felt Alex tug gently on her hand, and, following his lead, she knelt before Père Jean-Paul to receive the host on her tongue.

In the instant that the consecrated wafer touched her mouth the thought came to her: *I am no longer a child. I am no longer Adam de Marisco's daughter. I am Alex Gordon's wife. No—I am no longer Velvet de Marisco. I am Velvet Gordon. I may love my parents, but I can depend upon them no more for my every need. I must now depend upon myself and upon Alex, and soon we shall have the responsibility of our own children. This is what growing up means.*

The enormity of her thoughts stunned her briefly, and for a frightened moment she wanted to flee. Was she really ready for all of this? Was she ready to grow old? Where had her youth gone? Why had she not appreciated her freedom when she had had it?

Then Alex's arm slipped about her, and she felt his warm breath in her ear as he whispered softly to her, "Dinna fear, lass. Suddenly I'm nae sure I'm ready for all of this myself."

She cast him a startled look and swallowed back a bubble of laughter in her throat. "'Tis what you wanted, my lord," she whispered back, "and 'tis now too late to back out, for the deed is done!"

He squeezed her hand reassuringly, and Velvet squeezed his back. Life was never going to be easy with this man, her husband, but neither was it going to be dull! Forcing her mind back to the here and now, she tried to follow the service.

In short order Père Jean-Paul had given them his blessing, and with a smile he half-turned the Earl and Countess of BrocCairn about to present them to the congregation of the chapel. With another smile to Alex, he said, "I think you might kiss your wife, my lord."

Alex gladly complied, sweeping Velvet into a bear hug of an embrace, his mouth molding against hers in a warm kiss that left her weak-kneed, while about them the Gordon clansmen and the de Marisco retainers cheered lustily.

Velvet felt marvelously happy, and then Alex took his mouth from hers and looked down into her face with an equally happy smile. With a burst of joyous laughter, her green eyes sparkling with mischief, she smiled back at him and said, "*Now*, my lord husband, now we are most truly wed!"

"Ye're sure?" he teased back.

"Very sure!"

"I love ye, Velvet," he said.

"You're sure?"

"Aye," he drawled, "very sure." Then before the delighted spectators he pulled her back into his arms and kissed her once again, lifting his head but a moment to murmur against her trembling mouth, *"Very, very sure!"*

Chapter 6

Late autumn of 1588 was an incredible social whirl for those who followed the court of Elizabeth Tudor. Capping the season, on November 17, the queen left Somerset House in a state procession for St. Paul's. The great parade was headed by palace officials, followed by London's aldermen and judges all done up in their finest clothes. Next came the Lancaster, York, Somerset, and Richmond heralds introducing the dukes, marquesses, earls, and viscounts. It was among these that Lord Southwood and his brother-in-law, the Scots Earl of BrocCairn, mingled.

Then came the lord treasurer of England, William Cecil, Lord Burghley, in his fur-trimmed black velvet gown, his heavy gold chain of office about his neck. With him was the lord chancellor of England, Sir Christopher Hatton, resplendent himself in black velvet with gold lace, his own badge of office shining in the November daylight. These two worthies were followed by the archbishop of Canterbury, John Whitcliff, the archbishop of York, the French ambassador, the lord mayor of London, and the nobleman chosen to carry the Sword of State, who was surrounded by the sergeants-at-arms.

Finally came the queen's *Gentlemen Pensioners*, and at last Elizabeth Tudor herself, riding in her open chariot with its canopy sporting waving white plumes, and gilded crown resplendent. The queen was magnificent in a cloth-of-silver gown embroidered with tiny diamonds and pearls so that she glittered with the slightest movement in the cold lemon-colored light. The sleeves of the gown as well as the hem and the overskirt were trimmed in purest white ermine. She wore no cloak, but beneath her voluminous skirts her ladies had insisted upon her wearing flannel petticoats and a fur-lined underblouse. Upon her head was a fiery red wig topped by a sparkling diamond, pearl, and sapphire crown. The crowds on Fleet Street and Ludgate Hill went wild with shouting. She was their Bess.

Arriving at the west door of St. Paul's Cathedral, the queen stepped out of her chariot and entered the great church. Once inside, she knelt in the aisle to pray silently. Then she was led to her place of honor in the choir where the litany was chanted to her. The great Armada victory was graciously attributed to the winds and the tides sent to aid a just English cause by a beneficent God. No mention was made of the valiant English seamen who, though low on rations and ammunition, had by their sheer courage and skill wrought this miracle. Lord Howard, the lord admiral, listening to the pious prelates and their chanting, thought it was ironic that the English survivors of the great victory had been paid their wages by the crown only when he had finally threatened to take the money from his own pocket. As it was, he had had to go among the English coastal villages begging shelter for many of the wounded seamen who otherwise would have been left in the streets, for now that the danger was past, the people were quick to forget.

Crowded into a pew with some dozen people, Velvet and her sister, the Countess of Alcester, and their sister-in-law, the Countess of Lynmouth, shifted uncomfortably and wondered if their gowns would be ruined in the crush. The entire day was to be one great fête. After they left St. Paul's they would return to Whitehall where there would be jousting in the tiltyard, followed by feasting and dancing. On the morrow Velvet's officially sanctioned English wedding to Alex was to take place, this ceremony to be performed by the archbishop himself. Velvet smiled to herself as she once again wished her parents here, but this time for a far different reason. How Adam and Skye would laugh, seeing the delicious humor in all these many weddings, Velvet thought.

At last the ceremony of thanksgiving was finished, and the queen left St. Paul's for her return to Whitehall Palace. The court began to file out behind her in one enormous, if somewhat confused procession, as they made their way down Ludgate Hill. The day that had begun bright and clear was now, as the afternoon wore on, growing gray and cloudy, and there was a sharp wind off the river. It was not cold enough for snow, but rain was a very distinct possibility.

"I hope the rain holds off long enough for the jousting," said Velvet, for she had never seen this type of entertainment.

"Unless it pours they'll joust," remarked Willow.

"In the rain?" Velvet exclaimed.

"The spectator seats in the tiltyard are covered," said Angel. "And the queen loves the sport. There was no time for such frivolity this past summer with the Spanish threat."

"Thank God that's over and done with!" was Willow's brisk reply. "The Spanish will think twice before they come at us again. I far prefer peace for my children. I should not like to think I was raising Henry, Francis, and Adam for cannon fodder! Then, too, if there continues to be all these wars there will be no suitable husbands for Cecily and Gabrielle."

"Or for Elsbeth, Catherine, or Cecily," replied Angel.

Willow's amber eyes grew warm with her approval. "You like Robin's girls, don't you?" she said.

"How could I not like them!" Angel cried. "They are such adorable little creatures, and, Willow, you will never guess! They call me Mama!"

"It means that they've taken to you," Willow replied. "They'll never remember Alison as they were far too young when she died, though they'll, of course, be told you're only their stepmother. Yes, they're young enough for you to train in your own ways, but remember to spare not the rod else they be spoilt."

Velvet smiled to herself as she listened to her oldest sister who only a short while ago had been so suspicious of Angel's motives for marrying Robin. And Angel! What had happened to that wordly-wise and impudent royal ward? Velvet's smile broadened. Willow and Angel were two of a kind. They were family-oriented, loving, strong women who would always put husband and children first and foremost above all. Velvet admired them though she didn't think that she would ever be like them. How strange, she thought, that she, the youngest of all her mother's children, should be the most like her in spirit. She would have liked to have shared that new knowledge with Skye, too.

They finally reached Whitehall where, to their vast relief, Angel told them that she and Robin had a small apartment where they could go to refresh themselves and repair any damages done to their coifs and gowns. When they reached it, Jane, Angel's tiring woman, hurried to fetch warm water so that they might bathe their hands and faces. Then she helped them to redo their hair and brushed their gowns free of wrinkles and dust.

Each woman was wearing a gown of velvet as it was far too cool to wear silk outdoors now. They looked like rare gems in their colorful dresses: Willow in a deep ruby red, Angel in a magnificent sapphire, and Velvet in a rich amethyst color. Refreshed by the pleasant golden wine that Jane offered them, they refastened their fur-lined cloaks, which matched their gowns, and prepared to find their way to the tiltyard for the jousting. There they would meet their husbands, and all of them had been invited to sit near the queen.

To their intense embarrassment Elizabeth Tudor was already there when they arrived, but with a gracious wave of her hand she overlooked their tardiness. "The crowds were mighty," she remarked, offering them the excuse, and they nodded and agreed with her. The queen gazed briefly at them, then noted, "You're a pretty trio of jewels, I vow."

"Your Majesty is too kind," said Willow, smiling.

Elizabeth chuckled. "Willow," she said, "if you were a man you'd be the perfect courtier. It amazes me each time I remember who your mother is."

"My mother," said Willow, "has ever been Your Majesty's loyal servant."

"Only, my dear, when it suited her," said the queen, laughing, "but I have no quarrel with my dear Skye. Perhaps the reason we have always chafed at each other is that we are basically alike. What have you heard from her of late? When may we expect her back in England? I am anxious to learn if her voyage has been successful."

"There has been no word of late, Your Majesty, which in itself is unusual, for Mama usually keeps a ready line of communication open between herself and London. We only know what she wrote last. From that letter we expect they will be home in the spring."

The queen nodded, then said softly as if to herself, "It is vital that she succeed!" Then she fixed her glance on Angel. "Tell me, my lady Southwood, is married life all that you envisioned it would be? Are you happy?"

"Aye, madame! My lord husband is the kindest and most loving of men. I can never repay Your Majesty for allowing me to be his wife." Angel's beautiful face was radiant with her happiness.

"You are very fortunate then, my little Angel, for it is not always so. Is the rumor true that you're already with child?"

"I believe it is so, madame."

"In that, too, you are fortunate," the queen remarked.

"We should name it after Your Majesty, but we already have an Elsbeth."

The queen's laughter was a sharp bark. "Nay, my lady Southwood! 'Twill be a boy, I am certain, and you should name it Geoffrey after your husband's father! There was a man now! I hope your son will be his like!"

"I shall tell Robin that Your Majesty wishes it," responded Angel sweetly.

The queen now turned her gaze to the tiltyard. The joust was one of her favorite forms of entertainment, as it had been her father's. Greenwich, Hampton Court, and Whitehall all had tiltyards. There were three styles of jousting. The first was the Tilts, where horsemen used blunted spears. The second was called the Tourney in which they used swords. The third form of the joust was called the Barriers, and here the opponents fought on foot, alternating between pike and sword. Mock jousting was often the highlight of banquet entertainment and court masques.

Since jousting was the only other type of organized sport in Tudor England apart from archery contests, many came to watch the pageants. A seat in the stands could be had for twelve pence. A courtier not invited to the queen's box had to fend for himself. Thus it was that many a nobleman and his lady found themselves sharing space with the London public.

The champions, each wearing his own distinctive color, brought their horses into the arena to the sound of trumpets, and the pageant was begun. The servants of those jousting were also dressed in colorful garb, some like savages, some like ancient Britons with long hair hanging to their girdles, and others wore horses' manes. Some of the knights entered the arena first in carriages, their horses made to look like unicorns with finely wrought, twisted gold horns centered upon their foreheads. Others had their vehicles drawn by blackamoors garbed in balloonlike scarlet pantaloons and cloth-of-gold turbans. The proudest of the knights arrived already in full shining silver armor upon their own spirited and beautiful horses, proudly showing off their mounts' skills.

Each knight with his servant, upon reaching the barrier, stopped at the foot of the staircase leading to the queen's box. The servant, in pompous attire of his master's special pattern would climb the steps and offer the queen a little speech in well-composed verse or a silly jest that would make her and her ladies and guests laugh. When the speech was ended, the queen was presented with a costly gift in the name of his lord, and Elizabeth then gave her permission for the knight to take part in the tournament. When all the knights had presented themselves thusly to the queen, the jousting began.

Among the knights this day was the Earl of Lynmouth, the Earl of BrocCairn, and the Earl of Alcester. Although Willow fussed noisily about her husband's taking part in the sport—"James must remember that he is no longer a boy!"—

she was, in truth, very proud, for he carried her colors, midnight blue and silver silks. He was to ride with Lord Southwood while Alex had been paired with Sir Walter Ralegh.

The tournament began, and two by two the knights rode against each other, breaking their lances across a beam. Gradually the two hundred or so men taking part in the tilting were weeded out until only four were left. The Earl of Essex rode with the Earl of Oxford against the Earl of BrocCairn and Sir Walter Ralegh. Essex carried Elizabeth Tudor's favor upon his lance, the bright green and white ribbons blowing in the wind. He looked supremely confident for he fully expected to win.

Alex carried Velvet's favor, silver and scarlet ribbons. He was also confident, for he felt he rode for the honor of Scotland. He didn't particularly like Robert Devereux, still suspecting him of taking more than a brotherly interest in Velvet. Essex and Ralegh, though companions during the Armada crisis, had once again become enemies, for each was jealous of the other's influence with the queen. Alex decided that he could not have had a better tournament partner than Ralegh.

Edward de Vere, the Earl of Oxford, looked at his opponents and said to Essex, "That wild Scot fights well, and so does Ralegh. We will not have an easy victory, Robert."

Essex looked down the field. "Strange," he drawled, "I think we will. 'Tis only luck and Ralegh's skill that have brought the Highland savage this far. They will be easy pickings, Ned. My word on it!"

A few minutes later the Earl of Essex's handsome face registered pure surprise and shock as he saw that his lance was broken and the queen's colors dumped rudely onto the ground. Oxford's lance had also suffered an unkind fate due to Ralegh's skill. The Earl of BrocCairn and Sir Walter Ralegh were declared the champions of the joust that day. They would present their shields adorned with their mottoed emblems to be hung in the Shield Gallery, which was situated by the Thames.

Alex and Sir Walter knelt before the queen to receive the victor's prize, which this day turned out to be emeralds, one to each gentleman. "You may rise now, my brave gallants. 'Twas a battle well fought! Very well fought!"

"For you, madame," replied Ralegh, and Elizabeth smiled.

"The cask of Malmsey is well appreciated, Wat-er," she said, "but you, Lord Gordon! What a fine gift you have presented me with. What breed are the dogs your wicked-looking servant gave me? I have not seen their like before."

"They are dogs of my own breeding, madame. Good hunting setters. I have given ye a pair, male and female, should ye wish to breed them yerself. They are excellent in heavy cover and retrieve well, especially woodcock and grouse."

"I like their coloring, the black and tan," said the queen. "I have no others like them. If they do well in the hunt I shall expect you to send me another pair, for you owe me that, having stolen my godchild and compromised her honor." She eyed him archly.

"They are yers, madame, and Velvet is well worth the price," came his quick answer.

"Humph." The queen snorted. "I do not know what I shall say to Lord and Lady de Marisco when they return home in the spring. I have failed in my duties as godmother, and all due to your impatience, my lord!"

"I shall accept full responsibility, madame, and ye need have no feelings of guilt, for did ye not send after us post-haste? Ye did yer duty as I see it."

"But I was not quick enough, was I, my lord?"

"Madame, accept my apology," Alex said sincerely. "I admit to allowing my temper to overrule my common sense and thereby placed Yer Majesty in a compromising position. For that I beg yer forgiveness, but I love Velvet so deeply that I could not wait . . ." He shrugged helplessly.

"Damn me, but you are an honest man, Alexander Gordon! You've spoken fairly and plainly to me, which few would do for fear of me. I like you! You have my forgiveness, but you must give me your word that after tomorrow's ceremony with the archbishop you will remain in England until my godchild's parents do return. I know that you long to return to your own home, but this I must insist upon. Skye O'Malley is protective, nay, she is a veritable lioness where her children are concerned. The last time I fought with her over a matter involving one of her children she pricked me sorely. Her sting is too sharp for me to tolerate at this time in my life."

Alex laughed. "Strange," he said. "I have met my mother-in-law only one time, at the time of my betrothal to Velvet. I remember her as a beautiful woman and a gracious hostess. Yet everything I have heard about her indicates that she is a warrior of the fiercest temperament. But ye have my word, madame. Neither Velvet nor I shall leave England until after we have been properly reunited with her parents in the spring."

On the following day, November 18, 1588, Velvet and Alex were married one last time in the same chapel at Greenwich where Skye had married Geoffrey Southwood. When the queen had learned during the tournament at Whitehall that the gown the bride would wear was the same one in which Skye had wed the *Angel Earl*, nothing would do but that the ceremony be in the same place. This necessitated a quick move by the entire court downriver to Greenwich, which was the queen's favorite palace. There at half past four o'clock in the afternoon Velvet and Alex stood before John Whitcliff, the archbishop of Canterbury, and were wed legally and lawfully for a fourth and final time.

Afterwards there was another wedding feast, this one with a wonderful wedding cake complete with a spun-sugar bride and groom atop it. Then there was a marvelous masque in which members of the court took part along with Christopher Marlowe and his company of players.

Afterwards Marlowe managed to corner Velvet, who eyed him warily. The actor-playwright laughed wickedly at her.

"Tell me, my beauty, have you kept your ideals of love, or did you marry him because you were forced to it? If it is the latter then I hope I may offer you a bit of comfort now." He grinned at her.

"I love my husband, you arrogant buffoon!" she snapped back at him. "Now let me pass, or I swear I'll set the dogs on you!"

Marlowe laughed uproariously. "Jesu, you're a hot piece! I'm sorry you'll not accept my offer, sweetheart. I'm sure both of us would benefit by the experience." Nonetheless, he stepped aside to allow her by.

Velvet and Alex were now forced to remain at court, which, fortunately, due to the onset of winter stayed in the Greenwich and London area. Robin had turned over their mother's house on the Strand to his sister and her new husband. Greenwood, he knew, was to have been part of Velvet's wedding settlement, and although he would have been happy to have the newlyweds in Lynmouth House with him and Angel, he knew the couple needed their privacy. Besides, he and his own bride were far more compatible it seemed to him. Any slight thing was apt to set Velvet and her husband to battling. Robin, like his uncle, Lord Bliss, was a man who appreciated his quiet.

On December fifth Velvet and Alex gave their first small party, a family affair to celebrate Angel's eighteenth birthday. The young countess of Lynmouth was now quite certain that she was expecting a child in the springtime, and Robin treated his wife as if she were made of delicate crystal instead of flesh and blood.

Angel bloomed beneath this treatment and even happily confided to Velvet, "Robin was so right! I have learned to love him! I love him so much that I cannot imagine what life would be without him!"

Velvet's own heart warmed at Angel's words. She loved her brother dearly and was glad of his happiness. "When do you think the babe is due?" she asked.

"Sometime in the ninth month of our marriage," Angel answered with a charming blush. Then she lowered her voice. "It must have happened on our wedding night. I only wish you the same good fortune, dearest Velvet. You will stand godmother to our son, won't you?"

"You're certain 'tis a lad you carry?" teased Velvet.

"Oh, yes!" Angel said positively. "I am most certain!"

Velvet laughed merrily, and Alex asked, "What is it, my love?"

"I cannot help but think of the surprises awaiting Mama upon her return. Our marriage, and a new grandchild from a daughter-in-law she doesn't even know she has. She will not go away and leave us soon again!"

Since All Hallows' Eve on the last day of October, London had been celebrating the winter holidays. There had been St. Martin's Day with its traditional roast goose, St. Catherine's Day to celebrate the end of the apple harvest, the queen's Armada thanksgiving, and St. Clement's Day, and December hadn't even begun. A Lord of Misrule had been appointed for every Inn of the Court in London, for every wealthy nobleman's house, and at the Tudor court itself. When Angel's birthday came as well it seemed as if every day was a feast or a festival of some kind with good food, wine, and merriment of every description.

Since it was to be the first Christmas that the two newly wedded couples had ever celebrated together it was decided that Christmas Eve would be held at Greenwood, and on Christmas Day they would adjourn across the garden to Lynmouth House. The servants employed at Greenwood decorated the house joyously, for it had been many years since one of the family had been in residence on this holiday. Some of the retainers had been there since the time when Skye had lived at Greenwood, others were their children. Happily they had hung the holly and the ivy, the bay and the laurel, in the hall of Greenwood.

The Yule log had been sent from *Queen's Malvern*, but Velvet and Alex's invitation to Dame Cecily had been refused, for, she claimed, she was too old to make the trip, and, besides, her joints would ache with the damp cold from the river.

Velvet thought differently. She is a sentimental old lady. She wants us to have our first Christmas together by ourselves and, besides, I suspect she doesn't want to leave the servants alone without their Christmas, for the holidays at *Queen's Malvern* have always been celebrated gaily.

The Yule log was dragged into the hall by the male servants, but even some of the women came boldly forward to help. The fireplace was banked in greens, and upon the mantel great candles in enormous silver holders flickered at their mates on the sideboards and tables. The log was pushed and pulled with much good-natured groaning and grunting into the center of the room. Then each member of the household, master and servants all, were invited to sit on it while singing a song to ward off any evil spirits that would prevent the log from burning. When each person in the room from Alex down to the little potboy had had a turn, ale was served to everyone and they toasted a merry Christmas along with a happy New Year.

The log was then rolled into the great fireplace, and the kindling carefully set about it. Alex took a brand and, handing it to Velvet, said, "'Tis yer house, madame. A woman is keeper of the hearth and home. It is therefore up to ye to light our first Christmas fire." Their eyes met and in his she could already see a fire burning.

Taking the brand from him, she smiled a slow smile. "May it be the first of many fires, my lord!" And then she thrust the brand into the kindling where it caught with a sharp snap.

Within minutes the Yule log was crackling brightly, and as the first orange flames shot up the chimney, the doors to Greenwood were opened to all who would come to share Christmas Eve with the Earl and Countess of BrocCairn. Yule dough and cakes, and bowls of steaming hot frumenty swimming in creamy milk and sweetened with a sugar loaf were served. Musicians hired for the celebration began to play upon pipe and reed, drum and tabor, and soon everyone was singing carols. It was one of the few times of the year that master and servant sat at the same board and ate and drank together.

Curiosity had brought a number of the villagers from Chiswick-on-Strand into Greenwood's hall that night. They well remembered Velvet's generous mother and were eager to see her daughter and to find out if that generosity had been passed on to the child.

Velvet did not disappoint them. The men were all presented with a purse containing six silver pieces; the women with a colorful bolt of cloth; and the children with little bags of brightly colored sugar candy. The poor who entered the hall that night all departed with full bellies, warm cloaks and slippers, and a purse apiece. The health of the lord and lady of Greenwood was drunk again and again.

At midnight the church bells all over England began to ring, a symbol to the devil that Christ was born and Satan was vanquished.

It had been a long evening. The villagers departed to their homes and the servants to their beds for a short rest before they must be up again to see to the running of the house. The two young couples walked through the gardens that separated Greenwood from Lynmouth House. Velvet, Robin, and Alex each carried in their arms one of Robin's little daughters who had been brought up from Devon for the holiday season. Since it was not advisable that Angel travel in her condition, she had sent for her three young stepdaughters rather than leave them alone in the care of the servants at *Lynmouth Castle*.

Angel was proving to be a doting mother. She remembered too well her own motherless childhood, and she intended that Elsbeth, Cecily, and Catherine should have a loving and caring mother in her. This new side of her sister-in-law was proving to be a revelation to Velvet, for she herself felt no such maternal longings. In time she and Alex would have children, and she would love them, but not yet.

On the terrace of Lynmouth House servants materialized to take the children, and Velvet and Alex bid Angel and Robin a good night.

As they walked back across the garden, their hands entwined, Alex spoke with longing. "They're bonny wee lasses, aren't they?"

"Aye," she answered him, for there was no doubt her nieces were pretty children.

He stopped just past their side of the low wall with its little wicket gate and, pulling her into his arms, murmured against her mouth, "Are ye certain ye're not wi' child yet, lovey?" Then his lips brushed her brow.

"Aye, Alex. Not yet. With some 'tis quick, and with others it takes time," she said feeling just the tiniest twinge of guilt for she knew well that there would be no babes just yet.

Just before the wedding ceremony at *Queen's Malvern* Daisy had spoken to her in private, and although at first her words had shocked Velvet, she had listened, fascinated.

For the first time in many years Daisy had felt at a loss as to whether or not she was doing the right thing, but thinking how upset her Mistress Skye would be upon learning of her daughter's marriage, she decided a grandchild in addition would be far too much to tolerate, and so she spoke out. "I know that this is something that your mama would tell you if she were here," she began, "but she ain't, and so I feel it my duty to do so. Years ago your Aunt Eiblin, your mother's sister that's the doctoring nun in Ireland, gave your mama the recipe for a potion that prevents you from having babes. I know you ain't too happy about this marriage—not that you don't love the earl," she hastily amended, "but I know you hoped to wait until your parents returned. I know you also wanted to be courted like a princess in a story, and I know you're far too young to be a mother right now even though your mama had your brother, Ewan, at sixteen. She was too young herself, and many's the time she's said it, though she'd not wish Master Ewan away." Daisy held out a small crystal goblet. "Drink it," she said, "and you'll be safe this night." Then she pulled back her hand. "You're not already with child, are you?"

"Nay," said Velvet, her eyes round with surprise.

"Then drink this," replied Daisy, holding the goblet out again. "I've a vial of it already made up for you and I've entrusted the recipe to Pansy with careful instructions. As long as you don't want babes, take it daily and you'll be safe. When you're ready to start your family, stop the potion and let nature take its course."

"Would Père Jean-Paul approve?" Velvet queried nervously. "I cannot think it is permitted by the holy church."

"Father Jean-Paul is a good man, but he's never borne a babe, nor is he likely to. Remember this potion was given your mama by her own sister, a holy woman. Would the good nun go against God's law, child?" Daisy counted on Velvet's innocence to win her over. If Mistress Skye disapproved when she returned, it was Pansy who had the recipe, not Velvet, and on her mother's orders Pansy would destroy the formula.

For only the briefest moment Velvet hesitated. She wanted children, but not so quickly like Angel. Marriage to Alex could be delightful if only she could be sure there would be no baby right away. So she reached out and, taking the little goblet from Daisy, drained it. Each day since then she had taken a small dose of the golden-green potion that smelled of angelica, and it had obviously worked, for her monthly flows came regularly.

"I want to put a bairn in yer belly," Alex whispered. "When I see how rich with life Angel is, and Rob's three wee girlies, I ache for a child of our own."

"'Twill be in God's own good time, my lord," she answered, hoping her guilt did not show. Dammit, must he harp so on babies?

"Aye, in God's own good time, but think of the fun we will have in the meantime trying to execute the Lord's will," he teased her, and Velvet giggled.

"Fie, my lord! Do not be sacrilegious!" she scolded him, but he heard the laughter in her voice. While she spoke she surreptitiously scooped up a handful of snow from the stone balustrade that flanked the steps to the terrace of Greenwood, and, whirling about, she pelted him with a downy snowball.

With a roar of mock outrage he fought back, pulling her back down the steps and chasing her through the garden. With a shriek, Velvet fled him, stopping every few seconds to toss handfuls of snow at him. They raced about the garden like a pair of unruly children until, attempting to make a run for the steps to the house, Velvet was caught and pulled down into the snow by her husband, who rolled her onto her back and tickled her until, giggling uncontrollably, she begged him to stop.

"Stop? Impudent wench, ye deserve much more punishment for this disrespect of yer lord and master!" Straddling her, he bent to kiss her, but Velvet turned her head aside.

"Master?" She pretended outrage. "Master, is it? Are we back to horses and dogs again? Which am I, pray, sir?"

"A kitten!" he answered quickly. "A hissing, spitting, ferocious kitten!"

"Meooow! Fssst! Kittens respond best to warmth and affection." Her emerald eyes sparkled mischievously.

"Indeed, madame?" Swinging himself off her, he pulled her up. "Then let me take this small, bedraggled kitten into the house," he murmured. "Into my bed to cuddle it and make it more amenable."

She shook her skirts free of the snow. "Purrrr!" she responded, and then she darted away from him and up the steps into the house.

With a burst of laughter he was after her, chasing her through the library, into the main hall of Greenwood, up the stairs, and down the passageway to their apartments. They burst into the rooms, startling Pansy, who had been dozing by the anteroom fire. Seated by her side upon the floor, his head in her lap, was Dugald, who leaped to his feet.

"M'lord! M'lady!" He poked at the sleepy Pansy, hissing, "Get up, lass!"

Bleary-eyed, Pansy stumbled to her feet, and Velvet realized the lateness of the hour. "Just undo me, Pansy," she said, "and then find your own bed."

Pansy nodded but said, "I'll put your gown away, m'lady. 'Twill only take a minute." She followed her mistress into her bedchamber.

The gown removed, Velvet stood in her silken undergarments thinking dreamily back on the lovely evening. Pansy fumbled at her neck and removed first her necklace and then her earbobs. Clutching the gown and the jewelry, she departed for the dressing room, to return a few moments later.

"Good night, m'lady," she said, bobbing a curtsy, "and a Merry Christmas to you!"

"Merry Christmas, Pansy!" came Velvet's reply. The door shut behind the young tiring woman, and slowly Velvet began to remove her petticoats, underblouse, shoes, and stockings, which she flung upon a chair. Naked, she walked to the small silver ewer holding the warm water that Pansy had prepared and, taking up a little cake of fragrant soap, washed her face and hands and then rinsed her teeth. In the bedroom fireplace the red-orange flames crackled sharply as a log slipped in the grate, sending up a shower of golden sparks. Velvet stretched lazily in the warmth of the room.

"Jesu, ye're beautiful!" Alex stood in the doorway that connected their two bedchambers. "I never tire of seeing ye this way, as God has created ye. Yer creamy skin, yer eyes, yer hair! 'Tis all pure perfection, lovey." He moved up behind her and, sliding his hands around her, cupped her breasts in his two hands.

The pier glass was before them, and, fascinated, Velvet watched as he caressed her. Her breasts were in perfect proportion to her size, yet as she watched him play with her it seemed as if his big hands made her appear smaller. Her nipples began to tingle with sharp sensations and shriveled into tight little love knots. The rounds of her breasts swelled under his soft, mesmerizing touch.

Velvet sighed deeply and said softly, "Don't stop, my love. I adore it when you touch me so!"

He smiled at her over her shoulder in the glass. "I'm glad ye're not one of those icy wenches who undresses in the dark and must have all the candles out," he said. "I love to pet my kitten and see her purr with pleasure." He bent his head and dropped a kiss on her smooth shoulder.

One of his hands slipped down her satiny skin and moved in a circular motion around her belly while the other remained in possession of a breast. Velvet's whole body was becoming atingle with a myriad of delightful sensations. She relaxed against her husband and, closing her eyes, murmured contentedly. His long fingers slipped to her Venus mont and, parting the plump lips, found sweet sensitivity. Velvet drew her breath in sharply as her eyes flew open. She couldn't resist looking into the mirror, and she was half-shocked, half intrigued by what she saw.

Suddenly everything in the deep, half-golden gloom of the room was richer and lusher. Her body seemed more voluptuous than she could ever remember it being. There was a tautness to her belly that gave her skin a silken sheen and belied the melting passion she felt within her. Slowly her eyes dropped to his teasing fingers, and then they widened as she saw her own flesh, pink and glistening with pearly drops of moisture. She was unexpectedly aware of his manhood, hard and insistent, pressing between her tight buttocks. Lifting her eyes, she caught her breath a second time as she saw his face dark with the hot passion he felt for her. He ceased his dalliance and, turning her about, drew her gently into his embrace, his mouth covering hers with a hungry kiss.

The pressure of his lips was hard and fierce, forcing the breath from her. She parted her own lips to catch a breath, and he invaded her mouth with his tongue. Velvet shivered but was not yet ready to give quarter. Together their tongues, those two sleek organs with seeming lives of their own, danced madly back and forth in the dark caverns of their mouths. Then, never lifting his lips from hers, he lifted her up and carried her to their bed. Gently he lowered her, his own body following hers down upon the mattress, which sagged under their combined weights. His fingers tangled in her thick hair holding her head still.

It was a fiercely passionate kiss that drained her totally of whatever will and strength she might have had. Her whole being was attuned to but one thing: to receive pleasure, and to give it.

His mouth now moved from hers to travel a route that took him to her quivering eyelids, her cheeks, her chin, her soft throat with its violently leaping pulse that told him the depth of her own passion. He let his lips linger on that pulse, kissing it softly until it quieted a small bit; then he moved onward down to her lovely breasts. With a sigh Alex took the nipple of one breast into his mouth and sucked it lovingly for several long minutes before saluting its mate as tenderly.

Velvet felt a strong tug of desire deep within her. Why was it that he could make her want him so very much? With a deep sigh of her own, she caressed his head and neck, her hand gradually moving to his shoulders then sliding down his back to fondle his buttocks. He groaned with the pleasure she gave him, and then with a fluid movement he parted her thighs and slid his loveshaft into her fevered body.

Velvet felt tears sliding down her cheeks in a totally uncontrolled fashion as he moved upon her. "I love you!" she whispered softly. "Dear God, how I love you, my wild Scots husband!"

He kissed her tears, tasting their saltiness upon his tongue, and then he took her face between his hands, saying as he did so, "I love ye, Velvet! There has never been any other woman who engaged my whole heart, and there never will be! I will always be faithful to ye, sweetheart. Always!"

Then they sought love's perfection in each other's arms, their souls as well as their bodies blending until there was nothing for either of them but the other in every moment of their love.

Christmas Day dawned with the sound of voices singing carols beneath their windows. Tousled but happy, Velvet and Alex smiled at each other and then arose from their bed, carefully sliding into the night garments that had been laid out for them but never used. Then going to the windows of their bedchamber, they flung them open and cried "Merry Christmas" to the children who were so sweetly serenading them. The children beamed delightedly at the lord and lady's approval, and then scrambled for the coppers that Alex tossed to them.

"There's cakes and ale at the kitchen door," Velvet called to the small songsters who, curtsying and bobbing bows, scampered around the side of the house and out of sight.

Alex slipped his arm about his wife and pinched her mischievously. Then he buried his face in her warm bosom, inhaling her sweet fragrance.

"Oh, no, my lord!" Velvet pushed him away. "We have services to attend in the chapel. The priest is due at eight! Would you cause a scandal?"

"Yes!" He grinned and grabbed for her.

Skillfully she evaded him. "My lord, fie! As your wife I am the moral arbitrator of this family. We will begin our Christmas properly. What would the holy man think if we are late?"

"He will undoubtedly think of the fine breakfast of brawn with mustard and Malmsey he'll receive afterwards," muttered Alex, but obedient to his young wife's wishes he repaired to his own room to dress.

Christmas dinner was the main event of the day, and it began at three in the afternoon at the Earl of Lynmouth's great mansion. The invited guests were few, consisting of the earl's newly married sister and brother-in-law; the earl's elder sister and brother-in-law, the Earl and Countess of Alcester, and their five children; Sir Walter Ralegh; and Bess Throckmorton. These last two had been invited separately, and had each managed to get their mistress's approval for their absence providing they appeared back at court in time for the dancing that night. The queen had no idea that one of her favorite gentlemen and Mistress Throckmorton would be at the same table this Christmas Day.

The meal was a lavish one consisting of several courses each preceded by music from the minstrels' gallery. They began with great platters carried into the hall by footmen, led by the Earl of Lynmouth's master of the revels. Upon the platters were seafood of all kinds: sea trout served whole and surrounded by carved lemons and garnished with chervil; sole in a sauce of eggs, heavy cream, and dill; prawns that had been steamed in white wine and stuffed with lobster; a great oaken tub filled with ice and, amid the ice, oysters ready to crack open and eat whole. There was an enormous side of rare beef that was brought in and placed on the sideboard to be carved by an underchef; several fine hams; succulent capons stuffed with dried fruit; an enormous turkey stuffed with both oysters and chestnuts; a pheasant, roasted whole with all its feathers replaced and served on a golden platter; several large pies, one of rabbit, one of pigeon, one of goose, each wheeled in upon its own specially made cart as they were far too large to be carried by hand. There were bowls of carrots glazed in honey, peas cooked with leeks, and lettuces steamed in wine. There was fine white bread, butter, and salt aplenty, but the highlight of the meal was the bringing in of the boar's head.

The honor of carrying in the beast had been given to young Henry Edwardes, Willow's eldest son. One day, Robin thought after he had very much pleased his eldest sister by his choice, I shall have my own son to delegate this task to, but for now Henry will more than do. Proudly, the lad, his father's young image, came forth, led by the master of the revels and preceded by musicians and songsters. Upon a huge silver salver, almost too large for the boy, rested the boar's head, crowned and garlanded with laurel leaves and rosemary, a lemon in its mouth to suggest plenty. At Henry's entrance the assembled family arose from the table singing:

"*Caput apri defero,*
Reddens laudes domino.
The boar's head in hand bring I,
Bedecked with bays and rosemary;
I pray you all sing merrily,
Quot estis in convivio . . .

Then, set in its place of honor on the board, the boar's head was greeted with much cheering.

The Earl of Lynmouth and his guests ate heartily and drank deeply of fine Archambault wines. Even so, the leftovers would easily feed all the beggars who came to his door that night and feed them generously at that, especially when the servants' leftovers were added.

When the last course of wine-soaked cakes, rich custards, fruit tarts, candied angelica, rose petals, and violets, sweet biscuits, and Malmsey was cleared from the board, the Christmas mummers were let into the hall to perform the time-honored play with St. George, the Saracen, and the Dragon. Along with the three major performers were lesser ones, consisting of Father Christmas with his holly bough, a doctor to cure the "wounds," a handsome young boy carrying a wassail bowl, and a pretty little girl with warm brown eyes and golden brown hair who carried the mistletoe.

The children, Willow's five and Robin's three, were enchanted by the rather simple performance. Bess Throckmorton turned and smiled at Walter Ralegh who, free of royal restraint, gazed passionately back at her.

"It is almost like my childhood at home," she said wistfully.

"And do you find it preferable to your life at court, Bess?" he asked.

She sighed. "At court, or so I am told, I serve the best interests of my family who have ever been in service to the crown. I love the queen, my mistress, but that does not mean I do not long for a simpler life in the country, a husband, children, and my own hearth. That life I should prefer to the court." Then she smiled sadly. "I am, however, past my prime in the marriage mart, and, lacking a dowry, who will have me?"

"I would have you, Bess," he declared softly. "I have more than enough wealth for us both!"

"And how long would you have it, Walter, should you cease to be Her Majesty's loyal and loving knight?" she asked.

"I would not be the cause of your downfall, not after all you have done to gain your position."

"She forgave Leicester."

"Robert Dudley was, as we all know, a special case, Walter. They shared the same birthdate and had been friends since childhood. In the days when the queen was but the Princess Elizabeth and sent by her sister, Mary, to the tower, it was Robert Dudley, also imprisoned, who spent his own small hoard of silver to make her life more bearable by bribing the guards to bring her small luxuries such as firewood so that she might be warm. She loved Dudley, truly loved him. I believe she would have forgiven him anything, Walter, but the rest of us are vulnerable to her wrath. 'Tis a fine compliment you have paid me nonetheless, and I shall always cherish it."

"I love you, Bess," he said quietly.

Elizabeth Throckmorton blushed becomingly. "I love you, Walter," she replied as softly, then she turned from him to watch the children, who were now engaged in a game of shoe-the-mare amid much giggling and scampering.

Robert Southwood sought out Walter Ralegh. "I hope you do not mind the simplicity with which we are celebrating," he said with a smile as he watched the children. "Angel did so want you and Bess to share our Christmas, but unlike many of my station I prefer a family gathering."

Walter Ralegh smiled back, nodding. "Both Bess and I were just saying how we missed the simpler times. I hear, however, that you will revive a custom of your late father's and hold a great Twelfth Night masque for the court in the new year."

"Aye! The queen requested it, and I cannot refuse her. Afterwards, however, I shall attempt to withdraw from the society of the court until after my wife has been delivered in the spring. It is her first child, and I am told she must have quiet. If it is possible, we shall try to return home to Devon so that the baby may be born at *Lynmouth*."

As the hour grew late, the children were all taken away to their beds and the musicians began to play a lilting lavolta.

The Earl of Lynmouth led his wife into the center of the hall, and they began to dance. They were joined by the others in quick order, but when the lavolta ended and a Spanish canary was played, Angel retired from the floor, the lively jig being too much for her in her current state. Finally as Christmas Day slipped nearer to St. Stephen's Day the evening drew to a close.

Sir Walter Ralegh and Mistress Throckmorton had taken their leave earlier, both mindful of their duties to the queen. Willow and her husband were staying at Lynmouth House for the next few days, but Velvet and Alex now made their way across the snowy garden, both well satisfied with their first Christmas together.

Once again within their chamber Alex spoke lovingly to his wife. "There has been no time today for us to exchange gifts, lovey. Look beneath yer pillow."

Velvet's green eyes grew round with anticipation, and she flew across the bedchamber to their bed. Slipping her hand beneath the plump pillows, she drew forth a flat, white leather jeweler's case that opened to reveal a magnificent necklace of diamonds and rubies, the center stone in the piece being a heart-shaped jewel of a deep red hue. "Oh, Alex!" She lifted the necklace from its nest of white satin and held it up to the light. "Oh, Alex!"

He chuckled with delight. "I am pleased to have finally rendered ye speechless, Velvet. May I assume then that ye like it?"

"Oh, yes, my lord! I love it! I adore it! It is the most beautiful thing I have ever possessed!" Still clutching her present, she flung herself at him and hugged him.

His arms slid about her, and he breathed in the warm scent of her elusive perfume. His face buried itself in the fragrant hollow of her neck and shoulder, and he sighed. "Dammit, lass, I do love ye so! I never knew that love would be so all-consuming, but by God I don't regret a moment of it! In fact I despise myself for being such an arrogant fool that I missed all those years with ye."

Velvet nestled against Alex's shoulder, her heart filled with a new and wonderful warmth. So this was love, she thought. It was not an unpleasant feeling. It was, in fact, most tolerable. She sighed happily as he drew her closer.

Alex's face, which had been a study in all-consuming passion, now took on an expression of amusement. He wondered what she was thinking and came close to the truth. He felt his heart expanding within his chest until he thought it would burst with the incredible depth of his feeling for this woman. Jesu, how he loved her! Still, it would do her no good to know his full emotions. Women who were too sure of their men often became unruly. Best to end this soft moment before he said something further he would have cause to regret. He spoke with a nonchalant tone.

"Have ye nothing for me, lass?"

"Oh, Lord!" she exclaimed. "I do!" She ran across the room. Flinging open a large chest by the door, she bent down and lifted out a muffled object. Pulling the cloth wrappings from the seemingly bulky lump, she triumphantly unveiled a small painting. Turning the carved and gilded wooden frame about, she revealed the subject, herself in her mother's creamy silken wedding gown.

Alex stared in surprise, his jaw slack. "How?" he demanded. "How could this be? There hasn't been time!" His eyes devoured the portrait delightedly.

Velvet smiled triumphantly. "It is by Master Hilliard," she said proudly. "He did my miniature when I first came to court. It was to be a Christmas gift for my parents. When we returned to court from Scotland, I went to him and begged him to re-create from the miniature a larger painting that I might give you for Christmas. He doesn't often do full portraits, Alex. 'Tis quite an honor. He copied the head from the original, and then I sat for him twice in the gown so that he might, as he put it, rough it all in. After that I simply left the garment and he copied the details from it. You never guessed, did you?" she crowed delightedly.

He turned from the painting a moment to look at her. "Nay, lass, I never suspected."

It was a wonderful painting, he thought as he looked again upon his wife's portrait. She stood flanked on one side by two of his setters, her slender hand resting on one of the dog's heads. Her other hand was at waist level and held a small, ornate gold pomander ball. Velvet stared straight out from the canvas, her jeweled green eyes clear with the innocence of her youth, yet curious; in fact, very much as he remembered her when they had first met only several months ago. She was not really smiling, and yet the corners of her mouth were faintly turned up as if any minute she would burst into laughter. She seemed to be hugging some secret to herself that she had absolutely no intention of sharing with anyone, and her expression told the viewer that she delighted with her private knowledge. The background of the painting was a simple blue sky, but as Alex looked more closely at the picture he noticed in the lower left-hand corner, on the Turkey carpet that his wife stood upon, a badger wearing a bejeweled collar.

She saw his eyes widen and chuckled softly. "Am I not the badger's wife, Alex?" she teased him.

"Badgers dinna have wives, they have mates, and 'tis a certainty that ye're mine, Velvet," came his reply.

"Aye," she drawled. "I am yours, but you are also mine, my lord. Four times have I pledged my fidelity to you in various marriage ceremonies, but as I have pledged my faith and loyalty to you, so have you pledged yours to me. Remember it well should you be tempted to stray from my bed, my lord. I will tolerate no slight upon my honor."

He stared at her, astounded. "What in hell has made ye say a thing like that?" he demanded, outraged not only by her words, but by the threatening tone she seemed to use.

"Angel tells me that Robin has been forced to include Lord and Lady de Boult on his guest list for the Twelfth Night masque. Lord de Boult has recently done the queen some small but vital service and stands in her favor at the moment. To exclude them from the masque would be insulting."

"Ye think I would accost the lady publicly?" His tone was dangerously low.

"She was once your mistress," Velvet said sharply.

"Never!" He spat out the word with equal ire, his eyes dark with his outrage.

"Never?" she looked doubtful.

"Never, madame! 'Twas done only to make ye jealous, but never did I bed that viper! How dare ye presume that I did, and how dare ye presume that now wed to ye I would renew such a liaison had there ever been one in the first place!"

"I will accept your word, Alex, that naught took place between you and Lady de Boult, but you must admit that you played the lover well before me, and as I recall our first marriage took place because I found you with your hands all over the bitch in the queen's gardens! What was I supposed to think, pray, my lord? If I have offended you, I beg your pardon, but I could not know that you were not really involved with that creature!"

"Whether I was or not, for ye to dare to set conditions for my conduct is inexcusable, madame!" he shouted.

"Indeed, sir? Do you not attempt to set standards for my conduct?"

"Ye're my wife!"

"You're my husband!"

Suddenly the incongruity of the situation hit him and he began to laugh. "I think we're back to horses and dogs again," he chortled.

"Villain!" She laughed back. "Dear God, Alex, what a proud pair of peacocks we are! I wonder if there will ever be peace between us?"

"I dinna mind the little battles, lassie," he murmured softly and, reaching out, drew her back into his arms. Nuzzling her fragrant hair, he kissed the top of her head and said, "I dinna mind the battles for I so enjoy the peace-making."

Velvet felt her bones turning soft with his words. She felt warm and safe in the haven of his arms. Perhaps this marriage business would work out after all. They loved each other, and she was wise enough to know that he was a good man for all his pigheaded ways. She smiled to herself. For all her pigheaded ways, too, for the truth of the matter was that she was no better than he. Slipping her arms about his neck, she murmured huskily, "'Tis cold in here, my lord. Shall we repair to our bed to negotiate this latest treaty?"

Wordlessly, he swept her up, walked across the bedchamber, and pulling back the covers, tucked her beneath them before joining her. They spent the night in heavy bargaining, but when the dawn finally came both the Earl of BrocCairn and his countess were well satisfied with the results of their dickering.

Chapter 7

The new year of Our Lord fifteen hundred and eighty-nine was ushered in with relief in England. No longer did the threat of the Armada hang over Elizabeth Tudor's realm.

The queen and her court looked forward eagerly to the Earl and Countess of Lynmouth's Twelfth Night masque. It had been over twenty years since Lynmouth House on the Strand had opened its doors to the festivities made so famous by Robin's late father, Geoffrey Southwood.

Angel, just beginning to thicken slightly at the waistline, had appealed to her sisters-in-law to help her with the many preparations. The young countess, having been raised at court, knew exactly what needed be be done, but such an enormous undertaking required several cool heads. Willow, whose approval of Angel grew daily, was delighted and threw herself into the melee with enthusiasm. Velvet, on the other hand, was as untried a hostess as Angel, and far more interested in what she would wear than all the many tasks to be done in order to entertain the queen and the other guests.

"You'd best pay attention to all of this," the Countess of Alcester scolded her youngest sister. "After all, you may be called upon to entertain King James once you're in Scotland."

"Their court isn't as formal," responded Velvet.

"Does that mean you'll forget your upbringing?" Willow looked shocked. "Mama may be Irish, but she never forgets that she bears an English title, and she behaves accordingly."

"Mama behaves as it pleases her to behave." Velvet laughed. "You can't deny it, sister. Even the queen says it!"

Willow harrumphed, but the corners of her mouth twitched with private amusement. She always wondered how it was that she, the daughter of an Irish rebel and a Spanish nobleman, had turned into such a proper Englishwoman. Then she remembered her own upbringing, which had been overseen for the most part by Dame Cecily. Her poor mother with her adventurous life had had very little to do with Willow despite the fact that Skye adored her firstborn daughter. There had been a strong bond between Dame Cecily and Willow from her birth, and Skye, loving her daughter enough to want what was best for her, had given Willow over to the childless Englishwoman who loved the girl as if she were her own.

Willow looked at her sister again. Sweet, spoilt Velvet, who had been so very much loved and so dearly cosseted by both her parents, was really far too young to be a wife. She had no real sense of responsibility, but there was no malice in her at all. Well, Willow thought, she's not a stupid girl. She'll learn quickly. Then she said, "Tell me about your costumes. You first, Angel, for you're the hostess. Lord, how I remember Mama's gowns and Geoffrey's elegance. No one could ever learn what they were to wear in advance, and then the following year there would be at least half a dozen imitations of their previous year's costumes." She laughed at the memory.

Angel smiled. "Robin is to come as the sun, and I shall be his sky. My gown is the most exquisite shade of blue!"

Willow clapped her hands delightedly. "Perfect!" she said. "Blue is definitely your color, Angel." She turned to her sister. "What of you, Velvet? What will be your costume?"

"Nay, you first," countered Velvet. "I can well imagine how James feels about a costume masque, being more a country gentleman than a courtier."

Willow nodded ruefully. "Aye, 'tis true, but I have managed to persuade him, and he has given in with good grace to me. I shall come as a perfect English spring day, and James will come as a perfect English spring night."

"What does a perfect English spring night wear?" Velvet giggled.

"Black velvet," came the practical reply. "James's doublet, however, will be sewn with silver thread, pearls, and small diamonds in a design of stars and the moon."

"How clever you are!" exclaimed Angel.

"Aye," agreed Willow. "The very simplicity of the costume was what decided him. One has to know how to handle a man. It is all really quite easy."

"Depending upon the man," said Velvet. "Now your James and certainly our brother, Robin, are biddable men. But my lord Gordon is surely the most stubborn male ever created by our Lord God. He refuses to wear any silly folderol, as he has put it to me. He says he will wear his plaid instead, as he suspects that none of the queen's court will have seen full Highland regalia. That is the best I can do with him. He is impossible."

"What will you come as then, Velvet?" said Angel.

Velvet smiled mischievously. "I shall be fire," she replied. "Blazing, furious fire! I have had it planned for weeks, of course, and knowing it, Alex presented me with the most marvelous necklace and earbobs of rubies for New Year's. Every woman in court will envy me, my dears, perhaps even the queen herself!"

"He's most generous, isn't he?" noted Willow. "Diamonds and rubies for Christmas, and now more rubies for New Year's. It would seem you're a woman who inspires jewelry, like Mama."

For a moment Velvet's face grew somber. "I do miss Mama, Willow! Will this winter never end? How I look forward to the spring and the return of my parents! There is so much that has happened since they left for the Indies two years ago. There is so much I have to tell them, to share with them. Is it really so childish to love one's parents as I do, Willow?"

Willow put a comforting arm about her sister. "Nay, Velvet. I suppose it seems strange to the rest of us because we never had both of our parents around for very long. Do you realize that you're the only one of Skye O'Malley's children to grow up with her always nearby? And you're the only one who has grown up with both a mother and a father. If your devotion to your parents seems excessive to us, perhaps that's the reason why. When we were growing up we were lucky to have Mama to ourselves for any period of time. You've had her your whole life. Of course you're close to her, Velvet, and even if you're Alex's wife that closeness will remain, but you must accept the responsibilities of womanhood now. Why you could be a mother yourself within the year!" She kissed her sister's cheek. "What color is your gown?"

"Colors, Willow, not color! 'Twill be all the colors of the fire. Scarlet and red and gold and orange! Wait until you see! 'Tis most original!"

It sounded rather vulgar to Willow. Scarlet and red and gold and orange? Even a gypsy wouldn't dare such gaudiness, and with Velvet's auburn hair, too! Still, it was the girl's first elegant masque. If her costume wasn't quite as marvelous as the others, then she would be disappointed for certain, but she was quick and would learn from her unfortunate experience, thought Willow.

On the night of the masque, however, Willow had to revise her opinion of her youngest sister's taste.

The three women met in the main hall of Lynmouth to compare gowns. Angel was pure perfection in a sky blue silk creation: the skirt's center panel was sewn with pearls and moonstones to create the effect of puffy white clouds. Here and there, scattered across the blue silk, were small jeweled pins fashioned to represent birds in flight. Angel's golden blond hair was hidden beneath a headdress of fluffy white lawn and lace that represented a large cloud that was topped by a multicolored jeweled rainbow glittering with rubies, emeralds, topazes, amethyst, and peridots. Since her neckline was high and no skin was exposed, it was not necessary that she wear a necklace.

By her side stood Robin, resplendent in a costume of cloth of gold and twinkling with golden beryls. Atop his head was a large headdress fashioned like a sunburst. Looking at him, Willow couldn't ever remember her late stepfather, Geoffrey Southwood, looking more resplendent.

Willow had come, according to her word, garbed as the perfect English spring day. Her gown was of spring-green satin, the center panel of the skirt a meadowful of colorful yellow and white flowers. Across her skirt gamboled small silver lambs, and in her dark hair rested a small, golden bird's nest complete with a bejeweled inhabitant. By her side stood her husband dressed, as she had said, in black velvet.

Alex, true to his word, had come decked out in his full Highland dress, his one concession to the festivities the golden mask on a gilt wand that was carried by all the guests. It was Velvet, however, who caused gasps from her sister and sister-in-law. She had indeed come dressed as fire, but not garbed as the other women in full dress. Velvet had instead chosen to wear a wild assortment of flowing draperies whose rather savage hues of scarlet, red, gold, and orange flowed and blended themselves so cleverly that it was difficult to decide where one ended and another began. About her neck glittered her fiery ruby necklace, and from her ears bobbed the matching earrings.

"You can't be seen like that!" protested Willow. "'Tis the most indecent costume that I've ever seen. Blessed Mother! You can see your legs!"

"Don't be such an old woman, Willow," retorted Velvet. "I'm wearing scarlet silk stockings." She held out a rather shapely red leg. "See!" Her garters, covered in twinkling red garnets, flashed wickedly.

"That's worse!" shrieked Willow.

"I can't be fire in a gown over vertingale and hip bolsters, Willow. It would have been far too awkward. Fire must leap and flow gracefully."

"I think she looks rather original," said Robin, his lime-green eyes sparkling with amusement. "I certainly have no objection to her costume, and I must assume, Alex, that you have no objections either, else we would not see Velvet here before us now in her delightful garb."

Alex let his eyes slide lazily and appreciatively over his wife. "She's more covered than ye are, Willow, with yer rather low neckline."

"Indeed," said the Earl of Alcester, looking pointedly down his wife's décolletage. "Besides, I think Velvet looks rather fetching."

Willow threw up her hands in despair. "I cannot imagine what the queen will say," she fussed, and then drawing her lips together in a severe line grew silent.

The queen, however, was enchanted by the originality of Velvet's costume and praised her greatly. There wasn't a gentleman at court who didn't agree with Her Majesty's entirely astute judgment, and Alex found his temper sorely tried on far too many occasions that evening. The women were divided between those who agreed with the queen and those who hid their jealousy behind disapproving frowns and pretenses of shock at the Countess of BrocCairn's outrageous garb.

Mary de Boult was one of the latter. She had come dressed as an English rose, but had chosen a dusky pink for her gown, and not until it was too late had she realized that the deep color rendered her milky skin sallow. She would have been far better off had she chosen the clear pink her dressmaker had tried to press upon her. Added to this was the fact that her gown lacked originality—there were at least two dozen other roses in the room—and Lady de Boult's unhappiness was complete, particularly in the face of Velvet's much-talked-about costume.

"I am appalled that Lord Gordon would allow his wife to appear in such an outlandish garb, but then he's naught but a rude and savage Scot," she said spitefully.

The Earl of Essex turned and fixed the lady with a rather fierce look. "Madame," he said, "I fear that your disappointment stems rather from the fact that Alexander Gordon used you to bring Velvet around. But then how could he have possibly had any serious interest in you when he was betrothed to her?"

Mary de Boult gaped, struck dumb by the insult, but before she could reply, Essex had turned away from her, and the few people who had been gathered about her melted away with mumbled excuses. Angry and ashamed, she vowed vengeance. Essex had been right. Alex had used her. He was the most exciting man she had ever known, but he didn't know that she was alive. He had simply used her to gain his own ends. She hadn't even been able to bring him to her bed, an unheard-of thing in her experience. Men were ever eager to get into her bed. He would pay! God's bones, he would pay dearly! And that proud, arrogant bitch he was married to would pay as well!

Mary de Boult sought out her husband. "Take me home," she commanded him. "I am ill."

Clifford de Boult was some twenty years older than his wife. His first wife had died childless after some fifteen years of marriage, and he had had no illusions about Mary when he had married her. She had been fifteen at the time and came from a large family. He had noted that she was quite healthy, and he had hoped she would prove fecund, which she quickly did, birthing him four healthy children in four years. He now had three sons and a daughter. She had done her part, and now he did his by allowing her to spend a portion of each year with the court and turning a blind eye to her little flirtations as long as they were discreet. He had not, he believed, been made a cuckold by his wife, and he would have called out any man he believed had had intimate knowledge of his Mary, for in his own way he loved her.

Bending, he inquired solicitously of her, "What is the matter, my dear?"

"My head aches unbearably with all this noise and the stink of the fireplaces," she whined. "You'd think Lynmouth's fireplaces would draw better."

He had not noticed any excess smoke and had thought that, quite to the contrary, the ballroom was quite well ventilated. Still, it was not like Mary to leave a good time, and so he could only assume that she was telling the truth. "I will beg the queen's leave for us to withdraw," he said and hurried off.

Mary de Boult looked across the room to where Alexander Gordon stood next to his wife. The open look of love on the earl's face as he bent to speak to Velvet made Mary almost physically ill, so great was her jealousy. Why should he be so happy when he had made her so miserable? she fumed bitterly. Her hatred rose, almost choking her, and she whispered to herself, "I wish you were dead, Alexander Gordon! I wish you were dead!"

Velvet shivered suddenly.

"Are ye cold, sweetheart?" Alex inquired worriedly. "Those silks ye're wearing cannot be very warm."

"Nay, Alex. 'Twas just a rabbit hopping across my grave." She was puzzled herself. For the briefest moment she had felt some terrible, fierce hatred directed toward herself and Alex, and, looking around, she had seen no one who might be their enemy. She shook off the anxiety and concentrated on having a good time. Was she not the highlight of this evening, the center of attention? There wasn't a person in the room this night who hadn't either admired or disapproved of her costume.

The queen did not leave Lynmouth House until the first pale light of dawn was beginning to gray the skies over London. She had danced every dance that evening, eaten of the finest food, and drunk the best French wines. Elizabeth Tudor felt more relaxed and at peace with the world than she had felt in many months. She had even, for a few brief moments that evening, not missed her Dudley.

The young earl's Twelfth Night masque was declared an enormous success by all who had attended it, and even Robin himself admitted to having had a good time. So much so that he had promised the queen that from now on he would continue his late father's custom of keeping Twelfth Night. Well-satisfied, Elizabeth Tudor had stepped into her barge and, waving gaily, departed.

Now began another round of fêtes and parties prior to the beginning of the Lenten season. Feeling better than she had felt in weeks, Angel persuaded Robin to remain in London at least until Candlemas, and perhaps beyond. The Earl of Lynmouth, his beautiful wife, and his sisters became a familiar sight at all of the galas.

Velvet could not ever remember being happier. It was true that she and Alex still quarreled over the slightest thing, but she sometimes wondered if they both remained stubborn only because their reconciliations were so wonderfully passionate. Yes, she was very happy and certainly not prepared for the sudden arrival home of her brother Murrough O'Flaherty.

Murrough was the second of Skye O'Malley's children and perhaps the one most like her, for as much as he loved his wife and children he also loved a good adventure. He had spent his early years in Ireland, and later followed the Tudor court where he had been a page to Geraldine FitzGerald Clinton, the Countess of Lincoln. Growing bored with it, and realizing that with no lands of his own or title he could not go very far at court, he had asked his mother to send him to Oxford where he studied diligently both there and later at the university in Paris where his father had studied. No one had been more surprised than Skye when Murrough announced his intentions of going to sea.

Taken in hand by his mother's best captains, he had shown a true O'Malley talent for the sea. By the time Murrough reached the age of twenty-five he had his own ship, and was one of Skye and Robbie Small's most trusted captains.

"Of them all, he's the only true O'Malley you spawned," old Sean MacGuire, Skye's senior captain, had observed to her.

Murrough's had been one of the eight vessels accompanying Skye and Adam to the Indies. Now suddenly he was back, sailing not into his home port of Plymouth, but up the Thames into the pool of London itself. By chance, one of the Earl of Lynmouth's retainers was on the docks seeking a ship with oranges, for Angel craved them desperately. Recognizing the *Sea Hawk* and her master, the earl's man spoke to Murrough.

"Welcome home, Captain! The earl is in London at his house along with the lord and lady of Alcester, the lady Velvet and her bridegroom, the Scotsman. Shall I tell my lord that you'll be coming?"

Murrough's brain only registered that Robin and two of his sisters were here. "Do you have a horse, man?" he demanded of the servant.

"Aye, Captain. Over there. The bay with the Lynmouth livery."

"I'll need the loan of her," Murrough replied, and without even waiting for an answer he hurried over to the animal and, mounting it, rode swiftly away.

Only when he was on his way did the words spoken by his brother's servant penetrate his mind. "The lady Velvet and her bridegroom, the Scotsman." Velvet married? When had that happened, and what would her parents have to say when they learned about it? He hurried the horse along the river road. It was early, and fortunately there were few people out and about as it was a raw and chilly day. Lynmouth House finally came into view, and he barely acknowledged the greeting of the gatekeeper as he galloped his mount through and up the driveway.

"Welcome home, Captain," said the majordomo, hurrying forward as he entered the house. "His lordship is not up yet, but I shall inform him that you're here."

"Don't bother," came Murrough's quick reply as he ran up the staircase. "I know my way to Robin's apartments."

"But, Captain . . ." The majordomo's voice trailed off as Murrough disappeared at the top of the stairs.

"Captain O'Flaherty!" Robin's valet bowed briefly as Murrough came through the door of the earl's apartment. "Welcome home, sir."

"Thank you, Kipp. Is his lordship still abed?"

"Aye, sir. 'Twas rather a late night."

Murrough only chuckled. He put his hand on the bedchamber door.

"Captain!" Kipp looked uncomfortable. "His lordship isn't alone."

A smile split Murrough's face. "I would hope not, Kipp!" He flung open the door and, striding in, called loudly, "Robin, you slugabed! Up with you now, and let's have a look at the lass you've spent the night debauching." Walking over to the bed, Murrough yanked back the bedcovers.

With a roar the Earl of Lynmouth leaped from his bed. Angel shrieked loudly and sought to cover herself. Murrough's startled gaze took in her condition, her blond beauty, and the wedding ring on her finger. Then his brother hit him. "Ouch!" grunted Murrough, rubbing his jaw. "Is that any way to greet me, you young pup?"

Robin was now on his feet, and he stared at the big, shaggy man who stood before him. "Murrough? Is it you? Jesu, man, you gave us a start!"

"Did you think it was her husband then?" Murrough chortled.

"*I'm* her husband, you randy old seadog!" The earl laughed. "You've been away too long, big brother. I was wed last August by the queen's own chaplain and in Her Majesty's presence. This is my wife, Angel."

Murrough O'Flaherty had the decency to look abashed, and he actually blushed. "Madame," he began, "I do beg your pardon."

Angel's beautiful face was serious. "I do not know if I shall ever forgive you, sir," she said, but her eyes were dancing with merriment, and, unable to restrain herself, she giggled mischievously, which turned Murrough's woebegone expression back to a merry one.

"Oh, brother, I can see I shall have to get you aside so that you may tell me all about my husband's bachelor adventures. Welcome home, Murrough O'Flaherty! Your sisters have told me much about you, but I can see that they don't know the half of it!"

Murrough laughed. "Nay, madame, they don't! Nor my good wife either! When is the babe due, for I can see my little brother has done his duty well by you."

"In May," she replied, and Murrough raised his eyebrows. "You didn't wait, did you, Rob?"

"For what?" came Robin's laughing reply, and then the earl turned serious. "Murrough, what are you doing home? Are Mother and Adam with you?"

"Nay, Rob, and that is why I sought you out first when I learned you were in London. I had originally planned to go to the queen, but now that I think on it 'tis better we make our own plans before speaking with Her Majesty. Mother and Adam are being held captive by the Portuguese viceroy in Bombay. The only reason they aren't dead is that they can pay a fat ransom to the Portuguese, and Mother made a huge fuss as well about the fact that she and Adam are members of the holy mother church. She made it sound like our uncle Michael O'Malley is about to be elected the next pope. The viceroy is surrounded by Jesuits, y'know, and the Jesuits are far too clever and political to offend a high churchman. Besides, they'll get a goodly share of the ransom for their missionary work in India."

"Can the viceroy be trusted to release Mother and Adam unharmed once we pay the ransom?" Robin asked.

"From what I could see of the viceroy, he's a snake of the lowest order," Murrough remarked, "but the Jesuits are honest enough as long as the ransom is paid." Here Murrough allowed himself a small chuckle. "Mother's piety is quite something to behold, Rob. I never knew she even possessed a rosary, and yet it is most visible on her person in Bombay, and she never misses an opportunity to finger it publicly. The viceroy's chaplain is both enchanted and fascinated by both her and her beauty."

"Is she all right, Murrough?"

"Aye, and quite in her element, too, little brother. I do believe she has been pining all these years for another high adventure, and none of us ever knew it. As for Adam, he's ten years younger in appearance. They have lived the quiet life for Velvet's sake, but I believe now that it was only for her that they gave up the sea."

Robert Southwood smiled fondly for a moment, and then he was all business. "How much ransom are the Portuguese demanding?"

"Fortunately, they have no real idea of mother's wealth," Murrough replied. "They want two hundred and fifty thousand coins' worth of pure gold in exchange for her, Adam, and their ship. They also don't realize there were other vessels in our fleet, for only Mother's ship and mine entered Bombay harbor. Our original destination was the mughal's port of Cambay to the north, but we were blown off course by a storm and Mother's ship was damaged slightly. We needed water, too. The others in the fleet stayed several miles off the coast with orders to remain there until they were given the signal that it was safe to come ashore. Mother has sent them on now under Robbie Small, who has friends among the East Indies sultans. They should be able to obtain their spices in the islands, and the trip will be worthwhile for us even if we were not able to accomplish the queen's mission."

"The queen did not expect to meet with success this time, but she and Mother felt it was worth a try at least. The important thing now is that we get Mother, Adam, and our ships back safely," said Robin.

Murrough nodded, then asked, "What is this I hear of Velvet's marriage? I thought the child was not to be wed until after her sixteenth birthday, which, if I recall aright, isn't until this spring."

"Lord Gordon suddenly found himself the only direct male in his family line due to the sudden death of both his father and younger brother. He found it necessary to come to England to claim Velvet a year early. Unfortunately, no one had bothered to remind Velvet that she had a betrothed husband. And Mother had been filling her head for years with tales of going to court."

Murrough chuckled, imagining his little sister's outrage, and his chuckles grew into delighted laughter as Robin continued the tale, particularly when he told of the four weddings the couple had had.

"Of course," said Robin, gazing over at his wife who sat up in their bed, the coverlet to her chin, her blond curls peeking adorably from beneath her lace-edged nightcap with its silk ribbons, "had Velvet not come to court I should have never met my beloved Angel."

She beamed at her husband.

"I would say then that you owe our willful little sister a great debt, Robin," observed Murrough, and then he stood up. "I must get me to court now and tell the queen of what has happened. It is Whitehall at this time of year, isn't it?"

"Aye, and, Murrough, return here afterwards, for I will not keep this secret from our sisters. Both Willow and Velvet are here in London. Velvet in particular must know, for the queen, believing Mother would return this spring, ordered Alex to remain here until she came so that she and Adam might give their official blessing to the marriage. Now it will be at least twelve months or more depending on wind and tide, before we will see Mother and Adam; Alex will not want to stay in England for that long a time. He has been away from his lands almost a year and he will want to go home. The queen will understand that, but it will take some doing to convince Velvet of her duty. She far prefers life at court with all its divertissements and amusements to the thought of being a proper wife and mother."

"She is very young, my lord," Angel defended her friend. "You must not forget that her parents sheltered her so much that she knew little of life before she came to court last May. She is merely making up for lost time, and once she has had her fill of fun she will settle down and be an admirable mate for Alex. Besides, he loves her deeply."

"No man is really content to wait for sons," came Robin's reply.

"You have waited," Angel said calmly.

"You have assured me that it is a son you carry, madame," teased Robin.

"And so it is," she proclaimed, "yet you have three daughters already, my lord." She turned to Murrough. "Now, my newly met brother, how long will you be in London?"

Murrough considered. "The ship has to be revictualed before I can return to India and the ransom collected from the goldsmiths. I must have a complete change of crew, for the men with me have been at sea two years now and need more shore time than I can give them. But I must be gone within two weeks, else I will not be able to make the Indian Ocean crossing as the winds will be against me. There is a certain time when one can come easily around the horn of Africa and travel northeast across the Indian Ocean to Bombay; and there is a certain time when one can travel back. At all other times the winds are unfavorable."

"We will expect you for the evening meal then," said Angel, "and I hope you'll make this your home ashore while you're in London. It would please me greatly."

Murrough moved to the bedside and, taking Angel's hand, kissed it graciously. "Thank you," he said simply, and then with a nod to his brother he was gone from the apartment.

Murrough O'Flaherty was supplied with a fresh mount and rode for Whitehall where he found Lord Burghley, and through his good offices was admitted to Elizabeth Tudor's presence almost immediately. Bowing first, he then knelt before the queen.

"Rise, Captain O'Flaherty," she said, "and tell us your news." She seated herself in a high-back chair and waited.

Murrough outlined what had happened, and the queen's face darkened with outrage.

William Cecil, standing by her side, grew grim, but remained silent until the captain had ended his tale. Then he said, "There can be no question of our allowing so much gold out of England."

"The decision is not yours, m'lord," snapped Murrough. "It is O'Malley gold, not English gold. It has been earned by us, and it is ours to do with as we wish. I might say to you that had we not agreed to do the queen this service my mother and stepfather would not at this moment be in such a position, and there would be no need for us to use our gold for ransom. This venture has cost England not a penny piece, but it has cost us dearly." Murrough's fair face was flushed above his dark beard.

"Madame," responded Burghley, "I must protest Captain O'Flaherty's logic. That gold could be used against us in future wars by the papists!"

"Bah!" Murrough countered furiously. "Half of it will go directly into the viceroy's own pockets, and the rest the Jesuits will use to continue their campaign of conversion amongst the natives. The Portuguese government will never see one gold piece. Were Lisbon aware of our presence in Bombay, they would have seen us all executed and our ships confiscated. They want only one thing, total control over the East Indian trade."

"He is right," said the queen. "Lisbon knows nothing of their viceroy's activities."

"Then let us protest to them!"

"No, my lord," Elizabeth chided Burghley. "They must not be made aware of our presence in what they consider their private pond. This mission has failed, but there will be others, and eventually we will succeed. One day the riches of the Indies will be ours. Now, however, our paramount wish is to get Lord and Lady de Marisco safely home to England." She turned to Murrough and smiled. "I only wish that we could help with the ransom, Captain O'Flaherty, but the expenses in defeating Spain's mighty Armada last summer were great, and it will be several years before our treasury recovers."

"I rejoice with you, madame, in beating King Philip's might," Murrough said, "and I fully understand your position. You have all of England to consider. You need not worry though, for we will be able to manage the ransom demanded ourselves."

The queen smiled and held out her hand for him to kiss, which he did. "Then go with God, Murrough O'Flaherty," she said, "and return home safely with your mother and her husband. You have both our permission and our blessing."

"Thank you, madame," was his reply, and Murrough bowed and backed his way out of the queen's chamber.

"Two hundred and fifty thousand coins' worth of pure gold!" exclaimed Lord Burghley disgustedly when the door had shut behind the captain. "Do you know what we could do with that money, madame?"

"She is my friend," said Elizabeth Tudor quietly.

"That Irish bitch?" exploded William Cecil. "How many times has she defied you, and fought you, madame?"

"Aye, William," the queen said calmly, "she has indeed defied me and fought me over the years, but never, my lord, *never* has Skye O'Malley betrayed me. Not once, and 'tis certainly more than I can say for my own conduct with regards to her."

"You are England's queen, madame, and your conduct as such has always been above reproach," came his answer.

"Aye," the queen agreed, "but there are few people other than yourself, my dear *Spirit*, whose conduct and code of morals is steady and never-changing. Skye O'Malley is one of those people. She did not have to put either herself or her ships in jeopardy in order to gain a toehold in India for England, but when I asked her to she agreed to try."

"She would have gained greatly by it," Lord Burghley said sourly.

"But there was the greater chance that she would lose, William, and indeed she has. This venture has cost her dearly, but it shall not cost her her life or the life of her husband. I will speak no more on it!"

William Cecil, Lord Burghley, clamped his lips shut. Ever since Dudley's death the queen had grown sentimental, and at the damndest times. He would wager that Lady de Marisco, left to her own clever devices, would escape quite handily from the Portuguese, and without the loss of all that gold to England's economy. Skye O'Malley wasn't a woman to sit idle.

Murrough O'Flaherty, making his way back to his brother's home, would have agreed with the queen's closest confidant. Ever since his youngest sibling's birth his mother had been content to remain at home, which was totally unlike her. Murrough admired Skye, and now that Velvet was married and settled he expected to see Skye take complete charge of the O'Malley empire again.

"Murrough!" Willow hurried toward him with outstretched arms.

"Murrough!"

Jesu! Was that exquisite beauty really Velvet? The two women hugged him warmly and planted wet kisses on his ruddy cheeks. A burst of contentment ran through him, and he hugged them back, one arm around a supple waist and the other around one less supple, but comfortable. "Damn me if you're not a pretty pair of pigeons to come home to, my darlings!"

"Have you been home yet to Joan and the children?" his elder sister demanded.

"Nay, Willow, I came directly to London, for I have news of Mother and Adam."

"Are they long behind you?" Willow demanded. "We did not expect them until spring."

Robin appeared at the top of the main staircase. "Come up," he said, "and Murrough shall give you the news at once."

Realizing that his brother didn't want him to speak until they were all together, Murrough mounted the stairs with his two sisters. Entering Robin's library, he saw his brother-in-law, James Edwardes, the Earl of Alcester, and another man who Robin quickly introduced as Velvet's husband, Alex Gordon, the Earl of BrocCairn. Alex's handclasp was firm and his gaze unwavering. Murrough liked the look of him.

"Now tell us your news!" Velvet demanded impatiently as she settled herself in a chair by the fire.

"Aye," said Willow, for once echoing her younger sister. "Tell us of Mother and Adam. Were they well when you last left them? And what of Uncle Robbie?"

Calmly, Murrough explained the situation as he had left it, and was relieved to see that neither of his sisters fell into a swoon.

"How long before you leave?" Willow asked bluntly when he had finished.

"Two weeks at the most," was his reply.

"How long is the passage to India?" Velvet was more to the point.

"Several months, depending upon the winds."

She nodded. "Robin should have at least one child and another started by the time Mama and Papa get back."

"And what of us?" demanded Alex.

"'Twill be as God wills it, my lord," said Velvet airily, and he scowled.

"Is the money a problem?" Robin asked. "Did the queen offer to aid us any?"

Murrough laughed. "The queen apologized for her purse, which she claims is empty from the expense of the Armada victory. Lord Burghley tried to prevent our ransoming Mother and Adam on the excuse that the loss of our monies to the Portuguese dons could hurt the English economy. The queen refused his reasoning and wished me Godspeed. Don't fear, Rob. We can well afford the gold though I hate to see it go to the viceroy."

"No one must know," said Robin.

"Of course," agreed Murrough.

"Why?" questioned Velvet.

"If word got out as to the amount of gold our ships are carrying, we would be a prime target for pirates. There are many miles of water between London and Bombay. We must travel in a small fleet, in a tight formation, without hailing any other vessel before we reach our destination. We'll be transporting several thousand pounds of gold in five ships. Even one of those ships would be a tempting prize. That, Velvet, is why no one must know."

"In that case I can only hope no one saw you at Whitehall," remarked Willow.

Murrough laughed. "Only the queen and Lord Burghley. 'Twas too early in the morning for the high and mighty to be up and about. Besides, the fact that I am back is no reason for anyone to be suspicious. It looks like I simply came ahead."

"You will get them home safely, won't you, Murrough?" Velvet's voice was slightly unsteady. "The Portuguese won't harm Mama and Papa before you return with the ransom?"

"If I know Mother, Velvet, she will have wagered some mad bet with the viceroy and won back every penny of the ransom before I arrive. Do not fear, little sister. The viceroy is only interested in becoming a wealthy man. Harming Mother and Adam would gain him nothing. They may sail beneath an English flag, but they are Catholics. There is no reason to harm them. By this time next year our family will be back together, I promise you!"

She believed him. He was Murrough, her Murrough, the big brother who had carried her on his shoulders when she was a wee girl. This was the brother who had sneaked sweetmeats into her bed when she had been sent to her room supperless for some long-forgotten infraction. Murrough had never failed her, and Velvet knew that he wouldn't now.

In the next few days Murrough set in motion the revictualizing of his ship and the provisioning of the ships that would accompany him. The gold that was secretly brought from goldsmiths in three different countries would be placed aboard at the last possible minute, hidden among the trading cargo that was even now being placed in conspicuous locations on the O'Malley-Small docks in order to allay any suspicions. All the captains and the crews involved in the mission were handpicked and trustworthy. Murrough was pleased to discover that his own crew didn't want to be replaced. Despite their many months at sea and their short stay at home, they had begun to love this adventure, and to a man they were determined to finish it. Once everything was well underway, Murrough departed for Devon to visit his wife and children.

Although she was concerned for her parents, Velvet knew now that come spring Alex would request the queen's permission to return to *Dun Broc*. Under the circumstances she suspected that the queen would give him that permission. Velvet might get Alex to remain in England until her sixteenth birthday on May 1, but she knew that soon after that they would be on their way. So she would have only a few months more at court, and the Lenten season would shortly be upon them with its fasting and prayers. There would be no gaiety or parties during the six weeks between Ash Wednesday and Easter. She debated the wisdom of allowing Alex to get her with child now, but discarded the notion for she knew it meant a great deal to him that his heir be born at *Dun Broc*. Better to wait until they returned to Scotland than to attempt pregnancy now and force Alex to remain in England until the baby was born.

There was to be a final masque on Shrove Tuesday night at court.

"On the morrow 'twill be fish and ashes," mourned Essex, and the queen rapped him sharply on the knuckles with her fan.

"Fie, sire!" she scolded. "A six-week penance will do you no harm, and I've no doubt that come Easter Sunday you'll begin to make up for lost time!"

The queen had ordered that the ladies come to the masque garbed in either silver or gold, the gentlemen in red or black. The celebration would end precisely at midnight. Until then there would be music and dancing and feasting at Her Majesty's expense.

"What will you do in the next six weeks?" Angel asked Velvet as they lunched on the day of the masque. "We are leaving for *Lynmouth* tomorrow. My health is excellent, and Robin feels that if we travel slowly there will be no danger to the baby. Surely you don't mean to stay in London. 'Twill be so dull!"

Before Velvet could answer, Alex broke into their conversation. "We are leaving for Scotland in several days' time," he said quietly.

"Scotland!" Both Velvet and Angel gasped, and then Velvet cried, "'Tis winter! The roads will be terrible, if not im-

passable! I did not think we would leave until after Easter, my lord."

"I have been away from my lands ten months now, Velvet. I have an enormous group of retainers that is costing me a fortune to feed and house here in London. They are restless, and restless men grow troublesome. They long for their homes and families. It may be cold, but the roads are passable here in England. I cannot say what they will be like in Scotland, but we are going to try to get through. With luck we will be at *Dun Broc* within the month. I have already asked the queen's permission. Yer parents will not be back for a full year or more. With luck we can greet them with a fine grandson."

"Which is just as it should be!" said Willow briskly. "Why James and I are for Alcester once Lent begins. With your permission, brother Alex, we shall ride with you. For once I'll have no fear of getting home safely, for no one will even consider trifling with that wild-looking band of Highlanders who owe you loyalty. If you wish the hospitality of *Hill House* before traveling on, you're most welcome to it."

"I'm most happy to have you travel with us, Willow," responded Alex courteously. "As for yer hospitality, we shall see. If the weather is good we shall press on without delay."

"When did you intend to tell me of your plans, my lord?" said Velvet. Her voice was ominously calm at first, then it began to rise angrily. "Tonight is the queen's masque, and then how many days was I to be allowed to pack up my life before being dragged into the wintry Highlands? Or perhaps, my lord, you meant to drag me off again with nothing but the shift on my back as you did the last time we traveled north together!"

"Ye don't need to take everything ye own now," Alex replied foolishly. "Pansy can pack the rest and come in the spring."

"What?" Velvet shrieked. "First you propose to deprive me of my family, then my clothing and personal effects, and now my tiring woman! Is it that you have duplicated everything at that Highland stone heap you call a castle? Have you a maid waiting then for me who can speak the queen's English to keep me company, or will I be faced with some half-savage girl who'll not understand me, nor I her? I'll not go! If you're so anxious to return to Scotland, then go yourself, but you'll go without me if I cannot have the time to pack my things and if I cannot have my own tiring woman!"

"Will ye disobey me then, Velvet?" he shouted back at her, and everyone in the room jumped at the threatening tone in his voice.

"Is it the horses and dogs again, Alex?" she demanded, hands upon her hips.

He glowered blackly at her, and then Robin spoke. "You cannot expect my sister to go to her new home without her own things and servants about her, Alex. How soon do you want to leave?"

"Within the week."

"Plenty of time," soothed Robin, "for Pansy and my servants to pack everything up for transport. Can you use my traveling coach?"

"As far as Edinburgh," muttered Alex.

"Excellent!" enthused Robin. "Velvet and Pansy will be most comfortable and well-rested for the ride from Edinburgh to *Dun Broc*. It's settled then, eh?" He looked at his sister and brother-in-law.

"Well," said Willow, "I for one will be delighted to ride to *Hill House* in your fine coach, Robin. You've never offered it to me, and 'tis the best-sprung vehicle I've ever ridden in. But how will you and Angel get home?"

"We are leaving tomorrow," came Robin's reply. "There will be time enough for the coach to get us to *Lynmouth*, and then return to London for you and Alex and Velvet."

"In that case," said Velvet sweetly, "I shall be quite content to leave for Scotland." She smiled mischievously at her husband.

"Ye'll drive me mad, woman, if I don't kill ye first," Alex grumbled at her darkly.

"Have you grown tired then of the making-up?" she murmured.

Alex's eyes suddenly grew warm again, and his mouth, which had been compressed into a thin, angry line, softened. Crossing the space that separated them, he swept her up laughingly and walked from the room carrying his precious burden. Behind him he heard the gasps of surprise from Willow and Angel and the indulgent chuckles of his two brothers-in-law.

Velvet nuzzled her husband's ear as he exited Lynmouth House and moved across the garden that partitioned it from their own house, Greenwood. He stumbled a little as she nibbled thoughtfully on his tender earlobe.

"Wanton," he growled. "Ye're naught but a shameless wanton."

"And you'd have me no other way, my lord," she whispered boldly as he entered their house and mounted the stairs to their private apartments. Two young housemaids dusting in the hallway gaped, stunned, after them. Velvet ran her tongue around the shell of his ear, and he shuddered.

"I'll drop ye," he threatened, but she only laughed.

"Nay, you won't, Alex. You're too hot to take your pleasure with me and too much the gentleman to do it here before the servants." She blew softly into his ear.

"Ye're as hot to fuck as I am," he muttered thickly, kicking their bedchamber door open and entering the room.

"Aye, my lord," she drawled slowly, "I am."

He put her down and, hooking his fingers into her low-cut bodice, yanked the fabric downward, tearing her gown away to bare her breasts. Pushing her back upon their bed, he deftly tossed her skirts up with one hand while loosening his own clothes with the other. Then, falling atop her, his mouth found a tender and tempting nipple. Slowly his tongue encircled it while his left hand imprisoned her hands above her head, and his right hand found the sensitive little jewel of her womanliness. Gently he stroked it, his mouth all the while suckling her breast. Beneath him, Velvet quivered with excitement, loving his touch and his insistent lips on her nipple.

"Aye, ye're naught but a shameless strumpet," he muttered against her flesh, "and were I not sure 'twas I who took yer maidenhead, I should wonder about yer unseemly eagerness. Knowing the truth, however, I can only assume yer wild passion for me is the cause."

Velvet laughed low. "Aye, my lord, but I wonder if my passion will ever be satisfied with all your talk. Ahhhhh! Oh, Alex, yessss!"

His mouth descended on hers as he thrust deep within her warm sweetness. He moved upon her with maddening slowness, teasing her lovingly until Velvet sank her teeth into his muscular shoulder to ease some of her swiftly roused passion.

"Vixen! My hot, honeyed little vixen," he crooned.

Amid the tangle of her bunched-up skirts, she strove to meet his every downward stroke. She almost laughed remembering how fearful she had been of this marvelous part of marriage. Then she wondered if all women craved the loving their husbands gave them or if she were indeed the wanton he teased her about being. But suddenly it didn't matter, for she was being swept up in the powerful and magnificent storm that their lovemaking created. With a soft cry she clung fiercely to him as their rapture built in intensity until finally the raging fire between them hurled both Alex and Velvet into an exquisite world of perfect pleasure from which neither was anxious to return too quickly.

"Ah, lass," he finally said, "never will there ever be another woman for me but thee. I adore ye!"

"And I thee, my lord husband, my beloved lover!" she responded.

They lay quietly for a time, entwined together upon their bed. The shadows of late afternoon lengthened, and soon the room was dim. Finally Velvet said softly, "'Tis another gown you owe me, my lord, and I'll have it before we return to Scotland."

He laughed lazily. "Ye're well worth the price of a new gown, lass." Then he leaned over her and kissed her bared breasts again with slow, warm kisses.

Velvet felt a delicious tingle race down her spine, but then she caught at his hair and pulled his head away. "Oh, no, Alex! You're forgetting the queen's masque!"

"To hell with the queen's masque," he muttered and captured a pert nipple between his teeth, worrying it gently.

"No! No!" she fussed at him, laughing now and helpless in the face of her own rising desires.

"Yes," he insisted. "We've time for one more sweet tumble, madame, before I must dress myself in some silly fanciful garb and dance the evening away simply to amuse an aging queen."

"Alex! You must not speak so against the queen!"

"Aye, lass, ye're right," he said, and blew softly in her ear as his strong hands caressed her breasts and moved down to stroke her silken belly. Then his mouth found hers once more in kiss after long, sweet kiss until Velvet's lips ached with his loving. His body hovered over hers but a moment and then he was entering her gently.

She sighed deeply, her hands frantically clutching his back as he moved upon her. She could feel him within her, loving her fiercely and strongly, his hardness fanning a fire that raged totally out of control. The queen's majesty, the queen's masque, the coming trip to Scotland were all forgotten in the midst of their passion.

Once again Alex and Velvet lay together sated with their love, but this time a knock came upon the door. "My lady! My lady!" called Pansy. "I must bring the bath or else you will be late."

"That bloody wench has no proper sense of timing or of decency," grumbled Alex. "If Dugald weren't so taken with her I should leave her behind!"

"Nay," said Velvet, laughing, "you wouldn't. She means much to me, and well you know it." She sat up. "Quickly, Alex, help me get out of the ruins you've made of my gown. Pansy will be far less shocked to see me in a chamber robe at this time of day than to witness the tatters you've made of my bodice."

Alex made a noise that to his wife sounded as if he were quite pleased with this afternoon's work and not in the least repentent. With swift hands he undid her gown, his fingers teasing mischievously, and chortled gleefully as she frowned at him and slapped his hands away.

"Where shall we hide it?" He grinned at her, holding up the rags that had been her gown.

Velvet looked frantically about the room, and then, leaping off the bed, she stuffed the unfortunate garment into a small trunk by the window. Then, turning, she grinned saucily at him. "I'll give it to the sewing woman tomorrow so that she may repair it if that's possible." She laughed again, seeing the dangerous look smoldering in his eyes as he gazed upon her nudity.

"Put something on this instant and let Pansy into the room, lass, or I'll not be responsible for my actions!" he threatened.

"The bath water is here," called Pansy through the door.

Velvet opened another small trunk and drew forth a chamber robe. "Open the door, Alex," she said. Her beautiful green eyes were sparkling with mirth, and he gritted his teeth in frustration, for he found to his amazement that despite their two couplings he wanted her once again.

With a gusty sigh, he crossed the room and opened the door to admit Pansy and several footmen who came in bearing jars of hot water for his wife's bath. There was no way for him to avoid taking her to court tonight. It was the last of the pre-Lenten festivities and after midnight all would be fasting and solemnity for the next six weeks. He grimaced. The queen, sharp-eyed female that she was, would know precisely who came and who did not. Since he had already obtained her gracious permission to remove his wife to Scotland before Easter, Alex knew he was bound to put in an appearance tonight with Velvet by his side. The queen could rescind her permission as easily as she had given it.

"Is my lady the only one to get hot water?" he growled surlily at the footmen and then stamped off into his own bedchamber.

Her tub filled to the brim and its warm steam smelling sweetly of gillyflowers, Velvet removed her chamber robe once the footmen had departed and settled herself daintily in, sighing happily.

"Did you get your tub, my lord?" she inquired of him in sugared tones through the open door that connected their rooms.

"I got what hot water was left over, and 'twas precious little at that, but 'twill serve, madame," he responded sourly.

"My tub is simply delicious." Velvet purred. "I think I shall soak awhile." She splashed delicately and sighed noisily.

"No soaking!" His voice was outraged. There was but three inches of water in his own tub, and he was already chilled. "We'll be late if ye soak, and ye know how Her Majesty dislikes tardiness. I'll not get on her bad side now!"

"If we're late," teased Velvet, "I shall tell Her Majesty 'twas all your fault, *and* I shall tell her just how you kept me dallying the afternoon away, my lord."

He laughed aloud, his mirth warm with the memory of their long and lovely afternoon of lovemaking. "If ye tell on us, madame, we'll never be allowed back at Elizabeth Tudor's court again. Are ye prepared to spend yer lifetime at *Dun Broc?* Not, mind ye, that I should mind that."

Velvet returned his laughter. "God, no!" she said with deep feeling.

"Then I suggest, madame," he replied with a chuckle, "that ye hurry yerself or else prepare to spend a lifetime in the Highlands."

Pansy grinned at her mistress conspiratorily, and Velvet chuckled as her tiring woman bent to scrub her back. Two little undermaids fussed and bustled about the room laying out the clothing that their lady would wear tonight. Her silken, lace-trimmed underthings, exquisitely perfumed, were spread upon the bed. Her silk stockings, in a gold-and-silver diamond pattern, were carefully placed next to her petticoats. Lastly her gown was brought forth and laid across a chair. It was a magnificent confection of cloth of silver and silver lace. The bodice was sewn all over with transparent green amber in a pattern of waving ferns and butterflies, and the sleeves of the gown were lush with silver lace.

Velvet stepped from her tub and was enveloped in a large bath sheet. Seating herself next to the fire, she sat patiently while the two little undermaids dried her and Pansy brushed her dark auburn hair with a perfumed brush. Then she arose and was dressed by the three servants. Bending, she drew her garters up each leg, admiring the large silver butterflies with the green antennae on each.

"Ain't they shockingly wonderful!" enthused Pansy. "'Tis almost a pity you can't show them."

"Only to his lordship if I plan to get us safely to *Dun Broc.*" She looked at her tiring woman. "Do you mind that we will live in Scotland, Pansy? Our new home is to be deep in the country far from the Stewart court. 'Twill be most dull, I've not a doubt. Perhaps you would prefer to remain in service here in England."

"Nay, m'lady! Like you I'm used to the country, having grown up at *Queen's Malvern* with you. London is exciting, I'll admit, but I prefer a quieter, more stable life. Dugald is seeking me hand in marriage, and he's a good man. I couldn't do better."

"I would hope that you love him if you would marry him, Pansy," said Velvet softly.

Pansy smiled happily. "Aye," she admitted. "I love the rogue!" Then she turned on the two undermaids. "Speak a word of what I've said this evening, and you'll not live to see the spring, either of you! I'll not have that Dugald knowing all me feelings!"

Both of the two other servant girls nodded vigorously in agreement with Pansy. "Aye," said the one called Sarah. "It don't do for a man to get too sure of you. I'll speak nay a word, Mistress Pansy, and neither will Millie. Will you, Millie?" The girl named Millie shook her head. "Nay," she said. "I'll not chatter."

Velvet was now ready for her gown to be put on, and Pansy spoke sharply to the others. "Don't stand there dawdling! Bring m'lady's dress this instant!"

The gown was brought, and within a few moments Velvet stood gazing at her reflection in the tall pier glass. Her costume, she decided, was a triumph, and she preened, a small smile upon her face. Her breasts were dangerously close to bursting over the silver lace that edged her bodice. About her neck and spilling onto her chest was a magnificent necklace of transparent green amber and yellow diamonds that had matching earbobs. Pansy had brushed Velvet's hair back so that it hung loose down her back, and above her left ear the maid affixed an arrangement of silver roses.

"M'lady, your jewel case," said Pansy, holding open a box filled with rings.

Velvet paused a moment, thinking that this time last year she had nothing in the way of jewels, and now she was the proud possessor of several cases of necklaces, earbobs, bracelets, rings, pins, and various other geegaws. Alex enjoyed showering her with beautiful jewels. Then, a tiny frown of concentration between her brows, she chose several rings: a yellow diamond, an emerald, a violet-blue spinel, and a large creamy pearl. She quickly slipped these on her elegant fingers.

"Madame, ye're magnificent!"

She turned to find that her husband had entered the room. He was garbed in red velvet from his head to his toes, his doublet embroidered with gold beads in a geometric pattern.

"You, milord, are also magnificent!" She returned his compliment with feeling, thinking how damnably handsome he was and how very much she had grown to love him.

"'Tis a pity we must go, isn't it?" he teased her, his amber eyes warm with love.

Velvet sighed. "Aye, 'tis a pity, but 'twould be a greater pity to disappoint my godmother, the queen, who has been so very loving and good to us both." Her eyes were modestly downcast, and he chuckled at her demure demeanor.

"Very well, madame, then go we must, but 'twill be on yer head if I have a dull evening."

"Then I need not fear, milord, for you never have dull evenings. We shall be at court but a few minutes before you'll be totally surrounded by giggling, giddy women who barely tolerate my existence. I have watched you, sir, and you become like a pampered, fat tomcat under such attention. Nay, 'twill be no dull evening for you!"

"Nor ye either, madame," he countered. "If I am surrounded by the ladies, ye're as quickly surrounded by the men."

She laughed merrily, knowing his jealousy. Pansy placed a full-length cloth-of-silver cape lined in sable about her mistress as Dugald came through the connecting door with his master's cape and bonnet. Then together the Earl and Countess of BrocCairn departed for Greenwich in their comfortable barge, for although it was cold, the river was not yet frozen over and a channel was open. Fur robes were tucked about them, and hot bricks wrapped in flannel were placed at their feet.

Velvet loved traveling on the river, and she settled back comfortably as their barge glided along. The sun had just sunk, and slightly to their right they were treated to the magnificent orange-and-gold traces of the winter sunset above which, in the darkening evening sky, shone one clear, pristine star. The Thames flowed calmly about them, smooth and dark, for it was that short period between the ebb and flood tides, and the BrocCairn barge cleaved the waters neatly, leaving virtually no wake behind it. There was no wind at all, and wrapped snugly beneath the fur robes neither of the Gordons felt the February cold.

"Are ye still distressed about leaving for Scotland?" he asked her quietly.

"Nay, not really," she answered. "It is true that I wanted to see my parents before we left England, but since they arranged our marriage in the first place, they can have no objections that we have wed in their absence. Besides"—and here a small smile played at the corners of Velvet's mouth—"'tis past time we had a child, milord, don't you think?"

His mouth fell open in surprise at this sudden change in her attitude. "Dammit, lass, isn't that what I've been saying all along to ye?" he demanded.

"Aye, milord, but then it wouldn't do for the heir of BrocCairn to be born in England, would it?"

"Once again, madame," he grumbled at her, "ye drive me to the point of violence. Tell me, though, ye're sure now about not waiting for yer parents?"

"I have thought long on it, Alex," she said, "and I have decided that if they are still spry enough to travel thousands of miles to India, then Scotland will be but a tiny trip for them to make in order to see us and our children." Her gloved hand slipped into his and she squeezed it. Then she turned her head and, gazing up at him, smiled happily. "I think I am beginning to grow up, Alex, and I want to go home."

He felt a lump deep in the base of his throat, which he quickly swallowed back. At the same time he felt great relief surge through his entire being. He wanted her to love Scotland, and most of all he wanted her to love *Dun Broc*, which would be her home from now on. He loved her too much to have been able to bear the thought of her being unhappy. Now it seemed that his prayers had been answered.

He also had the strong urge to put her over his knee and spank her bottom until it was pink. She had driven him mad with her stubbornness these past months, ever since their very first meeting. All this emotion was very visible in his face, and Velvet, gazing adoringly at her husband, couldn't restrain the tiny giggle that slipped forth.

"Lass, ye try me sorely," he growled low at her, "but damn me if I don't love ye to the point of distraction."

"I seem to be afflicted with the same malaise, milord. Besides, London out of season is dreadfully dull, I am told."

He laughed, unable to contain himself. "So, Velvet de Marisco Gordon, Countess of BrocCairn, ye go adventuring to Scotland to ease yer boredom, do ye?"

"And my curiosity," she teased him back. "Ever since you arrived in England last spring, Alex, you've been anxious to return to your precious Scotland, even to the point of kidnapping me! I am curious to see what lies beyond Edinburgh that draws you so."

"*Dun Broc* is what draws me, lass, and I hope ye'll love it! Ah, Velvet, my love, the forested mountains surround us, and the castle perches like a gyrfalcon on the crest of a high hill. Even on days when there are mists in the glen below, the heights on which we stand are clear, for *Dun Broc* soars with the eagles!"

She felt a small thrill run through her at his words, for his deep love of his home was so obvious. "I am sure I will love it, Alex," she said sincerely. "How can I not, for it was from *Dun Broc* that you sprang and from *Dun Broc* that you came into my life."

She loved him! With a sudden burst of clarity it penetrated his bemused brain. She really loved him! She actually loved him! His head dipped to find her sweet, sweet lips, and they kissed passionately for a long, tender moment.

As their mouths parted he gazed deeply into her emerald eyes, and Velvet realized that now he finally knew and understood her heart, which came close to bursting with her gladness. For the life of her she couldn't comprehend why she had been resisting him all these months.

"Greenwich, milord," their bargeman called, and ahead of them they could see the gaily twinkling lights of the palace.

"Ye'll miss it," he said softly.

"Aye," she conceded, "I'll miss it, but we'll come back someday when our children are grown enough for us to leave them safely, Alex. My home, I am realizing, is where you are, my love. Yes, I am most certainly growing up!"

"So am I," he answered her with a grin.

Their barge slipped into the long line of other vessels waiting to land at the royal quay. In the darkness of early evening it was not possible to recognize the occupants of the other boats despite the lanterns that bobbed from them all. At one point a new arrival attempted to push its way in before the BrocCairn barge.

"Make way for Lord de Boult," snapped a surly-looking waterman.

"The Earl and Countess of BrocCairn give way only to the queen herself," countered the Gordons' bargeman. "Get to the end of the line and wait your turn!" He punctuated his remarks by shoving the offending vessel with his oar.

About them the other bargemen lined up on the side of the earl's man, equally annoyed at the pushiness of Lord de Boult's servant.

"'Ere now, move to the rear!"

"Aye! Who the 'ell is Lord de Boult next to my Lord Lincoln?" roared the Earl of Lincoln's man.

There was more outrage voiced by the various servants of the waiting barges, some of them not at all kind, and with a mumbled oath the offending bargeman moved his boat to the end of the line.

Within a few minutes the Earl and Countess of BrocCairn landed and, climbing from their vessel, moved up the stairs to the palace of Greenwich, where the queen's Shrove Tuesday fête had already begun. They could hear the musicians tuning up their instruments, and as they entered the building they were surrounded by their friends who had been awaiting them.

"Aha!" cried Essex, "at long last. What kept you?" He was dressed in black velvet, and his doublet twinkled with diamonds.

"Need you ask?" Ralegh chuckled, equally resplendent in a red doublet sewn with sparkling garnets and gold beads.

"Walter!" chided Bess Throckmorton, her dark blond beauty enhanced by her gold brocade gown, the fabric of which had been Velvet's Twelfth Night gift to her. But Velvet only laughed.

"The marriage bed, Sir Walter, is one of the nicest prerogatives of wedded life should you ever decide to try it." She looked but for an instant at her friend, who blushed furiously.

"Come along," Bess said, in an attempt to cover her embarrassment. "The queen has already been asking for you both, and I was sent to fetch you to her the moment you arrived."

Gaily, they followed the queen's favorite Maid of Honor, trooping up the stairs to where the festivities were noisily in progress. Elizabeth Tudor was ensconced in a large, carved, gilt throne that sat atop a small carpeted dais. She was magnificently gowned in a dress of white velvet with cloth-of-silver stripes sewn all over with diamonds, pearls, and small golden bows. About her neck was a necklace made of six strands of perfectly matched pink pearls with an emerald clasp. Upon her head was a wig of the fieriest hue of bright red. Her gray-black eyes were sparkling with pleasure, and as she spoke she used her beautiful hands with their long, beringed fingers gracefully to punctuate her point. Seeing Velvet and Alex, she smiled warmly and gestured for them to approach her, which they did, moving easily between the rows of chattering courtiers. Reaching the dais, the Earl and Countess of BrocCairn made a respectful obeisance to the monarch.

The queen stood, then shouted over the din, "*Silence!* We would speak and have everyone hear what it is we have to say." The room quieted, even the musicians falling silent. The queen smiled, well pleased at them all. If she had taught them one thing over the years, it was obedience to her will. "Tomorrow," she began, "is the start of the penitential season, and shortly thereafter my dearest godchild, Velvet, will depart with her husband for their home in Scotland. Since it is to be hoped that my goddaughter, once in her new home, will do her duty by her husband. . ." Here the queen paused, and there were several loud, appreciative chuckles from those present. "It is not likely that we will see them again for several years, for *Dun Broc* is many long miles from London. *Queen's Malvern*, where Velvet grew up, was a grant from my own estates to Adam de Marisco. Since he has no son to carry on his line, we would have it known that upon his death the estate of *Queen's Malvern* is to be deeded to Alexander Gordon, the Earl of BrocCairn, and his heirs forever. This is my gift to you both, for I love you well."

Velvet's eyes filled with tears of pleasure. To know that someday *Queen's Malvern* would be hers and her children's was almost too much to bear. She wished her parents not one moment less time on earth than God ordained for them, but in preparing to leave England for the north she had felt so cut off. Now the queen had remedied that feeling as if she had known exactly what Velvet was thinking. The young Countess of BrocCairn fell to her knees. Taking the hem of the queen's gown, she raised it to her lips and kissed it. "Thank you, madame," she said, her voice thick with emotion. She could say no more.

Elizabeth bent and raised the girl up, her own eyes wet with honest tears. Pulling a silken scrap from her sleeve, she wiped her godchild's cheeks. "There now, child, I but sought to please you."

"Oh, you have, gracious madame! You have!"

"It is a most generous gift, indeed, Majesty," said Alex, who had finally found his voice.

The queen shot him an amused look. "It is unlikely that we shall have heirs of our own body," she said with great understatement. "Perhaps someday the son of my traitorous cousin, Mary Stewart, will inherit this throne." She smiled coldly. *"Perhaps.* If that should be the case, then it cannot hurt for you to have English estates, my lord. It cannot hurt you at all."

"Nay." He nodded gravely. "It canna hurt me, madame."

"We intend to live a long life"—the queen chuckled—"and we have no doubt that Adam de Marisco and his wife will also live long. It may be many years until you come into your inheritance, sir. Many years, indeed."

"But when I do," said Alex with great deftness, "I will remember with respect and affection England's great queen, Elizabeth Tudor."

"Hah!" chortled the queen. "God's nightshirt, what a waste! You should stay here at court, Alex Gordon, for you've a courtier's tongue in your head for certain. You could go far. Aye, you could!"

"The queen is most gracious," replied Alex, "but with all due respect to ye, and to yer court, I long for the hills of my home."

Elizabeth smiled. "I understand," she said quietly. "You love your *Dun Broc* as I love my Greenwich. I let no one deny me my home, and I shall not deny you yours, my lord. Our permission for you to go stands. Go safely with God, but return to us with your wife in time."

Alex bowed low and, taking the queen's hand, kissed it.

The queen's eyes sparkled again. "Now away with you, sir, and enjoy the evening! There are several pairs of eyes that have not left your person since you entered the room. Bold, immoral wenches, they are. Are you jealous, Velvet?"

"Nay, madame, for my lord gives me no cause. I weep for these ladies, for unlike an Eastern sultana, I cannot find it in my heart to share my husband."

The queen laughed once more, for she was in high good humor this evening. "Methinks somehow that my lord BrocCairn has all he can handle in you, my child!"

"Aye, madame, and that's a truth," came Velvet's mischievous reply, and she curtsied prettily to the queen. Then, taking her husband's arm, she moved out into the room again.

"You're a bold jade," said Sir Walter Ralegh as he moved to join them. Bess had returned to her place by her mistress's side, as had the handsome Earl of Essex.

"The better to breed up bold sons, sirrah!" came Velvet's pert reply.

Ralegh grinned and thought how very much Velvet had changed in the eight months since she had joined the court. The musicians began to play a spritely country dance, and as quick as a wink he claimed Velvet from under Alex's surprised nose. Slipping his arm about her waist, he skillfully wove her into the figure and they were swiftly gone.

With a chuckle Alex made his way back to the queen's dais. Asking and receiving her permission, he partnered Mistress Throckmorton in the dance as the queen went merrily off with Lord Essex.

Although the evening was scheduled to end at midnight with the entire court gathering in the queen's chapel to receive ashes, it seemed as if the masque fête would never end. The musicians played with great liveliness and almost without stopping. Toward mid-evening the dining-room doors were thrown open, and the guests were treated to a huge buffet that had been set up for their pleasure.

The royal cooks, painfully aware of the six weeks to follow, had outdone themselves in their preparation of the feast. There were sides of beef, lamb, venison, stag, and boar. There were game birds: ducks, swans, and peacocks, these last two with their feathers restored to them; as well as partridges, quails, pigeons, and larks. There were capons roasted to a golden, juicy turn and geese, succulent and browned—both with their stuffings of dried fruits bursting from them. There were large pies of rabbit and songbirds; whole suckling pigs with lemons in their mouths set on golden platters filled with cress; large pink hams; barrels of icy oysters from the North Sea; whole salmons; and dishes of prawns, some prepared in white wine and others broiled simply in butter with herbs. There were bowls of beets and carrots, platters of baby lettuce steamed in wine, great loaves of fresh baked breads, and cheeses: great wheels of Derby, Stilton, and Cheddar from the surrounding countryside, and soft, subtle Brie from France.

On a separate table rested all manner of sweets for the queen's guests. There were colored jellies in various shapes, cakes soaked in sweet wine, great fruit tarts with bowls of clotted cream, sugar wafers, marzipan, bowls of winter apples and pears, and firm golden oranges from Seville. The wines; a heady, dark red Burgundy and a fruity pale golden wine, flowed in a never-ending stream from the silver pitchers of the royal footmen.

The queen's guests streamed in and out of the dining rooms, helping themselves to the bounty spread before them. They ate with great concentration, stuffing the various foods into their mouths as if the fasting was to last forever rather than a simple forty days' time. The dancing had stopped temporarily, and Elizabeth Tudor sat easily on her gilt throne with its red velvet cushion, watching through hooded eyelids her court as they feasted to excess.

There was a faint smile upon her lips, but whether it bespoke merely amusement or scorn even the most observant could not tell. Many were now falling prey to the excellent wine the queen served, and there was some slight evidence of drunkenness among several of the courtiers. Elizabeth watched it all.

It pleased her immensely that the marriage she had permitted between her royal ward, Angel Christman, and Robert Southwood, the Earl of Lynmouth, was a happy one. The young countess, now visibly enceinte beneath her gown, was radiantly happy, for her husband was obviously deeply in love with her. The queen's mouth softened a little. There, at least, her instinct had been correct. How she would have loved to experience such happiness herself, but she had realized early on in her life that if a man was given the upper hand over a woman he could destroy her in either body, mind, or spirit, if not in all three. The world demanded that one pay for one's weakness of character. She had learned that lesson young. Still, occasionally she saw in some marriages a happy equality that pleased her even if she instinctively knew that such happiness was not for her. One could not be blissfully happy and be a successful queen of England, she thought wryly.

Her eyes moved to Velvet, who had finally granted a dance to her husband. Elizabeth's lips quirked with delight. Eight months ago the chit had been a mere child. Now she capered merrily with her handsome lord, a naughty smile upon her face, her tongue no doubt sharp with some saucy quip. Dearest Skye will be mightily surprised when she finally returns from her voyage to find herself a grandmother by her youngest child, thought the queen, for I have not a doubt that once home in Scotland the girl will breed successfully. I shall miss the wench, for she is sweet of nature and good fun, Elizabeth realized.

The object of the queen's thoughts danced happily with her husband, flirting outrageously with him until he threatened to kiss her before the entire court unless she ceased. In answer Velvet laughed up in his face, trying his patience quite sorely.

The stately pavane came slowly to an end, and the musicians began the waltzlike lavolta. Velvet was claimed by Lord Essex, and Alex moved off to find himself some chilled wine.

Taking a goblet from a passing footman, he sought a quiet corner away from the dancing. There was no doubt in his mind that Elizabeth Tudor had the most elegant, witty, and urbane court in all of Christendom, but he had to admit to himself that as much as he had enjoyed his stay in England he would be glad to return home again. He longed for the smell of clean, fresh air in his nostrils instead of the stink of Londontown. He longed to roam the hills about *Dun Broc* with his dogs at his heels, instead of the streets of this city with his men about him to deter the cutpurses. He longed for his castle, for simple food, to have Velvet all to himself without her family or their friends. There was so much he had to show her, so much he wanted to share with her, but until they left England none of it would be. Aye, he was eager to be quit of the place.

"Alone, m'lord? How fortuitous for me." Mary de Boult stood in a gown of gold and silver stripes before him, her hands upon her hips. There was something almost blowsy about her, he noticed now. Had her hair always been that flat shade of black?

"Madame." His greeting offered her no encouragement. If anything, the tone of his voice was discouraging.

"Madame," she mimicked him unpleasantly, and he saw that she was drunk. "There was a time, Alexander Gordon, when it was 'darling' and 'sweetheart,' not 'madame.' You have insulted me, m'lord! You have offended me beyond all, and I intend that you pay for it!"

"Indeed, madame, and how have I offended ye? By refusing to become yer lover? By declining to travel a path already so well traveled by so many others? Ye offered yerself, madame, and although I was willing to flirt and play the gallant, never did I lead ye to believe it would be anything else." His expression was icy with disdain.

"You used me to entrap that auburn-haired bitch you're wed to!" she hissed angrily at him.

"Ye used me, too, madame! Ye loved the idea that ye had taken me away from one of the queen's young Maids of Honor. Ye loved the thought that ye had captured the Scots earl, and ye paraded me like a lapdog throughout the entire court to the point of indiscretion. Ye were well paid for yer services, madame. I was, as I recall it, most generous with my gifts. Ye should have no complaints, Lady de Boult. My treatment of ye was fair and honorable by all accounts."

"You bastard!" she snarled and, raising her hand, struck out at him.

Alexander Gordon caught her arm in midair, his fingers tightening about her wrist. His voice, when he spoke, was dangerously low. "Nay, madame, and were ye a man ye'd stand challenged already."

Their eyes locked in deadly combat. Then, without warning, Mary de Boult tore her bodice open with her other hand, grasped one of her bare breasts, and shrieked, "Ahhh, no, my lord! How can you seek to shame me so! Stop! Stop! I pray you!" Her generous breasts spilled wantonly from her gown, and for the briefest moment her eyes sparkled in triumphant defiance at him. Then she began to caterwaul at the top of her lungs while a small crowd gathered about them. "He tried . . ." She hiccoughed several sobs. "He tried to dishonor me!" She wept for the assembled audience, pointing at the marks upon her bosom.

Lord de Boult pushed his way through the crowd of amused and curious courtiers. "What is this, my lord? What have you done to my wife? I demand that you answer me!"

Alex was only just beginning to recover from his surprise at Mary de Boult's action. Then Velvet was at his side and Essex with her.

"What has happened, my lord?" she asked gently, realizing his shock.

Alex struggled to find a reasonable explanation, for it went against his nature to attack a woman. Still, upon quick reflection, he could find no other way to extricate himself from this very difficult and embarrassing situation. Taking a deep breath, he said, "Yer wife, my lord de Boult, felt she had a quarrel with me. When I refused to allow her to strike me, she tore open her gown in an attempt to make it appear as if I had forced my attentions upon her and therefore have her revenge."

"Nay, Clifford! Nay!" pleaded Lady de Boult. Then she sobbed wildly. "He attempted to have his way with me here in this very alcove, and when I refused him he attacked me! I swear it!"

"Hah!" snapped the Earl of Essex. "More than likely *you* tried to have your way with him, madame, and *he* refused! I suspect that it is Lord Gordon's honor that has been damaged in this affair and not yours."

The assembled onlookers laughed.

"Are you calling my wife a liar, my lord Essex?" demanded Clifford de Boult, drawing himself up.

"Use your head, man," argued Essex. "Lady de Boult is fair enough, but next to the Countess of BrocCairn she is like a colored stone to a fine pearl. I believe Lord Gordon. Take your wife home and give her a good beating for causing this trouble in the queen's presence."

The Earl of Essex's words rang with practicality, and secretly Lord de Boult believed him. For him to admit it, however, was impossible, for it would bring shame upon his good name. His honor had been besmirched by this matter, and until that honor was appeased he would not be able to hold his head up at court. Coldly, he looked at Lord Gordon and said, "Tomorrow morning just past dawn in Brightwaters field, my lord?"

Alex nodded. "As you will, sir," he answered.

"Nay!" cried Velvet. "I will not permit it! Nay, Alex!"

Alex turned to Essex. "Will ye be my second, Robert?"

Esssex nodded slowly, but he could not resist saying, "Is it worth it for that jade, Alex?"

"It is for my own honor, Robert, which has been impugned by this evening's uproar. In several days' time Velvet and I leave for Scotland. How can I someday return to England with this hanging over my head? I cannot, and therefore the affair must be concluded honorably before we leave for Scotland."

"Nay!" Velvet almost shouted. "You would endanger yourself and our future over this lying trull! No, I say! No!"

Mary de Boult was very much enjoying the scene she had so skillfully engineered. A duel was to be fought, and over her! Her anger and disappointment at having been rejected by the Scotsman was fast fading in light of this delightful development. Then she heard Velvet's words. Gathering the tatters of her bodice, she glowered at her rival and said angrily to her husband, "Did you hear her? I have been mortally insulted, Clifford!"

Wearily he turned a cold face to her. "Would you also have me challenge the Countess of BrocCairn to a duel then, madame?" His fingers grasped his wife's arm, and, turning to Essex, he said, low, "Tender the queen our apologies, but my wife has been taken ill." Then he hustled his spouse from the ballroom.

"This is madness!" Velvet nearly shouted. "We all know, even poor Lord de Boult, that she is lying. We know it, and yet you will duel tomorrow over nothing?"

"We will duel to satisfy the code of honor," Alex said quietly.

"I will go to the queen! You know she has forbidden dueling," Velvet threatened.

"Ye will go home, madame, and ye will say nothing to Elizabeth Tudor," he said softly.

"I will!" Velvet couldn't remember ever having been so angry.

"Nay, Velvet," said Essex soothingly. "There are things a woman does not understand, things she cannot comprehend easily, and dueling is one of those things."

"The queen understands men better than you think," snapped Velvet, "and so do I! Men are naught but little boys!"

"No one will get hurt," Essex promised, smiling his most winning smile at her. "You're right when you say de Boult knows his wife is lying. The bitch has put him in an untenable position. But to admit it would dishonor him even more. It would be like saying he can't control his own wife. He had to challenge Alex. I will see that they fight with their swordpoints tipped. Honor will be quickly and easily satisfied, I promise you."

Velvet looked at her husband, and Alex nodded.

"I agree, lovey. No blood will be shed, and especially not mine." He smiled down at her.

The crowd had dissipated, returning to the dancing, and the queen, if she was aware of the scandal that had exploded in her ballroom, gave no sign of it. The principals involved hoped that by the time she received a full account the duel would be over and done with. Essex had gone back to Elizabeth's side, and Alex and Velvet found themselves surrounded by their family. The incident was retold, and while Willow and Angel expressed their indignation over Lady de Boult's terrible behavior and comforted Velvet, James Edwardes and Robin Southwood, along with Captain Murrough O'Flaherty and Lord Burke of *Clearfields Priory*, agreed with Alex that the duel must be fought.

"I offer myself as your second," said Robin quietly.

"I also!" enthused Padraic Burkc.

Velvet glowered at her brothers, but her annoyance was particularly reserved for Lord Burke. "When did *you* arrive in London?" she demanded. "'Tis a strange time to come calling when at midnight Lent begins."

Lord Burke, the master of *Clearfields Priory*, even handsomer than his late father, Niall, grinned down upon his youngest sister. His silvery eyes twinkled at her and as he spoke he brushed back an errant lock of black hair that tumbled over his high forehead. "I arrived but this evening with Murrough, who sails on the tide tomorrow morning back to India, sweet sister. My signature was necessary upon certain documents, y'see, else I should never have come to this stinkhole of a city." He turned to Alex. "We've not met, my lord. I am Velvet's brother, Padraic Burke of *Clearfields Priory*. You look none the worse for wear having been married to this wench these last few months."

With another engaging grin Padraic held out his hand, and Alex grasped it, a smile upon his own face. He instinctively liked this young man who stood almost as tall as he himself did and had the graceful body of an athlete.

"Ye feel about London as I do, eh, younger brother?" Alex said.

"If you mean by that that I prefer my lands, then you're right," came Padraic's quick reply.

"Then come visit us in Scotland next summer," said Alex. "We've good hunting and fishing."

"I'll do that!" agreed Padraic. "And perhaps I'll even be the first of our family to see my new nephew—or niece, whichever the case may be."

"I am not with child yet!" snapped Velvet.

"Being home will remedy that, madame," said Alex maddeningly.

"My lords and ladies," came the stentorian voice of the queen's majordomo, "'Tis midnight. The feasting is over, and the penitential season is upon us. Her Gracious Majesty commands that you all join her in the chapel to receive ashes."

With an almost audible sigh the court trooped forth from the queen's ballroom. The tables lay almost empty and wasted behind them; the musicians had already departed. The solemnity of Lent had fallen about them like some dark cloak, and they were suddenly anxious to be home.

The church service was mercifully brief, and the children of Skye O'Malley quickly found themselves descending the river stairs to the wharf where their barges were lined up and waiting. Velvet had insisted that Padraic stay with them, and Murrough, too, this last night before he sailed. There was more than enough room for them all in the BrocCairn barge, and as the tide was now with them the boat quickly moved upriver to the Strand. The Lynmouth and BrocCairn vessels raced to see which would get home first. They were fairly matched, for while Velvet and Alex carried her two brothers, Robin and Angel had Willow and James as passengers. Both boats finished in a dead heat, which was a disappointment to the bargemen, those on the winning vessel having been promised a purse. The two earls, however, in a burst of generosity, awarded their men their prizes despite the tie. Then calling good night to each other as they passed up their adjoining gardens the Southwood and Gordon parties entered their respective homes.

Murrough's rooms awaited him, and an apartment was quickly prepared for Lord Burke who, kissing his sister good night, whispered, "Don't fret, littlest one, nothing will happen to Alex I promise. Besides, de Boult is not said to be any sort of a swordsman."

Velvet made a little moue with her mouth. "The whole thing is foolishness, and that dreadful jade will brag for weeks afterwards about having caused a duel. Thank God we shall not be here to listen to her."

Murrough hid a smile. Velvet became more like their mother every day. "Shall I bid you farewell now, Velvet?" he asked. "Or will you arise from your snug bed in the morning to see me off?"

"What time will you go?" She looked dubious.

"I must leave Greenwood by half after seven at the latest. The tide is just after eleven in the morning."

"What time is the sunrise?" she said quietly.

"Half after six," said Alex, and he took her hand in his to reassure her.

"I will be up, Murrough. I shall see you off myself."

He nodded and then, bending, kissed her good night.

When Velvet and Alex were undressed and in their own warm bed, she asked him, "Is this duel really necessary? It is foolish of me, I realize, to be frightened, but I cannot help it. No one I've ever known has fought a duel."

He drew her into his arms. "There is no danger, Velvet, lass. Now be a good girl and kiss me, sweetheart."

She gave him her lips in a sweet and tender kiss, but when his hands began to roam lasciviously about her lush body, she slapped them away, saying severely, "Nay, my lord! You need all the sleep you can get! It is past two now, and you must be on your damned field of honor in four hours!"

He swore a mild oath and then chuckled. "Very well, lass, but I hope ye'll not have cause to regret turning me away. Think of the beautiful child we might start this night."

"And shall I explain to him how his father lost an ear in a duel several hours after his conception because he could not resist rutting like a stallion when he needed his sleep?"

Alex laughed outright. "Little Tartar," he scolded. Then, kissing her full on the mouth, he turned her so that her body curved into his, spoon fashion, and, clamping a hand about one of her soft breasts, he fell asleep.

Velvet smiled in the darkness of their room and thought with a contented sigh that she would not find it necessary to take her potion any longer, at least not until after her first child was born. She did regret the fact that she had not let him make love to her, but despite everyone's reassurances and the fact that they all made light of the matter, this duel frightened her. Then she decided she was being foolish. Even if they fought with naked swords, Alex would triumph. De Boult was a much, much older man. She relaxed and snuggled closer into her husband's embrace.

When Velvet awoke, dawn was smearing color across the horizon. She reached for Alex and then, with a frown, remembered. That damned duel! The door to her bedchamber opened and Pansy hurried into the room.

"You're awake then, m'lady? You said you wanted to see Captain O'Flaherty off, and 'tis almost seven o'clock." She held out her mistress's quilted apple-green chamber robe.

Velvet swung her legs from the bed and thrust her feet into her slippers. Standing, she slipped into the robe. "When did his lordship leave?"

"At least half an hour ago. 'Tis only a few minutes' ride to Brightwaters, but no gentleman likes to be late to a duel. 'Tis considered quite rude."

Velvet was forced to smile. "I wasn't aware that you were familiar with the courtesies of dueling, Pansy."

"Oh, you'd be surprised, m'lady, what I heard from the other servants when we was at court. They're a chattery bunch."

Velvet laughed. Pansy could always put her in a good mood. "Has Captain O'Flaherty broken his fast yet?"

"Nay, m'lady."

"Then ask him to break it with me in my dayroom and see that the food is brought quickly, for he did say he had to leave by half after seven o'clock."

"Yes, m'lady," came Pansy's answer, and the servant hurried off.

Within a very few moments both Murrough and the meal arrived. Murrough was dressed for travel in well-made, serviceable but expensive garments. He had but recently celebrated his thirty-second birthday and was a fine figure of a man who looked very much like his mother with his dark hair and his Kerry-blue eyes. The only thing of his sire about him seemed to be his squared jawline, which, though it had been weak in the long-dead but never lamented Dom O'Flaherty, had a firm strength in his younger son.

Smiling, Murrough greeted his youngest sister with a kiss and then sat down. "I still can't believe that you're a properly settled matron," he said with fond indulgence. "I can't wait to see the look on Mother's face when I tell her, not to mention Adam's."

"Don't tell them!" begged Velvet. "I want to surprise them with a grandchild when they return. Can you imagine Papa if I greet him at the docks with a baby in my arms?"

Murrough howled with delight as he pictured the scene. Adam de Marisco absolutely doted on his daughter, his beloved only child. It had never bothered him one whit that Alex Gordon had ignored Velvet from the day of their betrothal, for Adam had preferred to be the most important man in his daughter's life, only barely tolerating her half brothers who were equally enamored of her because she was so like their adored mother in character. Willow had been a prim and proper English miss from the start, always motherhenning them, and Deirdre had been a shy and insecure little mouse of a girl. It had always been Velvet who was the imp.

Murrough wiped his eyes, for he had laughed so hard that he'd begun to cry. "I should like to indulge you, poppet, but Mother, having been penned up these many months in a hot city, will be anxious for the open sea and might decide to go adventuring once more unless I can offer her an incentive to return home. Your marriage will be just the incentive. I'll wager that when Mother hears you're already a wife, even possibly with child, she will wish our ships had wings. You're very dear to her, Velvet."

"And she to me, Murrough. Aye, you had best tell them. It will give Papa time to calm his famous temper. 'Twill no doubt be winter once again when you return to England, dearest brother. You'll send a messenger by the fastest horses, won't you? I will feel so much better just knowing that Mama and Papa are safely home again."

"Aye, dear one," he answered her, reaching across the table to squeeze her hand.

"How are Joan and the children?" she inquired as she served him a large plate of eggs poached in marsala and cream, which had been placed on a thick slice of pink ham. "It was thoughtless of me not to ask you last night." She poured a tankard of brown ale and handed it to him.

"They are fine, but I left Henry angry at me for leaving him behind this time. Joan, however, is grateful. We promised the boy he could go off with the O'Malley uncles this spring, which has mollified him somewhat. He'll not find the Spanish Indies too tame, I'll warrant, although I will admit I made it sound safer to Joan than it actually is. Still, the O'Malleys will see that he comes to no harm, and the lad has to learn if he's to make the sea his life. He has no great love for book learning like our brother Ewan."

Velvet nodded and attacked her own plate with vigor. For several minutes they ate in silence, for neither were considered poor trenchermen by those who knew them. They ate with enjoyment and an obvious appreciation for the subtlety of the sauce that covered the eggs. Both were therefore surprised when the door to the room burst open and Padraic stumbled in, white and drawn.

Velvet looked at Lord Burke and then her hand went to her throat as she spoke but one word. "Alex?"

"An accident," burst out Lord Burke. "Oh, God! It was awful!"

The room dimmed before her eyes, but with a monumental burst of willpower Velvet refused to faint. Her voice, when she managed to find it, was ragged with fear. "What happened, Padraic? For God's good mercy, tell us!"

"We arrived at Brightwaters just as Lord de Boult did. Essex was already there with the queen's physician. The doctor said the queen had told him to go with Robert Devereux that morning. God's nightshirt! Is there nothing she doesn't know?"

Velvet's eyes were round with shock.

"What happened, Padraic?" repeated Murrough tensely. "Get on with it, laddie!"

"Both Alex and Lord de Boult agreed to Essex's suggestion that the swords be tipped with wax balls. The duel began, and both men fought well, but soon Lord de Boult began to tire. Suddenly the wax ball flew from his blade tip, and he stumbled. There was no time for Alex to get clear. It was an accident, but the blade pierced him. Oh, God! I've never seen so much blood! Essex cried out, 'Jesu, man, you've killed him!' When they carried him from the field, I rode back to tell you, Velvet. I couldn't let them bring him home to you like that. . .not without warning you." He began to weep. "Oh, God, littlest one, I am so sorry!"

Velvet sat very still in her chair, her beautiful face devoid of both expression and color. Neither of her brothers spoke, and the only thing that could be heard in the silence was the slow and reassuring tick of the mantel clock. Then suddenly, without warning, she began to weep wildly. The tears surged down her face in an abundant and fast flow. Within moments her eyes were swollen with her unassuaged grief. "Mama," she wept piteously. "I want my mother!"

For a moment Murrough was shocked. Was Velvet still just a child that she called for their mother? Then it hit him. She was no child but a woman finally grown. Alex was dead, and she had already accepted it. Now she called for someone she loved as deeply to comfort her in her unbearable grief. He was quickly at her side, and she cried into his shoulder as he murmured soft, unintelligible sounds in an effort to comfort her.

After a few minutes her tears ceased, and, looking up at him, she whispered brokenly, "Take me with you, Murrough. Please take me with you!"

"Velvet!" Padraic Burke was finally coming to his senses. "Have you no respect for Alex? You must bury your husband, Velvet. You can't leave him!"

She turned her head to look at him, and he saw the terrible grief in her green eyes.

"Why can I not leave him, Padraic?" she said bitterly. "He left me! I pleaded with him not to involve himself in this meaningless duel with Lord de Boult, but no! Honor must be served, which I could not possibly understand being but a simple woman." Her voice was thick with pain and scorn. "Well, this much I do understand, Padraic. I am widowed three months after my marriage, and for what? Because two grown men could not admit either to themselves or to each other that a whoring jade had lied?" She began to weep once more.

"You must bury him, Velvet," Padraic repeated helplessly.

"Bury him?" Her voice was suddenly hoarse with horror. "I can't bury him, Padraic! Enclose him in some dark tomb? Dear God, no! Besides, he would not want to be buried here in England. Let his men take his body back home to *Dun Broc*. He was the last of the Earls of BrocCairn. There will be no heirs of his body, and that much is all my fault!" She looked desperately at Murrough and begged once again, "Take me with you, brother! I won't make the long trip to Scotland, and what is there for me here? I cannot face the pity of our family or the court. I will go mad for certain! If there is any kindness in you, Murrough, take me with you.

I will die here alone. Oh, Alex, why? *Why?* I do not understand, and I never shall!" Then she wept once more, falling back into her chair, her face in her hands, her slender shoulders wracked by heartbroken sobs.

Murrough watched her, and a deep sigh rent his frame. It was imperative that he leave this day. It was already a week past his intended departure date. He would just reach the Indian Ocean in time to catch the favoring winds before they reversed their course, making it difficult, if not impossible, to cross that body of water. Still, how could he leave her? He made an attempt to reason with her. "Velvet, I would take you with me, poppet, but I must go now, today. Mother's life depends upon my swift return. If I delay even another day I could lose the favorable weather I need to get across the Indian Ocean safely. I cannot wait for you!"

"I can go now, today," she said. "My things are already packed for the trip north."

"But you'll need lightweight garments for the Indies, my dear. The climate is terribly hot and steamy."

"Pansy knows where everything is," she reassured him. "Please, Murrough, I beg of you! Don't leave me behind. I need Mother!"

He glanced at the clock upon the mantel and then made his decision. It was madness, but her frame of mind was precarious just now, and he believed she would be better off with him away from all that was familiar. The pain of her grief would be no less, but it should ease faster in a different setting. "Can you be ready in an hour?"

The tension drained momentarily from Velvet's body. "Aye, I can be ready," she said.

"You're mad, both of you!" Padraic shouted, but Velvet had already run from the room, calling for Pansy.

Murrough shrugged helplessly. "How can I leave her under these circumstances?" he demanded of his younger sibling. "You don't understand her, but I do. She is just like Mother in that she feels things with greater intensity than the rest of us. She loves with all her being, and she hates and grieves the same way. This grief will consume her here with all her memories of Alex, and if she returns to our dear Dame Cecily at Queen's Malvern that good worthy will baby our sister into a wasting sickness." Then he glared at Padraic. "You're sure?" he demanded. "You're absolutely certain that Alex received a mortal wound, Padraic?"

Padraic Burke looked offended. "Of course I'm certain," he snapped. "There was blood all over him, and Essex said most distinctly that he'd been killed. They carried him to a nearby house so that the queen's physician could do his duty in comfort as it was beginning to snow. It's stopped now," he finished helplessly.

Murrough put his arm about his brother. "I'm not sure how wise you were to hurry here with the news, but 'tis done now, and I've no other choice than to take Velvet with me."

A short while later a barge pulled away from Greenwood's small dock and steered a course for the London pool where Murrough's vessel, *Sea Hawk*, stood awaiting the outgoing tide. From an upper window Padraic Burke watched the barge go and felt a deep sorrow in his heart. Velvet's chambers were now empty and silent. Then something caught his eye, and, bending, he picked up a dainty glove. Crushing it to his cheek, he smelled the fragrance of gillyflowers and a tear slid down his cheek.

Slowly Padraic turned from the river and, walking to the sideboard, poured himself a goblet of *Archambault* Burgundy. He downed it in three deep gulps and poured himself another. Sitting before the banked fire with both decanter and cup, he drank himself to sleep, for he had had little enough rest the night before and his exhaustion, coupled with the shock his system had suffered that morning made him all the more vulnerable.

Awaking with a sour mouth some time later, his temples throbbing hurtfully, he saw by the mantel clock that it was well after one in the afternoon. Stumbling to his feet, he made his way downstairs. Alex's body would undoubtedly be placed in the main room for the mourners.

Willow would probably lay Padriac out in lavender for allowing Murrough to take Velvet, as if he could have stopped either of them. Willow would be furious at Velvet's lack of decorum, but they would simply have to tell everyone that the widow was too prostrate with grief to attend the funeral and, besides, the body was going home to Scotland. It was a perfectly plausible explanation.

Reaching Greenwood's lower level, Padraic saw Dugald, the earl's man, just entering the house, and he hurried toward him. "Have you brought the earl's body home then?" he asked.

"He's too badly injured to move right now," replied Dugald, "but the queen's physician says he'll live to be an old man yet."

Padraic Burke suddenly felt sick. He heard his older brother's voice demanding, *"You're sure?"*

Finding his voice, he gasped, "Alex is alive? He's not dead?"

"Dead?" Dugald looked surprised. "What in hell made ye think that, my lord?"

"The blood," said Padraic helplessly. "All that blood, and Essex said de Boult had killed Alex. He said it."

"Essex!" Dugald said scornfully. "What the devil would that gallant know about death? 'Twould take more than just a sword's prick to kill the Gordon of BrocCairn."

"Where is Alex?"

"They carried the earl to the nearest house, one owned by a Master Wythe, a silversmith. They dared move him no farther, and he must remain there until his wound is closed so that there will be no danger of it opening and bleeding again. We believed ye came on ahead to tell her ladyship, but when she did not come I was sent to fetch her and to reassure her that my lord will survive though he is sleeping now with the draught the queen's physician gave him."

"Jesu!" groaned Padraic Burke. "What have I done?" And then he was calling for his horse and running through the door, while behind him the Earl of BrocCairn's man stared after him in open-mouthed confusion.

Part Three

THE MUGHAL'S ENGLISH ROSE

How delicious an instrument is woman, when artfully played upon; how capable is she of producing the most exquisite harmonies, or executing the most complicated variations of love, and of giving the most Divine of erotic pleasures.

—*Ananga Ranga*

Chapter 8

It was a hot afternoon, and Jalal-ud Din Muhammad Akbar, emperor of the Mughal empire, sat upon his throne conducting his country's business. He was feeling bored and irritable. The air in the audience chamber of the Diwan was heavy with humidity, and from the rumblings outside the building another storm was due soon. He sighed as a bead of perspiration rolled down the side of his face from beneath his small, tightly rolled white turban, which had been fashioned to combine both the Muslim and the Hindu modes. It was the season of the monsoon. He could feel the dampness on his wheat-colored skin even through his peacock blue sarcenet trousers, and his gold tunic, which was called a cabaya, was limp. His personal bodyslave leaned over and wiped the moisture from his face. The emperor smiled his thanks to the man, even as he longed for a bath and a cool breeze.

"And now, Most High, a final item," said Ramesh, the khan-i-saman of his household. "Today there is newly arrived a train of gifts from the Portuguese governor in Bombay. They were routed to your capital in Lahore, but learning that you were visiting here in Fatehpur-Sikri they came directly to you."

Akbar raised his expressive, fine dark eyes heavenward. "Let me guess," he said, somewhat wryly. "Several just passable horses, a few second-rate fighting elephants, at least one brace of moth-eaten hunting cats, another painting of some Christian saint or martyr, *and* a pouch of inferior gemstones." He sighed deeply. "Why *do* the Portuguese insist on sending me bad fighting elephants and worse gemstones, Ramesh?

They have absolutely no taste in either. Am I right, old friend?"

Ramesh, the lord high steward, smiled affectionately at his master. "You are correct, Most High, but this time the Portuguese have added two additional gifts. One should please you, but as for the other . . ." He shrugged.

"There is more?" Akbar was surprised, for Portuguese generosity toward him was generally scant. The Portuguese were far more interested in what they could take from India than in what they could give to it. "Well, Ramesh," he said, "what have the Portuguese added to their caravan of delights this time to please and amuse this barbarian king?"

"What will please you, Most High, is a jeweled clock that chimes the hour," was the lord high steward's reply.

Akbar's eyes lit with pleasure, for he very much enjoyed mechanical objects. *"And?"* he queried.

Ramesh's face grew concerned. "The Portuguese have sent you a woman, Most High."

"A woman?" The emperor was astounded. "Do the Portuguese think my zenana is not full enough?" Then he grew curious. "What kind of a woman, Ramesh? Have they sent me one of their dwarfs for my amusement or perhaps some other female freak of nature?"

"I think she is a European, Most High. She is certainly not of our land or from Cathay," the lord high steward replied.

"What frets you about her, Ramesh?"

The lord high steward hesitated a moment, and then said, "I believe that the Portuguese meant to please you, but this woman is, I am absolutely convinced, stark, raving mad. I question that she has not been sent here to assassinate Your Majesty, and I fear for your safety."

Akbar's interest was piqued, and he found that he was much less bored. During this whole afternoon in the oppressive heat of the monsoon season he had sat patiently listening to various, long-winded complaints from his subjects and mediating delicate disputes between the many fiery factions, both religious and political, that made up his realm.

He needed a diversion, and here, at last, was something different.

"Have the woman brought to me," he commanded. "I would see her now."

"My lord," protested Ramesh, "I fear for you, and, besides, I promise you she is like the gemstones and the elephants, nothing special. Her skin is very white but for her hands, face, and feet, which have been sunburned in the trek from the coast. The Portuguese governor did not even think enough of her to provide her with an elephant or a camel or even a simple litter. I cannot make out the color of her hair because it is so dirty—I suspect it is filled with lice and fleas. Her eyes seem to be of a light hue. I have never seen anything like them before. She is an ugly creature. Let me send her to the kitchens. Perhaps they can make use of her."

Akbar laughed. "I cannot send a gift from the Portuguese to the kitchens," he said. "At the very least I must see her, and then she shall be sent to my zenana. Now stop fussing like an old woman, Ramesh, and bring me this female!"

The khan-i-saman signaled to one of his underlings, who hurried from the audience chamber. A few moments later an unearthly shriek rent the air, startling all within the steaming chamber. They could hear a woman's voice angrily raging, a sound that drew nearer and nearer until the double doors to the audience chamber burst open and two servants dragged in a naked, struggling creature who screamed and fought them wildly, her heavy, lank hair thrashing about her body.

"Take your filthy hands from me, you evil baboons!" she angrily shouted, but they no more understood her protests than she comprehended their sharp commands.

"Kneel, woman! You are in the presence of the emperor!" They attempted to force her to her knees, but the woman, in a most surprising maneuver, broke free and, snatching a cape from one of the servants who was trying to restrain her, attempted to cover her nudity. Then with her bare foot she kicked out at the other servant, catching him in a most vulnerable and tender spot.

"Arrrrgh!" cried the wounded one, falling to the floor and clutching at himself.

In the chaos that followed the woman bent and swiftly relieved her victim of his dagger, then, turning, she backed quickly into a corner, pointing the weapon outward toward her tormentors.

"Come near me, any of you, and I swear I'll kill you!" she threatened.

"Aiyee!" wailed the khan-i-saman, rolling his head from side to side. "I knew this creature would bring disaster upon us all! She has the evil eye, I am sure! Call out the guard lest she harm the emperor!"

"Remain in your places, all of you!" Akbar sharply commanded. "Can none of you see? The woman is terrified." He himself felt no fear. Watching the drama unfolding before him, he found he was rather fascinated and curious as to what the woman looked like beneath her many layers of dirt. He had never seen a European woman before, and he couldn't tell a great deal at the moment about the filthy, crouching female. "Has anyone tried to speak reasonably with her?" he asked.

"No one can understand her barbarian tongue, Most High," quavered Ramesh.

"How like the Portuguese not to teach her even a few words of our language," murmured the emperor. "But then, knowing their lack of subtlety of intellect, they probably assumed the simple Mughal would find no need to speak with the woman. He would simply fall upon her and sate his lust."

"Do you think she is Portuguese?" wondered Ramesh.

Akbar shook his head. "It is doubtful they would send one of their own women to me," he said.

"The holy fathers taught you their tongues, Most High. Could you not speak to this woman in them?"

"Yes, my old friend," said the emperor. "I have learned two languages from the holy fathers. If this woman understands one of them, then perhaps we can calm her fears."

"What can she possibly be afraid of?" fussed the lord high steward in a somewhat aggrieved tone of voice. "This is a civilized land. Our cultures—Moslem, Buddhist, even Hindu with its caste system—are ancient and venerable. Older, in many instances, than the Europeans, and certainly more civilized.

Akbar smiled. "Yes," he agreed, "but do the Europeans know it, Ramesh?" He turned to the woman who was still crouched defensively in her corner. None of the others had noticed, but he could see that she was trembling slightly. Still, she gave no other indication of her fear and that intrigued him. Although he knew of brave women by reputation, he had never before faced one. Her eyes—intelligent eyes, he noted—had been following the conversation between himself and Ramesh as she attempted to ascertain some indication of her fate.

"Are you Portuguese, *senhora?*" he inquired of her in that tongue.

She stared blankly at him.

"Êtes-vous français, mademoiselle?" he asked, switching to the French language. He could see relief wash over her in that moment.

"Non, monseigneur, je ne suis pas français, mais je parle français comme ma grandmère est une Française," came the woman's reply. Then uncontrolled tears began to slide down her oval face, making dirty runnels in her skin as they went. For a moment she was in a quandary as to what to do. One hand held the dagger, the other the cape that covered her. Finally she reached up with her weaponed hand and brushed her tears away with the heel of her palm, further smudging the dust on her face.

"Why do you weep?" Akbar asked softly, finding that desperate, feminine gesture both charming and vulnerable.

"Because, *monseigneur,*" she sobbed, "this is the first time in weeks that someone has spoken to me in a tongue that I could understand. Your accent is heavy, but I can comprehend you. Have you any idea what it is like to be in a strange place, unable to communicate with the people around you, not knowing what is going to happen to you?"

"No," he said quietly, "I do not, but if I found myself in such a position I think I would be afraid." The emperor could see that the woman was near the breaking point, and not wishing to frighten her further he asked gently, "Would you like it if I sent all these people away, *mademoiselle*?"

She nodded, saying, "Can you do that? Are you the lord of this place?"

"I am."

"What are you called, *monseigneur?* How shall I address you?"

"I am Akbar, called the Grand Mughal. I am the emperor of this land, *mademoiselle*. Who are you?"

She drew herself up in a proud little gesture, and he was surprised by her height. "I am the Countess of BrocCairn, *monseigneur*. I am Velvet Gordon."

"Are you hungry, my lady? Thirsty, perhaps?"

"Oh, yes, my lord! I am both hungry and thirsty. It is so very hot."

The emperor turned back to his people. "Leave us," he said to them, "but, Ramesh, see that a servant brings cool wine and some fruit. This woman is not quite the villainess you imagined. From what I can gather so far, she is a noblewoman in her own land. I suspect treachery on the part of the Portuguese, and this poor creature has been their victim."

"Is she Portuguese then, Most High?"

"No, my friend. I do not yet know her native land, but she is able to speak with me in the tongue of the Franks. I shall soon learn all, and you need not fear for me. She is no danger."

Ramesh nodded. The emperor had a magic about him when it came to dealing with people. Had he not virtually single-handedly united this great land, which for years had been divided by warring factions that set family against family? Neighbor against neighbor? Was he not the first Moslem emperor to bring Hindus into the government and the army? Ramesh nodded again to himself and, leading the way for the others, he left the room.

Velvet relaxed a tiny bit now and quickly studied the man who sat calm and cross-legged amid colorful pillows upon the raised dais before her. She suspected that when he stood he would be of medium height for a man, and not a great deal taller than she was herself, but then she was considered tall for a woman. He was beautifully dressed and jeweled. Beneath the sheer fabric of his tunic she could see his broad, smooth, muscled chest tapering down to a narrow waist. He had a golden complexion, and was clean shaven but for a closely trimmed, small, dark moustache. His brows were thin and black; his bright eyes were also black but despite their narrow shape, which revealed the Mongolian strain in his blood, they shimmered and danced in the light. His forehead was broad, his nose somewhat short though slender, and between the left nostril and his upper lip was a mole about the size of a small pea. The emperor's mouth was a sensual one, but his expression was serene and full of dignity.

Akbar gave her a moment to collect herself, and then said, "I would reassure you, my lady, that no one here means you any harm. Will you come and sit on the steps beneath me here? You would be far more comfortable than you are now in that corner."

"I will not give up my weapon," she replied.

"If it will make you feel more secure, then keep it." He smiled in a kindly fashion at her. "Come," he said, holding out his hand.

Instinctively Velvet trusted him, though she knew not why, and so she slowly came forward from her refuge and sat gingerly upon a long comfortable pillow that was set on the marble step just below the emperor's throne. "Thank you, my lord," she said simply.

A servant silently entered the room bearing a tray upon which were two goblets of frosty wine and a plate of a juicy, sliced fruit that Velvet could not identify. Bowing low, he offered the contents of the tray first to Akbar and then to Velvet.

"What is that fruit?" she questioned him. It was pale orange in color and looked very good.

"It is melon," Akbar answered. "It is very good and very sweet. I have these particular melons brought down from my capital of Lahore in the north. Try a slice," he suggested and took one himself.

Following his lead, she took a piece and bit into it. It was delicious and, along with the cool, light wine, revived her spirits.

When she had eaten half of the melon and drunk part of her wine, he began to question her gently. "Tell me, my lady," he began, "you are not Portuguese and you say you are not French, though you speak that language. What then is your native land?"

"I am English, my lord," she answered him, daintily licking the juice from the melon off her grimy fingers and suddenly becoming aware of just how dirty her hands were, particularly her nails.

Akbar was not a man to miss anything, and it amused him to see such a typically female reaction come over her in the midst of all her troubles. He could still not tell a great deal about her looks beneath the dirt and the mass of lank hair, but the one thing he could see as she glanced up at him was that her features were fine and that her eyes were the color of emeralds. "You are English," he repeated, and she nodded. "I had some Englishmen here several years back. They brought me a letter from your queen. Does she still reign?"

"Yes, my lord, Queen Elizabeth yet reigns, and will continue to do so, God willing. The queen is my godmother, my lord! The expedition you speak of was that of Master John Newbery and Master William Hawkins. They and their assistants, a jeweler named Leedes and James Story, a painter, along with a friend of my mother's, a London merchant named Ralph Fitch, left England when I was twelve. Nothing was heard of them after they landed in Goa. In England it was thought that they died," Velvet told him.

"Three of them reached my court a few years ago at just this time. The artist had married a half-caste girl and remained in Goa, but the others I knew. The jeweler I took into my service, and he served me well until he died of a fever. The other two departed Fatehpur-Sikri to return to their homeland and I never heard from them again."

"They had not returned to England when I left several months ago, my lord," Velvet said.

"It was unusual that three Englishmen reached my court at all," said Akbar. "Tell me now how it is that you find yourself here, my lady. Where is your family? Why have the Portuguese taken it upon themselves to deliver you to me? You do understand that they have sent you to me as a gift? Why did you not arrive as befits your state in a jeweled palanquin?"

"The Portuguese have not the right to 'gift' you with me, my lord. I am a great noblewoman in my own land! I stand high in the queen's favor!" Velvet's voice rang out angrily with her indignation.

Fascinating, he thought. In his whole life only his mother had ever raised her voice at him. The Englishwoman was different from the women he knew, and he was becoming more and more intrigued. "Do not be angry," he soothed her. "I merely seek to learn how you came here and in such a frankly disgraceful state."

"There was no jeweled palanquin, my lord, for as I was told before we left Bombay, the caravan master wished to travel quickly before the rains set in. I was made to walk, and my only shelter was beneath a cart at night. Two weeks ago my tiring woman became ill, and they wanted to leave her behind. I do not speak Portuguese, and I do not speak your language, but I conveyed to the leader of the caravan my distress at being separated from Pansy. I screamed and I cried and I clung to her, all the while shaking my head and saying 'no.' Finally I offered the caravan master my jeweled mirror as a bribe, and they put her in one of the carts. I have been nursing her ever since, but she is very sick, my lord. Have you a doctor who can make her well? She is all I have." Velvet's voice quavered at this last.

Akbar clapped his hands twice, and a servant materialized seemingly from nowhere. The emperor spoke quickly and firmly to the man who, when his master had finished speaking, bowed low and hurried from the chamber.

"Your servant will be well cared for now, my lady," Akbar said. "I have given instructions that the physician see to her. He will report to me as soon as he has made his examination and can render a diagnosis."

"Thank you!" she exclaimed, smiling at him.

Allah! he thought. Beneath all that dirt she is pretty. He was suddenly even more curious than before to learn just *how* pretty. "Your journey of the last several weeks has been long, and hard" he said, "and I do not doubt that you are exhausted. Let me have Ramesh take you to a comfortable place where you can bathe and eat. Then I will come, and you will tell me of your travels and how it is you have come to Fatehpur-Sikri."

"You are kind, my lord, and I thank you," said Velvet. She had been very frightened, but now her fears had lessened for this king did not seem a cruel man.

Once more the emperor clapped his hands, and then ordered the answering servant to fetch Ramesh. Then he turned back to Velvet. "Ramesh is the khan-i-saman of my household. You would call him a lord high steward. You need not fear him, and he will see that you are made comfortable."

His words were barely finished when Ramesh hurried into the audience chamber and bowed before Akbar. "How may I serve you, Most High?"

"The woman is English, Ramesh, and I suspect the Portuguese have done something that they ought not have by sending her to me. Still, she is here now, and she has suffered. I have already given orders that her beloved servant who is ill be cared for, and now I would have you take her to the women's quarters so that she may bathe and eat. Give her her own room and be sure she is kindly treated, for I do not want her frightened further. Then see if you can find someone among my servants who can speak the tongue of the Franks. If there be a eunuch or maidservant who knows it, then transfer them from their current duties to serve this woman. I will visit her later to learn her full history."

"It will be as you desire, Most High," replied Ramesh, bowing low again. He looked at Velvet and gestured her to follow him.

"Go with him," said Akbar. "He has been ordered to treat you gently." He smiled reassuringly at her, showing strong, very white teeth.

Velvet stood and, clutching her cape about her, followed Ramesh from the room. She followed him down a wide corridor and out into the hot, cloudy afternoon, then across the square to a beautiful, two-storied, carved sandstone building. Ramesh gestured her inside. Velvet hurried through the doors. It had now begun to rain.

I wonder where I am, she thought. Thanks to the emperor she knew that the name of this town was Fatehpur-Sikri, but *was* it a town? There didn't seem to be any townspeople in evidence. What was this building to which she had been escorted? To her amazement she saw that there were women soldiers guarding it. As she followed Ramesh up a flight of stairs and through the building, she caught glimpses of other women and at least one small child, a little girl with big dark eyes who seemed startled at Velvet's appearance. The building did not have windows as she knew them, but rather arches, some fitted with carved screens and some open, through which she could see the rain falling in sheets across the great square.

Ramesh stopped before a door and, opening it, gestured for her to enter through it. For a moment Velvet hesitated. Why was he not entering the chamber? Then as she fought back her rising panic she remembered Akbar's promise that Ramesh would treat her gently. Taking a deep breath to calm her nerves, she entered the room and heard the door close behind her. Turning, she saw that she was alone, and, frightened again, she ran to the door and tried the handle. It turned. With a sigh of relief she left it shut and set about to explore her new surroundings.

It was a large single room, the walls of which were painted with wonderful scenes of Indian court life. There were hunting scenes that showed the king upon an elephant, with all his court, the beaters fanning out in the tall grass to ferret out the tiger, a wonderful creature of fierce proportions who hid not too successfully from them. There were scenes showing dancing girls performing before the king, their colorful skirts whirling gracefully so that their brown legs showed. Then there was the king upon a horse, his hunting cats loping by his side; the king upon his dais listening to petitioners; and the king seated with his women about him. The colors were bright and fresh upon the sandstone walls.

The rest of the chamber was just as lovely. Upon a red-painted platform with square gilt feet was a mattress covered in sky blue silk, and above it, held up by delicate, twisted red posts at each corner of the platform, was a blue and gold canopy. There were colorful pillows strewn at one end of the bed, which had been placed in the center of the room to catch the breezes. Beyond the platform was an open doorway that led out on to a veranda that was filled with plants of all descriptions, including two red rose trees. The greenery grew in crockery planters of all sizes and shapes. Velvet could only stand and look at it through the gauze curtains as the rain was heavy.

Turning back to the room after a moment, she saw that there was a large, engraved brass table, actually an enormous tray that was set upon wooden supports. About it were more pillows. Other than that and the bed the room was empty.

The door opened, and a woman beckoned her toward the hallway with an impatient motion. Without even thinking twice, Velvet followed her. She had no other choice, and she was once more beginning to feel frustrated by her lack of ability to communicate. The woman, obviously an upper servant, led her to what she quickly realized were the baths. As more women hurried forward to aid her, Velvet blushed at their nudity. Her cape was taken from her, and the women immediately set about to make her presentable once again.

For a brief moment the bath mistress stared at Velvet as if she couldn't decide where to start. Then with a sharp order to her helpers she pointed to Velvet's head, and they mercilessly went to work washing her hair and scrubbing her scalp until she feared that they meant to make her bald. One washing was not sufficient, nor was two. Not until they had soaped, scrubbed, and rinsed her head three times did the bath mistress evince any sign of satisfaction. Next Velvet found her skin being washed vigorously, and before she could protest a rose-colored paste smelling of almonds was smeared beneath her arms, on her arms and legs, and, to her mortification, upon her Venus mont, which she had been unable to pluck free of hair these last weeks.

By means of hand signals they indicated to her that she was to stand still, and while she did a girl began to towel her hair damp-dry. When the bath mistress deemed it time, the almond paste was rinsed from her skin, and to her surprise she found her entire body now hairless. Velvet was quite fascinated, for although she had never thought to denude her arms and legs of their body hair, it was a tiresome chore to pluck her Venus mont free of its silky growth. Still, Mama had always said that no lady would allow such a growth upon her private person.

Once again she was washed, but this time they scrubbed her gently, using soft cloths and scented soap. Nothing was overlooked, and several times Velvet found herself reddening with embarrassment, but protests were useless. They could not comprehend her words, nor could she understand them. In the end she bore the treatment stoically.

Afterwards she was led to a marble bench and gestured to sit. While one girl cleaned and pared her fingernails, another, kneeling before her, sighed and *tsk*ed over the condition of Velvet's feet as she pumiced and cut the calluses from them, then finally cleaned and pared the toenails.

Smiling now, the bath mistress herself led Velvet into another room that contained a large pool. Gesturing her toward the wide steps that led down into the pool, she waved her into the water. Velvet gladly complied and to her delight found the pool both warm and deliciously scented. "Oh." She sighed, her pleasure evident, and the bath women giggled behind their hands, happy that she was pleased with their treatment of her. Feeling better than she had felt in months,

Velvet swam and paddled about the bathing pool like a little girl released from tedious lessons.

Above her, hidden behind a carved screen, Akbar watched her frolic, gaining pleasure from the sight of her firm, young breasts, her sleek flanks, and wonderfully long legs. "Well, Ramesh," he said to the steward who stood by his side, "what do you think of the Portuguese gift now? The woman is beautiful! Look at that skin! It is as white as the snows of Kashmir! I want her kept from the sun, and see that lemons are brought from the bazaars in Agra to bleach her hands and feet and face. Never have I seen a woman so fair! Never have I possessed a woman so fair, but possess her I shall!"

"She will not be easy to win over, Most High," observed the lord high steward. "She is a European and not familiar with our ways."

"I want her kept from the other women for the time being," said Akbar. "I don't want her becoming like them. Her value to me is in her very difference. See that every effort is made to cure her servant, for if she remains lonely she will be easy prey for the other women of the zenana for a woman needs another woman to talk with. In the meantime, is there anyone in my service who can speak the tongue of the Franks?"

"When you asked me, Most High, I thought you had set me an impossible task, but I have actually found someone. He is a young eunuch of the lowest rank. His mother was a girl of Cambay and his father a French sailor. The boy is one of many children, and in the last famine was sold into service and gelded for a eunuch. His name is Adali. He claims to speak good French."

"Bring him to me and we will see. I do not want to send him to the woman only to disappoint her. She is very brave, but I do not think she can take much more."

Ramesh nodded. "The eunuch could be merely seeking to advance himself. If he has lied I will personally see that he is flayed alive."

"Let us hope he has not," returned Akbar, and then with a final glance down at the bathing pool he regretfully turned away and hurried from the zenana, Ramesh at his heels.

Because the emperor would not trust himself to test the eunuch personally, a French Jesuit who traveled with the court was sent for to speak with Adali. "His French, Majesty, is of the lower classes, but intelligible," the Jesuit announced and was thanked for his trouble.

Akbar looked at the eunuch. Adali was short and already plump as many were in his position, but his brown eyes were intelligent. "You have been chosen for a very special assignment," said the emperor. "You are to care for a European lady who has entered my zenana and cannot speak our language. Answer all her questions and be loyal to her. She has a female servant, but the girl is ill at this time, and the lady has had no one to speak with during most of her trek from Bombay. She is still fearful, and you will reassure her that no one here will harm her. Do you understand?"

"Yes, Most High," the eunuch said.

The emperor turned to Ramesh. "Take him to the English woman's quarters."

Velvet had been fed a light meal of tender baby lamb, saffroned rice, melon, and a light fruity wine. She was slightly uncomfortable in her new clothes, which consisted of a pale green skirt, its hem edged in gold, which hung to her ankles and a matching blouselike top. When the women had put the blouse on her she had at first thought the garment too short, for despite its modest, high, round neckline, it fit her tightly and only covered the tops of her breasts to the nipples, leaving the fullness of her lower breasts bare. The bath women had laughed, however, and putting on their own blouses had shown her that the garment was as it should be.

Velvet sighed at the strangeness of it all, but meekly followed one of the women back to her own chamber where, to her surprise, a short, plump little man in white Turkish trousers and a sleeveless white vest awaited her.

"I am Adali," he said in careful French. "I have been assigned to serve you, princess."

"I am not a princess," said Velvet.

"You must be," said the smiling eunuch, "for I could only serve a princess."

"I am Velvet Gordon, the Countess of BrocCairn, Adali."

"I do not know what a *comtesse* is," he returned, "but I do know what a princess is, and you are as beautiful as any princess I have ever seen. You must therefore be a princess."

Velvet laughed. She liked this fat little man with his snapping, merry brown eyes. "And how many princesses have you seen in your life, Adali?"

"Well," he considered, "there is the Amber Princess who is the emperor's favorite wife. Then there is the Princess of Khandesh, the Princess of Bikaner, the Princess of Jaisalmer, the Princess of Puragadh, to mention but a few of the lord Akbar's other wives. It seems that every time a king makes a treaty of peace with another king there is a nubile princess involved in the transaction! Now why was I not born a king also?" He gave a watery chuckle that was so infectious in its mirth that Velvet laughed again.

She settled herself in the middle of the pillows upon the bed and looked at Adali. "Your French is terrible!" she scolded him. "Where on earth did you ever learn it? I am going to have to teach you to speak properly, Adali."

"Oh, yes, princess! I should very much like to learn whatever you can teach me. My father was a simple sailor from Brittany who married my mother, who is a Muslim, and settled in the city of Cambay. They own a small shop on the waterfront where they repair sails. It is from my father and his sailor friends that I learned to speak the tongue of the Franks. They are simple men, princess."

For a moment Velvet felt ashamed at having teased him. She was fortunate that Adali spoke French at all. "Forgive me, Adali," she said humbly. "I have been unkind, and the truth is that I am very grateful you can speak to me."

"It is nothing, princess," he answered her graciously. "I am your slave, and you may do with me as you will." Her honest apology had won him, and he would serve her with loyalty always.

Velvet found his words rather startling. She had never owned a slave before. To cover her confusion she said, "Sit down and answer the many questions that I have, Adali. What is this place, this Fatehpur-Sikri? It seems a city, and yet it does not."

A smile split his round face. "When the rains stop I shall show you Fatehpur-Sikri," he said, "for it is indeed a city. It was built by the lord Akbar, and for over ten years it was his capital. He abandoned it five years ago in favor of Lahore to the north. Many say it was because Sheikh Salim, the holy man who lives here and who predicted the birth of the lord Akbar's three sons, disliked the bustle and noise of the capital. It disturbed his meditations, they say.

"That, however, is not so. The lord Akbar abandoned Fatehpur-Sikri because of a water shortage. We are on the edge of the great Indian desert here, and as there are not enough natural springs to supply a city we have to depend upon reservoirs and catch basins. And it does not rain enough here except in this the monsoon season. There isn't really enough water to supply the city, to keep the gardens, and to supply the fountains. That is why the lord Akbar left Fatehpur-Sikri. Still, it is his favorite place, and occasionally he cannot resist returning. The last time was over three years ago."

"So that is why it seems deserted," said Velvet.

Adali nodded. "There is no longer a large population here," he replied.

"Does the lord Akbar's whole court travel with him like our English queen's does?"

Adali chuckled. "Sometimes and sometimes not. This is one of those times when the lord Akbar wished to be by himself for a short while." The eunuch grew somber and lowered his voice. "It has not been a good year for my master. His eldest son, Prince Salim, is now twenty and chafes against his father's control. His two half brothers are nineteen and seventeen. They are the princes Murad and Daniyal. They, too, resent their father, but they resent each other as well.

The two younger sons have too great an addiction for sweet wines, and it is said that Prince Salim is an opium-eater as well. None of them are really like their father. He loves them, but I think they sadden him.

"He is a great king, the lord Akbar. Under him almost all of India is now united. The laws, the judgments, and the taxes are finally fair. The roads are safe to travel. He loves and encourages musicians and artisans. He is a man of great intellect and curiosity. He built a house here in Fatehpur-Sikri and then invited priests of all religions, including the Christians, to come here and discourse with him and with each other. He holds no prejudices like our past rulers. He even lifted the special tax from the Rajputs! He is a wonderful and good man, but he has not been well, and so he has come to Fatehpur-Sikri once again to regain his strength."

"Tell me of his wife," said Velvet innocently, forgetting the eunuch's reference to Akbar's many princesses.

"*Wives*, princess! The lord Akbar has thirty-nine wives at last count, and several hundred concubines. In all, the zenana of my master contains close to five thousand women, including female relatives, slaves, and others!" He chuckled. "Wife! Ha! Ha!" Then he turned serious. "You, my princess, I suspect, shall be the lord Akbar's new favorite. You do not look like our women, but you are very, very beautiful. He cannot fail to love you."

Velvet looked positively shocked. "*I was* a married woman, Adali," she said seriously. "I am only here because the Portuguese kidnapped me!"

Before the eunuch could reply, the door to the chamber opened and Akbar entered the room. Adali threw himself to the floor in a gesture of total and complete obeisance. "Rise, Adali," said the emperor, "and fetch us refreshment."

The slave scrambled to his feet and scampered out the door. Then to Velvet's surprise the emperor settled himself upon the bed facing her. He studied her carefully for a long moment, bringing a deep blush to her cheeks.

"I do not mean to embarrass you," he apologized, "but you are incredibly fair. Never have I seen such exquisite beauty in any woman, and I have certainly seen many beauties in my lifetime. I have never, however, seen eyes like emeralds or hair the rich reddish color of newly turned earth."

"Most of the women in my land have fair skin, sire," Velvet replied, "and many, though not all, have light-colored eyes. My mother's eyes are the blue of the sea."

"And your mother, does she have hair the color of yours?"

"Oh, no, sire. My parents both have dark hair. I have inherited my hair color from my *grandmère*, the Comtesse de Saville."

He smiled at her. "Tell me about your homeland, your England."

"It is a cool, green land of hills, orchards, and fields, lakes and rivers, and a great city called London. The queen is most wonderful, and the wisest and bravest of rulers. All the kings of Europe stand in awe of her."

"Not the Portuguese." Akbar chuckled.

"The Portuguese!" Velvet sniffed, outraged. "Lackeys of Philip of Spain who would usurp our queen's rightful place. A place even her sister, Queen Mary, who was King Philip's wife would not deny."

He was enchanted; enchanted by her obvious intelligence, her quick speech, and the way her straight, little nose wrinkled in scornful distaste of the Portuguese. He wanted to know more about her; a great deal more. "You love your England, I can see. Tell me then how it is you came to India."

Adali reentered the room, bringing with him wine and cakes, which he placed on a small footed tray by the bed. Then he tactfully departed.

Velvet's face had grown sad. Where could she begin? she wondered. She took a deep breath. "The queen very much wants to trade with India, sire. When the Newbery-Hawkins expedition did not return after a reasonable time, Her Majesty asked my mother if she would send some of her vessels to Cambay. My mother, who in her youth amassed a great trading empire, and my father mounted an expedition and set sail. As they neared the end of their journey they were blown off course in a brief but fierce storm and, losing their rudder, were forced to land at Bombay. There the Portuguese took them and my older brother into custody, and were my family not members of the holy mother church, they would surely have been killed. Instead, the Portuguese demanded a heavy ransom, which my mother and father agreed to pay. My brother sailed back to England to raise the ransom, and when he returned here I came with him."

"Why?" demanded the emperor. "Was such a trip not dangerous for you?"

"Sire, my husband had just died, and I could not bear to stay at court with all its reminders of my Alex." A single, bright tear slipped down her face, and without realizing the intimacy of the act he reached out and brushed it from her cheek.

"Don't weep," he said quietly.

"It was a useless death, sire. My husband was killed in a duel of honor that neither he nor his opponent wished to fight. He came from a country to our north, Scotland. We had only been married a few months and had no children. Because of me his line has died, and I must live with that the rest of my life!" Her beautiful eyes brimmed with tears, and, unable to contain himself, Akbar reached out and took her hand in an attempt to soothe her.

"It was not the will of God, else your husband would have left you with a child in your womb," he comforted her.

Velvet was too overwrought and ashamed to admit to him why she had not conceived, and so, regaining control of her emotions, she continued her tale. "We did not follow the route the Portuguese usually take in their sea travel to India," she said. "My mother's ships are protected in their southern travel by the Dey of Algiers, and so we were able to hug the coast of Africa without fear. It cuts a month off the voyage, you know. We were a fleet of several ships, and we sailed under most favorable conditions. The storms we encountered were mild, and we reached Bombay easily.

"Murrough, my brother, is a very clever man, and he had our fleet wait just over the horizon while we entered Bombay on the flagship to be certain that Mother and Father had not been harmed and were alive before we handed over all that gold to the Portuguese."

"Do you know how much gold?" asked the emperor casually.

"It was, my brother told me, two hundred and fifty thousand coins' worth of pure gold. It was distributed among the fleet so unless you had all the ships, you didn't have all the gold." Velvet smiled a small smile. "Murrough is very clever," she said. "He is very like our mother in that."

"What happened when you got to Bombay?" asked Akbar.

Velvet shivered despite the heat. "Before we even docked," she said, "we could see a small group of Portuguese soldiers upon the docks . . ."

Her eyes clouded with the memory. The day had been incredibly hot, and the bright sun mirrored the heat of the busy harbor. The noise and the smells were varied and overwhelming as virtually naked, sweating men secured the heavy lines from the ship to the pier.

"You're to stay in the cabin," Murrough had warned her. "I'll not have the Portuguese seeing you. There aren't too many European women here. I want to make sure Mother and Adam are safe before I signal the others to come ashore."

"We'll die of the heat in here," Velvet protested. "Why can't I go with you? I want to see Mother and Father!"

"There will be some hard bargaining first, poppet, and Adam would have my hide if I put you in any danger. I want you and Pansy safe."

"Very well." She sighed. "If we must stay here, then we must. Get the chess set out again, Pansy, and we'll play a game while we wait."

"Yes, m'lady," replied Pansy. "Would it be safe for us to open the bow windows, Master Murrough? Perhaps there might be a breeze. Lord almighty, I've never felt such heat before. I feel positively weak in me knees."

"Aye," Murrough agreed with her. "'Tis debilitating, lass, and that's a truth. Open the windows, and it will help, I promise. Now that we're landed you can drink all the water you want, too." He smiled at both women as they reluctantly settled themselves, and then hurried from the cabin. When he was gone, Velvet rose and crossed quickly to slip out after him. Once on deck, she hid behind a barrel that gave her a good vantage point.

The ship had been made firmly secure and the gangway lowered so that the severely correct Jesuit priest might board.

"You have returned quickly, Captain O'Flaherty," said Esteban Ruy Ourique, the governor's personal advisor, as he gained the deck.

"Where are my mother and her husband?" demanded Murrough. "That was part of the bargain, that they would be awaiting me on the docks of this pesthole so that I might be certain that they were alive and safe. I do not see them anywhere."

"There has been some difficulty," began the Jesuit smoothly, "but did I not personally give you the church's word that no harm would come to them, Captain?"

"Then where are they, Father Ourique?" Murrough's gaze swept the pier and as it did something suddenly struck him. When he had sailed for England his mother's damaged vessel had been moored at this very dock. Now it was nowhere to be seen. In a flash he knew what had happened. They had escaped! His mother and Adam had seen some opportunity and had seized it! "They are gone!" he said triumphantly.

"Yes," the priest returned. "Three months ago." There was a small smile upon his thin lips. "Your mother is a formidable woman, Captain. As you know, we imprisoned the bulk of her crew, leaving only a small force aboard to repair the ship. Nonetheless, she somehow managed to gain freedom for her entire crew, overpower those soldiers guarding her vessel, and escape to the open sea. His Excellency, the governor, is most unhappy."

"I've not a doubt he is," said Murrough, a huge grin splitting his face.

"There is much, however, to be said for your honor, Captain, in returning here to pay the ransom nonetheless," murmured Father Ourique.

"Ah, now, Padre," said Murrough, "I see no reason to pay for something you don't have." He was immensely tickled that his mother had scored such a coup over the Portuguese. This would make grand telling back in England, and if he could return with the entire ransom intact, there might even be a knighthood in it for him. Sir Murrough O'Flaherty! Aye, his Joan would like that!

"A bargain was made," said the priest.

"Nay," returned Murrough. "Your governor, disregarding all the laws of hospitality, did unlawfully seize my mother, her husband, and their disabled ship when they entered this harbor in search of aid. Then he demanded ransom like a common pirate. A bargain with a pirate is not one that need be honored."

"I am sorry you feel that way, Captain, for half the monies are marked for the church's work here in India, and I cannot see it lost. As a faithful son of the church you must understand that."

"There is nothing that you can do to prevent it, Padre," came Murrough's quiet reply.

"But there is," returned the Jesuit, languidly raising his hand.

Murrough's eyes followed the direction in which the hand waved, and to his horror he suddenly found his ship surrounded and being boarded by a large force of Portuguese soldiers who must have been waiting in the shadows of the buildings on the docks. "You're wasting your time, Padre," he said in an attempted bluff. "There is no gold upon my ship."

"I cannot believe you returned without the ransom," said Father Ourique. "If there is no gold upon this ship, then it is upon the ships you undoubtedly have awaiting your signal just beyond the horizon, Captain."

"That, Padre, you'll never know, for I shall say neither yea or nay upon the subject."

"You will not object then if we search the ship," was the reply.

Murrough shrugged. "Do I have a choice?"

Velvet slid from her hiding place and slipped back into her brother's large cabin to tell Pansy the news. She felt as elated as her brother at their mother's cleverness.

Pansy was delighted as well, but for other reasons. "Then we'll not have to stay here, m'lady? We can turn right around and go home? Good! Lord, this heat is killing me. I wouldn't last a month here."

"Poor Pansy," Velvet sympathized. "This has not been an easy trip for you, seasick the first few months and now this heat. I will ask Murrough to obtain for us some fresh fruit and vegetables before we sail. We haven't had any in some weeks."

"Aye, 'twould be nice, m'lady. Maybe it's the salt air, but I do have a fancy for fruits. I wonder how me dad bears it being at sea for months at a time year after year."

"He was home long enough to get all those children with your mother," teased Velvet.

Pansy giggled back. "Aye, and that's a truth! Still, I don't know how he or any other sailor bears it. If it hadn't been for that route your brother took, sailing just off the coast of Africa, going ashore every now and then for water and fresh foods, I don't think I could have stood it, m'lady. I hope you've not developed a taste for travel like your ma."

"Nay, Pansy, I haven't. I will be glad to get home to England. The shock of Alex's death has now worn off, although I shall never forget him, and I will spend my days mourning him. 'Twill be a quiet life we'll lead, Pansy, for I do not want to return to court or see London again. I will spend my days at *Queen's Malvern* with my parents, caring for them as they enter their old age."

Practical Pansy swallowed her laughter, for it would not do for her to make mock of her mistress. Velvet might think she was going to spend her life a widow, but Pansy suspected she would eventually remarry, for she was far too alive a person to remain alone and unloved. As for Master Adam and Mistress Skye gaining their old age! Those two will never be old, thought Pansy. "Aye, m'lady," she answered simply, "'twill be good to get home."

Her words had not even died away when the door to the cabin burst open, and the room was filled with soldiers who began to poke and pry into everything, opening chests and pulling out garments.

"How dare you!" Velvet cried. "Stop at once! Get out of my cabin!"

They did not understand her words, and so continued on with their mission. Velvet, however, attempted to stop them physically, pushing at them, yanking back her garments from their hands, the outrage plain upon her lovely face. The soldiers began to grin as they recognized her womanly fury, though it became obvious that there was no gold hidden in the captain's cabin. European women were very few here, and surely their superiors would not deny them a few moments' sport with this heretic Englishwoman.

Pansy, seeing their change in mood, slipped from the cabin and ran quickly to find Murrough.

With a roar of outrage Murrough rushed to his cabin, followed by Father Ourique. Velvet, however, was defending herself quite well against the governor's soldiers. She had flung a perfume bottle at one, hitting her target squarely in the middle of his forehead and rendering him unconscious. About him his comrades clustered worriedly.

"Who is this angry young woman?" demanded the Jesuit.

"My sister, Velvet Gordon, the Countess of BrocCairn," said Murrough with a relieved chuckle. "Velvet, poppet, may I present to you Father Esteban Ruy Ourique, the governor's aide."

"*Mon père*, your men are unruly and have made an unholy disaster of my trunks. Not only that, but they have made rather obscene advances to me. Although I do not understand your language, I most certainly understood their intent. I am shocked! I am a most respectable Catholic gentlewoman, a widow in mourning."

"You have my apologies, madame, and those of His Excellency for whom I speak. I can only say that women of our race are rare in these climes, and my men in their enthusiasm at seeing a beautiful European woman were overzealous in their admiration."

Velvet laughed, a clear, sweet sound. "Padre, I have never before met a Jesuit, but you do their reputation for diplomacy great honor."

"I see much of your mother in you, madame," came Father Ourique's reply, and he smiled thinly. Then he turned to Murrough. "Such a long voyage has undoubtedly been hard on your sister, Captain. She and her servant must be the governor's guests for the next few days until our business is completed."

"My sister is quite comfortable here, Padre, and, besides, we have no further business," said Murrough.

"Ah, but we do, Captain O'Flaherty. Just beyond our horizon lies your fleet, and until it anchors here in Bombay and disgorges its cargo to us, Lady Gordon will remain our guest."

"I cannot allow that," said Murrough tersely.

"But I insist," came the Jesuit's steely reply. "You really have no choice, Captain. My soldiers far outnumber your crew."

"This is outright piracy, Padre!" protested Murrough.

"To whom will you complain, Captain?" mocked the Jesuit. "The Portuguese government will not chastize us for extracting monies from those who seek to dislodge us from our place here in India. Neither can you, as the good Catholic you are, deny the church a contribution for its work here."

"Padre, I think you should know that my sister is the queen's godchild. She is particularly dear to Elizabeth Tudor."

"The English queen means nothing to us, heretic that she is."

"My sister's other godmother is France's queen," was Murrough's quick reply. "She is also cherished by that lady. I am sure if England's queen is naught to you, France's must be, for that is where, if memory serves me, the Jesuits have their headquarters. I might also remind you that our uncle is a bishop."

"You need have no fears, Captain. We mean your sister no harm, but we do need some sort of bond for your good behavior as you have shown yourself to be impetuous," Father Ourique insisted.

"I will complain to the queen when we return to England, Padre!" said Murrough angrily.

"Of course," murmured the priest smoothly, and then he turned to Velvet. "Take only a minimum of personal necessities, madame. I do not expect you will be with us long."

"You're damned right she won't be!" exploded Murrough.

"Don't fret, Murrough," said Velvet calmly. "There is nothing we can do about this situation. I am merely surprised that Mother could not get some sort of message to you before we reached Bombay. It was inevitable that once we reached here the ransom would have to be paid."

The Jesuit smiled coldly, but his eyes were beaming with approval. "Your sister understands the game, Captain O'Flaherty," he said, "far better than you do."

Velvet smiled back at Father Ourique. "Will you see that my cabin is cleared of your men, Padre, so that my tiring woman and I may pack? We will not be very long."

"There is time, Countess. I will send for a carriage to transport you." He bowed, and then with a paucity of motion shooed the soldiers from the cabin, leaving Pansy, Murrough, and Velvet alone.

"You mustn't be frightened," began Murrough.

"I'm not," said Velvet. "It will give me a chance to see the city, and then I shall have something to talk about when we return to England."

"You surprise me more every day," said Murrough quietly. "What happened to the hysterical young woman who boarded my ship five months ago?"

"She grew up a little more, brother. Alex's death was a terrible shock to me for many reasons, but perhaps mostly because it was so unnecessary. Being away from everyone and everything, out on the sea with only the elements for companions, I have been able to come to terms with myself, for I really have only myself to rely on in the end. I will never forget my marriage, short though it was. I will never forget Alex. I, however, am alive, and I must go on for whatever purpose God intends. When we return home, I will retire to *Queen's Malvern* and spend the rest of my days there with Mama and Papa. They were my life before Alex, and so shall they be once again."

"There will be someone else for you one day, poppet," Murrough said. "Has not Robin found new happiness with Angel? And our mother? Did not life treat her harshly time after time until she wed with your father?"

"There will be no one else for me," said Velvet with all the dramatic certainty of a sixteen-year-old, and Murrough, knowing better, did not bother to argue with her further. One day another man would come along who would capture her heart.

"I will go on deck and arrange for the water casks to be refilled so that we may set sail for the fleet as quickly as possible after you've left the ship," he told her.

She stepped forward and hugged her brother hard. She loved him greatly, and he had been so good to her.

Remembering it now, in Akbar's zenana, fresh tears began to slide down Velvet's face. Until this moment she had not realized how painful the memory was.

"I see now how you came to India," said Akbar, "but there is more. I would not distress you, but you must finish your story for me."

"I'll be all right." Velvet sniffed. "It was just that I was thinking of my brother. I love him very much. Are you sure, my lord, that I do not bore you with my tale?"

He smiled warmly at her. "No, you do not bore me. I feel very much like Sultan Schariar with his Scheherezade."

"Who were Sultan Schariar and Scheherezade?" asked Velvet.

"Schariar was a ruler of Persia many centuries ago who, having been deceived by his wife, executed her in accordance with the laws of his land, and then decided that all women were wicked as she had been. Vowing never to be deluded again, he ordered that a new bride be brought to him each night and on each following morning he had her executed.

Up until then Schariar had been much loved by his people, but now they feared him, and they feared for their daughters. Finally the elder daughter of the sultan's grand vizier, a maiden named Scheherezade, was determined to put a stop to the tragedy and, despite her father's distress, offered herself as the sultan's bride.

"That evening Scheherezade begged the sultan to allow her sister, Dinarzade, to spend the night with her as it was her last night on earth. The sultan acquiesced, which was fortunate since Scheherezade's plan required her sister's cooperation. An hour before the dawn, Dinarzade awoke and begged her sister to tell one of her fabulous stories as it would be the last time she ever heard one. With the sultan's permission Scheherezade began her tale. At daybreak she ceased speaking, though the tale was nowhere near finished, but she knew the sultan arose at dawn to attend his council. Dinarzade protested, and the sultan, who at this point was very much caught up in the story himself, delayed Scheherezade's execution for a day.

Each night for a thousand and one nights Scheherezade told the sultan fabulous tales of geniis, ghouls, and jinns; of Peris, who are fairies; of princesses who worked magic spells; and of handsome princes, flying carpets, and horses that flew. In the end the sultan fell in love with her, made her his sultana, and when his reign of terror stopped, he was once more loved by his people as was Scheherezade."

Velvet was intrigued by his story. "Will you order me executed after I have finished my tale?" she said with a little smile.

Akbar's black eyes fixed themselves on her face, and he said in his deep, satiny voice, "I could never destroy such rare beauty as yours. I am more likely to make you one of my queens."

Velvet's cheeks pinked prettily. "You have many queens, I am told," she said pertly.

A chuckle rumbled from his chest. "Continue your tale, my Scheherezade," he said, thinking again that he liked her spirit.

"I was transported to the Portuguese governor's house late that afternoon," she began, remembering as she spoke the terrible, damp heat of Bombay that left her feeling totally limp. Beside her in the stuffy, closed carriage, Pansy was looking green again.

"Lord, m'lady, first 'tis the sea that makes me sick, and then no sooner am I upon dry land than I feel even worse. God help us, but I will be glad to go home."

Secretly, Velvet agreed with her young tiring woman, but it was up to her now to keep their spirits up. "I'm sure that once we get to the governor's house we will be able to have something cool to drink, and that should help."

Pansy didn't look particularly convinced, but she grew quiet again, and Velvet couldn't decide which was worse, the silence or her maid's complaints. The governor's residence looked promising, a two-story white-brick building built around a large, flowering courtyard. They were settled into an airy suite of rooms overlooking the courtyard and given cool, scented baths, which after the months at sea was a great treat, but it was not until evening that Velvet met the governor, Don Cesar Affonso Marinha-Grande.

He was a tall, spare man, his skin bronzed by the relentless Indian sun, his eyes cold and flat, and his hair dark. He had a beautifully barbered small beard and a narrow moustache. To her amazement he was dressed in the height of fashion, in black velvet and white lace, which she couldn't help thinking must be very warm considering the heat of the day. She herself had chosen to wear a simple brown silk gown with an open neckline in order to be as cool as possible.

Father Ourique moved to introduce Velvet as she entered the dining chamber. "Your Excellency, may I present Velvet Gordon, the Countess of BrocCairn, who will be your guest until her brother returns to complete our business. She is the only child of Lord and Lady de Marisco."

Velvet curtsied politely. "Your Excellency," she said.

He bowed, but his eyes were instantly fastened upon her breasts. "You are a widow, madame?" was his greeting.

"Yes, m'lord."

"Children?"

"No, m'lord. We were not blessed, and our union was short."

"You remind me of your mother, though you don't really look like her," the governor said. "A most beautiful woman, Lady de Marisco."

"My father is her equal, for he is the most handsome man I have ever known," said Velvet proudly.

"A troublesome man, your father, madame, but then your mother for all her beauty is a troublesome woman."

The dinner was served. Velvet ate automatically, not even remembering what it was she consumed. The governor spoke no more to her, instead conversing in his own language with the Jesuit. When the meal was over, she politely bid the two good night and, escorted by a servant, turned to make her way to her chambers. She could feel the governor's eyes boring into her back as she left the room.

Pansy was feeling better, having stuffed herself with fresh fruit. "I haven't got the foggiest notion what half of them was, m'lady." She laughed. "But it all tasted delicious, and I decided if they brought it for you, it must be all right."

Both the young women were exhausted, so they retired early, Velvet sleeping on the bed and Pansy on the trundle.

Velvet didn't know exactly what it was that woke her during the night, but she suddenly came wide awake and saw Don Cesar standing over her bed, flanked by several of his native servants. Before she could cry out, she was pulled up from the bed. Her first reaction was one of anger. How dare they lay hands upon her! But the anger turned to fear when the governor calmly reached out and ripped the thin silk of her night rail from her. Her eyes widened, and her throat tensed in a shocked scream of outrage and embarrassment.

"Beautiful," he murmured almost worshipfully, ignoring her cry. He stood before her, cupping her breasts, and then his hands smoothed down to fit the curve of her waist. "I hope you realize that I am denying myself greatly by sending you to the emperor, madame. He has never, to my knowledge, had a fair-skinned European woman in his harem, and you shall be the first." He ran his hand across her belly, and then slid it around to fondle one of her buttocks. "Glorious! Absolutely glorious! What tender, young skin you have!" He fingered her freshly washed auburn hair. "How soft it is," he said, almost to himself, "and perfection with your emerald eyes. You are really quite magnificent, madame, perhaps even more beautiful than your bitch of a mother."

Velvet stiffened angrily. "How dare you, my lord! How dare you speak of my mama in such a fashion!"

"Your mama!" He hissed, and at the corner of his lips a tiny foam of spittle appeared. "I offered your mama the honor of my protection. Unlike your father and his heretic crew, whom I housed in my dungeons, I brought your mama here to my palace and put her in rooms next to my own apartments.

"She flaunted her beauty before me in lascivious fashion, taunting and tempting me beyond reason." His dark eyes were haunted by the memory and filled with pain. His face grew almost frenzied with his hatred. "I desired her, and she refused me! She said I was incapable of true desire, a poor excuse for a man, that she would rather be in a filthy prison than with me! The bitch! She dared to spit in my face!"

"Good for Mama!" Velvet cried out bravely, and Pansy silently cheered her mistress.

Outraged by this echo of her mother's defiance, the governor slapped Velvet across the face as if to gain some measure of revenge on Skye. Then he smiled, showing small, pointed, yellowed teeth. "Perhaps such a show of spirit will intrigue the Grand Mughal, my dear."

"Are you mad, sir?" she demanded. "How dare you enter my chamber and behave as you are doing!"

The governor laughed. "You English! Always so cool in a crisis. Have you not heard a word I have said to you?

"Tonight you will begin a journey across this incredible land to Lahore, the capital of Akbar, the Grand Mughal himself," Don Cesar told her. "You are a gift to him from me. He has several thousand concubines in his harem, but if you are lucky you will attract him. Akbar, has, I am told, a great appetite for beautiful women. He has never had a European concubine before. What a rarity you will be for him! He will be in my debt, thanks to you! And I will have settled my score with your shameless mother."

Velvet was shocked by the governor's words. "You are mad, sir!" she cried out to him. "I am under the protection of the church. You cannot do this!"

Cesar Affonso Marinha-Grande laughed heartily. "I can do whatever I want for I am the governor here. No one, not even Padre Ourique, will know what I have done with you until your unsuspecting brother has paid the ransom. Do you think the Jesuit will ride after you then, after he learns what I have done? Do not be foolish, madame! The Jesuit only seeks the gold your brother brings. His share will help him to do great things among the heretics, and perhaps in time word of it will get to Paris and he will be recalled with honors to civilization. No, he will not help you. As for your brother, he will not be able to go after you. What does he know of this land? He will be expelled immediately upon his delivery of the ransom. You are no virgin to weep and whine. Resign yourself to your fate, madame!"

Velvet was horrified, and then her eyes met Pansy's frightened ones. "At least leave my servant here to return with my brother to England. This heat will be her death, sir."

"No! The girl goes with you! Or else she dies!" He reached for the dagger at his waist.

"No!" Velvet cried, thinking, we are at the mercy of a madman!

"Then you must both make ready to leave. My caravan of gifts departs within the hour. The moon will light your way, and it is cooler traveling at night. Unfortunately, there will be no palanquin for you. You will travel faster on your own two feet. I will send a woman to you who will show you how to dress so that your skin will not be marred by exposure to the sun. Farewell."

"Please, sir!" Velvet called after him, and he turned back to her. "Why are you doing this? Think on it! I am the god-child of two queens, not some poor, defenseless girl with no family. Cease your actions now and I will say nothing, and neither will Pansy."

Suddenly his face went dark with rage, and he almost spat the words at her. "You are just like your mother," he said venomously. "A proud, defiant wench. Well, we will see how defiant you are after a year in the Grand Mughal's harem!" Then, whirling, he was gone with his servants, and a dark-skinned woman in native dress was entering the room.

"I am Zerlinda," she said. "The governor has sent me with garments for you and your servant."

"Zerlinda! You must help us!" said Velvet desperately. "I am the Countess of BrocCairn. I am under the protection of the Jesuits. What the governor is doing is wrong. Help me and I will reward you well. My brother will give you whatever you want!"

"What I want is to be the wife of Don Cesar, and he has promised me that if I help him," came the woman's frightening reply. "I have loved him for three years, but what chance did I, a half-caste of Portuguese-Jewish-Indian blood, have to be his wife? There is nothing that you can give me, madame, to aid you. After tonight I will have everything!"

She handed Velvet and Pansy enveloping robes that covered them from neck to ankle. The garments were of cotton gauze and striped in several colors. After they had put them on, Zerlinda said, "I have hooded capes for you also. The nights are sometimes cool, and if it should rain you will need them. Be sure you take sturdy shoes. It is a long trek to Lahore. You will be on the road well over a month."

Numbly Velvet donned her cape. She could not believe what was happening to her. Suddenly she grew very angry. "I am not going to be kidnapped like this!" she said. "Neither my servant nor I will leave this room until we have seen Father Ourique. He will not permit this outrage!"

Zerlinda said nothing. Instead she opened the door and spoke quickly in Portuguese to the soldier who waited outside. He entered the room, and, walking swiftly up to Velvet, he hit her on the jaw, catching her as she collapsed unconscious into his arms.

"Get shoes for yourself and your mistress, and any other small thing you can carry that will make her comfortable," said Zerlinda. "I will wait outside, but be quick."

Pansy gathered up Velvet's hairbrush, some hairpins, ribbons, handkerchiefs, a tiny jeweled gold mirror, and a small silver paring knife that Velvet carried on a delicate matching chain. Carefully Pansy wrapped the whole bundle in a large silk square. Sturdy shoes, Zerlinda had said. Pansy almost laughed. Sturdy shoes were all she possessed, but her lady was another matter. All she had were silken slippers. Sighing, Pansy unwrapped her bundle and, adding three pair of the delicate footwear, retied it. Then hoisting it into her arms she left the room.

Pansy followed Zerlinda down into the courtyard where a formidable-looking caravan was assembled. "Your mistress is there," said Zerlinda, pointing at a cart. "This entire caravan is made up of gifts for the emperor. It is well protected. Neither you nor your mistress will come to any harm. The caravan master understands that your mistress is a special gift for the emperor himself." Then as an afterthought Zerlinda said, "Tell your mistress that the lord Akbar is a kind and good man well loved by his people."

Pansy clambered into the cart where her mistress lay. Gently she fingered Velvet's jaw. Thank God there would be no bruise, and that was a miracle for the brute had hit her hard enough.

The caravan departed the governor's palace and wound through the silent streets of the city onto the northwest highway. A bright moon shone down on them, illuminating their way.

It wasn't until morning that Velvet began to rouse. By then the caravan was well north of the city. Pansy, who had been walking next to the cart that carried Velvet, was glad to see her mistress awake and apparently unharmed.

With the sun came the heat, and finally toward midmorning they made camp in the shelter of some large rocks. Water and fruits were passed around, the animals cared for, and then everyone but those guarding the caravan fell asleep.

"I know you've slept all the night, m'lady, but you'd best sleep today as well. Tonight you'll be walking, and you're not used to it," Pansy said.

"I feel awful," Velvet admitted, "my head hurts."

"I'm not surprised," the tiring woman fussed as she braced her mistress's shoulders and gently fed her some brackish water. When Velvet had sipped her fill, Pansy offered her slices of a soft, reddish fruit with a sweet taste. "I ain't got no idea what it is, but it tastes good," she said.

Velvet laughed weakly, but she nibbled on the fruit eagerly.

They slept the day away in the stifling heat, which toward midafternoon was broken for a short time by a rainstorm. Huddling in a small, open cave made by two large rocks, they were better protected with their hooded capes than the others.

Then in the late afternoon as the rain ceased several cookfires sprang up, and a lamb was butchered and roasted. Together the two women waited their turn as the meat was finally carved, and were given pieces of lamb and a ladleful each of rice on a tin plate. There were no utensils, and so, following the lead of their captors, they used their three middle fingers to scoop up the rice. The meal over, the trek began again as soon as the campfires were put out and everything packed away.

It was in the middle of the third week of their trek that Pansy fell ill of a fever. What caused it Velvet did not know, but when the tiring woman could walk no farther and collapsed onto the road, the caravan master was for leaving her. Frantically Velvet clung to her servant, her friend. "No! I won't let you," she protested, her green eyes filling with tears.

Angrily, the caravan master shouted at her and tried to pull her away, but Velvet clung to Pansy like moss to a rock. "No!" She sobbed desperately, and then suddenly an idea struck her. Falling to her knees, she frantically scrabbled through the bundle Pansy had hastily packed at the governor's palace. Finding what she sought, she stood and held it out with one hand while pointing first to Pansy and then to the cart with the other.

The caravan master's eyes grew round with greed at the sight of the dainty, bejeweled gold mirror. There was a girl in Lahore that he was courting, and this was a finer gift than anything he could ordinarily give her. He reached for the mirror, but Velvet shook her head and pointed again at the cart. The caravan master nodded and reached out once more, but Velvet dropped again to her knees and began to draw in the dirt with her finger. Fascinated, he watched her, and when she gestured him over he knelt to see a rather crude rendition of the cart, a long road, and finally a city. When his eye had reached the end of her message, she laid the mirror down on the city portion and looked at him.

He gazed at her, wondering if he could trust her and admiring her cleverness in bargaining with him despite the language barrier. As if she sensed his thoughts, Velvet detached the filigreed gold chain she used to hang the mirror from her belt and offered it to him. Taking it from her, he nodded his agreement. The chain now, the mirror when they reached their destination, and in return the sick girl could ride in a cart. He gave the order, and Pansy was lifted from her place upon the ground and into the cart beneath which they had been sleeping at night.

Velvet breathed a sigh of relief, not realizing that the caravan master fully expected that Pansy would be dead long before they reached Lahore. She might have been, too, had word not come that Akbar was at Fatehpur-Sikri and the caravan altered its route. In the meantime Velvet worked frantically nursing her servant, terrified lest she lose her friend and her last link with England. She knew very little of what to do, for the herbal medicine she had learned from her mother and Dame Cecily involved herbs and roots that she had no idea how to obtain here in this unfamiliar place. If only she could find some fennel leaves, which, brewed as a tea, would help to lower Pansy's fever. Violet tea was another decoction that could help, but she suspected that violets were not native to this hot land. How could she find marrows, another fever remedy? She simply didn't know, and her inability to help Pansy fully was both frightening and frustrating. The most Velvet could do was to bathe her servant's hands and head, and to get water, mashed fruit, and juices into her, a task that became increasingly difficult as Pansy spent more and more time unconscious.

By the time the caravan reached Fatehpur-Sikri, Velvet was terrified both of Pansy's fate and of the unknown fate that awaited her.

"And does your fate seem so awful now, my Scheherezade?" Akbar asked her as she stopped speaking.

"I do not know what my fate is to be yet, sire," Velvet answered him.

He looked at her a long moment, and then said, "I think you do know."

Again her cheeks filled with color, and she lowered her eyes. Velvet was no fool, and she knew quite well why the Portuguese governor had sent her to the Grand Mughal. She was not a virgin, yet still she was afraid. In her mind she yet remained Alex's wife.

"And Pansy?" she said, finding her voice and attempting to change the subject. "Has your physician been able to determine what is wrong with her?"

"It took some time, I am told, to bathe her in her unconscious state. The physician should be with her now. Would you like to go and see?" He rose easily from his seated position on the bed and held out his hand to her.

Shyly she put her hand in his and stood to go with him. He led her from her chamber, down the corridor to another smaller room. Within, Velvet saw a very pale Pansy lying on a bed, an elderly, bearded gentleman standing over her.

The physician turned as they entered the room and, bowing, spoke to Akbar.

"My lord, I have been able to render a diagnosis. It is really quite simple. The woman is suffering from the effect of our heat to which she is obviously not accustomed, and from a swelling of her hands and feet, which have been brought on by her advanced state of pregnancy. She should deliver her child within a month to six weeks. She must remain in bed until that time. I have prescribed a diuretic, which should reduce the swelling. With rest, shelter from the sun, and cool baths her fever will shortly abate. Should the swelling not go down within the next few days I will induce her labor. Delivery of the child will cure her if nothing else will."

"Thank you, Zafar Singh. This lady is the woman's mistress, and she loves her servant dearly. She will be greatly relieved."

"What is it?" Velvet asked anxiously, for the conversation had been held in Akbar's native tongue. "Will Pansy live?"

"Most likely," he said, and then, "Are you aware that your servant is expecting a child?"

"*What*?" Velvet was astounded. Pansy enceinte? "It isn't possible," she said, but in the back of her mind she knew that if it were Dugald was the father.

"Will you ask the physician if he is certain, my lord?" she said.

"He is most certain. Your servant will deliver within a month or so."

"When can I speak with her? She has been unconscious these last few days." Velvet gazed worriedly down at Pansy's drawn features.

"When will the girl be able to speak? She has been unconscious for several days," Akbar demanded of the doctor.

"Her rest is a natural one now, my lord. She should awaken tomorrow."

"You should be able to speak with your servant tomorrow," Akbar relayed to Velvet. "Her sleep is now a natural one."

"Thank God!"

He was touched by her emotion. He found her concern for her servant charming. Taking her again by the hand, he led her back to her own quarters.

"She doesn't look enceinte," Velvet mused. "When we left England my sister-in-law was with child, and not as near to term, yet she was big. I hope Pansy's baby is all right."

"Each woman carries her child in a different fashion. Some grow large early, others late, and some not at all. Some women carry high, some low. She seems a hardy girl."

"She is." Velvet looked at him and smiled. "You are so very kind, sire. Tell me how it is you know so much about babies."

"I should. I have fathered enough." He smiled sadly. "Only six, however, have lived. I have three sons and three daughters."

They stood awkwardly silent for a few moments. Then Akbar said, "You will want to rest now. I will come tomorrow and see you. Good night, my English Rose. Sleep well."

Adali arose from the corner where he had been awaiting her. "Aiyee! You have pleased him, my princess! Yes! Yes, I could tell it! He is pleased with you!"

Velvet shook her head. "He is simply a kind man, Adali. Tomorrow I will ask him to return me to my own land."

The eunuch said nothing further. He knew that Akbar would do no such thing. He had seen the look in his emperor's eyes as they caressed his new mistress. It had been many years since the Grand Mughal had looked with passion upon a woman. Most of his liaisons were either out of political necessity or physical need. This, however, was a different matter.

Adali remembered the story of Akbar and one of his wives, the beauteous Almira. Almira had been thirteen when she had caught the eye of the Grand Mughal. Unfortunately she was the wife of the elderly Shaikh Abdul Wasi. Akbar, however, desired her greatly, and Almira was equally enamored of the emperor. Since neither could control their passions,

Akbar forced the shaikh to divorce his wife so that he might have her. Almira was the mother of Akbar's second son, Prince Murad.

It was the only time Adali knew of that his master had wed out of his own desire and not expediency. The eunuch himself had not been with the court then, being just a small boy in Cambay, but the tale was a famous one. After Adali had joined the Mughal's court he had learned that Akbar was fond of all his wives; the mother of his heir, Prince Salim, Princess Jodh Bai, being highest in his esteem. Never, however, had Adali ever heard it said that the emperor was in love. Adali believed, though, that this was about to change. Akbar desired the foreign princess, his mistress, that much was plain, but there was more to it than that. The eunuch could tell by the emperor's patience and gentleness to the woman that Akbar thought her special. She was very different, and the emperor knew it. Had he not instructed Adali to keep her from the others lest they change her? Adali realized that by virtue of his French father he had just taken a giant step forward in the hierarchy of the household eunuchs. If his mistress could hold the Grand Mughal's heart, his fortune was made. To that end he intended to work.

"You must rest now," he said. "It has been a frightening time for you, but you are safe here." He turned her about and pulled open the ribbons that held her little blouse closed.

"What are you doing?" Velvet cried.

"You must prepare for sleep," he answered her. "Here we sleep without garments."

"You cannot undress me," exclaimed Velvet in a shocked tone.

"I am your servant," he answered.

"You are a man," she replied.

Adali laughed. "No I am not, princess. I am a eunuch. Oh, I resemble a man, and I was born a male, but when I was gelded I ceased to be a man." He whisked her blouse off and reached to loosen her skirtband. "I have none of the feelings and desires of a normal man." The skirt slipped to the floor, and Velvet automatically stepped from the silken circle as Adali bent to pick up the garment.

Realizing that she was naked, Velvet quickly climbed onto her bed and drew a silken coverlet over herself. "I am really quite capable of undressing myself," she said in a small voice.

"You are a princess," he answered, "and it is my duty to serve you. You will be used to me in a few days." He chuckled. "And then you will think nothing of my presence." Taking a hairbrush from his pantaloons, he sat down next to her and began to brush out her luxuriant hair quite expertly, gently but firmly removing the tangles. When he had finished, he replaced the brush within thc voluminous folds of his pantaloons and walked to the door. Turning, he smiled and said, "I will sleep outside in the hallway. Should you need me you have but to call."

"Where are you taking my clothes?" she asked. "They are all I have."

"I must give them to the laundress to wash," he said. "Do not worry. In the morning there will be a trunkful of beautiful garments for you, I promise. Good night."

She was alone. Alone for the first time in many months. For some minutes she sat in the middle of the silken bed staring through the open arch that led to the terrace. Her eyes were not really focused on anything, but her mind was very active. She was hundreds of miles from a coast that separated her by thousands of miles of water from her own land. It was a sobering thought. Would her family—could her family—ever find her? And if they did, what was really left for her in England? In the months following Alex's death she had consoled herself with the thought of caring for her aging parents, but the truth was that neither Adam nor Skye would ever be old in a conventional sense, and they had each other. She had no one. Even Pansy had Dugald, and that was something that she had to think seriously about now.

The baby that Pansy carried was certainly Dugald's, and he had just as much right to his child as she did. Pansy was eventually going to have to be returned to England with her child to be reunited with Dugald. It was only right. Velvet was relieved, however, to realize that it would be many months before Pansy could even consider going.

Velvet sighed deeply and stretched out, flinging the silken coverlet off her. There was the tiniest of breezes coming through the arch, but it was warm and scented with a hauntingly sweet fragrance that was not familiar to her. She wondered what it was and decided to ask Adali tomorrow. What is to happen to me? she thought. The Portuguese have attempted to curry favor with the Grand Mughal by sending me to grace his bed. He is a kind man, but is he a patient one? How can I submit to him? How can I be his concubine? I am so afraid. They were disturbing thoughts that swirled around in her brain, but despite the distress they caused, Velvet, exhausted both emotionally and physically by her travails of the last month, without realizing it fell into a deep sleep.

The moon rose and silvered the landscape of Fatehpur-Sikri, preening itself vainly in the city's artificial lake and fountains. The reddish-and-white sandstone glistened as the moonlight touched the whimsical domes, turned columns, and the carved sandstone panels on the exterior of the palaces. All was still and quiet, but for the occasional cackle of a hyena out scavenging beyond the city's walls.

In the emperor's zenana the female guards, nodding sleepily at their posts, straightened momentarily as Akbar moved by them. He paused before Velvet's doorway, and instantly Adali was on his feet quietly opening the portal to him. Silently Akbar moved into the chamber and, standing before the bed, gazed down at the sleeping girl. Slowly his eyes traveled the length of her, taking in the delicacy of her fine-bone structure; her lovely, smooth, round breasts; lithe waistline; long, slim legs; and slender feet. In the moonlight her creamy skin was faultless. She had spread her hair over the pillow before falling asleep in order to be cooler, and, reaching out, he fingered a silky curl. Then he sighed. She was flawless, a perfect beauty, and he longed to possess her body. Yet there was more.

The women of his land were taught meekness from the cradle, and though some were strong of character, few would go against their breeding. Those who did generally did it for their sons or husbands who were either young or weak, or both. Indian women did not converse intelligently with men, considering such behavior forward and rude. In the privacy of the bedchamber a woman spoke of love, or of her children, or worried about her lord's health.

This young woman, however, was vastly different. It was apparent from the moment she was dragged, shrieking, into his presence. An Indian woman would have submitted meekly, but not this English rose. She was highly educated, he could see, for her French was even better than that of the Jesuit who had taught him.

Akbar, though he could neither read nor write, was a highly educated man. In his youth he had escaped his tutors for hunting and riding, pursuits he far preferred, but because he was infinitely curious, he now had scholars of all subjects surrounding him, reading to him, discoursing with him, lecturing to him. There was very little of the world's knowledge that he did not know, and he was forever seeking to learn more.

This girl who lay here in her innocent, troubled sleep could be something more to him than simply a beautiful body to enjoy, to slake his desires upon. She could be his companion and his friend as well. It was a novel idea, and he pondered it as he turned away from Velvet and exited her chamber to return to his own. It was a thought he would never share with anyone else, for his friends would be shocked and amused and the women of his household would be horrified.

The English woman was going to ask him, he knew, to return her to her own people. It was something he could not do for many reasons but mainly because he would not offend the Portuguese. He was going to have to work very hard to make Velvet happy so that she would want to stay with him, so that she would not pine for her own people. He found it an interesting challenge.

. . .

In the morning as Velvet sat wrapped in the silk coverlet on her bed eating something cool, tart, and smooth that Adali called yogurt, sipping a pungent hot drink he told her was tea, a knock came upon the door. Opening it, Adali gave a small cry of delight and stepped back to allow entry to a line of slaves who entered the room carrying all manner of things.

"What is this?" Velvet's eyes widened.

"Just the beginning, my princess," said the eunuch. "The lord Akbar honors you with gifts. Did I not tell you that you had caught his eye?"

She watched as two men carried in and out onto the rooftop terrace a large, stuffed, silk-upholstered piece of furniture. It was shaped in a semicircle with a medium-high back and rolled arms. Upon its seat they placed many cushions. Next to it went a small table inlaid with mother-of-pearl.

"What on earth is that for?" she asked Adali.

"For reclining," he answered her.

"It is very big," she replied.

"Big enough for two." He smiled broadly.

"Oh!"

"Aiyee! Look, my princess! Look!" Adali was almost dancing with delight as two matching trunks—each painted with exquisite designs of pink, blue, and red flowers with yellow centers and green leaves upon a shiny, black-lacquered background, and bound with bright polished brass bands—were brought into the room. He did not wait for the trunks to be opened by the bearers, instead eagerly lifting the lid on the one nearest to hand himself to reveal that it was filled with clothing, a rainbow of skirts and dainty blouses that he lifted out with tiny exclamations of pleasure. They were all of the finest, softest silk: some decorated with gold or silver designs, some bejeweled, some plain. The colors were bright, but only those shades that would flatter her: blues, greens, pinks, mauves, purples, tawny oranges, and creams.

Velvet was honestly stunned by this unexpected bounty and, looking at Adali, said, "Why?"

"Foolish woman," he answered her in a scolding tone, "I keep telling you that you have found favor with the lord Akbar."

"I have done nothing," she said, bewildered.

"He is wooing you, my princess. Have you never been wooed?"

She shook her head, realizing that she and Alex had fought and battled through their courtship, but never had he wooed her in a traditional sense. He had loved her, but he had certainly never courted her. Velvet's female soul was touched.

"Open the other trunk," she commanded the eunuch, and when he had she stared in surprise at its contents. There were carved jade bottles containing lotions and scents all with the same fragrance that Adali identified as jasmine.

"Is that what is growing outside on my terrace?" she questioned him.

He nodded. "Jasmine is a flower of love, my princess."

Velvet said nothing, instead looking farther into the second trunk to find a lovely, pearl-studded, gold brush for her hair and a miniature of the larger trunk filled with hair ornaments made from both precious metals and jewels. There was another box carved from a solid piece of lavender jade, mounted with silver hinges and a silver-filigreed lock that, when opened, revealed a small fortune in jewels. If there was one thing Velvet knew it was precious gems, for her mother had one of the most incredible collections of jewelry in all of Europe. As a child she had delighted in playing with the sparkling gemstones and Skye had explained to her child what each stone was and where the finest examples of each came from. In the jade box were Ceylon sapphires, Burmese rubies, Indian Ocean pearls, incredible yellow diamonds, fine, deep purple amethysts, light blue aquamarines, emeralds, olive green peridots from the Red Sea, and honey-colored zircons. They were set in necklaces, chains, earbobs, and rings; and there wasn't a flawed stone among them.

Adali was almost beside himself with joy. He doubted that his master had done more than hold the English woman's hand so far, and yet he was already showering her with valuables. While Velvet sat stunned, gazing at the contents of the lavender jade box, the eunuch directed the parade of slaves that continued to enter the room bearing more gifts. Magnificent red and blue wool rugs were spread upon the floors; tall, brass vases filled with flowers were placed upon the floor throughout the chamber; several small tables were placed strategically, and then lamps of silver studded with colorful gemstones were brought and put on the tables. Finally twin girls of approximately ten years of age, with long, straight black hair, expressive dark eyes, and golden skin, entered and prostrated themselves before Velvet. Behind them came Ramesh, who spoke quickly to the eunuch, handed him a small, covered reed basket, and then left.

Adali's eyes grew round with importance. "The lord high steward brings you greetings from our master, the lord Akbar. The little girls are to be your handmaidens. They are identical but for one thing. Toramalli has a birthmark by the corner of her right eye, and Rohana has the mark by the corner of her left eye."

He was positively puffed up with new importance, Velvet noted with amusement.

Shooing everyone but the handmaidens from the room, he presented Velvet with the reed basket. "This is something that the lord Akbar thought you might particularly enjoy," Adali said.

Velvet lifted the lid of the basket, and then her mouth formed a small O of delight. "It's a kitten!" she said, smiling delightedly. "Oh, Adali, look! A kitten!" She lifted from the basket a tiny, long-haired black kitten with just the teeniest bit of white at the very tip of its tail. "Is it a male or a female?" she asked the eunuch.

"It is a gentleman cat, I am told, my princess."

For a moment the kitten looked about, wide-eyed, at his new surroundings, then he leaped from the bed, and with his tiny tail swishing gracefully set about to explore the room.

"I shall call him Banner," Velvet said, "for his little tail with its white tip is just like a floating banner."

The eunuch nodded with a smile. "Perfect," he agreed.

Suddenly Velvet realized that it was close to midmorning, and she had not yet been to visit poor Pansy. How frightened and confused her faithful tiring woman would be waking up in this palace and not knowing where she was. "Adali! My poor maid will wonder where I am. Give me something to wear! I must go immediately to her!"

As Adali had predicted, Velvet on this her second day in Fatehpur-Sikri was no longer concerned about his gender or rather lack of it. Her mind was on Pansy, and, leaping from the bed, she accepted the clothing he handed her, slipping her feet into the delicate sandals Toramalli and Rohana held out for her. Then with Adali bustling after her she hurried from her chamber and down the corridor to Pansy's quarters.

As Velvet entered the room Pansy's eyes lit up with relief, and she smiled weakly. "M'lady! Oh, thank God!"

Velvet bent to hug her maid, and then sat down on the edge of the girl's bed. "Pansy, why didn't you tell me that you were with child? It's Dugald's child, isn't it?"

Pansy looked very shamefaced. "How did you find out, m'lady?"

"The physician who examined you to determine your illness told me. You'll have to remain in bed for a while, for it is the babe and the heat that have caused your fever and the swelling. You'll both be all right, however, if you'll abide by the physician's instructions."

Pansy looked relieved. "That's a mercy," she said, and then, "I didn't tell you because I didn't know until we were well at sea that I was with child. At first I didn't believe it myself, for Dugald and me was only together once, on Twelfth Night. In the beginning when me moon link was broken I thought that it was perhaps because of the great upset we suffered leaving England. By the time I realized that it wasn't that at all, I was too ashamed to tell you, and I didn't seem to be showing so I kept it to myself."

"Did I not warn you about Dugald, Pansy? Your mother and father will not be very happy when they learn about this. I thought you meant to save yourself until you and Dugald were married. A man will not buy the cow if he can obtain the cream for free, as Dame Cecily has so often said," Velvet scolded.

"Dugald and me pledged ourselves in handfast before the earl's men on Twelfth Night, m'lady. He said that in Scotland 'twas legal, and since you and the earl had done it, and we were going to live in Scotland, too, 'twould be all right. He promised me a church wedding when we got to *Dun Broc.* I was only with him that one time, for it seemed a shame to deny him his wedding night, but afterwards I told him we'd cuddle and grope no more until we had stood before a proper preacher."

Velvet sighed. That devil, Dugald! she thought. Well, there was no help for it now, and she didn't want to fret Pansy about it further. She patted her tiring woman's hand. "It will be all right, and our main concern must now be your safety and the baby's."

The tension drained from Pansy's face. "Where are we?" she said.

"We are in the royal city of Fatehpur-Sikri, Pansy, and I have met the Grand Mughal himself. He is a kind and good man."

"How long have we been here, m'lady?"

"Just since yesterday," Velvet answered. "When Zafar Singh, the physician, says you are well enough, you must come with me to my apartment. It is only one room, but it is enormous, and there is a lovely terrace that is mine. The Mughal has given me a eunuch named Adali, who is kind and funny, and two dear little girls, Toramalli and Rohana, for maidservants."

Pansy looked somewhat put out. "There'll not be much for me to do then, will there, m'lady, with all your new servants."

"Oh, Pansy, no one can take care of me like you!" Velvet protested. "As Daisy is to my mother, so are you to me, but don't forget that in less than two months you'll have a child to care for, and then you'll have little time for me."

"You're me mistress," said Pansy in an aggrieved tone. "I'll nurse my babe, but I'll let one of the others care for it so that I may care for you. 'Tis my duty, and me ma would have my head if I acted otherwise!"

"We'll all take turns with the baby, Pansy," soothed Velvet.

"What's to become of us, m'lady?" Pansy suddenly asked. "Will we ever go home? This place is so very, very hot. Does it never get cool?"

"I don't know if it ever does," was Velvet's answer. "I am trying not to think about it. I'll ask Adali about the weather. Surely it won't be this stifling all the year round." She smiled encouragingly at Pansy.

"But when are we going home?" Pansy repeated.

"I don't know," said Velvet. "I have not had the opportunity to speak with the lord Akbar about it, but I will. You can't leave now, Pansy. You must first finish your confinement, and then we must be certain that the baby is strong enough to make such a long trip. I am afraid that it will be several months before we can even consider leaving India."

Pansy nodded, beginning to look tired again.

Velvet arose from her sitting position. "I will return later, Pansy," she said. "Rest, and do not fear. We are safe here, I promise you." Bending, she kissed Pansy's brow. The tiring woman's eyes were already shut.

"Your servant is better?" inquired Adali as she exited the little room.

"Yes, I believe so," said Velvet. "I will want to see her again later."

"Of course, my princess. You are free to see her at any time." As they reentered Velvet's chamber, he continued, "Now, however, our schedule calls for a trip to the baths."

There was no protest from Velvet. She had to admit that she enjoyed all the pampering that seemed to go on here. With Adali walking ahead, and flanked by Toramalli and Rohana, she made her way through the zenana to the baths. The little maids carried fresh clothing for her and a basket of lotions and perfumes. As they entered the baths a party of women was exiting. One, a tiny elegant woman with the most beautiful, long dark hair Velvet had ever seen and wonderfully expressive golden-brown eyes, stopped a fraction of a second to stare quite openly at her. The woman's glance was without malice. It was simply curious. Some deep instinct told Velvet that this dignified lady was of great importance, and she bowed her head politely. A small smile touched the woman's lips, and she gave a little nod in return before passing on out of the baths.

"Who was that?" Velvet demanded of Adali.

"That was the Princess Jodh Bai, mother of the heir and a favorite of our lord Akbar. You did well to make your obeisance, my princess. She was, I could tell, well pleased by your good manners."

The bath mistress greeted Velvet effusively. Zenana gossip had already informed her of the train of gifts that had arrived at the foreign woman's chambers this morning. Gifts! And the lord Akbar had not even slept with her yet! The bath mistress had also seen Velvet's modest and correct behavior toward Jodh Bai, who was a great favorite within the zenana. She hummed with approval as she supervised Velvet's morning ablutions.

"She has pretty manners, the foreign woman. You have fallen into a pot of honey, Adali." She chuckled.

"Of course she has fine manners, Raokhshna. She is a princess in her own land." The eunuch lowered his voice and confided in the bath mistress, "Our lord Akbar calls her his 'Rose.' Have you ever seen such rare beauty before?"

Roakhshna nodded in agreement. "She is wonderfully fair, and her temper seems pleasant enough. If she becomes his favorite, your fortune will be made. If she bears him a child, you will be a rich man, Adali. I hope you will remember old Roakhshna then, eh?" She poked him playfully.

"Help me to make her the most beautiful woman he has ever possessed, and I promise not to forget you in my good fortune," he assured her.

Velvet listened to them chattering back and forth and suspected that she was their topic of conversation. She wished she knew what it was they spoke of, but she would not ask in this instance. After she had been scrubbed, pumiced, bathed, and lotioned she was led to a padded bench and placed facedown. For the next hour Adali's skillful fingers massaged every inch of her body until she was so relaxed that it was an effort to stay awake. Then dressed in fresh garments she was led back to her chamber where she did indeed fall asleep, her soothed body and spirit unable to resist in the heat of the day.

Toward late afternoon she awakened and was brought more yogurt, fruit, and tea that had been minted. She was wet with the heat, and it all tasted very good to her. She had just finished her meal when her chamber door opened, and Akbar entered the room.

"You are feeling more rested?" he asked.

She rose from her table to face him, realizing as she did that he was no more than an inch taller than she. She could look directly into his dark eyes. "I am much better," she answered, "and if you have the time I should like to speak with you on a serious matter."

He held up his hand, and she fell silent. "Before you do let me ask you, is it true that the noblewomen of Europe ride horses?"

"Yes, my lord, it is."

"Do you ride horses, my Rose?"

"Yes, my lord, I do. I can ride both sidesaddle, which is considered correct for ladies, and astride, which is thought of as somewhat hoydenish but is far more comfortable in my own estimation. Since my mother agrees with me, I usually ride astride. Why do you ask?"

"Would you like to ride with me later? I ride when the sun is low, just before the sunset."

"Oh, yes, my lord! I should very much like to ride with you, but is such a thing permitted?"

"You will have to dress like a young Rajput prince to disguise yourself, my Rose, but it shall be arranged."

"Thank you, my lord! I was so afraid I should not be able to have my freedom. The women of my land are used to roaming at will."

"I understand that, my Rose, and so I will try to see that you do not feel confined, but you will still not be able to move about as easily here as in England. The reason, however, is because this is a far more savage land than your green island. You might be set upon by bandits or wild animals." He smiled at her. "I will return for you in an hour," he said, and then was gone from the chamber.

It wasn't until he had left that she realized that she had not spoken to him about returning her to her own people when Pansy was once again able to travel. I shall do it when we ride, she thought.

Shortly after Akbar had departed from her presence there was a soft knock upon the door, which was quickly answered by Rohana. A eunuch placed in the maidservant's hands a white bundle, which, unwrapped, turned out to be Velvet's disguise. Delightedly she dressed herself in the white silk trousers and knee-length tunic. There were soft, red leather boots that amazingly fit her like a glove, and she wondered how that had been managed, but then had the sandals not also fit her perfectly?

Toramalli carefully pinned up Velvet's long auburn curls, and Adali wound a small turban about her head, little puckers of worry and disapproval upon his face. He did not know whether to rejoice that she was to be alone with the emperor or to weep because should word of this adventure be made public his princess would surely be disgraced.

Confused, he could say nothing, and Velvet was too excited to even notice his distress. When she was finally ready he led her out onto her terrace and pointed to a narrow staircase in the corner that she hadn't even noticed before.

"Our lord Akbar awaits you at the bottom, my princess," Adali told her.

"I shall want to bathe when I return," she told him. "I'll stink of horses after a ride in this heat." Then she bounded off down the staircase, leaving him to shudder with disapproval behind her.

Akbar was prompt and awaiting her as Adali had promised. He looked at her, his eyes admiring. "You make a most fetching prince, my Rose."

"I did not stop to look at myself in a mirror." She laughed into his face. "I was far too anxious to ride. I would have sold my soul a hundred times over during our trek from Bombay to have had a mount beneath me. As it is I do not think my feet will ever be the same again, and I fear my dancing days are over once I return to England."

From the shadows a groom appeared leading two horses, one a big-boned white stallion, the other a dainty golden mare. The stallion snorted and pranced and attempted to reach over to nip at the mare, who danced skillfully out of his reach, almost pulling the groom in two.

Akbar chuckled. "The age-old battle between male and female," he noted. "He would take, but she is not yet ready to give, and he will not have her until she is." He offered Velvet his cupped hands as a mounting block, and, putting her foot up, she vaulted easily into the saddle and gathered up the reins.

"Where do we ride, my lord?" she asked.

"Just outside the city along the Agra road," he answered her, then mounted the stallion.

She saw that they were alone and was puzzled. "Do we ride without an escort, my lord?"

"There is no need for an escort, my Rose. You will be safe with me."

Velvet was amazed. She had never known a king or great lord who dared to ride his lands without some sort of escort. She said nothing further, but followed him from the courtyard out through the city, her eyes wide at all that she saw, for the day before as the caravan had arrived in the city she had not been of a mind to really look about her. Now, however, she could not refrain from turning her head this way and that, each moment that passed bringing a wonderful new sight.

The thing that struck her as the strangest was that the city was so very quiet, unlike any city she had ever known. She realized this was because few people actually lived here anymore, and that was the most peculiar thing of all, for the city seemed to be in perfect condition. Still, she could see it was really a royal city with no place for the common people. Only Akbar and his court had inhabited it, and so when they had left it to move to Lahore, Fatehpur-Sikri had become truly deserted, having no merchants and beggars to remain and keep it alive. The city was like a sleeping princess waiting only for the return of her prince to bring her back to life. Akbar's small entourage now visiting it simply wasn't enough. Velvet found that rather sad.

The city was beautiful in a stark, yet highly decorative way. It was built entirely of native sandstone. The broad streets and squares were paved with wide square blocks of it. All the buildings were built of it, from the former seat of government, the Diwan-i-Khass, to the Great Mosque, to the various palaces, to the Panch Mahal, an amusing structure of no particular use. Most of pillars were carved, some with vines and leaves, some with flowers, others fluted, yet others with great whorls that entwined themselves seemingly without end around the columns. The buildings contained porches and domes, latticed windows and carved panels, all as perfect as the day their creators had finished them. The entire city was like that, and it gave Velvet an eerie feeling.

They rode through one of the city's gates out onto the Agra road, and Velvet took this opportunity to broach the subject of her return with Akbar. "Knowing how I came here," she began, "and knowing that the Portuguese kidnapped me, will you not arrange for my return to my own people, my lord?"

"I cannot, my Rose," he said quietly. "To do so would be to insult the Portuguese, and I will not do that."

"Then send me back overland by caravan. The Portuguese need never know."

He shook his head. "It is much too dangerous. You would likely end up in some slave market, or worse, in some Mongol hetman's yurt. No, my Rose, the fates decreed that your path bring you to me. I will take care of you. Besides, what is there for you to return to now that your husband is dead?"

"I have my family . . ." she began.

"Your family," he interrupted, "would arrange another marriage for you and send you from them. Your fate would be the same as what has actually transpired. You will be safe and cared for with me, my Rose."

"I want to go home," she said, her voice wavering.

"This land is now your home," he replied. "Do you know how to hunt?" he asked, changing the subject. "Would you like to go on a tiger hunt with me?"

The matter, she realized, was closed. For a moment she stared ahead in shock as she comprehended her situation. He had no intention of allowing her to go. There was no way in which she might flee. They were hundreds of miles from the coast, and even if she could surmount that hurdle, the O'Malley fleet would not be there waiting for her. How would she get home? *There was no way*. Suddenly angry and frustrated by a fate not of her own making, Velvet kicked her mare into a headlong gallop, careening blindly down the road in a desperate attempt to escape the overwhelming reality of the situation.

Akbar galloped after her. He was not afraid of her escaping him—he actually understood her anguish—but the road was no longer the best, and he was worried that the mare might stumble and throw her.

She saw nothing through her tears. It was over. Her life was finished and over. Alex was dead. Never again would she see her beloved parents. Murrough, Ewan, Robin, Willow, Padraic, and Deirdre were all lost to her! Like a child suddenly finding herself alone in an empty and strange room, Velvet could see nothing familiar in her future and despaired bitterly. Her sobs shook her entire body, and when the mare did stumble she was totally unprepared for it, tumbling headlong from her saddle.

By some miracle she was not hurt. Indeed she lurched to her feet and continued her flight, running down the Agra road, totally unaware of where she was and what she was doing.

Akbar raced after her. As he passed the mare his Mongol soul was relieved to note that she was not injured. He galloped on and, controlling his stallion with his strong legs, reached out to catch Velvet up into his arms. Suddenly conscious of him she struggled wildly, flailing at him with her fists, hitting out blindly in an effort to exorcise her pain. He cradled her body against his, her head held firmly against his broad chest.

"Shh, my Rose," he soothed her over and over again. "Shh, shh. It will be all right. It will be all right, I promise you."

Velvet began to cry in earnest now, weeping huge, salty tears that streamed down her face making dirty ribbons through the dust on her cheeks. She sobbed and sobbed until he thought his heart would break for her, so piteous was the sound of her keening. He had never heard such grief. It was total and lonely beyond all, and, slowing his horse to a walk, he let her wear herself out crying. He continued to walk his stallion until she finally quieted, and only then did he turn the animal back toward Fatehpur-Sikri.

Velvet realized suddenly where she was; that she had not only dirtied his silk tunic but wet it clear through. Beneath her ear his heartbeat thumped with steady monotony, and the manly smell of him filled her nostrils with the warm fragrance of sandalwood. She was very aware of him in all his maleness, and her own thoughts startled her greatly.

"Is the mare all right?" she ventured softly, embarrassed and almost wishing the earth would open and swallow her whole.

"The mare is fine and awaits us just up ahead. You will, of course, want to ride her back to the city."

"Yes, my lord."

"Do you feel better now?"" he asked.

"The shock is over," she answered thoughtfully, "but I shall never stop wanting to return to England."

"What is there for you now, my Rose?" he asked again.

"I have my memories," she said quietly. "Would you take them from me?"

"Look at me," he commanded fiercely, and, startled, she obeyed him, her emerald eyes gazing up into his face. "I will make you new memories, my Rose," he said. "I cannot take your old memories from you, nor would I want to, but I can make you new memories, and I intend to, my beautiful English Rose."

Velvet felt her pulse leap. He could not have made his intentions any clearer. "I cannot be your concubine," she said. "I simply cannot."

"I have not suggested such a thing," he returned. "Though I know that is why the Portuguese governor sent you to me. For some reason he wished to debase you, and, given your background, gifting me with you as a concubine would do just that, I understood that once I learned your history. In my un-Christian and evil barbarian lust I was supposed to fall on you not even suspecting his motives. I have learned a great deal about the Portuguese. They, fortunately, have not learned a great deal about me, possibly because they have not even bothered to try. They have two interests here in India: to convert as many of my people to their religion as they can, and to remove my country's riches to their land. For both I am expected to be grateful." He chuckled. "I only wish I might be a fly on the wall when Don Cesar Affonso Marinha-Grande receives my message informing that I was so delighted with his gift that I immediately did him honor by marrying her. He is quite apt to have an apoplectic fit."

"You have not married me," Velvet said.

"But I have," came Akbar's startling answer.

"What?" her voice squeaked. "How could you have married me when I knew nothing about it?"

"I was born to the faith of Islam, my Rose, and although I long ago realized that no one faith is the only true faith, I do marry my wives, and you are the fortieth, in either Islam's faith or that of the Hindus. I felt that since Islam is closest to Christianity you would prefer it. In the Muslim faith it is neither necessary to have the bride's consent nor to have the bride at the wedding. Only the consent of a woman's guardian is needed, and in this case it is me. We were wed this morning."

She was stunned, and, remembering the comedy of her four weddings to Alex, she almost laughed. She had refused to acknowledge that they were married until they had been wed in a church; and now here she was once again being told that she was a married woman. But this time she knew there would be no Catholic ceremony. "If you have wed other women in their own faith, why can you not wed me, if you must wed me, in *my* own faith, my lord? There are Jesuits here, I have been told." God's bones, I am so calm, she thought.

"This is India, my Rose, and I am considered a Moslem ruler. I have already outraged half my subjects by marrying my Rajput wives in their Hindu faith. If I wed a woman in a Christian ceremony I could easily start a civil war. I have fought hard to unite this land, and not even you are worth its dissolution. Besides, such a Christian union would be considered my only legal marriage by your Christian Jesuits, and I would have trouble from that quarter as well."

Why did I even suggest it, she thought. His answer was the only one he could give in such a situation. Was she losing her wits in all this heat?

They had reached the place where her own mount waited, and with strong arms he lifted her from his mount back into her own saddle. Taking up her reins, she rode by his side again. "I will need time," she said, "to adjust myself to this situation. It is all a great deal to face." What an understatement! She almost laughed at herself again. What was the matter with her? Why was she so calm? Then it came to her that her intelligence had already accepted what her emotions had not.

"You may have time," he said. "I am not some animal who will ravish you. I have a zenana filled with willing women. I have no need to resort to force. I want you, but I will wait."

"It is all so strange to me," she said. "I never imagined a life like this existed. And I was not wed to my husband very long."

"How long?" he asked.

"Two and a half months," she said softly. "There was so little time. He was my parents' choice, and until we met I knew no man."

"We have much time," Akbar said. "It is foretold that I shall live a long life, even as it was foretold that I should have only three living sons. I believe you are here to bring me happiness in my last years, as Jodh Bai brought me happiness in my youth. In turn I shall endeavor to make you happy, my Rose. No woman will be as cherished or as loved as you shall be, O youngest and fairest of my wives."

"My lord, you barely know me," she ventured.

"What man ever really knows a woman, my Rose? I know that you are intelligent, beautiful, and brave. Each is a fine attribute, but for one woman to possess all three is a miracle, and you are truly a miracle coming into my life when I thought there was nothing left for me but the long road into infinity."

They were once again passing through the city gates and back into Fatehpur-Sikri. Velvet was touched and amazed by the words that the Grand Mughal had spoken to her. A tiny flame of hope was kindled deep within her heart, and she realized that perhaps life was not so unbearable after all. After all, she was her mother's daughter, and the desire for survival burned strongly within her. She had come through the several weeks' trek from Bombay to the interior, and without knowledge of the language she had successfully bargained for Pansy's life. Her fate had been to attract the loving attention of a great ruler. If she must remain in this fierce and hot land, then there were worse fates than the one she was living.

I am young, Velvet thought, and it is true, I am beautiful. I want to live! This man offers me life. He offers me love. Has my mother not always told me that when one door closes another opens?

"You are so kind, my lord, but I do not know you. I will learn about you, though, and I will learn how to please you." She turned her head and smiled tentatively at him.

"You please me now, my Rose. Do not change, for it is your very uniqueness from other women that intrigues and fascinates me. Be yourself, nothing more. Once the wheel of love has been set in motion, there is no absolute rule." He reached out and took one of her hands, turning it over to place a kiss upon the palm. "I *will* make you happy," he promised, and in that moment Velvet knew that he would.

Chapter 9

Velvet's days took on a comfortable sameness that suited her for the time being. Sometimes, though, she remembered that it was late September in England now, and she thought back to how a year ago at this very time she had been the queen's Maid of Honor and a darling of the Tudor court. She and Alex had been feuding then prior to his wild abduction of her. Such memories usually brought tears, or at the very least a deep sadness that would sweep over her, casting her into such dark depths that it was all Akbar could do to cheer her again.

That the Grand Mughal was a man in love was apparent to everyone at his court, a fact that amused his two younger sons who were both older than Velvet, and for some reason increased the bitter feeling of Prince Salim toward his father. Akbar, thought Salim, was at a time in his life when he should behave in a more circumspect manner. Was he not a grandfather? Was he not about to become one again? Instead his father played the fool with a beautiful young woman. Why had he not given the foreign beauty to Salim, as Sultan Selim of the Ottoman empire had given his heir, who had now come into his inheritance as Sultan Suleiman, a beautiful young princess sent to him from Baghdad as tribute? At twenty Salim was much closer in age to Velvet than was his father, who was in his late forties, and having seen Velvet riding with Akbar the young prince truly envied his sire. No one, Salim included, was aware that the union of Akbar and his English Rose had yet to be consummated.

Each day toward sunset they rode together, and sometimes he would take along his hunting cats, two sleek, spotted animals who loped by their sides, occasionally streaking ahead to bring down a rabbit or plump game bird, then returning with it to the emperor who more often than not allowed them to keep their prey.

One day he arranged for her to see an elephant fight, and Velvet was both fascinated and repulsed by the barbarity of it all. Akbar was very proud of his fighting elephants. In his stables were the most prime examples of elephant flesh to be found in all of India. There were also elephants used for breeding, for traveling, and for other work within the stables of the emperor. One day Akbar ordered that a conveyance he called a howdah be placed upon one of the great beasts so that he might take her for a ride.

Velvet was as excited as a child and her delight knew no bounds when the elephant arrived, for the beast had been decked out in the most incredible finery. It was a young male, she was told, for the male elephants native to India sported long ivory tusks. Upon the animal's tusks, however, long golden fitted sheaths studded with rubies had been placed. A magnificent red satin coverlet decorated with gold bangles and diamonds was drawn over the great beast's head. It had openings where his eyes were, and upon the two bumps that the elephant had high up on its forehead were gold shields. The coverlet narrowed between the tusks to cover the trunk and was fringed with gold on either side. Even the elephant's small ears were encased in satin, and a matching coverlet was spread across his back and fell down his sides in two strips over his chest.

Strapped atop the animal's swayed back was an octagonal-shaped golden howdah with a domed top and fitted with silk cushions. As Velvet settled herself inside it, Akbar told her that the driver would ride before them where the elephant's neck joined its head.

She enjoyed the rolling gait of the beast as they moved through the city. His back was a wonderful vantage point from which to see the countryside about them, but unfortunately height did nothing to improve the flat, monotonous landscape surrounding Fatehpur-Sikri. For miles and miles it seemed that everything was dun-colored and dull.

"I miss my green hills," she said one day to Akbar.

"Is all of your land green?" he asked her.

"Yes," she answered. "Is all of your land brown?"

He laughed at her quick retort. "No, not all, but a good part. We have our forests, and toward the north is Kashmir, a lovely land of lakes and mountains that I will soon make completely mine."

"Then *that* is where I would live," she said.

"We will soon journey to Lahore, my capital," was his reply.

"Is it green?" she begged him.

"Greener," he promised, "and I shall give you your own palace there with gardens and fountains, and you will never complain to me again about your England." He smiled at her, and Velvet smiled back.

He loves me, she thought. He has never even kissed me, and still he loves me. It was strange and wonderful and frightening all at once. This was no boy but a man well versed in passion. He had said he would be patient, and he certainly had been true to his word.

"Will you play chess with me again tonight?" he asked her.

"Oh, yes, my lord! I shall beat you this time, too!" she threatened, and he laughed delightedly. Those of his other women with whom he had occasionally played the game had never beaten him. Even had they been skillful enough, he doubted they would have dared. This adorable creature, however, not only dared, but on two occasions she actually had bested him, clapping her hands and shamelessly crowing with glee at her victory. Tonight, though, he had a rather interesting surprise for her.

He ordered the elephant driver to return them to the palace housing the zenana, and there she left him, to bathe, eat, and rest.

When he rejoined her several hours later she was attired in a deep blue silk skirt decorated with golden dots the size of coins that had a wide hem of gold. Her dark silk blouse with its low, scooped neckline was short-sleeved and molded her figure to its best advantage. About her neck Velvet wore a long double strand of pearls, the outside strand being decorated with pure gold rounds edged in tiny sapphires. Each ear sported a round sapphire to which was attached a cluster of pearls. She wore arm bands of gold that were decorated with colored stones or raised gold work, and rings on every finger but her thumbs. Her hair was loose and wavy and very full about her shoulders, and atop her head was a circlet of pearls and sapphires. Rohana had taught her how to outline her eyes in kohl, but neither her cheeks nor her lips needed further color.

"I have the chessboard already set up for us, my lord," she greeted him.

"No," Akbar said. "I have a surprise for you. Adali, attend your mistress and follow me."

He led them from her chamber to a small balcony overlooking a wide, square courtyard. "This, my Rose, is how we shall play chess tonight!" he said with a wave of his hand over the courtyard.

With a gasp of delight Velvet looked out to discover that the square below her was in actuality a giant playing board. Standing upon the board were live female chess figures: the pawns nude maidens with long dark hair and ropes of pearls about their waists; the knights naked but for cloth of gold turbans each adorned with a good-sized diamond from which sprouted a gold aigrette and white feather. Each of the "pieces" was unclothed for the most part but for the costly jewelry, with the exception of the king and the queen "pieces," who were positively resplendent in silk garments sewn over every inch of their surface with pearls and rubies, their golden crowns studded with emeralds.

"Beat me," Akbar challenged, "and you may keep the jewels from the pieces you win."

"And if I lose," she demanded, "then what will you have in forfeit?"

"A kiss," he said quietly.

Velvet looked at him, her face serious. "A kiss?" she repeated.

"Do you agree, my Rose?"

For a moment she hysterically contemplated the possibility of answering him with a no. Then she simply nodded her head.

"I will allow you to begin the play," he said.

It was a serious game they played that night; Akbar calling out his moves to be carried out by the bejeweled players below, and Adali translating Velvet's commands to the human pieces. Velvet did not really care that she might keep the gems adorning the playing pieces if she won. She sought to win for the joy of knowing that she could outwit him if she was skillful enough in her strategy. Akbar quickly understood that. Another woman would have played recklessly and rashly in order to gain the jewels, but not his Rose. She pleased him greatly, and he thought about the kiss that she would give him when he won their game because he knew he would triumph. She was an excellent opponent, better than some men he knew, but he was still the better player. What would her lips be like? He knew from his vast experience that each woman's mouth was different.

"Ha!" She took his rook, watching the glittering player, her shoulders drooping, walk from the board, then laughed into his face with her small victory.

A smile touched his lips at Velvet's enthusiasm, and he mentally chided himself for thinking of other things and not concentrating on the game at hand. It was a mistake he did not make again, and after an hour's play, Velvet was forced to concede defeat, doing so reluctantly as she carefully studied the great board below her in hopes of finding another move she might make that would prolong the game.

"Checkmate!" he said. "I win!"

"Indeed you do, my lord," she admitted.

"Are you ready to pay your wager?" he asked her.

She turned to face him, and, closing her eyes, she lifted her face slightly and in childlike fashion puckered her lips at him. For a brief moment Akbar studied her, knowing that she fully expected him to give her a brief kiss. He had, however, waited too long for this opportunity, and, slipping an arm about her waist, he drew her close to him. For a moment his fingers caressed her cheek, and then, taking her chin between his thumb and his forefinger, his lips descended upon hers.

Strange thoughts flitted through her consciousness as she felt his fleshy mouth upon hers. *I haven't been kissed in seven months. Not since Alex died. Akbar does not kiss me like Alex kissed me. I didn't realize that men kissed differently. Alex possessed me like a wild and wonderful storm. This man kisses me with tenderness. It is almost as if he is trying to please me.*

The gentleness in Akbar's caress induced Velvet to relax. He sought not to open her lips at this time, instead savoring the firmness of her lovely mouth. Then, unable to restrain himself, his hand crept to her breast, and he fondled her. She murmured softly against his lips, the little nipple of her breast suddenly hardening and pushing itself forward. Taking that little point between his fingers, he pinched it firmly.

A stab of pure desire shot through her body from deep within the core of her very being. With a small gasp she steadied herself, placing her palms against his chest. His skin was like fire, but for a moment she could not draw away. He kissed the corners of her mouth slowly and sweetly with lingering regret as their embrace came to an end.

Velvet opened her eyes to find him looking at her with open desire. She knew what it was he asked her so silently. Tears sprang to her eyes. "I cannot!" she whispered desperately, and then she fled him.

With a groan Akbar placed his head in his hands. *He wanted her!* And he had every right to take her! Had he not done her the honor of making her his wife, knowing her European sensibilities? And yet despite it all she still denied him! He groaned again for he knew he could not force her. That would be an admission of defeat, and he would not be defeated in any battle, let alone a battle of love, by a mere girl!

"My lord!" Adali had remained at his side. "My lord, she

is yet tied to her old life. She will come around soon. I know it!"

With a snort of impatience Akbar stamped from the balcony. He needed to speak with someone who could give him sound advice on how to handle this skittish young mare. His steps led him to the lavish apartments of Jodh Bai, the Amber Princess, one of his favorite consorts. He found her having tea and cakes with the first of his wives, his cousin, Rugaiya Begum. Both women rose to greet him, bowing politely.

Rugaiya Begum was plump and big-boned with marvelous smooth skin and bright black eyes. Her once dark hair was now silvered, and he thought her still most handsome. Beside her was the petite Jodh Bai, doll-like in comparison to her companion. He was enormously fond of them both. They were loving, good women and neither had ever given him a moment's unrest. He valued their judgment in domestic matters above all others.

They settled him comfortably amid the soft cushions and pressed refreshments on him. He had come for a purpose, they both knew, but they would wait for him to broach the matter that concerned him. Akbar breathed a momentary sigh of contentment and sipped the smoky, dark tea from Assam that they had given him. Jodh Bai held out a plate of tiny cakes made from ground nuts, honey, and sesame seeds. Akbar took one and chewed it slowly, enjoying the lingering sweetness of the honey. When he had finished, a slave woman handed him a moistened towel to cleanse his sticky hands. Calm now, he sat back and looked at his wives.

"I need your guidance in a rather delicate matter," he began.

"How may we aid you, my lord?" questioned Jodh Bai.

"It is my new wife, the English girl. She is a charming companion, but she is reluctant to come to my bed. I do not want to force her, but I grow irritable in my desire for her."

"I had heard that she was a widow," remarked Rugaiya Begum. "Since she is not a virgin I cannot understand this demurring."

"Does she still mourn her last husband, my lord?" said Jodh Bai.

"Yes, I believe so."

"Then you must turn her thoughts from him to you, else you'll never possess her."

"But how can I?" he demanded of her.

"I shall help you, my lord. I will send your English Rose a Pillow Book. I have just had one made that I intended to give to my brother's daughter who is to be married next year, but there is time yet for another Pillow Book to be done for my niece. Tomorrow I shall send the one I now possess to your Rose. When you visit her tomorrow evening, you will tell her that you learned I sent it and wish to view it with her. Once she is reminded of the love between a man and a woman I am certain that her shyness will vanish."

"Unless she is cold by nature," put in Rugaiya Begum. "These Europeans are very different from us."

"She isn't cold," he said. "She is warm and sweet, but her marriage lasted less than three months before her husband was killed. She had been most sheltered by her parents, and although she has never said it, I believe that she was never even kissed until he married her."

"Her parents were good people to protect her virtue," approved Rugaiya Begum. "She is an interesting-looking creature, not at all like us. I have seen her in the baths several times. Her skin is like heavy cream."

He smiled. "I know," he said, and Jodh Bai smiled behind her hands.

"I will inform you when the book has been delivered," she said.

He left them feeling the situation was now once again under control.

After he was gone Rugaiya Begum and Jodh Bai signaled to a slave woman to freshen their teacups.

"He is as eager as a youth," remarked the older Rugaiya Begum.

"He was eager once with all of us. Remember when he desired Almira?" Jodh Bai sipped her tea delicately.

Rugaiya Begum chortled. "What I remember is the look upon the face of her first husband, the old shaikh, when Akbar told him he must divorce Almira." She cackled lewdly. "The old devil had watched Almira from childhood planning on the day when he would pierce her tender young yoni with his lusty old lingam. He had nurtured her like a gardener nurtures his favorite rosebush, and then to discover he'd nurtured her for someone else! It broke his heart, and he died before he could divorce her. What irony! He had even married her when she was still a child in order to see that no one else possessed her!" She popped a pastry into her mouth and chewed it vigorously.

"It is different this time," Jodh Bai said. "This time I think he is in love. Some he has lusted after, others he has lain with out of sense of duty, some like ourselves he is even genuinely fond of, but never do I believe that Akbar has been in love. Never until now."

"Do you fear she will have a son who will supplant yours?" Rugaiya Begum inquired slyly. She herself had had no children.

"No," replied Jodh Bai. "The old Moslem saint who predicted Salim's birth also predicted that Akbar would only have three living sons. So it has been. First my Salim, then Almira's Murad, and finally Roopmati's Daniyal. Daniyal was born over seventeen years ago. Since then there have been no more sons, only daughters. I don't fear for Salim especially since he already has one son of his own."

"Perhaps then it is for yourself that you fear, Jodh Bai. Perhaps you fear that Akbar's new love will supplant you in his affections."

Jodh Bai smiled ruefully. She and Rugaiya Begum were good friends of long standing; if anyone knew her as well as she knew herself it was Rugaiya Begum. "Perhaps I am jealous," she admitted.

"Then you must do what I did in my youth to overcome the jealousy I felt each time Akbar took a new wife—particularly you."

"Me?" Jodh Bai was surprised. "You were jealous of me?" She had been Akbar's wife for twenty-seven years, and she had never even suspected such a thing.

Rugaiya Begum laughed. "I was indeed. Remember that I am Akbar's first wife. I was married to him when I was just nine years old. He was the cousin that I adored, and has been the only man I have ever known. When I was fifteen he married another of our cousins, Zada Begum, and when neither of us produced children he wed with Salima Begum, Bairam Khan's widow. She was already the mother of a son, but she could only give Akbar his eldest daughter, Shahzad-Khanim Begum.

"Then you, Princess of Amber, were wed to our lord. Zada and Salima were outraged for you were a Rajput and not a Moslem. Remember how they shunned you when you first entered our zenana?"

Jodh Bai nodded, her dark eyes remembering the hurt of their rejection. She had been so young and so very frightened, marrying a powerful man who was of a different culture than hers. "You were kind to me, Rugaiya."

"I was the senior wife. It was my duty, but do not think because I was kind that I was not jealous. I am big and plain and have always been so. Neither Zada nor Salima are beauties; pretty enough, but not beauties, and both were tall. The difference between us seemed little. You, however, were different. You were tiny and exotic and so lovely. It was clear to us all that Akbar was drawn to you in a way he had not been drawn to any of us. I lay awake during the nights that Akbar visited you and finally decided that I would rather be your friend if Akbar cared for you than be your enemy. I was glad afterwards for I shared in the joy of your first pregnancy with you."

"And you shared my sorrow when my twin sons, Hasan and Husein, died at only a month old," remembered Jodh Bai. "What you are saying to me, Rugaiya, is that I can conquer my fears of this English girl by making friends with her. How can I, though? She does not speak our language."

"She will learn," said Rugaiya Begum. "She will eventually have no choice but to learn, and we will help her because she will need our friendship. How fortunate we are in comparison to this girl, Jodh Bai. This is our land. We have our families about us; you have your son, Salim. What has this girl? She is virtually alone but for her servantwoman. She is in a strange land, and it is unlikely she will ever see her own people again. How hard it must be for her."

"You are so good, Rugaiya!" said Jodh Bai. "You can always see the other person's side of an issue. I can't. Yours is a rare virtue. No wonder all our children love you!" She smiled at her friend. "Very well, we shall make friends with the foreigner. I only hope she will want to be friends with us."

"The women servants have brought us reports of how loving and attentive she is to her serving woman, and of how that young woman loves her mistress," Rugaiya Begum reminded Jodh Bai. "She has been polite to us both whenever we have chanced to pass her in the zenana. Her character, I can tell, is a good one. This last year has been a bad time for Akbar. He has not been well, and there have been other problems. This girl is the first thing I have seen him take a deep interest in for many months. He is happy again."

"But for his inability to bed her," Jodh Bai giggled.

Rugaiya Begum chuckled richly. "A little chase and tussle does not hurt a love match. She unknowingly whets his appetite by her reluctance. The Pillow Book you plan to send will do the trick, I have not a doubt!" She chuckled again. "Poor girl! I imagine she has never seen a Pillow Book before. Remember how shocked the holy fathers of the Christians were when Prince Murad purloined Shahazad Khanim's Pillow Book after her wedding and showed it to them? I cannot understand why the Europeans do not accept what is natural between a man and a woman."

Jodh Bai joined her friend in laughter. "The holy fathers were not so upset that they did not look long at that Pillow Book. Remember how their robes thrust forward with the rising of their lingams as they turned each page?"

Rugaiya Begum was now laughing so hard that the tears were flowing freely down her face. "And Akbar said that seeing it he saw that they were like other men, and he was relieved to find that they, too, had unruly lingams! Ah ha ha ha ha!"

"Perhaps the English girl will not want to be our friend when she learns what a Pillow Book contains," said Jodh Bai, sobering.

"More than likely she will thank us when she learns how magnificent is our lord's passion," said the more practical Rugaiya Begum. "I have never known another man, but I am certain that no other could be the lover that Akbar is."

Jodh Bai nodded her agreement, and the two women began to gossip on another topic of interest to them: Prince Salim's soon-to-be-born second child. Both were certain that it would be another prince.

They also looked forward to returning home to Lahore. Fatehpur-Sikri depressed them with its dusty landscape, and they longed for the gardens and fountains of the royal palace farther to the north. They both wanted to be there for the birth, which would take place before the year's end.

While Akbar's favorite wives chatted amicably, the subject of their previous conversation tossed restlessly upon her silken mattress. Velvet could not sleep. She was in a quandary once more about her position in this strange world. What should she do? Was there any chance at all of her leaving India? She pondered the question for some time, finally deciding there was no hope at all. She would spend the rest of her days in this land. There was simply no choice.

Akbar was in love with her. Even Velvet with her small experience knew that. He was not unkind, but he was not going to be patient forever. Her only chance of happiness and of survival—hers, Pansy's, and that of Pansy's unborn child—lay in her accepting the inevitable. He had even married her according to the laws and a religion of this land. She was the Grand Mughal's wife. If she was to have any life at all she must build it around that certain fact.

He wanted to make love to her. Velvet trembled at the thought. No one had ever made love to her but Alex. *Alex.* She tried desperately to remember his face and found to her horror that it was difficult to recall. Not because she loved him any the less in death, but because it had been so long since she had last seen him and she had no miniature to remind her. Silent tears ran down the sides of her face. This sudden realization made her feel disloyal and guilty. Rising from her bed, she wrapped the silk coverlet about her body and, softly opening her chamber door, stepped over the sleeping Adali and slipped down the hall to Pansy's small cubicle.

"M'lady!" Pansy whispered as Velvet entered the room. "Can you not sleep either?"

Velvet shook her head, and then said as she settled herself on the floor next to her tiring woman, "Can you remember what Dugald looked like, Pansy? I mean *really* remember?"

Pansy looked unhappy. "Nay," she answered her mistress. "I cannot, m'lady, not his features—just the fact that he had a mop of red hair, blue eyes, and was as freckled as I am. The rest is gone, but perhaps if me baby is a lad he'll look like his pa, and I'll remember then."

"I cannot remember Alex," Velvet said sadly. "Like you I remember that his face was a strong one, his hair black, and his eyes amber. The rest is gone!"

"Maybe it's better for us that way," Pansy said wisely. "Maybe it's best that we not remember. We ain't going home neither of us, m'lady. You ain't said it to me, I know, for fear of harming my child, but I know it to be true. We're going to have to make our lives here, or we ain't going to have no lives at all." She struggled to sit up on her pallet, and as her gown tightened across her stomach Velvet could see the movement of the child so near to its birth. "Lord Akbar, the emperor of this land, now he loves you; even I can see it when you come to visit me each morning. I don't think he'd be an unhappy man if you made your life with him."

"He has already made me his legal wife," Velvet said softly, "though the marriage had not been consummated yet."

"And he wants to, but you don't?" Pansy questioned her outright.

"Yes."

"I think in the end, m'lady, if you'll not be angry with me for being so bold, you really haven't any other choice. Besides, it appears to me that you could have done worse than to have the ruler of such a rich land fall in love with you and make you his wife. I always remember me mum saying that her Mistress Skye survived by facing the situation honestly. What's past is past, m'lady. 'Tis here and now, and we've got to go on. I'm not happy about never seeing me Dugald again, but I've had time to think about that these last few weeks, and I've faced it. I'm going to have me bairn, raise it, and maybe even find me another husband! I don't hold no illusions that Dugald ain't going to find another woman for hisself."

"Another husband! Oh, Pansy, you are so much wiser than I am, and you are right. We cannot wish away what is. I thought it was so awful of me not to be able to recall Alex's face, and I grew frightened. Now I had better return to my chamber lest Adali awake and rouse the watch looking for me." She stood up. "I shall ask my lord Akbar to move you to my chamber as quickly as possible. I miss you!" She smiled at Pansy and then slipped from the room to return to her own.

Laying back down upon her bed, she thought of all Pansy had said. The tiring woman was only a few months older than she was, and her experience hadn't been any greater than Velvet's. Still, she had her mother's practical nature, and Velvet was glad that she did, for Pansy's words had comforted and reassured her. She had to admit that she was a little afraid of Akbar's making love to her, but it was, she thought, only because she was not particularly experienced. She had to admit when he had kissed her and fondled her this evening she had not found it unpleasant. Her distress had mainly stemmed from her guilt. All she had been able to think of was that she was Alex's wife. Now she was ready to face the fact that she was Alex Gordon's widow and the Grand Mughal Akbar's bride.

These things now clear in her mind, Velvet slept. She did not hear, nor had she heard in all the nights she had lain in this room, Akbar's entry into the chamber. Bare-footed, he came across the floor to stand by her bed and gaze down upon her, his face alive with the love and the passion he felt for her. Reaching out his hand, he gently drew the coverlet aside so that he might look upon her nude beauty. For some time he drank in her loveliness, aching with his desperate need to possess her. Then with a deep sigh he turned and left the room. Behind him, she stirred slightly as the door clicked shut, but she did not awaken until the morning.

Adali had been briefed by Akbar himself that this night would be the night that the Mughal would consummate his marriage to the English Rose. Since she needed coaxing, the lady Jodh Bai was sending her a Pillow Book, which would arrive sometime that day. The bride was not to be forewarned lest the anticipation distress or frighten her. Her day would be as usual.

Velvet awoke at midmorning and, after her usual meal of yogurt, fruit, and tea, went off to the baths, which she very much enjoyed. It was there that Jodh Bai and Rugaiya Begum made their first overtures of friendship. Having been bathed, Velvet was swimming about the pool happily relaxed when the two other women joined her.

"What is your name, eunuch?" Rugaiya Begum demanded of Adali.

"I am called Adali, gracious lady," he answered her.

"Tell your mistress that we bid her good day," said Rugaiya Begum.

Adali was almost beside himself with joy. Recognition by the Mughal's first wife *and* his most favored wife was an incredible social step forward in the tight little world of the zenana. "My princess," he called to Velvet, who swam to the pool's edge.

"Yes, Adali?" She smiled at the two women.

"My princess, Rugaiya Begum bids you good day!"

Realizing the importance of the situation, Velvet replied, "Tell the lady Rugaiya Begum that I return her salutation and am honored that she has deigned to notice me."

Adali translated, and Velvet could see the great approval in the older woman's eyes as he spoke.

Then Jodh Bai said to Adali, "Greet the Rose Princess for me also, Adali, and offer my felicitations to her upon her marriage to our lord Akbar."

The eunuch was quivering with excitement. As he spoke in his improving French to Velvet, he knew that the bath mistress and her attendants were already spreading word about the baths that these two senior wives of the lord Akbar were in conversation with the youngest and least important of his women. Velvet's stature would now rise a thousand-fold.

"Greet the Amber Princess for me, Adali, and tell her that her kindness and that of Rugaiya Begum mean much to me, a stranger in what is for me an unknown land. Would it be impolite for me to invite them to tea one day, Adali?"

"No, my princess, it would not. I must first ask the Mughal's permission and tender your invitation based on his approval. I shall invite them for several days from now." He then turned to the two older women and repeated Velvet's message. Rugaiya Begum spoke back to him, and then Adali returned to his mistress. "They will come!" He tried to keep the excitement from his voice, but his eyes were dancing and his smile was broad.

Rugaiya Begum and Jodh Bai nodded politely to Velvet, who nodded back with a smile, and then the two women left the baths.

Velvet stepped from the pool, and two bath attendants hurried up to pat her dry. She was lotioned and massaged, and with Adali chattering nonstop in her ear she returned to her own chamber to rest in the midday heat.

Toward sunset she and Akbar rode out from the city, and he told her then that they would soon be leaving for his capital of Lahore.

"But Pansy has not yet borne her child, my lord. I do not like to leave her alone as she has not even the advantage of speaking French as I do. She would be very frightened."

"It is strange that a mistress and servant would be so close, my Rose. You seem to care for her as you would a sister."

"Her mother has been in my mother's service for over thirty years, and her father is one of my mother's captains. She is a bit older than I am, but we were raised on the same estate."

"Is she the only child of her parents?"

"No." Velvet laughed. "She is one of ten. Each time her father came home from a voyage he got her mother with child until Daisy finally put a stop to it. Please do not make me leave Pansy my lord. She is a strong girl, and as soon as her child has come she will be able to travel."

"If it pleases you," he answered her, "then I shall wait for your Pansy, should her child not come before my planned departure."

She smiled her thanks at him, and as the sun dipped lower with each moment they turned their horses back to the city, where Velvet left Akbar at the foot of the steps that led to her chamber's terrace. She bathed once more as she did every day after her ride, and then Adali and her two handmaidens brought her a supper of baby lamb and rice with fruit. A small carafe of sweet and heady wine was placed by her elbow.

Velvet ate slowly, enjoying the well-prepared meal and wondering if Akbar would play chess with her again this evening. Would they play here in her chamber or would it be on the balcony above the great playing board? She had not quite finished her supper when Adali answered a knock at her door. Velvet heard him murmuring in his soft voice to someone outside that she could not see, and then the door was shut and the eunuch came to her side bearing a box in his hands.

"What is it, Adali?" she asked.

"It is a gift to you from Her Highness, Jodh Bai, my princess." He couldn't conceal his delight as he handed it to her.

Velvet accepted the beautiful sandalwood box, its edges bound with gold-filigreed corners. There was a matching filigreed lock, but it was only decorative. Lifting the lock, she raised the lid to reveal the contents. The interior of the box was lined in beaten gold and held a scarlet satin pillow upon which rested a book.

"She has sent you a Pillow Book!" exclaimed Adali.

Velvet lifted the volume from the box. It was beautifully bound in peacock blue silk, its edges of pure gold studded with tiny pearls and diamonds. "What is a Pillow Book?" she asked him, opening it to reveal the first ivory-vellum page with words written in gold upon it. "What does that say, Adali?"

"A Pillow Book, my princess, is a book of paintings revealing the postures of love. It is believed among our people that such books aid a bride in overcoming her natural fears. As for the writing upon this page it is a saying from our most famous book of love, the *Kama Sutra*. It says: 'Once the Wheel of Love has been set in motion, there is no absolute rule.'"

"And the lady Jodh Bai sent this to me?"

"Yes, my princess. It is very good luck to receive one. You are most fortunate to have gained the favor of Jodh Bai. She is the mother of the heir, and one day when our lord Akbar heeds Allah's call and steps aside for his son, it will not hurt to be his mother's friend. Particularly if you have children of your own then."

Children of her own! She had barely begun to accustom herself to the fact that she was Akbar's wife! Velvet turned to the next page of the book and stared at the picture. Upon a marble terrace, its balcony edged in colorful foliage, were two people on a piece of silk-upholstered furniture similar to the one on Velvet's own terrace. Beside them on the floor was a tray with two decanters and two goblets. The beautifully dressed woman sat on the man's lap, her back to him, her head back so that she might gaze lovingly up into his eyes, her arms about his neck. He, in turn, gazed down into her liquid eyes, his hands cupping her round breasts.

"Oh!" Velvet blushed and shut the book. She took a long sip of her wine and handed the volume to Adali. "Perhaps I shall look later," she said.

"Yes, my princess," he said quietly, taking the book from her and returning it to its box, which he placed upon a nearby table.

What on earth is the matter with me? Velvet wondered. I'm no virgin. I'm not totally inexperienced.

Still, she had never seen anyone making love before. One *made* love. One did not view it. She was curious, however, about what the rest of the book contained. She would view it later when Rohana and Toramalli had gone to their quarters and Adali slept across her doorsill. She wanted to be alone before she opened Jodh Bai's gift again.

The remnants of her meal were cleared away, and a basin was brought to her so that she might wash her face and hands and rinse her mouth with rosewater. A tray containing a decanter of wine and two goblets was placed by her bed, but Velvet didn't notice. She was too busy setting up the chessboard that Akbar had given her. The board was fashioned from small squares of mother-of-pearl and red marble. The figures were carved from ivory and dark green jade. Carefully she placed each piece on its place, never noticing Adali as he directed her two maidservants by means of hand signals. A bowl of fruit with a knife was placed by the tray; the bed neatly remade, its coverlet smoothed, its pillows fluffed.

"Let Rohana brush your hair, my princess," said Adali. "The lord Akbar will soon be here."

Velvet sat upon a stool while the little maid carefully brushed her auburn curls until they shone with elusive golden lights. She was looking particularly beautiful this night, Adali thought. Her silken blouse was mauve pink, and her skirt, which was edged in silver, was a pale purple.

At the knock upon the door Toramalli hurried to allow Akbar entrance into the room. Rohana gave her mistress's hair a final pat, and then the two girls hurried from the room followed by Adali.

"How lovely you look this evening," Akbar complimented Velvet, and he held out to her a dainty golden chain that was sprinkled with small pink diamonds. "For you, my Rose."

"Why do you always call me your Rose?" asked Velvet. "You know my name."

"You remind me of the roses in my gardens at the palace in Lahore. Your skin is like the white roses that grow by the spraying fountains, your lips like the red roses that bloom along the pathway to my chamber, and your beautiful eyes are the green of their leaves. I have never known a woman like you. Still, you are correct. You should have a more suitable name. I will think on it."

"What a lovely thing to say, my lord. You are indeed kind to me." She slipped the chain about her neck. "And generous, too."

"It pleases me to be kind and generous to you," he said. "I should like it if one day you would also be kind and generous to me."

Velvet lowered her eyes as she felt her cheeks grow warm. His meaning was very clear. "Will you play chess with me tonight, my lord?" she asked him, attempting to change the subject.

He laughed softly. "Of course, if that is what you wish." He turned toward the chessboard when suddenly his eyes lit upon the sandalwood box that Adali had placed so that his master would see it. "What is this, my Rose?" Akbar said.

She answered without thinking. "It is a gift from the Lady Jodh Bai."

"What is it?"

"A . . . book, my lord."

"A book? Let me see it, my pet. I greatly fancy books and have an enormous library of them at Lahore."

"My lord, it is a book for a woman, not a man," Velvet replied, her cheeks turning pink again.

"Has Jodh Bai sent you a Pillow Book, perchance?"

Velvet nodded blindly, not daring to look at him.

"A Pillow Book, my Rose, is for both the bride and the bridegroom. It is believed that by viewing paintings of the postures of love together they will be reassured." Akbar opened the box and lifted the book out. "Come," he said to her. "Let us sit outside upon the terrace and view the book together. Bring a lamp so that we may fully enjoy the art-work, for much care and talent goes into the making of such a book."

It was impossible to refuse him, and so with a sinking heart Velvet followed him onto the terrace. The night was warm, the slate-black sky sprinkled with bright stars. Akbar settled himself with his back against the cushions. He wore a white silk gown that was belted about his middle with a cloth of gold sash and his customary white turban, but his feet were bare as they usually were within the privacy of the zenana.

"Sit next to me, my Rose," he invited, patting the cushions at his side.

Reluctantly she sat by him, and, placing the book where they both might see it, he opened to the first of the paintings.

On second glance it is not so shocking, Velvet thought. "The colors are very fresh, aren't they?" she noted.

"Yes," he answered her seriously. "Note that the prince portrayed wears a lotus crown. That would indicate that he has reached a high level of spiritual attainment." He turned the page, and Velvet sucked her breath in sharply. The beau-tiful consort was now bare-breasted, and the prince's crown was gone. Akbar chuckled. "I do not believe the prince now thinks of the advancement of his soul, but rather the sweet flesh of his consort." He turned to the next page.

The prince firmly clasped one of his lady's breasts in his hand while his other hand roamed her bare belly. Velvet trembled, and Akbar's hand closed over hers while he moved on to the next page. Here the prince and his consort were both unclothed, and she lay in his arms as he gazed lovingly down at her, his masculinity fully engorged and thrusting forward in anticipation. Velvet's breath caught in her throat, and then she began to breathe rather quickly. Feeling Akbar's fingers gently undoing the ribbons that held her blouse together, she tensed.

"No, my Rose," he breathed warmly in her ear, "don't be afraid of me. I have sworn not to force you, and I will keep my promise. I only wish to caress you. Surely you will not deny me that?"

"N-no, my lord," she whispered, her throat tight as she forced the words out.

The ribbon ties undone, he pushed the silk blouse off her shoulders and then with swift fingers removed it completely, laying it to one side on the couch. His breath hissed softly. "Allah! Allah!" he murmured, "your breasts are like twin moons." Reaching out, he began to stroke her with a light and gentle touch.

His caress sent a small shiver of pleasure racing through Velvet's veins, and she was unable to restrain the small "ohhh" that slipped forth from between her lips.

Akbar moved her from her position at his side so that she sat between his legs. Drawing her back against his chest, he cupped both her breasts in his hands, his thumbs softly but insistently rubbing against her nipples. "Turn the page, my Rose," he commanded her, and Velvet obeyed him.

The picture before her both shocked and excited her, for now the beautiful woman lay upon her back, the prince between her legs, his tongue gently probing at her deepest secret. She stared, fascinated, at the little painting. The woman wore a look of pure ecstasy, her eyes half-closed in her passion. Velvet shivered uncontrollably.

"Did your first husband do that to you, my Rose?" came Akbar's deep voice. "Are you remembering your own pleasure?"

"Alex never d-did that to m-me," she whispered. "I did not know that a man did such things to a woman." She was still shivering.

"It is a way to give a woman sweetness, my love. A woman's pleasure only adds to a man's pleasure. I want to love you like that, my Rose. I want to give you joy."

Velvet quickly turned the page, unable to bear it any longer. The paintings were frankly exciting her. If she could just get through the Pillow Book, then everything would be all right. But the next painting showed the woman between the man's legs, her mouth caressing his sex. With a cry of despair she turned the page once more to discover the two lovers now joined in a conjugal embrace, his mighty shaft plunging deep into the beautiful consort, who was quite openly encouraging his efforts. "Oh, God," she sobbed, closing the book with a slam.

Releasing his hold upon her breasts, Akbar pulled Velvet into his arms, and his mouth crushed bruisingly against hers. Unable to restrain her inflamed emotions, she wrapped her arms about him and returned the kiss as passionately. For some time they kissed hungrily and without ceasing, one deep kiss blending into another. His tongue made its first penetration of her, plunging between her lips and into her mouth to meet with her tongue, which leaped with shock at his touch and fled, only to be pursued until the two were entwining together with ever-mounting ardor.

Finally their lips parted, and he gazed down upon her with burning eyes. "I want to make love to you," he said in his deep voice. "I want to plunge my lingam deep within your sweet yoni! Can you honestly tell me that you do not want me, too, my beautiful Rose? Can you honestly deny us the bliss that our bodies so desperately crave?"

"No," came her reply, "I cannot, for I want you even as you want me!"

"Is this then to be our night of nights, my love?"

"Yes," she said softly, sitting up so that she could loosen his golden sash and open his robe. Her hands trembled as she worked, but she was soon successful and the sash fell away. Velvet knelt and gently pushed away the white silk of his long robe, drawing it over his shoulders until it fell about his waist. Beneath it he was naked, his golden body smooth and hairless.

He watched her, charmed by the mixture of shyness and passion that seemed to control her. When she had worked his robe free, he reached out and undid the waistband of her sheer silk skirt, slipping it down over her slender hips. Then his lips brushed her belly with sweet fire, and she gasped with delight as his hot mouth worked over her satiny skin. Swinging himself off the couch, Akbar lifted Velvet into his arms and, walking into her chamber, gently placed her upon the bed.

Velvet opened her arms to him. Her heart was hammering wildly, but she was no longer controlled by any common sense. All that mattered to her now was that he love her, love her as Alex had once loved her.

No! He was nothing like Alex! God! She didn't want to think of Alex now. It was her wedding night with this man who was now her husband. Her mother had lived through six such nights and survived. Had she thought of the others? Velvet wondered. Had she ever thought of her old husbands as her new husband roused her to passion? I'll never know, Velvet realized.

Akbar stood for a long moment gazing down at the beautiful young woman on the bed. Her skin seemed even whiter against the sky blue silk. She was offering herself to him, and he relished the sight, for he had waited so patiently for it. If age had taught him one thing it was patience. How long her legs were, and how shapely. Kneeling, he took her slim foot in his hand and tenderly kissed each pink toe. His lips traveled slowly up the warm length of first one leg and then the other. Her skin was soft and fragrant with jasmine. He sighed.

"How absolutely perfect you are in both face and form," he said in his wonderful, rich voice. "I never knew that such pure beauty existed, but you, my Rose, surpass all others." Then he joined her on the bed, removing his white turban as he did so, and Velvet was surprised to find that he had shoulder-length hair. She had assumed that his hair would be short as was that of the other turbanless men she had seen. He spread her thighs and then, lowering his dark head, pressed a soft kiss upon her quivering flesh. Opening her tenderly with his two thumbs, he gazed upon her tiny jewel and then with a low cry of desire began to love it with his tongue.

Her body leaped with shock at the sensation, and for a moment she grew dizzy. Reaching out, she touched his head and was amazed at the softness of his hair, which spread like a black stain across her white thighs. The touch of his tongue against that most hidden part of her offered her a feeling she likened to boiling wine flowing through her veins. At first she couldn't breathe, and then when she was finally able to she gasped the air in great gulpfuls as she felt his tongue darting over her hot moistness, touching her here, touching her there with tantalizing madness. A tiny tingle began within her very core, and it grew until it was almost unbearable. Velvet felt herself sliding into a wonderful, whirling pit of pure passion. In a brief second of sanity she tried to fight it back, but then with a soft cry she gave in to it, feeling herself soaring for what seemed a long moment, and then she floated back to earth with a long sigh.

Akbar moved upward on her body now, kissing and stroking as he went until he had reached her breasts. There he stopped and loved her again with exquisite skill and tender caring. His fingers caressed and molded her flesh until it grew taut and firm within his hands. His lips found her nipples, and he tongued them with vigor until finally her little, mewling cries told him that she needed a release of sorts. He took one of the hard, little spear points into his warm mouth and suckled upon it.

"My lord! My lord!" she whispered frantically, her slim fingers threading themselves through the silken length of his dark hair with growing desperation. The need within her for him was growing with each passing minute. Would he never take her? Would he continue this divine foreplay until she died from the very wanting?

He positioned himself so that she was caught between his muscular thighs. Taking her face in his hand, he bent, kissing her, and then commanded, "Look at me, my Rose."

Velvet raised her eyes to him, blushing as she did so, for she knew her desire was as plain to him as his was to her.

"Are you willing, my beloved Rose? Do you hunger for me as I do for you? Would you have me consummate this marriage between us?"

"Oh, yes!" she whispered.

"Say my name!" he demanded. "I have never heard my name upon your sweet lips."

"Take me and make me yours, my lord Akbar," she murmured, "I long for you, my darling! Oh, Akbar! I can wait no longer!" She sobbed, and with bold hands she caught at the length of him and guided him to her throbbing body.

The touch of her hot, little hands upon his pulsing lingam caught him by surprise and almost caused him to spill his seed. He groaned, wanting to encase himself in her then and there, but age had taught him the wisdom of patience, and even in the midst of his passion Akbar knew that Velvet would be tight from her abstinence and lack of marital experience. Gently he pushed her hands away and carefully guided himself to the portal of paradise, inserting his swollen manhood just a tiny amount. She sobbed with a sound that sounded almost like relief to him. Already her green eyes had closed, and her lashes were quivering against her cheeks.

"Please," she almost sobbed against his lips, "please!"

"Shh," he whispered back. "Shh, my sweet love. I don't want to hurt you."

Frantically she thrust herself up at him, trying to drive him deeper, and he realized that she was too caught up in the throes of her own rapture to care any longer. A groan of delight escaped him that she was so very ardent in her nature and he shoved himself deep within her waiting yoni. With rhythmic motions he drove himself in and out of her again and again and again until he, too, was engulfed in the fiery ardor. He could not, it seemed, satisfy his intense desire for her even now that she lay beneath him giving him her body and her soul. Her own passion peaked several times before he finally could no longer contain himself, and he spilled his seed into her burning womb, falling across her breasts with a cry of fierce pleasure.

This first passionate encounter exhausted them both, and without a word they fell into a peaceful sleep, his dark hair mingling with her auburn curls upon the pillows.

Awakening several hours later, Velvet lay quietly for several long minutes. Comparisons were inevitable, she thought. Alex had been a wonderful lover, quick, passionate, and demanding; but Akbar was every bit as proficient. Not only that but he had been so very patient, so careful that she obtain her portion of pleasure, too. Instinctively Velvet knew that she was very fortunate in both of her husbands. Within her heart there would always be that secret, special place that would be inhabited by Alex Gordon, her first love, but if she continued to think of him, refused to let him go from her life, she would spend her days in misery. She had been given a good and loving man to care for her now, and she was grateful for it.

Propping herself up on an elbow, she gazed down at Akbar. He was handsome in a much different way than Alex had been. She did not know his age, but she did know that his sons were all older than she was, as were two of his three daughters who were already married. Only little Aram-Banu Begum was still a child. Akbar could be her father, and yet the feelings that were growing inside her for him were not those of a daughter for a father.

Reaching out, she gently touched his cheek. His golden skin seemed so dark next to her fairness, and his silky hair was so very black and straight. His eyes, she saw now, slanted a tiny bit upward, yet he had not the look of an Oriental about him. He had a good body. It was sturdy and well formed, though he was not really any taller than she was in his bare feet. Well, perhaps an inch, but certainly no more. She could look him right in the eye when they spoke. Jodh Bai could not be any higher than his heart, and Rugaiya Begum came only to his shoulder, Velvet thought. Beneath his left nostril just above his lip was a mole the size of a pea. It gave him a rather distinguished look.

Unable to resist, Velvet bent and kissed that mole, and Akbar, who had merely pretended to be asleep during her careful inspection of him, surprised her by wrapping his arms about her tightly.

"Oh! You are awake, my lord Akbar."

"Awake and hungry for you, my adorable sweetmeat!" he growled at her.

Mischievously she escaped his hold and, slipping from the bed, knelt to pour them some wine. "First you must drink to our love," she teased him, handing him a cup.

"Only if you drink with me," he answered, knowing that this particular wine had certain herbs and spices added to it that would not only stimulate their desires once more but aid him in retaining his prowess with his young and passionate wife.

"A man should never drink alone," she agreed with him, and filled her own cup.

"I have made you happy," he said with simplicity.

"Yes," she answered, rejoining him upon the tumbled bed. "You have made me happy, Akbar. I have been so frightened and lonely. I never expected my life to take the direction that it has." She smiled. "None of my fine friends at the queen's court would believe that, as they follow Her Majesty upon her annual progress this autumn, thousands of miles to the south in the land of the Grand Mughal, Velvet Gordon now resides as the monarch's new consort."

"Does it make you unhappy that you shall never see your land again, my Rose?"

"Of course it does!" she answered without hesitation. "You must understand that everything I have held dear my whole life is in England. Perhaps in time I shall accept India as my land, but I cannot say it now."

"You will give me a child, and then it will be better for you," he said.

Velvet laughed. That reminded her of Alex. "Why is it," she asked him, "that you men seem to think that all we women need is babes to make us happy? Is there no more to life than just that?"

"What is it you want?" he asked her.

"I don't know yet," she said with complete candor. "I have not lived long enough to be sure. Perhaps had I remained in England I should have wanted to be like my mother, who has built an enormous trading empire. Or perhaps I would be happy living like my sisters, Willow and Deirdre, who are content with their houses and children. Until a year ago I had seen very little of life, sequestered as I was upon my family's estates in England and France. I have not the experience to be certain what it is I want."

Her answer astounded him. He had been intrigued by her because of the fact that she was different from the other women he had known, and yet he had mentally attempted to place her in the same position as Jodh Bai and the others, to enclose her world with the walls of the zenana. He realized that he didn't want such a thing to happen to his beautiful Rose. Releasing her from his embrace, he sat up and Velvet sat cross-legged facing him.

"I will give orders that whatever questions you have should be answered, and when we return to Lahore my library will be yours. Whatever you desire I will give you if it is in my power," he promised.

"I will have to learn your language, or at least one of your languages for I can see there are many here in India."

"I shall teach you your first two words," he said. "Look by the side of the bed and see if Adali has left a basin of perfumed water and soft cloths." Leaning over the edge of the bed, Velvet found the items, and he said, "Wring one of the cloths out, my love, and give it to me." She complied, and taking the cloth, he began gently to wipe her free of the evidence of their recent lovemaking. "This, my Rose, is called the yoni," he murmured, rubbing her secret softness with tantalizing and delicate strokes. Velvet began to quiver with his loving touch. When he had finished, he said as he handed her the cloth. "Discard it, and take a fresh one, my love. You must now serve me as I have served you."

She obeyed him, and as she began to sponge him her soft touch roused his manhood, which until then had been sleeping peacefully.

"This randy fellow," he said with a mischievous smile, "is called the lingam, and it is already very fond of your sweet yoni that just a short while ago made it so very welcome."

The love cloth fell from her hand, and Akbar picked it up and deposited it with the other one. Then he reached out and touched her yoni with delicate fingers while his other hand began to tease one of her breasts. Following his lead, Velvet, sitting opposite her husband, began to stroke his mighty lingam, which grew greater and longer with her honeyed touch. She took her cue from him, feeling no shame or shyness in what they were doing. She wanted to do to him what he had done before to her, and suddenly she was kneeling before him to take the ruby head of his manhood into her mouth.

"Use your tongue, my Rose," he said softly.

Slowly she encircled the knob of him with her tongue, and then she grew bolder, taking more of him into her mouth and licking at the shaft with sure and bold strokes. He groaned, and she felt his hand on her head.

"Stop, my love," he begged her, and Velvet, having no experience in these matters, obeyed him. "I want you to kneel, resting upon your forearms, with your adorable bottom facing toward me," he commanded. "I will not hurt you, my Rose."

Trusting him, she followed his instructions and felt him as, clasping her hips in his hands, he entered her burning yoni with his lingam from behind her. She gasped as he plunged deep inside her, thrusting farther than he had before. Again and again he drove himself within the warmth of her quivering body. His passion began to build to an incredible crest. He had never before felt this way with any woman, and he fought to control the shout of exultation that struggled to burst from his throat.

It has never been like this for me, Velvet thought, as he pounded against her. *Dearest God, I shall burst with the desire that rages through me for this man.* She made a low animal sound, for he seemed to swell and grow within her, filling her so full that she did not think she could bear much more of the incredible pleasure. Then one of his hands reached out to tease her little jewel, and Velvet cried out as her passion crested wildly.

He could wait no longer and flooded her with his essence as together they collapsed onto the bed. For a moment he lay atop her, and then, fearing that he might crush her delicate bones, he rolled off her and gathered her into his arms. "I love you," he said. "I love you!"

She heard his passionate declaration through the haze of her own receding passion and sighed deeply. He loved her! For a moment the knowledge that this powerful man loved her was too intoxicating. She was beloved of a king! Then she remembered that she was his fortieth legal wife, and there was a zenana full of lovely women, some of whom had even borne him children. Once they, even as she, had held his favor, but the favor of a king was often a fleeting thing. She had best remember that, she thought. Rolling onto her back, she reached up and caressed his face with her hand.

"I love you," he repeated.

She smiled up at him. "You are so good to me, Akbar, but my experience is so little. I will never lie to you, and therefore I will not now say that I love you. Perhaps in time I will. What I do know is that I like you and am fond of you. I am grateful for your kindness to me."

"Had you told me you loved me, my Rose, I should have been very disappointed in you. It would have shown me a lack of sincerity."

"Yet you claim to love me," she challenged him.

"I do love you, my darling! My experience is as great as yours is little. I know quickly my feelings for a woman, and you have utterly bewitched me with not only your beauty but your intelligence."

Velvet had to laugh. "You," she declared, "have a very quick tongue, my Akbar, which matches your quick mind! I do not know that I should not be afraid of you."

"Perhaps you should," he said with a gentle smile. It was not good to ever let one person become too sure of another, he thought.

They made love twice more that night, and Akbar was frankly astounded by his own prowess. He had not performed so vigorously in at least ten years. This beautiful English consort he had taken into his bed and his heart seemed to have renewed him physically. He found that a very flattering thought as he finally fell into a satisfied sleep.

When Velvet awoke she found that her husband had left her side. The day was already hot, and she stretched in a leisurely fashion, flexing her feet and wiggling her toes. She felt, she realized, better than she had in months! She smiled, suddenly comprehending that women had certain needs even as men did. Why was it that they never talked of them?

A light rap came upon her door. "Come in," she called, and Adali entered the room.

"I have come to tell you that your serving woman is at this very moment attempting to give birth to her child, my princess."

"Fetch my clothing," Velvet commanded. "I will go to her."

Dressing quickly, she pondered the fact that she knew little about the act of birthing a child. She had been considered too young by both her parents to attend Deirdre, the closest of her sisters, when Deirdre had borne the first of her babies. Still, Pansy would need a friendly and familiar face to cheer her along. Her tiring woman herself had seen many a birth, being one of Daisy's older children.

Hurrying down the corridor, Velvet could hear Pansy's groans as she neared her tiring woman's small cubicle. Within the little chamber a midwife sat waiting for nature to take its course. Pansy was a big, healthy girl and should have no problems.

"Come inside with me, Adali. If the midwife tries to give Pansy some direction, we will need you to translate," Velvet said.

"I will remain, my princess."

Velvet knelt by her friend's side. "Adali will stay nearby in case the midwife needs to communicate with us."

Pansy smiled and said wryly, "I'd hate to disobey the old crone. She looks like a tough one. Lord, Mistress Velvet, I ain't ever felt such pain before. I remember me ma yelling plenty each time she had one of me brothers or sisters. It ain't easy birthin' a babe, but I ain't afraid."

"I know you're not," said Velvet, and she took Pansy's hand in her own.

"It does get a bit messy though, m'lady," Pansy grunted. "I'm not sure you want to be around me right now."

"Pansy, unlike most girls my age I have never seen a baby born. What if I have one of my own? Do you think it should come as a surprise to me?"

Pansy was forced to chuckle although it was uncomfortable for her to do so. "Are you planning on having a baby soon, m'lady?" she teased her mistress.

"My lord Akbar says he wishes to have a child by me, Pansy. I think I should like children of my own."

In the brief minutes between her labor pains Pansy looked closely at her mistress. Velvet had lost that guarded look she had worn these many weeks. There was a glow about her this morning, and Pansy immediately knew the reason. Her mistress's marriage to the Grand Mughal had been consummated at last. Pansy breathed a sigh of relief. She had frankly been frightened that Velvet's long resistance would finally pall on the lord of this land, and then they would be lost. What would have happened to her and her about-to-be-born child if Velvet had lost the master's favor? Pansy's thoughts were interrupted by another pain that seared through her straining body.

The midwife shuffled to her feet and motioned Pansy to rise as well, cackling words at her that neither of the young women could understand.

"She says your servant is ready to give birth and must squat down over the birthing cloth she has set out," said Adali.

Velvet translated Adali's French into her own native tongue for Pansy, then helped the girl to her feet. "I hope she knows what she's doing," Velvet fretted.

Pansy gave one of her many impudent grins to her mistress. "I don't have no other choice, m'lady do I? 'Twill be all right, I'm sure." Clumsily she got to her feet and, walking slowly across the room, squatted over the brightly colored cloth the old woman had spread out.

With Adali translating, Velvet relayed the midwife's instructions to her tiring woman and friend. "She says you must push as hard as you can, Pansy."

Pansy gritted her teeth with the next pain and then bore down with all of her might. The effort almost tore her in two, and large beads of moisture stood out upon her forehead. "Gawdalmighty!" She groaned. "That was the worst."

"Again!" Velvet ordered.

Pansy repeated her labor, remarking, "The littler bugger had better be born soon. I'm growing tired with all of this." Her lower regions felt stretched beyond their limit.

"Once more, Pansy, 'tis almost over, dear one!" Velvet encouraged.

Pansy obeyed a third time, pushing as hard as she could, and sudddenly she felt something slide from her body, and the pressure was gone. A mighty howl broke the hot stillness of the morning, and she strained around in her awkward position to see the child.

"'Tis a boy, Pansy! You've given Dugald a fine son!" Velvet cried happily.

Pansy expelled the afterbirth from her body with a matter-of-fact nonchalance and said, "He'll never know it, m'lady. 'Tis a pity, but that's the way of it. At least I'm a proven breeder of sons, and maybe I'll catch some lusty soldier's eye."

The midwife cleaned first the infant and then his mother, finally tucking them both back upon the low pallet bed. She smiled broadly, saying a few words they could not comprehend, and then with a final cackle of laughter exited the little room.

"She said your servant was made for birthing, and that both mother and son are in excellent shape and should live to be a hundred. She wishes your Pansy many more such fine sons," Adali translated.

"But not too soon," Pansy said wryly, and then she turned to get the first good look at her son. The sight brought quick tears to her eyes. "Lord, don't he look just like his father," she said, her voice somewhat quavery. "I only wish Dugald was here to see him, m'lady."

"So do I, Pansy!" replied Velvet. "Oh, Pansy, I will try to get you home! I will!"

"Don't break your heart, m'lady. Your family don't know where we are. If I was allowed to return home I would tell them, and then they would want you back, and there would be all kinds of an unholy trouble. Be honest with yourself. Do you think the lord Akbar would really release me?"

Velvet didn't even need to consider the matter seriously. She knew the answer and it was no. Akbar would certainly never let Pansy or her go, and frankly, after the passion she herself had experienced in his arms last night, she did not believe she wanted to leave. Eventually after she had had children she would get him to allow her to communicate with her family. If they knew that she was well, and loved, and happy with a husband and babes there would be no problems. That, however, would not be for at least several years. It pained her to think of their agony and heartbreak over her disappearance in the meantime, but what else could she do? Someday she would be able to explain it to them, and they would understand. Till then there was nothing she could do to relieve their unhappiness, and it was up to her to see that she, Pansy, and Pansy's son survived.

"What are you going to call the lad?" she asked Pansy, who was beginning to nod upon her pillows.

"Dugald, after his pa," came her friend's sleepy reply. "Maybe someday he'll be able to go home even if we cannot." Pansy's eyes closed.

Velvet bent down and kissed the girl's forehead and that of the baby's. With his fuzzy crown of carrotty hair and very pronounced little nose, he did look very much like his father, she thought as she quietly left the room.

"It is a fine boy," Adali noted. "She is a good strong girl, your Pansy."

"Yes," Velvet said. "She is very strong."

"What did you talk about?" he asked her. "You both looked as if you would cry at one point."

"We just thought it sad that Pansy's husband could not know that he had such a beautiful son. She did not realize she was with child until we were several weeks into our voyage. Dugald did not even know he was to become a father."

"Then he will feel no loss," replied Adali wisely.

"No," said Velvet sadly. "He will feel no loss."

"Then all will be well with you." Adali beamed with his approval.

Velvet could not resist a small smile, for she could not stay unhappy long. "Yes, Adali, all will be well with us from now on!"

Chapter 10

Murrough O'Flaherty made the passage from India back to England in record time. Thus it was that he anchored his ship in the London pool on a snowy day in late January, 1590, slightly less than a year after he had left. Putting ashore at the O'Malley warehouses, he learned that his mother and stepfather were in residence at Greenwood, having arrived back in England some three months earlier. A horse was immediately put at his disposal, and Murrough rode as quickly as he could to his mother's house. The blustery weather gave him one small advantage in that the streets were fairly empty as late-afternoon darkness began to claim London town. The bitter cold had sent even the hardiest beggar seeking shelter. He galloped through the gates of the mansion's grounds and up the sweeping driveway. Immediately the door was opened, and a groom ran to take his horse as he leaped from it.

"Welcome home, Captain O'Flaherty!" said the elderly majordomo as Murrough strode into the main entry.

"Where is my mother?" Murrough demanded.

"At this time of day she would be in her apartments resting with Lord de Marisco," came the servant's reply.

Murrough took the stairs two at a time, moving from the main level of Greenwood to the third floor where the family's private apartments were located. His knock brought Daisy to the door of Skye's chambers.

"Captain O'Flaherty!" Daisy fell back, and then she flung herself forward to hug him mightily. "Come in, Captain! Oh, I just knew that you'd get home safe. Where is Mistress Velvet and my Pansy? Have you come on ahead?"

"So many questions, Daisy," he chided her gently. "Tell my mother that I am here, please."

"There is no need, Murrough," said Skye O'Malley de Marisco as she came through the door of her bedchamber into the dayroom. Taking him in her arms, she kissed him. "My dearest son, I am so thankful to have you back. Where is Velvet? Will she be coming along shortly? We've been so worried. It has been all I could do to prevent Adam from taking one of my ships and sailing back out to sea to find her." She held him away from her, looking at him closely, and then her marvelous Kerry-blue eyes clouded. "What has happened, Murrough?"

"How could you escape, Mother, and not leave us some word, some sign? I arrived back in Bombay in less than six months!"

"What has happened, Murrough? Tell me this instant!"

"Tell us both," came Adam de Marisco's terse words as he came out of the bedchamber. "Where is my daughter, Murrough? Where is Velvet?"

Murrough took a deep breath. 'Twas best, he knew, to get the worst over with first. There would be time later for the full explanation. "Velvet is at the court of the Grand Mughal, Akbar. In his harem, to be precise."

Daisy gave a little shriek of dismay even as her mistress cried out, "Dear God!" Skye's eyes closed, and she swayed where she stood as a thousand memories came flooding back to her. She was too strong a woman, however, to faint, and Adam's arms about her steadied her enough to open her eyes. She could feel him trembling against her, and immediately her total concern was for her husband. Turning, she took his face in her hands. "I'm sure 'tis not as bad as Murrough has made it sound, my darling, but nonetheless I think I need to sit down. Sit by me, Adam. *Please.*" She looked at her son as she settled herself next to her husband. "What happened?" was all she could say.

"We reached Bombay in good time, Mother. I had not delayed a moment in gathering the ransom and returning with it. The Jesuit was awaiting us. He attempted to elicit the gold from me, but I reminded him that our bargain had been that you and Adam would be waiting for us on the dock so that we might be certain that you were both safe. He was finally forced to admit that you had escaped. He demanded the gold, nevertheless, and I told him that I had nothing to pay for. Naturally Father Ourique was not particularly pleased. He had come well prepared, Mother, with a goodly troop of soldiers who lay hidden on the docks. The Jesuit took Velvet and Pansy from the ship to the residence of the Portuguese governor, agreeing to return them when we delivered your ransom. I had no reason to believe that he would not keep his promise, and I could not endanger my sister by haggling. We put back to sea immediately, and the following day I returned with our fleet and the Jesuit saw to the unloading of the gold.

"When it was off our ships, Father Ourique and I rode to the governor's palace to get Velvet and Pansy. When we got there, the bastard who is their governor told us that he had sent Velvet and her servant to the Mughal as a gift. I thought the Jesuit was going to have a fit where he stood, for he is an honorable man; and had it not been for the governor's bodyguards, Mother, I would have killed Don Marinha-Grande then and there! I will give Father Ourique credit. He threatened the governor with excommunication, but the Portuguese bastard just laughed at him. It was no sin, he claimed, to send a heretic Englishwoman to Akbar's harem. When the Jesuit reminded him of Velvet's faith, that she was not a heretic but a loyal daughter of the church, the governor laughed and said that the Spanish king would not punish him for ridding the world of an English bitch.

"We left the palace then, and I spoke with the padre about retrieving my sister. He told me quite frankly that it was impossible. We could not remove Velvet from a caravan meant for the Mughal without an army, and once she arrived in his capital of Lahore it would be impossible to see her ever again. The Muslims are jealous of their women, and although the Mughal is more civilized than most, he is still a man of

India. Father Ourique said we must face the fact that Velvet is lost to us."

"The Jesuit is a fool then if he thinks I will allow my daughter to spend the rest of her life in some Muslim's harem!" snapped Adam de Marisco. He turned to his wife. "How soon before we can set sail, my love?"

"Not soon enough," said Skye. "Velvet is already a part of this ruler's life. We have dealt with this sort of thing before, Adam. We must plan carefully, for we will get only one chance to retrieve our child. We have an advantage in that they will not suspect we are coming."

"Their capital is hundreds of miles from the coast, Mother," said Murrough. "We might get there, but could we get back? It will not be as simple as your escape from Fez once was."

She nodded. "I know. This will have to be different, and I will need time to consider it."

"Every minute we waste brings Velvet closer to that devil's bed!" exploded Adam.

"My darling," Skye said matter-of-factly, "if Velvet was sent as a gift to the Mughal, he has already most certainly bedded her. It is not the worst fate that can befall a woman."

"You were older, stronger, more worldly," Adam replied. "My precious little Velvet is barely a child."

"Your precious Velvet is an impossible minx who led me a merry chase at court before finally being brought to the altar," said Alexander Gordon, who had only heard the end of Adam's sentence as he entered the room. "Murrough! What the hell possessed ye to take my wife off to India, and where is the wench? I've a score to settle with her, leaving me wounded and half-dead to be nursed by strangers!"

Murrough O'Flaherty's jaw dropped open in his complete and utter shock. *"You're dead!"* he said.

"If I am there's none who's yet dared to tell me so," came back Alex's amused reply.

"Murrough," said his mother, realizing that there was very definitely something amiss, "I want you tell me why you took Velvet with you when you left London. Alex, sit down."

"First tell me where Padraic is," demanded Murrough.

"What the hell has Padraic to do with this?" asked Adam.

"Where is he?"

"Why do you want Padriac?" asked Skye. "What can he possibly have done? He has been down at *Clearfields* for months now, and I was only able to get him to come to London for Twelfth Night because I told him you should be back from India before the end of the month."

"Exactly how long has he been at *Clearfields*, Mother?"

For a moment Skye's brow furrowed in thought, and then she said, "I don't really know, Murrough. Is it important?"

"Get him!" said his elder brother grimly.

"Daisy," said Skye. "Fetch Lord Burke. Murrough won't continue his story until you return."

Daisy hurried out the door, and an uncomfortable silence descended upon the room. Skye looked at her husband of over seventeen years. He would be sixty this year, and his dark hair was already well silvered, but it only had the effect of making him more handsome and distinguished, she thought. His dark blue eyes were still lively. If he had a weakness it was his only child, their daughter, Velvet. How often over the years had she deferred to him in the raising of their child and all because she could not bear that he have any less than a perfect relationship with Velvet. She realized now that she loved them both too much. She wondered if Velvet would be able to cope with what life had forced upon her, for despite her short-lived marriage Skye knew that her daughter was still innocent at heart. Skye reached out and took Adam's hand, squeezing it reassuringly.

He managed a weak smile at her and squeezed back, but then his eyes fogged over as his thoughts returned to his only child. In his mind she was still a little girl. Oh, granted she had been twelve and a half when they had left on their voyage, and many a girl was not much older when wedded and bedded; but he and Skye had arranged that she not have to marry until she was sixteen. They had intended to give her a little time at court under their careful supervision. He sighed. They had protected her and sheltered her so carefully, perhaps too carefully, he was now beginning to think. How would she survive the ordeal of being incarcerated within a harem? What did Velvet know of love except perhaps the little Alex Gordon had taught her in their short time together? He let his glance rest on the son of his old friend.

Alexander Gordon, the Earl of BrocCairn, sat stiffly and grimly in his chair. For close to a year he had been without his wife. *His wife!* That cunning, willful jade had deserted him in his hour of need to run off to find her parents. She had had him convinced that she was content to return to Dun Broc with him and behave like a proper wife. Instead she had taken the first opportunity she'd found to desert him. His hand itched to make contact with her delightful bottom. When he got his hands on her, she was going to learn what it meant to be *his wife*, the Countess of BrocCairn.

The door to the apartment opened and Lord Burke and Daisy hurried into the room. Murrough leaped forward, his face a mask of fury as he hit his brother a clout that sent the younger man sprawling to the floor. Everyone else in the room gaped in surprise as Murrough reached down to haul his brother up and hit him once again.

"You're certain?" I asked you! Do you remember, Padraic? I asked you if you were sure that Lord Gordon had been killed. You assured both Velvet and me that he had been. As I remember it you even became insulted that I should dare to question your veracity! Do you know what you've done, Padraic? Do you have any idea what you've done?"

"You're back safe!" blubbered Padraic. "I made an error, Murrough. I'm sorry, but you're back safe, and 'tis all right now, isn't it?"

"Your sister is at this moment the prisoner of India's Grand Mughal!" roared Murrough. "She's locked away in his harem, and we've precious little chance of ever seeing her again! Would you call that all right?" He pushed his youngest brother from him disgustedly. "Jesu! You're just like your father, Niall. You're charming but totally heedless of your own selfish actions! You didn't even stay long enough to tell Alex what really happened, did you? You ran back to *Clearfields* and hid away. Why didn't you own up to your error and save him the anxiety? I could kill you with my own two hands!"

Padraic Burke, sprawled upon the floor, looked up apprehensively at his elder sibling. Murrough was totally right, and he knew it. Desperately he tried to explain his actions. "How could I tell Alex what a fool I had been running back to Velvet to announce his death, when if I had waited a few more minutes I would have learned he was merely badly wounded?"

"My death?" exclaimed Alex, who had gone white when Murrough had said Velvet was in a harem. "Ye told Velvet I was dead?"

Now the earl looked as if he wanted to hit Padraic as well, and the young man, seeing the dark look on his brother-in-law's face scrambled to his feet and moved closer to his mother.

"You sneaking little coward!" snarled Murrough, stepping threateningly toward Padraic again.

Skye leaped up and stood between her sons. "Am I to understand that Padraic told you and Velvet that Lord Gordon had been killed? Why would he do such a thing?" She looked at Alex. "What do you know of this, m'lord?"

"'Twas a duel," he muttered.

"A duel that needn't have been fought!" snapped Murrough. "And my sister begged you not to, but would you listen? Nay!"

"Stop this bickering!" snapped Skye, who was becoming irritated and anxious to learn exactly what had happened. "You were injured in a duel, Alex, and Padraic, believing you dead, took it upon himself to inform Velvet. Is that correct?"

Padraic nodded.

Skye turned back to her elder son. "What I would like to know, Murrough, is why *you* took it upon yourself to remove your sister from London and take her on such a hazardous journey? You didn't even allow her time to bury her husband. Why?"

"Because she begged me," he said weakly.

"Because she begged you?" Skye was astounded. "Murrough! You're a grown man, the father of children yourself. Your eldest son is only a few years younger than Velvet! How could you do such a thing?"

"Mother," he said brokenly, "you don't understand. She was totally hysterical when she learned Alex had been killed. Hysterical and unreasonable. Robin and his wife weren't here to help me, nor were Willow and James. My little sister begged my aid, and I could see no other way of handling it than the manner in which I did. She believed that Alex would want to be buried at *Dun Broc*, and she could not bear to make her first trip to what was to have been her home in order to bury her husband. She kept sobbing that Alex's line had ended and that it was all her fault because she was not with child yet. There was simply no reasoning with her! I thought it better to take her with me than to leave her to God knows what mischief."

Alex's mouth compressed itself into a grim line. How typical of Velvet to run to her parents in a crisis. She hadn't grown up at all.

Skye slumped back onto the settle next to her husband. She didn't know whether to laugh or to cry, and she could tell from his face that neither did Adam. People could make the most ungodly disasters of their own lives and those around them by their headstrong actions. Murrough thought he had done the right thing for Velvet, but it was, in the end, the wrong thing. He should have checked Padraic's facts, for he knew his younger brother was often careless in his reports. Though Murrough had not waited, she knew, for fear of losing another day and missing the favorable winds across the Indian Ocean in his rescue mission of herself and Adam. How could she possibly upbraid him for what he had and hadn't done? If anything she blamed Alex Gordon, who would fight a duel that needn't have been fought, and Padraic, who had run off to his sister like Henny Penny to shout the sky down.

"All right, my sons, I believe I now understand this ridiculous muddle, and I blame all of you, including Velvet, whom I believed I had taught to face life better than that. Now we must consider what we have to do to regain her release and that of Pansy. At least the girls are together, for I know the people of the East and they would not separate Velvet from her tiring woman."

"What will happen to them, m'lady Skye?" quavered Daisy, and Skye, looking at her faithful servant and friend, was shocked. Never in her entire life had she seen Daisy lose heart, but then this time Daisy's fears were for her child, not for herself.

"Velvet, I imagine, has already been made a concubine of this Akbar," Skye told her. "As for Pansy she will not be harmed. She will simply continue to serve her mistress, Daisy. You need have no fears for her."

"My wife, some Turk's concubine? You speak about your daughter's fate quite matter-of-factly, madame," said Alex grimly.

"Akbar is the Grand Mughal of India, Alex, not a Turk," said Skye in an amused tone of voice. "If I speak matter-of-factly it is because I have been at one time in my life in the same position in which Velvet now finds herself. It is not always an envied position, Alex, but Velvet is my daughter, and she will survive! It could be far worse. We might not know where she was, or she might even be dead."

"Perhaps it would be better if she were dead than in another man's bed," said Alex bitterly.

Adam was at his son-in-law's throat in an instant. "You young whelp!" he snarled at the startled Scot, his knee on Alex's chest pinning him in his chair. "Your father was my friend, but you've turned into a smug, selfish bastard. You came out of your Highlands when our backs were turned and forced my child into your own bed. Don't think I don't know the *whole* story of your scandalous courtship of my daughter, for I do!

"Once long ago I watched my beloved Skye be bartered into marriage with a stranger. Then I saw her almost destroyed by another man in her attempt to rescue Padraic's father, her first love. At no time did I stop to consider that she had known other men. It was not important to me as long as she loved me, and it wouldn't be important to you either if you really loved my daughter, but I'm not certain that you do. I believe you consider her naught but a possession, some sort of brood mare. I'll not have it! If when we get her safely home you don't want her, and frankly I'm not sure you deserve her, then an annulment will be arranged!" He stood back and glowered fiercely at the young earl, and Alex shifted uncomfortably.

"Adam!" Skye chided her husband gently. "Alex is upset as well he might be. In his own way he has been as sheltered as Velvet." She gently separated the two, then took Alex's hand in hers. "I understand your distress, Alex, but whatever has befallen Velvet I know she still loves you. She is not a girl to give either her heart or her body wantonly, but I don't have to tell you that for you know it, don't you?"

"I can't bear the thought of any other man touching her, madame," he said, low.

"Yet you've known other women, Alex."

"'Tis different, madame,"

Skye smiled wisely. "Any man can have her body, Alex. Only you can possess her heart."

He looked down at her and thought that she was probably one of the most beautiful women he had ever known. The beauty, however, was not simply limited to her face and form. She had a great heart. He sighed. "We Scots are hard men, madame. I don't know if I can be as generous of spirit as Adam."

"Let us bring Velvet home first, Alex," she said, "and then we will see." He was very concerned with his own feelings, she thought. He did not stop to consider that Velvet, believing him dead, could easily fall in love again. She looked at Murrough once more. "You say that the Jesuits have some influence with Akbar?"

"Aye, there are two at his court, and he has allowed the order to have several priests in the country who work toward converting the huge population. Of course the two priests at court hope to convert the emperor himself. Father Ourique told me Akbar is amazingly intelligent, an enlightened ruler, and quite kindly in his character."

Skye pondered her son's words for several long minutes. The situation did not sound too discouraging. Praise from the Jesuits was not lightly given. They were a young order, having only been founded fifty-six years ago, but already they were wealthy and powerful. The motto of the order was *Ad Majorem Dei Gloriam*—To the Greater Glory of God—and their primary object was to spread the faith of the church. Working through the Jesuits, it just might be possible to regain Velvet's freedom. Skye turned to her tiring woman.

"Daisy, find Bran and tell him I want him to go to Ireland and fetch my brother, Michael."

"What can Michael do?" demanded Adam.

"As bishop of Mid-Connaught, Michael will go to the Jesuits in Paris where an old friend of his is high in the order. We need to gain their cooperation in the rescue of our child. After all, my darling, 'twas it not a Jesuit who demanded that outrageous ransom from us? A ransom that was paid. Was it not a Jesuit who placed our child in the care of that dreadful man, Marinha-Grande, who then sent her, a good and loyal daughter of the church, to an infidel lord for immoral purposes? Adam, my darling, if the Jesuits hadn't meddled, then our child would be safe today.

"The way I see it is that the Jesuits owe us for this terrible travesty. We shall, of course, show our further gratitude once Velvet is safely returned to us, but they must first use their influence to get Michael to the Grand Mughal; and once he is there, they must aid him in convincing Akbar to release Velvet into her uncle's care so that she may be returned to her family, and to her husband whom she believed dead."

"It is possible," pondered Adam. "It's just possible that such a thing might work."

"What if it doesn't?" asked Alex.

"To my knowledge," said Skye, "Akbar is a Muslim. No true believer would keep in his harem the wife of a living man. I am certain that once Akbar is told that Velvet's husband lives he will give her her freedom."

"I want to go with your brother," said Alex.

"No," said Skye quietly. "Velvet will have suffered more in the last year than she has ever done in her entire life. She will need the time during the voyage home to rebuild her physical and emotional strength, Alex. She will need to be alone. Your strong presence would only result in a heavy burden of guilt upon her. I will not allow you to do that to my daughter. Go home to Scotland. You have been gone from your lands for well over two years, and your people need to see you. We will send you word when Velvet's arrival is imminent. It will be well over a year from now, Alex.

"The voyage itself is of several months' duration each way. Once Michael is in India, he must travel hundreds of miles inland to Lahore and the Mughal's court, present his plea, and travel back to his ship. Yes, it will take well over a full year if not more. Go home to your Scotland. It is better that way. Here there is nothing for you to do."

What Skye did not say to her son-in-law was that she was more than aware that he had taken a mistress, pretty Alanna Wythe, the daughter of the silversmith whose house the wounded Earl of BrocCairn had been carried to after his duel and who had nursed him in Velvet's stead. Skye believed it would be best to separate Alex from his *chère aime* before her daughter returned home. Oh, Alex might amuse himself with the girls on his estate, something he had no doubt done in the past, but Alanna Wythe could become a much more serious threat to her daughter's happiness should Alex become attached to her. Sending him back to Scotland would end the relationship, and Mistress Alanna would look for another protector.

"I'll go," said Alex finally. "My men are anxious to be home again and have waited almost a year for me to make this decision. You are right. There is nothing for me to do here in London. There is one thing your Daisy should know, however. My man, Dugald, pledged himself in handfast to her daughter Pansy a month before she disappeared with Velvet. He'll be happy when we learn the lass is safe and coming home. He really loves that saucy little wench."

Skye smiled. "I'll tell her and Bran. I think, too, that Dugald should speak with them, to ask their blessing out of courtesy. Bran Kelly loves all his children, but Pansy as the eldest girl was always a particular favorite with him."

Alex nodded. "I'll see to it, *belle-mère*."

"Go along with you now, all of you. Murrough, make your peace with Padraic. I'll have no more of your brawling. What's done is done."

"There'll be no more fighting, Mother, but I'll not make any peace with Padraic until Velvet is safely home," growled Murrough, glaring at his youngest brother.

"'Twas not me who rushed Velvet out of the country," muttered Padraic, flushing hotly.

"'Twas not me who gave her a fit of hysterics by insisting that her husband had been killed," countered Murrough, his fists clenching and unclenching at his sides.

"Enough!" roared Adam de Marisco at his two stepsons. "Your squabbling isn't going to bring my daughter back. Get out, the pair of you!"

The two brothers bowed politely to their stepfather and then, still throwing black looks at each other, quickly left the room.

Skye opened her arms to her husband, and for a long moment they stood clinging to each other. If they had made one mistake with Velvet it was that they had loved her too well, and had overprotected her. Finally Skye said quietly, "She'll survive, my love. Is she not made up of a little bit of us both? Are we not survivors ourselves, my darling Adam? Velvet will come home to us! I know it!"

"Do you know what she's going through?" He groaned. "My God, Skye! She's so innocent!"

"She's a married woman, Adam," Skye reminded her husband. "She's no longer totally innocent."

"My little girl," he murmured, "my poor little girl."

"Adam!" Skye's voice pierced through his distress.

He looked down at her, and there were tears in his smoky blue eyes.

"Oh, Adam," Skye said softly, "she's my little girl, too, and as precious to me as any of my children, perhaps even a little more so because her birth was such a miracle for us. She will come back to us! I am certain of it!"

A knock upon the door brought Bran Kelly, Skye's senior captain, into the room. "Daisy's told me," he said, looking every bit as haggard as Adam did. "It'll be quicker if I ride for Devon and ship from there, m'lady."

Skye nodded. "Agreed!"

"I'll be on my way then, m'lady," said the captain, and, bowing to them both, he was gone.

Bran Kelly rode without rest from London to Bideford where he took command of one of the ships of the O'Malley-Small fleet to sail across the Irish Sea, around Cape Clear, and up the western flank of Ireland to Innisfana Island where he knew he would find word of Michael O'Malley, who was now bishop of Mid-Connaught as his late uncle Seamus had been before him.

As luck would have it, the bishop was visiting his stepmother at his ancestral home. Learning of his niece's fate and that of Bran Kelly's daughter, Michael O'Malley packed at once, and two weeks after he had left London, Bran Kelly returned with Skye O'Malley's younger brother.

The bishop of Mid-Connaught, once a tall, thin youth with pink cheeks and an earnest air about him, had grown into a bluff, hearty man with twinkling blue eyes, his dark hair very closely cropped as befitted a churchman, and a worldly air of assurance about him. His cheeks, however, were still pink from his heritage. His sister Skye had, fifteen years earlier, passed on her title "the O'Malley" to him despite his clerical standing. It always amused Michael that he had ended up with the responsibility that had actually been rightfully his all along. His father had died when he was just a small boy and, knowing Michael's desire to be a priest, had passed him over in favor of his sister, Skye. Skye, however, had given him back his inheritance after bearing the family responsibilities upon her own shoulders for many, many years. Michael, in turn, had chosen a nephew who would eventually supplant him, but which nephew he would not tell for fear that the boy would become big-headed by knowing his future position. Privately he had discussed his choice with Skye, and she had agreed that their half brother Brian's second son, Ahern, was the perfect choice. Michael O'Malley would pass on his authority when he thought his nephew ready, but for now he retained it and allowed the boy the opportunity to grow and to savor life.

"Don't you ever change?" he now demanded of his sister, giving her a bear hug that suddenly reminded her of their father.

Gazing at him, she realized that his increased girth made him look very much like their father as well, although she had never noticed it until now. "You suddenly resemble Da," she said.

"Aye, so Mother Anne tells me. Our stepmother sends you her greetings." He paused. "I hear I'm to go to Paris."

"And afterwards to India, brother," she said quietly.

"For a man who's never been out of Ireland but for a bit of study in Rome and Paris 'tis a big leap, sister Skye." He plumped himself down into a comfortable chair by the fire and took a goblet of wine from the servant who proferred it.

"You're our only hope, Michael. If the Mughal's capital were on the sea, or even near it, I should not need your help; but 'tis hundreds of miles inland. The Jesuits are in great favor with Akbar. They must understand that 'twas one of their order who involved my child in this disaster, and now they must aid us in retrieving her."

"You'll be expected to pay, Skye. You know that?"

Skye raised an eloquent eyebrow. "I always pay for what I seriously desire, Michael, but I'll pay not a penny piece into the Jesuit coffers until I know that my child is safe! Make sure your friends in Paris understand that, Michael."

"What of my niece's husband? Is he anxious to have his wife back from what is certain to be a very carnal captivity?"

"Yes," said Skye tersely, in a tone that decided Michael O'Malley to press his sister no further on that point.

"I am not quite certain," he said, "that I fully understand how Velvet got herself in this position. What was she doing in India with Murrough, and where was her bridegroom?"

"The situation in which Velvet finds herself was brought about by a mixture of stubbornness, pride, gossip, misinformation, and the usual sort of general mayhem that in another case could have caused a war!"

A deep rumble of laughter rocked the bishop. "In other words, sister, the human condition. Say on!"

Skye launched into the tale of Velvet's troubles. Michael listened with rapt attention, not interrupting until she came to the Portuguese governor's act of sending Velvet to the Grand Mughal as a gift.

"What possessed the governor to do such a terrible thing?" wondered Michael aloud.

"When Adam and I were imprisoned in Bombay by the Portuguese, they separated us for a time. The governor placed me in his house, where he made indecent overtures toward me that I most firmly rebuffed. I was then put back with Adam in the local prison, a disgusting place, but far preferable!"

"Your rebuff of that proud don must have been a fierce one that he would take such a revenge as to send your child, a Catholic noblewoman, into such a degrading situation."

"My rebuff of him was no more than he deserved!" snapped Skye.

"I've not a doubt," replied her brother, his bright blue eyes atwinkle. "Well," he said, sighing, "now I see the matter clearly, sister Skye, but 'twill take a great deal of clever negotiation on our part to get the Jesuits to aid us. To begin with they will deny any responsibility."

"Michael, I don't care how you do it! You're the youngest bishop Ireland's ever had, and I've always contended that you're wasted there when your talents could be put to better use in Rome. You've a friend, I remember, who is high up within the Jesuit ranks, and I know that he's in Paris."

"Bearach O'Dowd." Michael smiled with the memory. "His aunt was married to a distant O'Malley cousin who lived on Innisfana, and he used to come to visit in the summers with his sister, Caitlin. We used to take her fishing with us and then make her clean our catch. Bearach and I studied for the priesthood together in Rome. Aye, he's a Jesuit, and he is in Paris. Bearach always had a taste for the finer things."

"Will he help us?" Skye asked.

"Aye. He's an honest man, though clever. He'll be shocked by Father Ourique's behavior, but I'll wager he'll end up with at least part of your Portuguese ransom for the Paris order, probably from the Portuguese governor's portion, as well as whatever we pay him!"

"Do not delay, Michael. Every day that passes Velvet is further lost to us. She believes Alex is dead, and the Grand Mughal, I am told, is a kind man. If she falls in love with him, she will suffer not only from losing him, but from her guilt at returning to Alex with knowledge of another man."

"Perhaps you worry needlessly, my sister," the bishop counseled. "Do not Eastern potentates have vast harems? In all likelihood Velvet has lost herself in the crowd."

"As a European woman Velvet would be a rarity to the emperor of India, Michael. I will wager he has never seen one before. To ignore her would be to insult the Portuguese governor's gift, and he would not do that. No, my child has already been in his bed. I can only hope she does not love him so there will be no pain in leaving him. Any guilt she may feel I will assuage and help her to overcome, but first you must get her back for us, Michael!"

Michael O'Malley heard the agony in his sister's voice. He had to accept her words as accurate, for if anyone knew the East it was Skye by virtue of the two periods in her life when she had lived in Algeria and Morocco. "I'll get her back," he said quietly. "Never fear, sister. I will bring our Velvet safely home. Poor child! How she must be pining for her homeland!"

But Velvet had not given a thought to England for several weeks now. Pansy had recovered quickly from the ordeal of her childbirth, and they had left Fatehpur-Sikri with Akbar and all his household to return to the capital of Lahore.

Velvet felt a small pang as she passed by the great chessboard with its red sandstone squares for the last time. The huge court of the Panch Mahal gleamed brightly in the morning sun as they passed beneath the lovely entrance gate. From the vantage point of her gaily decorated howdah atop a plodding female elephant, Velvet turned to catch a final glimpse of the former capital of the Mughals in all its abandoned splendor. Then with the resilience of youth she looked only ahead.

They traveled in a crescent-shaped formation, Akbar followed by his cavalry and then his elephant corps. Mounted archers and pikemen guarded the enormous convoy. Before Akbar went drummers and trumpeters upon elephants; only one sounded his drum at specific intervals. In the middle of the caravan rode those wives and favorites of Akbar who had accompanied him from Lahore. The consorts were all mounted upon elephants, their serving women riding behind upon camels. The women were guarded by armed eunuchs who drove all away from the line of march. Behind them came the treasury and the baggage train, which included the tents and furnishings, all packed into mule-drawn carts and accompanied by soldiers, water-carriers, carpenters, tentmakers, torch bearers, leather workers, and sweepers.

Velvet quickly realized that she should have no fear of attack, for no one would dare to accost Akbar. It was simply to be a tedious journey, but at its end he had promised her gardens and fountains. The monsoons were over, and the cold season was coming. In Lahore, he said, her life would be perfection, and so she dreamed the hot days away snug in her howdah. When the evenings came, however, she was escorted from the women's tents to the large two-story pavilion where Akbar slept to partake in exquisite nights of passion with this powerful man who had become her husband.

She was no longer segregated from the other women, though only Jodh Bai and Rugaiya Begum approached her. They had begun to teach her Persian and a little Hindi so that she might communicate with those about her. With Adali acting as her translator, Velvet struggled to learn, though not with too great a success. She managed enough vocabulary so that she could gossip with the two women, but often Adali was called upon to explain words Velvet could not comprehend.

"I feel so stupid," she complained to her two friends one evening, "but the sounds are so different from the tongues of Europe."

"We think you clever," answered Jodh Bai. "We cannot learn any of your language. It confounds our brains!"

Velvet chuckled. "I think you are just being kind, Jodh Bai."

Jodh Bai smiled back at Velvet. "It is not difficult to be kind to you, Candra. Your nature is most sweet."

Candra. It was strange, Velvet thought, to have been given a new name at this time in her life, but indeed she had been. Before they had departed Fatchpur-Sikri, Akbar had spoken to her of it. "The women in my household do not know what to call you, my Rose. You must have a name that they can understand. I have therefore taken it upon myself to rename you Candra. You will answer to it from this time forth."

"I will do what pleases you, my lord," she replied sweetly, "but does the name have a meaning?"

"It means moon, or moonlike, in the ancient Sanskrit language. Your skin is so white that it can be compared to the moon, and therefore I consider it very fitting that you be called Candra."

So she became Candra Begum, the Rose Princess, among those who lived at the court of the Grand Mughal. The women of the zenana treated her with respect for the most part, but kept their distance. With Jodh Bai and Rugaiya

Begum for friends she felt no lack of companionship, but she often saw some of the other wives eyeing her with jealousy.

Zada Begum, Akbar's second wife, was a gray-brown mouse of a woman with no children to keep her company. She was close friends with the third wife, Salima Begum, mother of the Mughal's eldest daughter, Shahzad Khanim. Both women were haughty and held the rest of the zenana's inhabitants in contempt. They were much avoided by the others.

Jealousy, however, held in its grip four of the more important consorts: Almira, mother of Prince Murad; Leila, the Princess of Khandesh whose daughter was Shukuran Nisa; Roopmati, the Princess of Bikaner, mother of Prince Daniyal; and Kamlavati, the Princess of Jaisalmer, who had miscarried twice. Akbar no longer visited Kamlavati's bed, which embittered her greatly, especially considering that a mere concubine named Waqi had borne the last of Akbar's children, the little Princess Aram-Banu. Each of these ladies eyed Velvet constantly with black, unfriendly glances and gossiped meanly amongst themselves.

"She has eyes the color of a cat's," said Kamlavati.

"And her hair," murmured Almira. "It is the shade of the plowed earth. I certainly never saw hair that color! It's disgusting."

"'Tis her white skin I find so ugly," piped up Roopmati. "It looks like a fish belly."

"She is enormous in size," said Leila. "Why, she can look our dear lord directly in the eye. That is most unfeminine. I cannot understand what it is about her that he finds so attractive."

"Perhaps it is her sweet nature." Rugaiya Begum, who had overheard the others, chuckled. "None of you can lay claim to that particular nicety of character. Candra is as sweet as honey, and Akbar, a wise old bee, has grown tired of your sour fruits."

As Rugaiya Begum was Akbar's senior wife they did not dare to turn their backs on her or to refute her words. The older woman offered them an arch smile and then strode away.

It took a month for them to reach Lahore, and as Velvet viewed the surrounding landscape she was not encouraged. The region was positively parched and grim. Her heart sank. How could there possibly be gardens and fountains in this barren brown place? She sighed and for a moment was melancholy for her beautiful green homeland.

Pansy, however, had recovered her former robust health and seemed to thrive as she cared for her son, who grew larger daily on his mother's rich milk. Velvet had seen several handsome soldiers eyeing her tiring woman with a look akin to lust. Pansy had seen them, too, but she just shrugged and said dryly, "Eventually I'll take another husband. There's many a likely lad amongst them, I can see, and virginity ain't so much to a man as a woman who can have sons. But now is not the time. Besides, as your tiring woman I don't have to let myself go cheap."

Finally Lahore loomed before them, surrounded by a great fortifying wall and accessible only through its thirteen gates. It was set upon the banks of the Ravi River, which had its birth high in the purple Himalaya Mountains. They could see the mountains to the distant north. As they came closer to the city, the landscape grew greener the nearer to the river they got, and, looking closely, Velvet saw that the land was irrigated by narrow canals that drew water from the river inland a short distance. From their howdahs they could see in these fields the peasants with their bullocks plowing the tall rows of grain to remove the weeds and keep the topsoil turned.

The Mughal's great caravan was now strung out along the main road into Lahore. The single drummer thrummed his monotonous cadence as they moved steadily toward the city. Forced to the side of the road by Akbar's passage were great commercial caravans of heavily ladened camels, smaller caravans that were donkey-borne, peasants, merchants, and nobles astride fine mounts, their women in carefully curtained palanquins. Past them all rode the Grand Mughal and his household, moving majestically through Lahore's main gate and into the city, where the caravan wended its way through narrow streets, past great mosques and minarets, past the Mughal fort, to the northwest corner of the city where the palace was located.

Here the section of the caravan carrying the women and their servants was brought directly through the main courtyard of the palace and into the women's portion of the building. The camels knelt so that the occupants of the palanquins could disembark. The elephants, however, were brought one by one to a high mounting block where each howdah's occupant was assisted out. As Akbar's newest wife, Velvet was the last to leave her elephant.

"I should be glad," she said, laughing to Jodh Bai and Rugaiya Begum as she joined them, "that our lord did not bring all his wives else I would have been here the entire night!"

"Youth and beauty are not always first and foremost." Rugaiya Begum chuckled. "It is a good lesson for you to learn, Candra."

"Are you as eager for a bath as I am?" asked Jodh Bai. "Those birdbaths we were permitted along the way were only frustrating. I wonder if I shall ever get the dust out of my hair and off my skin. I am certain it has bored right into my face!"

"Must I be the last to the baths as well?" asked Velvet with a mournful face.

"Not if we hurry while the others are busy greeting their friends and relations," said Rugaiya Begum with a mischievous twinkle in her dark eyes. "Each wants to be the first to spread the news of Akbar's bride and new favorite. Look! Already you are being cast envious looks." She took the others' hands and hurried them into the palace. "Come! We will be steaming and soaking before they can decide which one of them is clever enough to take Akbar from you."

"Oh, Rugaiya! I should die if my lord deserted me now," wailed Velvet nervously. This was something she had not thought of, and suddenly she realized it could happen. She cast a backward glance at the clustering women behind her. 'I have not half the beauty those women have," she said, worried.

"Little silly!" said the practical Rugaiya Begum. "He loves you! Do you not believe it? I do, and I have been with him longer than any of the others. There will be times he will turn to the others to assuage his manly lusts and desire for variety, but that is only natural in a man. Not yet though. You occupy his thoughts constantly, Candra. Remember you were the only woman he called to him each night along our line of march, except for the nights you were unclean."

"There are few he really cares for although he is kind to them all," put in Jodh Bai, understanding Velvet's need to be reassured. European women, Velvet had told them, did not share their men. The Christians permitted their men only one wife, something Jodh Bai personally thought appalling. How could one woman be all things to a man? It was barbaric and impossible, not to mention very unfair to the poor wife who must be at her lord's beck and call at all times. Once sweet Candra saw the advantages in being one of many wives she would appreciate it greatly. Jodh Bai smiled to herself, her smile broadening as they reached the baths. "Ah, at last," she said as a cloud of perfumed steam hit her.

The three women were divested of their dusty clothing by clucking, fussing bath attendants and were halfway through their ablutions by the time the other travelers arrived. The latecomers eyed the three sourly.

"Hah!" teased Rugaiya Begum. "How did you manage to pull yourselves away from the other gossips?"

"Someone had to explain who the ugly foreigner was," replied Almira. "After all, a woman with skin like sour milk and hair the color of cattle dung is unusual."

Velvet flushed, understanding enough of Almira's words to comprehend the insult, but before either of her two friends could defend her, she said slowly in Persian, "In my country . . . we know how to . . . make . . . strangers welcome . . . even if they do not look . . . like us. You are very . . . rude,

Almira." Then she turned her back upon the woman and continued her bathing.

Almira gaped in surprise at this rebuke, her face growing mottled as the women with her tittered behind their hands, and both Jodh Bai and Rugaiya Begum grinned openly, pleased with the success of their new friend and protégée. Then they, too, returned to their washing.

"Well done, Candra," whispered Jodh Bai. "She is over-proud despite the fact that Akbar grew tired of her long ago!"

"Aye, his passion cooled quickly with her." Rugaiya Begum chuckled. "She was fortunate that she was with child and bore Akbar his second son, else he would have never looked at her again."

"His passion could cool just as quickly with me," Velvet remarked.

"His passion for Almira cooled because she was greedy and carping, Candra. You are not at all like her. Akbar will never grow tired of you," said Rugaiya Begum.

Clean and refreshed, the three women left the baths and returned to the zenana where both Rugaiya Begum and Jodh Bai had spacious apartments, but before they could reach them Adali hurried up and bowed.

"My princess," he said to Velvet, "You are to come with me. Our gracious lord had caused your own palace to be prepared as he promised you. If you will but follow me."

"Come with me!" Velvet begged her friends, and they nodded their agreement, looking meaningfully at each other, frankly very curious to see the home Akbar had ordered readied for Candra.

"Your own palace," said Rugaiya Begum. "You are most honored. In Fatehpur-Sikri we had our own palaces, but no one has had their own home here in Lahore. Large apartments in the zenana have been the best we could hope for here."

"You will be very envied," murmured Jodh Bai.

"I don't care as long as you two remain my friends," said Velvet. "The others are nothing to me."

"Even in paradise one must have friends," counseled Rugaiya Begum wisely.

"Perhaps this is not paradise," teased Velvet, and the two other women laughed.

"Candra, you are really unpredictable," said Jodh Bai. "One moment you are all sweetness, the next you are spice!"

"The better to keep my lord fascinated, dear friend," came Velvet's saucy reply, and once more the two older women were forced to laugh at their young companion.

The three women followed the eunuch through the women's quarters, down a narrow flight of stairs to a short corridor, and out into the vast palace gardens. Hurrying behind Adali, they moved deep into the gardens along paths of chipped white marble lined with tall, graceful orchid trees. The warm air was filled with the richly fragrant scent of the light purple flowers, which had deeper purple centers streaked with cream and carmine. In the flower beds bordering the orchid trees were tall stands of white and rosy-red Crown Imperials, their large pendant flowers arranged in rings at the top of each plant's stem and topped by tufts of green leaves. The path led past a beautiful turquoise blue tiled fountain that had pale green marble basins set in tiers, with crystal water dripping from the top basin down into the second and finally into the pool itself where bright orange goldfish swam, darting between the shafts of sunlight that dappled the waters of the pool.

Following Adali a little farther, they came upon a small palace of creamy marble, a perfect little dome centered on the roof, set like a perfect jewel amid the greenery of the garden.

"What a beautiful building!" exclaimed Jodh Bai. "I did not know such a building existed here in the palace grounds."

"It was originally built for a favorite of Babur," replied Rugaiya Begum. "Akbar and I played here as children. It has not been used for many, many years."

"I was not aware Akbar lived here as a child," replied Jodh Bai.

"He didn't, but I did," said Rugaiya. "He came once to visit me as we were betrothed. We spent most of our time here. I thought he had forgotten it even existed."

"Come along, ladies! Come along!" fussed Adali, turning back to hurry them with gestures.

Velvet said nothing, but followed behind her two friends. She was touched that Akbar had kept his promise to her. She had really dreaded living in the zenana with all the other women. She would never get used to the lack of privacy, but her own little home would certainly help. Both Rugaiya and Jodh Bai had said that living in a spacious apartment as they did she wouldn't even know that the other wives existed, but nonetheless she had been very uncomfortable with the idea. How caring of Akbar to have sensed her feelings. He really was the most marvelous of men.

They entered the little palace through an arched doorway that led into a two-storied reception room that ran the length of the building. Above them rose the dome, light coming in through thin sheets of latticed jasper set in at its bottom. A golden chandelier hung down into the area to light it in the evening. About the long room were decorative tubs of cardamom with their long leaves and sprays of yellow-green flowers that had blue and white lips. There were also tubs of sweet-scented ginger lillies, the long-tubed flowers of cream, white, and yellow perfuming the air.

Velvet was enchanted, but Rugaiya and Jodh Bai clapped their hands and exclaimed with delight.

"How exquisite!" Akbar's eldest wife said. "Trust Akbar with his artist's eye to fashion a perfect setting for a perfect jewel."

"Oh, look!" Jodh Bai pointed with a graceful finger to the long reflecting pool that ran along the entry hall to the far arches that led into the gardens at the rear of the palace. At the corners of each side of the pool were silver cages filled with colorful birds that shrieked and called now that they had been noticed.

"I will be happy here," said Velvet softly. "It is so green and cool."

"Come, come!" called Adali. "Come and see the rest of this wonderful house, my princess!" Bustling with importance, he led them about the main floor of the small palace, which had two wings: the right one housing the kitchens and the baths; the left one a dining room and a salon that looked out into the rear gardens with their beds of flowers and several fountains and pools. Returning to the entry hall, they climbed one of the graceful little marble staircases that led to the upper floor. An open corridor with delicately carved wooden railings that overlooked the main hall ran the length of each wing and connected the two wings to each other. On the left side of the building was a large bedchamber for Velvet, and a smaller room for Pansy lay next to it. On the right side of the palace was a big room with only one piece of furniture in it at the present time. It was a bejeweled cradle, and it had been placed in the exact center of the floor.

Rugaiya Begum chuckled richly as Velvet's cheeks turned a deep rose. "There is no mistaking our lord's wishes for the use of this room. May God grant you are able to fulfill Akbar's desire in this matter."

"I would like a child," Velvet said. "I never had one with my first husband. I should like a strong son."

"There will be no more sons for Akbar," said Jodh Bai quietly, and Velvet looked at her, surprised.

"My son would not be a threat to yours, Jodh Bai. Your son is already grown, and has children of his own."

"There will be no more sons for Akbar, Candra, because it has been foretold that he would have only three living sons, and so it has been all these years. The first two, twin boys, lived less than a year. Then came my Salim, Murad two years later, and finally Daniyal two years after that. There have been no further sons for Akbar in almost twenty years, Candra. If you are fortunate to bear Akbar a child, it will be a daughter, but I myself should have far rather had a daughter. Sons only grow up to break a mother's heart."

Rugaiya Begum put a comforting arm about her friend. "Salim is a good boy, Jodh Bai. Truly he is. He only chafes against his father's will because he is an intelligent man who desires to show his own mettle."

"He places me between his father and himself," Jodh Bai said sadly. "There are still those who say his father was wrong to marry a Rajput."

"They are fools!" snapped Rugaiya Begum. "I am a Moslem, and you a Hindu. Candra is a Christian. These are doctrines created by men, which, although good in intent, have divided God's peoples all over the earth, and there is nothing good or holy about that. I have learned from our lord husband, and he is right. He could not have united this vast land had he not put old prejudices aside."

"You flatter me, my dear wife," Akbar said, sweeping into the room. He stopped to kiss both Rugaiya Begum and Jodh Bai on their cheeks, and then his eyes found Velvet. "You are pleased, Candra?"

"You are so kind, my lord," she said softly.

"I want you to be happy, my English Rose." His look told her that he also wanted to be alone with her.

"I cannot help but be happy as long as I am in your favor, my lord," she replied, her cheeks once more pink for his glance was burning.

Rugaiya Begum almost laughed aloud. Akbar's desire was so wonderfully obvious. For the first time in his life she saw vulnerability in the man, and it pleased her. He was a great ruler, she knew, but like all great men he needed to be a bit more human. "We must go," she announced. "I am exhausted from our travels and Adali brought us directly here from the baths."

"Yes," agreed Jodh Bai, envying her young friend just the tiniest bit.

"You will come tomorrow, won't you?" Velvet asked. "I would like to share my good fortune with you both."

"We will come tomorrow," replied Jodh Bai, "and I shall bring you a wonderful cook for your kitchens as a gift."

"I hadn't thought of that!" Velvet cried. "Oh, my lord, how shall I feed you tonight?"

"Can he not live on love alone?" teased Rugaiya Begum, and they were all brought to laughter by her wryness.

"No!" said Akbar, settling the matter. "*He* must have his supper, and at the appropriate moment it will arrive from the main palace by Candra's own servants. For now, however, I would like to see the house and the gardens. I sent orders ahead as to what should be done, but this is the first chance I have had to come and see myself. Since I am here we should begin with this room."

"But the room is empty and devoid of decoration, my lord," said Velvet. She gracefully waved her hands about the space, noting as she did so that her two friends had withdrawn and that she was now alone with Akbar.

"There is a cradle."

"It has no occupant."

"We will remedy that lack, my Rose."

"Come and see the rest of the house," she said, and quickly drew him from the nursery. "I have not seen the rooms next door."

"They are for the servants," he answered, leading her down the hallway and across the connecting corridor to the opposite side of the building. "I have looked into the salon. It is simply furnished, and you must do whatever you desire with it for this is your home. You may want to obtain furniture from England, which can be done through the Portuguese. You have only to make a list for Adali." They had reached the gallery, and Akbar turned to the right. "If I remember, the main chamber is here," he said, opening the carved door to the room. Then, turning back, he picked her up in his strong arms, saying as he did so, "The holy fathers tell me it is a Christian custom to carry a bride over the threshold of her new home." He carried her into the room.

For a third time that afternoon Velvet felt a blush suffuse her face and throat. To cover her sudden shyness she exclaimed, "What a lovely room! I only glanced at it before when Rugaiya Begum and Jodh Bai were with me. Please put me down, my lord, so I may explore farther."

An amused little smile touched the corners of his sensual mouth, but he complied with her request. "If the room pleases you, Candra, then I shall be content. I gave very careful instructions as to its decoration. It must be a beautiful garden to house my perfect English Rose." He then stood silently as she carefully studied the chamber.

The floors of the room were of highly polished teakwood and glowed with a soft warmth. There were dark open beams in the wooden ceiling carved with flowers that had been painted in reds, blues, and golds. The walls were divided by a narrow wooden molding that ran horizontally approximately a third of the way up from the floor. The molding was covered in gold leaf, and the portion of wall below it was painted a dark blue. Above the molding the walls were decorated in an incredible painting depicting a jungle where a magnificent tiger lurked and brightly colored parrots shrieked from the trees. The jungle gradually gave way to a fertile plain populated by animals done in the most exquisite detail, including a small herd of elephants with babies, young bulls and cows, several older females, and a grizzled patriarch with magnificent tusks. There were, Velvet observed, a trio of mischievous squirrels in a plane tree; a wonderful mother leopard teaching her two cubs how to hunt; a tribe of rather amusing monkeys; sheep; goats; gazelles; and a fantastic peacock and its hen. Velvet was dazzled by the marvelous painting that spread from one wall to the next until it reached a panel showing two lovers on an open terrace. She recognized Akbar at once and then, looking closely, saw that the beautiful woman portrayed had white skin in contrast to the man's wheaten hue and that her long hair was auburn.

"I think that Basawan did very well considering that all he had to work with was my rather lyrical description of you," Akbar observed.

Velvet was speechless for the moment. It was a beautiful painting that depicted behind the lovers a clear blue lake. On the other side of the lake the snowcapped purple mountains rose into an early morning sky of molten gold and peach. A green rug, its gold and orange designs quite distinctive to the eye, had been spread on the terrace, and there on colorful pillows the lovers knelt, gazing into each other's faces. Akbar was dressed in white pantaloons, his chest bare, a small turban upon his dark hair, a rope of milky pearls about his neck reaching to his navel. Velvet, portrayed as his consort, was garbed in sheer turquoise silk gauze pantaloons through which her slender legs were quite visible. She was decked in strands of long pink pearls and gold chains, but her torso from the decorative waistband of her pantaloons upward was quite bare.

"I told the artist that you had delightfully saucy little breasts," said Akbar. "I am not satisfied with the way they are drawn. He will have to redo them, but this time he can paint from life."

"My lord!" She was mortified. "Would you have me exposed before another man?"

"He is an artist, Candra. Besides, here in my land we do not hide the body, nor cry false modesty. If it will make you easier in your mind, however, I will be with you when Basawan redoes the painting."

Velvet fell silent again and studied the painting once more. It was really quite charming. The lovers were not alone upon their terrace. Indeed there were two maidservants, one to fan the royal pair, the other engaged in preparing refreshments, and a pretty musician who strummed upon what looked to Velvet like a lute but for its long neck. The last occupant on the terrace was a large, fat cat with long black fur and a somewhat pleased expression on its face as it eyed a small bird perched upon a tubbed tree. It was her own kitten, Banner, grown up. She turned and saw that even now he was already curled up sleeping upon a corner of the bed.

Velvet then focused attention on the furnishings in the room. The large rug upon the floor, she noted, was identical to the one in the painting. There was a low, rectangular table of polished teak against one wall of the chamber. About it were strewn plump, silken pillows in shades of blue, green, and purple with gold stripes. Along another wall were two carved and decorated chests, which would be used for Velvet's clothing, and against the wall opposite was a cream-colored marble platform veined in gold upon which rested a magnificent bed with a canopied wooden top that was domed. The exterior of the dome had been laid over in gold leaf; the interior, as Velvet was soon to find out, had been painted a deep blue with shining gold stars, some of which twinkled with diamonds that had been imbedded in them. The four posts holding up the canopy were gilded and carved with vines and flowers that had been painted most realistically. The bed was hung with blue, green, and golden gauze draperies, and upon the wall at its head a large shamsa had been painted; in the center of this sunburst design was a rosette of abstract and arabesque designs in gold, red, and bluc. In the very middle of the rosette was a circle, the outer ring of which was gold, followed by rings of first blue and then red, inscribed with several verses in Arabic script.

Akbar translated for Velvet knowing the words by heart since he had ordered them specially. "The first verse is from the *Kama Sutra.* It reads: *Once the Wheel of Love has been set in motion, there is no absolute rule.* The second verse says: *Your being contains mine; now I am truly part of you. Together as one, we form an unbroken circle of love.* The last verse is from the Mahabharata and says: *The wife is half the man, his priceless friend; Of pleasure, virtue, wealth, his constant source; A help throughout his earthly years; Through life unchanging, even beyond its end.* These words, Candra, speak of my love for you. My joy at having found you. Alas, I am not a poet and must rely upon the words of others to tell you what's in my heart."

For a long moment Velvet could not speak. Her throat was tight, and quick tears filled her eyes. Then she turned to look into his dark ones. "I do not understand," she began softly, "why I should be so fortunate as to have your love, my lord Akbar, but my own heart is filled to overflowing. I told you once I should not tell you that I loved you unless it were so, but now I believe that I do love you. I cannot imagine my life without you, and I long for a child of your loins and my body. We come from totally different worlds, different cultures, and yet if I can truly make you happy, then I shall be content." She reached up and touched his face gently, her fingers softly trailing down his cheek and across his sensual lips.

Passion blazed in his eyes, and, catching her hand, he kissed her palm ardently. "I adore you," he murmured. "Of women I have always had my fill, and I have made love to many. Some I have even cared for in my way, and they have become my friends. But you, my beautiful Rose, I love with my whole heart. Never before has there been one like you, and there shall never be another to fully engage my heart!"

Velvet's heart hammered wildly at the extravagance of his tribute. She was totally overwhelmed by this love of his, which enveloped and surrounded her. Her emerald eyes caught his dark ones, and she could actually feel the love flowing between them. Her lips trembled with the fierce emotions that buffeted her, and she swayed. Akbar's strong arm immediately shot out and wrapped itself about her slender waist. Slowly he drew her toward him and then their mouths met in a tender kiss. His warm lips gently caressed her quivering ones, pressing delicate little kisses across her entire mouth.

Then he stepped back from her, still holding her in his embrace, and said, "You are tired from your long journey, my love, and I am not insensitive to that. Rest now, and I will come to you tonight. I want to make love to you, Candra. I should like to do it this very minute, but in your exhaustion your own pleasure, and therefore mine, would not be complete. Our coming together will be better for the anticipation."

With a smile he released his hold on her and together they walked to the door of the chamber. Reaching it, Akbar kissed her again lightly. "Pansy and the others should have arrived by now. I will send them to you." Then he opened the door and was gone.

Moving back to the bed, Velvet flung herself down upon it, not even noticing the coverlet that had been embroidered in jewellike hues of blue, green, and gold in a peacock's tail pattern. She gazed again at the wall behind the bed. There were so many things she had not seen before; magnificent golden phoenixes and other birds soaring around the central figure of the sunburst. Her eyes went again to the Arabic lettering in the very center. The verses he had quoted her were so beautiful, so wildly romantic.

She thought about the first verse he had spoken to her. *Once the Wheel of Love has been set in motion, there is no absolute rule.* There was certainly truth in that statement. Had she not expected after her marriage to Alex that they would remain together for the rest of their lives? She had certainly never thought that her husband would be killed in a foolish and prideful duel, leaving her bereft. How strange life was. How many women lost one love to so easily find another?

The chamber door opened and Pansy rushed in, chattering. "What a wonderful home, my lady! The lord Akbar certainly thinks highly of you. None of the other ladies have their own house. When we was in the baths just a little while ago, Toramalli and Rohana said that the other serving women were gossiping something fierce about it. Some of their mistresses are jealous of you, and others afraid of the power they think you wield over Akbar."

"I have no power over my lord," Velvet replied.

"He's a man in love and that always gives a woman power," said Pansy wisely. Then she looked about the room. "Lord! If this ain't the prettiest place I've ever seen, I don't know what is! The walls are simply beautiful with all those paintings, and I just love the blues and greens and golds. 'Tis so rich. I'll wager the queen herself doesn't have such a beautiful room in all of her palaces!"

"I wouldn't know, Pansy, having never visited all of the queen's castles. This house, however, suits me admirably. My lord has said I may buy whatever I desire for it." Velvet smiled at her tiring woman. "You're refreshed now? How is the baby doing?"

"Happy as a little pink pig in the clover, he is, m'lady. That black slave girl, Sari, that Adali found me to help with the baby is a good soul, bless her. She's going to spoil him completely and that's for certain, but without her how could I serve you?"

"You're more like your mother every day, Pansy. As sorry as I am to have taken you from your family, and from Dugald, I am so glad you are with me! What would I do without you?"

"Quite well, m'lady, and I've not a doubt. You're just being kind," demurred Pansy.

Velvet didn't press the issue any further, for it would have only embarrassed the loyal Pansy. Instead she said, "I want to rest for a few hours. I'm not certain what to do about food yet, for we've no cook, though Jodh Bai has promised me that she will send me one tomorrow."

"It's all been taken care of, m'lady," Pansy assured her. "His Majesty gave orders before he left the house that you were to eat without him. He will return late. Adali has sent Rohana to the kitchens of the zenana to arrange for a meal for us all. Let me make you comfortable, and then I'll bring your food. You can rest afterwards."

The meal arrived quickly and was hot and delicious. Velvet was hungry, and she greedily devoured the charcoal-broiled lamb kebobs with tiny sweet white onions, seasoned with pungent ground black pepper. There was a rice pilaf, a small dish of green vegetables, and little sweet cakes made from alternating layers of crisp dough, chopped almonds, and honey. Adali had also brought her a peacock blue carafe of sweet wine.

Finished with her meal, she bathed her hands and face in a basin of rosewater that Pansy brought her, and after the tiring woman had drawn back the silken coverlet on the bed, Velvet lay down and fell into a deep sleep.

It was close to midnight when Adali awakened her. "The master comes," he said, gently shaking her from her slumbers.

Slowly she arose from the silken cocoon that was their bed. The eunuch whisked her blouse and skirt from her, leaving her totally nude. Hurriedly Rohana sponged her with water into which jasmine oil had been poured, while Toramalli brushed Velvet's long auburn hair with a similarly scented brush. The room was then quickly neatened, the basin and brush put away just seconds before Akbar entered the room.

He opened his arms, and Adali swiftly removed his master's white robe with its silver sash and the matching silver turban. Beneath his robes Akbar was nude, but he showed no embarrassment at displaying his fine body before his wife's eunuch and slave girls. As Adali discreetly withdrew from the room, the emperor joined Velvet upon the bed. Rohana brought them each a cup of wine and then seated herself in a corner with Toramalli, who began to play a romantic Persian love song upon a stringed instrument.

"You are rested now, my Rose?"

"Quite, my lord," Velvet replied.

"Good," Akbar said with a smile, "for I intend to drive you hard this night."

"My lord!" Her tone rebuked him gently.

He chuckled. "I must if we are to fill that cradle in that sad and empty room across the hall." The look he sent her was a smoldering one.

"I would please you in all your desires, my lord," she teasingly answered. How handsome he is, she thought. He is so totally different from Alex with his craggy face. My lord Akbar's features are like those of a bird of prey, and yet when he looks at me those features soften and grow kind. It cannot be easy being a great ruler.

Akbar reclined on his side, his head propped up by his hand. "What are you thinking, Candra?" he asked her.

"I was thinking of how different you and Alex are," she answered him honestly.

"He was fair of skin?"

"Oh, yes, very! The men of my country are fair naturally, though they are known to brown in the sun."

"Does the fact that my skin is darker than yours bother you?" he asked.

"Oh, no, my lord! And except for your eyes, which slant just the tiniest bit, your features are quite like ours."

"We will make a beautiful child, my Rose." Then he reached out and caressed one of her breasts. Almost immediately the little nipple quivered into a point. He smiled and, leaning forward, stroked it with his warm tongue, circling it until it was rigid. Then his mouth closed over it, and he sucked hard, sending darts of painful pleasure to her very core.

Velvet fell back upon the bed, her breath coming in quick, little pants. Her fingers entwined themselves in his soft, black hair, sliding down to massage the nape of his neck. He rumbled with pleasure at her touch, and, having satisifed himself at her one breast, he moved his mouth to its twin. The deserted breast was not be neglected, however, for while his lips wreaked havoc on one, his free hand kneaded the other breast strongly, his fingers taunting it until Velvet was unable to lie quietly, so tantalizing were his actions.

"Keep still!" he commanded her. "If you give in too quickly to pleasure you lose half of it."

"It is too sweet," she protested.

"This is only the beginning, my Rose. It will be far sweeter before we are through." He shifted his weight now so that he was lying almost atop her, and his hands caught her face, his lips finding hers. They kissed until Velvet was forced to tear her head away from his, gasping for air, but he forced her back to his will, his mouth coming down again bruisingly upon hers. She felt his tongue moving insinuatingly along her lips, and she parted them so that he might penetrate her. Boldly she pushed her own tongue into his mouth, and he sucked upon it, savoring her sweetness. Sated now with her lips, he kissed her shadowed eyelids, the corners of her eyes and mouth, the sensitive place where her jawbone met her ear.

"There are many paths to pleasure," he murmured to her. "I would explore them with you, Candra. You are yet so innocent that the mere thought of your ignorance fires my blood."

"Teach me everything," she whispered back to him. "I would know all, my husband."

He smiled to himself at the naiveté of her words. "Not all, my Rose, for there are those who find pleasure in pain, and I do not believe you are one, are you?"

"Pleasure in pain? That is mad!"

"I agree, and yet there are people who cannot gain the summit of joy without it."

"That could never be my way, my lord."

"No," he agreed, "but there are other paths I would take with you, Candra. Perhaps they will not please you, and if that is so then we will not travel those paths again. Will you trust me to school you?" She nodded, and he continued, "Is the virginity of your bottom still intact?"

Velvet was puzzled. "The virginity of my bottom?" she said. "I do not understand, my lord."

"There are three passages by which the lingam may find pleasure. Within your mouth, your yoni, and the rose hole of your bottom," he explained. "You have learned the delights of the first two, and now I would instruct you in the third."

While Velvet pondered his words, Akbar spoke a swift command in Hindi to Rohana, who obediently arose from her seat and, going to one of the carved trunks, removed a rolled, quilted mattress of emerald green velvet, which she spread upon the floor. She then returned to her place by Toramalli's side and began to sing softly to the other girl's accompaniment.

"Come, my love," said Akbar, rising from the bed and drawing Velvet up after him. He led her to the mattress upon the floor. "We will need a firmer foundation for this than our marvelous bed."

Velvet looked at her two servant girls. "Must they remain?" she asked her husband.

"To make love is a natural thing," he answered her, "and their music will inspire us. Besides," he teased her gently, "they will not look. They are slaves, and it is not their place to watch, only to serve us. They know that should I see them staring I will have them blinded with hot coals so that they will never spy again upon their master."

Velvet shivered. He said the words so matter-of-factly. The differences between their cultures were staggering in some instances, and she wondered if she would ever get used to the contrast.

"Now, my Candra," Akbar began, "I want you to kneel, your legs spread just slightly, your head resting upon your folded arms." While she followed his instructions, Akbar took a small flask that Rohana had left by the mattress and opened it. Dipping his finger into the flask, he oiled the finger well. Then spreading the twin moons of her bottom, he began a gentle insertion of his finger. Velvet squealed and tried to twist away, but he quieted her, saying, "I will not hurt you, my love. Do not be frightened." He could feel her relax at the sound of his voice, and smoothly he moved his finger into her to the first knuckle. "Am I hurting you?" he questioned her.

"N-no, my lord, but I find the sensation strange," she said, low.

"Only because you are unfamiliar with it," he answered, and began a gentle rhythm with the encased digit. When she had become quite accustomed to this action, he withdrew his finger and re-oiled it along with a second finger. Rubbing the tight little pucker of her rose hole, he inserted both fingers. Velvet shrieked softly and once again attempted to evade the pressure of his fingers, but Akbar would not let her. Within her tight passage he veed the two fingers in an attempt to open her wider. When she realized that she wasn't being harmed, Velvet quieted once again. Slowly he moved his fingers back and forth until he felt she was ready to receive him fully. He was already hard with anticipation and the wine he had drunk, which was well laced with stimulants in order that he might perform well with his young wife. Removing his fingers, he now oiled his great shaft, and, holding her bottom open with one hand, he used the other to position himself.

"The first entry is the hardest as it was when your yoni was first penetrated. I will go very slowly, and although you will feel pressure, you should not really feel any pain."

"I am a little frightened," she admitted.

"New ways are always frightening, and this may not be to your taste, my Rose. Should that be so, we will not do it again. The pleasure should be for us both."

"Do you gain pleasure from this way, my lord?"

"Diversity has its advantages as one grows older," he answered her. Then he began to press firmly against her back passage. At first it would not give, but then as he increased the pressure the little opening began to blossom against the force of his eager shaft, which suddenly broke through. The head of his mighty lingam was firmly imbedded within her.

"Ohhhh!" Velvet cried softly, and she bit her lower lip.

"Am I hurting you?" he asked anxiously.

"N-n-o."

He gave her several moments to become used to the sensation, his hands now firmly grasping her hips. Then he began very slowly to move deeper within her. She was wonderfully tight, her little bottom passage seeming to almost suck him deep inside her each time he moved farther forward. He was finally lodged completely, and it took every ounce of his self-control to prevent himself from spilling his seed.

Velvet had never felt so filled in her entire life. She was not certain that she liked this manner of lovemaking. His weight pushed down upon her as he reached forward to crush her breasts within his hands. At the same time he began love's rhythm, drawing himself almost completely out of her back passage, then pushing himself back into her at an increasing rate of speed. His warm hands moved from her breasts downward to her very core, and he gently stroked her. Now Velvet began to grow restive and squirmed beneath his touch. To her surprise she felt the tension beginning to build within her, and she moaned softly. He quickened his pace, his own desire now building and growing as he plunged within the tight sheath. Her hips were now moving in tempo with his, thrusting upward to meet his own movement. Akbar could feel the storm of passion fast rising within his own body. Unable to control it any longer, he let it burst forward as with a cry Velvet collapsed beneath him.

For some minutes he lay, his weight pressing her down, and then, rolling off her, he pulled her into his arms.

"Tell me, Candra. Was it to your liking?"

She sighed deeply. "I gained some pleasure from it, my lord, but I do not think that given the choice I should choose to make love in this fashion often."

"Then we will not do it again, for pleasure should be the only outcome of our union."

"The *only* outcome?" she teased him.

He smiled to himself. She had not really enjoyed the last half-hour and yet she joked with him. He liked her spirit. Another woman would have wept and reproached him. "I cannot impregnate you every time we make love," he protested, and she laughed.

"I also do not believe you can give me a child in such an act as we have just performed, my lord."

Akbar chuckled, genuinely amused. God help him but he loved this fair-skinned girl with her wonderful reddish hair and her emerald green eyes. "Then we shall have to begin again at the beginning," he answered her. He called to the two serving girls who ceased their music and brought a basin of warm, scented water and love cloths to cleanse their master and mistress. Velvet bore with this stoically although she was still uncomfortable when the servants handled her so intimately.

When the girls had finished, Velvet spoke gently to her husband. "Send Rohana and Toramalli to their beds, my lord. It is late, and I will care for you myself. I prefer it. It is the way of my people, that women sweetly serve their men."

"How meek you sound, my Rose," he teased her. "I cannot believe it is you to whom I listen." Then he spoke quick words to the two serving maids, and they bowed themselves from the room. "Now," he said with mock seriousness, "you may serve me sweetly, my Candra."

"You have but to command me, my lord," she teased him back.

Standing, he drew her up and led her back to their bed. Then his arms tightened about her, their lips met in a fiery kiss, and they fell back onto the soft, silken mattress, their limbs intertwined. "I love you," he murmured against her mouth. "In the spring I will take you to Kashmir and build you a palace beside a blue lake. We will live forever in the shadows of the great mountains and raise our child in peace. Together you and I will hunt the ibex, the stag, the markhor, and the bear. You will like Kashmir, for its beauty is a perfect frame for your own. I will make you happy, Candra. By the great God who created us all, I swear it!"

"I am happy just being with you, my lord Akbar. How can you rule your kingdom if you exile yourself from its capital? I cannot let you do that for me. It would be wrong. Keep me by your side, my dearest husband. It is all I ask of you."

"I am growing older," he answered her. "I have not been well in the last several years. Let Salim have it, for by God he longs for the power. Already he sows rebellion against me in order to claim his birthright. I will give it to him and depart. I will only take with me the wives whose company I actually enjoy. The others will remain here in Lahore. The fewer of my women I have with me, the less I will have to listen to their complaints. Now that I think on it I shall take only Rugaiya Begum and Jodh Bai with us."

"No, my lord Akbar. If you attempt to do this thing you will endanger me. You are not old and feeble. You are a great leader, a great king. You are loved and respected by all who know you. Abdicate your throne for a rash boy and you will plunge your country once again into a civil war. Salim cannot hold together the princely states as you do. If you love me, you must promise me that you will not leave the throne. Build me a palace in Kashmir, and each year in the hot weather we will journey forth there to enjoy the mountains and the waters."

"This is truly your wish, Candra? You are content to live in Lahore, to follow me across this land when I must go?"

"I am content, my husband, as long as I am with you."

He kissed her once again, this time his mouth fiercely taking possession of her soft lips. His hard body bore down upon hers, and she opened herself to him, sighing as he slipped his hard shaft within her silken sheath.

"You are mine," he whispered, raising his head to look down into her eyes. "Tell me you are mine, my beloved wife."

"I am yours, my lord husband. I am yours for as long as God will give us life, and afterwards I will be yours into eternity." Then taking his head between her hands she kissed him sweetly, kissed him until he could bear no longer the honeyed passion she aroused within him. With a ferocious cry he ground himself savagely into her, flooding her throbbing body with his essence, and together they created a child in that wonderful and blinding moment.

Chapter 11

The coach that carried Michael O'Malley, the bishop of Mid-Connaught, from the French coast to Paris was a large and comfortable vehicle. Four strong horses guided by an expert coachman galloped along the snowy, midwinter roads that by virtue of the hard-packed snow were actually in much better condition than the rutted, potholed earth beneath. The landscape was mostly black and white, the leafless trees stretching their barren branches skyward, the smoke from occasional cottages and farms dark against the gray gloom.

Looking out through the coach's very expensive glass windows, the bishop shivered. He himself was quite warm and comfortable amid the dark green velvet upholstery, covered by a thick gray fox coverlet, a brazier of hot coals at his feet. Gold, he thought with a soft smile, certainly had its uses. Leaning forward, he drew the back of the front seat down and removed a willow basket from the niche there. Opening it, he took out a leather decanter of dark red Burgundy and filled the silver cup that was also in the basket. Closing his eyes, he inhaled the heady fragrance of the wine with a connoisseur's palate before taking his first blissful sip. Fitting the goblet between his knees, he recorked the decanter and, having replaced it in the basket, drew forth a little crock of goose-liver pâté and a small, crisp loaf of bread, which had been wrapped in a rough linen napkin and was yet warm. Breaking a piece of bread off, he used it to scoop up a dollop of the pâté and popped the entire thing into his mouth, chewing delightedly. The pâté was excellent, and the bread had a wonderful crust on it.

The inn at which he had spent the night had been a charming one, and since they were still a half-day's travel from Paris, the innkeeper's wife had packed him the basket to tide him over. He had done her the honor of hearing her confession and pronounced only a light penance for her few but troublesome sins. Finishing his meal with a crisp pear, he packed the basket away behind the seat again and gazed back out the window. A light snow was beginning to fall, and Michael O'Malley did not envy either the coachman or the men-at-arms who escorted his coach. In the distance, however, he could see the spires of Notre Dame poking through the grayness. It would not be too long now.

He would be staying at the Paris town house of Adam de Marisco's mother and stepfather, the Comte and Comtesse de Cher, which was located in the rue Soeur Celestine on the Rive Gauche. It was a small house, having only six bedchambers, but the bishop would be quite comfortable and well taken care of by a staff of servants who had been sent up from the comte and comtesse's estate at Archambault in the Loire.

Michael O'Malley turned his thoughts to the task ahead of him. It would not be an easy one, and even though he would be dealing with an old friend, the utmost diplomacy would be required. The truth of the matter was that he understood the logic behind Father Ourique's actions. God help the man! Exiled from Europe and expected to work miracles of conversion for the holy mother church without, Michael wagered with himself, any monies sent him. Desperate to do well, to be brought to the attention of his superiors in Portugal, in Paris, and in Rome—and desperate, Michael suspected, to be brought home—the Jesuit had undoubtedly seen his future disappearing over the horizon in the same direction as Lord and Lady de Marisco. He had done the only thing he felt he could in taking Velvet hostage in exchange for delivery of the ransom. Michael believed, however, that Father Ourique had been unaware of the Portuguese governor's brooding desire for revenge. The whole matter was an unfortunate combination of bad timing and worse luck, with his niece the innocent victim. Poor little Velvet! The bishop's face darkened with his concern. What tortures was she enduring in what must be for so sheltered a lass a terrifying captivity? He sincerely prayed that she would survive to be released from her bondage.

The coach came to an abrupt stop, and, focusing his eyes on the outside world, Michael saw that they were already in Paris and, in fact, were awaiting the gatekeeper of *Chez Cher* to open the gates so that they might enter the mansion's courtyard. The snow was falling heavily now, and the bishop could just make out the shambling figure of the porter as he pulled open the entry. The coachman, eager to see the end of his journey, and doubtless thinking of a warm fire and a good pint, almost toppled the gatekeeper over as he hurried his horses into the courtyard and pulled up before the house's double doors, which swung wide magically. Two liveried footmen ran down the three steps and, opening the carriage door, pulled down the steps and helped Michael O'Malley descend.

"Merci, merci!" the bishop said, signing them with the cross in thanks, and then he moved hastily into the building.

A thin, spare man came quickly forward. "*Bienvenue, Monsieur le évêque.* I am Alard, the majordomo." He drew a tiny, plump woman forward. "My wife, Jeannine, who is the housekeeper and cook. We have been sent by Madame la comtesse to see to your needs, and we will try to make your stay a pleasant one. Is it possible that you can tell us how long you plan to be in Paris?"

"Not for more than a week or two at the most," Michael replied.

"Thank you, my lord bishop. Let me show you to your rooms now, and you must tell me if there is anything that we can do for you at this moment."

"I'll need someone to take a message to a friend of mine, Father O'Dowd, a Jesuit."

Alard bowed. "Of course, my lord bishop. As soon as you're settled, I'll send a footman to you."

The messenger was dispatched and returned within another hour. He had found Father O'Dowd, who sent back word that he would be delighted to see his old friend, and would the evening meal be too soon? When Michael passed this query on to Jeannine, the plump little woman smiled mischievously and, bobbing him a curtsy, promised an excellent dinner.

When Bearach O'Dowd arrived, Michael O'Malley could not help but think how little his friend had changed. Of medium height and plump of figure, Bearach O'Dowd had the round, innocent face of a choirboy. He was fair of skin with fat, pink Irish cheeks and deceptively bland light blue eyes with long sandy-colored lashes that matched his close-cropped sandy hair. He was dressed as a Jesuit, but, Michael noted, his robes were of the best materials and well cut.

"You've brought a bit of peat whiskey, Michaeleen?" was his greeting. "I've not been able to think of anything else since your messenger brought me word you were in Paris."

The bishop laughed. "Aye, I've got it. How else would two old friends toast each other, Bearach?" Walking to the library table, he poured them both a dram of the smoky whiskey and, handing his friend one, raised his own goblet. "Ireland!" he said.

"Ireland, God help her!" came the Jesuit's reply.

When the whiskey had been downed by both men, Michael led the way into a small dining room, and they sat down to the dinner table. True to her word, Jeannine had prepared a wonderful supper for the two clerics. Bowls of mussels, braised in white wine and garlic, with individual bowls of Dijon sauce de moutarde began the meal, which was served family style as there were only two diners. The broth surrounding the mussels was as delicious as were the delicately flavored shellfish themselves.

When the bowls containing the thoroughly pillaged shells had been removed, Alard directed the footmen to pass various platters and bowls. There was a lovely, fat duck, its skin burned black, its flesh rare, stuffed with apricots and prunes, and served with wild plum sauce. There was a fine savory ragout of beef, fragrant with red wine and fine herbs, and served with fluffy little dumplings; a bowl of tiny potatoes, another of onions, and one of celery and carrots. The last dish presented in this course was a small ham baked in a flaky pastry that had been glazed with egg.

Both Michael O'Malley and Bearach O'Dowd were men of great appetite. They handily finished Jeannine's offerings as well as a loaf of crusty bread and a crock of sweet butter from Normandy that had been placed upon the table. A large decanter of Burgundy from the Archambault vineyards was emptied as well.

Jeannine smiling from ear to ear at the priests' flattering appreciation of her culinary skills, served the sweet herself. It was a large tartlet of pears set within a delicate, cakelike crust that had been filled with a sweet custard. The goblets were refilled with a light, fruity white wine. Both clerics raised their goblets to Jeannine who, already flushed from the heat of her kitchen, turned a deeper pink in her pleasure.

Their meal completed, Michael and Bearach adjourned back to the library. Their glasses refilled, they settled themselves cosily before the fire. Outside the winter storm howled noisily, rattling the windows.

"What brings an Irish bishop to Paris, Michaeleen?" The Jesuit's curiosity was finally aroused.

"'Tis a family matter," came Michael's calm reply, "and 'twas thought that since your aunt is an O'Malley and you're therefore a part of the family that you'd like to aid us."

"If I can," was Bearach's canny answer.

"Aye, you can."

"Well, out with it, man! Unless you're planning to keep me here all night."

"You'll remember my sister, Skye," began Michael.

"And who could forget that beautiful creature?" demanded Bearach. "Has she outlived another husband, then, Michaeleen? Or is she still wed to that big man, de Marisco, was it?"

"Adam de Marisco, and, aye, they're still happily married. 'Twill be eighteen years this Michaelmas."

"Well, what's the problem, then?" asked Bearach O'-Dowd.

"I'd best begin at the beginning," said Michael. "Several years ago my sister and her husband departed England for a voyage to the East Indies. As you'll remember Skye and her partner, Sir Robert Small, have had a profitable relationship for many, many years with a number of the island sultans. Their ship was damaged in a storm and blown off course. They ended up becalmed just off Bombay and were taken in tow by the Portuguese."

Bearach O'Dowd nodded, all the while thinking to himself that Skye O'Malley's destination had probably been India all along, and that she had likely been on an expedition for the English with an eye toward opening trade with the Grand Mughal himself. He doubted the Portuguese, and their Spanish masters, would have liked that.

"The Portuguese governor took my sister, her husband, and their ship and crew hostage, forcing my nephew, Captain Murrough O'Flaherty, to return to England in his own vessel to fetch the ransom demanded," Michael continued. "The governor was under the direct influence of, and guided by, his Jesuit advisor Father Ourique."

"Are you holding the Jesuit order responsible then for the irresponsible act of one man, Michaeleen?"

"Wait, Bearach, there is a good deal more. Hear me out, and then we will discuss our differences."

The Jesuit nodded, then listened intently as his old friend told the tale of Velvet's misadventures.

"Jesus Christus!" exploded Bearach O'Dowd when Michael had finished. He could now see what his old friend and playmate was getting at. The O'Malleys were holding the Jesuits responsible for the kidnapping of one of their own. Here was a fine kettle of fish! In their own small way the O'Malleys of Innisfana, though but a minor branch of the great seafaring family, had a certain amount of influence, and a great deal of money behind that influence.

Bearach O'Dowd's nimble mind scrambled to remember what he could of Velvet de Marisco. Her father was not of an important family, but de Marisco's stepfather, the Comte de Cher, was highly thought of by the French royal family, and despite the fact that there was currently a civil war raging in France over the succession, royal connections were not to be sneezed at. Holy Father! The girl's godmothers were Queen Margot herself and Elizabeth of England! Was it possible that the actions of one greedy priest could destroy the Jesuits' reputation and ruin their years of hard work?

Gathering his wits, Bearach O'Dowd said in a voice that belied his thumping heart, "How is it you think the Jesuits might help you, Michaeleen? I don't quite understand what it is you want."

Michael O'Malley hid a smile. Bearach, his old and good friend, was no fool. His position within the order was that of banker. He had a knack for increasing wealth through investments that endeared him to his superiors. That talent gave him a certain amount of power. "There are Jesuits at the Emperor Akbar's court, Bearach," he said. "The emperor, I am told, was born a Moslem, and my sister, Skye, who knows these things says that no honest Moslem will take unto his bed the wife of a living man. Skye, has sent me to you, Bearach. She holds the Jesuit order responsible for Velvet's plight, but she also believes that you can aid her, aid me in getting to Akbar's court to present our case before the emperor. The O'Malleys would be most grateful, Bearach."

"How grateful?" The two words were sharp and clear.

"Very grateful," was Michael's equally enigmatic reply, but the two men understood each other. The O'Malleys would not settle upon a price until they got what they wanted, but they would be very generous in the end.

"It is possible that we might be able to help you, Michaeleen, but mind you we cannot accept responsibility for the actions of one foolish priest."

"A *Jesuit*, Bearach. One of your own, not just some random priest. Otherwise I should be in Rome and not Paris," Michael O'Malley gently reminded him.

"Of course, old friend, and you have but to tell me what it is that you want."

"The Jesuits are welcome at Akbar's court, Bearach. I have even heard talk of his conversion."

Bearach O'Dowd snorted. "A dream of glory-seekers, but never say I told you so, Michaeleen. 'Tis my opinion that they'll never convert him, and that opinion is held by those in the higher strata of the order than I, but 'twill never be admitted aloud. Still, he welcomes us to his court and does nothing to hinder our conversion of the population."

"Then a letter of introduction from the Jesuits will obtain me an interview with the emperor, Bearach. It will keep the Portuguese from hindering me in my mission. I do not intend to land at Bombay at any rate, but rather I shall debark at Cambay. That port is under the emperor's control. After that it will be a journey of at least six weeks overland in order to reach Akbar's capital of Lahore."

"If he is in Lahore, Michaeleen. It is said that the emperor, like Elizabeth Tudor, travels his land regularly."

"I will find him, Bearach, and I will gain the release of my poor niece," Michael said quietly.

"Pray God that she is still alive, Michaeleen."

Michael O'Malley laughed aloud. "She's Skye O'Malley's daughter, Bearach, and if she's half the woman her mother is then she's survived. I've not seen her since she was eleven years old, but she was a winsome little lass."

"I will have to present this dilemma to my superiors, Michaeleen, but rest assured they will see the matter even as I do and be most eager to play their part in obtaining the release of this virtuous young Catholic noblewoman," Bearach vowed.

Michael hid a smile. The Jesuits were well served by Father Bearach O'Dowd, who did not admit to the order's duplicity in Velvet's plight, and at the same time made it sound as if they were doing the O'Malleys a great favor out of pure Christian charity and not because of the fine profit they would make. "Ah, Bearach, what would we do in this life if we could not rely upon our friends?" he said. "The family will be so relieved to learn of your aid in rescuing Velvet."

Rescue was the farthest thought from Velvet's mind. She was far too happy now, and as her memories of Alex had faded into the dark corners of her heart, her joy at the love that she and Akbar shared filled her soul. He loved her as no other man could ever love her. He shared more of himself with Velvet than he had ever shared with his other wives and concubines. He used her as a sounding board for his thoughts and ideas, which was something he said he had never done with anyone before. Velvet listened to her husband and learned a great deal about politics and strategy from him. Occasionally she even offered her own suggestions or disagreed with him, which no one had also ever done, but he listened to her, and if her reasoning was sound, he would take her advice. It was a love built upon mutual respect as well as passion, but the passion was certainly there as well. Akbar had never loved a woman as he loved Candra Begum, his English Rose, and their love was a fruitful one.

Yasaman Kama Begum was born in her mother's lakeside palace in Kashmir, which her father had built during the nine months she spent in her mother's womb, on August 9, 1590. Velvet had a relatively easy time and although normally the birth of the Mughal's child would have entailed the participation of the entire zenana, only Rugaiya Begum, Jodh Bai, Pansy, and Velvet's slave women were present. Most of Akbar's others wives were not welcome in her Kashmiri home.

The little princess was placed in her bejeweled cradle and guarded by two fierce female warriors. She was a strong, healthy infant from birth, which was a great relief to her parents. Each day that passed saw her growing and thriving as she suckled eagerly on her mother's breasts, anxious to extract every bit of nourishment that she could. Yasaman was an extraordinarily beautiful baby and had been from the moment of her quick entry into life.

She was not as fair-skined as her mother, but neither was she as bronzed as her father. Her skin color was that of very rich, heavy cream; her thick curls dark as her father's black hair, but with her mother's auburn highlights. Most startling of all her features, however, were her eyes, which went from a baby blue at her birth to a vibrant turquoise by the time she was almost six months of age.

In personality Yasaman was most decidedly her parents' child. Her mother's sweetness was quickly apparent in the normally sunny-natured infant; but when crossed she was quickly the imperial Mughal's adored daughter, screaming at the top of her tiny lungs until totally satisfied that her will had been done.

Most children have one mother, but Yasaman Kama Begum had three, for both the childless Rugaiya Begum and Jodh Bai, who had lost her only daughter several days after the baby was born, doted upon her totally. Little Yasaman was fortunate to have two such powerful allies within the zenana, for Akbar's other wives were jealous of both her and her beautiful mother. It was also in her favor that she was the light of her father's life, the rich harvest of his love for her mother.

It was hard for Velvet to imagine that it was winter once again in England. She had explained the twelve days of Christmas and the feast of Twelfth Night to Akbar once the month of December was well underway. He had found it an interesting custom and said, "Our little Yasaman comes from two such different cultures. She must know of them both as she grows up." Velvet agreed. She might be the wife of a powerful Eastern potentate, but she was still proud of her own heritage. She had already given her daughter the first link in the chain that was to bind mother and child.

It had been done quietly, of course, almost secretly. Akbar had enough difficulties between the Moslems, the Hindus, and the Buddhists without encouraging further rebellions. His youngest child had, therefore, been baptized by the Jesuits in her mother's house in the presence of only her parents, Pansy, who was designated her godmother, Rugaiya Begum, and Jodh Bai. Velvet had also taken the opportunity to have her tiring woman's son, now a year old, baptized, too. The two Jesuits who had performed the ceremony, one acting as godfather to both of the children, had been amazed to learn that Akbar had a Christian wife.

"My child," exclaimed Father Xavier, the elder of the two, a man with a kindly, worn face. "How is it you have come to this place? When did you last make your confession? When was the last time you received the sacraments? Do you not fear for your soul? Who are you? You have not the look of a peasant girl."

"Who I am is of no importance to you, Father," replied Velvet, "but to satisfy your curiosity I will tell you that in my own land I was a Catholic noblewoman. I was betrayed into captivity by those in high places and sent here to my lord Akbar. Those who sought to harm me, however, did me a great service instead. I have found true love and happiness as my lord's wife."

"But it is not a Christian marriage, my lady," fretted the priest.

"What does it matter in this land?" said Velvet. "Once, not so long ago, such things were important to me. I have since learned that it's what is in a person's heart which God judges him by, not by the way in which he worships."

The two Jesuits looked scandalized, but nonetheless they baptized the children, then went about their business sworn to secrecy. Velvet was well satisfied.

On the first day of Christmas Akbar gave his favorite a strand of bright green emeralds with matching earrings. On the following days he presented her with a chestnut-colored Arabian mare, a carved ivory box containing several strands of pink pearls, and a chess set with a board made from alternating squares of green and white marble with playing pieces carved from ivory and green jasper, each piece studded with multicolored gemstones. On the fifth day, he presented her with a beautifully decorated, gilded barge with crimson velvet cushions so that she might sail on the man-made palace lake. The sixth day brought a diamond necklace and earrings. The seventh morning saw a beautiful female elephant with cloth of gold trappings sewn with pearls and precious jewels standing beneath her windows, its graceful trunk raised in salute. On the eighth day of Christmas, Akbar presented his wife with the revenues from the lands upon which her palace in Kashmir stood; on the ninth day, a solid silver litter with purple cushions and mauve hangings with four slaves to bear it; on the tenth day, a necklace of priceless rubies and two gold and ruby bracelets were her gift; and on the eleventh day, a pair of spotted hunting cats. Finally on Twelfth Night Akbar gave Velvet the most opulent gift of all. She was weighed three times, the first time receiving her weight in silver, the second in gold, and the third time in precious gems.

"Lordy, lordy!" gasped Pansy. "You must be the richest woman in the world now, m'lady! They wouldn't believe this back home if we could show them!"

Akbar laughed when Velvet told him what her tiring woman had said. "It is I who am rich in your love," he said gallantly.

"And it is your love that means more to me than all of this wealth of gold and jewels," she replied, kissing him sweetly.

He pulled her into his arms. "You are my world, Candra! Before you I did not live. I existed." Gently his lips caressed her forehead, then moved to find her mouth.

I never grow tired of his kisses, she thought. *He lifts me from the everyday world into a magic realm.*

The kiss deepened as he explored the texture of her lips as if for the very first time. Her mouth was always warm and welcoming. He felt as if he were floating and from her little murmur of pleasure he knew that she was experiencing a similar delight. His hands moved downward over her nude form, caressing, stroking, cupping her willing flesh. He fondled her breasts, marveling at the texture of them. They were so wonderfully firm and silky, and full with the milk she fed their daughter. It gave him a marvelous feeling of deep physical enjoyment to gaze upon those twin globes of smooth, moonlight-colored flesh. He bent his head and nuzzled a dark pink nipple, already puckered with her own pleasure. A tiny bead of milk burst forth from it, and Akbar leaned over and caught it up with his quick tongue.

Velvet shivered and, falling back amid the pillows, drew him with her. He lay for several long minutes, his head pillowed against her heart, listening to its rapid beat, gaining an almost boyish enjoyment from being able to make her heart race when he slipped his hand between her legs to tease her little jewel.

His own breath caught in his throat as her slender fingers caressed first his dark head and then slipped beneath his hair to brush softly the nape of his neck, sending shivers down his spine.

"I love your hair," she said. "It is so incredibly soft. I never knew a man could have such soft hair. I hope our Yasaman's hair has such a texture."

"I want Yasaman to be like you," he insisted as, parting her legs, he entered her body in one smooth motion.

"Ah, my darling," she cried out softly, not from pain but rather pleasure. There had been little foreplay between them this night, but she had been ready for him. She was, she thought for a brief, lucid moment, always ready to make love where he was concerned.

Her legs were firmly between his thighs. Now he put his arms about her and drew her up against his chest. Together they rocked back and forth, their arms and legs now entwined, their tongues caressing one another in sweet embrace. Her breasts were pressed hard against his smooth chest, and his hands moved down to cup her buttocks, raising her up just slightly. Velvet cried out with delight as she found the first peak of pleasure. For many long minutes they sat face to face, their bodies entwined, making passionate love, each giving the other sweet, lingering moments of delight. Then came one flaming minute when the lovers soared together only to slide back finally to reality.

With a sigh Velvet lay her head upon Akbar's chest. With a matching sigh he slipped a loving arm around her. They lay together, slipping in and out of a light sleep for at least an hour, and then Velvet had the desire to make love again.

Slipping from the bed, she fetched a basin of warm, perfumed water and several cloths. He grumbled at the sudden loss of warmth.

"If you would permit Rohana and Toramalli to attend us . . ." he began, only to be silenced by her.

"I want no one, even a slave, to be present during our most intimate moments. You may say what you wish about their powers of observation, but they are still human beings and cannot help but see and hear us even if they dare not acknowledge it. Our love is for us alone, my darling. I will not share my time with you!"

She carefully cleansed him free of all evidence of their prior lovemaking, handling his lingam now without any show of embarrassment, even when it began to rise and stir beneath her delicate touch. He watched as she then quickly bathed herself, and removed the cloths and basin. When she returned to him she was freshly perfumed with jasmine, now her favorite scent as gillyflowers were not grown here. It surrounded her like an invisible cloud, and he could see that her hair had been brushed with a jasmine-scented brush, for it was slightly damp and shining with fiery lights.

Velvet saw the desire in his dark eyes as she walked toward him, each step deliberately slow to entice and arouse him. It was a small trick that Rugaiya had taught her, and she had learned it well. She moved upon the balls of her feet, her body long, her buttocks tight, her breasts thrust forward.

Lying on his back amid the pillows, Akbar watched her. She was the most desirable and graceful woman he had ever seen. She almost slithered onto the bed, her slender hands sliding up his legs ahead of the rest of her. Her warm hands massaged first his feet, then his calves, and finally his muscled thighs. Swinging her body over his and leaning just slightly forward, she caressed his smooth chest, her fingers moving in a circular motion over his skin.

"Does this please you, my lord?" she murmured provocatively.

The corners of his mouth twitched just slightly, but he answered coolly, "It pleases me," and nothing more. He did not even look at her, his impersonal gaze staring over her shoulder.

Her hands moved upward to cup his face between them, and bending forward just a wee bit more, she covered his mouth with her own, running her little tongue over his lips and then thrusting it boldly into his mouth. She caressed his tongue with her own until he thought his blood would surely boil, and then she sucked upon it lingeringly. It took every ounce of willpower that he had not to take her then and there, but he was very much enjoying having her act the aggressor. Only since Yasaman's birth had she occasionally begun to make love to him, and he frankly enjoyed it. Still, he could not resist clasping her delectable bottom in his two hands and fondling the deliciously springy flesh of its twin cheeks.

Releasing him from the kiss, Velvet sat back just slightly but not quite enough to dislodge his hands. Then cupping her breasts in her own palms she began to play with them, fondling the sensitive flesh, teasing the nipples until a little moan escaped from between her lips. When he tried to release her bottom, she would not let him, seating herself firmly upon his hands and looking straight into his eyes while she continued to play with herself.

She could feel his lingam growing large and hard beneath her, and the very thought that he would soon possess her excited her further. Unable to help herself, she began to squirm slightly upon him. Bending forward again, she brushed the nipple of one breast over his cheek, a softly taunting smile upon her face. He was ready for her, however, when she rubbed the other breast over his mouth. Capturing the nipple in his lips, he encircled it with his tongue, licking the sensitive flesh until it tingled, and she shivered. It was then that Velvet raised her lower body and impaled herself upon his staff.

"Little bitch," he growled at her, loving the way her tight, sweet yoni encased his throbbing lingam.

At first her rhythm was excruciatingly slow and teasing, but gradually her pace quickened, and suddenly they were both lost in the fiery madness of their shared passion, flying together to that paradise known only to true lovers, never even remembering their descent from the heavens into blissful sleep.

In the days that followed, life took on an almost unreal happiness for Velvet. She could not remember ever having been so content, feeling so loved. Her parents had, of course, adored her, but even when she'd sat in one or the other's lap, she could feel them loving each other with their eyes, oblivious to her, or to anything else for that matter. How often had she been told of the great love that had led to her very existence? The love she now experienced, however, was that same kind of love that her parents had for one another, and she finally understood their constant preoccupation with each other. She hoped that little Yasaman would not feel shut out by the love she and Akbar shared, but she vowed to herself it would not happen.

She smiled. Akbar was really determined to spoil their daughter, but then she thought how fortunate it was that he loved their child so very much.

She had to take him to task, however, the very next day for bringing the baby along with him in his howdah when he went on a tiger hunt. When she scolded her husband, he looked quite hurt and replied, "Yasaman was quite safe with *me.*"

"Safe?" Velvet cried. "Safe upon that rogue elephant you insist on riding?" She made a marvelous picture of outraged motherhood standing before him and clutching her infant to her breast.

"The elephant simply cannot tolerate anyone but me," he explained.

"Do not take *my* daughter from her nursery again without *my* permission," Velvet said. Rugaiya Begum and Jodh Bai agreed with her, chattering at Akbar furiously, one in Persian, the other in Hindi.

Laughing, Akbar held up his hands in a gesture of surrender.

"I give up," he said. "I cannot argue with you all. Very well, Candra, my darling, I shall not take Yasaman tiger hunting until she is at least five."

It was at this point that Ramesh was granted entrance into the room by Adali. "My lord Akbar, so this is where you are hiding yourself. Have you forgotten the interview that you promised to give the traveling Christian father who has been brought to you by Father Xavier?"

With a sigh the emperor stood up, bid his wives farewell, and left them to return to the audience chamber of the main palace. It was a beautiful room, though not as grand as the great audience hall at Fatehpur-Sikri. The floors were made up of squares of red and gold marble, some areas of which were covered in magnificent red, blue, and gold rugs. The walls of the room were painted with scenes of triumphs in the emperor's life. There were tall gold censers burning fragrant oils on either side of the wide aisle leading to the raised dais with its golden throne, which was studded with sapphires, diamonds, rubies, pearls, emeralds, beryls, and corals. Akbar had quickly dressed himself in the Persian fashion: white silk trousers, a matching coat embroidered with gold, diamonds, and pearls, and his usual turban with a huge pigeon's-blood ruby in the center. Seated cross-legged upon his throne, he made an impressive picture.

Michael O'Malley could hardly keep himself from staring. It was the most incredible room he had ever seen, and he longed to be able to examine more closely the wonderful paintings upon the wall. How Skye would love the thick carpets! They made what she had in London seem poor stuff indeed. Forcing his eyes back to where they belonged, he glanced from beneath lowered eyelashes at the emperor himself. Akbar's bearing is most regal, he thought. Put him at any civilized court in Europe, and no one would not recognize him for the king he is.

Father Xavier gave him a quick poke, and, realizing that the Jesuit was bowing low before the enthroned figure, Michael O'Malley did the same.

Akbar hid a little smile. He had not missed the tall Christian priest's overawed examination of the room. Languidly he raised his hand in signal to Father Xavier that he might speak.

"Most High Emperor, may I present to you Father Michael O'Malley, a bishop of the church. He brings with him a request from my superiors in Paris that he is to have a private audience with you. He is quite fluent in French."

A private audience? Akbar was most curious. Usually the Christian priests loved to make quite public their attempts at his conversion. "Clear the room," he commanded Ramesh. When only he and the tall man remained, he said, "Speak, priest. I am listening."

"My name is Michael O'Malley, and I am the bishop of Mid-Connaught, in the country of Ireland."

Akbar held up his hand. "What is a bishop?" he asked. "And where is this place you call Ireland? Why have I not heard of it before?"

Michael cudgeled his brain. Finally he said, "A bishop is a nobleman of the church, a man of some authority, usually responsible for a small territory." Akbar nodded in understanding. "Ireland," continued Michael, "is a captive country of the English, an island kingdom to the west of England."

Again Akbar nodded his comprehension. "Continue," he said.

"My lord, it has been brought to my attention that you are a Moslem."

"No longer," said Akbar. "I was raised in the faith of the prophet Mohammed but I was curious as to the other faiths of the world. I built in my former capital of Fatehpur-Sikri a place where I invited holy men of every faith to come and expound upon the virtues of their own way of worship. What I saw angered and saddened me. Men of religion, priests of every sect, squabbling and arguing amongst themselves as to which faith was best, which of them worshipped the true God, actually even coming to blows with one another. It was then I devised my own form of worship, taking from each what I deemed the best. It is my faith, and that of some of my closest friends. I do not expound my faith even among my own people, for I have decided that each person must find his own path to God's salvation."

"You say," said Michael, "that you have taken the best from each faith. Do you still believe it is against God's law to take the wife of a living man for your own?"

"Of course!" said Akbar without hesitation.

"Then, my gracious lord, I must continue. Some many months ago you received at your city of Fatehpur-Sikri a train of gifts from the Portuguese governor in Bombay. Among these gifts was a young Englishwoman, the Countess of BrocCairn, Velvet Gordon."

Akbar stared at the priest, his face and his eyes expressionless, but his heart was beginning to pound nervously. Suddenly he knew that the man before him was going to bring him great unhappiness. He wanted to shout at the priest to stop, but he knew that he could not. His own strong conscience forbade it.

"Lady Gordon," Michael continued, "is my niece, the youngest daughter of my sister. My lord, I beg you to tell me. Does she yet live?"

"Yes," said Akbar in a toneless voice.

"Praise be to God and his blessed mother, Mary, who have heard my prayers!" Michael said joyfully. Then he went on, "My lord, I have come to bring my niece home to England. Her family will pay whatever ransom you deem necessary."

"I am not holding your niece for ransom, Father O'Malley. Has it occurred to you that she might not want to return to England? Have you considered that perhaps she has found love and favor in my eyes?"

"My lord, her husband lives."

"I am her husband," said Akbar.

"No, my lord, I meant that her husband, the Earl of BrocCairn, is not dead as she believed, but alive and eager to have his wife returned to him. If you believe as you say you do, Most High, then you must release my niece to me so that I may bring her back to her rightful lord."

It was as if a hammer blow had been dealt to Akbar's heart. For what seemed like an eternity he could not draw his breath. His chest felt as if it were being crushed by several bands of iron. I am going to die, he thought, and it is better that I do so than to live without my beloved Candra. But then he found that he was breathing, and his head cleared, and he said, "First we must be sure that we speak of the same woman, priest. Come with me!"

Rising from his cross-legged position upon his throne, he led Michael O'Malley through a door hidden behind the throne. They were in a cool, well-lit but narrow stone corridor, and Michael had to hurry to keep up with the emperor though Akbar was much shorter than he was. Finally they stopped and the Grand Mughal drew Michael forward. To the priest's surprise he stood before a peephole.

"Tell me if you recognize anyone within the room, priest. Look carefully, for far more is involved than you know."

There were three women in the room, but Michael recognized her almost instantly. His hesitation was only caused by the fact that he had carried in his mind a picture of Velvet as he had last seen her at eleven years of age. She had been tall and leggy with an unruly mass of auburn curls then. Her face had just been beginning to change from a child's to a young girl's, and her body had been basically still formless.

The woman in the room was probably one of the most beautiful he had ever seen. In a strange way she surpassed even her own mother in loveliness. She was slightly taller than Skye, and the auburn hair was now totally under control, parted in the middle and drawn smoothly back over her ears into a chignon at the nape of her graceful neck. Her face was serene, and her nose had grown, he noted, from the little bit of flesh that it had once been into a straight nose of elegant proportions. The formlessness, too, had given way to a feminine shape of delightful proportions. He considered her turquoise blue and gold clothing most immodest, showing her legs through the thinness of the flowing skirt and at least half of her breasts due to the shortness of her blouse. Still, it was Velvet. Without a doubt, it was his niece.

"It is she," he said to Akbar. "The girl with the auburn hair." He thought he heard a sound, almost the groan of an animal in pain, but when he turned to the emperor, Akbar's face was an impassive one. Still, he could not help but ask, "Are you all right, my lord?"

"You have just told me that my favorite wife, the mother of my daughter, is another man's wife, priest. Were I not a moral man, were I not a man of strict conscience, I would kill you here in this secret corridor where we now stand."

Michael felt an icy chill run over him, for he saw the mixture of despair and anger that had suddenly appeared in the emperor's eyes. "My lord, this is a tragedy, I will grant you, but what can I do? I, too, am a man of morals and strict conscience," he said.

Akbar nodded. "Give me time to make certain arrangements, priest, and then I will have you brought to me again, and we will settle this matter."

Michael O'Malley nodded. He instinctively knew that he could trust this man. Together they exited the corridor, and then in the company of Father Xavier he left the palace. To his surprise he was recalled several hours later.

"They tell me you will not return to us," said Father Xavier who brought Michael back to the palace gates. "Can you trust these people, my lord bishop? We are, after all, responsible for your safety."

"Rest assured that I shall be safe, Father Xavier," said Michael O'Malley. "I am most grateful to the Jesuits here in Lahore for all their aid. Remember, however, that my visit must go unrecorded in your journals. That is the wish of Paris and Rome."

The Jesuit nodded. "Go with God," he said, and turned back toward his house.

Michael O'Malley was not taken into the main buildings of the palace. Instead he was brought secretly through the gardens to a smaller building where Akbar awaited him. There his escort disappeared, leaving him with the emperor.

"This is Candra's house," said Akbar. "Candra is the name by which your niece is known here. It comes from the ancient Sanskrit language and means 'Moonlight.' I have told her only that I wish her to meet a visiting Christian priest. I have arranged that you will leave Lahore toward dawn. You will travel to the coast under my own personal protection as quickly as possible."

"You said there was a child . . ." began Michael.

"Our daughter, Yasaman Kama Begum," said Akbar.

"I am not sure about taking the baby, my lord. I do not know how Velvet's husband will take the news of another man's child."

"Do you think I would expose my daughter to your European bigotry?" thundered Akbar. "*Never!* My child remains here with me."

"How will my niece take such a plan?" Michael was worried.

"We will convince her, priest, you and I. Come now. Candra awaits us."

Seeing her close up, Michael was once more astounded by Velvet's beauty. Her creamy skin was flawless, and he could understand why the emperor had renamed her Candra.

"This is the priest I was telling you about, my Rose," Akbar said.

She looked up at him with her emerald green eyes, and then as recognition dawned her eyes widened with disbelief. "Uncle M-Michael?"

"Yes, Velvet, it is I." Michael O'Malley held out his arms.

"Dearest uncle!" She flung herself at him. "I had never thought to see any of my family ever again! Oh, how wonderful that you are here!" She hugged him hard and then stood back to look up at him. "You are the answer to a prayer, Uncle! Now I can send my poor Pansy and her little son home! She has tried so hard to adjust, but she really misses her Dugald, and it isn't at all fair that he not know his son."

"Sweet child, I have come to take *you* home," said Michael O'Malley.

Velvet laughed merrily, and then, reaching out, she drew Akbar to her side. "No, Uncle Michael. I am not returning to England. When you tell my parents how happy I am they will understand, and I know that my lord husband will allow them to come visit me here at Lahore or at my palace in

Kashmir. They must see their granddaughter. Pansy! Pansy! Come quickly!"

Another young woman hurried into the room, and Michael vaguely thought that she resembled Skye's Daisy. "Yes, m'lady?"

"Pansy, this is my uncle, Michael O'Malley, the bishop of Mid-Connaught. He is going to take you and little Dugie home! Isn't that wonderful?"

"Oh, m'lady, I can't leave you!" Pansy protested.

"Yes, you can! Oh, Pansy, you're not like me, widowed and beginning a new life. Dugald is alive, and you both have the right to your happiness together. Little Dugie has the right to know his father. You have tried for my sake, I know, but you are not happy here. I want you to go home with Uncle Michael."

"Oh, m'lady . . ." Pansy began to sniffle.

"She's Daisy's daughter," said Velvet to her uncle. "She is as loyal to me as her mother is to my mother. It will pain me to part with her, but it is for her own good. Her little boy does not tolerate well the heat of our summers."

"Velvet, my child, you have not heard me," said Michael O'Malley. "You, too, must return with me to England. Your husband is alive and anxious for your coming."

"My husband is by my side, Uncle."

"It is not this great king to whom I refer, Velvet, but to your lawful husband in the eyes of our church. It is Alexander Gordon who awaits you."

"Alexander Gordon is dead, Uncle Michael. He died two years ago. He wasted his life for the honor of a strumpet," Velvet said sharply.

"No, my child, Alexander Gordon is very much alive. He was only badly wounded, but in the excitement that followed his injury someone was heard to say he was dead, and your brother, Padraic, without verifying the facts, rushed to tell you that you had become a widow."

"No!" Velvet's hand flew to her mouth in shock. "No! He is dead! *He is dead!*"

Akbar caught her to his chest and held her close. "Don't, my beloved, do not make this harder than it already is. This man is your uncle, the brother of your mother. Has he ever been a man of deceit, of subterfuge? Would he lie to you about something so important?"

She shook her head and then, looking up at Akbar asked, "What does all this mean to us? I was only wed to Alex Gordon three months. I have been your wife for over a year. We have a child. I will not leave you!" Her eyes were filled to overflowing with her tears.

"I cannot take the wife of a living man for my own wife, Candra. You are no longer mine. You are *his*, and I must send you back to your own people, to your own land. I must do it though it be my death blow."

"No! No! No!" She shook her head violently, and her hair came loose, the pins flying in all directions. Clutching him, she slid to her knees, her arms about his legs. "Do not send me away, my lord. I will be your concubine if I cannot be your wife. I will be the humblest slave in your palace, but do not send me from you! I love you! I love you too much to be separated from you." Her eyes pleaded with him as eloquently as her voice did. "Ah, I cannot bear the pain!" She wept.

Once again Akbar felt the shortness of breath that had afflicted him earlier. She was breaking his heart, for he loved her above all other creatures in this world, even his own children. He did not know how he would survive without her, but he would have to, for God had decreed that she not be his. Gently he raised her up, brushing the hair from her face. Then signaling for Michael O'Malley to remain behind, he led her into their bedchamber where Yasaman lay sleeping in her cradle near their bed. He poured two goblets of fruity, sweet wine, and when he was certain she could not see him, he flipped a secret catch on one of his rings and dumped an instantly dissolving white powder into one of the goblets. Then, turning, he handed it to her. Drawing her down, they reclined together upon the bed.

Looking into her wonderful eyes, he toasted her, and they drank. "Fate has played us a cruel trick, Candra, but if we did not obey God's laws, then we should be no better than the animals, should we, my Rose? We must both be very brave, but you, my darling, will have to be the bravest, for I cannot let you take Yasaman."

"You cannot mean to separate me from my baby?" she whispered piteously. "She is not even six months of age yet. How will she know me if you take her away from me?"

"*Think Candra!* Your clever mind is the first thing about you that attracted me. What kind of a life would she lead in your England? Would your husband accept her? I think not. I have studied your Christianity, and my child would be considered a bastard in your land. Could all your love make up for the cruel taunts and the wicked whispers that would surround her all her life? How would your other children feel about a bastard sister? No, Candra. Yasaman has the right to grow up surrounded by love and security. She is an imperial Mughal princess, and I will raise her as one! I will allow no one to hurt her, and though I am forced to part with you, my dearest English Rose, I shall not part with the fruit of our love for one another."

She heard his words, and she understood the sense of them, but still her heart cried out for her child. "Do you not think I feel the same way? If I am to be torn from you, why can't I have our child to comfort me?"

"You will love again, Candra. You will learn to love your Alex again as you once did, and there will be other children of your body to fill that void in your life. There will be nothing for me, my beloved. Without Yasaman you would be only a dream to me. Besides, for the child's sake it is better that she remain with me." His tone was determined.

Velvet wanted to protest further, but suddenly she could not gather her thoughts into a coherent pattern. Gazing into her wine goblet, she saw dregs in its bottom and realized what he had done. Marshaling every ounce of her strength, Velvet pulled herself out of his embrace and slid her body off the bed. Her arms and legs were fast becoming leaden, and she could barely keep her eyes open. Still, she fought her way along the few feet separating her from the cradle where her infant daughter lay peacefully sleeping. Gaining her objective, she pulled herself up and stared down on the child.

Oh, Yasaman, you are so beautiful, she thought. *I have been a good mother to you the short time I have had you, but you will never know that, my baby. I love you, Yasaman! I love you!*

Then Velvet raised her eyes to Akbar and said distinctly, "I shall never forgive you for this."

He was by her side in an instant, his arms tight about her. "Remember that I love you," he said. "That has not stopped, nor will it ever."

"And I, God help me, love you, my lord Akbar." Her eyes were beginning to close. "Do not forget me," she whispered to him.

"Never!" he promised.

Her eyes fluttered open just a moment more, and she gazed at the wonderful design he had created on the wall behind their bed. Then she drew his head down to her lips. "Once the Wheel of Love has been set in motion," she murmured against his mouth, "there is no absolute rule." Then her lips touched his in farewell as she slid into her drug-induced sleep.

He sat for several long minutes holding her slumbering form, memorizing every line of her face and body. His sorrowing dark eyes went from her to their child. How like her the baby was. Would Yasaman forgive him someday when she learned that he had separated her from Candra, her mother? With a sigh Akbar stood, lifting Velvet in his arms. Slowly he walked to the door that Adali, who had been hidden in the shadows, hurried to open.

"When you return from Cambay, Adali, you will become head eunuch to Yasaman Kama Begum. You will have charge of her whole household."

"My lord is gracious," came the eunuch's reply, but Adali's face was sad as he opened the door, then took the precious burden that Akbar gave him.

"She is drugged into sleep," said Akbar to Michael O'Malley, who was waiting in the corridor. "This is Adali, her eunuch, who will accompany you to the coast. He is fluent in French. Go now before my heart overrules my conscience!"

"I will tell them of your greatness in England, Most High," Michael said.

Akbar allowed a small smile to break through his heartache. "Two last things, priest. Tell Candra that I have given Yasaman to Rugaiya Begum to bring up. It will ease some of her sadness to know her daughter is safe with her close friend. Then when you return to England, tell your queen that I will soon allow England to trade with my country. I grow tired of Portuguese arrogance."

"Thank you, my lord." Michael could scarcely believe the emperor's generosity and England's luck at such an outcome.

Akbar nodded, then gently touched Velvet's cheek a final time. "Farewell, Candra, my English Rose, my heart and my life." Then he turned and left them.

The Grand Mughal climbed to a tower room at the highest point of the palace, a room overlooking the coastal road to the port of Cambay, some several hundred miles away. There he stayed, watching as Velvet's caravan departed in the early, gray hours of first light. He watched until his eyes ached with the strain, imagining her fair form behind the gauze curtains of the litter, until finally the procession was no more than a puff of distant dust upon the horizon. About him the sky was golden with the promise of a new day, but Akbar saw it not. He remained alone, locked in the tower room without either food or drink for the next three days, coming out at last only so as not to encourage his sons to new rebellions. And when he reentered the world of the living, his long dark hair and his moustache had turned snow white, and he was suddenly an old man.

Part Four

VELVET

But true love is a durable fire
In the mind ever burning,
Never sick, never old, never dead
From itself never turning.

—*Sir Walter Ralegh*

Chapter 12

The wind, which had been blowing all day from the north-northeast, suddenly shifted to the east. It was almost as if it wanted to aid the *Sea Hawk* as she ploughed her way through the deep swells of the English Channel up into the Strait of Dover, around Margate Head, and into the Thames estuary. The sky was as flat and as gray as slate, and a fine mist of rain had begun to fall. England! As green and lush as only it could be in early August. How Velvet had dreamed of the soft green hills of her homeland those blazing hot days in Lahore, and now that she was faced with the reality it was like bitter ashes in her mouth. She was glad that Alex had not wasted his life in the foolish duel, but, oh, what unhappiness that prideful action had wrought, and he would never know the real truth of it.

Leaning over the ship's rail, she looked down at the dark, swiftly moving water. How easy it would be, she thought, and then the mewling cry of a gull made her raise her head to the sky, and the softly falling rain mixed with the tears on her cheeks. How could she even consider such a thing? Death would change nothing for her. She would still be separated from Akbar and her daughter, Yasaman. It took far more courage to live, and she was, after all, her parents' child.

Velvet remembered little of her departure from India. After Akbar had drugged her, Adali had kept her in a sleeping state for most of the several weeks it took to reach Cambay and the coast. The eunuch had seen her aboard Murrough's ship, settling her in her quarters as his last service to her. She had been awake then, but very weak.

Tucking her into bed, he had said to her, "My lord has told me several things to say to you, things to ease your fears. The little princess has been given to Rugaiya Begum who will raise her as if she were her very own. She will be instructed secretly in your faith, for our lord Akbar thought you would want that. I am to be Yasaman Kama Begum's eunuch and head of her household. He thought that would please you. Among your belongings you will find a thin gold chain upon which there is one pink pearl. Each year to celebrate the little princess's birthday another pink pearl will be delivered to your father. In this way you will know that the child lives and thrives."

"Make sure that she knows I did not want to leave her," Velvet whispered weakly. "Make sure that she knows that I love her."

"I will not let her forget you," he promised.

"Uncle!" Velvet called out.

Michael O'Malley hurried to his niece's side. "What is it, my child?"

"Give me the miniature that you carry of me. I am certain you have one that you planned to show my lord Akbar."

"I do," he said, reaching into his robes where it had been all these weeks. Drawing it out, he handed it to her.

"Give it to my daughter when she is old enough," Velvet said to the eunuch, and then she fell back against the pillows.

Adali nodded his head, his eyes filled with tears. Kneeling, he kissed her hand, and then rising once more he hurried from the cabin, not even daring to turn as he said, "Farewell, my princess," lest she see the tears upon his cheeks.

Velvet was exhausted and worn. Her will to live had been badly sapped. For the next three months she slept constantly, only rousing for Pansy, who spoon-fed her mistress soup made from chickens that had been brought aboard and were kept caged on deck. It was only in the fourth month of her journey that Velvet began to rouse from her torpor.

They sailed in a convoy of six ships, for the de Mariscos would take no chances in bringing their child home safely. They had stopped in Zanzibar to take on fresh water, more chickens, fruit, and vegetables; and later when they had rounded the horn of Africa, they stopped several times to trade for these items with the natives, most of whom were wary when they saw the ships, fearing slavers. Halfway up the African coast, Murrough put well out to sea, for although he and his fleet could outgun any Barbary pirates rash enough to attack them, he preferred to avoid such danger with his sister in such a weakened condition of both body and mind.

Velvet, however, improved daily, for her basic will was to survive. Her body responded to Pansy's tender nursing and her uncle's and brother's concern, even if her conscious mind did not.

Pansy, although she attempted restraint before her mistress, was totally overjoyed to be going home. Velvet overheard her tiring woman one day as she sat upon the deck, little Dugie in her lap.

"You're going to meet your father soon, Dugie. You'll like him, for he's a wonderful man. Did I tell you that you look just like him? And you'll see your grandmam and your grandpa, too, my lamb. Oh, you'll like England, me darlin'!"

Dugie stared up at his mother, bright-eyed, taking in every word she said. At first he'd been afraid of the sailors who looked so very different from the emperor's soldiers who had courted his mother and played with him in an effort to please her. He was, however, unable to resist the ship's elderly sailmaker who sat cross-legged sewing upon the deck almost every day. The sailmaker, a man without chick or child, was flattered and happily demonstrated his craft to the tiny boy, watching over him when Pansy was serving her mistress. Gradually the child began to win over other sailors on the vessel, many of whom rarely saw their own children, if in fact they even acknowledged them. Dugie, to his delight, found himself being petted and spoiled quite royally.

"He's going to be impossible when I get him home," Pansy said indulgently.

Tonight they would anchor in the London pool, and Velvet would see her parents for the first time in five years, and her husband for the first time in two and a half years. Alexander Gordon. "*Alex*," she whispered his name into the wind. What kind of chance for happiness did she have with him now? Perhaps he would want their marriage annulled, and that, thought Velvet, would suit her quite well. She would go back to Akbar. She had, after all, been unfaithful to Alex even if she hadn't known it. She couldn't believe Uncle Michael when he said that Alex wanted her back. Her parents wanted her back, but Alex? She did not think so, proud bastard that he was.

Did she want to be his wife? No! Yes! At this point she simply didn't know. How could she love again the man who had ignored her pleadings and fought a duel over nothing? His alleged death had caused her to flee, had brought her to Akbar, had given her Yasaman, and now his resurrection had stolen her happiness and taken her child from her. It was all his fault, and she was not certain that she would or could ever forgive him.

"You look so serious, little sister." Murrough was by her side, throwing an arm about her.

"I am afraid of the future," she said truthfully.

"Come, poppet," he said in an attempt to cheer her up, "Mother and Adam are anxiously awaiting your arrival at Greenwood. Be happy! You are finally home."

"And Alex? Will he be anxiously awaiting me, Murrough?"

"Mother sent Alex home to Scotland before I left. She said she would send for him when you returned. Since she couldn't know exactly when we would arrive, I do not believe she has yet dispatched a messenger to Scotland."

"Good! I am not ready yet to see him."

"Velvet . . ."

"He is as much to blame for this situation as I am, Murrough. Had he not involved himself in a duel with Lord de Boult, none of this would have happened. I have lost far more than my husband in this matter."

"He's a proud man, Velvet. Be generous," Murrough counseled.

"Why?" she demanded. "Should we both not be generous and forgiving of *each other?*"

God's boots, he thought, how she has changed. I wonder how wise we have been in bringing her back. "Sometimes," he said aloud, "a woman must show a man the path, sister. Remember that in your dealings with Alexander Gordon."

"What is today's date?" she asked him.

"It is the ninth of August," he replied.

"Today is my daughter's first birthday," she said, and then, turning, she left him to return to her cabin.

He felt as if she had hit him. The timbre of her voice had been calm, almost matter-of-fact, but how he had felt the raw pain in it. A loving father himself, Murrough O'Flaherty could not help but wonder about his sister's child, the infant princess she had been forced to leave behind. She had not talked of her daughter until now, and frankly he had not been brave enough to ask her. He had spoken to Pansy, who had told him of his little niece's early beauty, of her rare turquoise eyes.

"I ain't never seen a baby so pretty," Pansy had allowed, and then she had said, "It weren't right making m'lady leave her baby behind, but the bishop feared that Lord Gordon would not accept the lass, and the lord Akbar wouldn't let his daughter go anyhow. He said 'twas all he had left of his love for m'lady. They said in the zenana that they never saw him so taken with a woman as he was with Mistress Velvet." Then Pansy, as if remembering her place, had stopped speaking for a moment before saying, "I shouldn't talk so much. You're not going to tell on me, Captain O'Flaherty, are you?"

"No, Pansy, I'll not tell on you if you'll not tell Velvet that I was asking."

Murrough shook his head. It was a tragic situation. All he could hope was that Alex and Velvet would make their peace and that Velvet would have another child as quickly as possible. She would never forget the child in India, but perhaps in time with other children around her the memory would fade and her lost daughter would seem like a child stillborn. Remembered, but not known.

He gave orders that a boat was to be lowered over the side of the *Sea Hawk.* With luck the family barge would be awaiting them when they docked. For once his plans were executed like clockwork, and the barge was indeed at the appointed place. Velvet, Pansy, Dugie, Michael, and Murrough boarded it, and it began its trip up the river to Greenwood. It was already dark, and the night was cool. Velvet drew her cloak about her.

When she had been well enough to care, she'd learned that some of her clothes had been packed by Daisy and sent with Murrough to India. Although there were several pretty gowns among her things, she had chosen that morning to wear a black silk dress with a low neckline and plain sleeves with simple white lace cuffs. There was something spare, almost severe about the gown. The matching cloak was lined in white silk.

The barge bumped the Greenwood landing and was made fast. Looking up, Velvet thought she had never seen her mother run so quickly, and Daisy easily kept pace with her. Behind them came Velvet's father and Bran Kelly. Murrough jumped out of the barge and, turning, lifted his sister onto dry land.

Skye stopped short and stared at the young woman in the black cloak. In her mind she was remembering the child of almost thirteen years she had last seen, and the woman before her did not fit that memory. This was a beautiful woman, a woman who had known love and suffered for it. What had happened to her little girl? Then, as quickly as the thought flew through her head, the answer came behind it. Time. Time had passed. Time she and Velvet had not shared together, and in that time the child had become a woman. Her eyes filled with tears, but whether they were for the lost moments she and her daughter had missed or for Velvet's own pain, she knew not.

Opening her arms, she said, "Welcome home, my darling!" And Velvet, enfolded in her mother's embrace, knew that nothing had changed between them.

Skye hugged her daughter tightly, instinctively knowing her child's greatest fear, and whispered reassuringly to her, "I have not yet sent for Alex, my love. First we must talk." Feeling Velvet relax, she knew that she had said the right thing. She caught her daughter's face between her hands. "Oh, how beautiful you have become!" Then she kissed Velvet once on each cheek.

"There is so much to tell you, Mama. Things I haven't talked about since I left India. They cannot wait! I need to talk with you!"

"Yes! Yes!" Skye agreed. "Tonight! I promise!"

"Velvet!"

She turned from her mother and ran into her father's arms. With a groan Adam de Marisco buried his face in his daughter's neck. "I thought never to see you again!"

"It's all right now, Papa," she reassured him.

"The thought of your suffering, my poppet . . ."

"I did not suffer, Papa."

"But you were sent to the harem of the Grand Mughal," he protested.

"It is called a zenana in India, Papa, and my lord Akbar loved me. He took me for his wife. I did not know that such happiness existed."

Beside them, Daisy wept tears of relief at the sight of her daughter, Pansy, and her first grandchild. Bran, however, the more practical where their children were concerned, seeing his child in good health, relieved Pansy's most immediate fear.

"That bandy-legged Scotsman you handfasted yourself to promised to wait for you. He even asked my permission to formally marry you. I hope you're still of a mind to do so if only for my fine grandson's sake."

"Aye, Da! The more little Dugie looked like his pa, the more I missed Dugald. He'll be mightily surprised to learn he's got a son."

"And what were you doing tumbling into bed with the man before you were properly wed?" demanded Daisy, recovering and reaching out to give her daughter a smack.

"Ma! 'Twas only once!"

"Once is enough!" snapped Daisy.

"Do you think we might adjourn to the house?" Michael O'Malley asked plaintively from the barge where he still sat, blocked from disembarking by the crush upon the quay. "Night air from the Thames is not particularly salubrious and is known to harbor bad humors."

"Oh, Michael darling, yes!" Skye said. "I've not even thanked you for all your help!"

"Thank me inside, dear sister, and I can but hope you have some good peat whiskey to take the chill from my bones. I ran out months ago."

"Aye," replied Adam de Marisco, pulling his brother-in-law up from the barge. "I've a barrel, and for all you've done for us, Michael, you can bathe in the damned stuff if you want!"

They moved up the lawn from the river into the house, and Bran and Daisy took Pansy and her son off to their own rooms, while Adam, kissing his daughter good night, promised to come and see her first thing in the morning. Then he escorted his stepson, Murrough, and brother-in-law to his library for some of the promised whiskey.

Taking her daughter's hand, Skye led Velvet upstairs to her apartments.

In Velvet's room a large oak tub stood steaming with the hot water emptied into it by a line of footmen. "I thought that you would prefer to bathe yourself tonight," Skye said quietly. "Pansy and Daisy need their time together, too. When was the little boy born?"

"Shortly after we arrived at Akbar's court in Fatehpur-Sikri, Mama. I didn't even know that Pansy was with child. She carried small, and she was afraid to tell me. The court physician informed me. Dugald had cajoled her into bed the night they were handfast." Velvet removed her cloak and, turning her back, had her mother aid her with her bodice and skirt. "Have they brought my things from the barge yet?"

"They are in your dressing room, my darling."

Velvet walked into the smaller room and, opening a leather-bound trunk, rummaged until she found what it was she sought, a small stone vial. Moving back into her bedroom, she uncorked the little bottle and, climbing up the steps to the tub, poured a stream of pale gold liquid into the hot water. Immediately the room was filled with an exquisite fragrance. Descending from the steps, Velvet pulled off the rest of her clothes.

"What is that?" Skye asked. "It's absolutely lovely!"

"Jasmine, Mama. I prize its perfume above all others." She rolled her stockings off her shapely legs.

Skye could not help but look at her daughter. She was simply gorgeous in her nudity. Velvet's long legs rose up into a wide span of hips and taut, round, silken buttocks. Velvet had had no breasts to speak of when her mother had last seen her, but the dainty buds of childhood had become full and voluptuous with five years' passing. Her belly was faintly rounded, not as maiden flat as it should have been. Suddenly Skye looked closely at her daughter, and Velvet, caught unawares, could not hide the sadness in her eyes. In that moment, Skye realized the truth.

"Was my grandchild a boy or a girl?" she asked.

"I have a daughter, Yasaman Kama Begum, Mama. Yasaman means Jasmine. She is one year old today." Velvet climbed into her tub, leaving her mother speechless.

When Skye managed to recover from her surprise, she said, "Why is she not with you, Velvet?"

"Because her father and Uncle Michael would not let me bring her. Uncle Michael feared that Alex would never accept my bearing another man's child. My lord Akbar said that Yasaman was all he had left of our love, and he would not allow me to take our daughter from him. They were quite agreed, if for different reasons."

Skye nodded mutely, understanding but suffering for her beloved child, who was obviously in great pain over the loss of her own daughter, even if she hid it behind a calm and brittle exterior.

"How did you do it, Mama? How did you manage when you were my age to run your own life without interference? If there is a way, I want to know it, for never again will I allow anyone, man or woman, to rule *my* life! I will be mistress of my own fate, for I can live no other way," Velvet declared.

Skye sighed deeply. "I could tell you to grasp your destiny by the throat, Velvet, and in a way that would be true, but the real answer lies in my wealth. Wealth is power for a woman of independent spirit. But in the end everyone must answer to a higher authority. My authority has been Elizabeth Tudor."

"She has used you shamefully, Mama."

"And she has paid a high price for it, Velvet. The queen has had to answer to England all these years. I have served this English queen, but never have I been subservient to her."

Velvet nodded, fully understanding her mother's words. "I think I am rich," she said, "although I have never bothered to learn about trading and investments as Willow has. I have brought back from India jewelry worth a king's ransom. Those jewels, however, I shall not sell. They will be returned to India one day for my daughter when she is married. Akbar, however, did send with me certain items which I believe should make me a wealthy woman."

"What are they?" Skye was frankly curious.

"There are five trunks of spices, one each of peppercorns, cinnamon sticks, nutmegs, cloves, and cardamoms; as well as three caskets of gems, one of Indian Ocean pearls, one of Ceylon sapphires, and the third of rubies, some of which come from Mogok and some from a mine near Kabul. I want to sell these things. Will they make me a rich woman, Mama?"

Skye nodded slowly. "Yes, my darling, they will make you quite respectably rich in your own right. The market for spices is, because of the Portuguese monopoly, quite high here in England. Spices are very much in demand. As for the jewels you have brought back, I will have to see them, of course, but your gems come from mines that are considered the best. Lord Akbar obviously held you in great esteem."

"We loved one another, Mama. He is like no man that I have ever known." She then ducked her head beneath the bath water and, coming back up, began to wash her hair.

Skye bit her lip. Her child was hurting, and there was nothing she could do to ease that hurt. In time, of course, the pain would lessen, but right now the wound was much too fresh. How was Velvet going to receive Alexander Gordon? Skye knew that she was going to have to send for him within the next day or two.

Finishing her bath, Velvet climbed from the tub and wrapped herself in a large towel. Seating herself by the fire, she began to dry her hair. "I do not want Alex to know that I possess great wealth. He will claim it for himself, and then I shall be powerless against him. Will you help me, Mama?"

"Yes, my darling, but I will aid you only if you promise me you will do nothing rash or foolish. Come what may, you are married to the Earl of BrocCairn, and unless he seeks to annul your union you will remain married to him until death. I know about the rash act that led to your separation. There is blame on both sides, and as Alex must accept his responsibility in this matter, so must you. Then you must both put the past behind you and start afresh, Velvet."

"Does he really want me back, Mama?" She took up a hairbrush and began brushing her damp tresses.

"I believe so. He is hurt, and he is angry, but he might have sought an annulment before this, which he hasn't done. I have not seen him since your uncle left for England some months ago. He has written me on several occasions inquiring as to the status of our search, but never has he suggested ending your marriage. I will send a messenger to him first thing tomorrow morning."

"So soon, Mama?"

"We're going to leave for *Queen's Malvern* tomorrow, Velvet. The word of your return will be quickly around court circles, and I do not want you to have to face the gossips until you and Alex have settled your differences. Besides, I believe the country is a better place for you to recuperate. It will take our messenger at least five days, riding at top speed, to reach *Dun Broc.* Then it will take Alex time to return with him. I do not expect you will have to see your husband for two weeks."

"It does not seem so long," Velvet replied.

"There is something that you should know, Velvet, and I do not want you to become angry when I tell you. When Alex was wounded, he was carried to the house of one Peter Wythe, a silversmith. Master Wythe had a daughter. I don't know how it happened, but Alanna Wythe became Alex's mistress. I thought to separate them by sending him home to Scotland, but he took her with him. She is at *Dun Broc* now."

Velvet laughed bitterly. "He did not wait long to replace me in his bed, Mama, did he? Does he love her?"

"That is something that you will have to ask him yourself, Velvet, but I doubt it. Men seldom really love their mistresses. They consider them playthings and secretly hold them in contempt."

"Is that how Geoffrey Southwood felt about you when you were his mistress, Mama?"

"Velvet! Where on earth did you ever hear such a thing?" Skye demanded.

"Don't forget, Mama, that I spent some months at court while you were away. There were those who couldn't wait to tell me of your adventures while you were young."

"I am not yet old," Skye retorted dryly. "Very well, Velvet, certain men love their mistresses more than their high-born wives. I do not believe, however, that this is the case with Alex."

"Then why is she still with him, Mama? Frankly I hope he is in love with her. Then perhaps he will free me, and I can return to the man I love and our daughter." Velvet stood up and shrugged the towel from her body. Her auburn hair was now dry, and it billowed about her shoulders. Walking to the bed, she donned the simple nightshift that was laid out and climbed into bed.

Skye plumped the goose-down pillows behind her daughter's back in motherly fashion and sat down on the edge of the bed. "Have you cried any?" she asked Velvet.

"Would crying change all of this, Mama? Would crying bring me my little Yasaman? Tears are a waste of time."

"Tears help to wash your pain from your soul, my darling."

"No, Mama. The pain will keep me strong when Alex attempts to weaken me with his bullying."

"Oh, Velvet, was your marriage to Alex that awful? I never meant that you should marry him unless you really wanted to. The betrothal was to please your father, but even he agreed that if, when you were grown, you did not suit, the match would be called off. I had hoped that perhaps you would love him."

"I thought that I did, Mama, but still we fought constantly from the moment that we met."

"About what?"

"Everything! Anything!" Velvet smiled softly, but then her mouth grew grim again. "He does not know how to treat a woman, Mama. I was forever reminding him that I was not one of his dogs or his horses to be ordered about. Sometimes I thought that he was beginning to learn, but then we would be back to the old 'I am the master and you're merely my wife.' I cannot live under such domination."

"Was not the lord Akbar a dominating man?" Skye inquired.

"Not with me. He said that all the women he had ever known were fawning creatures who would not dream of questioning anything he either said or did. I was the first, he said, the very first woman who ever challenged him. He talked with me a great deal about his conquests, of religion, of his eldest son, Salim, who was so rebellious and resentful that his father still ruled when he wanted to seize the kingdom for himself. My lord Akbar said that actually his younger son, Prince Daniyal, was better suited to rule, but Daniyal is a drunkard. He loves wine more than power."

Skye was fascinated. Velvet had obviously captured Akbar's heart that he would unburden himself to her, speaking with her as he would an equal. "You loved him very much, didn't you, my darling?"

"I shall always love him," Velvet said quietly.

"You must try and rekindle your love for Alex, Velvet. That is obviously your fate or you would not be here now. Once when I was your age and very mutinous about the way life had treated me, my dear friend, Osman the Astrologer, told me that I must not fight against my fate; that what was ordained would be even if I did not like it. It took me a long time to realize the truth of his words. You and Alex have been through a trying time. You have each coped in your own fashion, but now, however, fate has ordained you be reunited. Don't fight your fate, Velvet. Give your marriage a chance."

Before Velvet could reply, the bedchamber door opened and Daisy came in bearing a tray. "Welcome home, Mistress Velvet. I thought you might want a bite before you go off to sleep." She placed a tray containing a small bowl of clear broth, a plump capon wing, some fresh bread, a slice of runny Brie, and a fat peach upon Velvet's lap.

"Thank you, Daisy! I think I actually am hungry, and I have not had Brie in so long!"

"It is I who should be thanking you, Mistress Velvet!" Daisy had tears in her eyes as she turned to Skye. "She saved my Pansy's life, m'lady! She nursed her herself when Pansy got ill in that heathen land. Pansy could have lost her life, and that of little Dugie, had it not been for Mistress Velvet." Daisy looked again at her mistress's daughter. "God bless you, Mistress Velvet!"

Velvet flushed. "Oh, Daisy! Pansy makes much ado over little. Her pregnancy was advanced, and the fierce heat of India bothered her. I just saw that she was comfortable and had enough to drink. I didn't even know she was enceinte."

"I know what Pansy told me, m'lady. I won't ever forget it either, Mistress Velvet." Then Daisy bobbed a curtsy to the two women and departed.

"What really happened?" asked Skye, intrigued. She was beginning to see her daughter in a somewhat new light.

"The heat disagreed with Pansy to the point where her legs grew swollen, and she couldn't walk. She was unconscious, and the caravan master wanted to leave her behind. I couldn't understand his language, and he didn't understand me, but his meaning was very plain. I bribed him with my gold mirror, the one on the chain that Papa gave me for my tenth birthday. In return, he allowed Pansy to ride in one of the baggage carts, and I was able to care for her until we reached Fatehpur-Sikri where my lord Akbar's physician took over."

"How on earth did you ever get the caravan master to understand you?" Skye questioned.

"I drew a map in the dirt with a road that ended in a city. I placed the mirror by my drawing of the city. The chain I gave him immediately to show my good faith," replied Velvet.

Skye shook her head. "That, my darling, was very, very clever! You did indeed save Pansy's life and that of her little son. I am so proud of you, my daughter. Now use that same brave spirit to heal the breach in your marriage with Alexander Gordon."

Velvet sighed and pushed her tray aside. She had eaten every crumb of food and felt enormously better. Now, however, all she wanted was to sleep. "Let me go home to *Queen's Malvern*, Mama, and catch my breath for a little bit. You have said yourself that Alex will not be there for at least two weeks."

Skye stood up and, taking the tray, bent for a moment to kiss her daughter's cheek. "Good night, my love. I am so glad that you are home again!" Then she left the room.

Raising herself up, Velvet blew out the bedside candle, leaving only the light from the dying fire to brighten the room. *Home*, she thought, leaning back upon the pillows.

Where is my home? Certainly not with my parents any longer. Nor with my beloved Akbar in my dear little white palace in Lahore or my beautiful, airy marble palace in Kashmir. Is my home at *Dun Broc* with Alex? Dear God, the very name sounds so harsh. *Dun Broc.* Is my place there? She sighed. I don't have to think about it for at least two weeks, and, she decided, I won't.

By midmorning the following day, Greenwood had been closed, and the de Marisco family was on their way to their estate near Worcester. Joan O'Flaherty was already there with her children waiting to greet her husband, Murrough, and the returning Velvet. Willow and James along with their family, Deirdre, John, and their children, and Padraic would all be at *Queen's Malvern*, Skye told Velvet.

"What of Robin and Angel? Gracious! I have not even asked about Angel's baby! Was it a boy?"

"Angel has borne Robin two sons." Skye laughed. "The first was born on the fourteenth of May two years ago. In accordance with the queen's wish he was christened Geoffrey. Their second son, John, was born just two weeks ago, which is why they cannot come to *Queen's Malvern* right now. Angel is still recovering from the birth, and the baby is over young to travel. Deirdre had another son last year. His name is Peter. The biggest surprise of all, however, is Willow. She and James had a daughter last year. Little Johanna."

"Willow had another baby?" Velvet was astounded. "She always said five was quite enough."

Skye chuckled. "It was very much a surprise to her. In the beginning she showed none of the usual signs of a woman with child, and when she finally realized what her 'illness' was, she didn't know whether to laugh or to cry. Johanna, however, is a lovely child."

"How fortunate my sisters and sisters-in-law are," Velvet said softly.

Adam reached out and patted his daughter's hand. "Don't grieve, poppet. You will have other children." Skye had told him the previous night of Velvet's little daughter, Yasaman.

For the first time in months Velvet spoke of her child. Looking directly at her father, she said, "It was such an easy birth, Papa. She was so eager to come into the world that she was born almost before I realized what was happening. Most of my lord's wives were jealous of me but for Jodh Bai, the mother of the heir, and my lord's first wife and cousin, Rugaiya Begum. They were my friends, and it was they who aided me.

"There was a golden cradle, all bejeweled, ready for Yasaman, and after her birth she was placed in it. My lord came, praised me, and acknowledged the baby as his own true child. Then the others were sent away, and when we were alone my lord Akbar presented me with this." Velvet held out her hand to display a large pigeon's-blood ruby carved into a heart shape and set into a gold ring.

"She is the most beautiful child, Papa. She was never scrawny like some newly born babies are. She was plump and dimpled. Her eyes are turquoise blue, and her hair as black as night, yet in the sun it has reddish lights in it. She will be very smart, I could tell. She always turned her head at the sound of my voice, or of her father's, and she could laugh. She was just learning how when they took me from her.

"Oh, Papa! I shall never see my child again, and I do not think that I can bear it!"

Adam de Marisco thought that his heart was going to break. Whenever things had gone awry for Velvet in her youth he had been there to make it right. Now he could not There was absolutely nothing he could do to spare his only child this terrible pain. Reaching out, he lifted her from her seat in their coach and cradled her in his lap. "I am so sorry, my poppet," he whispered, his usually strong voice ragged and torn with his own emotions. "I am so very sorry! I would do anything in my power, Velvet, to spare you this anguish, but I cannot. God help me, I cannot!" And then he began to sob, great, wracking sobs that shook his whole body, and Velvet, stunned by her father's grief, was, after six months, finally able to cry herself.

Skye felt her own tears slipping silently down her cheeks, and she impatiently brushed them away. It was enough that Velvet was now purging some of the bitterness from her soul.

After a time, Velvet's weeping dissolved into little hiccoughs, then finally ceased altogether as she fell asleep in her father's protective arms. Adam raised his head and looked across the coach at his wife.

"I feel as if I have failed her," he said quietly.

Skye shook her head. "No. You have helped her greatly. Neither of us can change what has happened to Velvet, but we can see that she is happy from now on, and that means that Alex Gordon must honestly want her back. It would be a tragic mistake to allow him to take Velvet back to Scotland if he does not love her."

Adam nodded. "I agree, my love, but she is legally his wife. There is little we can do to stop him, whatever his attitude. I am sure, however, that he would have demanded an annulment before this had he not wanted her back. Angus Gordon, his father, was a strong but gentle and good man. He raised his son to manhood before his untimely death. I am certain Alex will show his father's ways once he sees Velvet again."

"I hope you're right," said Skye, but in her heart she fretted, for from what she had seen of her Scots son-in-law he was a proud, stubborn man. Still, he had not demanded an annulment. She closed her eyes and allowed the rocking motion of the coach to lull her into sleep.

As she slept the de Marisco messenger galloped north, stopping only to change horses, to eat, and to relieve himself. It took him five days to reach *Dun Broc*, where he was immediately ushered into the earl's presence. Kneeling, he handed Alexander Gordon his packet.

"My wife is safe in England?" Alex questioned the messenger before even opening the packet.

"Aye, my lord. She landed in London on the ninth of August. The family left for *Queen's Malvern* the following morning. Lady de Marisco asks that you join them there."

"Alanna!" The earl's voice was sharp. "Take this man to the kitchens and see that he is first fed then sheltered for the night." He turned back to the messenger. "Ye will carry my message back to Lord and Lady de Marisco tomorrow."

"Thank you, my lord," said the messenger, rising.

Alanna Wythe pouted prettily at the man who had been her lover, but the effect was lost, for Alex was not even looking at her. He was far too busy tearing open the packet he had just received. With a little huff of indignation she rose from the floor before the fire where she had artfully sprawled herself. The de Marisco messenger eyed her boldly, thinking that she was a prime young bitch.

Alanna gave him a haughty look and stalked from the room. With a chuckle he followed after her, noticing as he did so that he towered over her, for she was but five feet tall. Her hair, which when unbound looked like it would cascade to just below her hips, was a pure sunshine yellow. She wore it in two fat braids that fell over her very full bosom. The de Marisco messenger leaped around her in the corridor and, with a grin, stood blocking her way.

"I've traveled far, sweeting. I don't suppose you'd have a kiss for a tired man."

"So much as touch me, and my lord earl will have your randy pizzle cut off and fed to the wolves!" she snapped. "I'm not for the likes of you."

"Your pardon, me lady," he said mockingly, and then stepping aside continued, "I wasn't aware you saved your whoring for only the earl."

Alanna's brown eyes flashed with anger. "The earl loves me," she hissed at her antagonist. "You'll soon see!"

The messenger laughed harshly. "I've yet to know a man who'd leave his rich and beautiful wife for his doxy, sweeting. You're riding for a hard fall. Now that my lady Velvet's home you'll be sent packing quick enough. Now get me something to eat like your master ordered you!"

Outraged, Alanna ran down the hallway on her short legs, the messenger easily keeping up with her.

In his library Alexander Gordon carefully opened the packet. Within the protective wrappings he found the heavy parchment message sent to him by Skye. He unfolded it and read.

To Alexander Gordon, Earl of BrocCairn:
My lord. My daughter, Velvet, arrived home yesterday evening. Although she appears to be in good health, she is exhausted both emotionally and physically. If the last two and a half years have been difficult for you, the last six months have been equally hard for Velvet who, believing herself a widow, had allowed the Grand Mughal, Akbar, to woo and win her only to learn that you were alive. She is, as you may well imagine, quite confused. For my daughter's sake, I beg that you be certain you wish your marriage to continue. You will need patience, a quality of which I am not convinced you possess a great deal; and you will need to love Velvet with your whole heart. If you cannot, then I beg of you to release my child from your marriage vows, lest you destroy each other. We shall await your arrival at Queen's Malvern.
(Signed) *Skye O'Malley de Marisco, Countess of Lundy.*

Alex reread Skye's letter several times over, realizing as he did so that now that his wife had returned he was going to have to make some serious decisions. The first of those decisions involved his wife, and the second, Alanna Wythe.

Velvet de Marisco. Did he love her still? Did he *really* love her, or did he simply want to revenge himself upon her for leaving him? God only knew that he had once loved her, once promised her that there would never be another woman to engage his heart. That much at least was true. He had never seriously loved a woman before Velvet, and he loved none now. The question remained, however: Did he yet love Velvet herself, or was his anger deeper than his love?

He gazed up at the portrait above the fireplace. There she stood in her wedding gown gazing down at him in all her youthful innocence. How excited she had been to surprise him with the portrait their first and only Christmastide together. She was the most beautiful woman he had ever seen, and she was his wife. A wife who had deserted him, leaving him for dead, not even staying to give him a Christian burial. He had not understood it when it happened, and though he knew more of the facts, he did not comprehend it now. *Why?* It was a question that had haunted him these past two and a half years. He would see her again if only to learn the answer.

That brought him to his other problem, Alanna Wythe. She had already borne him a daughter, Sybilla, but he had never loved her. She had been there in her father's house to nurse him, and she had one night, when he was particularly drunk with self-pity, climbed into his bed to ease his pain in a far pleasanter way. She had not been a virgin, and so he had felt no regret. It had amused him to bring her to Scotland, for he was well aware that his mother-in-law had sent him home in order to separate him from his light-o'-love. That had been a mistake, for it had led to Sybilla's birth and to a tie he could not easily break. Alanna was an overproud girl with a greed for possessions and position. Even so, however, she cheated on him, although he had not told her that he was aware of her infidelity.

He had learned about it quite accidentally, going to her tower apartment one night to see his daughter. Sybilla's cradle had been placed in the hallway outside Alanna's bedchamber, and the door was ajar. Hearing voices, he had peeped around the door, feeling very foolish to do such a thing in his own castle. The sight that greeted his eyes was an astounding one: a naked Alanna entertaining two of his men-at-arms. He had quietly departed. He had avoided her bed after that, and had set Dugald to spying on his mistress to learn that, as Dugald so pithily put it, "The woman fucks more than a doe rabbit in season, m'lord."

He should have confronted her with his evidence then and there and sent her back to England, but he worried about the child he had fathered on her, if indeed the child were his. Alanna Wythe, it seemed, was a born whore. So she had remained at *Dun Broc* because that was easier than making a decision. Now he was going to have to take some action.

He could hardly have his mistress living here in his wife's home.

Suddenly she was there, though he had not even heard her come into the room. Wrapping her arms about his neck, she kissed his mouth, and her perfume was almost that of a feral beast, heavy and ladened with musk. He detached her.

"I'm going to England to bring my wife home, Alanna. Ye have a choice. I will either take ye back to your father's house and settle a goodly amount on ye and the child, or ye can have a cottage and income in the village in the glen." He fully expected her to return to England, as she had done nothing except complain about the Highland climate since he had brought her to *Dun Broc.*

"You'd send me away, Alex?" She pouted again and looked saddened. "How can you send me away when you know how much I love you? What will happen to our little Sybilla without her dear father?"

He had to laugh. It was really quite a wonderful performance, but he knew that now was his chance to settle this matter once and for all. "Alanna, I have recognized Sybilla as my child even though I am not entirely certain that she is mine. Nay, lass, dinna protest. Ye've got a healthy appetite for men that ye've been indulging in my west tower these past three months. I've said nothing because there was no need for ye to leave, but now there is. Make yer choice. Either way, I'll take care of ye both."

"I'll not go back to England! Sybilla is your child, and if we were wed she'd be your heiress."

"God's cock, lass! Dinna tell me ye ever expected marriage from me because ye didn't. I am married. Sybilla's my bastard, nothing more."

"Married!" Alanna said scornfully. "Married to a wench who ran and left you dying! She's as big a whore as I am."

His face darkened. "Ye know nothing of my Velvet! Get out! Get out of my sight, bitch!"

"Which cottage am I to have then?" Alanna was quite unperturbed by his anger.

"It will be built new. I'll have ye out of here long before I return from England. I don't want to see yer face again, Alanna. Keep from my sight, or as God is my witness I'll give Sybilla to a decent woman and have ye driven from my lands."

When she had left him, Alex poured himself a dram of peat whiskey from his own still and sat down before his fire. His argument with Alanna had taught him one thing he hadn't previously been certain of. There was still something in his heart and soul for Velvet. He needed to see his wife and, come the morning, he would send the de Marisco messenger back to England announcing his impending arrival within a few short days. He would not delay the reunion between himself and Velvet any longer. Whatever had happened between them, they had to resolve their differences now.

Chapter 13

"She has changed!" declared the Countess of Alcester. "She has changed greatly." Her voice held a hint of disapproval.

"She has grown up," replied Lady Blackthorn. "Do not forget, Willow, that we have not seen Velvet for two and a half years."

"I am more than well aware of the passage of time, Deirdre, but our sister is not the same girl."

"No," Deirdre had to agree, "she isn't."

"Did you expect her to be?" inquired their mother. Skye looked at her two older daughters. God's nightshirt! Was it actually possible that she was the mother of daughters aged thirty-one and twenty-four?

"What has happened to her, Mama?" asked Deirdre.

"Believing Alex dead, she fell in love with another man. Now her heart is torn between the two. She has no choice in the matter and must return to her husband. It makes the forbidden fruit, in this case the Indian emperor, somehow more attractive, and being an independent girl, she chafes at being *forced* to a decision. She would like to feel that the choice is hers to make."

"Poor Velvet," said Deirdre, who was a compassionate and gentle woman.

"Humph!" snorted Willow. "If she had stayed where she belonged, instead of running off when she believed Alex was killed in that ridiculous duel, none of this would have happened."

"You are too hard on your sister, Willow," replied their mother. "In your whole life nothing has ever gone awry for you. You cannot know how you would have acted under similar circumstances."

"Well, I most certainly would not have left my husband's burial to others!" Willow appeared to be outraged, but the truth of the matter was that she was made somewhat uncomfortable by her mother's reference to her charmed life. She had, she thought, been born practical, and most of her upbringing had been supervised by Dame Cecily, who had raised Willow to have all the English goodwife's virtues of thrift and loyalty to duty first. She felt secure with her values, and only once or twice in her life had she entertained the thought of a life as filled with adventure and passion as her mother's had been, only to push such a wild notion aside with a shudder. Willow, Countess of Alcester, was the perfect example of a high-minded English noblewoman, and she would have had it no other way.

"Has not Velvet led a charmed life, too, Mama?" she countered. "She has certainly had much more time with you than the rest of us did, and is the only child you really raised yourself."

"That is true," agreed her mother, "but you must remember that both Adam and I were forced to leave her at a time when, as it turned out, she needed us very much. She had no one to really guide her. Be patient, Willow. Velvet has been home only two weeks, and she is very worried about her reunion with Alex."

"She doesn't seem comfortable with us," grumbled Willow. "I told her that I had made her little Johanna's godmother, and she was not the least bit thrilled. All she wants to do is ride that damned stallion of hers from dawn to dusk!"

Skye said nothing more, her eye catching a glimpse of Velvet through the window as she mounted her big-boned chestnut and galloped down the drive. How could she explain to Willow about Velvet's own daughter who was only a month younger than Johanna? She couldn't. Before they had even reached *Queen's Malvern*, Velvet had insisted that nothing be said to anyone about Yasaman. Pansy had already been sworn to secrecy, as had Daisy and Bran.

"What of Alex?" Skye had queried of her daughter.

"No! If I cannot have my baby, then why should Alex have the knowledge of her with which to reproach me, Mama? I will never tell him of her."

Then they had reached *Queen's Malvern*, and the family had joyously hailed her safe return, thrusting their new babies upon her to admire. It had not been easy, and Skye had devoutly wished in the days that followed that her children and grandchildren would all depart for their own homes if only to give Velvet some peace. When they didn't, Velvet sought her own solitude upon her horse, feeling no guilt at all in making her escape for she knew that her mother understood.

This particular afternoon, she had eagerly sought refuge from her elder sister who persisted in dandling her youngest child at her. Velvet had tried to enjoy little Johanna, who was a most charming baby, but each time she held her niece it brought her to tears remembering her own daughter. Finally this afternoon she could stand no more and had rudely thrust Johanna back into her mother's arms, snapping at Willow, "Her bottom is wet, and she is drooling all over me! Do not give me the child again unless I ask for her. I dislike being soaked!" Then she had stormed from the room.

Now, as the late-summer wind blew her auburn hair about her face and shoulders, Velvet felt the weight lifting from her. Leaning forward, she kicked her horse into a gallop and raced up into the hills, feeling freer than she had in weeks. It was almost as it had been five years ago when she was yet a child and could not remember the name of Alexander Gordon, Earl of BrocCairn. She had been in such a hurry to grow up. Why was it, she wondered, that children were always in such a damned hurry to get older? Childhood was so very brief. If only children understood that and enjoyed their time in that safe and innocent world. She sighed, then laughed softly to herself. That was knowledge that came only with age.

Reaching the crest of the hill, she stopped and, turning her stallion back for a moment, gazed down upon her home. *Queen's Malvern*, so called because it had been built for a queen and was situated in the Malvern Hills in an almost hidden valley between the Severn and Wye rivers, sat like a jewel in a perfect setting. She had never thought to see it again. There was a faint late-summer haze over the valley, and everything was so very lush and green. There was peace here; the kind of peace she had never been able to find anywhere else. She would miss it when she went to Scotland with her husband.

Then her eye caught a movement on the road below, and, gazing down, she could make out a large party of men approaching the manor house. Even from a distance she could see they were Scots, their plaids fluttering bravely in the light breeze. *Gordon plaid.* He had come, and she could not take her eyes away from the scene below. He rode at the head of his men, but suddenly they stopped, and then Alexander Gordon broke away from the main group and headed his horse directly up the hill toward her.

Panic gripped Velvet's heart, and, wheeling her own stallion sharply about, she galloped blindly off. It wasn't long before she heard him behind her, his own horse relentlessly coming onward. Inwardly she cursed herself for being caught like this. In the valley below she was certain she could have outrun him, but here the ground was so uneven and dangerous. Should her mount step into a rabbit hole he would break a leg, and she could break her neck.

Then she felt herself being lifted from her saddle, and, surprised, she didn't even have the presence of mind to struggle.

Bringing his own horse to a stop, Alex lowered her to the ground and then, dismounting himself, asked her in a none-too-gentle voice, "Just what is it about me, madame, that sends you fleeing almost every time we meet?" He towered over her menacingly, his golden eyes blazing.

If he had expected tears or anger, he was totally surprised when, looking up at him, she burst into laughter instead. "I have never thought about it," she said with complete candor, "but I do seem to spend a great deal of time going in the opposite direction from you, my lord."

He gazed down at her. Had she always been this beautiful? He shook his head, surprised at his bemused thoughts, and then said, "Welcome home, Velvet. I've missed ye."

She would almost rather he had shouted and railed at her, but that, she was certain, would come later. "Did you, Alex? Did you really miss me? You didn't wait overlong to replace me in your bed with Mistress Wythe."

"Nor did ye wait overlong to desert me. My body wasn't even cold, Velvet, and ye were hurrying off to India to yer parents."

"Padraic swore you were dead! I was in shock! I was in agony, for I loved you, and you had wagered our future for the false honor of a strumpet in a ridiculous duel! I begged you not to go! I begged you, Alex, but you would not listen!"

"Could ye not at least have stayed long enough to bury me, Velvet?"

"Did you want to be buried on English soil, Alex? I gave orders that you be taken home to *Dun Broc* because I believed you would have wanted that."

He was surprised again. In the back of his mind he remembered Murrough saying something like that. So she *had* cared. He was relieved. And yet . . . "But ye weren't going to accompany the body, were ye, my dear wife?"

"No, I was not! You broke my heart, you bastard! Did you want me to follow you into the tomb, for I would have been dead of grief long before we reached *Dun Broc!* Would that have pleased you, my lord? Perhaps your little mistress would have done it, but not I!"

"Alanna Wythe means nothing to me, Velvet. I took her to my bed, I will admit, but what of ye? Ye were as quick to replace me."

"*Never!* I spent a six-month voyage mourning you, Alex. When I was kidnapped and sent to the Grand Mughal I mourned you yet."

"Not long enough, obviously, madame. He made ye his wife in very quick order, I am told."

"Of course he did. It was the polite thing to do, for I was a gift to him from the Portuguese governor of Bombay. It wasn't me he was marrying, it was the gift!"

"Which one of ye did he fuck, Velvet?"

"Ah," she said, "that is what bothers you more than anything else, isn't it, Alex? In your mind 'tis perfectly all right for you to have taken a mistress because your wife ran off and left you; but for me, believing myself widowed, to remarry and love again, *that* is the crime!"

"Did ye love him, Velvet?"

"Yes!"

She looked straight at him when she said it, and it was he who flinched under her steady green gaze. She had changed, he thought, and he didn't know if he was going to like that change. Still, standing there looking at her, he realized that he still wanted her, perhaps even still loved her. There was a great deal to be settled between them, but only time could accomplish that.

Holding out his hand to her, he said, "I've come to take ye home, lass. Will ye come wi' me?"

He is as unsure of me as I am of him, Velvet thought, and yet he seems willing to try to rebuild the life together we both so heedlessly shattered. Slowly she put her hand into his, and his fingers closed over hers. "Aye, Alex," she replied to him. "I'll come home with you."

Her horse was grazing nearby, and they caught it easily. Giving her a boost, he aided her in remounting and then gained his own saddle. Together they quietly descended from the hills to the gentle valley below. Upon returning to *Queen's Malvern*, they found that Alex's men had already stabled their horses and were just now trooping into the house. They were in time to witness the reunion between Pansy and her Dugald.

Pansy stood in the doorway to the kitchen, little Dugie holding her hand with one of his own, his other thumb in his mouth as he stared wide-eyed at the troop of men with their plaids and bonnets. There was no doubt whose son he was, and as the Highlanders began to poke each other, chortling with delight, looking from their comrade to Pansy and her child, Dugald stopped and stared, open-mouthed.

Finally Pansy said impatiently, "Well, say something, you big oaf! You're going to scare the lad to death if you don't."

"What's his name?" Dugald ventured, shifting nervously.

"Dugald Geddes, the same as yours," she answered.

"How old is he?"

"He'll be two the day after Michaelmas," Pansy replied.

"But how . . ." Dugald shifted his feet again.

"Well, if you don't remember, Dugald Geddes . . .!" began Pansy indignantly, and the other men chuckled.

"But 'twas only once!" he burst out.

"Me ma says once is more than enough!" she answered, and Dugald's companions, unable to restrain themselves any longer, burst out laughing.

"Gawdalmighty, man," said one of them, "ye're not going to deny him, are ye? He's yer spit fer certain, and 'tis true!"

"N-nay, I can see he's my laddie," Dugald said slowly.

"And are you still of a mind to wed me?" Pansy demanded.

"Aye," he answered without any hesitation.

"Then wash your face and hands, Dugald Geddes. Father Jean-Paul is awaiting us in the chapel." She bent down and spoke to the child at her side. "Say hello to your pa, Dugie." But the little boy hid his faced in his mother's skirts, much to Dugald's disappointment.

"He's just shy," Pansy said. "He ain't used to men in plaids and bonnets with bony knees, but you'll win him over soon enough."

Unable to restrain himself any longer, Dugald wrapped Pansy in a fierce embrace.

Watching from his horse, Alex turned to smile at Velvet. It was the first smile he had offered her. "He's missed her very much. Pansy has a good man in Dugald," he told her.

"She loves him," Velvet said quietly. "She had many suitors among the Mughal's best soldiers, but, knowing that Dugald was alive, none would do for her."

Dismounting, he helped her down from her own stallion, and the horses were quickly taken away by two stableboys. They continued together into the house. Seeing them coming, Skye realized that they had already made some kind of peace between themselves.

"Welcome to *Queen's Malvern*, Alex," she said graciously.

He kissed her hand. "Velvet has agreed to come home wi' me," he said.

"But surely not for a few more days, my lord. We have scarce had time with our daughter these past five years as you well know."

"We would be pleased to remain with ye for a time, madame," he said quietly, and Skye saw that he was anxious to please Velvet.

"I want a bath," Velvet said. "'Twas hot riding this afternoon. I fear that we will have a storm before nightfall. Can you send Daisy to me, Mama? I don't want to disturb Pansy's reunion with Dugald."

"Of course, my darling. Alex, I would like very much to speak with you, and perhaps while Velvet's bathing would be a good time."

"Have Alex's things put in my room," Velvet said to her mother. "For propriety's sake we must share a bedchamber."

"For practicality's sake." Skye laughed. "All the other bedchambers are filled to overflowing with your sisters and brothers, their spouses, and their offspring. Go along now, my darling, and Alex and I will have a cosy chat." She smiled brightly at her daughter, and Velvet turned and hurried up the stairs. "Come with me, my lord," Skye said to her son-in-law. He dutifully followed her into the library where Adam was already waiting.

Once they were all settled, Skye turned to Alex and said, "You have made your decision then, my lord?"

"We have already talked, Velvet and I. She is willing to come back to Scotland wi' me as I have already told ye."

"Have you thought over what I wrote to you, Alex? Do you possess the patience to love Velvet?"

"I don't know," he answered her honestly. "What I do know is that I want her to come home wi' me. I am not certain that I love her, but I don't want to lose her again."

Skye nodded. She understood his quandary, but Adam was not so open-minded. He glowered at his son-in-law from the depths of his chair and growled, "You'd best not hurt her, my lad. Son of Angus Gordon or no, I'll kill you if you hurt my child!"

"Adam!" Skye gently admonished her husband.

"Nay, little girl, I mean it. She's suffered enough. I'd rather he sue for an annulment than give Velvet a moment's pain," Adam declared.

Strangely, Alex was not offended by his father-in-law's vehemence. "I am trying, my lord, but remember that I have suffered also. Still, given time, I believe that Velvet and I can work out the difficulties between us."

"How long before you leave?" demanded Adam.

"A few days, perhaps a week or more. I don't want to tear Velvet from her family too quickly after this long separation."

"Umm." Adam nodded. "'Tis wise."

"You see," Skye said, "Alex is indeed going to try to overcome the gulf that divides him from our daughter." She rose from her own chair and, walking over to Lord Gordon, put a hand on his arm. "I know it will not be easy," she said, "but I somehow believe that you and Velvet are meant to be together. Hold fast to that thought, Alex! It will aid you in getting over the hard spots."

He stood and smiled down at her, thinking as he had thought those long years ago when he had first become betrothed to Velvet that his mother-in-law was an incredibly beautiful woman. But then so was his wife, and he wanted to go to her now. "I will try, madame," he promised.

"I know you will," she said, reassured. "I will have a servant show you to your apartment, my lord."

When she had sent him on his way, Skye turned back to Adam. "Let them be, my love. You cannot make this all right for Velvet any more than you could the *other* matter.

She must work this out with her husband, and there will be bad times before it is all settled between them. Was it not that way with us?" She settled down into his lap, resting her head upon his shoulder.

"I always hated it when you were hurt as well," he grumbled.

"I know that, but you and I made a great mistake with Velvet. We spoiled her, and we overprotected her. She is a strong girl, Adam. Away from us she not only survived, but she saw to Pansy's safety. She will triumph in this matter also if we will but let her."

"'Tis not Velvet I worry about, but Alex," Adam grumbled.

"He is trying, my love, but he is not you. In his own way he has been sheltered, too. Do not forget that when we first met I had been widowed thrice, and you were a man who had grown up in both the English and French courts. Most of Alex's life has been spent at *Dun Broc* but for the years of his university schooling. He's a Highland chieftain, and the thought that his wife has lain with another man must be maddening to him. I am frankly surprised he is being as reasonable as he is." She leaned over and kissed her husband's cheek.

Adam turned his head and, finding her loving mouth, kissed it passionately. "The only thing that ever mattered to me, little girl, was that you were finally mine," he said.

She smiled. "You, my darling, are a very unusual man."

Adam de Marisco grinned wickedly at his wife and fondled her breasts. "And you, madame, are a *very* unusual woman."

"Sir!" she teased him with mock outrage, "we are grandparents! Will you ever stop being such a randy old billy goat?"

"Never, madame," he answered her, and, tipping her from his lap, he moved across the room to lock the library door. "Not as long as I have you, sweet Skye, to warm my bed."

Their eyes met, and then Skye threw her arms around her husband of nineteen years. "I am so happy with you, my darling! You did not lie to me when you promised to slay all my dragons and keep me safe."

"If I could but slay Velvet's dragons," he said, "but that is for Alex to do now." Then he bent his shaggy dark head and kissed her, far happier with his lot than his son-in-law was with his own right now.

Alex mounted the stairs almost reluctantly. Velvet had agreed to return to Scotland with him, but he fretted as to what kind of marriage they would have now. She had made no secret that she had loved Akbar. Did she love him still? Would she ever love him again? Could he love her again? Or had he never stopped loving her? Alex sighed deeply, hesitated for an instant as the footman opened the door to Velvet's apartments, then went in. As he closed the door behind him, he could hear voices in the bedchamber.

"May I come in?" he called politely.

Velvet, seated in her oaken tub in the next room, raised her eyebrows delicately. What had come over Alex? He was treating her as if she were made of fine crystal. "Come in, my lord. I am finished."

"Not until I get the back of your neck, you ain't," said Daisy.

Velvet laughed. "This is Pansy's mother, Alex," she said when he had entered. "Daisy, my lord of BrocCairn. Your man, Dugald, is now safely wed to my tiring woman, Alex. Pansy wasted no time."

"Considering the size of me grandson, it was none too soon, and I expect Bran and me will be grandparents again by those two before another year is past," Daisy said proudly. "Past time for you to have your own babies, Mistress Velvet. Now that you've been reunited with your fine husband, I expect you'll be starting your own family."

For a moment Alex thought the briefest shadow of sadness clouded Velvet's eyes, but when she spoke he decided he must have been mistaken. "Indeed, Daisy, it is past time for us to have a child," she said. Then she rose and climbed from the tub.

Alex caught his breath. He *had* forgotten how extraordinarily beautiful she was. Her creamy skin and rounded breasts! Her arms and long legs that were, he thought, fuller and fleshier. There was no boldness about her, but she was no longer the skittish child-bride he remembered. She never even gave him so much as a coy glance as Daisy dried her, powdered her, and finally wrapped her in a silken chamber robe of apple-green silk.

"Go along, Daisy. I will see to my own hair now."

"Pansy will come to dress you for dinner, Mistress Velvet."

"Nay, let her have her time with her bridegroom, if that is all right with you, my lord." Alex nodded his assent. "Just send me one of the undermaids to help, Daisy."

"Very good, Mistress Velvet." Daisy bobbed a curtsy and departed from the room.

For a long moment Velvet and Alex stood looking at each other, and then she said, "Let us sit by the fire, my lord. The day has grown chill, and the rain I predicted has already begun to fall." She waved a graceful hand toward the window as she seated herself in a chair. "It only rains in 'season' in India, and then it is as if someone had cut a large hole in the sky, so heavy is the downpour."

"What is it like?" he asked curiously.

"India?" She smiled. "A green, gray, and brown land. The sun would shine for months on end until I thought that if I did not see a cloudy day I would die from the wanting. I never knew that the weather could get so hot. One rarely wore clothing to bed. The heat hovered over the plains so that you could actually see it. It was better when we moved to Lahore. Still hot, but at least there I had gardens and greenery. Still, I missed the green of England."

"Scotland is green, and the sun will not shine for weeks on end until you will long for those sunny days," he said quietly.

She nodded. "I will not mind, Alex."

"Do ye really want to come home wi' me, lass?" he asked.

"Alex, what else is there for us? We are married. I should like to tell you that nothing has changed, and that we can pick up our lives from where we left them long ago on that snowy February day two and a half years past, but I cannot. I thought you dead. I have loved another man with my whole being. He filled my heart, and his touch made my body ache with joy. I cannot deny these things, and I will not, not even to please you, my lord. I know that the truth is hurtful to you, but if I lied to you, you would know it, sense it, and there would always be an element of doubt between us."

"Do ye love me, Velvet?"

"Once I did, Alex." She made no further promises, and he felt angry and rejected.

"Ye left me, madame," he said through gritted teeth. "I awoke in a stranger's house, weak from loss of blood, with yer name upon my lips, but ye were not there, Velvet. When they finally told me that ye had left England to find yer parents, I couldn't believe it."

"I didn't leave you, Alex. Not that way. When Padraic told me that you had been killed, I thought I would go mad. All my worst fears had been realized, for I had not wanted you to fight that duel. The pain was so terrible that, like the child I still was, I sought my parents to be comforted. I ran, not from you, Alex, but from the horrible reality of your death. What was left for me here in England without you? We had no children that might comfort me. We had nothing in common but three months of marriage and several months before that time when we fought each other almost constantly."

"I courted ye in those months before our marriage!"

She laughed. "Nay, Alex. You stormed me like a castle to be taken, and take me you did, but you know nothing of courtship."

"Did Akbar?" His look was angry and piercing.

"Yes," she answered him quietly, "but that has nothing to do with us here and now, Alex. That part of my life is over and done with, and I should as lief not speak of it any longer if we are to rebuild our life together."

"Are ye afraid, Velvet?"

"Aye," she said slowly.

"So am I," he answered her in a burst of candor.

"Let us go home to *Dun Broc* in two days," she said suddenly.

"What?" He was mightily surprised.

"*Queen's Malvern* is filled to overflowing with my relatives, and as long as we are here they will be here, standing about, looking at us with anxious looks, their children underfoot. Let us reassure my parents that we do not intend to murder one another, and then let us go home to *Dun Broc.* You're still of a mind to get yourself an heir, aren't you? We have lost several years, Alex. Why should we wait any longer?"

"But ye do not love me, Velvet. Ye have said it."

"Ours was an arranged marriage like so many others, Alex. How many marriages have the luxury of love between the mates? Once we loved, and we may do so again when the strain of our reunion is past, and we learn to know each other once more, but as long as we are surrounded by my well-meaning family, what chance do we have?"

Thinking about it, he was startled to realize that everything she said made perfect sense. "Ye're far more a woman than when I last knew ye, lass," he said seriously.

"Aye, Alex, I am," she answered.

Her reply, he felt, had more meaning than the simplicity of the words she spoke, but her gaze was a steady one as her emerald eyes locked on to his amber ones.

"We'll leave in two days' time then, lass. 'Tis a good time of year to go north."

They announced their decision at the huge family dinner that evening, and, as Velvet had anticipated, her parents and siblings were not anxious for her to go so quickly. She overrode their objections calmly and firmly, and Skye could see that her youngest child meant what she had said to her mother just a few days back.

"If a woman is weak, Mama, then she offers herself as prey to those who feed upon weakness. I shall never be a victim again in this life. *Never!* I shall be strong, for if I am not, the next time I shall shatter completely."

Adam grumbled, throwing his son-in-law of BrocCairn black looks, but Velvet said, "'Tis what I want, Papa. Alex is most willing to abide here, but I am anxious to see *Dun Broc.*"

Skye put a gentle hand upon her husband's arm, and with a sigh Adam ceased his arguments. "I'll miss you, poppet, but you're right. 'Tis past time you went home. Go then and know that you have our blessing and our prayers."

"Thank you, Papa," Velvet replied softly.

The air cleared, the family gathering proceeded, beginning with a wonderful feast that almost brought tears to Velvet's eyes, for it had been a long time since she had seen many of the wonderful dishes. A side of beef had been packed in rock salt and roasted to a turn. It dripped its juices onto the huge charger that contained it as it was carried into the room by four serving men. There was a large pink ham that had been glazed with honey; a roe deer; ducks stuffed with plums and peaches served with a sauce of cherries; and several lovely meat pies with delicate golden crusts, steam rising from the decorative vents in the pastry.

Alex had contributed to the feast in a wonderfully unusual way. Several of his men had led pack animals all the way from Scotland that had carried small barrels filled with cool water containing two live salmon apiece. Now the beautifully poached salmon, settled decoratively amid beds of cress upon silver platters, were presented to the de Marisco family.

From the manor farm came carrots, spinach, scallions, radishes, and lettuces. There were egg-glazed loaves of soft white bread, sweet butter, Normandy Brie, and a particularly fine pâté of goose liver. The goblets were never empty of the excellent dark Burgundy that came from Velvet's grandparents' vineyard at *Archambault* in France.

For the last course there were, as a special treat, pears stewed with cinnamon sticks, fat purple grapes from France, early apples up from Devon, a cake soaked in marsala, and dainty sugar wafers.

Afterwards, Skye's children entertained the rest of the family, which tonight included Sir Robert Small and his sister, Dame Cecily, with a musicale. Velvet was accomplished on the virginal, Deirdre on the harp, Padraic on the oboe, Murrough on the drum. Willow, of all Skye's children, had a clear, sweet voice, which she now raised in song. Soon she was joined by the rest of the gathered guests, and the old hall of *Queen's Malvern* rang with happy voices.

Afterwards, as their elders sat at the high board enjoying the last of the wine, the younger folk and their children joined in games of blindman's buff, hide-and-seek, and hide-the-slipper. There was much laughter and squealing. Watching, Skye smiled with pleasure. She enjoyed having her family about her, although it frankly amazed her that at almost fifty-one years of age she was a grandmother to twenty-seven children. No, she amended to herself silently, twenty-eight, if she counted Velvet's little daughter in India. At this moment fourteen of those children were in her house, and she suddenly realized that, despite the fact that she loved each and every one, she would be mightily relieved when they all went home. She laughed softly, and Adam raised a questioning eyebrow.

"I adore them," she said softly. "but I'll be glad when they've scattered again."

He nodded, smiling, but Dame Cecily, who had fox-sharp ears despite her age, mourned, "It'll be like a tomb."

"Deirdre has begged you to go and stay with her," Skye reminded her old friend. "She never feels happier than when you're with her."

The elderly lady preened with pleasure. "Well, perhaps," she allowed, "I might pay her a short visit. I do enjoy the children so very much."

"I suspect, although she has said nothing to me yet, Dame Cecily, that Deirdre is breeding again. You could be an enormous help to her," Skye said.

"I will speak to her, Skye, for she will tell me if I ask, and if there is a new baby coming in the spring then I shall most certainly be needed at *Blackthorn Priory* for many months to come."

Skye put her hand over Dame Cecily's and smiled warmly at her. "Yes, my dearest friend, we most certainly will always need you. You have been our rock these many years, and I pray that you will always be here with us."

Dame Cecily squeezed Skye's hand. "Not always, my dear. That is not possible, but for as long as the good Lord will allow. Remember that I was seventy-six this past May. If the good Lord will permit that I see Velvet's first child, then I shall count myself ready to leave this earth."

Skye looked across the room at her youngest child. Velvet sat quietly with her husband by the fireplace. When two of her little nieces, Cecily and Gabrielle Edwardes, tried to draw her into their game of hide-the-slipper, she refused, giving them a shake of her head and a wan smile. Yes, thought Skye, it is better that she go off to Scotland as soon as possible. Her child's loss is still too open a wound. She needs to begin her new life quickly. She should have another baby as soon as possible. Dear God, let her conceive quickly!

Velvet felt her mother's gaze upon her and felt uncomfortable. Standing, she said to Alex, "I am tired and want to go to bed now."

She looked so drawn that he was suddenly concerned for her. "Are ye all right, lass?"

"Just tired," she repeated.

"I think we can leave the hall without causing undue attention," he replied, putting his hand beneath her elbow.

Watching them slip quietly from the room, Skye prayed again for her daughter; prayed that she would be happy at long last, that her life would finally be a calm and contented one, and most of all that she would learn to love her husband once again.

Gaining their apartments, Velvet and Alex found Pansy and Dugald awaiting them, and Velvet was struck with a sense of déjà vu. While Alex and his serving man went into the smaller bedroom, Pansy helped her mistress to disrobe. Taking her gown away, she brought her mistress a basin of warm water scented with gillyflowers and a cake of Velvet's hard-milled soap.

"The jasmine is almost gone, m'lady, and we can't get it here in England."

"Don't use it," Velvet ordered tersely. "Put it away somewhere, for I don't want to be reminded of India."

"Yes, m'lady," said a subdued Pansy.

"Are you happy, Pansy? And what does Dugald think of little Dugie?"

"Proud as a peacock, he is, m'lady! You'd think he'd done it all hisself, and he's anxious to have another, he says." She chuckled. "Easy for him to say, ain't it?"

Velvet smiled. "He's a good man, Pansy, and I can see from the look in his eyes when he gazes at you that he loves you. Take good care of him, girl."

"Aye, m'lady, I will, for as God is me judge I never thought to see him again! 'Tis lucky I am!"

The little maid worked efficiently, taking her mistress's undergarments, stockings, and shoes and hurriedly putting them away. Picking out a gossamer silk night rail the color of apricots, she started to lower it over Velvet's head, but her mistress pushed it away.

"No," she said. "I am chilled, Pansy, and I will freeze in that gown. Give me a plain, white silk night rail."

Pansy raised her eyebrows but said nothing, instead obeying her mistress and handing her a simple, white silk gown with long, full sleeves that tied with blue silk ribbons at the neck.

Velvet bowed the ribbons prettily and then, having cleaned her teeth with a mixture of pumice and mint leaves, got into bed. "Leave me now, Pansy, and you needn't come until I send for you in the morning. I may sleep late, and 'twill give you time with your husband and child. Good night."

"Good night, m'lady, and God bless you!" Pansy curtsied and was gone from the room.

Velvet reached for the chamber stick on the table by the bed and blew it out. The low fire would light Alex's way. She snuggled down, drawing the covers well over her shoulders and head until only her nose was visible outside the coverlet. Still, she was cold, and she shivered. Then she realized it was not the late August night air that chilled her, but rather fear. She was afraid, and it fretted her to admit to it. She was no virgin bride awaiting her husband. She was a woman who had accepted two men as husbands in her short lifetime and had borne a child. Hearing Alex come into the room, she closed her eyes tightly and breathed slowly and evenly. Perhaps he would believe her to be already asleep.

She felt the cool night air as he raised the coverlet, and the bed sagged with his weight as he entered it. She stiffened slightly as his long, lean body moved next to hers. When he reached out to draw her against him, she panicked completely and cried out, *"No!"*

For a moment Alex was shocked. She was his wife, not some captive wench about to be ravished. His first instinct was to be angry, then he felt her shaking and said gently, "Velvet, lass, I only want to hold ye. It's been so damned long! If it distresses ye, however, I won't."

"I'm sorry," she whispered, but she did not deny him and gradually her trembling subsided to the tiniest of quivers.

He lay there in the darkness, for the fire had become only a small orange glow, his wife against him, spoon-fashion, obviously terrified that he would demand his *rights*, and he realized in a great burst of clarity the source of her pain. For two and a half years Velvet had been very much alive to him, while he had been dead to her. While he was biding his time amusing himself with Alanna Wythe, she had built a new life with another man, only to be torn brutally from that man and that life. She had great courage. He had already heard her praises sung by the usually taciturn Dugald, who had told him a wild tale of how Velvet had saved the lives of both Pansy and little Dugie.

"She's a great lady, m'lord! A great lady! She'll breed up fine sons for BrocCairn!" Dugald had said.

Alex smiled to himself in the darkness. There could be no sons unless Velvet's heartbreak healed, and he must be the one to heal it, for his stubborn pride had been a prime factor in breaking that brave, young heart. "Don't be afraid of me, Velvet," he said to her softly. "I understand. I truly do."

"I feel so foolish," she answered him, "but I am not yet ready for this part of our marriage, Alex. Please be patient with me. I am trying, I swear it!"

"I understand," he repeated. "I was dead to ye, but Akbar is not."

"Yes."

"Then I must woo ye from him, lass, and I will try to do so. I am not a man for the lute and love songs. I cannot compose a verse to save my soul, but I will show ye that I love ye in other ways if ye will give me the chance. Will ye, lass?"

She was silent a moment, and then she said, "Aye." Nothing more, but she turned in his arms so that she faced him, and, taking his head between her hands, she kissed him on the mouth before turning her back to him again.

Alex's heart soared! He felt like a young lad with his first lass. It would not be easy, he knew. He must swallow his pride to win back his wife's heart and soul from another man, but he would do it! He wanted her! Oh, how he wanted her, and whatever he had to do, it mattered not as long as Velvet would smile at him again with love in her eyes as she had those two and a half years ago. Pushing her thick hair from her neck, he placed a quick kiss on the soft skin at the nape. "Good night, lass," he said.

"Good night, my lord," was her reply.

Chapter 14

On the last day of August in the year 1591, the Earl of BrocCairn's party crossed over the Cheviot Hills and rode through the invisible gateway that separated England from Scotland. They had traveled slowly, for Velvet was still worn out from her long voyage. It had been a strange week for Alex since he reclaimed his wife. Velvet remained subdued in both manner and speech with him, but at least she had stopped trembling against him during the night. He knew that if he made love to her she would acquiesce, but it would have been like rape to him. He waited for her to want him again even as he wanted her. Patience, Skye had said, and she had been so very right. He only hoped that he had enough patience, for it was not easy to lay with Velvet night after night without loving her.

The air was yet warm in the Cheviots during the day; still, there were already signs of autumn around them. The heather had begun to bloom, and Velvet saw whole hillsides of the purple-pink flowers. The bumblebees loved the heather and flew busily from flower to flower gathering the nectar that would make their delicious honey. The whortleberry bushes were long stripped of their delicious fruit, but already the foliage had begun to assume its rosy-red autumnal tints. Here and there flocks of Cheviot sheep grazed the seemingly peaceful land, but the men of BrocCairn were ever-watchful for an unseen enemy who might attack without warning.

Alex had sent a messenger on to *Hermitage* requesting the hospitality of his cousin, the Earl of Bothwell. Bothwell was once again in his royal cousin James's bad graces, and Lord Home had been sent in early summer to arrest him. Sandy

Home, however, had decided that he preferred hunting and fishing with Francis Stewart-Hepburn to arresting him, and he had remained at *Hermitage* with his friend.

Most believed that the royal wrath against the Earl of Bothwell had been brought to a fine froth by the king's chancellor, John Maitland. Maitland had caused Bothwell to be imprisoned in Edinburgh Castle for several months, but on Midsummer's Eve the earl had escaped and publicly mocked Maitland at Nether Bow, daring him to come out of his house, where, rumor had it, the chancellor was cowering in a cabinet, to return the earl to prison. All of Edinburgh had enjoyed a good laugh at Master Maitland's expense, and he had not forgotten it. Learning from the king's chamber boy that James secretly coveted Catriona Leslie, the beautiful Countess of Glenkirk, Maitland allowed the king to learn that both Bothwell and Lady Leslie sought divorces from their spouses and planned to marry. In fact, Margaret Douglas, Bothwell's wife, had already been granted her decree. James had then used Bothwell's past misdemeanors and "his lewd conduct wi' a certain lady of the court" as excuses to outlaw his cousin. And he had prevented Lady Leslie's divorce. The lady, however, was not to be bullied by the king and remained with her lover in defiance of the Stewart's anger.

Under normal circumstances, Alex would have avoided Bothwell's hospitality at this time. He had no desire to bring the king's temper down on BrocCairn. Velvet, however, was simply not strong enough to ride too great a distance at a stretch, yet, and he had to break their journey at *Hermitage*. Perhaps, he hoped, the king would not learn of it.

The stone keep that was Bothwell's home had no sooner come into view when its great gates opened and a small party of horsemen rode out to meet them.

Francis Stewart-Hepburn's face was split in a huge smile as he greeted his cousin of BrocCairn. "Alex! 'Tis good to see ye!" Then he turned to Velvet, and his smile softened. "I'm glad ye're home safe, lass," he said quietly.

Velvet felt quick tears prick her eyes, and she blinked them away. "Thank you, Francis," she said, and for the first time in days Alex saw a small smile touch the corners of her mouth. "I am told the king is most put out with you, my lord. I would have thought you had outgrown your bad habit of teasing His Majesty by now."

Bothwell chuckled. "Jamie is too tempting a target, lass," he replied. Then he moved his horse just slightly so that the rider next to him was visible to them, and both Alex and Velvet were surprised to see that it was a woman. "This is Cat Leslie," Bothwell said simply. "She is to be my wife one day."

"Oh, Francis!" Velvet burst out, "you are finally happy! I am so glad! So very glad!"

Bothwell flushed, pleased by her words, but the beautiful Lady Leslie gave a soft, husky laugh. "Were she not yer cousin's wife, Francis, I think I should be jealous," she teased him.

"Velvet is the sweetest of lasses," Bothwell said, "but there is only one woman in the world for me, Cat, and 'tis ye, my darling."

Now Lady Leslie flushed becomingly, and Velvet thought that, next to her mother, she was the most beautiful woman she had ever seen. Tall, slender, and full-bosomed, Cat Leslie had fair skin like Velvet's, leaf-green eyes, and dark, honey-colored hair. Her face was truly heart-shaped, with a stubborn little chin. She was dressed in doeskin riding breeches, a creamy, open-necked silk shirt, and a leather jerkin with silver-rimmed horn buttons. Her boots came to her knees, and her long, heavy hair fell about her shoulders.

"It's not safe for us to remain outside the castle walls, Francis," reminded the earl's bastard brother, Hercules Stewart.

Bothwell nodded and, turning his horse, led them safely into *Hermitage Castle*. As they dismounted, he said, "Cat, take Lady Gordon to the apartments ye prepared for her. She looks fair worn."

"I am," Velvet admitted. "It's been a long time since I've ridden like this."

"Almost three years?" he ventured.

For a moment Velvet thought, and then another smile lit her features. "Aye, Francis, 'tis almost three years, isn't it?"

He chuckled. "Ye're a lot more docile now than ye were then, lass."

"I have but to regain my strength, my lord," Velvet answered mischievously, realizing as she spoke that she was suddenly feeling better than she had in weeks.

Cat Leslie slipped her arm through Velvet's. "Come, Lady Gordon, I will wager that ye want a bath, and if I don't get the water brought now, ye'll be out of luck, for 'twill soon be time for dinner."

The two women departed, and Francis ushered his cousin Alex into the Great Hall, signaling a servant as they went to bring them wine. When he had settled his guest comfortably, Bothwell said, "Ye take a great risk coming to *Hermitage*, Alex. I am put to the horn and outlawed. If our cousin Jamie should learn of your visit, it could go hard wi' ye."

"I must risk it, Francis. Velvet was simply not strong enough to go any farther today. Actually, I should like to bide wi' ye for a few days before going on north."

"Will ye stop in Edinburgh?"

"I must."

"Tell Jamie then that ye were here and why ye came. Then no one, Maitland in particular, can accuse ye of duplicity. He means to bring all the earls down, Alex. He begins wi' me, but beware, for I suspect he will turn on Huntley next. He is an ambitious man, Master Maitland. If he can break the power of the earls, then he can rule James himself without interference."

"Is it true what I heard as I came south? That James stopped Lady Leslie's divorce from Glenkirk?"

"Aye! The bastard! He forced her to his bed, and when she finally fled him she came to me. I have loved her for some time now, but she knew it not until she sought refuge wi' me. The queen had managed to keep James from stopping the divorce, to hold him off until Maitland found out and told him that Cat was wi' me. The queen, of course, has no idea that her lord and king desires Cat. She would be most hurt if she knew, and Cat loves the queen, which Jamie well knows."

"What will happen to ye, Francis?"

"I know not, Alex, but perhaps someday I shall seek refuge at *Dun Broc.*" He smiled. "Will ye gie it me?"

"Aye!"

The servant arrived with the wine, and the two men stood by one of the large fireplaces drinking together, while in another part of the castle Cat had brought Velvet to a comfortable, airy apartment.

Pansy and Dugald were already there, and, seeing them, Cat said, "I will give instructions to have a bath brought to ye, Lady Gordon. I shall see ye at dinner."

"Please, won't you call me Velvet?"

"If ye will call me Cat," came the other woman's reply, and then she was gone.

"Isn't she beautiful?" Velvet said to Pansy.

"She's caused a great scandal here in Scotland, Dugald says. She ran away from her husband to be with Lord Bothwell!" Pansy told her mistress.

"I can understand a woman falling in love with Francis," said Velvet. "He's devilishly attractive, but 'tis not just his looks."

"Aye," agreed Pansy. "He's got a way about him. They say there ain't a woman alive who can resist him."

"Fine talk for a couple of seemingly respectable married women," grumbled Dugald, and Velvet and Pansy giggled. "Laugh if ye will, but 'tis said the Earl of Bothwell is a warlock, a wizard."

"He can cast a spell on me anytime." Pansy laughed.

"Hush yer mouth, woman, or I'll take a stick to ye!" threatened her husband. "Such talk, and from my own wife!"

"Lay a hand on me, Dugald Geddes, and I'll turn right around and go home to England—and I'll take me son with me, too!" Pansy snapped at her spouse. "I birthed him without you, and I've raised him for two years without you."

"Now, lassie," wheedled Dugald, "'tis just jealous I am, hearing ye talk about Lord Bothwell. I dinna mean it."

Pansy sniffed, but said nothing more, and Velvet hid a smile. Her tiring woman certainly had the upper hand where her new husband was concerned. Dugald adored his wife and son, and Pansy knew it and used her advantage to great effect.

Within a few minutes the oaken tub was set up before the fireplace in the bedchamber, and a line of kilted Borderers brought buckets and buckets of hot water to fill it fully. Velvet bathed gratefully, hearing Alex come in and, attended by Dugald, bathe as well in the outer chamber before its fireplace. He entered the bedchamber, a towel wrapped around his loins, before she had climbed from her own tub. Pansy blushed, and he chuckled.

"Run along, lass, and see to yer bairn, who I've heard is wailing for both his mam and his supper. I'll attend yer mistress until ye return." He gently shooed Pansy from the room, closing the door behind her. Then taking the large towel that had been warmed on its rack before the fire, he opened it out and, holding it up, said, "Come on, Velvet, and let me dry ye. Ye'll get a chill."

She rose and stepped from the tub into his arms, which closed about her, enfolding her in the warmed bath sheet. For a moment they both stood very still, and then Alex began to rub her down briskly. She knew that he wanted to kiss her, and had he done so she would not have minded. Yet he kept his promise not to force her.

When he dried her, he threw the towel aside and, picking her up, walked over to the bed where he tucked her beneath the sheets. "'Tis several hours before dinner, Velvet. Rest while ye can. We are going to stay several days here at *Hermitage* before we move on to Edinburgh."

"Are we going to court, my lord?"

"Nay, but I must pay my respects to Jamie. We may not even stay overnight before pushing on to *Dun Broc*."

"Good," she said. "I don't want to go to court, Alex. I want to get to *Dun Broc*. I grow more and more anxious to see my new home. I remember you once told me that the castle stood on cliffs above the glen; that it soared with the eagles! I have never forgotten that. You made it sound so beautiful."

"It is beautiful, Velvet, and ye will see it first at the prettiest time of the year to my mind. The birches will make the mountainside appear to be covered in molten gold, and the mountain ash and rowan trees will be heavy with their red and orange berries. Ye will be happy there, Velvet, I promise ye."

She took his hand in hers, and, raising it to her lips, she gently kissed it. He looked startled, and she smiled. "'Tis just my way of thanking you, Alex, for your kindness and your patience." Then she closed her green eyes and seemed to fall asleep, yet she did not release his hand.

Gingerly he shifted himself onto the bed next to her, but lay on the outside of the coverlet. With a sigh Velvet put her auburn head upon his shoulder. He did not sleep. Indeed he lay by her side, awake, his mind boiling with a thousand thoughts. In the few days that they had been together again he had come to realize once and for all that he loved her. It pained him yet that she had given herself to another man, but he understood it even as he understood her difficulty in resuming their full married relationship. In her mind Akbar was yet her husband, and he the interloper. He wasn't sure how to overcome such a hurdle, but then he realized it was Velvet's battle to fight, and not his. She must be clear in her mind. He was ready. He understood how hard it must be for her.

Still, it was uncomfortable for him to face the plain fact that she had only lived with him as his wife for three months whereas she had lived as Akbar's wife for sixteen months. God's bones! Could she ever love him again? He found himself silently praying that she could.

The fine dinner that was served at the Earl of Bothwell's board that night caused his cousin to remark, "For a condemned man, Francis, ye eat well."

"Ye know my love of good living, Alex," came Bothwell's laughing reply.

"Aye," said Cat Leslie, "I worried myself sick when he was imprisoned in Edinburgh Castle, only to learn that he was living better than the castle warden himself, the rogue!"

One of the men in the hall now took up his pipe and began to play while several others raised their voices in song. Alex and Lady Leslie began to explore their degree of kinship, for his mother had been a Leslie. Bothwell stood up, pulling Velvet with him.

"Come and walk about the hall wi' me, lass," he said, seeing her beginning to grow sad from the music, an ancient Border tune that dealt with unrequited love. He led her away from the high board and slowly moved down the room, her hand tucked securely in his arm. "I will listen, Velvet lass, if ye want to talk," he said quietly.

"There is little to say, Francis. I have come home to Alex."

"Yet yer heart isna wi' him. Why?"

"Oh, Francis, I am so confused! I believed him dead. I loved again, but then I learned he was not dead and I had to come home. I love Alex even now, but I cannot, it seems, stop loving Akbar. To give myself to another man when I was a widow is far different than the position in which I now find myself. I want to begin anew with Alex. I must! Yet I cannot stop thinking of Akbar, of India, of. . . ." She stopped, looking stricken when he finished the sentence for her.

"Yer bairn."

"Oh, God," she whispered. "How did you know?" Her eyes were filled with tears.

"It is the only thing that could possibly bind ye so tightly to another man, Velvet."

"Alex must not know! It would hurt him so to learn that I had given another man a child, and yet not borne him one."

"Then gie him one, Velvet." Stopping, he drew her into a little alcove, and, taking out a silk handkerchief from his doublet, he gently wiped her tears away. "Did the bairn die?"

"Nay. She is in India with her father. He would not let me take her. He said she was all he had left of our love. I didn't want to leave her, Francis! She wasn't even a year old, my Yasaman!" Then she began to weep.

"Velvet!" The urgency in his voice penetrated her sorrow. "Velvet lass, ye mustna grieve so. Alex will see yer face and know that something is wrong. What will ye tell him?" Frantically he mopped her cheeks.

In the midst of her grief Velvet suddenly found humor. "I could tell him you spurned my overtures, Francis," she said, starting to giggle through her tears.

He grinned at her, both delighted and relieved. "Ye're a bad lass!" he teased her, and Velvet began to laugh. Pleased, he stuffed the dampened silk back into his doublet, and then he turned serious once again. "Yer secret is safe wi' me, Velvet, but heed my advice and get yerself with bairn as soon as possible. Ye'll nae forget the other, but ye'll be so busy with the new bairn ye'll nae have time for too much remembering."

"Alex has been so very patient, Francis. He has promised not to force me, and he has kept that promise."

"Are ye telling me, lass, that ye've nae made love since yer reunion? Christ, Velvet! Ye'll nae get yerself wi' a bairn that way!"

"I couldn't," she quavered, her lower lip beginning to quiver again.

"Ye damn well can, and tonight ye will! The longer ye wait, the worse it will be for ye, and my poor cousin has been patient long enough!"

"He consoled himself quite nicely while I was away!" snapped Velvet.

"So did ye!" Bothwell shot back.

"I did, didn't I?" Velvet considered. "Dear God, Francis, I've been wallowing so much in my grief over Yasaman that I've never stopped to consider that life goes on. Alex and I have chosen to remain together after all our difficulties. No one forced us. Oh, Francis! I have been so unfair to him, haven't I?"

"Nay, Velvet, ye haven't been unfair to Alex. Ye simply needed time to come to terms wi' yerself. Now, I think, ye have."

"Thanks to you, my lord. If I have a son, one of his names will be Francis!"

"God's nightshirt, lass, dinna go sentimental on me now! Ye know I can't abide milk-and-water lasses!"

She flung her arms about him and kissed him full on the mouth, much to Bothwell's surprise. It was a lovely kiss, and her mouth tasted of sweet wine. Standing back, she looked up at him and said boldly, "Take me back to my husband, my lord. 'Tis time for us to retire for the night."

Bothwell grinned. "I suspect Alex will never know the great debt he owes me, Velvet." Then he escorted her from the alcove back through the Great Hall to the high board where Cat and Alex were still talking, never having really missed them.

"I shall not tell him if you don't, Francis," she replied pertly, and he grinned at her again, winking conspiratorily.

The piper was now playing a livelier tune, and some of Lord Bothwell's men were dancing while others had begun to dice, kneeling upon the floor by one of the fireplaces. Cat now joined them, to Alex's surprise, but Francis only smiled.

"She's a great favorite wi' my men. They would die for her as would I," he said.

"Somehow it will resolve itself happily for you both, I know it," Velvet soothed him. Then she turned to Alex and said, "I am tired, my lord. Shall we retire now, or would you prefer to remain and dice for a bit?"

"I'll stay for a while, sweetheart," he replied, and she curtsied and left him.

Alex stayed only for a few minutes with his cousin drinking another cup of heady wine. Then the Border lord, claiming fatigue, took Cat off, and there was no excuse for him to remain. It would hardly do for the world to see him but newly reunited with his wife and avoiding their bed.

Dugald had waited for his master and quickly aided him to undress, being eager to gain his own bed and Pansy's company. Alex chased his serving man off when he had disrobed and, having completed his ablutions, tiptoed into the bedchamber. A fire burned low in the large fireplace, and the room was toasty warm. Slipping quietly into the big bed in an attempt not to disturb her, Alex was very startled when Velvet, fragrant, warm, and quite naked, slipped into his arms with a purr.

He was stunned. "Ye're not wearing a night rail," he gasped.

"Nay, Alex, I'm not," she teased him.

Instinctively his arms tightened about her. Jesu, he thought, her skin is so damned soft and smooth. "Velvet . . . " His voice was slightly strangled as he sought to keep himself under control.

"Yes, Alex?" Her tone was bland and innocent.

"What is it ye want of me, Velvet? For God's sake, lass, I'm only human!"

"What do I want of you?" She began to laugh softly. "Dear God, Alex, I should think that would be obvious. I want you to make love to me. Here. Now. Tonight, my darling."

She snuggled closer to him, pressing her round breasts against his furred chest, leaning over to nibble on his ear, and he groaned. She was driving him absolutely mad, and he suspected she knew it. What had happened to change her in these few short hours?

"You took my virginity in this castle almost three years ago, my darling. We began our marriage here. I want to begin it again in this place, Alex. Can you understand that?"

He hadn't suspected this sentimental side of her, but he didn't care any longer. All that mattered was that his beautiful wife, his wife from whom he had been parted for so long, was offering herself to him, and he wanted her. Pulling her hard against him, he found her mouth and kissed her with all the hunger that had been building up in him for the last two and a half years. He kissed her until she was breathless, and her mouth was bruised with his ardor. In defense she parted her lips beneath his, and his tongue plunged almost violently into her mouth to love hers with a fierce abandon.

Their tongues were like two burning silk banners that twined and intertwined over and over again.

Rolling her beneath him, he caught her face between his hands. "Look at me, Velvet!" She slowly opened her eyes and gazed directly at him. "I love ye, lass! Do ye understand that? I love ye!"

"I never stopped loving you, Alex," she answered.

The unsaid words lay between them, however: *I never stopped loving you, Alex, but I loved another also*. Still, she was trying, and in time he hoped he could erase the memory of Akbar from her heart and soul, if not her mind. "Ah, lass," he murmured, caressing her cheek with the back of his fingers while his other hand smoothed her forehead. Then his mouth descended on hers again, kissing her tenderly this time, re-learning her sweet lips. He trailed a line of kisses down her neck, lingering in the hollow of her throat where he could feel the pulse leaping beneath his lips. His slender fingers slipped up to tangle in her soft hair, while the finger of his other hand turned her face to him.

Gently he nipped her little chin with his teeth, then kissed the corners of her mouth. Velvet pushed her tongue forward to lick at him, and, delighted, his own tongue gave battle. They teased and played thusly for some minutes, enjoying the game and learning to relax once more with each other. Finally he nuzzled one of her ears, running his tongue around it.

"Ye're absolutely delicious, lass," he murmured with hot breath in her ear. Then one of his hands captured a breast, and, turning himself, he sought the other breast with his mouth. While the first hand kneaded and fondled, his mouth began a most delightful torture of the second breast. He sucked softly at the nipple, but gradually he began to draw harder upon it, then he nibbled tenderly, sending little darts of desire through her.

She shifted beneath him almost skittishly. It had been so long since she had been loved. For a moment she felt disloyal, but to whom? To Akbar who she was bound to by an Eastern marriage and a child, or to Alex who was her only husband before the God of her own faith? It was too confusing a puzzle to struggle with, she thought. She must concentrate on the here and now, not on what had been.

Wiggling away from him, she said, "I want to love you, my darling."

"Ye are loving me, Velvet," was his reply, but she laughed.

"Nay, my lord. *You* are loving me." She pushed him back against the down pillows. "Now, I shall love you!"

Before he realized what she was about, Velvet turned herself about, and, grasping the half-hard shaft of his manhood in one hand, she bent her head and took him in her mouth, while her other hand sweetly caressed the pouch of his sex. For a moment Alex was frozen in shock. He had never taught her such a thing! Where had she learned it? The next emotion to slam into him was a wave of raging jealousy. *Akbar!* She had learned this from him! She had taken him between her honeyed lips and driven him to madness as she was surely going to drive him.

"Jesu!" The word burst from his throat, and his anger dissolved as the enjoyment she was giving him mounted with each moment that passed. Her tongue licked his full length, teasing the ruby knob of him. His hand reached down to touch her head, to encourage her further, and she sucked strongly upon him while shafts of pleasure plunged into his brain and body like sharp knives, and his manhood hardened like marble.

When he could bear no more, for he was close to bursting with desire, he commanded her through gritted teeth, "Enough, lass! 'Tis time for turnabout." Then pulling her up, he forced her back against the pillows, his head moving down between her legs. He had never before tasted of her, but he realized that if she knew how to use a man as she had just used him, then Akbar had also introduced her to similar delights. He found the little pearl of her womanhood, and, reaching out with his tongue, he began to love it tenderly and was pleased to hear a soft cry of rapture escape from between her lovely lips. "Does that please ye, lass?" he whispered, and she cried "Aye!" but no more. His tongue worked the silky, pink flesh until she was moaning with desire.

It was too sweet, she thought, as her passion began to build. The feathery touches of his tongue, his mouth, against that greatest secret of her sex was driving her farther than she had ever been driven before. She didn't think she could bear much more of his loving, and yet she didn't think she could bear it if he stopped. She would lose her sanity shortly, but she didn't care. Briefly she remembered back to the beginning of their marriage. He had loved her sweetly and tenderly then, but never as he was loving her now. His own passion had such an incredible intensity that for a moment she feared it would incinerate them both.

Then he lifted his head and, with a soft laugh, pulled himself up and over her. Taking his pulsing shaft in his hand, he positioned it and then plunged into her almost violently. With another cry Velvet wrapped her legs about his torso, her arms about his neck, and together they moved back and forth, dancing to love's rhythm.

"I've waited so long, lass, to be inside of ye again," he groaned in his passion.

"Oh, my darling," she sobbed as all the memories of their togetherness flooded her soul, "love me well! You're so big, my wild Highland lord. How you fill me! Don't stop loving me, Alex! Don't stop!"

He didn't, and for several long, sweet minutes they lay locked in that most intimate of conjugal embraces. Then, unable to control themselves any longer, they attained paradise together as he exploded within her, his manhood bursting forth furiously to flood her with his creamy essence. "Ah, Velvet lass! Ah, sweet one!" He almost sobbed the words.

He had collapsed against her breasts, and she held him tenderly there as she floated down from her own heaven. Would it always be this intense with him, or was it but the excitement of their reunion? she wondered to herself. Her fingers slipped through his fine, dark hair, caressing him, loving him, and he felt her touch through his own daze.

Raising his head, he gazed at her, and Velvet suddenly felt warm and safe again. Smiling back, she gently teased him,

"And just what are you looking so pleased about, my lord husband?"

"What kind of a woman have I taken to wife?" he wondered musingly.

"A passionate one," she answered promptly, "and I shall not change, my darling."

"Christ, no! My God, Velvet, I never suspected yer depths! Ye intoxicate me, my love, and knowing yer passion now, I shall become the most jealous of husbands."

"I do not belong to you, Alex. I belong to myself, and you must remember that. I will never betray you, my love. I truly never have. But I will not be treated like a possession."

"Nay, Velvet, I have learned this night that ye're an equal. I may forget that from time to time, but ye will, I've not a doubt, remind me."

"Indeed, my wild Highland lord, I will!"

He chuckled and, lying back, tossed an arm about her. "Ye did not jest when ye said 'twas time to start our family, did ye, Velvet, but ye've fair worn me out. I will need to rest now for a little bit."

"Not yet," she said and, slipping from his embrace, arose. Going to the fireplace, she lifted a small kettle from the grate. Pouring water from the kettle into a silver basin by the hearth, she returned to the bed with it and several soft cloths. "In India a bout of passion is followed, my lord husband, by a careful cleansing so that when Eros's dart strikes again, the combatants are ready." Dipping one of the cloths in the basin, she wrung it out and began to wash his manhood. When she was satisfied, she bent and kissed it, sending a surprising flash of heat through him. "Now," she said softly, "you must do me," and she handed him the second cloth.

Bathing her sex as she stood before him was, he found, one of the most sensually stimulating things he had ever done. He found himself working slowly, carefully, going back over already traveled territory until she laughed softly, saying, "You will but arouse me again, Alex, and that is not at all the purpose of this exercise. Kiss me now, and then let us rest." Mesmerized, he obeyed her, kissing the puckered pink flesh, but unable to resist tweaking her once with his tongue, which caused her to shriek and jump away from him. Laughing, and content at having regained some measure of his self-esteem, he dropped the cloth and climbed back into their bed.

She slid into his arms, warm and sweet, and lay her head against his shoulder. Soon he heard her soft, even breathing and knew that she had fallen asleep. He, however, lay awake for some minutes. The girl he had married almost three years ago was so long gone that he could barely remember her. The woman who had replaced her was a delicious mystery that he suspected he would never quite solve, but in the ensuing years they had together he would enjoy seeking the pieces to the puzzle Velvet had become. Gradually Alex drifted into sleep himself.

Velvet awoke to kisses being lightly pressed over her torso. With a murmur of contentment, she stretched, saying, "Don't stop, my darling. 'Tis too delicious!"

He chuckled. "Ye've turned into a magnificent wanton, my young wife. Dinna change!" Then he was kissing her lips, his tongue pushing into the fragrant cave of her mouth to re-explore. Challenging his invasion, she played a game of hide-and-seek with his tongue. His passion was slow to rouse this time, the edge having been taken off of it by their last love bout. Sitting up, the plump pillows behind his back, he placed her between his open legs and began to learn once more the curves and lines of her body.

The lushness of her delighted him. Her lovely round breasts fit perfectly into his big hands; her waist curved in so deeply that he could span it with his two hands; her torso was long and smooth. Her hips flared beneath his seeking fingers, and she murmured again signifying her pleasure at his touch. She drew her legs up, allowing him to smooth his hands up her thighs, down her calves. Then he held her in a tight embrace against his chest. His lips pushed her thick auburn hair aside, finding the soft nape of her neck upon which he placed several warm kisses.

"Ye're the most beautiful woman I've ever known," he whispered against her ear.

She smiled in the firelight, but he could not see her. "Is your little mistress, Alanna Wythe, not fair, my lord?" she asked wickedly.

"Alanna hasn't been my mistress in months, Velvet."

"Yet she resides at *Dun Broc*, I am told."

"I gave her the choice of returning to England or of remaining in my village of Broc Ailien with her daughter."

"Her daughter?" Velvet stiffened.

"She claims the child is mine, and in all probability it is," he replied, dreading each word as he spoke it, but it was better that she know it now before they reached *Dun Broc*. Alanna was still enormously put out by her removal from the castle and would cause mischief given the chance.

"How old is the child?" demanded Velvet.

"A year or so," he answered.

She almost laughed at the irony of it. She had been forced to relinquish her precious daughter because it was necessary that she resume her role as a good Christian wife. Her husband's whore, however, was allowed to keep her bastard, and none thought the worse of her for it. Alanna Wythe might raise her daughter, but she, Velvet, the Countess of BrocCairn, must not even admit to Yasaman's birth for fear of offending her husband and their peers. For a moment Velvet thought her heart would break all over again with the unfairness of it, but, taking a deep breath, she said, "I'd as lief the girl were back in England, Alex. Is there no way you can make her go?"

"I'll try, sweetheart," he promised, relieved that she was not going to cause a scene, "but Alanna can be stubborn, and I do feel a responsibility for little Sybilla." He hugged her tightly. "Dammit, Velvet, I don't want to talk about this now! I want to make love to ye again, lass. It's driving me wild wi' desire being wi' ye like this!"

And indeed she could feel him burgeoning and swelling, pressing against her back. She took a deep breath so that her breasts swelled within his hands and moved provocatively against him, tipping her head back so that he could look into her face. "Do you know what I want, Alex?" she asked him. When he shook his head, she said, "Once you said that I reminded you of a kitten, but the kitten has grown into a sleek cat, and like a cat I enjoy being stroked. Stroke me, Alex. Stroke your wee cat," and she slipped from his grasp to lay upon her belly.

She was a most delicious temptation, lying upon her stomach, propped up on her elbows, her round breasts hanging like ripe apples, her adorable bottom thrust up like twin hillocks. He feasted his eyes upon her in the waning firelight that cast golden shadows over her luscious form. Reaching out, he pushed her hair aside and massaged her neck gently before sweeping down the long length of her back to fondle her buttocks. He found the springy flesh of her bottom almost as exciting as he found her delightful breasts.

Velvet lay flat now, stretching her arms and legs out. Unable to resist, he lay atop her and began to tease her by licking at the side of her neck and blowing softly into her ear until she began to squirm slightly. Then he whispered, "Admit that ye are hot to fuck me, Velvet."

She laughed. "You're too impatient, Alex. I see that I shall have to teach you that half the pleasure is in the wanting, my darling! The truth is that you are hot to fuck me!"

He was astounded by her bold words, and she knew it.

"Do you really want that sweet child back, Alex? The one who fought constantly with you and lay passively during your lovemaking?"

He thought a minute and then, laughing, said, "Nay, sweetheart, I don't. She was sweet, but Jesu! I far prefer the hot wanton that ye've become in our bed. It still disturbs me that ye learned these things beneath another man's tutelage, yet I love ye."

"Always remember, Alex, that I believed Akbar was my second husband. I do not ask where you learned how to be a man, nor do I resent the women who taught you. Do not resent the man who has taught me, for he is now without me, and you will have all the benefits of his skill. Now, dammit, get off of me, my wild Highland husband, for you're crushing me beneath your great weight!"

He rolled off her, saying, "Then crush me beneath yours, lass!" She neatly straddled him, laughing softly down in his face. Reaching up, he began to tease her nipples, rubbing them softly until they began to thrust forward like little thorns. Watching her passion rise through his slitted amber eyes, he firmly pinched each nipple, sending little thrills throughout her so that she rubbed herself against him in a most erotic manner, her breath coming in shorter gasps.

"Now, my wanton wife," he said softly, "I shall teach ye that ye yet have things to learn, things that ye will learn from me, and no other man. Lean back, Velvet, and brace yerself upon yer arms." When she had obeyed him, he lifted his heavy and hardened loveshaft and began to rub it against her throbbing little jewel.

Velvet whimpered deep in her throat as tiny flames of pure desire began to touch her. This was a most delicious torture. She quivered slightly as she felt him caressing her softly, sensually, but when she attempted to shift herself so that he might enter her body, he reached out and prevented her.

"Nay, lass. Not yet. I will say when this time."

"I . . . I can bear no more, Alex." Her voice was beginning to quaver.

"Aye, lass, ye can bear more, and ye will, or in the end I shall not gie ye that hot sweetness ye crave. Did ye not tell me that the wanting was a part of the lovemaking?" Then he began again to tease her.

Velvet thought that she would die with the pleasure that his touch evoked. Looking down, she saw the ruby head of his shaft, almost glowing with its passion, stroking at the fountain of her very desire, which was now pearly with her lovejuices. She felt poised upon a precipice, and each touch brought her nearer to the brink. Finally she could bear it no longer, and with a little cry she slipped over the edge to whirl away into pure pleasure.

"That's it, lass," she heard him encourage her.

When her head cleared, he was still playing with her, and she could feel her hunger beginning to rise once more. "Oh, Alex," she sobbed.

"Stop trying to gain control, Velvet," he said. "Let it happen, lass. Let me pleasure ye for ye'll soon pleasure me."

It was too much this time, and she fell forward, but he caught her in his embrace. Turning her onto her back, he spread her wide to him and drove into her throbbing, honeyed sheath. Her scream of satisfaction almost caused him to lose his careful control, but he held fast and began to pump into her with long, slow strokes of his manhood.

"Ah, Alex," she cried, "'tis sweet! 'Tis so sweet, my darling!" Her nails raked a path down his straining back.

His rhythm increased, and he towered above her, thrusting fiercely within her eager body. He felt all-powerful! She inspired him to the heights of passion such as he had never attained before, and she kept pace with him, thrusting her buttocks up to meet his every downward stroke. Wrapping her legs about him as she had done earlier, she smoothed her hands down his back, cupping his tight buttocks within her warm hands, sending hot thrills of delight through him.

"Christ, Velvet!" He groaned as he moved from sanity to total mindlessness.

"That's it, my wild Highland lord," she breathed in his ear, "love me! Love me well!"

Neither of them remembered the ending to this interlude, for Velvet, climbing passion's peak, found herself falling away into a state of unconsciousness, so great was her lust for her husband. As for Alex, he could not remember a great deal more than the fact that, unable to bear any more of the delicious combat between them, his throbbing body had dissolved into hers, and he had rolled away from her in his last conscious moment.

Velvet awoke, chilled and exhausted. The gray light of early dawn was beginning to creep into the room. Beside her, Alex was sprawled, his long legs and arms akimbo. Her eyes went to his sex, and she smiled to herself. One of God's great mysteries surely had to do with a man's cock. It was hard to believe that the cupid's bow now between her husband's legs was the mighty lance that twice the night before had pierced her so sweetly.

Slipping from the bed, she knelt by the fireplace and, finding several hot coals left there, fed them little pieces of kindling until she regained a small flame, which she then encouraged into a decent fire. There was still a half kettle of water left, and this she heated while emptying the cold basin out the window. Refilling the silver basin with the now warmed water, she took a fresh cloth and began to bathe herself.

"I thought that was my duty," Alex said sleepily, and with a smile Velvet brought the basin to the bedside and handed him the cloth.

"'Tis a nice way to wake up, lass," he teased her as he worked.

She grinned down at him. "I don't remember the end of it at all last night, Alex, do you?"

He had finished, and while she took up the cloth to bathe him, he shook his head ruefully. "Nay, lass, I dinna remember anything except the fact that ye're the most delicious piece of goods a man ever held in his arms. If I wanted to tell the world about yer perfection as a bedmate, I couldn't find the proper words, for I dinna think they exist."

"Why, Alex," she said, coloring becomingly, "that is most gallant." Finished with her task, she put the basin with its cloths aside and climbed into bed with him. "I'm cold," she complained.

He wrapped his arms about her, and she snuggled contentedly next to him. "Dinna get too comfortable, lass," he cautioned her. "I've promised to go fishing wi' Bothwell, and 'tis almost dawn."

"You'll need better bait than this," she said, tweaking his manhood mischievously. "What happened to that fine, randy fellow who entertained me so well last night?"

"Ye've worn him out, Velvet lass, but dinna fear, for he'll be calling upon ye again quite soon." Then he chuckled.

"Ye're a bold wench, Lady Gordon, and full of surprises, I'm learning. I think that living wi' ye isna going to be either quiet or dull."

"Never dull, Alex, my wild Highland lord! That much I can promise you," she said, and, leaning over, she bit his shoulder sharply.

"Little bitch!" he growled, smacking her bottom lightly. Then detaching her arms from about his neck, he arose from the bed and dressed himself while she lay watching him. Kissing her tenderly, he said, "Go back to sleep, my bonny wife. I'll bring ye home a fine salmon." Then he was gone out the door.

Velvet snuggled down beneath the coverlet, warm now and feeling better than she had in months. Bothwell had been absolutely right. It was time that she put the past behind her and rebuilt her life with Alex. She needed another child to love, not that she would ever either forget or stop mourning Yasaman. There was not a day that went by that she didn't wonder about her little daughter. Yasaman would be thirteen months old in a few days. Did she walk yet? Was she talking? For a moment Velvet felt the old sadness sweep over her. It was Rugaiya whom her baby would call mama. It was Rugaiya to whom Yasaman would entrust her childish confidences and run to when hurt. Velvet's eyes filled with tears for a moment, but then she brushed the moisture away. There was nothing she could do about Yasaman's loss. Yasaman was Akbar's child, too, and he had probably been right when he had said that she would face the stigma of bastardy in Europe, whereas there was no such taboo in India. How would Alex have reacted to Yasaman? Probably in the same way she had reacted to the news of Alanna Wythe's daughter. He wouldn't want her baby about any more than she wanted the Wythe woman and her child.

She and Alex had been successfully reunited last night. She intended to give of herself as generously while they were here, and in Edinburgh, too. By the time they reached *Dun Broc* she intended that her husband should be so totally enamored of her once more that Alanna Wythe would not, even with her bastard, be able to regain even the slightest bit of Alex's attention. It startled Velvet to realize that she was a jealous woman. She had never felt jealousy for either Jodh Bai or Rugaiya Begum with regard to Akbar, but then that had been an entirely different world. This was Scotland, and she'd throw the bitch off the walls at *Dun Broc* if Alanna Wythe ever came near her husband again. "Defend or Die," she remembered, was the motto of the Gordons of Broc-Cairn, and she was certainly becoming one of them quickly enough. With a chuckle, Velvet turned over and went back to sleep.

Alex stood next to his cousin, Francis, in a freezing, fast-running stream wondering what in hell had possessed him to agree to come fishing when he could be warm in bed with his wife. As if reading his thoughts, Bothwell chuckled and said, "She'll keep all the better for the waiting, Alex. Ye're looking a bit worn, however, this morning. Did ye nae sleep last night? I hope the bed was comfortable."

"Damn comfortable." He watched as his line drifted downstream, and then he said, "Does it bother ye that the king has known Cat, Francis?"

"Aye, but there's little I can do about it, Alex. She dinna want him, nor did she encourage him for all his lechery." Bothwell paused, then looked at his younger cousin. "'Tis Velvet we're really speaking of, Alex, isn't it? It bothers ye that she's known another man? For God's sake, lad, get a hold of yerself! Ye're lucky to have her back!"

"Yer Cat didna go willingly to the king, but Velvet went willingly to Akbar, Francis. Christ, I am glad to have her back, but I canna help think of her in another man's arms, doing to him the wonderful things she did to me last night that I certainly never taught her!"

"Did she do them well, Alex? These wonderful things?"

"God's bones, yes!" muttered the Earl of BrocCairn.

"Then be grateful to this Akbar, ye idiot. Besides, when ye begin to think about him, remember that Velvet believed herself a widow. She's too toothsome a morsel, yer wife, to remain alone and celibate should ye die, Alex. Best ye remember that and take care not to worry yerself into an early grave. If ye do, ye'll have to sit up in heaven and watch some other lucky man plow wi' yer mare!" At Alex's startled look, Bothwell punched him jovially and laughed.

"Ye're a bastard, Francis, but by God ye're right!" replied Alex, and then he chuckled, seeing the situation in a somewhat brighter light.

"Then, cousin, that's settled," said Bothwell. "Come now, and share wi' me the secrets yer wife brought back from the East. By God, I've got to know these 'wonderful things'!"

"Francis! I've got a bite!" shouted Alex, and in the stream a large salmon leaped at the end of his line. "Help me, cousin!"

"Merde!" swore Bothwell, but he reached for the net to aid his kinsman.

For several days Alex and Velvet partook of Bothwell's hospitality, the two men going off to fish early each morning; and one day Bothwell and Lady Leslie took both Gordons hunting. It was a peaceful time, the long, lazy days followed by equally long nights of incredible passion between Alex and Velvet. In the magical atmosphere of *Hermitage* so ripe and full with the love between Francis Stewart-Hepburn and Cat Leslie, Velvet and Alex found once more the love that had been just blossoming between them when they had been separated, and that love grew quickly with each day that passed.

Finally, they could stay no longer, for the trip to *Dun Broc* was yet a long one, and they knew that they must stop in Edinburgh to pay their respects to the king. Velvet had found in Cat Leslie a good friend and an admirable companion even though the Countess of Glenkirk was some eleven years her senior.

"Life is short, Velvet," Cat told her. "Take yer happiness, try to harm none, and let no man, even the one ye love, dominate ye. 'Tis my rule of life now."

"What will happen to you and Francis?" asked the worried Velvet, who now knew the entire story of their love wild and fair.

"'Twill work out, Velvet, I'm certain. I sense that I am meant to be wi' Bothwell through eternity." Then the Countess of Glenkirk kissed the young Countess of BrocCairn upon the cheek and, hugging her, bid her a safe journey.

Next it was Bothwell's turn, and he couldn't resist giving Velvet a kiss as he enfolded her into a bear hug of an embrace. "Take care of Alex, Velvet lass, but then from the smug look he's been wearing these last few days I suspect ye are doing so already."

She laughed wickedly, and as he lifted her to her saddle she gave him a saucy wink.

Bothwell whooped with laughter as well. "By God, Velvet, I think perhaps that Alex will have a hard time wi' ye in the years to come. I dinna know if I envy him or pity him."

"Time will tell, my lord," she said pertly, and then she grew serious. "Have a care, Francis, and if you should ever need our hospitality it is yours despite the king. You have my word on it, and I am mistress of *Dun Broc* now." Then she bent from her horse and kissed him on the mouth.

His bright blue eyes met hers for a long moment, and without words they understood one another. "Godspeed, lass!" he said. Then, saying farewell to Alex, he sent them off toward Edinburgh and their cousin, James Stewart.

The king knew of their imminent arrival. John Maitland's spies had brought word to the chancellor who had then carried it to James. The Earl of BrocCairn and his wife were visiting at *Hermitage*. James had gone into a rage, a rage that was fed to excess by Maitland. "I've warned Yer Majesty about the earls time and time again," he said mournfully. "I have been suspicious of the Gordons for some time now, Huntley in particular, and BrocCairn *is* related to Bothwell. Who knows what they plot together."

"They are so arrogant," complained the king bitterly. "They hounded my mother, my grandfather, my great-grandfather. There hasna been one James Stewart who has not been interfered with by them. They're always sowing rebellion when things dinna suit them! Well, Maitland, I'll hae no more of it, d'ye hear me? I'll hae no more of it!"

"Ye hae but to command me, Yer Majesty," Maitland replied smoothly. "Ye know that ye can trust me to do what is best for ye, for Scotland."

"Arrest BrocCairn when he arrives in Edinburgh!" commanded the king.

"Jamie! You cannot do such a thing," the queen interjected. "You have no reason to arrest Alexander Gordon. What has he done that has you so angered?"

"He has been wi' Bothwell this last week, Annie. No loyal Scotsman should be associated wi' Francis any longer. Have I not outlawed him?"

"Jamie, Lord Gordon returns from England with his wife who you know was lost to him for over two years. The girl has had a long and exhausting journey. I imagine Lord Gordon but stopped so that his wife might rest. It is possible, isn't it?"

James liked his queen. Anne of Denmark was blond, pretty, and basically feather-headed, and she had actually nothing in common with her husband but a passion for hunting. She did, however, have a strong streak of common sense, which on occasion she exercised. She also had, like almost every woman at the Stewart court, fallen under the spell of Francis Stewart-Hepburn and defended him, much to Maitland's annoyance.

Because James liked his wife, he was often influenced by her in small matters. "The Countess of BrocCairn had plenty of time to rest at her mother's," he grumbled.

"Nay, Jamie, she didn't," the queen replied.

"Ye're singularly well informed, madame," said the chancellor archly.

"Aye, *Mas-ter* Maitland, I am," replied the queen quickly. "Lord Gordon informed me of of his circumstances in a message that was delivered to me even as he hurried south for his reunion with his bride. He did so because he wished me to know that he would be stopping in Edinburgh on his return to present his wife to me prior to their homecoming at his castle in the north. His wife had only just returned to England, so I doubt very much, *Mas-ter* Maitland, whether she had a great deal of time to rest. You have never been on a long voyage, but, as you will remember, I have. There is no doubt in my mind that the Countess of BrocCairn and her husband stopped at *Hermitage* so that she might recuperate." The queen turned to her husband. "Jamie, you must at least give Lord Gordon the chance to tell you that he stopped before you assume the worst of him. Neither he nor his father ever caused you difficulties, did they?"

"Nay," the king admitted grudgingly.

"There, you see!" the queen said, smiling at him winningly. She put her head against his shoulder and looked up at him with her blue eyes. "Now promise me, Jamie, that you'll not arrest Lord Gordon?" Her rosebud mouth was inches from his, and he thought of how nice she had been to him last night.

Sliding an arm about her waist, he said, "Aye, Annie, I'll promise, but if he gies me no explanation, then I'll have to assume the worst."

"I suspect the worst is that he might fear to tell you because you're so put out with Francis right now, though why I will never understand," the queen replied.

"Lord Bothwell has flaunted the king's authority by escaping from prison where the king placed him," said Maitland, seeking to extricate James before he could give himself away.

"A lot of faradiddle over nothing," said Anne, and then she smiled warmly at her husband. "You'll come to see me tonight, Jamie?"

"Aye, sweetheart." He smiled back at her, giving her a quick kiss, then loosing his hold upon her.

The queen curtsied prettily to the king and then left the room. "Until tonight, sir," she said as she went.

"Yer Majesty must not allow the queen to wheedle ye," the chancellor began, but he was cut short by James.

"She is right, Maitland. Let us see what Lord Gordon has to say for himself. I dinna want to act rashly, for Annie is correct. Neither Alex nor his father, nor any of their family, has ever given me any difficulties. I canna afford to make enemies."

"Of course not, sire," said Maitland sourly, forced to let the matter rest.

Two days later, the Earl and Countess of BrocCairn arrived from the Border country and went directly to the town house of George Gordon, the Earl of Huntley, the most powerful of all the Gordons and the head of the clan. They planned to stay but one night as both were anxious to reach *Dun Broc.* Since the Earl of Huntley was not in residence at the time, there was plenty of room for all of Alex's retainers. A message saying that the Earl of BrocCairn and his wife wished to pay their respects was sent immediately to the king. It was quickly answered, and they hurried off to *Holyrood Palace.*

They had taken the time to bathe and change, and Alex was enormously proud of his beautiful wife. The young Countess of BrocCairn was attired in a gown of rich, dark brown velvet. The dress had a very low square neckline, and with it she wore a starched cream-colored, fanshaped lace neck whisk. The sleeves of her gown were full to the elbow but fit the arm tightly below it, and the skirt was a pleasing bell shape. About her neck Velvet wore a necklace of red Irish gold from which hung a large, oval-shaped, golden-brown topaz surrounded by yellow diamonds. Her hair was parted in the center and caught in a caul of thin gold threads, drawn back over her ears so that her red gold necklace and topaz earbobs might be shown to their best advantage. As the day was warm, she wore neither hat nor cloak, but she did have delicate, pearl-embroidered French kid gloves of a beige color to protect her hands when she rode and to hide her rings from the cutpurses. It was altogether a simple but rich look and Alex knew that she would once again win over the king, and most assuredly the little queen.

Alex had debated as to whether or not he should tell James of their visit to *Hermitage*, but when he came face to face with his sire, he immediately realized from the king's suspicious attitude that James knew of it already and was but waiting for Alex to say something. Before he could, however, Velvet spoke up ingenuously.

"We saw Francis at *Hermitage*, Your Majesty. Do you remember the first time that we met, when Alex and I had just been married at *Hermitage*, and you were forced to return me to England because Alex had stolen me away from the queen's court?"

James Stewart was forced to smile. "Aye, Lady Gordon," he said, "and if I remember correctly ye were refusing to acknowledge yer marriage because it had not been performed by a priest of the old kirk. Do ye now admit to being married to this very disobedient earl of mine?"

"Aye, sire, for when we returned to England we were married twice more. But, sire, if I may ask a question of you?"

"Aye, madame?" James replied.

"Why do you call Alex disobedient? He is your most loyal servant."

"That, Lady Gordon, is a matter of opinion. Yer husband knows full well that Francis has been outlawed, and would even now be languishing in prison were we able to catch him. Yet knowing this, Lord Gordon still stopped at *Hermitage*. I should like an explanation of yer behavior, Alex!"

"There is nothing complicated about it, Jamie," Alex drawled, his very tone making the king feel foolish. "Velvet is but newly returned from India. It was a long voyage, but nonetheless her mother notified me immediately upon her return, and I hurried south to be reunited with my wife. Since we didna wish to stay in England under her entire family's watchful eye, we left almost immediately for Scotland. Velvet isna used to riding cross-country after two years away, and by the time we had passed over the border she was exhausted. Ye know the quality of inns in the Border, Jamie. They're full of petty thieves and whores. I couldna take my wife to one of them. There was no choice but to stop at *Hermitage*. I made no secret of my visit, nor did Francis. Had he wanted to hide it, then yer spies wouldna hae already brought ye word that we were there. Francis sends ye his most loyal greetings and says he wishes to make peace wi' ye."

"Francis can go to hell!" snapped the king. "He already has my terms for peace between us, but he willna comply. He has but to gie me back what is mine." Then the king, realizing that his wife was in the room, hurried on to say, "I'll forgive ye, Alex, for I dinna really believe ye would join any rebellion. Come now and present yer wife to the queen."

Alex hid a smile, for he had caught the king's little slip although the queen apparently had not. "As always, Jamie, yer graciousness is welcome." Then he turned his head to the queen, and, bowing, he lifted her hand to his lips. "Madame, it is good to see ye again. Ye're fairer than ever."

The queen dimpled prettily. "'Tis good to see you, Lord Gordon. Is this your bride then?"

"Aye, madame. May I present ye my wife, Velvet, the Countess of BrocCairn."

Velvet curtsied low to the queen, but it was the king's eyes that plunged to her décolletage, something that Alex did not miss.

"Welcome to Scotland at long last, Lady Gordon," said the queen.

"Thank you, madame. I am glad to have finally come home," said Velvet.

"Will you be staying in Edinburgh long?" asked Queen Anne.

"Nay, madame. I am not yet up to following the court. My voyage was of almost six months' duration, and although Alex and I have been married almost three years I have never seen *Dun Broc*. It is past time that I settled down to the business of being a wife and a mother."

"Yes," agreed the queen. "'Tis for that purpose God created women."

Before Velvet could reply, the king was raising her from her curtsy and saying, "Surely ye needn't continue yer journey so soon, Lady Gordon? Would not the gaiety of court gie ye pleasure?" He could scarcely take his eyes off her. How young she was, thought James. Young and tender and undoubtedly quite delicious. She had green eyes like his Cat's, not the same leaf-green, but more of a green-gold; and he would wager that her unbound hair fell to her hips in auburn waves as did Cat's dark gold locks.

Velvet had seen the king's look and was somewhat startled, yet her voice when she answered him was calm and friendly. "Your Majesty is so kind, just as I remembered you, but please understand that for all the time I was away I longed for *Dun Broc* and my husband." She sighed deeply. "Surely you will not forbid me my home when we are so very close? We will visit the court eventually, I promise Your Majesty, but for now I really do want to go home." She smiled at him sweetly, and James could not help but acquiesce.

"Very well, Lady Gordon," he said, "we shall let ye go this time, but the next time I shall not take a nay from ye." How prettily she pleaded with him, he thought. He would like to have her under him pleading for his love.

Later as they rode back to the Gordon town house in the Highgate, Alex complimented his wife on her behavior. "Yer performance, lass, was magnificent."

Velvet frowned. "Did you see how he looked down my dress, Alex? Poor Cat! The man is a terrible lech for all his pious mouthings. I wonder if the queen knows."

"If she does she'll say naught, for I believe she is basically intelligent for all her feather-headed ways. She's queen of Scotland, come what may, and Jamie is fond of her. So she'll have his bairns, and as long as he treats her wi' kindness and respect she'll tolerate his behavior provided it causes no scandal or embarrassment to her or the crown."

"I should not be as tolerant," muttered Velvet ominously.

Alex heard her words and knew that whether she had meant them as a warning or not, they were a warning nonetheless. He should, he thought, not have given Alanna Wythe any choice, but rather returned her to her father's house in London. Still, there was the child to think of.

They left Edinburgh the following day, beginning the last leg of their journey northward to *Dun Broc.* The countryside began to change, becoming wilder as they found themselves farther and farther from the city and entering the Highlands. The gentle hills of the south quickly gave way to the rugged mountains of the north, thick with forests of mixed conifers and hardwoods. There were trees of many kinds: alders, beeches, larches, sycamores, pines, firs, oaks, and birches. The mountain peaks were dark and granitelike, and fast streams of clear water tumbled over the rock-strewn streambeds. It was, to Velvet's eyes, an incredibly beautiful and lonely land; the only signs of life being occasional flocks of sheep, herds of cattle upon the moors, or a suddenly come-upon village consisting of a few cottages, perhaps a small inn, and a church.

They were not the picture-pretty villages of England with their whitewashed cottages and windowboxes of brightly colored flowers. The houses here were of dark stone, and the summer season, Alex told his wife, was not long enough to encourage flowers. Besides, such things took time, valuable time that was needed for more important things like helping in the fields of barley and oats or for keeping the kitchen garden free of rabbits so that there would be onions, leeks, and carrots through most of the winter.

"'Tis a beautiful land, lass, but often 'tis a harsh one for our people."

She was beginning to understand him through this. "At least the cottages are sturdy," she noted.

"Aye, but they dinna belong to the people who live in them. They belong to the lord of the land. Only the roofs belong to the peasants. If they move, the roof goes with them."

It took several days for them to reach *Dun Broc*, and, to Velvet's surprise, they stopped well before sunset each day and only at the houses of people who were bound by oath of fidelity to the great Gordon clan. Velvet and Alex were welcomed warmly there, fed simple suppers, and given beds from which they arose before dawn to eat bowls of hot oat stirabout with honey and cream, still warm from the cow, and then went on their way.

Velvet, having been advised by Cat Leslie, was now dressed very much like the Countess of Glenkirk. She rode astride, wearing dark green trunk hose and a cream-silk shirt over which she sported a leather jerkin with bone buttons belted with a wide, brown leather belt that had a silver buckle and showed her tiny waist off to perfection. Her brown leather boots came to her knees and her auburn hair was clubbed back with a black ribbon. Atop her head was perched a velvet bonnet with one eagle's feather in it, and she carried a Gordon plaid of warm wool should she grow chilly. Alex was dressed in his kilt as were all of his men, but in his bonnet he wore two eagle feathers denoting him as a chieftain of a cadet branch of the Clan Gordon. Only the Earl of Huntley, George Gordon, had the right to wear three feathers, and, in all of Scotland, only the king himself wore four.

Pansy was also dressed like a boy, to the delight of Alex's men and the belligerent annoyance of her husband, who, seeing his comrades eyeing his wife's shapely legs hugging her pony, became quite jealous. Before Pansy on her saddle rode little Dugie, although sometimes Dugald couldn't resist carrying his son himself to both his and the boy's delight.

Velvet's heart began to hammer with excitement when on the third afternoon Alex suddenly said to her, "We're now on BrocCairn land, lass."

"Where is *Dun Broc?*" she asked, looking about.

He smiled at her innocence. "'Tis several miles away over the next ridge of hills, but ye canna see it yet."

They rode on through the forest, sunlit this afternoon, and around a small lake he told her was called Loch Beith, meaning birch. Indeed, the loch was surrounded by them, their leaves bright gold with the autumn sun, reflecting themselves vainly in the blue, blue loch. The sight took her breath away.

On they rode up the hills surrounding the loch, through the pine forest, and once Velvet thought she saw a fox, and another time a family of pine martens. Alex told her that the area was home to weasels, wolves, and wildcats as well. When they reached the top of the small mountain that Alex insisted on calling a wee hill, the sight that met her eyes as they stopped to rest the horses was one of incredible beauty. Below them was a small glen where the village of Broc Ailien was located as well as the manor house of his brother-in-law, Ian Grant, Alex told her. She could see a great herd of cattle grazing in a meadow near the village.

"Cattle, lass, is the sign of a man's wealth here," he said. "A good deal of our wealth comes from them. We raise the cattle, and then each autumn a portion of the herd is slaughtered, then pickled, and barrels of it shipped to France, Holland, Denmark, and certain German states. I have a permit from the king to take salmon from my waters, and these, too, are exported either smoked, salted, or dried. My wealth comes from my cattle mainly, however."

"Who ships your goods?" she demanded, ever her mother's daughter.

He chuckled. "In my youth I convinced my father to let me invest in the purchase of several ships, and we now ship our own goods rather than pay another to do it. Before that time we had to contract out to a middleman who usually took too great a fee and still cheated us." He pointed. "Look across the glen, Velvet, and then look up upon the mountain above it."

Velvet's eyes followed his finger, and suddenly she saw it, a castle that seemed to spring up from the very rocks of the mountainside.

"Dun Broc!" he said.

A small thrill raced through her. *Dun Broc! Her home!* It was not a large castle, but, oh, how beautiful it was with its battlements and towers soaring high above the glen. It would be practically impregnable, she thought. She could not even see how one could reach it, and she asked Alex.

He smiled. "Look carefully, lass. There is a very narrow, walled road that leads from the glen up to *Dun Broc*."

"Then the castle cannot be attacked, can it? You couldn't get enough of an army up that narrow road at one time to make an attack, could you?"

"Nay," he answered, "but we are not totally impregnable, lass. The north side of the castle sits atop the mountain on a narrow plain. Although we are walled, like any castle walls they are breachable in certain instances. Still, only once in the history of *Dun Broc* were those walls scaled successfully, and that was during the reign of James IV. A castle serving girl who was in love with one of the opposing soldiers let a ladder down to her lover one night, and he, after rendering her unconscious, opened the main gate to the king's soldiers."

"Why was the king besieging *Dun Broc?*" asked Velvet.

He smiled. "'Twas a small dispute over a pretty lady. The lady, however, preferred my ancestor and married him after he had carried her away. The king broke in and found them honeymooning, but instead of being angry he is said to have laughed, admitted he was well bested, and given them a wedding gift of a golden candelabra, which you will see on the sideboard in the Great Hall tonight."

Velvet laughed. "'Tis a very romantic place that is to be my home." Then she turned, her face radiant. "It's beautiful even from here, Alex, and I know that I'm going to love it!"

"Let's go home then, lass," he said, and they began their descent into the glen.

"The earl is coming!" A barefooted boy ran at top speed through Broc Ailien shouting, "The earl is coming!" He was proud to be the first one to trumpet the news.

The cottage doors flew open, and the residents of the village poured forth to welcome their lord and his wife. Broc Ailien, Velvet noted, was more prosperous-looking than so many of the other villages that they had passed through. Some of the cottages had front gardens that did indeed boast flowers, and those that didn't had boxes of herbs on the windowsills. The faces were smiling and filled with welcome; the men casting approving looks at Velvet, the women nodding slyly at one another.

"Welcome home, m'lord!"

"Welcome to yer lady, m'lord!"

"God bless ye both, m'lord!"

The greetings came thick and fast, and Velvet couldn't help smiling. Alex, who knew each and every resident of his village, had a word for them all. "Allan, I thank ye kindly! Gavin, ye've gotten fat while I've been gone. Hae ye been poaching in my woods again, man? Jean, another bairn? This will make three in three years, won't it?" They looked absolutely delighted to see him, to be acknowledged so personally. He knew all about them, their problems, their strengths, their weaknesses, and Velvet could tell that they loved him for it.

There was a small village square with a Celtic cross to mark it, a small inn, and a little church in Broc Ailien. This is a good place to live, thought Velvet. Then a woman stepped directly in front of Alex's horse. She was petite and blond, and she was holding up a child, a little girl.

"Will you not bid your daughter a good day, Alex? Have you brought her a fine gift as I promised her?" the woman asked boldly.

"Ye should nae promise what ye canna give, Alanna," Alex said quietly, and attempted to move his horse by her and her child.

Alanna poked her daughter, and as if on cue the child cried out, "Papa! Papa!" She was too tiny to say much more, but it had its effect.

Unable to help himself, Alex reached down and took the child up into his arms. "How are ye, Sibby?" he asked, his face was tender. It was obvious that he loved his daughter.

It was as if someone had thrust a knife into her vitals so sharp was the pain. Velvet turned her head away, and quick tears filled her eyes, but only Pansy saw them. The tiring woman glowered at Alanna Wythe, but the blond English girl merely tossed her head and smiled boldly.

"Is this your wife, then Alex?" she said.

Without answering her, the earl handed her back the baby, then turning to Velvet said, "We're almost there now, sweetheart. Ye're beginning to look tired." Then they moved on and rode out of the village.

Jean Lawrie, the goodwife to whom Alex had spoken, looked archly at Alanna Wythe. "Ye'd best beware, ye bold baggage! I've known Alex Gordon my whole life, and I can tell ye that he'll nae put up wi' yer forwardness, nor will he allow ye to offend his bride."

"You've two daughters, don't you, Mistress Lawrie? If you want that fine son you're carrying to be born safe, I'd not offend me." Alanna's eyes narrowed.

Jean Lawrie crossed herself. "Oh, ye're a bad one, ye are! Ye'll nae frighten me though. I dinna believe the tale that ye're a witch. Perhaps ye can fool some of the younger girls in this village wi' yer love charms and potions, but ye canna fool me. If ye're so all-powerful, then why has yer witchcraft not kept the earl's favor?"

"Alex loves me," Alanna Wythe declared firmly.

"Humph," snorted Jean Lawrie. "Ye're a fool if ye believe that, lass. I saw the look he gave his beautiful wife. He'll hae her belly filled in nae time at all, and when her son is born, he'll nae gie ye another thought. He wouldn't now except for wee Sibby." Then she flounced off, satisfied at having bested the Englishwoman.

Angrily Alanna stared after her, but then she turned to look after Alex. She had given him a child, and what was her reward? A cottage in this backwater village and a pension that could barely keep them. She detested keeping house, and no woman in the village would work for her. Sybilla was forever hanging onto her skirts, whining for this or that. Alanna hated it here, but eventually she would be back at *Dun Broc* with a servant to care for her and another to look after her brat. She had already begun casting charms that would bring Alex back to her and away from the proud bitch who had not even bothered to look at her.

"I'm sorry, sweetheart," Alex apologized as they reached the narrow, walled road that led up to *Dun Broc*.

Velvet took a deep breath. "'Twas not your fault, Alex, but now perhaps you'll see why she must go. She'll not give you up, and she uses the child to gain your attention."

"If I send her away, God only knows what will happen to wee Sybilla, and she's a bonny little bairn, Velvet. Surely ye saw that?"

"I did not notice, Alex, but you could give the child to some kindly village woman to raise. Surely she would be better off, and I suspect that Mistress Wythe will be happy to accept a bag of gold from you and her passage home to London."

"God, Velvet! I dinna think a great deal of Alanna, but what kind of woman would leave her child? She'll nae do it, I'm certain, but gie me a little time and I will try to have her gone before the winter sets in here. Be patient lass. Ye need nae see her again."

He couldn't know how his words wounded her, but she would not tell him of Yasaman. Instead she said, "I will see her each time I go down to the village, Alex, you may be certain of it."

"She'd nae be so bold," he said, and Velvet thought how little her husband knew women.

"You cannot be sure what she will do, Alex. Remember Mary de Boult," she warned. Then she changed the subject entirely, asking, "Where is your sister's house? Did you not say 'twas in this glen also?"

"'Tis on the other side of the village," he answered. "We'll go there in a few days, but I am certain that we'll find both Annabella and Ian awaiting us at *Dun Broc*. Dinna invite her to spend the night or we'll nae get rid of her for a week."

"Alex! She's your sister, your only sister!"

"She's a spoilt and willful minx," he answered her. "When Mother and Nigel died, she moved herself and that weak-kneed husband of hers right into *Dun Broc*, and it wasn't until Father passed away that I was able to rid myself of her. She was already telling her bairns that they would inherit *Dun*

Broc one day because I wasn't married or likely to be so. She herself could have made a better match than the one she made, but for some reason she wed wi' Ian Grant. I have never been able to understand it."

They were close to the head of the road, and Velvet could see the lowered drawbridge and the portcullis raised to welcome the castle's master. Suddenly upon the battlements appeared a lone piper whose bagpipe wailed a spirited tune that Alex told her was called "BrocCairn's Triumph." The sound of the pipe hovered in the air over the glen, the notes blending one into another until the last of the melody was played in a victorious burst. Velvet could feel the hair on the back of her neck rising in excitement.

"'Tis how the chief is welcomed home," Alex said, "and today is a most joyful homecoming for my people because ye're with me, Velvet. They've long awaited their Countess of BrocCairn, lass. My mother's been dead close to five years now."

They passed over the drawbridge, the horses' hooves drumming on the heavy wood, and beneath the portcullis arch into the castle courtyard. On the south wall was the stables, with its blacksmith shop and its armory . Directly before them across the courtyard was the castle itself with its walled garden. The double-arched main doors of the castle were open, and waiting on the stone steps leading to them were a man and a woman.

"'Tis Bella and her weakling," muttered Alex.

Velvet giggled. "Alex!" she admonished.

"Nay," he replied. "Look at her standing so proudly as if 'twas she who was the lady of the manor. The minx should be on the lowest step awaiting us, nae on the top!"

They rode up to the foot of the steps, and Velvet got her first good look at her sister-in-law. She was wearing a deep crimson silk dress, one of her best, Velvet suspected, which flattered her dark hair and gray-blue eyes. She had a pretty, fair-skinned face, but she did not look particularly like her brother, and Velvet suspected she favored their late mother.

Alex slid easily off his horse and, turning, lifted Velvet down from hers, kissing her on the nose as he did so. She laughed up at him, and he couldn't resist a chuckle himself. She looked so damned adorable in that outrageous riding outfit. Then, slipping an arm about her, he walked up the steps to where his sister and her husband awaited.

"Welcome home, brother," said Annabella Grant, but her very disapproving gaze was upon Velvet.

Alex kissed his sister in a perfunctory manner. "How nice of ye to be here awaiting us, Bella." He loosed his grip on Velvet and drew her forward. "My wife, Velvet Gordon, the new Countess of BrocCairn."

Annabella Grant was forced to curtsy, but as she inclined her head, Velvet, in return, said graciously, "You need not curtsy to me, sister." Then, taking the surprised woman by the shoulders, she kissed her upon both of her cheeks. "I do hope we will be friends," she finished.

"Of course," said Annabella, quite flustered by this young and beautiful woman in her outlandish garb. This was not how she had imagined this meeting would go. She was, after all, her new sister-in-law's senior by eight years, yet Velvet made her feel positively awkward.

Velvet tucked her arm through Annabella's. "I want to know everything about *Dun Broc*, and since it was your childhood home, I am sure you can tell me. When I ask Alex, all he can talk about is history and architecture."

Bella felt a burst of warmth suffuse her slender frame. Why Velvet was very much like herself. How wonderful! "Men," she said importantly, "simply dinna understand the running of a household, sister." She looked archly at her brother and her husband, and then, as if remembering something, she said with a wave of her hand, "This is Ian, my husband." But before Ian could open his mouth, she was chattering on again about the numerous details necessary to running a castle like *Dun Broc*, quoting her dear, departed mother frequently as they walked into the castle.

Alex couldn't help but grin. Bella was incorrigible. He turned to his brother-in-law. "How are ye, Ian? Is all well at *Grantholm?* And wi' my nephews?"

"Aye, Alex. The cattle ye gave us last spring hae prospered, and we've just slaughtered them. They'll bring a pretty penny, and I'll finally be able to make repairs to the roof."

"Ye dinna slaughter all the cattle, did ye, Ian?"

"Aye," came his brother-in-law's reply.

"God's nightshirt!" exploded Alex. "How in hell do ye expect to build yer herd if ye hae no cows to breed to my bull?"

"Bella said we couldna afford to keep the cows this winter if we were to make all the repairs needed. She said ye'd gie us new stock in the spring. That it was her right."

"*Her right?* Christ almighty, man, the only rights yer wife has are those ye gie her! I warned ye that I would not help ye again, Ian. Bella has no claims to *Dun Broc*, and ye both well know it. Ye should hae seen that ye couldna make all the repairs necessary to yer house this year. The roof would hae been a good start. If ye'll take my advice, ye'll repair it and save the rest of yer money to buy fresh stock in the spring."

Ian nodded. "I'm nae wise like ye, Alex, but I'll take yer good advice. Bella is nae easy to live with, ye know," he finished apologetically.

"She needs a stick taken to her," snapped Alex, "and until ye do it ye'll nae be able to control her. She's a willful wench, Ian. For God's sake, man, show some backbone!" He stamped up the steps into his home and, turning back to Ian, said, "Now take yer wife home, Ian. Ye know that the road is difficult in the dark, and 'tis gettinig close to sunset."

"Are we not to stay the night, then? Bella said we were to stay."

"The hell ye're going to stay! It's taken me three years to bring my wife home to *Dun Broc*, and I dinna intend to spend our first night at *Dun Broc* entertaining ye and my sister."

Annabella was outraged at her brother's behavior, and though Velvet pleaded sweetly, Alex held firm. Within a few short minutes the Grants of *Grantholm* were trotting down the narrow, walled road toward the glen and their own home. The portcullis was lowered, the drawbridge raised, the men-at-arms paced upon the castle heights, and *Dun Broc* was secured for the night. With a self-satisfied grin, Alex returned to his wife.

Velvet loved *Dun Broc* from the first moment she saw it. It was not a large castle. Indeed, there was an almost cosy air about it. The building was set firmly against the north wall of *Dun Broc* and ran along a portion of the northwest and northeast walls as well. The windows on these particular walls were high enough to prevent entry through them by an enemy, for it was this area of the castle that was the most vulnerable. Most of the views from *Dun Broc* faced south, west, and east.

The gardens on the west and southwest walls of the castle were badly overgrown, except for the small kitchen garden. It was still warm enough, Velvet thought, that something could be done there before winter set in. At the very end of the gardens, and directly off the castle itself, was a small chapel.

Dun Broc had been begun two centuries before when a laird of BrocCairn had fortified the mountaintop and started to build upon it. The first Earl of BrocCairn had been created by James IV as reward for his support in his war of insurrection against his father, James III. The last laird had fought against his son, the first earl, and died with his king, James III, at Sauchieburn along with his two younger sons. It was said that James Gordon, the first Earl of BrocCairn, was punished by God for his rebellion against not only James III but his own father as well in that he had but one child, his son, Alexander. The second earl was also childless but for a single daughter.

Lady Alexandra Gordon, the heiress to BrocCairn, was a wild and willful girl with flaming red hair and black eyes. At fourteen she had attracted the attention of James V, the handsome and unmarried king. For close to a year Alexandra had held the king at bay, only yielding to her liege after a handfast marriage that James Stewart afterwards denied. Alexandra had died in childbirth at sixteen, bearing the king a son, Angus Gordon, the third Earl of BrocCairn. Young Angus, though recognized by his father, was raised by his grandfather and bore his name, not the king's. Angus was matched with Isabel Leslie who bore him two living sons and a daughter, of which Alex and Annabella were the survivors.

Since the time of the creation of the earldom, *Dun Broc* had grown: its walls going higher; sprouting round towers from which the land below might be viewed; its manor house giving away to the small jewel of a castle that now held sway over the bailey.

Within the castle Velvet found a fine, good-sized hall containing two large stone fireplaces to heat it. There were several large, beautiful tapestries hanging upon the walls, the stone floors were swept clean, and the tables were well polished. Bella's handiwork, Velvet thought, and reminded herself to thank her sister-in-law. The air was fragrant from the applewood fires and bowls of sweet herbs that had been discreetly placed about. The main level of the castle also contained the steward's office, Alex's private library, the kitchens, storage rooms with their casks, barrels, and boxes, as well as the granaries and the servants' hall. There were more storage rooms, as well as the castle's dungeon in the cellars below. On the upper level of *Dun Broc* were the family quarters, consisting of the earl's apartments, which adjoined the countess's, guest chambers, and the nursery. The servants slept in the attics above.

Alex led his wife to the kitchens so that she could meet *Dun Broc's* cook. A big-boned woman came forward at their entry, a smile upon her handsome face. Her dark hair was liberally streaked with gray, and she carried herself proudly.

"So here she is," the woman declared in a deep voice. "Welcome home, m'lady!" Then she curtsied.

Alex smiled at the woman. "Velvet, this is Morag Geddes."

Velvet looked closely at the cook and, suddenly seeing the resemblance, asked, "Are you Dugald's mother?"

"I am," came the reply, "and my son tells me that we both owe ye a great debt of gratitude, for ye saved the life of my only grandson."

"But how could you know that already?" demanded Velvet, astounded.

Morag Geddes laughed. "There's nae witchcraft about it, m'lady. Dugald rode on ahead of the main party to prepare me for the wonderful surprise. He says the lad is the spit of him. Is it true, then?"

"Aye," said Velvet, smiling, "and he's a fine little boy, too."

"Well, then," replied the big woman, "perhaps I'll take to the English girl my son's wed wi'."

"I've known Pansy all my life," Velvet said, hiding her smile, "and I am certain that you'll like her, but, more important, she loves Dugald."

"'Tis something to be said for that," replied Morag.

The kitchens smelled wonderful, reminding Velvet that she was very hungry, but nothing would do until Alex had showed her the upper level with their quarters. "I had the countess's apartments redone before I first came to England to fetch ye," he said, his voice holding an almost boyish note, anxious and seeking her approval.

"I'm sure they will be lovely," she said in reply, but secretly she wished he had not presumed to do such a thing without even knowing her first. When, however, she went through the door into her chambers, she was stunned and delighted.

It was not a large apartment, but both rooms overlooked the gardens below and a view west-southwest over the mountains. Each room had a large fireplace: the one in the dayroom flanked by carved stone dogs, the one in her bedchamber guarded by two winged angels. In both rooms wooden floors had been laid over the stone, and upon the floors were beautiful, thick, wool India rugs of acceptable quality. With a pang of remembrance, Velvet felt her feet sink into the carpet, and she wondered where he had obtained them and when but she did not ask. She never would.

The dayroom's main window was bowed, and there was a window seat within it. The drapes and the upholstery were coral-colored velvet sewn with threads of gold. There was a lovely rectangular table of polished oak in the center of the room, and upon it sat a blue and white porcelain bowl filled with heather. Two carved chairs with their plump cushions were before the fireplace, one on each side. At one wall there was an oak sideboard with carved legs, its polished top reflecting the candlelight from the twin candelabra on either end of it. At another wall stood a tall, two-door oaken chest. The walls were paneled, and the ceiling was of coffered oak. Above the fireplace was a magnificent tapestry depicting a handsome hunter closing in with his dogs on a big stag. There was something familiar about the man.

"The tapestry was worked by my grandmother, Alexandra Gordon. She did it in the two years that she knew King James V. It is his face ye see on the hunter."

"Were these her rooms, Alex?"

"Aye. 'Tis said the king used to visit her here."

"That's very romantic," Velvet mused, "and I love the room, Alex!"

"Come and see the rest of yer apartments, lass," he invited.

To Velvet's further delight her bedchamber was as lovely as the dayroom. Here, however, the draperies were of peacock blue velvet. There was a fine, big bed with hangings on silver rings that could be pulled around to enclose it. Upon the bed was a coverlet of red fox. There was a candlestand on one side of the bed and a large carved oak chest against one wall. The bowed window, the mate to the one in the dayroom, also had a window seat, and beside it was a round table containing a pewter bowl of late roses. Above the fireplace was a second tapestry, this one showing a seated pair of lovers embracing upon a hillside.

Velvet looked up at it. "Surely the lady Alexandra didn't do that tapestry as well as the one in my dayroom?"

"My mother did this tapestry," he replied. "These were her rooms also from the time she married my father. She worked the piece early in their marriage. She found the story of my grandmother a very romantic, if sad one. The lovers are supposed to be James and Alexandra. Two years after I was born my mother lost a set of twins and was ill for some months afterwards. She had a great deal of time upon her hands, and she spent a good bit of it designing and weaving the tapestry." He slipped his arms about his wife and drew her back against him. "I dinna want to think of past lovers, lass," he murmured in her ear. His hands slid up to cup both her breasts. "Ye're so damned tempting, Velvet Gordon."

She tingled deliciously beneath his seductive fondlings, but then she sighed and said, "I'm hungry, Alex!" and tried to squirm away.

"So am I," he answered, holding her fast. Then he turned her so that she faced him and, looking down at her, said softly, "I want to make love to ye, my bonny wife." His fingers undid her clothing as he spoke. "We are home at last, my beautiful Velvet. *Home!* I have dreamed of this moment for more than two years, lass! Dreamed of our being here, together, in this room." His lips brushed her temple, and her silk shirt slipped to the rug. He had already managed to remove her jerkin and belt.

Velvet's eyes closed unbidden as a lovely languorous feeling filled her veins. She could feel his hands undoing her chemisette, and then her breasts were bared. His head dipped to take a soft nipple in his warm mouth. She murmured softly, a pleased little sound that encouraged his boldness, and her hands stroked his head. Food was forgotten as hunger for another pleasure swept over her. She helped him to remove her lower garments, and then nude, she began to undress him.

Passion devoured him as she teasingly unbuttoned his silken shirt. He could feel himself hardening as her soft fingertips feathered themselves over his broad chest. Her touch was almost painful, so intense was his desire to possess her.

He couldn't wait for her, and with an impatient snort he almost tore the rest of his clothes off.

With a smile Velvet took his hand and drew him over so that they could see themselves reflected in the tall, silver-edged pier glass. "Are we not beautiful, my wild Highland husband?" she whispered as they stared at their naked forms in the mirror.

They were turned sideway, his arms about her waist. Her lovely full breasts pushed provocatively against his furred chest, and the rounds of her bottom were temptingly exciting to his eye. When she slipped her hand between their pressed bellies to catch him in her grasp, he groaned aloud; but she paid him little heed, caressing his length instead with a gentle, teasing touch that sent bursts of blazing desire flaming into his body and brain.

"Dear God, lass!" he managed to say through gritted teeth. "Ye're driving me wild!"

"Am I?" she teased him. "I love it when you grow so hard in my hand, Alex." Standing on her tiptoes, she bit his ear, whispering into it, "And I love it when you push yourself deep into me, my darling. You want to now, don't you?" she taunted him.

"What a vixen ye are," he said softly, and, sweeping her up, he moved swiftly to deposit her upon the bed. For a short moment he was startled by her creamy beauty upon the fox fur, and then he lowered himself down to join her. "A wicked, wanton vixen, my wild Highland wife; a vixen in need of taming."

Her emerald eyes glittered at him, and her little tongue swirled over her lips, moistening them. "Are you man enough to tame me, Alex?"

A lazy smile traveled all the way to his amber-gold eyes. "Aye, lass," he said slowly. "I think I'm more than man enough." He bent and kissed each of her breasts in turn. Then, sliding between her thighs, he surprised her by pulling her legs up and over his shoulders while his head found its way to her secret treasure.

Velvet felt her breath catch in her throat, and for a moment she couldn't breathe at all as she felt his tongue on her flesh. Slowly he licked the quivering insides of her satiny thighs. His tongue ran along the crease between each leg and her plump, pink Venus mont, traveling across the top of that temptation, finding its way to the moist cleft that hid even more secret delights. Shameless, she eagerly awaited his touch, her breath coming in short gasps, her fingers kneading the back of his neck. When at last his tongue found that sensitive little jewel, it was as if a fireball had burst within her. The pleasure was both unbearable and seemingly unending. She whimpered with pure bliss as his mouth wreaked havoc upon her tender body.

The first wave of rapture washed over her, and she cried his name in her wild passion. He raised his head slightly, a small smile upon his face, then returning to his sweet toil, he brought her to a second and third peak before drawing himself back up to find her mouth.

Her lips parted yearningly beneath his, and, filling her mouth with his tongue, he caressed hers for a long moment before drawing away and whispering softly, "That's how ye taste, my darling!" Then he pushed himself slowly into her warm and waiting body.

Velvet almost cried aloud as she felt his bigness filling her, so full that she couldn't believe her young body would be able to contain and satisfy him. "Ah, my love!" she finally sobbed, and knew in that moment that she was his once more. In her secret heart she called her *"farewell"* to Akbar. She would never allow what they had had together to haunt her relationship with Alex again. That time was over!

"Look at me!" His voice was fierce and demanding.

Her eyes opened, and he could see that they were filled with her passion for him, and her love. "Tame me, my wild Highland husband!" she challenged him.

Slowly he began to move on her, and then his tempo increased as he thrust faster and deeper, deeper and faster, into her burning sheath. He could feel her fingernails raking down his straining back, digging into his shoulders as he fanned the fires of her wild desires. Finally he could bear no more. "Ah, lass!" he cried aloud, "'tis ye who've conquered me!" But Velvet didn't hear his confession, for he had taken her to the heights of their love, and then she plummeted down into a whirlpool of passion, sated.

In the village the following morning the goodwives gathered outside the kirk after morning prayer and gossiped with glee at the stories already coming down from the castle of how the earl had taken his wife to bed last night before they had even eaten dinner, that Morag Geddes's good meal had gone uneaten altogether!

"There'll be an heir for BrocCairn within the year," said Jean Lawrie, chuckling, "and that's certain!"

"Aye," the other women agreed, pleased.

"But how will the English witch take this news?" asked a young girl.

"Humph! She's nae a witch even if some silly gooses believe it. If she's a witch, then why did Lord Alex desert her for his bride? She has no power, girl," Jean Lawrie scolded. "When she's willing to admit the truth, Alanna Wythe will return to England."

"I hope the earl will nae let her take her bairn. Poor wee girlie. She doesna hae an easy time wi' a mother who's nae really a mother to her at all," said another older woman.

Alanna Wythe heard it all, hidden in the shadows of the church she would not enter. Her anger was a black and bitter one. How she hated Velvet! If that woman had only stayed where she was, Alanna told herself, Alex would have eventually married her, and she, Alanna Wythe, would have been the countess of BrocCairn, not that red-haired bitch! They will pay for my pain, both of them, Alanna vowed. She didn't know how she was going to punish them, but she would indeed see that they suffered. She slipped silently away from the hurtful words of the women of Broc Ailien and hurried back to her own cottage where her daughter had awakened to find herself alone and was now wailing fearfully. Irritably Alanna slapped the baby.

"Be quiet, Sibby!" she snapped, but the child only howled louder. Annoyed, Alanna pulled her blouse down and pushed a nipple into her daughter's mouth. That at least would quiet the brat for the time being. She had been trying to wean Sibby for several weeks now. Her breasts were going to be ruined if she continued to allow the brat to keep tugging and sucking on them every day. God, how she hated children! She had only had Sibby in order to bind Alex to her. Even there she had been disappointed, for the baby turned out to be a girl and not the hoped-for son. No matter, she thought. He did have a certain weakness for the child, and that had certainly bettered her position with him even though his wife had returned.

She heard the back door to her cottage open and close, and she looked up, curious. A man stood in the shadows a moment, watching her nurse the child. Sibby had fallen back asleep against her mother's breast, and carefully Alanna returned her to her cot before she whirled and hissed at the intruder, "Are you mad to come here in daylight? What if one of those village biddies saw you?"

"Well, they didn't," he said. "I was careful, Alanna. Very careful. Besides, I needed to get out of the house this morning. I needed to see ye."

"What has happened?" She was instantly wary. This big fool of a man could ruin everything with his lack of caution.

"Bella started at me, demanding an accounting of the monies I received when I sold the cattle Alex gave us. I could hardly let her know I spent some of that gold now, could I, Alanna?"

"What did you tell her, Ian?"

"Nothing," he said with a smirk. "Instead I took my good and wise brother-in-law's advice on how to handle my wife."

"What did you do?" She was very worried now.

"I took a stick and beat her bottom until she begged me for mercy, reminding her all the while that 'twas I who was master of Grantholm. God's cock, how she howled and struggled! If I'd known that beating Bella was so pleasant I'd hae done it years ago."

"You fool!" Alanna spat at him. "If she tells her brother, then Alex will ask those same questions. Couldn't you have just lied to her?"

"She'll nae go to Alex," Ian said with certainty. "It excited me so to beat her that when I finished I couldn't help fucking her. She'll nae sit or walk for several days, Alanna, and by that time she'll hae decided to say nothing. She won't want her brother and his wife to know what happened. Annabella is a proud little bitch."

He licked his lips, and his eyes glazed with the memory of his recent victory. Alanna could see that he was still quite hot with lust, for his cock thrust itself out against his red and green kilt. She marveled to herself that she had somehow managed to find the biggest cock she'd ever seen, in this damned Highland backwater, in this barbaric so-called country. It was Ian Grant's only redeeming feature, for he hadn't a brain in his head. She suspected it was his monster cock that had won him the hand of the fair Annabella Gordon. She somehow didn't think Alex's sister still relished her bargain.

"Alanna," he murmured hungrily to her, and came forward to turn her around and bend her over the cottage table. Tossing her skirts over her head, he thrust into her without any preliminaries. She grunted softly at his entry, but accepted his bigness as his hands fumbled to find her breasts, large breasts for such a tiny girl. He thrust with practiced regularity into her, and Alanna let the pleasure wash over her. When he had finished, her earlier irritation had been dispelled. Ian Grant knew enough about his one talent to know that the woman must also be satisfied if he was to be totally fulfilled.

Alanna straightened herself up and smoothed her skirts. Ian grinned down at her. "You're a good fuck," he said.

"Don't be seen leaving here," she said coldly.

"I'll be back tonight," he said smugly. "Jesu, I canna ever remember being so hot for a woman even after I've just had two." Then with a chuckle he was quickly gone the way he came.

"Fool!" she muttered after him, but she knew she'd welcome him back that night.

Chapter 15

The young Countess of BrocCairn was quickly and easily accepted by her husband's people. Her beauty drew them first, but they soon discovered her to be an intelligent, kindly, and caring woman for all that she had been born English. They protected her from Alanna Wythe, and life for the silversmith's daughter became even harder than it had been before Velvet's arrival. Little Sybilla, however, was not included in the ostracism of her mother, for the people of Broc Ailien considered that as Alex's child she was one of them.

Velvet spent the autumn restoring the gardens of *Dun Broc* and learning everything she possibly could about Alex's lands, people, and the way of life in the Highlands. In this Pansy was a great help to her, for as Dugald's wife and Morag Geddes's new daughter-in-law, she was accepted everywhere. The naturally cautious inhabitants of Broc Ailien couldn't help taking to Pansy with her deliciously funny accent, down-to-earth ways, and fine sense of humor. Velvet learned a good deal of local color and gossip, which aided her in being a good lady of the manor.

The autumn faded into winter, and there was no sign of a child. On New Year's Eve, Velvet and Alex stood with Bella and Ian upon the walls of *Dun Broc* and watched fires spring up over the hillsides as far as the eye could see as the church bell tolled in the new year of our Lord 1592. Alex had given her a magnificent rope of pink pearls from which hung three teardrop-shaped diamonds as a New Year's gift. As Velvet shared the news of her bounty with her sister-in-law, she thought that Bella looked pale, and she noticed a particularly ugly bruise on her breast when Bella bent over to halfheartedly admire the jewels.

Still, Annabella had said graciously, "It's a beautiful gift, Velvet, and I can tell ye're happy wi' my brother. I think he's a lucky man."

"Are ye finally wi' child," demanded Ian rudely, "that Alex would gie ye such a rich gift?" Ian had eaten a fine dinner that night and was full of Alex's good wine and whiskey.

Velvet flushed and looked mutely at her husband, who said in a level voice, "I think ye've partaken a wee bit too generously of my hospitality, Ian. Ye may be my sister's husband, but that doesna gie ye the right to ask such questions. When 'tis time to make an announcement, ye'll be one of the first to know."

"Then my lads are still yer heirs," came Ian's drunken reply.

Now Annabella flushed. "Ian!" she remonstrated.

"Ian," he mimicked her, and then said threateningly, "Dinna tell me how to behave, woman, or 'twill be the worse for ye." His eyes narrowed, and Bella edged nervously away from her husband.

Later when she was tucked up in bed with her husband, Velvet said, "I think Ian is beating your sister."

Alex laughed. "He wouldn't dare, lass. He hasna the guts for it. Besides, Bella wouldn't stand for it."

"Haven't you noticed how quiet your sister is lately, Alex? Usually she's waspish and quick, but recently she has been very subdued. I saw an ugly bruise on her breast tonight."

"Perhaps Ian was simply a bit rough in his loving, sweetheart. Dinna worry about Bella. She's nae been shy about voicing her displeasure over anything."

The winter deepened, Velvet's first winter in the north, and it was a ferocious one. Careful planning on their chief's part, however, kept the people of Broc Ailien from starvation and freezing. The granaries of *Dun Broc* doled out careful measures of grain to all on a weekly basis, and the earl permitted firewood to be harvested from his forests.

It was fortunate that the lovers enjoyed each other's company, for the heavy snows precluded visits from even the master of *Grantholm* and his wife, which was no loss in Velvet's mind. She liked her sister-in-law, but Ian Grant was another matter. He made her uncomfortable, and she could see nothing about him that should have attracted Bella to him.

Velvet was growing to love this land of her husband's. It was lonely, and God only knew it could be bleak on gray days, but even then the Highlands had a beauty all their own; the green pine forests sweeping down the snowy mountainsides, the deciduous trees bare and black against the flat skies. On clear nights the stars were big and bright, offering the illusion of nearness so that one was tempted to reach up and pluck them down. And somewhere in the forests below the wolves hunted, the packs stopping occasionally to howl triumphantly at the white winter moon.

Then as suddenly as winter had come it was gone, and the snows began to melt away during the longer days of spring. They were able to ride out again over the hills together, much to Velvet's joy; she would accompany Alex when he went to check on his cattle herds, which had grown enormous this spring with all the births. Together they watched as the calves gamboled awkwardly with their mothers in the glen pastures.

She sighed deeply, so deeply that her mount grew restive beneath her. "They make me feel so guilty that I am not yet with child," she mourned.

"We'll just hae to try harder," he teased her.

Secretly, Velvet was worried. She had become pregnant so quickly with Akbar's child. Why was it taking so long with Alex? His seed was not barren, as Sybilla and the Gordon faces upon a number of older children in the glen told her. Why could she not conceive his child? It did not help to have anxious faces peering at her each time she entered the village, nor did she like the fact that Alanna Wythe was spreading the rumor that it was her witchcraft that was keeping Velvet from conceiving.

"If I believed that for one minute," muttered Alex when he heard it, "I should strangle the bitch myself."

"You wouldn't have to," said Velvet grimly, "for I'd have already done it!"

The word coming from the south where the king and Lord Bothwell were still at odds boded ill for Francis Stewart-Hepburn. In late May the parliament under the orders of the king, no doubt encouraged by Maitland, ratified the sentence of total forfeiture against the Earl of Bothwell. Francis Stewart-Hepburn, claimed the king, aspired to Scotland's throne, and that was treason.

It was a ridiculous charge, and everyone knew it. The Scots nobility, usually at odds with each other as well as the throne, now saw John Maitland behind the king's actions. Maitland wanted to destroy them in an effort to take their power for his own and thereby rule the king. Without a moment's hesitation, they rallied behind the Earl of Bothwell in an effort to reconcile him to the king.

Francis Stewart-Hepburn wanted peace with his cousin, James Stewart. A brilliant intellectual, a man whose mind was far in advance of the time in which he lived, the one thing he did not want was to be king of Scotland or of any other land. The painful example of his late uncle, James Hepburn, the fifth Earl of Bothwell and the last husband of Mary, Queen of Scots haunted him.

When a proclamation for the raising of a levy to pursue the Earl of Bothwell was issued in early July, it was ignored by all. The king retired sulkily to his palace at Dalkeith for the remainder of the summer. On August first the earl was smuggled into the palace where the queen was to attempt to effect a meeting between the two. The king, however, suspecting something of this sort, sent his wife a message saying that he would punish *anyone* who attempted to introduce his outlawed cousin into his presence. Disappointed, Bothwell retired, returning to *Hermitage* in despair.

All of this was duly reported to the chiefs of the various powerful families in the Highlands. The Earl of Huntley,

George Gordon, head of Clan Gordon, arranged for a secret meeting with Bothwell. If the Border lord fell, Huntley knew that Maitland would come after him next, for George Gordon was the most powerful man in the Highlands, the so-called "Cock of the North." Bothwell slipped away from *Hermitage* alone while his Borderers, led by his half brother, Hercules, and his mistress, the Countess of Glenkirk, continued to raid along the border giving the illusion that he was still there.

Bothwell was passed from safe house to safe house until he finally arrived at *Dun Broc*, his last stop before reaching *Huntley*. The Gordons of BrocCairn greeted him joyously, and as Bothwell swung Velvet up in an embrace she squealed to him, "Careful, Francis! I am with child! At long last I am to be a mother!" Lowering her carefully, he kissed her on both cheeks.

"Congratulations, sweetheart!" he said.

"Ye might at least hae told me first," grumbled Alex, looking somewhat aggrieved.

"I planned to tell you today, but when Francis swept me up I had to say something. Oh, Alex"—she hugged him—"I am so happy!"

Her delight was so infectious that he couldn't help but grin like a fool at her. It suddenly dawned on him that he was going to be a father! Velvet was to have a baby! He startled them all with a loud Highland whoop. Then, picking his wife up in his arms, he carried her into the castle.

"Put me down, you great fool!" Velvet protested. "I am not made of some delicate stuff that breaks easily. My mother bore eight children successfully. My sisters have never lost a child. Put me down!"

"I dinna want anything to happen to my son," he protested, but he gently set her upon her feet.

"I intend to take good care of *our* child, Alex," came her pert reply.

Bothwell grinned at them delightedly. Marriage had not changed Alex and Velvet at all. In an increasingly confused world he found that a comforting fact. "Madame," he said, looking at Velvet, "I stink of four days' hard riding, and I am ravenous! What do ye intend to do about it?"

"Why, Francis," she replied sweetly, "I intend to bathe you with my very own hands just like the good chatelaines of old bathed their honored guests. Then you will find that Mistress Geddes has prepared you a fine feast. Since I count Cat among my friends, however, you will have to make do with hot bricks between your sheets to warm your bed tonight."

"Let's start wi' my bath," Bothwell said wickedly.

"Come along, my lord," she said, taking him by the hand and leading him upstairs to a guest apartment. There in the bedchamber a large oak tub had been set up and filled with steaming hot water. Velvet whirled, hands upon her hips. "Well, sir, remove your clothing. I cannot bathe you with your garments on."

Bothwell tossed his cloak to a manservant and, removing his jerkin and belt, slowly unbuttoned his shirt. Velvet's face remained impassive as the shirt was removed, and he sat to have his boots taken off. He was beginning to grow nervous, for she showed no signs of leaving.

"Shall I help you with your kilt, Francis?" she asked him innocently.

A slow grin lit his face. "Ye would, too, wouldn't ye?" he demanded of her.

"Aye," she answered him. "You haven't anything I haven't already seen, my lord, or do you?"

The Earl of Bothwell howled with glee. "God's cock, Velvet! Ye're a wicked wench! I've always suspected it, but until now I wasna certain. Now get the hell out of here, madame, so I may bathe myself and regain my dignity."

With a wink and a chuckle, Velvet left the room and hurried off to see that the evening meal would be ready on time for her guest. Francis Stewart-Hepburn's laughter warmed her as she went. She did like him so very much, and it broke her heart that the king was being so cruel to him.

It was decided that night that Alex and a troop of his men would accompany Bothwell to Huntley the next day. Velvet wanted to go along, for she had not yet met Henrietta Gordon, the Countess of Huntley, who was a Frenchwoman and knew Velvet's grandparents, aunts, uncles, and cousins at *Archambault.* Alex, however, anxious about his wife's newly announced pregnancy, forbade it.

"Are you telling me I can't ride?" she exploded at him.

"Nay!" he quickly replied. "I simply dinna want ye riding such a distance as it is to *Huntley*. Besides, there'll be nae women there but for Henrietta. George has called together all the chiefs of the most important families in the Highlands to discuss a plan of action against the King. If we dinna aid Francis, then Maitland will pick us off one by one."

"Dinna underestimate Jamie," said Bothwell. "He plays the fool, and 'tis true he can be slow in some matters, but he is nae really stupid, and he is very wise about certain things. I believe he uses Maitland even as Maitland believes he uses the king."

"Are ye saying 'tis Jamie who wishes to take the earls' power from them?"

Bothwell nodded. "Aye, I do. Jamie has learned his lessons well, Alex. Look at the history of the Stewart family, man. Nae one of the Stewart kings has lived to reach old age, being either killed off by their rebellious nobles in wars or by assassination. They have not even been safe from their own sons in many instances as ye well know. James is the only logical choice to succeed Elizabeth Tudor. Who else has she got? Oh, there's Arabella Stewart, Jamie's English cousin, but after Elizabeth I will wager the English will want a king! Jamie intends to be that king, and he intends to live to come into his inheritance. English nobles are far easier to cope wi' than us Scots." Bothwell smiled ruefully.

"This land is always roiling wi' some turmoil or another," he continued. "Jamie knows he must control the nobility in order to live long enough to inherit England. What better way to control them than to destroy, or at least cripple, the more powerful earls both in the Border and in the Highlands? Our downfall would set a forceful example for the smaller clans. Hell, if the royal bairn can take on both Huntley and me, *and can win*, the others will believe that God Himself is on his side. In this, however, he hides behind Maitland, for though Jamie be clever he is nae too brave. Maitland, poor fool, is expendable, for chancellors are a groat a dozen. If Jamie fails in his efforts, he can blame the whole thing on Master Maitland, who, as we all know, is nae popular wi' the earls."

"Then we ride at dawn," said Alex quietly. "The king may have his power, but he canna hae ours, too."

Velvet was up to see them go, kissing Francis Stewart-Hepburn on the cheek and bidding him Godspeed. "When you return to *Hermitage*, give my love to Cat. I'm praying for you both that this thing will soon be settled."

He nodded his appreciation. "Keep well, sweetheart. 'Tis a precious burden ye're carrying for BrocCairn now."

Alex kissed his wife. "I'll be gone only five or six days, lass. Ye need hae no fear. We hae no near enemies, and the castle is impregnable against simple raids, and besides, we've hae no problems in recent years."

"Dugald can advise me," she said, and then kissed him back. "Go carefully, my lord."

She watched from the drawbridge as Alex's party made their way down the narrow road into the glen. It was the first time since their reunion a year ago that they had been separated. A year ago, she thought. Her daughter would be two years of age now. Velvet wondered what she looked like. She would be walking now. Her vocabulary would be increasing. Did she speak Persian or Hindi? Probably both. For a moment Velvet felt pain in the region of her heart, but she firmly pushed aside the temptation to feel sorry for herself. Yasaman was lost to her, but within her body a new child was growing. By the time another year had passed she would have another baby to love and worry over.

In the village below the people of Broc Ailien had come out of their houses to see Francis Stewart-Hepburn, for as careful as Alex had been to keep Bothwell's visit a secret, it was known that he would be passing. To the villagers he was a hero, and, knowing the danger in which he stood, they would not gossip about his presence or betray him to strangers. They would, however, enjoy this event amongst themselves.

Watching the earl pass, Alanna Wythe spoke to her lover, who stood hidden behind the doorway. "There is a reward on his head. God's nightshirt, how I wish it were within our power to collect it!"

"Dinna be foolish, Alanna. How could we possibly capture Lord Bothwell and get him to Edinburgh?"

"I know a way if only you had the retainers to accomplish it," she said, "but you don't, and so we can't. 'Tis a pity, Ian. I should like to go away with you as we have talked."

She had piqued his interest. "How?" he asked.

"Bothwell and BrocCairn are cousins, are they not?"

"Aye, they are. Cousins of the king as well," Ian replied.

"What is dearest to Alex in all this world, Ian? His wife! His precious Velvet Gordon!" Her voice was tinged with bitterness. "What if her ladyship were kidnapped, Ian, and the ransom for her safe return was the delivery of Lord Bothwell into the king's hands? Had we the men, we could arrange such a thing *and* bargain with Master Maitland for payment of the reward upon delivery of Lord Bothwell. We don't have the men, however, and so it is useless to even speak of it."

"Perhaps it could be arranged," he said slowly, "perhaps if I could find him it could be managed."

"Find who?" Alanna pounced on him. "We don't want to have to share the reward equally, Ian. There would be little left for us."

"The reward wouldna really interest him," Ian said. "He can hae Alex's cattle. 'Tis a huge herd this year and worth a good deal of gold. That would appeal to him."

"Who?" Alanna demanded.

"Ranald Shaw. They call him Ranald Torc, Ranald the Boar. He's an outlaw, a beast of a man, but he's just greedy enough to like the idea, and he's a man of his word."

"What's to prevent him from simply stealing Alex's cattle when he finds out that BrocCairn is away?"

"Ranald Torc is nae a fool, Alanna. He's afraid of Alex, as he should be. He realizes that his only security would be in having Velvet in his custody. He'll cooperate wi' us, dinna fear."

"We may not have much time," Alanna cautioned. "Find out how long Alex will be gone. Only then will you know. Jesu, Ian! What an opportunity this is for us! With the king's reward, we can leave this damned glen, that dank pile of stones that you hate so much, and Annabella! We'll be rich, and neither of us will have to owe our livings to the damned Earl of BrocCairn! Think of it, Ian!" She grasped his arms. "We'll be rich!"

He did think of it, and as he pondered it over and over again in his mind it occurred to him that he could indeed be very rich. It also occurred to him that he did not want to share that wealth with Alanna. He would rid himself of both his carping wife and his carping mistress, but first he would use Alanna to help him.

Riding up to the castle that morning, Ian intruded upon Velvet as she worked in her garden. "Is it true," he demanded without so much as a greeting, "that Alex has gone to Huntley wi' Bothwell?"

"Aye," she answered him, annoyed to be caught upon her knees pruning her roses.

He enjoyed towering over her. It gave him a feeling of power, a feeling of sexual excitement that surged through him. "How long will he be gone?"

Velvet rose to her feet, dusting her hands on her skirt. "What difference does it make to you, Ian?" she demanded irritably.

"None to me, but Bella wanted to know, for she is eager to invite you to *Grantholm* and needs several days to prepare. I'm only her messenger."

"Alex will be gone several days, five to six, he said." She smiled sweetly at Ian. "Tell Bella I have a fancy for sweet cakes. I simply cannot live without them these days."

He looked at her as if she had lost her wits.

Velvet laughed. "Why, Ian, as the father of two I would think you'd know what a craving for certain foods indicated. Did we not promise you that you would be one of the first to know when I became enceinte?"

"Ye're wi' child?" he said incredulously, unable to believe this stroke of good fortune. He could already imagine the golden reward he would gain from the crown for Lord Bothwell's capture, for Alex loved his wife, and would love her even better now that she was expecting his heir.

"Aye," Velvet confirmed proudly. "I am with child, but don't tell Bella. I want to be the one to surprise her."

Ian smiled toothily at Velvet. "Nay, my dear, I'll nae tell Bella. Ye'll have yer surprise." Then he turned and left her as abruptly as he had come, heading his horse for the patch of wild country to the west of *Dun Broc* where Ranald Torc held sway.

The territory actually bordered on lands held by the Gordons, the Grants, and Clan Shaw. Ranald Torc was a younger son of the Shaws who had gone wild, but he was not bothered by his relations, for he was too fierce a man to fight and he frankly frightened them. He might have had the family's entire holding but for the fact that he wasn't an ambitious sort. Relieved by this, the Shaws let him be, turning a blind eye when he raided their cattle and sheep or carried off an occasional woman.

Ranald Torc's mother had been the sister of Ian Grant's father. The two had played together as boys, and even though Ranald was politely ignored by his family, Ian still kept up the connection between them although he had never understood why. Perhaps, weakling that he was, he secretly admired the unorthodox ways of his rebellious cousin.

Ranald Torc's home was a dilapidated stone house deep in the forest. Ian knew that he was observed almost every foot of the way he traveled from the moment he stepped onto his cousin's lands. Still, he looked neither to the right nor the left nor behind him. He simply pressed onward until the house came into view.

"Hallo, the house!" he called as he stopped his horse. "Ranald Torc! 'Tis Ian Grant."

The door to the dwelling slowly opened, and then a figure stooped beneath the entryway and came forth into the clearing. Ian was, as always when he saw his cousin after a long period of time, amazed by the man's size. Ranald Torc stood close to seven feet in height with huge limbs and shoulders. His massive head was completely in proportion with his great body, his light brown hair cut straight across his forehead and hanging to his shoulders. His nickname, "The Boar," came from the fact that his light blue eyes were closely spaced, giving him the wary, suspicious look of a wild pig. That feature prevented him from being handsome, although he was certainly not an ugly man.

"Hallo, Mouse!" His deep voice boomed at Ian. "What brings ye into my lair?"

Ian flushed at Ranald Torc's use of the nickname he'd been given by his elder cousin during their childhood. His color was not lost on Ranald, who chuckled at Ian's discomfort.

"I've a proposition to make ye, Ranald. It'll bring ye a lot of gold if ye're interested."

"Come into the house then, *Mouse*." The giant ducked back under his doorway followed by Ian. Once his eyes became used to the gloom Ian could see about the huge room with its great fireplace. It was quite comfortably furnished. Ranald poured some whiskey into pewter goblets and thrust one into Ian's hand, motioning him at the same time to be seated.

"Well, speak up, Mouse! How can I get myself this gold ye're babbling about?"

"I'll need yer word first that ye'll aid me in a small undertaking of my own, Ranald. My undertaking will earn me a great deal of gold, too, but that gold I'll nae share wi' ye. Besides, it will take longer to get than the easy gold I hae in mind for ye."

Ranald Torc shrugged. "Ye were always the smarter of us, Mouse. If ye say I'll be satisfied, then I believe ye, for we're kin, and I know ye'd nae cheat me because ye know if ye did that I'd kill ye. I'll aid ye in yer undertaking, cousin. Now, say on!"

"Lord Bothwell is at this very minute on his way to Huntley wi' BrocCairn. There's a good price on his head, but no one can catch him. I know how to catch him, however. He and BrocCairn are cousins. He's very fond of both Alex and Alex's wife, who is expecting BrocCairn's heir. Help me to kidnap Velvet Gordon, Ranald. Bothwell wouldn't let anything happen to his cousin's wife and child. He's too much the gentleman. He'll turn himself in, and I'll gain the king's reward for his capture, and ye'll gain BrocCairn's cattle, for we'll steal them as well as his wife. He's got a huge herd, Ranald! Since we're at peace, most of BrocCairn's men hae gone wi' him, and the cattle's unguarded."

"Hae ye thought of how ye're going to get Lady Gordon out of that fortress, Ian?"

"Aye! Ye can capture her when she comes to visit my wife at *Grantholm*. Ye know the stretch of lonely road between Broc Ailien and my holding. It's the ideal place to take her!"

"And what's to prevent BrocCairn from coming after her and killing me and mine?" demanded Ranald Torc. "A good wife can't be replaced easily."

"Ye need not fear Alex, Ranald. He adores Velvet, and the bairn she carries will be their firstborn. He won't want anything to happen to her, and neither will Bothwell. They'll cooperate, and we'll both be rich men!"

"What does yer wife think of this, Mouse? Is she in agreement wi' yer plan?"

"Annabella doesna know, Ranald. I'm leaving *Grantholm* when this is over."

"Ah. The giant smiled, "There's another woman, is there?"

Ian laughed. "I'll be leaving her, too," he said. "I'm not of a mind to exchange one complaining woman for another. Here's the best part, cousin. My mistress was Alex's mistress! He brought her from England before his wife came, but he grew tired of her. She has his brat, a daughter. No one, not even my wife, knows that I've been using her."

"Is she pretty?" Ranald Torc inquired.

"Aye. She's got long yellow hair she wears in thick braids, and the biggest pair of tits I've ever seen on any woman, let alone one who just stands over five feet in height. Her skin is good, for she's nae pockmarked like so many." Then suddenly Ian had another idea. "Would ye like her, Ranald? I'll gie her to ye! Alex's cattle and Alex's whore! 'Tis nae a bad deal, is it?"

"Well," Ranald Torc considered, "I've nae had a woman in a long time. I dinna like hurting them, and ye know my problem."

Ian did indeed know his cousin's problem. Ian was himself very well endowed sexually, but his cousin was considered to be deformed, for his genitals were more like those of a stallion than those of a man. As young men are wont to do, the cousins had once compared the sizes of their cocks. To Ian's intense embarrassment, Ranald was almost twice his size, and it wasn't until Ian saw how he stood among other men that his confidence was restored. Ranald Torc was simply too big for most women, and even paid whores refused to risk injury when they saw his male parts. But he missed a woman's warmth. Ian's offer was a tempting one.

"If ye're sure ye dinna want the woman anymore, Mouse, then, aye, I'll take her. If I kill her it'll nae matter since she's an English whore, but won't she object when she finds out ye're leaving her?"

"Let me handle Alanna. I'll tell her ye'll nae help us unless she spreads her legs for ye. She'll do it. She's a greedy bitch."

"How long do we have before BrocCairn returns?" Ranald was now making his plans.

"He'll be gone five or six days, but we'd best do it quickly."

"Aye, I'd agree wi' that, Mouse."

"Will ye bring Alex's wife here?" Ian asked.

"Nay, cousin. That's too obvious. We'll drive the cattle south and sell them there. Then we'll go to Edinburgh to await yer reward. I'll hae my gold, and it'll be harder for the Earl of BrocCairn to find us in the city than here. I'd like to live to enjoy my ill-gotten gains." He chuckled.

"Lady Gordon is newly wi' child, Ranald. Ye canna endanger her life or that of the child. Alex would kill me if ye did. I dinna like the bastard, but I'm no murderer," Ian declared.

"Ye dinna think he'll kill ye for leaving his sister, Mouse?"

"Bella willna let him. I know her; she'll be hoping that I'll return to her."

"Will ye?" Ranald asked.

"Nay. I'm for France where I'm told a man can live well wi' a goodly pile of gold. I never thought to hae such a chance, but Alanna is a wise wench and 'twas her idea, all of this."

"I'm thinking then that ye're a fool to let such a woman go so easily, Mouse."

"A woman, Ranald, is a woman, be she wife or mistress. Keep one around too long, and they all begin to sound alike, to say the same things, to carp and complain without ceasing. From now on I intend to have a different woman every week, and that way I'll never be bored again!"

"I'll gie my men their orders then, Mouse, and ye and I will ride down to Broc Ailien. I'm anxious to meet this Alanna."

It was already nightfall when they slipped into Alanna Wythe's cottage. Alanna was in her nightshift, and the fire was low when they arrived. Sybilla lay asleep in her cot.

"And who is this giant?" demanded Alanna crossly. "I didn't give you permission to bring your friends here."

"This is Ranald Torc, Alanna. He's agreed to help us. We move tomorrow. I'm going home tonight to *Grantholm* to get Annabella to send a message to sweet Velvet to come and visit wi' her tomorrow afternoon. Ranald's men will take her on the road between the village and my home. Then they'll take BrocCairn's cattle, and we'll be gone."

"What happens when your wife gives the alarm because Velvet hasn't arrived, Ian? You'll have to send the message in Annabella's name so that she doesn't know there's been a message. That way we'll have more time. You can even send another message to *Dun Broc* later, saying her ladyship has decided to spend the night at *Grantholm.* That way there'll be no alarm until the following day, and by the time they reach Alex, we'll all be very long gone."

"By God!" Ranald Torc said, "I like a woman who thinks like a man. Now, mouse, tell the wench my condition for helping ye."

"Mouse?" Alanna looked at Ian and laughed. "Aye, I can see it! What condition?"

"He wants to fuck ye," Ian said bluntly. "He'll help us if ye'll let him."

Alanna let her eyes roam over Ranald Torc. Her gaze was bold and noncommittal. "He's got to wash first," she said.

"What?" Both men spoke in unison.

"He smells like a pig byre. I'll fuck him, but he's got to be clean." She didn't give either man the chance to think, instead saying, "Ian, get the tub I use in the pantry, and I'll start heating the water."

Ranald Torc was fascinated. He had expected a shriek of outrage, which he would follow with the rape of the Englishwoman's person. Instead she was ordering him to bathe, and, by God, he was going to do it! He had never met such a woman in his entire life. He gave a barely perceptible nod to his cousin, and within a short time the tub was filled with warm water and set before the fire, which Alanna had built up so that its warmth filled the room.

He handed her his shirt and his stockings which, she immediately threw into a smaller tub to wash. Ian, having yanked his cousin's boots off moments before, had already fled the cottage. He didn't want to be around when Alanna got a good look at Ranald Torc's private parts.

"Get into the tub," Alanna ordered the giant, pulling his kilt from him and turning to shake it out the back door. "Now," she said, "just sit there a few minutes until I get your shirt and stockings clean. 'Tis no good putting a clean body into dirty clothes."

It was obvious she hadn't taken a good look at him yet, he thought, or she'd be screaming the cottage down. He did as he had been told and sat himself in the tub, considering even as he did so how foolish he must look, his knees sticking up into the air. Within a few minutes, as she had promised, his shirt and hose were washed and spread before the fire to dry. Alanna now turned to the task of bathing Ranald Torc, and she showed no mercy as she wielded a boar's-bristle brush on him.

"Jesu!" he complained as she soaped him with a small cake of soap. "I smell like a damned flower."

"You smell clean, you great oaf! A rare departure, I don't doubt! Stand up! I can't bathe what I can't see!"

Ranald Torc stood and waited for her scream to come. For a long moment she was very quiet, and then Alanna said, "I thought that Ian Grant had the biggest cock in Christendom, but I was certainly wrong, wasn't I?" She soaped him, her hands lingering lovingly over his male parts. "God almighty, you're built like a bull, Ranald Torc!" She cupped the pouch of his sex in her hands, and it overflowed her palms. She ran her tiny fingers sensually down the long, long length of him, sighing voluptuously as she did so, and his manhood stirred violently in her grasp. "Sit down and rinse yourself," she said in a tight voice. "The sooner you're clean, the sooner you can fill me up with that great pole of yours!"

No woman had ever spoken to him like that. Usually they howled and wept with fear at the sight of him. He looked up at her. She really was a little bit of a thing next to him. He was suddenly afraid he'd kill her with his bigness, and for some reason he couldn't quite explain he didn't want to.

As if reading his thoughts, she said, "You'll have to go slowly until we see how much of you will fit."

He nodded and, standing up, stepped from the tub. She rubbed him dry with a small square of toweling, and when she had finished he found that despite his nudity he felt himself in full command of the situation, no longer so nonplussed by the small, blond woman who spoke so boldly to him. "Well," he said slowly, "ye've had a good look at what I hae to offer, now let's see yer goods, woman!"

With a slow seductive smile, Alanna dropped her shift, and her smile broadened at his intake of breath. She was very proud of her body. She might be tiny in stature, but her limbs were pleasingly rounded, and her breasts were big and full. Reaching out, he gently hefted one of those large breasts, and a smile spread on his face as the nipple puckered at his touch. Taking him by the hand, she led him up into the loft above the cottage's main room where her mattress was spread. They knelt facing one another, and he let his hands run eagerly over her lushness. Overwhelmed by the bounty offered him, he couldn't decide where to begin. His big hands reached around to squeeze her buttocks, which were plump and firm. Alanna lifted her breasts and rubbed them against his hairy chest. His whole body was, she saw, covered with darkish hair. For a few moments, they explored each other, but the truth was that she excited him tremendously, and, seeing it, Alanna lay on her back and spread her legs wide.

"Go on," she encouraged him, "stuff me with that monster cock of yours, Ranald Torc!"

With a groan, he fell on her and began to push himself steadily into her. At first Alanna felt she was being torn asunder, but she forced herself to relax, and he restrained himself from hurrying. Suddenly, to her surprise, he was buried completely within her. With a pleased grin he kissed her heartily on the mouth.

She pulled her head away, though, and said, "Now fuck me, you brute! We know now you can't kill me."

Ranald Torc complied with Alanna's request most willingly. She was the first woman he'd ever taken who accepted him easily *and* at the height of her passion begged him for more. He spent a long and happy night loving this tiny Englishwoman. If the truth had been known, she actually wore him out, and he loved her the more for it. When the dawn came, she arose to cook him a large breakfast of porridge, ham, eggs, and scones.

Ian Grant, creeping back and expecting to find his mistress dead, instead found her eating quite contentedly with his cousin.

"She's my woman now," Ranald Torc said bluntly.

"Ye fucked her?" Ian was astounded.

"Aye," came the reply.

"But ye usually kill them wi' yer cock," said Ian.

"Aye, but this time 'twas different," Ranald answered.

"How?"

"There's nae doubt that I've the biggest cock in Christendom, but, Alanna"—he smiled broadly at Ian—"well, it seems that she has the biggest cunt in Christendom! We're a perfect match, Mouse! Now sit down, man, and hae something to eat. We've a long day ahead of us."

Bemused at this unexpected turn of events, Ian sat down. Alanna slammed a bowl of oat porridge in front of him. "I sent the message to Velvet first thing this morning," he said. "I've the other message ready to send to *Dun Broc* once we hae her in our custody."

Ranald Torc grunted approval.

"What are ye going to do wi' Sibby?" Ian asked Alanna. "Ye canna take her wi' us, can ye?"

"I'll ask Mistress Lawrie to take care of her," Alanna replied. "The brat spends most of her time with that woman anyhow, and the bitch seems to have a weakness for her despite all her own children. When they see I'm gone, you can be certain Jean Lawrie will take Sibby in. If she doesn't want another mouth to feed, she can give her to her father when he returns. It makes me laugh to think of her high-and-mighty ladyship returning home when this is over to find she has to raise *my* child. She'll do it, too, for she's softhearted. I've seen her with the children here in the village."

"Ye'd leave yer child to another?" Ranald Torc asked.

"Would you take me with you if I insisted upon bringing her along?" Alanna countered.

"Nay, 'tis no life for a child," he answered.

"Do you want to leave me, Ranald Torc, until this is all over?" she demanded. "I thought you liked fucking me."

"I'll nae leave ye ever again, Alanna," he replied. "That itch of yers needs my scratching, but be warned: If ye so much as look at another man, I'll beat ye senseless. Leave the brat. Ye're my woman now, and I'll gie ye more bairns to raise."

"Not unless ye marry me, ye won't!" she snapped.

"In Edinburgh, I will," he promised her, "and those who know me know my word is good."

Ian Grant was completely amazed by the conversation that was taking place as if he weren't even there. He was somewhat aggrieved that Alanna, having been his mistress for so many months, was so easily and effortlessly discarding him. He had forgotten for the moment that he had intended to leave her, that he had without a thought turned her over to his cousin whose mighty attentions could have either seriously injured or killed her. Ian fancied himself quite the lover, but Alanna Wythe seemed not to care. She was, he decided, an English bitch without the good taste to comprehend what she was throwing away in order to marry that monster of a cousin of his. Well, good luck to them both. They were going to need it if BrocCairn came after them. He, on the other hand, would be safe in France living as he was always meant to live.

Before the sun had sent its slender, golden rays into the glen, both Ian Grant and Ranald Torc were gone from Alanna Wythe's cottage. Not even little Sybilla knew that they had been there. The breakfast dishes were washed and returned to their cupboard before Alanna roused her child from her slumber. She bathed her and fed her lukewarm porridge with a scone that had a dab of honey on it. Dressing the child in clean clothes, she braided her reddish brown hair, then led her from the cottage and walked the few steps to Jean Lawrie's cottage.

Alanna entered the house without knocking, and Angus Lawrie, seated at his table, looked up, not quite able to hide the admiration in his eyes. "Good morning, Angus," she said sweetly, "I've come to see Jean."

"If ye could take yer eyes off my man long enough," snapped Jean Lawrie, "ye'd see me right here by the fireplace. What do ye want, Mistress Wythe?" Jean Lawrie was nursing her young son who was almost a year old now.

"I want to go into the forest today to look for roots," Alanna said. "I don't like bringing Sibby with me because she won't obey me and stay still. I'm always afraid she'll be hurt. Will you watch her until I get back? I'll make you a good medicine for coughs that you can use this winter if you do."

"I'd watch the lass in any case," Jean Lawrie said softening. "Go on. She's safe wi' me."

Alanna knelt down and looked into her daughter's face. "Be a good girl, Sibby, and obey Mistress Lawrie," she said, and then, standing up, she was gone.

At the very moment Alanna was leaving her daughter with Jean Lawrie, Velvet received an early-morning message from her sister-in-law. Annabella wanted her to come and visit today. Ian was going hunting, and as Alex was away at *Huntley* perhaps she would be free. She had to come. Annabella was so totally bored. This was Annabella in a far lighter mood than Velvet had seen her recently, and Velvet very much wanted to be friends with her husband's sister. Other than Bella, there were no females but the servants within visiting distance. Velvet was lonely for another woman's company. After her close relationship with Jodh Bai and Rugaiya Begum, and especially now that she was expecting a child, she needed female companionship. Pansy, bless her, was so involved in her own new life that Velvet didn't feel comfortable imposing on her.

"Pansy!" she called now from bed, and her tiring woman hurried into the bedchamber.

"Good morning, m'lady!"

"We're going to *Grantholm* today, Pansy. Can you still ride, or shall I have one of the maids go with me?"

Pansy, in the fifth month of her second pregnancy, patted her rounding belly, saying, "I'm good for a little while longer, m'lady. I'll go with you. With or without child, I still ride better than any of those flighty lasses."

Velvet hid her grin. Pansy was fiercely protective of her place in Velvet's life. She had no intention of allowing one of the local Scots girls the opportunity to steal it from her. Pansy was the Countess of BrocCairn's tiring woman, and she would let none forget it.

"Will you wear a gown or your usual riding garb, m'lady?"

"Not a gown, Pansy. The road is dusty. Bella will just have to take me in trunk hose."

Pansy agreed with her mistress and quickly assembled Velvet's hose, shirt, belt, jerkin, and boots. Then she arranged for her lady's bath, adding gillyflower bath oil to the steaming tub. When Velvet had bathed, Pansy helped her to dress. While her mistress ate her breakfast of eggs poached in cream and sherry, thin slices of newly caught and broiled salmon, freshly baked scones with honey and butter, and watered wine, Pansy hurried to exchange her own garb for one a little less conventional so that she might ride, too.

Learning that his wife was riding out with her mistress, Dugald fretted, "I dinna want ye losing the bairn, Pansy lass."

"Leave her be," snapped Morag Geddes, who seemed always to side with her English daughter-in-law. "Pansy's a good, strong girl, and she'd nae endanger her bairn. Didn't she bring our wee Dugie safely home from that heathen land? Go along wi' ye, Pansy," she commanded, and with a wave Pansy hurried to join her mistress.

As Dugald looked after his wife, his mother remonstrated him, "Ye're worse than an old woman, Dugald. 'Tis but two miles to *Grantholm*."

Velvet was already mounted upon her black mare, Sable, when Pansy joined her to climb up on her sturdy, black and white pony whom she had named Bess "in honor of Her Majesty," she had told her mistress. Half a dozen men-at-arms would ride with them, but only for show as these were BrocCairn lands, and there was peace in Scotland.

There was the faintest nip of early autumn in the air as they departed from the castle, their horses' hooves thrumming over the drawbridge and onto the road. They could feel a brisk breeze, and the sun was playing a game of peek-aboo with the bright, white clouds. As they passed through Broc Ailien, the villagers called their greetings to their countess who, like her husband, called back to them, using their names, knowing small bits of their lives, which she commented upon. As they loved Alex, the people of Broc Ailien loved Velvet now, too. She saw little Sibby playing before Jean Lawrie's cottage, and was for a quick moment reminded of Yasaman. She blinked the tears from her eyes, all the while thinking that something should really be done for Alex's daughter, who was a nice little thing despite her odious mother.

They left the village behind. It was only another mile or so to *Grantholm*, the manor house where Annabella and Ian lived with their two sons, James and Henry. The road wound through the woods, which were thick and green, and it was at the deepest part of the forest that they suddenly found themselves surprised and surrounded by a band of men wearing the green and blue tartan with the narrow red stripe that the BrocCairn men recognized as that of the Shaws. Instantly the six men-at-arms surrounded their countess and her tirewoman, but, badly outnumbered, they were quickly cut down.

"Go, Pansy!" shouted Velvet over the din of the short battle, and kicked Sable's sides. Her flight, and that of Pansy's, was quickly halted, however, by a giant bear of a man who, reaching out, yanked at both Sable's and Bess's bridles, successfully stopping them. Velvet lashed out at the man with her crop. "Let go of my horse!" she shouted. "I am the Countess of BrocCairn! How dare you attack me on my own lands!"

Ranald Torc burst into loud laughter. "BrocCairn's bride is a fire-eater, Mouse! Ye dinna tell me that her ladyship had spirit, but, by God, I like that in a woman!" The battle over and the BrocCairn men dead where they had fallen trying to protect Velvet, Ranald Torc turned to speak to the countess. "I am Ranald Shaw, called Ranald Torc, madame. Ye've been captured fairly. Will ye yield to me and gie me yer word ye'll nae try to excape?"

"Go to hell!" she shouted at him. "How dare you, you big ox!"

Ranald Torc laughed again. "Torc means boar, madame, nae ox."

"Very well, Ranald the Pig, I demand an explanation of your conduct! There is no feud between the Gordons and the Shaws."

Ranald Torc's face darkened at the word "pig." This was not going to be as easy as Ian had made it sound. The countess should be swooning with fright at this moment, begging for her life and her honor. Instead this auburn-haired hellion was spitting at him like a wildcat and asking for answers to difficult questions. Irritably he looked about. "Ian," he shouted. "This is yer place, nae mine."

It was then that Velvet noticed her brother-in-law for the first time. "Ian! What in hell is going on here?" she demanded.

Ian Grant moved his horse forward to come abreast of Velvet. He was very much in his element now and enjoying every minute of this drama. "Good morning, Velvet," he said cheerfully. "Ye would like to know what this is all about, wouldn't ye? Well, my dear, I am tired of being BrocCairn's poor relation, and so I hae decided to grasp fortune by the neck, as it were. There is a very large reward on the Earl of Bothwell, who at this very minute is wi' yer husband at Huntley. I should like to collect that reward, and since I doubt that either Alex or Lord Bothwell would like to see ye hurt, especially considering that ye carry BrocCairn's heir, I hae decided to offer them a bargain. I will return ye to Alex in exchange for Lord Bothwell. I dinna think they will refuse me, do ye? Now all ye must do is be a good lass for the next few weeks while this delicate exchange is arranged."

"Ian, I'd kill you if I could," said Velvet furiously, "and you'd best not to get too near me, you damned bastard, or I will!"

"Ho! Ho!" Ranald Torc chuckled. "I believe her ladyship would indeed slit yer throat given the chance, Mouse. Ye'd best be wary."

"Nay, cousin," said Ian calmly. "Velvet will behave herself, for her husband is as close to committing treason as any man, and if she doesna wish to see him executed for it, she will cooperate wi' us, won't ye, my dear?"

"What do you mean, treason?" Velvet demanded.

"Bothwell's been put to the horn, Velvet," said Ian. "Here in Scotland that means he's been outlawed, all his possessions forefeited to the crown. The king has accused him of treason."

"A ridiculous charge, and all of Scotland knows it," Velvet snapped back.

"Aye, but, nonetheless, James Stewart's word is law in this land, and by aiding Bothwell the outlaw, yer precious Alex is as guilty. Now shut yer mouth, yer ladyship! We hae a long way to travel before we'll be safe."

"You'll never be safe from Alex, you little bastard!" snarled Velvet. "And what of Bella?"

"I suppose she'll miss me," he said easily.

Velvet stared at him, outraged, and angry for poor Annabella. "I hope I'm there when Alex kills you," she said venomously.

Ranald Torc looked directly at Velvet, but her gaze never wavered. He knew Alex Gordon, and he thought that this woman was a fit mate for BrocCairn. She was canny, bonny, and very brave, he had not a doubt. "Enough of yer battling," he said firmly. "We must go now. There's still the cattle to take. Ian, ye bring her ladyship to safety wi' Alanna, and we'll meet ye."

Velvet could see that it was Ranald Torc who controlled this band of outlaws. "Let my tiring woman go back to *Dun Broc*," she pleaded. "She is five months gone with a bairn."

"She'd raise the alarm," said Ranald Torc. "We must go quickly, but we'll go carefully, madame, for I hae no wish to harm either of ye or yer bairns."

Ian leaned down and, taking Velvet's bridle, led her off, Pansy following along. Velvet recognized the route they were traveling as the same one that had brought her to BrocCairn. She had not been out of the glen in the year since her arrival. At the crest of the hill, she saw Alanna Wythe waiting.

"Is she your whore now?" Velvet demanded of Ian.

"She was for a while," he said easily, "but she seems to prefer my cousin, Ranald. They're to be wed in Edinburgh, although having declared their intentions before me, they're handfast and as good as married now."

Velvet glared at Alanna as they came abreast of the woman. "Where is your daughter?" she demanded of her.

"With Jean Lawrie, not that it's your business."

"You're leaving her?"

"She's better off in Broc Ailien with Jean," said Alanna. "My husband's an outlaw, or perhaps you didn't know that. 'Tis hardly the proper life for the Earl of BrocCairn's daughter, is it?"

"You're a cold bitch," said Velvet evenly. "When I return to BrocCairn, I'm going to take Sibby and raise her myself. I'll see she never even knows you exist!"

Suddenly Alanna found herself very discomfited by the situation and, with a toss of her head, said, "I'll come to see Sibby whenever it suits me, madame."

"If you ever come near *Dun Broc* again, I'll set the dogs on you, Alanna Wythe."

"Cease yer bickering," snarled Ian Grant. "We've miles to go before we meet up wi' Ranald Torc again, and I'll not waste the daylight hours listening to the pair of ye squabbling like two barnyard hens over a cock."

With surprising speed, Velvet lashed out at him with her riding crop. "Don't you even speak to me, you little bastard!" she shouted at him.

Stunned, Ian Grant ran his hand down the weal she had raised on his handsome face and was surprised to find that the side of his face by his left eye was bloodied. Anger poured through him. The bitch had marked him!

Velvet saw his anger, and a slow smile touched her lips. Her voice was low and even as she spoke. "Lay a hand on me, Ian, and you're a dead man where you stand. You know what Alex would do to you if you touched me, don't you?"

Several of Ranald Torc's men had accompanied Ian, and now the leader of the group leaned forward and said, "The earl will nae pay ye for damaged goods, Ian. Let it be."

Frustrated and furious, Ian Grant kicked his mount into a trot, and they were off. They did not meet up with Ranald Torc and the main body of his outlaws until close to evening. His band had successfully stolen the BrocCairn cattle and had driven them around the mountains on a deserted track. They were far enough from BrocCairn to discourage pursuit from the few men that had been left there, most having gone with their earl to Huntley.

Ranald Torc could not take the chance of being seen, and so they camped out in a meadow where the cattle could rest and graze the night away. Two small campfires sprang up, and a cow was butchered and roasted over the open flame, to be served with oatcakes that the men kept in their pouches and washed down with water from a nearby stream or whiskey from their personal flasks. Ranald Torc did his best to see that his two prisoners were comfortable, for Ian was still angry and would not go near Velvet and Pansy.

Alanna had passed on what had happened between them, and Ranald chuckled richly. "She's the badger's bitch all right," he said. "She'll breed up hell-raising sons and daughters for BrocCairn."

"You sound as if you like Alex," said Alanna, somewhat confused.

"I do," came the outlaw's reply. "He's a good man in a fight and a good lord to his people. I've nae quarrel wi' Gordon of BrocCairn."

"But you stole his cattle!" Alanna said.

"Stealing a man's cattle doesna mean ye dinna like him," said Ranald. "Cattle stealing is an old Highland tradition, Alanna. Ye've much to learn, lassie, but ye'll find me a good teacher." He rose to his full height. "I've got to see that Lady

Gordon and her woman are comfortable." Leaving Alanna to await his return, Ranald Torc walked over to where Velvet was seated and squatted down beside her. "I've given orders that ye not be disturbed, madame, and, believe me, none of my men will disobey me. I regret I canna offer ye more comfortable accommodations. There's a bit of a nip in the air tonight. Will ye be warm enough?"

"We've our plaids to wrap about us," replied Velvet. She was not afraid of this giant who was really not much taller than her own father. She was used to big men.

"Can I get ye anything before ye sleep?"

Velvet chuckled. "My husband," she said, and Ranald Torc grinned at her.

"Ye're nae afraid," he said. "Good! We'll nae hurt yer ladyship."

"Where are we going?" she demanded.

"South to sell the cattle, and then to Edinburgh. Has Ian nae spoken wi' ye?"

"Keep that little turd away from me!" Velvet exploded. "I swear if I get the chance I'll slit his throat with his own dagger! I'll not speak with him. You tell me."

He nodded, understanding her feelings. She was a Gordon of BrocCairn, and Ian Grant had been disloyal to the Gordons in the worst way: stealing from his brother-in-law, deserting his Gordon wife and his sons, attempting to betray Scotland's greatest nobleman as Judas had once betrayed his master. Ranald knew his cousin was no prize. Aye, he understood Velvet's anger and desire for revenge. "Tomorrow," he said, "two of my men will deliver a message to *Huntley* from Ian saying that ye're being held in his custody; the ransom being Lord Bothwell's person. Lord Bothwell will turn himself over to Ian Grant in Edinburgh at an arranged location. When Ian has given up his prisoner to the crown and received his reward, then ye and yer woman will be free to return to yer home at *Dun Broc*."

"And how much of the reward will you share?" she asked him scornfully.

"I'd nae betray Francis Stewart-Hepburn," said Ranald Torc. "He's naught to me or mine."

"Then why are you involved in this?" said Velvet.

"Because I promised my cousin, Ian, my aid before I knew what he had in mind. I am a man of my word, come what may. Yer husband's cattle were all I wanted, and because BrocCairn was so foolish as to leave his herds unguarded and because he will not come after me for fear of my harming you, I'll soon be a rich man. But dinna accuse me of betraying Bothwell. I hae no part in that."

"Without you, Ranald Torc, Ian could not accomplish his goal. The king accuses Lord Bothwell unfairly on the advice of his chancellor, Maitland. Do you want Maitland ruling Scotland through Jamie Stewart? Send me home tomorrow. You've gained the cattle, and if you speak the truth, 'tis all you really wanted."

"I hae given my word," replied Ranald Torc. "'Tis my most precious possession, Lady Gordon. I canna violate it."

"Then be warned, Ranald Torc, that I shall try to escape, for I would not want to be the instrument of Lord Bothwell's downfall." Then, wrapping herself in her plaid, she lay down, turning her back to him.

Neither she nor Pansy, however, was given the opportunity to escape. The following day, as they set out, the women found that leading reins had been attached to both sides of their mounts' bridles and armed men rode on either side of them, the leading reins in their grasp. Velvet was furious, but there was nothing that she could do, so she was forced to ride along quietly.

"We'll have our chance in Edinburgh," Pansy whispered to her in the night. "We'll escape the little toady in the city, and he'll not find us."

"But once Maitland learns of Ian's plan, even if I escape my bastard brother-in-law, I'll not be safe," fretted Velvet. "The king is not above using me himself to get at Francis. He simply never thought of it, Pansy. When Ian tells them of how he plans to capture Bothwell, the king and Maitland won't hesitate to use me. We must escape Ian Grant before he reaches them. If he doesn't have me, then perhaps Bothwell will be safe. Ian isn't stupid enough to go to the king and present his plan unless he has his hostage. Without me they'll throw him out of the palace."

Several days later Ranald Torc sold BrocCairn's cattle at a fair where, in light of the herd's excellence, no questions were asked. Then they were off to Edinburgh: Ranald Torc, Alanna, Ian, Velvet, Pansy, and half a dozen of Shaw's outlaws, the rest being sent back to their home for they were too expensive to maintain. Alanna insisted that Ranald Torc make good his promise to wed her, and at a small kirk near the city they were married, having declared before the preacher their state of handfast.

Then fate played into Velvet's hand, for Ian, beginning to realize the enormity of what he had done and was about to attempt, decided that if he was to make good his escape to France before Alex found and killed him, they would be safer staying in Edinburgh's port town, Leith. Knowing Bothwell's favorite tavern in Leith to be the Golden Anchor, Ian decided that the exchange would take place there, and one of Ranald Torc's men was dispatched to find the earl and tell him.

Ranald and Ian hid themselves and their captives in a slum near the waterfront, pretending to the landlady that they were two married couples—cousins they told her—and their servant. Ranald Torc had insisted that the rooms they rented be on the ground floor of the house to facilitate a quick escape should that become necessary. Ian was extremely irritated, for rooms at the top of the house would have cost him less.

There were only two rooms available, and at night the honeymooning couple closeted themsleves into the smaller room from which, much of the evening, there emitted a series of strange sounds. Added to this was the noise from the street outside, and the rats and fleas that infested their quarters. Ian spent his nights snoring loudly in a chair in the room with his captives, but Velvet did not get much sleep, and she began to fear that it would be impossible to escape, for neither she nor Pansy was allowed out of the apartment.

It was small consolation that Ranald Torc's men were not sharing their quarters, there not being enough room. Those five were forced to fend for themselves, usually sleeping in doorways, alleyways, or, if they were lucky, with a friendly whore. Alanna and her new husband spent their days sight-seeing, leaving Velvet and Pansy to bear Ian's dull company and that of one or two of Ranald Torc's men. Usually Velvet spoke with the outlaws, for they were simple men who, though they made their living in the world by robbery and occasionally killing, were basically friendly and respectful of the Countess of BrocCairn. They did not understand what was going on at all, but they obeyed their leader, and Ranald Shaw had brought them to Leith.

Their food came from a nearby cookhouse, Ian fetching it at midday, or if he was drunk, which happened more frequently, sending one of Ranald Torc's men for it. Ian was becoming increasingly nervous and irritable. It had been ten days since he had kidnapped his sister-in-law and aided in the theft of his brother-in-law's cattle, and they had not heard from BrocCairn, nor had the two messengers they had sent to *Huntley* returned. Until he heard from Alex, Ian dared not contact Maitland.

Velvet's calm began to annoy him, and one day he shouted at her, "Perhaps BrocCairn doesna want ye back, after all! Perhaps he has thought better of taking to wife an infidel's whore."

Velvet was not disturbed by his words. She knew her husband and she was certain she had his love. Looking at Ian Grant, she said wickedly, "Perhaps it's just that he's coming to murder you, Ian. This is Lord Bothwell's territory. Remember, he was once lord admiral of Scotland. They're looking for you, Ian, and when they find you, you're a dead man! I warned you!"

"Ye bitch!" he shouted at her, leaping to his feet a trifle unsteadily, for he'd been drinking most of the day. "I'll nae be cheated of my gold! I'm going to Maitland now! I'll turn ye over to him and be done wi' ye! I'm tired of yer face, and Maitland will gie me my gold. I'll nae be cheated of it! I won't!" And then he stumbled from the room and out into the street.

Surprised, Velvet and Pansy looked at one another. They were alone, their guards having gone to the cookhouse for the evening meal. Wordlessly, they grabbed their cloaks and fled the apartment before Ian realized what he had done, or their guards returned, or Ranald Torc and Alanna came back. Grasping her tiring woman by the hand, Velvet hurried her along, not quite knowing where they were going, but remembering vaguely that they were near the waterfront itself. It would soon be dark, and she was terrified that they would be caught on the streets in this strange place by men looking for whores.

"Where are we going, m'lady?" gasped Pansy as they ran.

"To the docks!" replied Velvet.

"But why? Can't we go straight home to *Dun Broc?*"

Velvet could smell the sea now, and, pulling Pansy with her, she rounded a corner. To her relief, she had somehow managed to find her way to the waterfront, and there was a fairly respectable-looking tavern, its sign a brightly painted golden anchor proclaiming its name. "Pull your hood up," she commanded her tiring woman, and Pansy obeyed. Together they entered the inn, and when the landlord came forward, Velvet said, "I am seeking passage for France for my servant and myself. Can you recommend a respectable ship?"

"Any particular port?" demanded the landlord.

"I am bound for Nantes," she said, "but if you know of a decent vessel headed for any French port that would accept a gentlewoman and her servant, I should like to book passage."

"There are several vessels leaving wi' the tide tonight, but only one I know is calling at Nantes. 'Tis an O'Malley-Small trading vessel headed for the Levant. It's captained by a young lad wi' his first command, a protégé of one of the owners. His name is Michael Small, nae relation to the owner, but he took his name, I understand, from the man who took him in as a boy. He's a good man, and I'll arrange it for ye if ye like."

"Thank you," said Velvet, "I would appreciate it, sir." She reached into her jerkin for her purse, but the landlord cautioned her severely.

"Dinna show me yer gold, madame, until I know whether he'll take ye or not. Ye dinna know who's watching."

Warned, Velvet removed her hand and asked, "Is there a private place where my servant and I might wait, and could you bring us some food?"

The landlord led them to a small private room, and shortly afterwards a rosy-cheeked serving girl brought them first warm water with which to bathe their face and hands, and then a hot meal that consisted of a roasted chicken, two small, steaming meat pies, bread, cheese, and baked apples with cream. There was good brown ale to drink, and both Velvet and Pansy stuffed themselves. The food that Ian had given them hadn't been very appetizing, and they had eaten it merely to stay alive long enough to be freed.

"God, I wish I could have a bath," Velvet said feelingly. "I'm beginning to smell, but without clean clothes what good would it do?" She sighed.

Pansy nodded mournfully. "Perhaps once we're on board ship and we tell Captain Michael Small who we are . . ."

Velvet did not let her tiring woman even finish. "No! We cannot tell him, Pansy. No one must know who we are, especially Captain Small. Uncle Robbie found Michael, beaten, in an alley many years ago," Velvet continued. "He was only a boy then. Uncle Robbie brought him aboard his ship, healed him, and made him a cabin boy. It was before I was born, Pansy. Michael couldn't even remember his last name, and so Uncle Robbie gave him his. We'll be safe aboard an O'Malley-Small ship, but Captain Small doesn't know me so he won't be able to tell anyone where we are."

"But why are we running away, m'lady?" asked Pansy.

"We've escaped Ranald Torc and Master Grant. Why can't we go home? Dugald's going to be having a fit for certain." She chuckled to herself and then shared with her mistress the cause for her humor. "Dugald didn't want me to ride with you that morning, but Morag sided with me, saying it was only two miles."

"Pansy," said Velvet seriously, "if you want to go home, you should, and the more I ponder it I think that you had better. But I cannot. Ian has gone to Maitland, and once Maitland hears his plan he will throw him out, for Ian is of no importance, but Maitland will use his idea. They will hunt me down and use me to get to Francis. I cannot let that happen! I daren't even send a message to my mother, lest it be intercepted, and who could we trust to even take such a message? No—in a few weeks' time the king will realize that I cannot be found, and they will forget me. Then I can return home secretly. In the meantime, I must be where the Scots crown cannot find me. They will look in all the obvious places, *Dun Broc*, and probably send agents to *Queen's Malvern*, but I shall not be there. I shall go where no one will find me; but you must go home, my dear Pansy."

"Go home?" Pansy looked horrified. "Leave you to run off on some wild adventure by yourself? Never, Mistress Velvet! Me mother would kill me, and that would only be after m'lady Skye and his lordship and yer husband and mine had had at me. Wherever we're going, we'll go together, m'lady. Who, I should like to know, would take care of you if I weren't around?"

"Oh, Pansy, are you sure? I don't want to endanger either you or the baby."

"You're with child, too, m'lady. You need me," came her servant's calm reply.

"Aye," Velvet admitted, "I do need you, Pansy."

"Well, then, 'tis settled," said Pansy. "Where are we going to hide in France? Surely not at your grandparents'? They'd get right in touch with your parents, who would tell the earl, and then the fat would be in the fire."

"We're going to *Belle Fleurs*, Pansy. It is my parents' home in France, but they rarely go there anymore. We will be safe there, and when James Stewart has decided that I am not worth bothering with, then we shall come home to our husbands and *Don Broc* again.

"Amen to that!" said Pansy reverently.

Chapter 16

Ian Grant had gotten no farther than a nearby tavern, however, where he proceeded to get himself roaring drunk.

Ranald Torc's men, returning with the evening meal, found both him and their two captives gone. Obedient to their leader, they waited until Ranald Torc and his wife had returned. Although Ranald had no idea where the two women were, he was fairly certain of where to find Ian and sent his men to the tavern to fetch his cousin back. Before he slid into a drunken stupor, Ian managed to disclaim any knowledge of what had happened.

"They've escaped, damn the sot!" said Ranald Torc to Alanna, "though how I dinna know."

"Could BrocCairn have found them?" said Alanna.

"Nay, Ian would be dead if he had."

"What are we going to do, Ranald?" For the first time since he had known her, Alanna sounded afraid. "If anything has happened to her ladyship, Alex is going to hold us all responsible."

"The only person who can possibly know anything about this is my drunken sot of a cousin," muttered Ranald Torc. "I'll nae wait around for Alex Gordon to wreak his vengeance upon us, my lass. I'll admit to stealing his cattle, but nae else."

"Then what are we to do?" Alanna repeated.

"I've kept my word to Ian, but our survival is at stake now," came her husband's reply. "Ian will sleep until sometime tomorrow, I'm certain. We'll take him to Edinburgh and leave him at Huntley's house with a message saying that he's the man BrocCairn is looking for, and that, my lass, will take care of everything. Then we're off for home. I'll nae be caught so far from my lands again, Alanna. We've gold enough to last us a goodly time. We'll go home and spend a long winter together fucking and eating, and fucking and drinking! Would ye like that?"

Alanna smiled up at him. "Aye," she said, "I would."

Fortunately, both Francis Stewart-Hepburn and Alex Gordon had kept their heads. Surrounded by Alex's men, they had made their way south, finding the place where Alex's cattle had been sold and moving on to Edinburgh where the trail had gone cold. Then Ian Grant was deposited on the Earl of Huntley's front steps by several brawny Highlanders wearing the kilt of Clan Shaw. All the note pinned to him said was that he was wanted by the Gordon of BrocCairn. Both Bothwell and Alex realized that Ian Grant had probably not gotten to Maitland.

On October eighteenth, Maitland attempted to lure Lord Bothwell into a trap of his own at the Gold Anchor in Leith, without any mention of Lady Gordon, and Alex and Francis knew for certain that Ian had never reached the chancellor. Bothwell, however, escaped and made his way back to *Hermitage*. His rendezvous in the Highlands had come to naught, for the various factions could not agree on a way to stand against the king without committing treason. Ian Grant had been very close to being a rich man.

Ian Grant, however, was by this time quite dead. It had been an ignominious death. Awakening from his drunken spree, he had stretched lazily, then suddenly realized that he was not in that disgusting apartment they had rented in Leith. His mouth tasted terrible, and he had an absolutely awful headache. Slowly he turned over onto his back, and his eyes met those of Alexander Gordon, the Earl of BrocCairn. Ian Grant's mouth dropped open in shock, and he drew but one gasping breath before his heart gave out from total terror at the dreadful look in the earl's eyes.

If he hadn't died then and there, Alex would have killed him, but only after he had found out what had happened to his wife. Ian's death robbed him of that knowledge. He had only one other direction in which to go, and that was north into the Highlands from whence he'd come; north to find Ranald Torc. The outlaw had to know what had happened to his wife, to Pansy, to the unborn bairns that they both carried. Alex didn't believe for one minute that his wife was dead. He would have known if she was dead, but he felt nothing, just an emptiness. Velvet lived! Of that he was convinced.

Ranald Torc's house was impervious to attack by virtue of the thick forest that surrounded it. Remembering Ian's sudden and unexpected death, Alex did not want to lose the only chance he had of finding out what had happened to Velvet by fighting his way in. Under a flag of truce, he met with Ranald Torc at his house in the forest.

"Ian is dead," Alex said bluntly to open the conversation, and then he went on to explain how the event had occurred. "I was unable to question the damned coward, and I dinna know where my wife and her tiring woman are. Ye can tell me."

"Nay," replied Ranald Torc, "I canna. The plot to kidnap yer wife was all Ian's. I only stole yer cattle, Alex. Ian insisted we go to Leith so that he might make his escape quickly when the exchange was made."

"Did he ever contact Maitland?" demanded Alex, too concerned about his wife to demand compensation for his cattle.

"Nay, not to my knowledge. Alanna and I were married outside of Edinburgh wi' yer wife for a witness. We were seeing the sights in Leith, that's all. We came back one day to find yer wife and her woman gone, and Ian off drunk. She must have escaped, and so we brought Ian to Huntley's house and left him for ye. I canna tell ye anything else or I would. Having found a woman of my own, I can sympathize wi' ye in yer double loss, especially since my own wife has only today told me that I'm to be a father."

Alex was stunned. Ranald Torc had been his only hope. What could have happened to Velvet? If she had escaped, why had she not returned home to *Dun Broc*? Perhaps she had been so frightened that she had fled south instead to her parents in England. He could understand that now, but why had the de Mariscos not gotten in touch with him? He returned to *Dun Broc* only long enough to settle an allowance on his widowed sister and orphaned nephews before heading south to England with Dugald and a troop of his men.

In the Loire Valley of France it had been a long and leisurely autumn. Velvet and Pansy arrived at *Belle Fleurs* safely to find her parents' little chateau still carefully and lovingly attended by Mignon and Guillaume, retainers from the great estate of *Archambault*, which belonged to Velvet's grandparents, the Comte and Comtesse de Cher. Mignon and her spouse, Guillaume, had attended Skye and Adam de Marisco, Velvet's parents, in the years that they had lived in France. The chateau had been left in their keeping. They were elderly now, and Velvet's simple story that wicked men sought to use her and her unborn child against her wonderful husband so no one, not even her *cher* grandmère and grandpère, must know that she was at *Belle Fleurs*, brought their immediate support and promise that Velvet's visit would remain a secret.

Safe now, Velvet sought news of Scotland, not easy to come by in this rural and bucolic setting. Still, with the help of Matthieu, Mignon and Guillaume's fourteen-year-old grandson, they were able to establish a small line of information, but the news coming from Scotland was not good. Velvet heard of Maitland's attempt to trap Bothwell and cursed Ian Grant for the bastard he was. It was obvious to her that they had tried to lure Bothwell into their hands by convincing the earl that they had her. She wished she could send a message to Alex telling him that they were safe. How he must be worrying! She missed him so very much, but she would not endanger him, or Bothwell, by revealing her whereabouts.

The news was slow in reaching her, so it was early November when she had learned about Maitland's attempted trap. Although Pansy was now within a month of giving birth to her second child, Velvet, whose child was not due until the spring, did not yet show her condition. It was a warm, late-autumn day that found her in the small kitchen garden pulling leeks for Mignon's ragout. Suddenly a magnificent, antlered stag leaped over the low garden wall and, dashing around the building, dove into the lake that surrounded *Belle Fleurs* on three sides, swam across it, and disappeared into the forest beyond.

Sitting back on her heels, Velvet laughed, but her mirth was cut short by the arrival of several huntsmen, one of whom demanded, "Have you seen a stag go by, wench?"

"It is *madame*," she replied, "and who gave you the right to hunt on my lands?"

"All of France is the king's land," came the arrogant reply.

"But for Paris," Velvet rejoined, "and a king without a capital is not much of a king. Besides, you don't look like a king to me."

"He isn't," said another voice, and a tall, lean man pushed his horse forward to the low garden wall. "He is the Marquis de la Victoire, but I, madame, am Henri de Navarre, at your service."

Velvet rose and curtsied politely. "Forgive my hasty tongue, Your Majesty," she said.

"I liked it better when you were scolding me, *ma belle*," he replied with a smile. "You have the advantage of me, *chèrie*. I do not know who you are." His eyes swept quite boldly over her.

"I am Velvet Gordon, sire," said Velvet.

"English?"

"My father is both English and French. My mother is Irish, and I, sire, am married to a Scot."

"You are too beautiful to be wed to a dour Scot, *chèrie*. You should be a Frenchman's wife! Tell me, where is your husband?"

"In Scotland, sire." She brushed the loose dirt from her velvet skirt. How embarrassing to be caught looking such a fright! Still, perhaps it was better that way, for Henri of Navarre was a notorious womanizer. Looking as dusty and unappealing as she did would encourage him to be on his way.

The king, however, was very adept at seeing the gold beneath the soil. "Return to the chateau," he told his companions. "We have obviously lost our quarry." Then with a small smile he lowered his voice and said, "I have other game in mind now, *mes amis*!"

The gentlemen riding with the king departed without a protest. Though civil war still controlled France, keeping him from his throne in Paris, they knew he was safe here in the Loire Valley.

The king dismounted, asking as he did so, "What is this chateau called?"

"*Belle Fleurs*, sire," replied Velvet.

"And it is yours?"

"It belongs to my parents."

"Ah," said Henri. "You have come to visit with your parents."

"My parents live in England, sire."

"Your husband is in Scotland, your parents are in England, and you, madame, are in France. I do not understand."

Velvet laughed at his perplexity. "Is it really necessary that you understand, sire? You do not even know me."

"A lover!" the king cried. "You have come to be with your lover!"

"I have no lover, sire. I am a respectable married woman, I promise you." This was becoming very uncomfortable. Velvet did not want to explain to the French king, who was an ally of the Scots king, why she was here in France. Henri of Navarre was a most exasperating man! Why did he insist upon going on like this? She would have to tell him something for he obviously would not go away unless she did. "I have come to France for my health, sire," she said. "The Scots winters are not easy, and as I was ill last year, my husband feared for my health and insisted that I spend this winter here at *Belle Fleurs*. He will join me when he is able."

"Then you are alone, *chèrie*?"

"I have my servants, sire, and my grandparents live nearby," she answered him demurely. She hoped that the mention of family would send him on his way.

"Did you know that your eyes are the color of the ferns one finds only in the deepest part of the forest?" the king asked.

Velvet flushed.

"And I can see strands of molten gold caught amid the auburn of your hair, which has the sheen of poured silk." He reached out to finger a strand. "It's as soft as silk, too, *chèrie.*"

Velvet found herself suddenly and totally mesmerized by Henri of Navarre's intense, lush tones, and his rich, deep brown-gold eyes held her completely captive. It was with a great effort that she fought free of his hold to say, "Your Majesty must remember me to Queen Margot, who is my godmother."

The king was indeed stopped in his intent for the moment. "My wife is your godmother?" he said.

"Yes, sire. Queen Margot and my own liege, good Queen Bess."

"I do not often see my wife," the king said. Then he smiled at her. "You have a mouth that was made for kisses, Madame Gordon," and so saying, he reached out to capture her in his grasp.

"Sire!" Velvet's palms pressed flat against the king's leather doublet. "I am a loyal wife to my lord."

"Loyalty," the king said, "is a valuable quality in a woman," and then kissed her, his lips pressing most expertly upon her own.

For a very long minute Velvet didn't know whether to be offended, flattered, or simply outraged. There wasn't a woman in Europe who didn't know the reputation for lechery held by the French king. He was a man for whom women held a supreme fascination. She didn't find his embrace unpleasant, but she was Alex Gordon's wife, and she loved her husband. Still, it was interesting being kissed by another man.

Taking her complacency for compliance, Henry gently forced Velvet's lips open and found her tongue with his own, meanwhile managing to pull her blouse down to fondle her full and firm breasts. It was that bold liberty that galvanized Velvet into action. Using all her strength, she wrenched free of the king's embrace, and, putting all her force behind the blow, she slapped Henri of Navarre.

"Sire! I am mortally offended by your conduct!" she raged. "I have said I am a loyal wife to my husband, and you then kiss me and fondle me in a most lascivious manner! For shame, Your Majesty! For shame! Surely your reputation for loving the ladies was not gained by means of force? I am with child, sire! I came to *Belle Fleurs* to seek peace during my confinement. Must I flee my home to return to a harsh Scots winter, thereby endangering my husband's heir, because you will not believe me when I refuse your attentions?"

The king was totally astounded. He had never in his life been rebuffed by a woman. Well, once he had been, but only once. For some reason this beautiful young woman reminded him of that time so long ago. It was a time best forgot, the night of the St. Bartholomew's Day massacre when his late but not lamented mother-in-law, Catherine de Medici, had arranged that he be detained by a woman he had fancied in order to keep him safe, or so she had said. Henri had always believed that his mother-in-law had arranged for that little divertissement in order to keep him from leading his soldiers into the fray.

He had just been married to his wife, Marguerite de Valois, the princess of France. It was a marriage meant to unite the ruling house of Valois with the house of Bourbon of which he was the heir. During the marriage celebrations, he had seen a magnificent Irishwoman with eyes the incredible blue-green of Ceylon sapphire and masses of black, black hair that tumbled against her fabulous white skin. He had wanted to possess her with all his soul, and as his bride had been far too busy with her own lover to notice, he had ardently pursued the woman whose name he now could not even remember. He had been most firmly rebuffed, but Catherine de Medici had seen his lust; and by fraud she had tricked the woman into an assignation with him. He had entered the room to find the object of his desire bound and helpless, and he had taken her without a moment's hesitation despite her furious protests, even as that wily old woman, his mother-in-law, had known he would.

And while he had dallied so delightfully, the Catholic League had butchered as many of the Huguenots assembled in Paris for his wedding as they could find. It had not sat well with the Huguenots that he had not been there to lead and protect them.

He shook the thought away. That religious division had caused France years of civil war—a war that, despite his conversion to Catholicism, still raged in sections of France.

How odd that he had been suddenly reminded of all that unhappiness by this beautiful woman who looked angrily up at him, attempting to somehow maintain her dignity while covering her lovely breasts. For some reason he felt guilty, although guilt was not a feeling that often touched him.

"Madame," he said solemnly, "I do beg your pardon." A small smile touched his lips. "You are very beautiful, and I am rather used to taking what I want. I can only remember being rebuffed by a woman once before in my entire life. Will you forgive me? I am staying nearby at *Chenonceaux*, and I should like us to be friends. It is very dull at *Chenonceaux*," he finished, and his face took on a mournful expression.

"Of course I shall forgive you, sire, providing that you promise me such a thing will not happen again."

"I give you the word of a king," he said.

"Why is it dull at *Chenonceaux*?" she asked, curious and thinking that the word of a king was not often good. "I had heard that *Chenonceaux* is the most beautiful chateau in France:"

"It is," he answered, "both inside and out. The chateau spans the entire river Cher, and there was a time when guests were greeted by the sight of beautiful young women garbed as water nymphs swimming in the river around the chateau. Now, alas, it is in the possession of Louise de Lorraine, widow of my predecessor, Henri III. She has draped the suites in black, and has painted many of the ceilings with skulls and crossbones and gravediggers' tools." He shuddered expressively. "It is a sacrilege to so defile such beauty."

A small giggle escaped Velvet. "You are teasing me," she said. "Louise de Lorraine did not really paint her ceilings with skulls and crossbones, did she?"

"She did." He nodded solemnly.

Suddenly Pansy, great with child, waddled out into the garden, calling, "M'lady! Have you got those leeks? Old Mignon says she cannot begin the ragout for supper without them. Oh, excuse me, m'lady. I didn't know we had a guest."

"This is my tiring woman," said Velvet to the king. "She does not speak French, being a good Englishwoman. Pansy, make your curtsy. This is King Henri."

Pansy gasped and, with some difficulty, curtsied to the king.

"She is enceinte, your tiring woman?"

"Yes, monseigneur. Her husband is my husband's servant. It is their second child."

"A mistress who is enceinte, a servant who is enceinte. I have obviously misjudged the Scots, who would seem to be a passionate race." The king chuckled.

"I had not heard, sire," replied Velvet quickly, "that the French had a monopoly on passion."

"You will never know the true comparison, *chèrie*, unless you allow me to demonstrate," he said mischievously.

"Monseigneur!" Velvet pretended outrage, but the king was not fooled, and they both laughed.

"Does this Mignon prepare a beef ragout, *chèrie*? A beef ragout with tender green leeks? I adore beef ragout with leeks!"

"Is Your Majesty seeking an invitation?" Velvet teased him.

"Yes, I most certainly do seek an invitation," he said, looking almost boyish. "The dowager queen Louise will serve up carp and plain boiled vegetables for dinner tonight as she does almost every night. She has made her mourning a fine art, and even her guests must suffer!"

"Then why do you visit her?" demanded the practical Velvet.

"Because it is my duty; because *Chenonceaux* is so incredibly beautiful and peaceful; and because the hunting is good," he answered her.

"I cannot feed your friends," she said. "It is not that I would be ungracious; it is simply that I have neither the food nor the staff for entertaining."

"I do not ask you to feed my men. What I hope for is a dinner *à deux*."

"Dinner, monseigneur, is all that I am serving," said Velvet severely to Henri of Navarre. "You must promise me that you understand that before I will tender you an invitation. I am not a woman to play the coy flirt. I love my husband and will not compromise either his honor or mine."

"Lovers," said the king, "should always begin as friends. It was unforgivable of me to behave as I did earlier. I can only excuse myself by saying that your beauty blinded me to reason. I promise to behave myself, *chèrie*, if you will invite me to supper."

"We are *not* going to be lovers!" said Velvet, somewhat crossly.

The king smiled sweetly at her. "I shall bring a fine red wine for us to drink with the ragout," he said as he mounted his horse.

"I have not said you could come!" Velvet protested.

"Do you think your Mignon would make me a pear tartlet for the last course, *chèrie*?" he asked her.

Velvet couldn't help but laugh. What a charming and impossible man he was. "I'll ask her," she said, "and now, sire, I bid you adieu, for if I do not bring these leeks in to Mignon immediately, there will be no supper for you."

The king kissed his fingers at her and, turning his horse, rode off.

"So that's what a king looks like," said Pansy matter-of-factly. "He's a bit big and gawky, ain't he? What was all that chattering you was doing?"

"He's invited himself to supper," said Velvet, still chuckling.

"He looks to me like he's got more than supper on his mind," said Pansy disapprovingly.

"He does," replied her mistress, "but I have been most truthful with the king. He understands me, though he will not yet admit that a lady could refuse his suit. There is no danger, Pansy, from Henri of Navarre. Besides, he is only visiting at *Chenonceaux*, and must be on his way in a day or so. France is still at war with itself, and he will not really be safe as its king until the country is once again united."

"You're going to throw old Mignon into quite a tizzy, m'lady. I don't expect that she's ever cooked for a king before."

Velvet's laughter renewed itself at that thought. "Wait until I tell her that he has requested a pear tartlet for the last course!"

Mignon, however, was not one bit nonplussed by the news that Henri of Navarre was coming to supper. When Velvet passed on the gossip about *Chenonceaux* to her, the old woman said, "Poor man! He grew up in the wholesome atmosphere of Navarre far from the French court. He is used to good country food and he misses it, I have not a doubt. I shall be pleased to cook for the king! I am only sorry that I shall not be able to tell everyone at *Archambault* about it. That fat Celine who cooks for your grandmother would be so jealous! After she cooked for Queen Catherine and Princess Margot at your christening, there was simply no living with her! Oh, how I would like to tell her!"

"In time, Mignon," Velvet soothed the old woman. "When I am with my husband, and King James no longer seeks me, then I can tell my grandparents that I was here, and you can brag to your heart's delight to Celine and the rest of the staff at *Archambault*."

"Celine will be so jealous," cackled Mignon as she threw the leeks, now peeled, into the steaming pot of ragout. "I think I shall put currants in with the pears," she mused. "It makes a tastier tartlet."

Velvet smiled and then, taking Pansy with her, went to prepare the table in the lovely hall where once her family used to gather when she was a tiny child. *Belle Fleurs* was not a large chateau. Built in the early fifteenth century, it sat in the midst of a garden, surrounded on three sides by a lakelike moat. Beyond it lay the forest, and four miles to the north, the great chateau of her grandparents, *Archambault*, which, like its neighbor, *Chenonceaux*, sat on the banks of the river Cher.

Belle Fleurs was a chateau out of a fairy tale. It was built of dark, reddish gray shist stone, and its four polygonal towers had slate roofs that were shaped like witches' hats. Since access to the chateau could be gained only through the *cour d'honneur*, it was easily defensible. It was the gardens, however, that had given *Belle Fleurs* its name. During the growing season, from spring until the late, late autumn, the gardens of *Belle Fleurs* were filled to overflowing with varied and colorful blooms of every known variety and hue. They were old Guillaume's pride, and he spent all of his waking hours amid the flowers, keeping *Belle Fleurs'* gardens thriving and orderly.

The chateau itself had a fine hall and kitchens, six bedchambers including the lord's apartment, and room for a dozen house servants. The outbuildings consisted of a stable for the horses, though there were only three, two that had been brought by Velvet and Pansy and an old mare that pulled a cart kept by Mignon and Guillaume. Velvet had hired a coach to bring them from Nantes to *Belle Fleurs*, but she had also purchased the two riding horses which had been tied behind the carriage. Transportation was vital in this isolated location. There was a dog kennel, but right now the only dogs at *Belle Fleurs* were an elderly spaniel and an even older hound. The falconry was empty now though the dovecote still housed a large family of gentle birds.

Velvet's father, Adam de Marisco, had bought the chateau furnished by its former owners, and the rooms were filled with attractive furniture and beautiful hangings. Though there would be but two of them at supper, Velvet knew that she must set the high board for the king. Carefully, she and Pansy laid the convent-made linen cloth upon the long table. There was but one pair of gold candelabra in the chateau, and Velvet cleaned them, placing them upon the table with the beeswax tapers. Pansy brought a bowl of flowers in autumn colors of yellow, brown, tawny orange, and gold, which was also placed on the table. Two place settings of silver knives and Florentine forks with matching silver plates and goblets studded with green jasper were set upon the table. The fires were laid in the two fireplaces on either side of the hall, and crystal decanters of wine, a pale gold liquid from *Archambault* and a crimson one the king had already sent ahead with one of the footmen from *Chenonceaux*, were placed upon the sideboard.

The hall ready, Velvet departed to her chamber to bathe in gillyflower-scented water and to dress in a dark green velvet gown that had once been her mother's. She thought it fortunate that Skye had left so many clothes at *Archambault*, else both she and Pansy would have been quite at a loss. They had worn the same clothing from the time of their kidnapping until they arrived at *Belle Fleurs*; clothing that Velvet immediately burned, for it was filthy beyond repair. Had they not had their cloaks to cover their stained and torn garments, Velvet did not know what they would have done.

It had taken almost two weeks for them to reach Nantes from Leith. Using Pansy's obvious condition as an excuse, they had kept very much to their cabin, coming out only once a day toward evening when the light was dim, and no one about, to walk about the deck.

Captain Michael Small did not usually take passengers, but an expected cargo had not been delivered in Leith on time, and since he had the room, he had decided to accept several passengers. They had been very lucky, for there had just been one small cabin left and only the intercession of the landlord of the Golden Anchor had gained it for them.

"They're respectable women, Captain," he had said. "There isn't another ship I would dare trust to transport them safely, and they can pay in gold."

"Very well," the captain had finally agreed, "but they must bring their own food. I'll supply drinking water, three cups each day, and one cup each of rum, but nothing else. There are two bunks in the cabin, but they must bring their own blankets."

Velvet had agreed to the captain's terms, and the landlord had negotiated the price for them and then helped them to quickly assemble their provisions, which consisted of oatcakes, dried and salted beef, a small cheese, and, at Velvet's insistence, a basket of apples and pears. There had been no time either to bathe or to purchase fresh clothing before they sailed, and so when they reached *Belle Fleurs*, they had been wearing the same garments for a month.

"We were forced to flee quickly," Velvet had explained to Mignon. "We could take nothing with us but what we had on our backs. I am certain that my mother has clothing stored here in the chateau."

"*Oui*, madame, indeed she does," replied Mignon. "I should know for was I not her tiring woman while she lived here in France? I myself packed everything away in cedar-lined trunks. They are stored in the attics. Tomorrow I will have Matthieu fetch them down."

The following day Velvet had opened her mother's trunks to find them filled with beautiful garments: gowns, skirts, and blouses; night rails of gossamer quality; petticoats; chemises; stockings; and shoes. There was even a small ivory box containing some rather magnificent jewelry. There were pink-tinged pearls with a matching ring set in gold; a marvelous necklace of large diamonds, blue-white in color, which also had matching earrings; several other pairs of earbobs of sapphires, emeralds, and rubies set in gold; bracelets; rings; and hair ornaments decorated with diamonds, pearls, and rubies.

"Were these my mother's?" she asked Mignon.

"Yes, madame, they were. She brought them with her when she came to *Archambault*."

Velvet was utterly intrigued, particularly in light of the yellowed parchment she found at the bottom of the ivory box. Its fading message offered yet a further mystery as it read:

Doucette, I had these made for you when I thought you might return to me. Since I will not give my wife jewelry made for another woman, I beg that you take this small offering that was meant only for you. Nicolas.

"Who was Nicolas, Mignon?" Velvet asked.

"Nicolas? Why, I do not know, madame," came the reply. "Is it important?"

"Nay," said Velvet. "I was but curious."

It was Pansy, however, who supplied the key to the mystery. "Nicolas," she said musingly, as if trying to remember something, and then her face lit up. "I know who he was, m'lady! Me mum told me many stories of Mistress Skye's adventures, some of them mum shared. I remember a Duke Nicolas that your mother was supposed to marry once. I can't remember why she didn't. He lived here in France somewheres. I will wager the note and the jewelry are from him."

Velvet was fascinated. It never occurred to her that her mother would receive jewelry from someone other than her father. Oh, all her life she had heard bits and pieces about her mother's adventures, and certainly at court there had been those who were only too eager to repeat the gossip about her mother. Skye herself, however, had never spoken a great deal of the past. She seemed to always live for the moment, for the morrow, and that was how her daughter saw her. Now, suddenly, her mother appeared in a different light; as a woman whom other men had adored and loved, and for whom men had jewelry created, a woman with a past. Why had the jewelry been left in France? Had the man who had given her the gems meant so little to her mother that Skye had carelessly left his gift behind? It was interesting, and she was going to have to ask her mother when she saw her again.

Velvet now picked up the diamond necklace and held it up against her throat. It really was quite beautiful, and it went very well with the green velvet gown. Clasping it about her neck, she admired herself for a moment in the glass and then added the earrings. Despite her somewhat old-fashioned dress she felt quite confident to receive the king.

If Henri of Navarre noticed that Velvet's gown was not of the latest fashion, he said nothing about it during their meal. Mignon had outdone herself, and on such short notice; Velvet herself was more than amazed at the meal that appeared on her table. The ragout was filled with chunks of tender beef that had been simmered in a brown gravy, which was fragrant with Burgundy and delicate mushrooms. There were small bits of carrot, too, and the green leeks that Velvet had picked earlier. To her surprise, there was also a plump, juicy capon that had been roasted to a golden brown and stuffed with a mixture of bread, sage, tiny white onions, and chestnuts; as well as a fine trout that had been caught by Matthieu in the chateau lake and poached in white wine and herbs. There was a bowl of turnips, and one of baby lettuce and watercress that had been braised in wine. Fresh bread still warm from the ovens was placed with a crock of sweet butter before them.

The king ate with great appetite, filling and refilling his plate three times. When the second course, which consisted of the pear and currant tartlet, apples baked in honey and dusted with cinnamon, a bowl of fat purple grapes, and a Normandy Brie, was placed before him, his eyes lit with delight. He decimated these offerings with equal gusto while Velvet was kept busy seeing that his goblet was never empty, for the king drank as heartily as he ate.

The meal finished, Velvet said, "Will you allow my housekeeper to greet Your Majesty? When she learned she was to cook for you, her delight knew no bounds. She can barely wait to gossip with the entire neighborhood, and your obvious appreciation of her culinary skills will give her much to talk about."

He nodded his assent, and Velvet sent to the kitchens for Mignon. The old lady came, her face flushed from excitement as well as the heat of her kitchens. Her white hair was neat, just peeping from beneath a fresh cap, and she had taken the time to remove her stained apron, replacing it with a clean one. Kneeling before Henri, she kissed his hand, and there were tears in her eyes.

The king was touched, and, standing, he raised the old woman to her feet, saying as he did so, "I cannot remember ever eating a finer meal, Madame Mignon. You have your monarch's grateful thanks."

Somehow Mignon found her voice, although later as she told it, she was surprised that she could speak at all to this wonderful, great man. "When my lady told me of the menu you suffer at *Chenonceaux*, I knew that Your Majesty longed for good country cooking as you once ate in your youth in Navarre. I cannot cook the elegant foods that your own chefs prepare, but I know how to cook for a *man*; and if the rumors that we hear are correct, Your Majesty is the best man in all of Europe!" Mignon chuckled.

"Mignon!" Velvet was surprised by her servant's boldness.

The king, however, laughed uproariously. "I will not deny those rumors, Madame Mignon," he said, and his golden brown eyes twinkled. "If I were but a bit older, I'm afraid I should have chased you around your kitchen for a kiss, thus shocking my young hostess even more."

"And were I a bit younger," cackled the housekeeper, "Your Majesty would have no trouble catching me! Alas, however, I am an old woman now."

"Madame Mignon," said the king, "a spirit such as yours never grows old!" And taking her hand, he kissed it gallantly.

Mignon drew herself up proudly. "I am pleased that I have been able to serve my king, even in so little a matter as this." She curtsied elegantly, and then said, "I have had a guest chamber prepared for Your Majesty, and when you are ready to retire, my husband, Guillaume, will valet Your Majesty. He once served the Comte de Cher in such a capacity."

"The king is not staying the night!" protested Velvet.

"He cannot leave now, madame," said Mignon. "There is a storm raging outside, and it has been raining very heavily for the past two hours. It will rain the entire night, Guillaume says, and he knows. The king will stay, and in the morning

I will serve him eggs poached in cream and marsala!" Bobbing a final cursty to both the king and the lady, she departed from the room.

"It would seem, *chèrie*, that the fates seek to plead my cause," said the king softly.

"I cannot send you out into the storm," Velvet said, "but I would remind Your Majesty of your promise to me to behave like the gentleman that you are."

Henri laughed. "You are very unfair, *chèrie.*"

"I did warn you that I am not a flirt," Velvet protested.

Henri of Navarre sighed dramatically. "If I am to be fair, then I must admit that you did. Still, if I were not to hope that you might change your mind, then I should not be the man I am."

Velvet could not help but smile. The king was most disarming. "Monseigneur, it is not that you are unattractive, it is just that I value the Gordon's honor above all else—even the attentions of a king. A man of such great honor as Your Majesty can understand that, I know."

"I understand it, *chèrie,*" he admitted to her, "but I do not have to like it. You are an outrageously beautiful woman. I am already wildly in love with you, and you are frank enough to dash my fondest hope with such innocent honesty that I cannot be in the least offended. Disappointed, *oui*, but not offended."

"It was never my intention to offend you, sire. I would far prefer that we be friends. I have never had a king for a friend." Even as she said it, Velvet was somewhat ashamed of the lie, for Akbar had been her friend first before he became her husband and her lover. Still, she knew that she must sweeten her rejection of the king, for it could be that she might need his goodwill one day.

Henri's gaze softened. "Ah, *chèrie,*" he said, "what a charming creature you are! Of course we will be friends. I would have it no other way."

Velvet arose from the table and curtsied to the king. "Will you then give me your permission to retire, monseigneur? I find in my condition that I seem to need more sleep than usual."

"Will you not show me to my chambers, *chèrie*?"

"If you are ready to retire, monseigneur, I shall call old Guillaume to escort you," said Velvet sweetly, and she was gone from the hall before the king could protest.

He watched her skirts disappearing around the corner, and he chuckled. How wise she was to entice him so. An easy quarry was usually unfulfilling and boring to bed. He far more enjoyed the hunt! If not tonight, it would be another night, but he would attempt to breach her defenses one more time this evening. There was a mystery about this beauty, and he was anxious to solve it. Who were these grandparents she spoke of who lived nearby? Where was her husband? He did not believe for one moment that the husband of such a beauty would allow his wife to live alone in such a remote place with only four servants to care for her. It was obvious to Henri that she was trying to hide something, but what he did not know.

The elderly Guillaume came to escort him to his apartment. He was polite and efficient, but the king learned little from him, for the old man was no fool, and *la belle* Gordon was obviously dear to him.

"Yes, sire," he said, "I once served the Comte de Cher. Not he who is currently the count, but his father who lived to be very old. I was with him from the time I was a young man. I went to court with my master and saw Henri II. We were there the day that he was killed in the tourney. Ah, that was a great tragedy. Both the lady Diane, the king's favorite, and the queen were terribly overwrought." Guillaume's eyes misted with the memory. "The lady Diane de Poitiers was such a beautiful creature. *Chenonceaux* was hers in those days, you know, but Queen Catherine took it from her once the king was dead. She gave her another chateau, but the lady Diane retired to her own home at Anet." He rambled on, and the king found himself quite fascinated by this little bit of France's recent history as seen through the eyes of a servant.

The king was quite surprised when Guillaume produced a man's silk nightshirt for him. "Where did this come from?" he demanded.

"It belongs to my master, Madame Velvet's father. There is a trunk of his things still here as well as one of his wife's."

So, thought the king, that was where she had obtained her gown for tonight. He had not mentioned it, but the dress had been somewhat out of fashion, and the aroma of cedar clung faintly to it. "How long has the lady Velvet been here?" he asked Guillaume.

"For several weeks now," said the manservant, and then he deftly switched the subject back to the old days when he had so loyally served his late master, the Comte de Cher.

The fire was banked, and as his final duty Guillaume tucked the king into bed. Henri said to the valet as he was leaving the room, "Sometimes I have bad dreams, Guillaume, and I cry out in my sleep. I should not like to frighten Madame Gordon in her condition. Is she nearby?"

"Madame's suite is across the hall, sire," said Guillaume. "The way the wind is blowing she would not hear you. I wish you, however, a good night's sleep with happy dreams."

"*Merci*, Guillaume," said the king, smiling, and closed his eyes. He heard the doors close, and then all was quiet but for the sound of the heavy rains against the windowpanes and the low moan of the rising wind. For over an hour the king lay resting, and then he arose from his bed and went directly from his chamber across the hall to Velvet's door. The floor in the passageway was cold, and he eagerly opened her door to step upon a soft carpet.

Inside the room was the largest bed he had ever seen. It was, to his eye, like an arena. What magnificent combats had taken place in it? he wondered. The velvet draperies were drawn across the windows, muffling the sound of the storm, and the firelight cast eerie, dark shadows upon the fabric. Then he heard it. The soft sound of her weeping. It was the saddest thing Henri had ever heard, and all thought of passion fled from his mind as his compassionate nature came to the forefront. Seating himself upon the edge of the bed, the king drew Velvet into his arms.

Instantly she stiffened, and he heard the outrage in her young voice as she said, "What are you doing in my room, monseigneur?"

"Why are you crying?" he answered her. "It breaks my heart to hear you so saddened, *chèrie*. What has made you so unhappy?"

She raised a tear-stained face to him, saying as she did so, "I miss my husband, and I miss my home."

"Then why do you not go home?"

"Because I c . . . , because my health will not allow it," was her stumbling reply.

"Forgive me, *chèrie*, but that is a terrible lie," the king replied. "I have never seen a healthier young woman than yourself. You are running from something, *chèrie*, and if I can help I will. Can you not trust me?"

Velvet was silent.

The king persisted. "At least tell me who your grandparents are. The ones who live nearby."

"I cannot tell you," Velvet said.

"Why not?"

"Because they do not know that I am here. If they knew, they would send me to my parents, and my parents would send me to my husband, and I cannot allow that."

"Why not?" the king demanded again. Suddenly he thought of something. "The child you carry! Is it not your husband's!"

"Of course it is Alex's!" Velvet cried. "Why on earth would you think such a thing of me!"

"Then why don't you want your husband to know that you are here, for despite your tale, I do not believe he knows where you are, does he?" Holding Velvet by the shoulders, the king looked down into her face. "Does he, *chèrie*?"

"No," said Velvet, and she burst into tears again.

Henri held her against his chest and allowed her to sob her misery out upon his silken nightshirt. When her weeping had abated somewhat, the king said, "Now, Velvet Gordon, I want you to unravel this mystery you have woven about yourself. I will not take no for an answer, and if you refuse me, I shall take you to *Chenonceaux* with me and keep you there until you have told me the truth. I am most resolved in this," he finished in a somewhat stern tone.

Velvet was silent again for some minutes, and then, sighing, she said, "I was forced to flee Scotland because enemies of my husband wanted to use me to entrap his cousin, a gentleman sought by the king for treason,—but there is no treason, monseigneur! My husband's cousin is King James's most loyal servant, if the king would but trust him. It is the king's chancellor, Master Maitland, who seeks to turn the king against the earls in order to further his own power!"

"François Stewart-Hepburn!" said the king. "It has to be my old friend François Stewart-Hepburn!"

"You know Francis?" said Velvet, amazed.

"For more years, *chèrie*, than I care to admit to, I have known François. It is he, is it not? François is the only man in the entire world who so terrifies and enrages James Stewart. Their relationship is a long and a very troubled one, for James Stewart has always been jealous of his cousin."

"He has outlawed him and confiscated all his estates," Velvet said, "and it has been done out of spite, for the king covets the woman that Francis loves."

"Ah," said Henri of Navarre, his voice echoing his total understanding. "It is a woman! I would not have thought such a thing of James Stewart. He does not seem the type, and I have never heard it said of him that he is overfond of the ladies."

"He pretends to be faithful to Queen Anne," replied Velvet, "but he has coveted this particular lady for some time, and she fled from him to be with Francis, who wishes to wed with her."

"Ahhhhh," said Henri of Navarre again, "so not only has this lady refused the king, she prefers his greatest rival. The insult is formidable! No wonder your king is angry, but how, *chèrie*, did you get involved in this tempest?"

Velvet took a deep breath. "Monseigneur, I can say nothing more unless you give me your word that you will not betray me to James Stewart. France and Scotland are allies, I know."

Henri smiled. "We are allies, *chèrie*, because it pleases us to occasionally aid the Scots against the English. It is the same with the Spanish. They enjoy aiding the Irish against the English. It is nuisance value. That is all. You have the word of a king, *chèrie*, that we will not betray you."

"I should far rather have the word of Henri of Navarre, monseigneur," returned Velvet. "The word of a king is not always reliable. Forgive me, for I mean no insult, but my mother has always said it, and she is the wisest woman that I know."

The king smiled ruefully. "Your mother is indeed wise, *chèrie*. Very well, then, you have the word of Henri of Navarre that whatever it is you tell me will remain secret. I will not betray you, and I would certainly not betray my old friend, François Stewart-Hepburn. One favor, however, I would ask of you."

"Anything, monseigneur!" Velvet vowed.

The king laughed. *"Anything?"* he said.

"Within reason," Velvet amended.

"May we please get beneath the coverlet, *chèrie*? I am freezing in this nightshirt, which you have soaked through with your tears. I must get warm or I shall have an ague come morning."

"Oh, dear! You must get out of that wet nightshirt, monseigneur!" said Velvet, her voice very concerned. Then she slipped from his arms and, running to a trunk at the foot of the bed, opened it and drew forth a second silk nightshirt. "This is my parents' chamber," she explained, "and my father's night garment." Handing him the shirt, she said, "I shall not peek. Tell me when you are ready."

Gratefully the king changed into the dry nightshirt and then, getting beneath the coverlet, said, "Come now, *chèrie*, and join me. A lady in your delicate condition should not be chilled."

It did not occur to Velvet to ask him whether he would behave this time. She simply assumed that he would. Settling herself comfortably next to him, she began her tale, "Francis secretly came north into the Highlands in late summer to meet with the Earl of Huntley. Francis stayed with us a night before going on to Huntley, with my husband and his men-at-arms riding along to protect him. My husband is Francis's cousin, but he is also a cousin of Huntley's and of the king, too."

"Who is your husband?" interrupted Henri of Navarre.

"My husband is Alexander Gordon, the Earl of BrocCairn," said Velvet. "Alex has but one sibling, his sister, Annabella, and it was her husband, Ian Grant, who decided that if he kidnapped me, he could force Francis into giving himself up. Ian would then turn him over to Maitland and collect the king's reward." Then she went on to tell him of her horrible captivity in Leith and lucky escape with Pansy from Ranald Torc and Ian. "I had to hide somewhere where the king could not find me until he grew tired of seeking me," Velvet wound up her tale, "or until he and Francis made up again, although this time I fear they will not reconcile. Because I am considered English, I knew that no one in Scotland would consider looking in France. They do not know of *Belle Fleurs*, and so I came here."

"Who are your grandparents?" Navarre asked.

"The Comte and Comtesse de Cher whose chateau, *Archambault*, is but four miles from here."

"Am I to assume that your husband has not known all these weeks where you are, *chèrie*?"

"How could he?" said Velvet. "I have not dared to communicate either with him or any member of my family, for fear that James Stewart would find me and use me in his war with Francis."

"Does Alex Gordon know he is to be a father?"

"Oh, yes!" said Velvet. "It is our first child, and I had only just told him before we were separated."

"Mon Dieu!" said Henri of Navarre. "This is an incredible tangle! I shall find out for you if your king still seeks you,

for if I were your husband, my adorable Velvet, I should be distraught beyond all not to know where my wife was, especially in your state."

"You will not betray me?" Her voice trembled.

"I have given you my word, *chèrie*. I will not betray you, but you cannot hide forever. Tomorrow, when I return to *Chenonceaux*, I shall make discreet inquiries about the difficulties between your king and our mutual friend, François. If you are sought by the Scots crown, *chèrie*, I shall learn of it, and then together we shall solve the problem, I promise you."

"You will really help me?"

Henri smiled to himself in the dark. She was absolutely charming. "Yes," he said, "I will help you, *chèrie*. How could I not?" Then, leaning over, he tipped her face to his and kissed her.

Velvet pulled away, suddenly very, very aware that the king's aid had its price. "You gave me your word," she said softly.

"I gave you my word not to force you, *chèrie*, and I will not. But if I offer you something that you very much want, is it not only fair that you offer me something that I very much want in return? Making love does not always have to involve the emotions. It is a delightful sport in which two compatible people may give each other pleasure."

"Your mind is much too sophisticated for me, monseigneur. I am a simple woman who finds it hard to visualize lovemaking outside of the bonds of matrimony."

"You have been most properly brought up, and I applaud your parents who have raised you to be a good Catholic noblewoman; nevertheless, there are times when even the most virtuous of women face serious decisions of this nature. You wish my help, and I wish to make love to you. The choice rests with you, *chèrie*. The ambassador from your country to mine can tell me what I wish to know. If James Stewart still seeks you, then I shall arrange to bring your husband to you secretly. You can live your life quite happily here in France until you are safe. When is your child due?"

"Early spring," said Velvet. "April, I would say."

"I can arrange that your husband be with you then. You would like that, wouldn't you? If James has already forgotten you, then you can contact your husband and he can join you here immediately. Is that not worth one brief encounter to you?"

Velvet bit her lip. She knew the story of her friend Cat Leslie and of how James Stewart had forced her to his bed. Would it be the same with Henri of Navarre? Somehow she did not think so, for the French king was a man who openly enjoyed women, and always had at least one acknowledged mistress. Being in the early months of her pregnancy, she could not become enceinte by him, and if Alex never knew of the incident . . . She could no longer bear this separation from him! She loved her husband, and she needed him!

"Promise me that my husband will never know of this shameful episode," she said.

"Madame, I am not a man to kiss and tell," he said, his tone offended.

"But you have not returned to *Chenonceaux* tonight, and surely the gentlemen with you will assume you have been in my bed."

"They would have assumed it even if I had not been, *chèrie*, and I would certainly not gainsay them their lecherous meanderings of the mind. Do not fear, my lovely Velvet, my gentlemen have no idea who you are, or even the name of this delightful little chateau. Even if you came to my court with your husband, there is not one amongst them who would betray your honor, for by doing so they would betray their own, and they are a proud bunch of milords."

"Then if I am to have your help, monseigneur, I have no other choice than to yield to you," Velvet said softly.

"Ah, *chèrie*," he said, the delight in his voice hard to conceal, "you have made me the happiest of men!"

He might be happy, she thought, but she certainly was not. Having committed herself to this course, one thought bothered her. She had never slept with a man with whom she was not in love. Would Henri of Navarre think her a good lover, or would he feel cheated and, considering her a bad bargain, not feel obliged to help her? "Monseigneur," she began, "I have virtually no experience in love other than with my husband." There was no need to explain Akbar. It would be too confusing.

"But I, *chèrie*, have great experience. You will learn at the hands of a master, and, to begin with, I should like you to disrobe for me." He himself arose from the bed and, going to the fireplace, built up the fire so that the room was bathed in a rosy glow. Then taking a taper, he relit the candelabrum on either side of the bed. "Love," he said, "should not be hidden away in the dark as if it were something to be ashamed of, *chèrie*. A woman's body is possibly the most beautiful of God's creations, and I am a connoisseur of beauty. I have always enjoyed watching the faces of the women I make love to. It is a weakness with me."

Velvet, too, had arisen slowly from the bed. She had been wearing a simple night rail of white silk with long, full sleeves that was decorated with pink ribbons at the wrists and high neckline. She suddenly felt very, very shy. Both Alex and Akbar had seen her naked, but this man was a virtual stranger, unknown to her except by reputation until a few hours ago. She began to tremble, and the king, who had already shed his nightshirt, saw it.

Coming up behind her, he slipped his long arms about her waist and bent his head to kiss her neck with delicate, feathery movements. "Don't be afraid of me, *chèrie*. I shall not hurt you or the child, and I promise to make you very happy even though your adorable, strict sense of morality will not let you believe such a thing is possible right now." Gently his slender fingers undid the ribbons at her neckline as he opened her night rail to the waist. Drawing the gown off her shoulders, he watched as it slipped down over her hips and past her shapely calves to puddle about her ankles.

Automatically Velvet stepped from the tangle of silk, and her heart began to beat faster at the king's sharp intake of breath.

"Ahhhh, *chèrie*," he breathed reverently, "you are beautiful beyond compare, beyond my wildest expectations! You should be sculpted in marble, but I do not believe that there is an artist living or dead who could do you justice! Come!" Catching her hand in his, he quickly drew her over to the pier glass. "Look at yourself, *chèrie*! Are you not magnificent? Look at us together! We are superb! I am a tall man, and it is not often that I have a tall woman. *Mon Dieu!* I must worship at your shrine, my exquisite goddess!" So saying, the king knelt and began to kiss Velvet from her feet upward, holding her firmly about the hips. She quivered beneath his touch.

His warm mouth wandered up her ankles to first her right knee and then her left. Slowly he turned her so that he might kiss her hips where they swelled out from her waist, her firm buttocks, the base of her spine. Turning her again, his mouth found its way up the fronts of her thighs, the rear having already been saluted.

Velvet could feel her legs buckling, and when his lips found the cleft in her Venus mont and his tongue ran along that cleft slowly, she almost shricked aloud, but then his mouth was suddenly at her navel. Now he was drawing her gently to her knees so that he could kiss her full, young breasts, her shoulders, her throat, her mouth, and her eyes. Velvet had to admit to herself that she had never been kissed quite as thoroughly as Henri of Navarre was kissing her, and it was not an altogether unpleasant thing.

He stood, drawing her to her feet again, and pressed her against his length. For the first time Velvet became aware of the king as merely a man. He was already rigid with his desire, but she did not dare to look down at him. She was quite close to fainting now, and her breathing was very shallow. He saw it, and, scooping her up, he laid her down upon the huge bed and, joining her, drew her into his arms.

"You are still afraid," he said, "and it distresses me to see it, *chèrie*." His big hand caressed her hair. "Such beautiful tresses," he murmured, the hand stroking her as if she were a beast to be gentled. Suddenly he buried his face in her hair and breathed deeply. "You smell of gillyflowers," he said. "It is the perfect scent for you—fresh and sharp, and even a trifle innocent. I shall never smell gillyflowers again without thinking of you, *chèrie*." Then rolling her onto her back in a single, deft movement, he found her lips once more.

For some reason she could never explain to herself, her lips parted quite willingly for him, and his tongue slipped in to find hers; to tease and play with it within the sweet grotto of her mouth; to stoke the banked fires of passion that lay hidden deep within her, waiting to be encouraged forth by this master of the erotic arts. Velvet felt the first stirrings of desire taking over her body, and with shock she realized suddenly that the king had been absolutely correct when he had told her that two compatible people could give each other pleasure despite their lack of emotion for one another. There was a word for such a thing. It was called lust, and though one part of her nature still denounced it, she perceived that lust could sometimes be an attractive thing.

Unable to help herself, she found she was kissing him back, her lips eager for his. He encouraged her further, his mouth lingering here, moving there, touching lightly at the corners of her mouth. The pressure of his lips on hers increased until she felt he was bruising her delicate skin.

"You are like the sweetest flower imaginable," he murmured against her mouth, "and like a gigantic bumblebee I could drink your honey all night, but there are other fountains from which I would drink!" His big head moved to her breasts, and, fastening his lips over one tender nipple, he began to suck on her.

The effect on her was so devastating that Velvet cried out softly. It was as if lightning had streaked from the top of her body to the very bottom. The tug of his lips upon her breast was suddenly the most sensual act, for her nipples were extremely sensitive with her pregnancy, and while his mouth worked upon one breast, his hand gently kneaded the other before switching sides to increase her delight.

Velvet felt herself beginning to lose control of her own emotions, particularly when the king moved his head even lower to explore tenderly that most secret shrine of her womanhood. Like a hummingbird seeking out sugary nectar, his tongue moved swiftly, touching her here, then there, then flicking maddeningly back and forth against the very jewel of her sex until she shattered into a thousand shards of honeyed pleasure—once, twice, three times in quick succession.

When she finally came to herself, he whispered, "You see, *chèrie*, I can indeed give you pleasure. Perhaps you will not admit it to me, but your beautiful face told me all. Ah, the face of a woman's passion! There is nothing more beautiful in this world!"

"I . . . I cannot deny your words, monseigneur," she said softly, "but loving without love is not for me quite the same."

"Sometimes it is better," he rejoined, "for only the senses are involved, unclouded by the emotion of love."

"I do not believe that you really think that," Velvet protested. "You cannot, and still be such . . ." She stopped, blushing.

"Such a what?" he demanded. "Tell me, *chèrie*."

"Such a magnificent lover," she finished. "I would lie if I said you were not. You have known love, monseigneur, whether you will admit it to me or not."

"You are so wise in some ways," he said, "yet so innocent in others, *chèrie*. Now, however, I wish to consummate our agreement." He caught her to him once again, kissing her lips, which were already swollen with his many kisses.

Her body was readily responsive to him. To her surprise the king drew Velvet toward him on her side, sliding one of her long legs beneath him, and the other over his own leg. With a swift and smooth motion he quickly penetrated her, thrusting deeply inside her. She gasped, but his mouth was already on hers again as his arms held her around her shoulders and about her buttocks. He moved with long, even strokes inside her, his rhythm well ordered and easy. His brown-gold eyes held her emerald ones in thrall, and as she felt herself sliding over the edge of passion's precipice she saw the swift light of triumph glowing, or was it merely reflected in those powerful eyes? Velvet cried out a piercing cry of sweet surrender that she clearly heard joined by his own voice.

Afterwards, he told her, "You, *chèrie*, are born to love. You must never, never be ashamed of the magnificent talent that *le bon Dieu* has given you. I only regret that you are happy with your husband."

Twice more that night he made passionate love to her, and Velvet finally slept, totally exhausted by their wild bout with Eros. When she awoke, the storm had passed, the candles lay melted in their silver holders, the fire was but glowing embers, and the sun was streaming through her windows. Upon her pillows was a single red rose—surely the last one of the season—and a folded parchment that she opened with trembling fingers to read:

> *Your hospitality,* madame la comtesse, *has been without equal. I shall not forget the debt that I owe you. Farewell,* chèrie! *Navarre.*

For a moment Velvet felt a sense of sadness, of deep and great loss. The king had behaved outrageously, taking advantage of her predicament, of her helplessness, and yet she felt no malice toward him. She had kept her part of their bargain, and she somehow knew that he would keep his part, too. So now, she thought, there are two secrets that I must keep from you, my darling husband. Perhaps, though, one day I shall be able to tell you about my daughter. Someday when you are completely in my love and surrounded by the children that I shall give to you, God willing. But I shall never tell you of this adventure with Henri of Navarre, Alex. Somehow I do not think you would understand that I had to barter my soul and my body so that we might be together again. There are some things, I have learned, that a woman never tells the man she loves, particularly if she really loves him. Love, I am learning, is the ability to bear pain silently in order to protect the one you love. Dear God, please end this separation between us quickly! Velvet silently prayed.

Chapter 17

Velvet's prayer had been echoed in Alex's heart a thousand times daily since he had learned of her kidnapping. Unable to gain anything of real value from Ranald Torc, he had returned to Broc Ailien where he sought out Jean Lawrie at her cottage. Her husband, Angus Lawrie, had been one of the six men with Velvet on the day of her kidnapping. Like his companions, he had been ruthlessly cut down by Ranald Torc's outlaws. The others had been young, unmarried, and untried men left behind due to their lack of experience because the mission to Huntley had held more danger than guarding the countess when she rode out. He had first visited the families of the other five paying them an indemnity for their loss, thankful there were no widowed mothers or single-son families amongst them. His visit to Jean Lawrie, however, was much harder, for he had known her since childhood when they had played together like brother and sister. Angus Lawrie had been her one and only love, and he had been, Alex thought with regret, a good man.

For several long moments he held his old friend in a close embrace and then said, "There is nae time now, Jeannie, but I promise ye that Ranald Torc will pay for Angus's death, and he will pay dearly. He owes us both a large debt."

She nodded, her eyes swollen from hours of weeping and worrying about her three children, now fatherless. "What of her ladyship, Alex?"

"She seems to hae disappeared off the face of the earth, Jeannie. I'm off to England tomorrow to her parents' home. Perhaps she fled there wi' Pansy. Dugald is as frantic as I am, and even Morag has expressed worry."

"Aye," said Jean, "'tis very possible that she fled to her mother's house. 'Tis the natural thought of a young woman carrying her first bairn. Ye'll find her at her mother's right enough!"

"I hope so, Jeannie," said Alex feverently, "but now I want to speak wi' ye about yer future and that of yer bairns. This cottage is yers now, whatever ye decide. I'd like ye to come up to the castle and be nurse to Sibby and to the bairn Velvet will bear in the spring. Yer children can be brought up wi' mine, even given an education if they show an aptitude for it. Can ye care for Sibby knowing that her mother is Ranald Torc's wife?"

"Och!" said Jean Lawrie. "The little lass is nae responsible for who her mother is. Will her ladyship allow the bairn in the castle, however?"

"Aye," he said. "Ranald Torc told me that she had already fought wi' Alanna about it, saying she would raise Sibby as her own, and that she'd set the dogs on Alanna if she ever showed her face at *Dun Broc* again. She has a bonny spirit, my lass!"

"Go south to England, Alex, and bring yer wife home," said Jean Lawrie, patting his arm comfortingly.

Giving her a hug, the Earl of BrocCairn did just that, traveling swiftly with Dugald and but a dozen men-at-arms. Reaching *Queen's Malvern* in record time, the first person he saw was his mother-in-law.

Surprise was written all over Skye's face as Alex and his men rode up the drive. She had just returned from a long ride with Adam, who had taken their horses to the stable. "Alex! Where is Velvet? Isn't she with you?"

He felt his heart sink, and he slid from his mount to take her hand. "Madame," he said, "I had hoped that you could tell me where Velvet is."

"What?" Skye's blood ran cold in her veins.

"Velvet was kidnapped several weeks ago and taken to Leith. She managed to escape her kidnappers, but we have not be able to find her. She's disappeared entirely. I had hoped she had come to you."

"Who in hell kidnapped her?" Adam de Marisco had come from the stables in time to hear his son-in-law's brief explanation.

"Please, Adam!" Skye put a restraining hand on her angry husband's arm. "Let us go into the house and hear Alex's explanation. Can you not see how worried he is?" She led her husband, Alex, and Dugald into the library to settle them down with goblets of dark red wine, all the while moving as if in a dream, though none of the men noticed it. Velvet was her baby, perhaps the dearest of her children, if a mother who has borne eight children can have a favorite. They waited tensely until she had joined them, and then Alex began his tale.

When he had finished, Adam exploded with rage. "You entertained James Stewart's sworn enemy in your house, you damned fool? What in hell ever possessed you to consort with a traitor? If anything has happened to my daughter, my lord, I'll settle with you myself!"

"Lord Bothwell is nae a traitor, Adam!" rejoined Alex. "None of us can help it that the king is and always has been both envious and afraid of Francis. Oh, 'tis true that Francis sometimes deliberately bedevils Jamie, but it has always been that way between them, and a more loyal subject James Stewart never had than his cousin, Francis Stewart-Hepburn!"

"Where did you look in Leith?" Skye interrupted, finally beginning to regain her wits.

"Where could we look, Skye? She was gone from the lodging. There was no place else."

"Leith is a port, Alex. Did it ever occur to you that she might have taken passage on a ship?" Skye asked.

"But why?" he said, surprised.

"I don't know why, Alex. We will have to find Velvet to learn that, but if she did, then she had a very good explanation, you may be sure, unless you are not telling me everything. Were you both happy? Truly happy? Or did you still hold her responsible for the separation that you both suffered?

"Nay, madame!" he cried. "We had long reconciled our differences. We were both happy. She loved *Dun Broc*, and everyone there loved her."

"Aye," chimed in Dugald. "The countess is beloved by our people, for she is kind and loving. She had nae enemies but for the English whore."

"Your . . ." Skye hesitated. "*That woman,* the silversmith's daughter, was still in the castle?" Her look was one of outrage.

"I hae not been involved with Alanna Wythe for three years," Alex said quietly. "When Velvet was to return, Alanna was yet living at *Dun Broc* although I had not slept wi' her for many months. I offered to send her back to London or to gie her a cottage in Broc Ailien. I dinna expect her to stay, for she hated Scotland, or so she claimed. When she took the cottage, I could not go back on my word. She was naught to Velvet but a nuisance, but that is all, I swear it!"

"She had your child," said Skye quietly.

"Aye, she did, and I will always care for the little lass," Alex answered honestly, "but Sibby is my bastard. The child Velvet carries is my heir."

"Velvet is with child?" Both Skye and Adam spoke in unison.

The bairn is due in early spring as near as Velvet could decide. Had she not written ye? But nay. She wouldna had the time, would she?"

"If my daughter was happy with you," said Skye, "then I cannot understand why she has left you, but before we can know for sure we must find her. I will send one of my own people to Leith. They will know the questions to ask and the places to ask them, Alex. Will you stay with us until we know something? If Velvet returns to *Dun Broc* on her own, your people will send for you."

"Aye," he answered her gratefully, "I'll stay, Skye, and I thank ye."

"My poor child, alone and friendless," muttered Adam.

"She isna alone!" snapped Dugald. "My wife is wi' her, and Pansy practically due again of a bairn. Yer daughter has the damndest sense of timing, if ye'll excuse me, m'lord, for each time my wife is to gie me a bairn, off goes m'lady, and Pansy wi' her!"

Skye couldn't help but laugh, and even Adam and Alex were forced to smile. "I'm sure that Velvet doesn't do it deliberately, Dugald," Skye said.

Dugald sniffed, sounding as if he wasn't too convinced.

"Will you go and explain this all to Daisy?" asked Skye of Alex's man. "She'll know you're here and will be anxious for word of her daughter."

"Thank ye, m'lady, and I will," said Dugald, rising from the bench where he had been sitting and hurrying from the room.

"It is too late in the day," Skye said, "to send my messenger out now, but he shall have his instructions tonight and leave in the morning for Leith."

"I'll send my men wi' him," replied Alex. "They can help him through any rough spots once he's over the border."

Adam de Marisco said nothing. Rather, he slouched in his big chair, his large hand gripping his goblet tightly, his eyes smoldering with anger. He was regretting ever having given his precious daughter to this Scot, for her life had been one crisis after another since the day Alex Gordon had come into it. All Adam wanted was for her to be happy. Why was it, he thought, that parents having learned from their own mistakes, could not make life perfection for their children? The autumn was almost over. Winter was near. Was Velvet safe? Was she warm and decently clothed? Was she hungry or thirsty? A thousand unanswered questions plagued Adam, and for the time being it appeared that there were no answers.

Upon his return to *Chenonceaux*, Henri de Navarre had smiled mysteriously at the jovial teasing of his hunting companions. Had he been successful in his hunt? they asked. Had he managed in one night to bring the pretty auburn doe to ground? Henri said nothing, but his gentlemen, many of whom had been close friends since his youth, knew that the king's look of satisfaction meant that he had gotten precisely what he wanted. They genuinely admired his great capacity for loving women, and they equally envied his tremendous success with the fairer sex, which strangely had little to do with his rank. When he had been a carefree boy in Navarre running barefoot like a goat over the hillsides, there wasn't a woman he couldn't have. So they teased him good-naturedly, and though he said nothing, they knew his night had been a far pleasanter one than theirs.

Now the king called his close friend, Robert, the Marquis de la Victoire, to him and instructed him to engage the Scots ambassador in conversation and told him what to say to him. The matter was to be one held in the strictest secrecy. The ambassador was not to know why the king was interested in the Countess of BrocCairn, or even that it was the king who was interested. And it was important that the information be extracted as quickly as possible.

The marquis, an old friend of Navarre's, asked no questions himself, but rather he did as he was bid, and, to the king's surprise, the answers he sought were quickly forthcoming.

"The Earl of BrocCairn is a cousin of the king's," said the marquis. "He lives in a castle in the Highlands. He is a Gordon by blood, but a small lordling. His wife is said to be a young Englishwoman, but the ambassador does not know either of them."

"That is all?" the king said.

"Yes, monseigneur."

"And what of my old friend François Stewart-Hepburn, Robert?"

"Ah, now that is a different story. Although the king has outlawed him and taken everything from him, he remains at his Border stronghold with, it is rumored, his mistress, a beautiful Scots noblewoman. The king fumes but is helpless to march on Lord Bothwell, for none of his earls will support him in his matter, and the common people adore the man. There the affair stands. The Earl of Bothwell cannot be caught, and the king will not make his peace with him though even the Scots ambassador admits that the earl is a loyal servent of James Stewart, and is very anxious to settle their differences."

"And nowhere in this situation is the Countess of BrocCairn mentioned?" demanded the king. "You are absolutely certain she is not involved in this tangle?"

"Monseigneur, I am as certain as I can be without asking the ambassador directly. He is a plain-spoken man, and we are friends. I helped him only recently with a rather delicate matter involving a lady of circumstance who had taken his fancy; but, alas, the ambassador's French is not of the courting variety. I interceded for him, and when the lady saw that the language this diplomat spoke was a universal one, she agreed to tutor him herself.

"I did ask him if the BrocCairns were involved with Lord Bothwell, saying that I had heard they were cousins. The ambassador laughed and said that most of the nobility are cousins of one degree or another in Scotland, thanks to James V, but that to his knowledge BrocCairn is a king's man even to the extent of taking an English wife so that he may one day follow James Stewart into England when he comes into his inheritance."

Henri nodded, satisfied, and dismissed the marquis. The lovely Velvet's fears were groundless. If at one point James Stewart had intended to use her as a pawn to bring Lord Bothwell down, that time was past and she was safe. He contemplated returning to *Belle Fleurs* and bringing her the news himself, but he quickly cast that thought aside. He did not really have the time, and, besides, if he saw her again, he would want to make love to her again, for she had been a most delicious armful. Velvet had been gracious enough to admit to his skill as a lover, to admit that she had taken pleasure from their coupling; but he knew that with the pleasure she had felt guilt as well, though she had yielded to him without complaint. The king would keep his promise to her and send for her husband, though the Earl of BrocCairn should never know from whence his summons had come.

In the night, that heavenly night he had spent in the silken arms of the Countess of BrocCairn, she had told the king of her home, the place in which she had grown up, a manor called *Queen's Malvern*, near the town of Worcester. She had spoken also of her home in Scotland, a castle with the improbable name of *Dun Broc*. He would send agents with messages to both places. If the earl was at neither abode, then he would simply have to search for him. A royal promise was a royal promise. Then he smiled to himself. The promise was not royal. It was the promise of Henri de Navarre. Calling his secretary to him, he dictated his instructions, including a simple message that he believed the earl would understand, but if the Scots ambassador had played him false and the message fell into the wrong hands, it would not be easily deciphered by anyone else.

At *Queen's Malvern* Christmas was bleak despite the presence of Skye and Adam's large family, who had descended upon them once more despite Skye's wish to be alone.

"You must not fall into the doldrums over Velvet's latest misadventure, Mama," scolded Willow, the Countess of Alcester.

"What Willow means, Mama . . ." began gentle Deirdre in an attempt to soften her elder sister's sharp tone.

"I am well aware of what Willow means!" exploded Skye. Then she rounded on her oldest daughter. "Do not talk down to me, madame! I have not reached my dotage yet. I have only just celebrated my fifty-first birthday. I have no need for wooden teeth, a wig, or a cane, and your stepfather and I yet make rather passionate love regularly!"

"Mama!" shrieked Willow, turning beet red.

Deirdre, however, could not help giggling at her mother's outrage, and Angel, far bolder, laughed outright at Willow's mortification. The men in the family were grinning openly, although Adam had only a hint of a smile about his lips.

"Please, Willow," continued Skye, "don't be the matriarch with me. That is my place now, though your time will come one day, I am certain. I requested privacy this holiday season because, my dear daughter, I am exhausted and worried sick over Velvet. As for Adam and Alex, neither has slept more than two or three hours a night in the last two months. Your motives are good, but your timing is deplorable. This is my house, Willow. Not yours. It is my place to invite guests, not yours."

"I only meant to make you happy, Mama," said Willow, very contrite.

"I know you did," said her mother with a deep sigh, "but will you please go home tomorrow?"

Willow nodded. "I thought the children would please you."

"They did," said Skye, softening. Dear Heaven, what would this proper English born-and-bred countess think if she knew that her deceased father had been known as the "Great Whoremaster of Algiers," thought Skye. She wanted to laugh, but she dared not, for she would have to explain her laughter, and Willow, overproud though good-hearted, would not like the explanation at all.

Robin put an arm about his mother. "Angel and I have to return to London anyway to oversee the preparations for the Twelfth Night masque. Come with us, Mama. You would enjoy seeing the queen, and she you. So many of her old friends have died lately. Walsingham last year, and Hatton this."

"She will outlive them all," said Skye. "Even that old spider, Cecil."

"Probably," agreed Robin, "but will you come?"

"Nay, love. If Velvet wants to get in touch with us, she will send to *Dun Broc* or *Queen's Malvern*. We must be here."

They departed the next day: the Earl and Countess of Alcester and their six children; Joan Southwood O'Flaherty and her five children; the Earl and Countess of Lynmouth and their brood of five; Lord and Lady Blackthorn and their three. Skye's oldest child and his family were on their estates in Ireland. It was unwise for the Irish gentry to leave their lands, for many returned to find they no longer possessed those lands. As for Padraic, Lord Burke of *Clearfields Manor*, he was at sea with his elder half brother, Captain Murrough O'Flaherty, for Skye had thought it was time that Niall Burke's only son have some experiences other than the quiet life he led on his small estate in Devon. And Velvet. Where was Velvet this Christmas season? Before Skye could dwell too deeply on this great worry, however, Daisy hurried into the hall where Skye sat before the fire enjoying the renewed quiet.

"A message for Lord Gordon, m'lady. Do you know where he be?"

"Here, Daisy," said Alex from the depths of the settle on the other side of the fireplace. "Who brought it?"

"I don't know, my lord. One of the stableboys brought it to the kitchen door. He said a stranger gave him a penny to deliver it to the house."

Skye sat up in her chair. "A stranger?"

"A man on horseback with a funny accent, the boy said, but you know that to these local lads any speech other than Worcester bred sounds foreign." Daisy handed the message to Alex.

"What does it say?" Skye demanded eagerly as Alex broke the thick wax seal and opened the heavy parchment to scan it quickly.

"I'm nae sure I understand it, Skye, for 'tis but one sentence."

"What does it say?" Skye had now risen from her seat.

"It says," Alex read slowly, *"'The treasure that you seek is at Belle Fleurs,'* but I dinna know what it means."

To his surprise Skye cried out, "Thank God! Thank God! Our prayers have been answered! Velvet is at *Belle Fleurs*, Alex! Velvet is safe in France at our chateau! *Belle Fleurs* is our home in the Loire. Velvet is the treasure! Who has signed the message?"

"There is no signature," he answered her, stunned. "Ye're sure that is what the message means?"

"Yes! Yes! It can mean nothing else, my dear Alex! Do you recognize the seal on the parchment?"

Turning the letter over, he looked down at the red wax, which was imprinted only with an N. "Nay," he said, handing it to her.

Skye looked down at the seal, but it was not familiar to her either. Clutching the message in her hand, she said, "We are going to France, Alex! I must find Adam! We are going to France!"

They sailed from Dover four days later bound for the port of Calais. Neither Skye nor Adam chose to chance an early January storm in the winter seas by sailing all the way to Nantes. They took with them their own coach with all its elegant comforts, but the horses would be waiting for them after their short passage in Calais and at various posting places along their route from the coast into the Loire. They skirted Paris, for the civil war yet raged within the city.

"It will not be long," Skye promised. "Just a few more days, Alex!"

Adam squeezed his wife's hand tightly. "We will be there by Twelfth Night with luck, and providing it doesn't snow!"

Alex said nothing. His heart was beating too quickly. Why had Velvet fled to France instead of returning home to *Dun Broc* when she had escaped Ian's clutches? Now he began to worry. Did she still love him, or had her weeks in captivity made her think twice about raising a child in such a wild land as Scotland? Knowing of his mother-in-law's ferocity with regard to her children's welfare, he expected Velvet to be no less fierce. Had she not threatened Alanna with bodily harm for being a bad mother to his bastard? Had she not said she would raise Sibby herself rather than allow Alanna to have the bairn back? That, however, was before she had fled. What had frightened her? The best Twelfth Night gift, he thought to himself, would be his reunion with his wife.

On Twelfth Night Velvet planned a small celebration for her little household. She even had gifts for them all, having raided the storeroom of the chateau. For old Mignon she had found a silver broach, which she had personally polished, removing years of black tarnish to reveal an engraving of raised flowers, each with a tiny ruby in its center. For Guillaume she had cut silver buckles off a pair of her father's old boots and polished them knowing that he would enjoy them greatly. For young Matthieu there was a puppy, for to everyone's surprise the old bitch in the kennels had given birth to a litter of two in mid-November. The boy had coveted a puppy, but dogs of breeding were usually reserved for the nobility. Since, however, the puppy's paternity was dubious, Velvet could see no harm in giving one to the lad. For Pansy, however, the best gift was saved. Velvet had been wearing a small pearl ring when they had been kidnapped. This she planned to present to her faithful tiring woman.

Mignon had prepared a little feast. There was a larded duck, a rabbit pie, and a small pink ham placed upon the sideboard along with a bowl of tiny white onions, a platter of mussels with Dijon mustard, artichokes that had been braised in white wine, a fat loaf of fresh bread, a crock of salted butter, and a hard yellow cheese. Velvet had insisted that Mignon and Guillaume eat with her on this occasion, and Mignon had accepted for her family with one provision. Matthieu would serve them, for his manners were not delicate enough to be seen at her ladyship's table.

The little hall had been trimmed with greenery, the fires burned merrily, and they were sitting down to their meal when the sound of a horse was heard outside. Old Guillaume hobbled to the door, opening it to admit the king.

"Ah, *chèrie,* you are ready to eat, and I am starving!" He kissed her heartily on both cheeks, holding her away from him to gaze at her. "Ah." He smiled warmly. "The little one is now showing! You are well?"

"Yes, monseigneur, I am very well." She looked helplessly at her servants, but the king quickly ascertained the cause of her distress.

"Sit, *mes amis*!" he commanded them. "Your mistress planned to share this meal with you, and now with your permission I will join you also. Madame Mignon! You have prepared another veritable feast. Your pretty mistress thinks I have come to see her, but you will note that I have arrived at the dinner hour! Who do you think I really came to see, eh?" He laughed uproariously.

Within minutes he had them all at their ease, though young Matthieu was goggle-eyed at serving the king. To his grandparents' nods of approval he did himself proud, so much so that Guillaume later promised to speak to the Comte de Cher about a place as a footman for the boy.

"What are you doing here?" asked Velvet as they ate.

"I came to wish Queen Louise a happy New Year," said the king. I am at *Chenonceaux* but one night. I also wanted you to know that my investigations of your difficulties reveal that if you had any cause for fear, it is now gone. I do not believe that your captor ever reached the chancellor, Maitland. I have sent word to both your home in Scotland and your parents' home in England on the chance that your husband is there, that you were to be found at *Belle Fleurs*. My agents have not yet said if the messages were delivered, but then they have not said that they were not. I suspect you will hear from your husband long before I hear from my messengers, *chèrie*!"

Velvet could feel the relief wash over her. "I can go home!" she said, and the smile on her face was the loveliest thing he had ever seen.

"You cannot travel in your state, *chèrie*. You will have to wait for your husband to come to you. He would not thank you if you endangered either yourself or the child."

"How can I thank you?" Velvet said with genuine feeling.

"You did," he said softly, so that only she could hear, "and most magnificently, madame la comtesse. It will be a long time before I forget that stormy night in November. I did not even plan to see you again, for I did not see how I could and not desire you. I am weak where women are concerned however, and being so near at *Chenonceaux* it was impossible to spend the evening with Queen Louise, her carp, and boiled vegetables when you were nearby."

Before Velvet could answer the king, however, there came the sounds of a coach outside. "Who can that be?" she wondered out loud as Guillaume haltingly hurried to open the door again.

"Madame!" Velvet heard him say. "Welcome home!"

She leaped to her feet as her mother came into the hall. "Mama!"

Skye caught her daughter in a fervent embrace. "Oh, my darling child! You have had us all so terribly, terribly worried!"

"Alex?" Velvet begged. "Is he with you?"

The king looked past the women to see the two men who had entered the hall. The elder he assumed was Velvet's father, the younger her husband. Skye released her daughter and stepped aside. For a long moment no one in the hall moved. It was as if they had been frozen in time. The Earl and Countess of BrocCairn had eyes for no one but each other, and the deep, passionate look that passed between them told Henri de Navarre that they were that most fortunate of married couples—one who loved each other. Then suddenly they moved toward one another: Velvet, a trifle ungainly, running; Alex closing the space between them in several long leaps, catching his wife into a fierce embrace, his mouth covering hers in a bruising kiss that left her somewhat speechless.

His amber eyes blazed down into her face. "Why did ye leave me, lass?" he said. "Why didn't ye come home to *Dun Broc* when ye escaped from Ian?"

She clung to him, weakened by his embrace, her heart pounding wildly. "I fought with Ian that day, and he slammed from the rooms where we were held captive saying that he was going immediately to Maitland and would turn me over to the king that very day. When Pansy and I realized that we were alone, we escaped. I didn't dare go home to *Dun Broc* for fear that the king would find me and use me to entrap Francis. I would have sooner died than been the cause of his downfall! I didn't dare go to my parents for the same reason. I feared the king would send to England for me. The only place that I knew Jamie wouldn't think to look for me was here at *Belle Fleurs*, Alex, and once I was here I couldn't even send you word that I was safe for fear my message would be intercepted; that the king would prevail upon his French allies to return me to Scotland. I could only wait and hope that James and Francis would resolve their differences so that I might return to you."

"But someone did know ye were here, lass. Someone sent a message to yer mother's home telling us where to look for ye," Alex said.

"'Twas I," said the king, stepping forward. "Henri de Navarre, at your service." He made an elegant bow. "I am relieved that you understood my somewhat cryptic message, for I did not wish to endanger your wife if my agent's information about James Stewart's lack of interest in her proved incorrect."

Skye and Adam de Marisco stiffened with shock as they recognized a somewhat older but nonetheless familiar face.

Alex, who knew the French king's reputation, said a trifle suspiciously, "How is it that ye know my wife, monseigneur?"

"She saved my life, monsieur. Several months back I was visiting Queen Louise at *Chenonceaux*. *Chenonceaux* is not what it once was, for Louise de Lorraine now lives to mourn my predecessor, even going so far as to drape the entire chateau in black crepe." He shuddered delicately. "It is criminal what she has done! Nonetheless, it is my duty to visit her several times a year, a sacrifice on my part, monsieur, I assure you, for she serves meals that reek of penance. The woman's life is a living Lenten season, but I digress. My gentlemen and I had gone hunting to escape the funereal atmosphere of the place, and as usual," Navarre said somewhat smugly, "I outrode them in the chase. *Mon Dieu!* That stag was magnificent! I only wish I had caught him!

"It grew dark suddenly, as it can do in autumn, and I could no longer hear my companions, the stag had disappeared, and I suddenly found myself lost. I fell into your lake in my wanderings. Your wife heard my cries for help and ordered lights to be brought. It was she who found me just as the storm broke and helped to pull me from the waters.

"The night was pitch black, and the storm wild in its intensity. Madame la comtesse graciously sheltered me, and Madame Mignon fed me a magnificent beef ragout. I was able to safely return to *Chenonceaux* in the morning, to the relief of all of France," he concluded. "Would you not say that I owed your wife a great debt? Before I left I asked her how I might repay her hospitality, not to mention the fact that she had saved my life. Swearing me to secrecy, she told me of her predicament and asked if I could help her. I was not certain that I could, but I offered to try. You see, Comte de BrocCairn, your cousin, François Stewart-Hepburn, is a very old friend of mine, and although France has allied itself with Scotland, I hold no love for James Stewart.

"I knew from Velvet of both her home in Scotland and her parents' home in England. I sent my agents with messages to both places. You saw my initial in the sealing wax, did you not?"

"N," said Alex. "N for Navarre!"

"Mais oui!" Henri grinned.

"How do I thank ye?" said Alex, and Velvet held her breath.

The king smiled charmingly. "By enjoying France's bounteous hospitality until your child is born, Comte de BrocCairn. Your wife cannot travel in her condition."

Alex turned back to kiss his wife as the king went politely to greet Velvet's parents whom he had not really looked at yet. As his eyes met those of Skye's, they widened. *"You!"* he said, stunned. "You are Velvet's mother?" His mind swung back almost twenty years to a night when he had possessed this fabulous woman; a night of the most incredible passion he had ever known; a night cut short by equally incredible violence; the night of the Saint Bartholomew's Day massacre.

"Velvet was born almost nine months after, monseigneur," she said very softly as she divined his thoughts.

Henri de Navarre went white with shock. Holy Mother! Was it possible that Velvet was his daughter, that he had unknowingly committed incest with his own child? Loathing surged through his body, and he could taste the bile in the back of his throat.

Skye watched the play of emotions on the king's face, and she knew precisely what he was thinking. She had never expected to be able to revenge herself upon Henri de Navarre for the rape of her person those many years ago, for the misery of the months that followed when she believed the child she carried was his. Now fate had played into her hands. She didn't have to say one word. He already believed it!

Then Adam spoke softly in her ear. "Forgive him, little girl, if not for my honor, for your own. He already has many blots upon his soul. Do not put this one upon yours."

She sighed, and then said, "Velvet is not your daughter, monseigneur."

"You are sure?" He still looked shaken.

"I was not until she was born," Skye said truthfully, "but she bears a birthmark that has been borne for centuries by the women in her father's family."

"The little black heart atop the left hip," said the king softly, his relief evident.

"You bastard!" hissed Skye, so low that only he heard it.

Henri de Navarre held his hands palms turned outward as he gave a little shrug of resignation. "*Chèrie,* did you expect any less of me?" he said.

Skye shook her head and laughed ruefully. "No," she answered him frankly, "I did not."

"You have not changed," he said. "You are still the most beautiful woman I have ever known."

"And you, monseigneur, are still, despite the civilized veneer of kingship that you bear, a rude boy!"

The king laughed. "I must go," he said, "before it gets dark, and I fall once more into your lake. It will be a cold ride to *Chenonceaux*, and last night I could hear the wolves."

"I always promised myself that if we ever met again I should kill you, monseigneur," said Adam de Marisco, "but it seems that having restored my only child to us I must count us even."

The king nodded. "*Adieu*, Lord de Marisco, Comte de BrocCairn," he said to the two gentlemen, and then he turned to Skye and Velvet. "It has been good to see you again, *chèrie,*" he said to Skye as he raised her hand to his lips and kissed it slowly. Then he took Velvet's hand and kissed it also. "Farewell, *chèrie,*" he said softly. "Be happy!" And, turning, he was swiftly gone from the hall.

Her eyes widening with surprise and sudden certainty, Velvet looked at her mother. "Mama?" she asked.

Skye's mouth turned up in a mischievous smile that acknowledged her daughter's unspoken question. "Yes, *chèrie,*" she said.

"Mama!" Velvet repeated, and then the delighted laughter of mother and daughter filled the hall at *Belle Fleurs* as they shared their newfound kinship.

Epilogue

His heart in me keeps me and him in one,
My heart in him his thoughts and senses guides:
He loves my heart, for once it was his own;
I cherish his because in me it bides.
His heart his wound received from my sight,
My heart was wounded with his wounded heart:
For as from me, on him his hurt did light,
So still methought in me his hurt did smart.
Both, equal hurt, in this change sought our bliss:
My true Love hath my heart, and I have his.
—Sir Philip Sidney

"Name this child," said Père Jean-Paul to the assembled company.

"James Francis Henry Alexander," said Scotland's king as he gingerly cradled his godson.

Velvet smiled proudly up at her husband, squeezing his hand in silent love. They stood quietly together amid her entire family in the chapel at *Dun Broc* as their firstborn son was baptized on this third day of June in the year of our Lord 1593. The child had been born at *Belle Fleurs* on the first day of April.

Velvet and Alex had lived in France with Skye and Adam from the time of their second reunion until just three weeks ago when they had returned to *Dun Broc*. The entire village of Broc Ailien had turned out to greet their returning lord and lady who brought with them their newborn son and heir, the next earl. It had been an incredibly joyous occasion for them all. At the castle Jean Lawrie awaited, holding little Sybilla by the hand. The child had been shy of her father and stepmother at first, but had quickly warmed when Velvet had drawn from the luggage cart a beautiful French doll dressed in silks and laces. Even if Sibby, who was almost three, remembered Alanna, which both Velvet and Alex doubted, it was Velvet who from that moment on became "Mama" to the little girl.

Jean was delighted with the new baby and took him proudly to the nursery, Sibby dogging her heels. Sybilla very much enjoyed being a big sister, and from the first was most adoring of her tiny infant brother. Seeing them together, Velvet sent a silent prayer of thanks to the God who, though he had taken Yasaman from her, had given her another daughter in return to raise.

Yasaman. Velvet's heart contracted at the thought of her first child. What did she look like now? Did she speak? Was she happy? She had been such a beautiful, contented baby. Velvet knew that Rugaiya Begum would love Yasaman as if she were indeed her own. What would they tell her daughter about her real mother? She sighed. There were already two pearls on the chain Akbar had given her; Skye had shown it to her in France. Velvet only needed to know that her daughter continued to thrive. Now her thoughts and energies must be with little Sybilla and Sandy, as the baby had already been nicknamed.

It had been decided immediately that the king of Scotland would be the baby's godfather and Velvet's sister-in-law, Angel, the godmother.

"I want the christening at *Dun Broc,*" Velvet had said. "He should have been born there, and but for our misfortune he would have been. He shall, however, be baptized there, and," she had said, looking at Skye, "we shall use the occasion to have a family reunion! Padriac and Murrough are already back from their voyage. Ewan can come with Gwyneth and their children from Ireland. Surely he can leave his estates long enough to come for little James's baptism."

"I will send one of your O'Malley uncles to oversee Ewan estates while he is gone. There will be no trouble. Do you really mean to have the entire family to *Dun Broc*, Velvet?" Skye asked.

"Yes, Mama! Everyone! Willow, Murrough, Ewan, Deirdre, Padraic, and Robin! All their families! Uncle Conn and Aunt Aiden and my cousins! Annabella and her sons! Daisy and Bran Kelly! Uncle Robbie and Dame Cecily! Everyone!"

The invitations had been sent even before they had left France, and, delighted at the prospect of their all being together again, the entire family had come, fifty-four of them in all. *Dun Broc* bulged with relatives, and there were children underfoot everywhere one turned.

"Are you aware that we have thirty grandchildren here?" said Adam de Marisco to his wife, somewhat overawed.

"I try not to think of it," said Skye. "If I did, my hair would go white!"

When the king had arrived, they had had to somehow make room for him and his entourage, though how they had done so Velvet didn't know. She only thanked God that the queen was breeding again, and therefore was unable to come. How she would have housed her retainers she shuddered to imagine.

When the king had heard his godson's name, he had frowned. "Francis," he said. "I dinna like the name Francis," and he glowered at Velvet.

"It is fortunate then, Your Majesty, that it is not your own son who is called Francis." She looked back at the king, her soft mouth set in a firm line.

"Must he be called Francis?" the king persisted.

"Francis is but his second name as Henry is his third and Alexander his fourth. He will be called by none of these other names, however. We shall call him James after Your Majesty." She smiled up at him, her mouth relaxing now as she sought to placate him.

"But why Francis?" the king asked again.

"Because he was always our good and true friend even as he has been yours," said Velvet boldly. "Because we first celebrated our marriage in his home at *Hermitage, and* because I am the baby's mother and I wish it!"

The king sighed, defeated. "There is nae arguing wi' a stubborn woman," he said in a somewhat aggrieved tone, but the matter was closed.

Now at last the baby was christened, and the assembled guests, having been blest by Père Jean-Paul, trooped to the Great Hall to celebrate the event, waiting until the king had changed his doublet to raise the toasts of long life to the infant. The future Earl of BrocCairn had not yet learned to respect his royal master and had wet him most thoroughly.

Pansy and Dugald had been invited to sit at the high board with the immediate family. After all their adventures together, the two young women had a closeness not unlike that of many sisters. Looking at her faithful tiring woman across the chapel that morning, Velvet had smiled to herself remembering what had happened after Henri de Navarre had bid them farewell.

As the king had left, Dugald, having stabled the horses with the coachman, had entered the little hall at *Belle Fleurs*. Pansy had stood up immediately and, reaching down to a cradle by her chair, had lifted her baby, born December third, up in her arms. Then she had walked over to her husband, saying, "His name is Bran."

"Is it now?" replied Dugald belligerently. "Ye named the first one. Dinna I get to name this one?"

"I named the first one after you," replied Pansy, equally feisty. "This one is named after my pa. Bran I calls him, and Bran he'll stay!"

"Then I get to name the next bairn, and would ye do me the kindness to at least let me be wi' ye when ye have him? Ye seem to delight in going off and spawning yer bairns without me, woman. At least I get to see this one when he's still a babe."

"Just be glad he's healthy!" snapped Pansy. "Now tell me, Dugald Geddes, are you just going to stand there arguing with me over trifles, or are you going to kiss me and say you're glad to see me?"

"I dinna think ye needed to hear it, woman. I thought ye knew it. God knows ye know everything else!"

"Well, I do need to hear it," said Pansy, smiling as he drew her into his arms and gave her a hearty buss, "and you're right, I do know everything else. After all, I'm a traveled woman!"

Velvet smiled again now at the memory. They were all so damned lucky, she thought, and she was grateful.

The party threatened to go on all night, but gradually as the children fell asleep where they sat, and the nursemaids carried them off to the dormitory that had been set up in the attics for them, even the adults began to show signs of tiring. Finally the king departed for his chambers giving the rest of the guests the excuse to find their beds.

Pansy prepared her mistress for bed, helping to bathe her in a warm, gillyflower-scented bath; brushing her long auburn hair free of snarls so that it rippled down her back in soft waves; and finally sliding a pale sea-green silk night rail over her lithe form. Velvet looked at herself in the pier glass. She had just had her twentieth birthday, and despite the fact that she had already borne two children her body was still good. She smiled a small smile of self-satisfaction and turned to dismiss Pansy.

"Don't come until I call you in the morning, Pansy. You could use some rest, too."

"Aye, but with two bairns I'm not so likely to get it, though Morag is wonderful with Dugie. His wee nose is still a bit out of joint over Bran."

"I think if you'd had a girl it would have been different," said Velvet.

"Perhaps"—Pansy shrugged—"but he'll get over it soon enough. Well, good night, m'lady." She bobbed a curtsy.

"Good night, Pansy."

The door closed after the tiring woman, and Velvet stretched and yawned. She was exhausted.

"Ye're tired?" Alex said, entering her bedchamber from his. Sitting down beside her, his arms slipped around her. "I had thought that we might play a bit after our long day."

"Did you now?" she teased him. "And what game did you have in mind, my wild Highland husband?"

His arms tightened about her. "Do ye know how very, very much I love ye, Velvet?"

"Aye," she said quietly. "Do you know how very, very much I love you, Alex?"

"Aye," he answered, and then, "I will never let ye out of my sight again, lass. Those months of not knowing where ye were, of people believing that ye were dead. I could not go through it ever again!"

"Did you believe I was dead?" she asked.

"Never!" he said. "I would have felt it, and I did not. Ye were simply lost, lass, but I've found ye, and I will nae let ye go ever again."

She looked up at him, locked within the protective circle of his embrace, her emerald eyes filled with the enormity of her love for this wonderful man who was her husband. "I will never leave you again, Alex, for this heart of mine could not bear the separation! You have become my life!"

"As ye hae become mine," he said. "Our love has been forged strongly, Velvet." And then kissing her passionately, he swept her into a lover's world from which neither of them would ever willingly emerge again.

About the Author

Bertrice Small is the bestselling author of *The Kadin, Love Wild and Fair, Adora, Skye O'Malley, Unconquered, Beloved* and *All The Sweet Tomorrows.* She lives in the oldest English settlement in the state of New York, a small village on the eastern end of Long Island. She is called "Sunny" by her friends, and "Lust's Leading Lady" by her fans; but her son insists that to him, she's just plain "Mom."

Mrs. Small works at an antique desk in a light-filled, pink, green and white studio overlooking her old-fashioned rose and flower garden. It is furnished in what she describes as a mixture of office modern and Turkish harem. Mrs. Small's companions as she works to create her handsome rogues, dashing renegades and beautiful vixens are her new electronic typewriter, Betsy (the faithful Rebecca having retired after many years of service), Checquers, now a large black and white cat, whose ears are still pink to match his collar, and her over-worked secretary, Judy Walker, who has recently joined the team.

Bertrice Small enjoys hearing from her readers, so, if you have enjoyed *This Heart of Mine* you may write her at P.O. Box 765, Southold, New York, 11971. Rest assured, she answers all her mail.